big
NATE
VERY FUNNY!

Complete Your *Big Nate* Collection

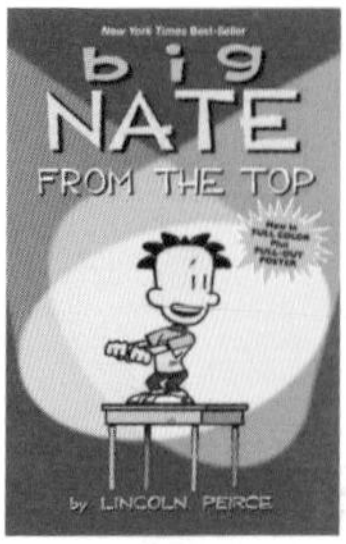
big NATE
FROM THE TOP
by LINCOLN PEIRCE

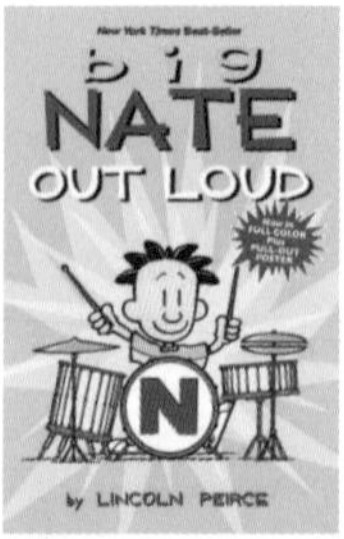
big NATE
OUT LOUD
by LINCOLN PEIRCE

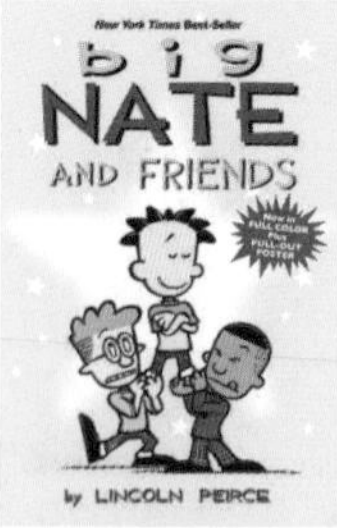
big NATE
AND FRIENDS
by LINCOLN PEIRCE

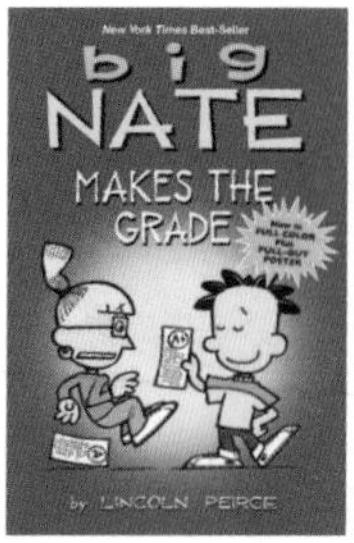
big NATE
MAKES THE GRADE
by LINCOLN PEIRCE

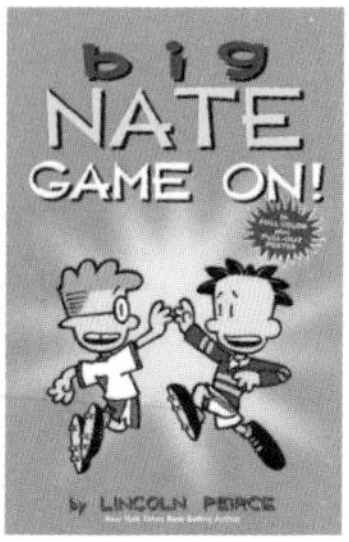
big NATE
GAME ON!
by LINCOLN PEIRCE

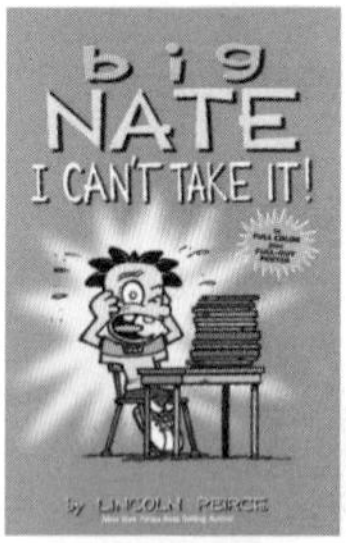
big NATE
I CAN'T TAKE IT!
by LINCOLN PEIRCE

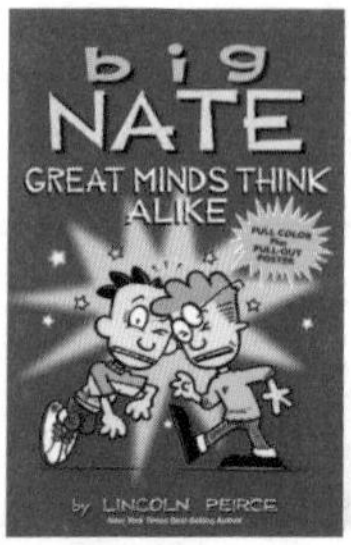
big NATE
GREAT MINDS THINK ALIKE
by LINCOLN PEIRCE

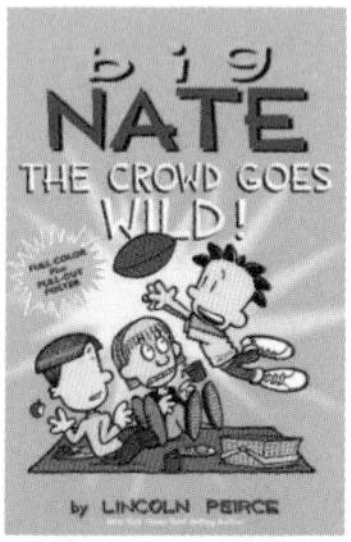
big NATE
THE CROWD GOES WILD!
by LINCOLN PEIRCE

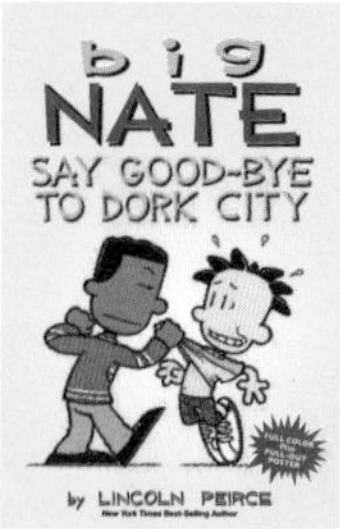
big NATE
SAY GOOD-BYE TO DORK CITY
by LINCOLN PEIRCE

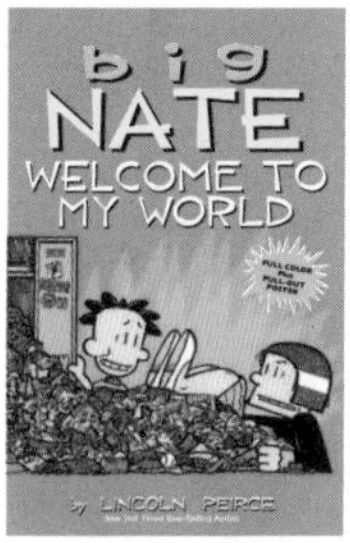
big NATE
WELCOME TO MY WORLD
by LINCOLN PEIRCE

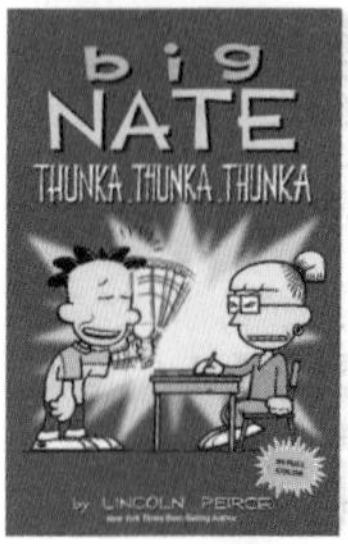
big NATE
THUNKA THUNKA THUNKA
by LINCOLN PEIRCE

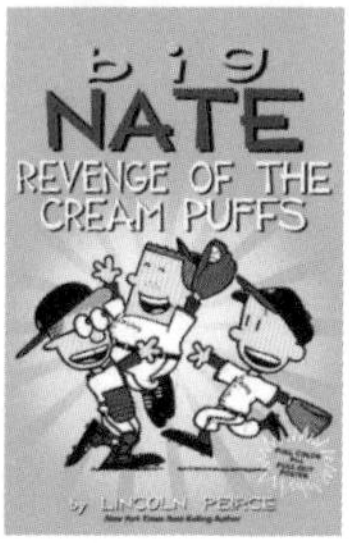
big NATE
REVENGE OF THE CREAM PUFFS
by LINCOLN PEIRCE

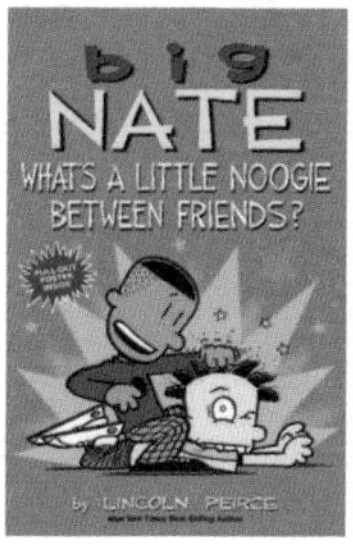
big NATE
WHAT'S A LITTLE NOOGIE BETWEEN FRIENDS?
by LINCOLN PEIRCE

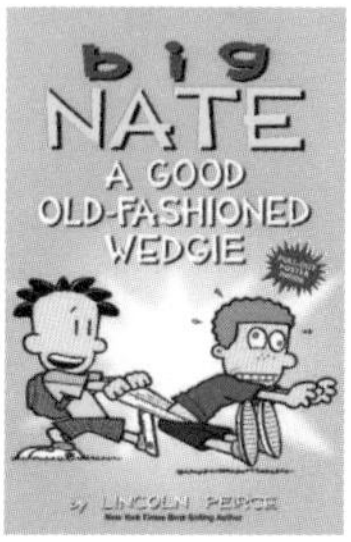
big NATE
A GOOD OLD-FASHIONED WEDGIE
by LINCOLN PEIRCE

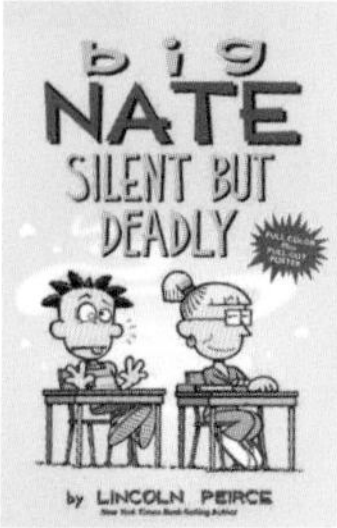
big NATE
SILENT BUT DEADLY
by LINCOLN PEIRCE

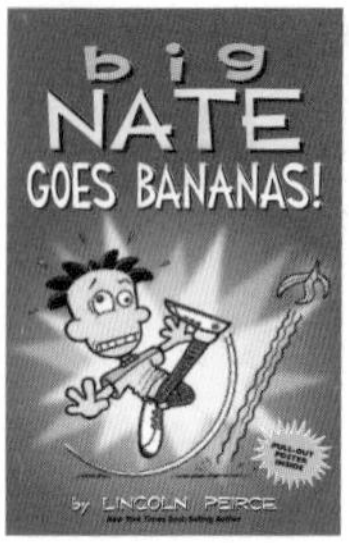
big NATE
GOES BANANAS!
by LINCOLN PEIRCE

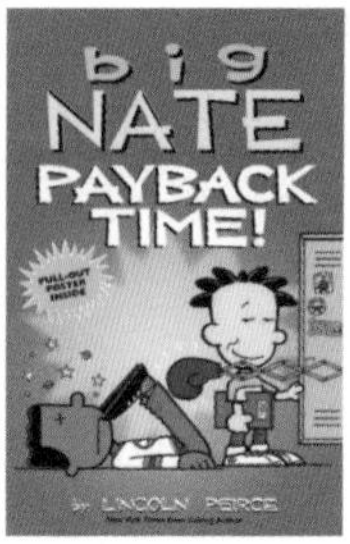
big NATE
PAYBACK TIME!
by LINCOLN PEIRCE

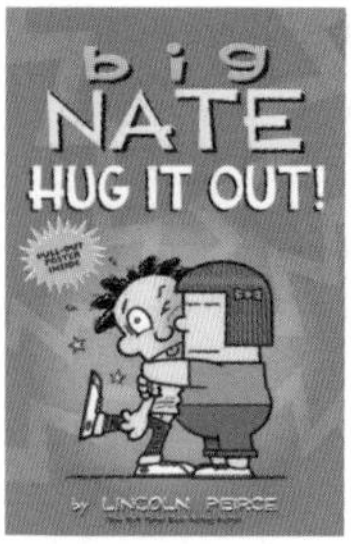
big NATE
HUG IT OUT!
by LINCOLN PEIRCE

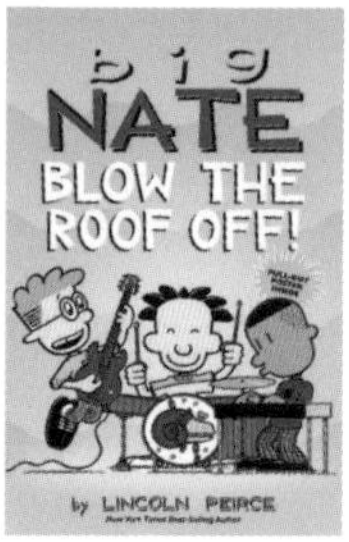
big NATE
BLOW THE ROOF OFF!
by LINCOLN PEIRCE

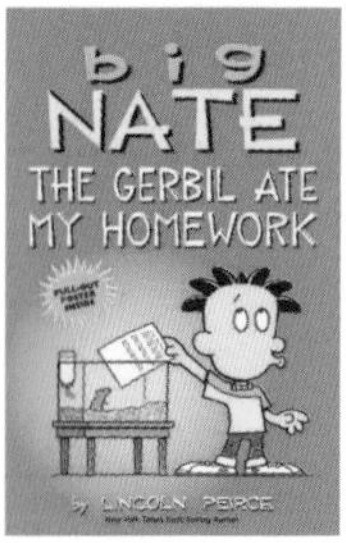
big NATE
THE GERBIL ATE MY HOMEWORK
by LINCOLN PEIRCE

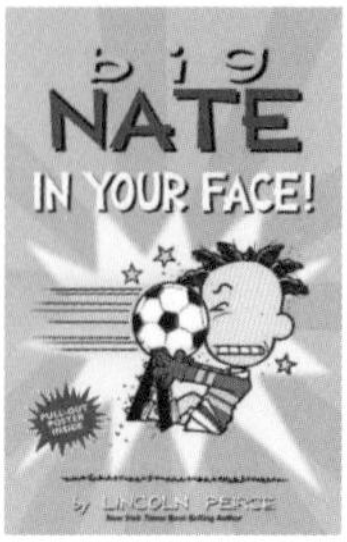
big NATE
IN YOUR FACE!
by LINCOLN PEIRCE

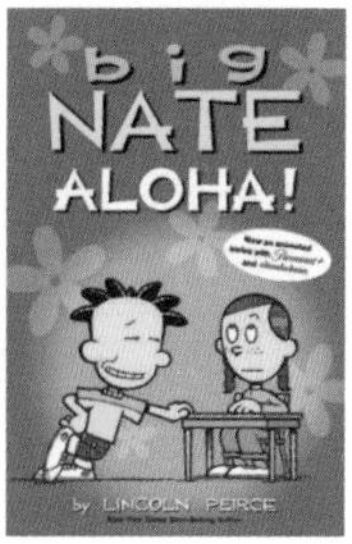
big NATE
ALOHA!
by LINCOLN PEIRCE

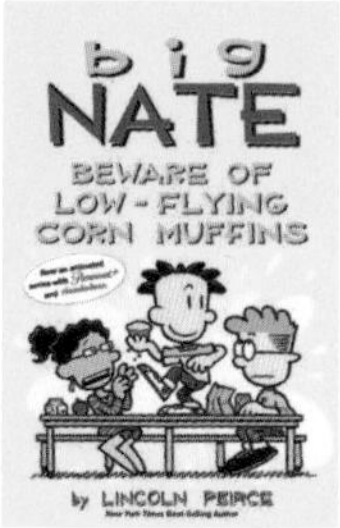
big NATE
BEWARE OF LOW-FLYING CORN MUFFINS
by LINCOLN PEIRCE

big NATE

VERY FUNNY!

by LINCOLN PEIRCE

A special collection featuring comics from
Big Nate: Welcome to My World and *Big Nate: Thunka, Thunka, Thunka*

Andrews McMeel
PUBLISHING®

Andrews McMeel Publishing
a division of Andrews McMeel Universal
1130 Walnut Street, Kansas City, Missouri 64106

www.andrewsmcmeel.com

22 23 24 25 26 SDB 10 9 8 7 6 5 4 3 2 1

ISBN: 978-1-5248-7695-1

Made by:
King Yip (Dongguan) Printing & Packaging Factory Ltd.
Address and location of production:
Daning Administrative District, Humen Town
Dongguan Guangdong, China 523930
1st Printing - 4/11/22

Big Nate can be viewed on the Internet at
www.comics.com/big_nate.

ATTENTION: SCHOOLS AND BUSINESSES
Andrews McMeel books are available at quantity discounts with bulk purchase for educational, business, or sales promotional use. For information, please e-mail the Andrews McMeel Publishing Special Sales Department: specialsales@amuniversal.com.

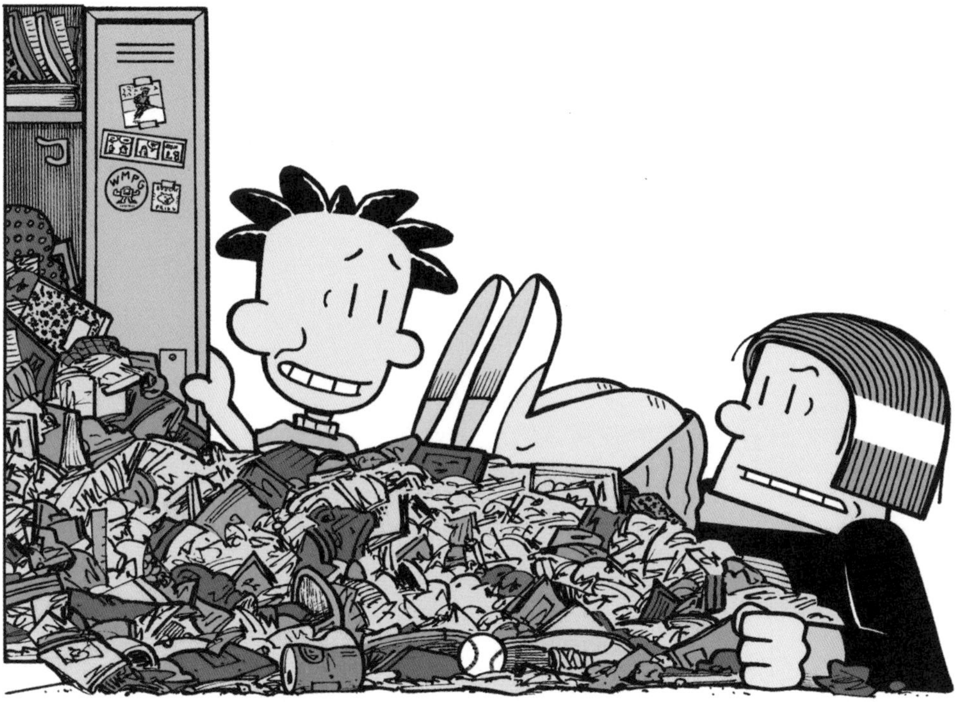
WMPG

big
NATE
WELCOME TO
MY WORLD

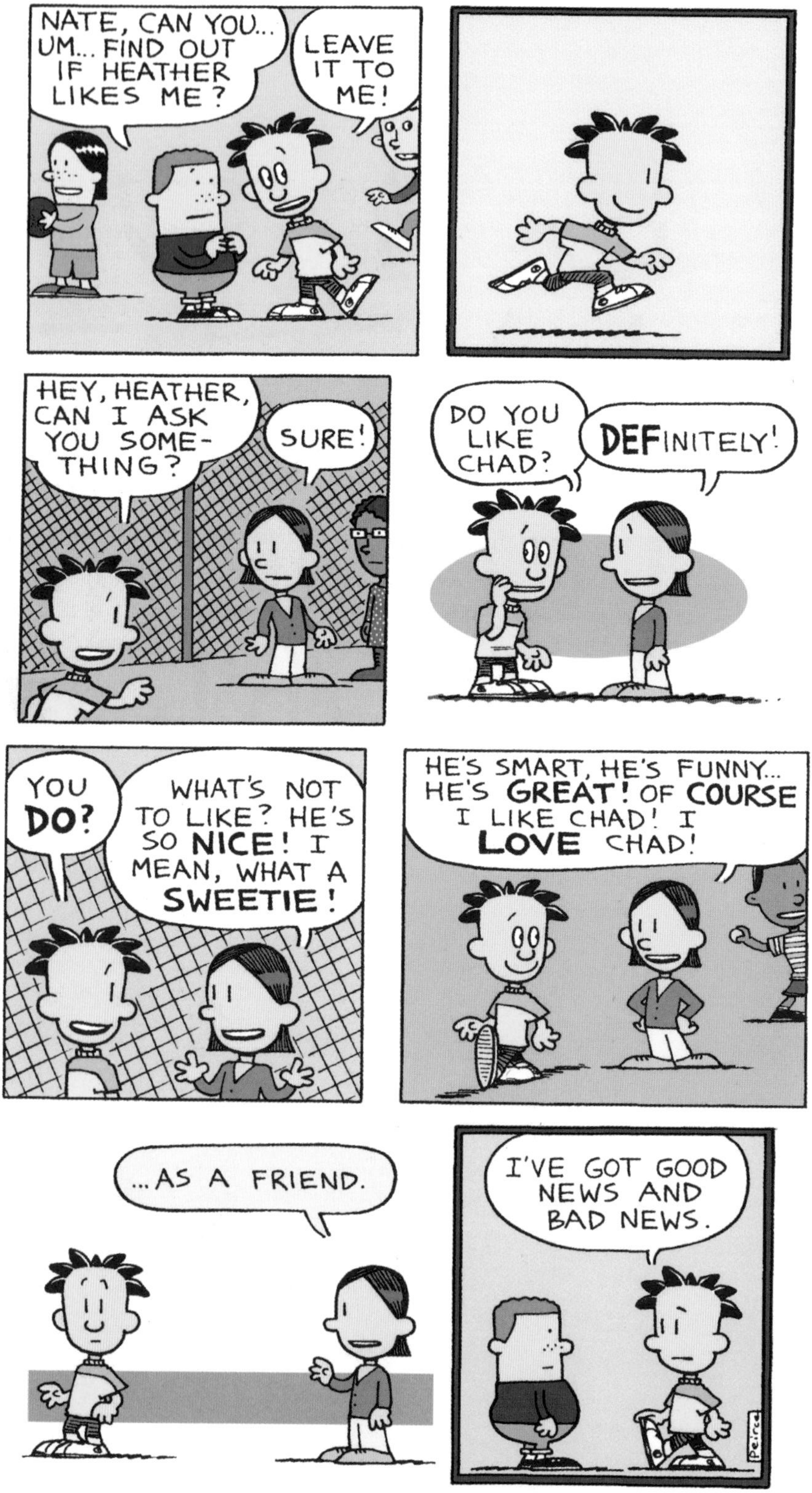
NATE, CAN YOU... UM... FIND OUT IF HEATHER LIKES ME?
LEAVE IT TO ME!
HEY, HEATHER, CAN I ASK YOU SOME-THING?
SURE!
DO YOU LIKE CHAD?
DEFINITELY!
YOU DO?
WHAT'S NOT TO LIKE? HE'S SO NICE! I MEAN, WHAT A SWEETIE!
HE'S SMART, HE'S FUNNY... HE'S GREAT! OF COURSE I LIKE CHAD! I LOVE CHAD!
...AS A FRIEND.
I'VE GOT GOOD NEWS AND BAD NEWS.
Peirce

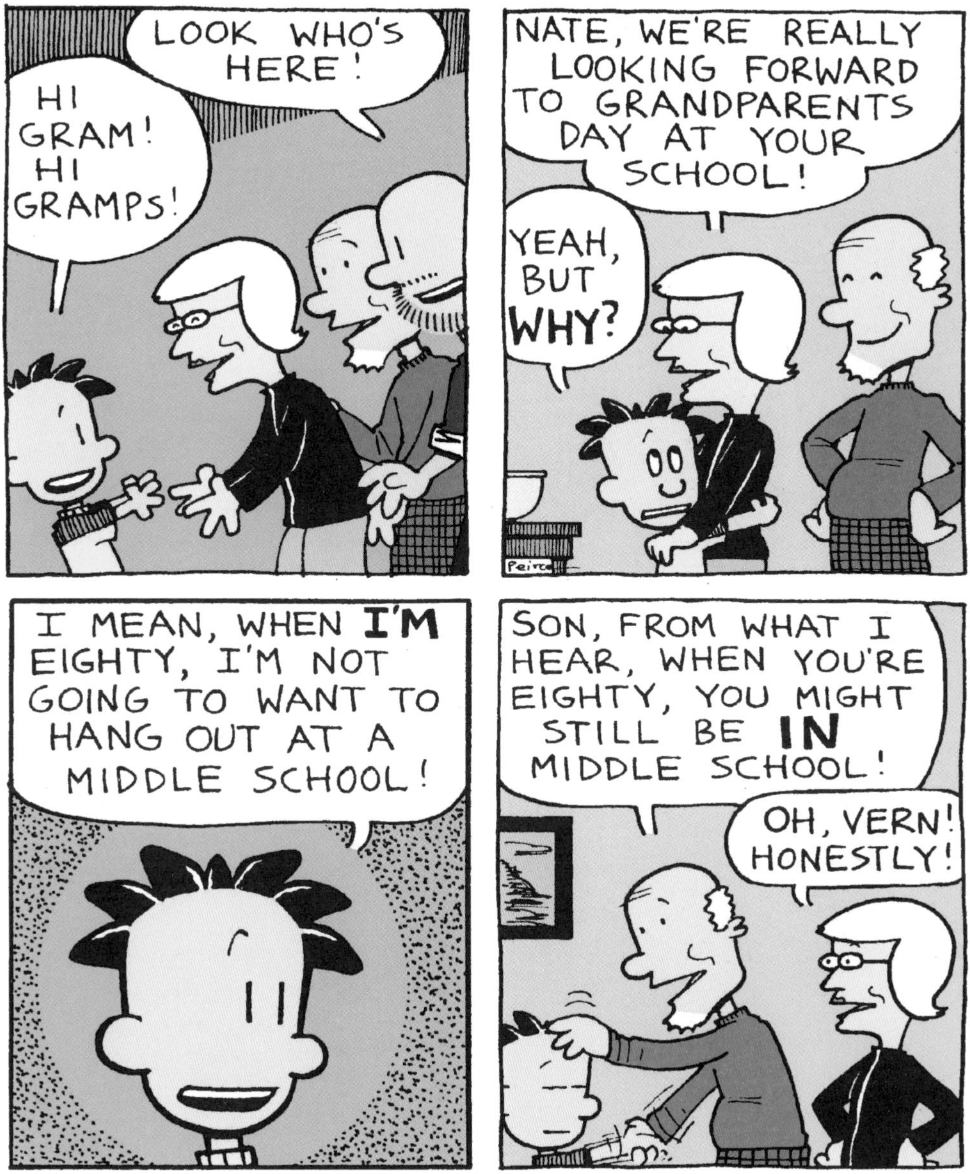
LOOK WHO'S HERE!
HI GRAM! HI GRAMPS!
NATE, WE'RE REALLY LOOKING FORWARD TO GRANDPARENTS DAY AT YOUR SCHOOL!
YEAH, BUT **WHY?**
Peirce
I MEAN, WHEN **I'M** EIGHTY, I'M NOT GOING TO WANT TO HANG OUT AT A MIDDLE SCHOOL!
SON, FROM WHAT I HEAR, WHEN YOU'RE EIGHTY, YOU MIGHT STILL BE **IN** MIDDLE SCHOOL!
OH, VERN! HONESTLY!

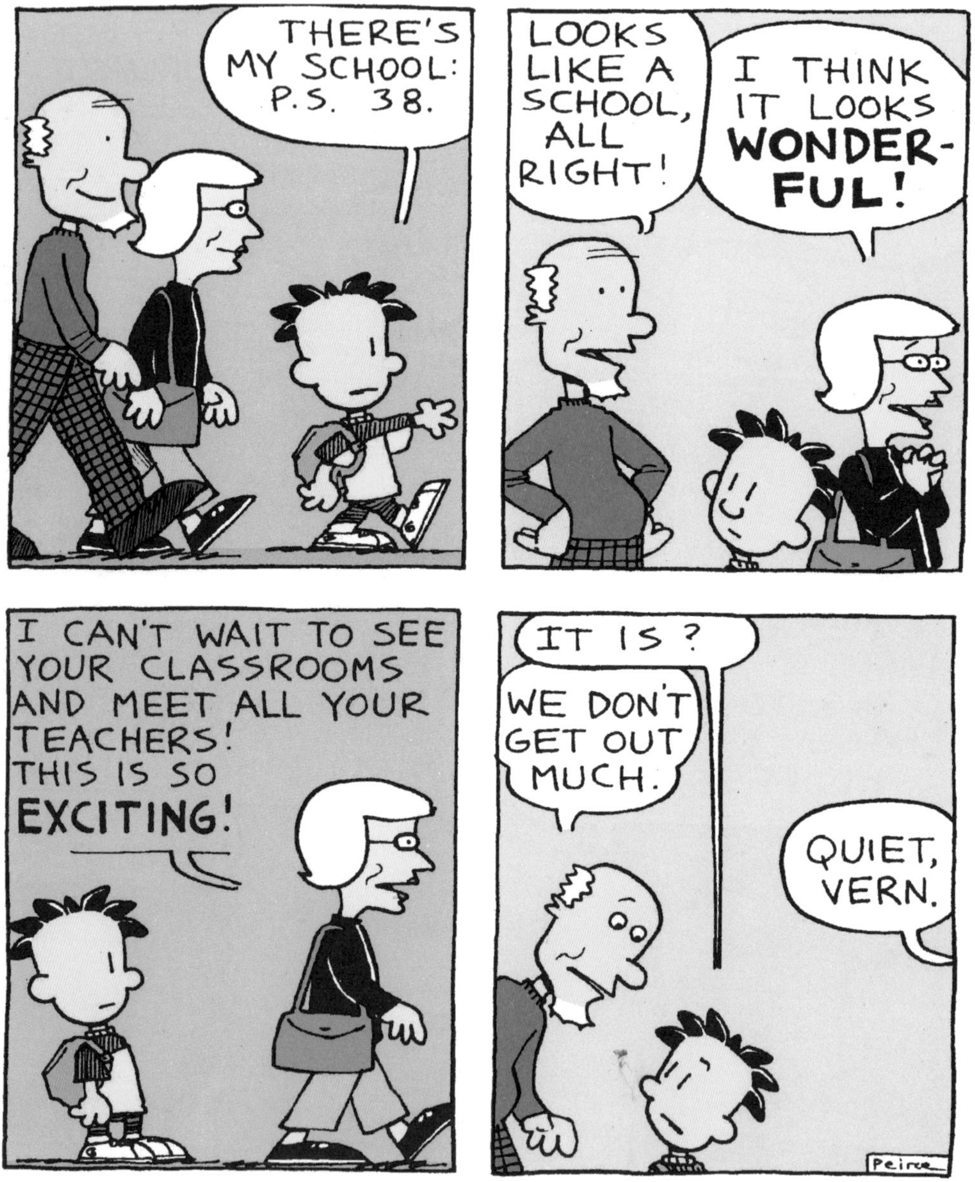
THERE'S MY SCHOOL: P.S. 38.
LOOKS LIKE A SCHOOL, ALL RIGHT!
I THINK IT LOOKS **WONDERFUL!**
I CAN'T WAIT TO SEE YOUR CLASSROOMS AND MEET ALL YOUR TEACHERS! THIS IS SO **EXCITING!**
IT IS?
WE DON'T GET OUT MUCH.
QUIET, VERN.
Peirce

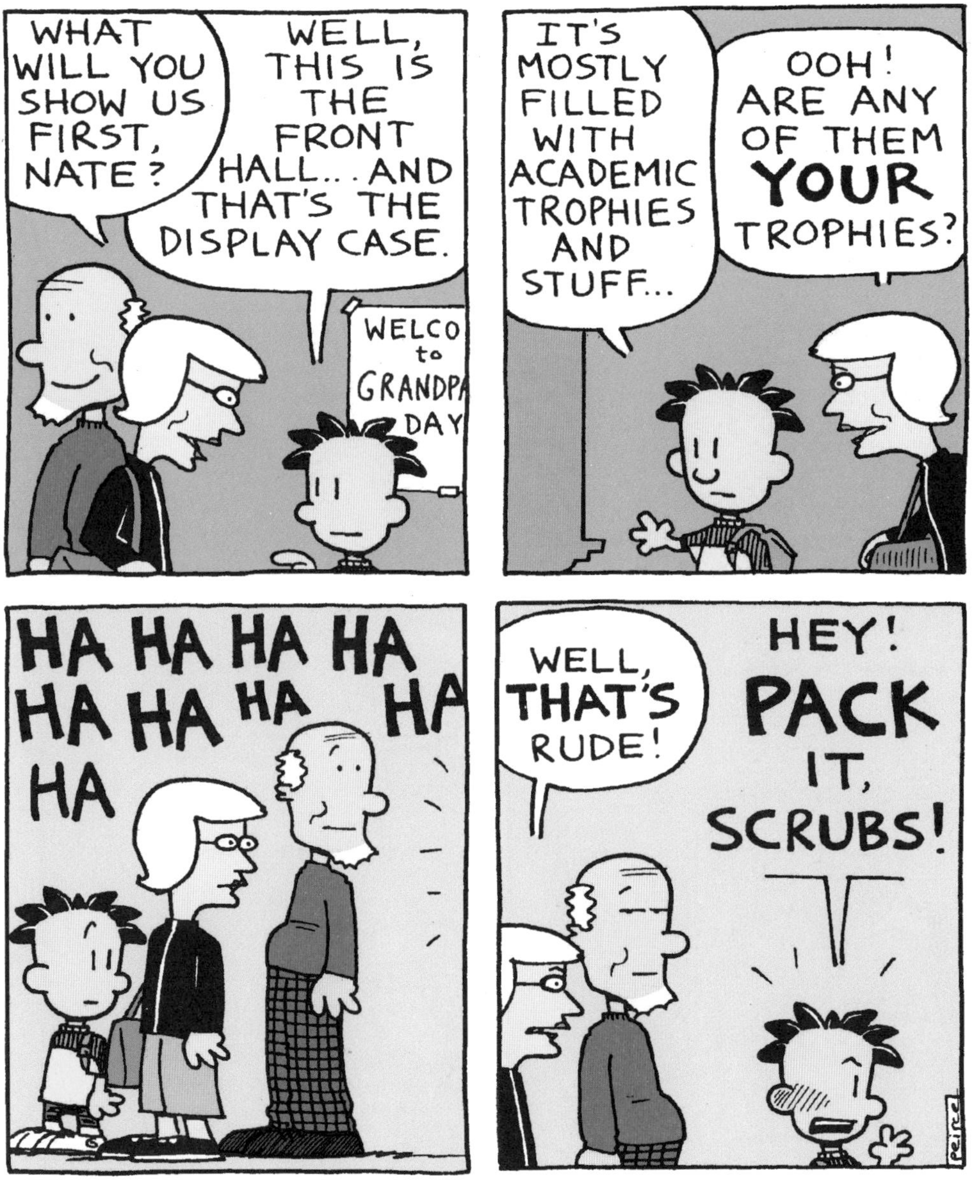
WHAT WILL YOU SHOW US FIRST, NATE?
WELL, THIS IS THE FRONT HALL... AND THAT'S THE DISPLAY CASE.
WELCO to GRANDPA DAY
IT'S MOSTLY FILLED WITH ACADEMIC TROPHIES AND STUFF...
OOH! ARE ANY OF THEM **YOUR** TROPHIES?
HA HA HA HA HA HA HA HA HA
HA
WELL, THAT'S RUDE!
HEY! PACK IT, SCRUBS!
peirce

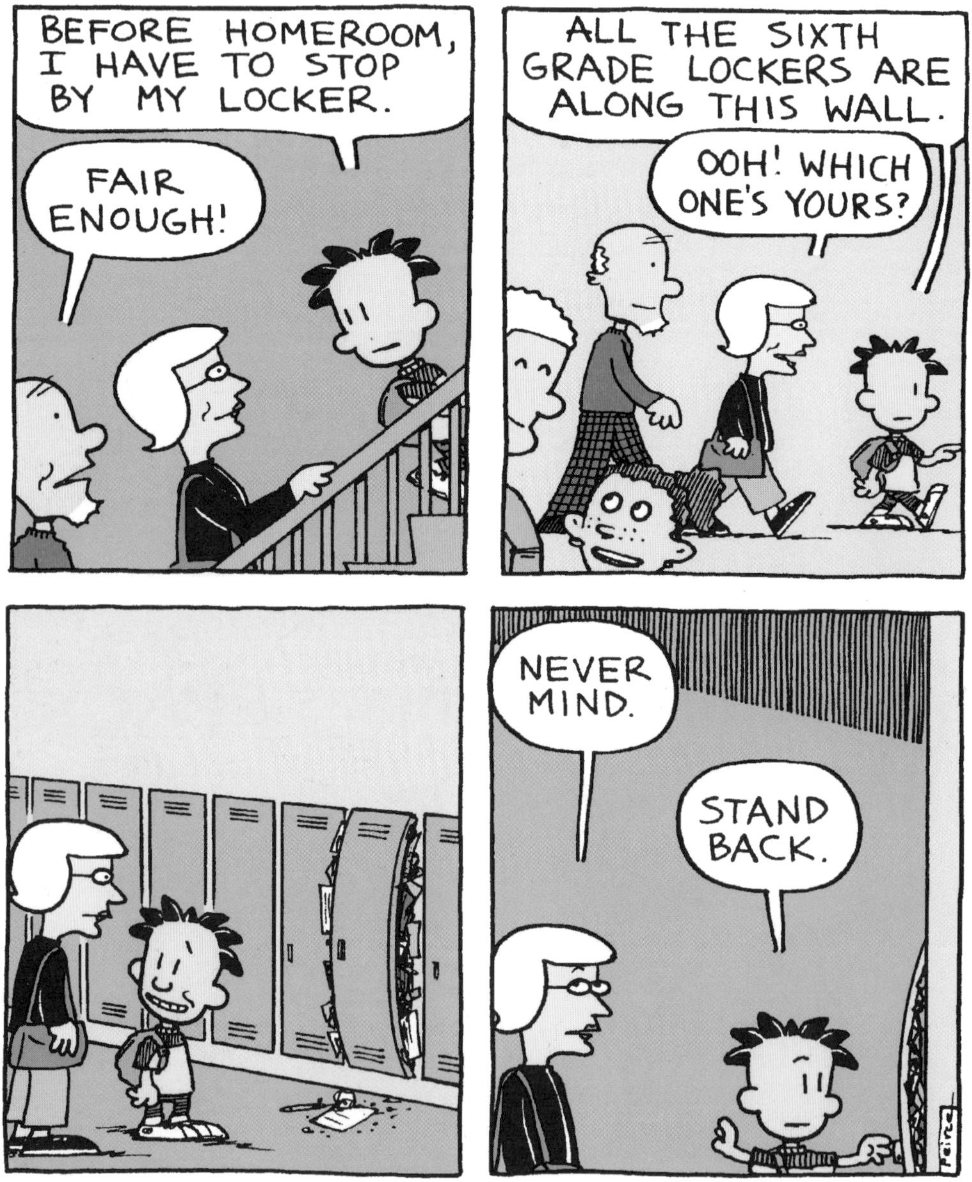
BEFORE HOMEROOM, I HAVE TO STOP BY MY LOCKER.
FAIR ENOUGH!
ALL THE SIXTH GRADE LOCKERS ARE ALONG THIS WALL.
OOH! WHICH ONE'S YOURS?
NEVER MIND.
STAND BACK.

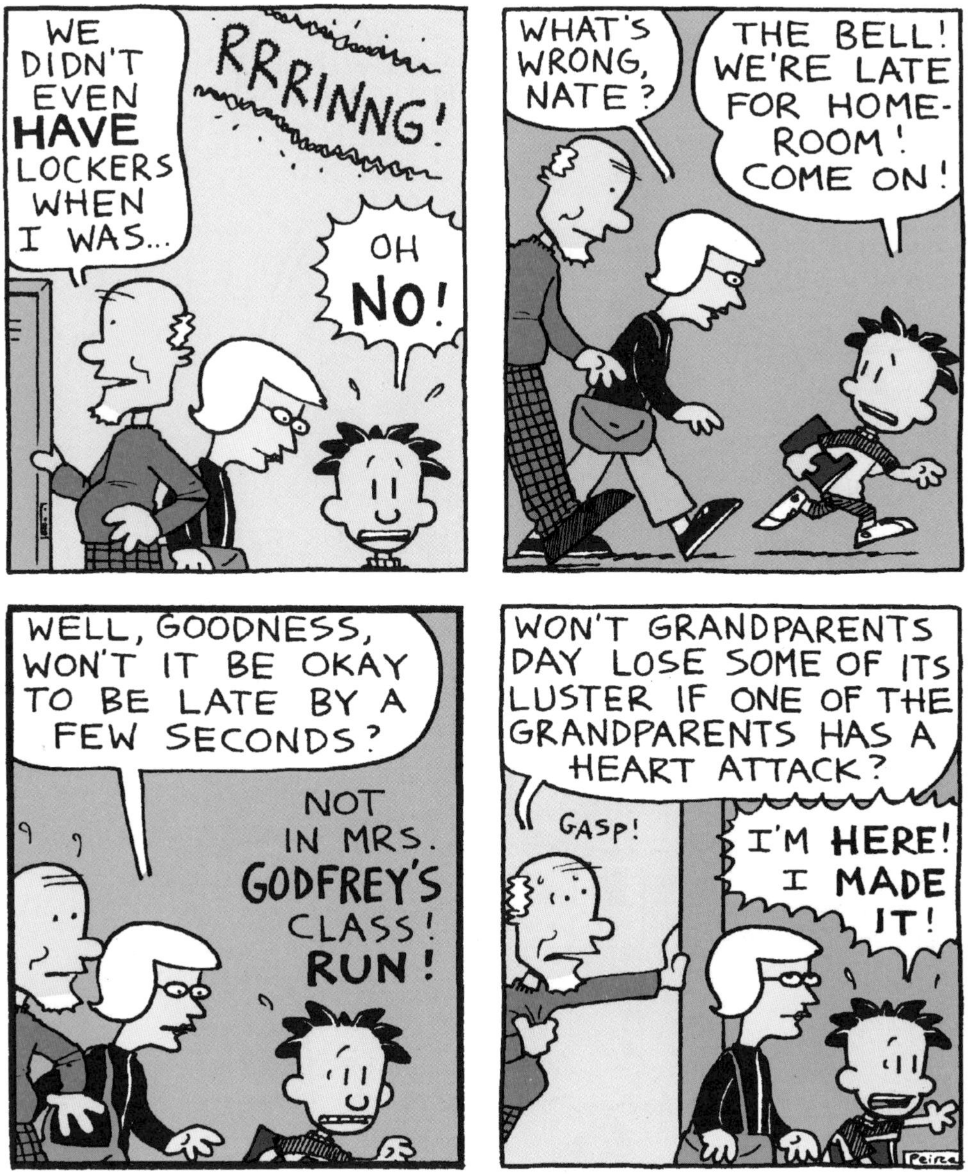
WE DIDN'T EVEN HAVE LOCKERS WHEN I WAS...
RRRINNG!
OH NO!
WHAT'S WRONG, NATE?
THE BELL! WE'RE LATE FOR HOME-ROOM! COME ON!
WELL, GOODNESS, WON'T IT BE OKAY TO BE LATE BY A FEW SECONDS?
NOT IN MRS. GODFREY'S CLASS! RUN!
WON'T GRANDPARENTS DAY LOSE SOME OF ITS LUSTER IF ONE OF THE GRANDPARENTS HAS A HEART ATTACK?
GASP!
I'M HERE! I MADE IT!
Peirce

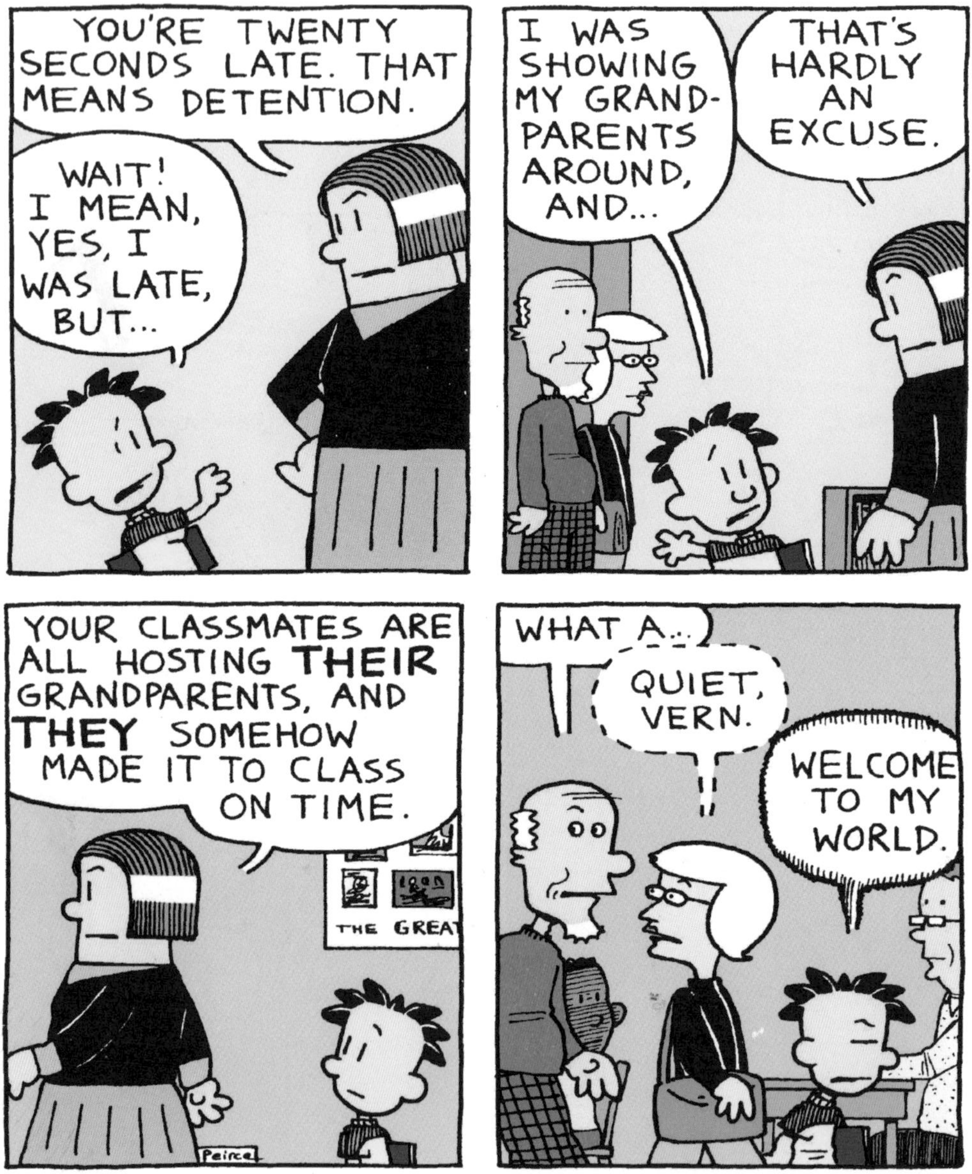
YOU'RE TWENTY SECONDS LATE. THAT MEANS DETENTION.
WAIT! I MEAN, YES, I WAS LATE, BUT...
I WAS SHOWING MY GRAND-PARENTS AROUND, AND...
THAT'S HARDLY AN EXCUSE.
YOUR CLASSMATES ARE ALL HOSTING **THEIR** GRANDPARENTS, AND **THEY** SOMEHOW MADE IT TO CLASS ON TIME.
THE GREAT
Peirce
WHAT A...
QUIET, VERN.
WELCOME TO MY WORLD.

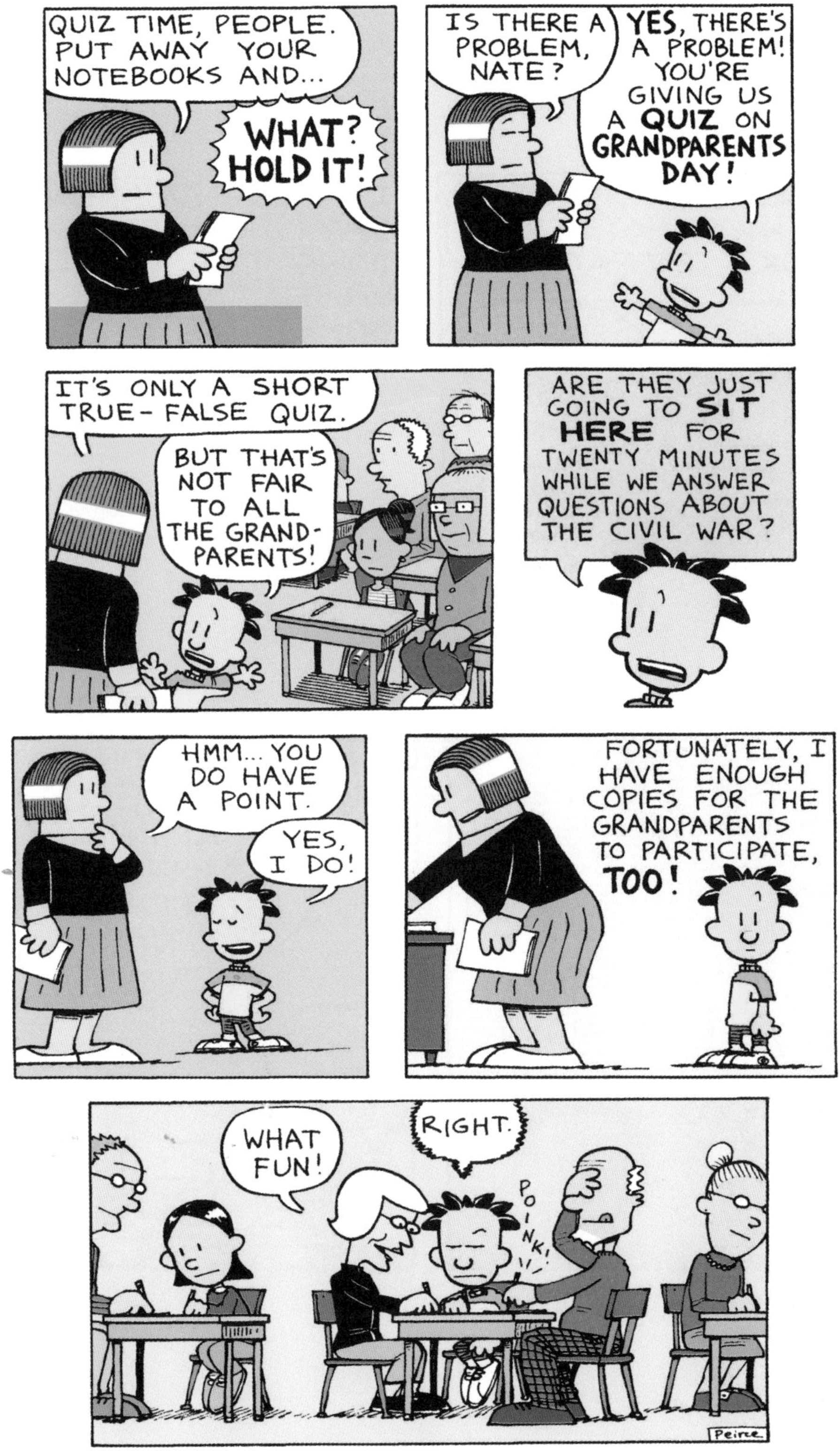

QUIZ TIME, PEOPLE. PUT AWAY YOUR NOTEBOOKS AND...
WHAT? HOLD IT!
IS THERE A PROBLEM, NATE?
YES, THERE'S A PROBLEM! YOU'RE GIVING US A QUIZ ON GRANDPARENTS DAY!
IT'S ONLY A SHORT TRUE-FALSE QUIZ.
BUT THAT'S NOT FAIR TO ALL THE GRAND-PARENTS!
ARE THEY JUST GOING TO SIT HERE FOR TWENTY MINUTES WHILE WE ANSWER QUESTIONS ABOUT THE CIVIL WAR?
HMM... YOU DO HAVE A POINT.
YES, I DO!
FORTUNATELY, I HAVE ENOUGH COPIES FOR THE GRANDPARENTS TO PARTICIPATE, TOO!
WHAT FUN!
RIGHT.
POINK!
Peirce

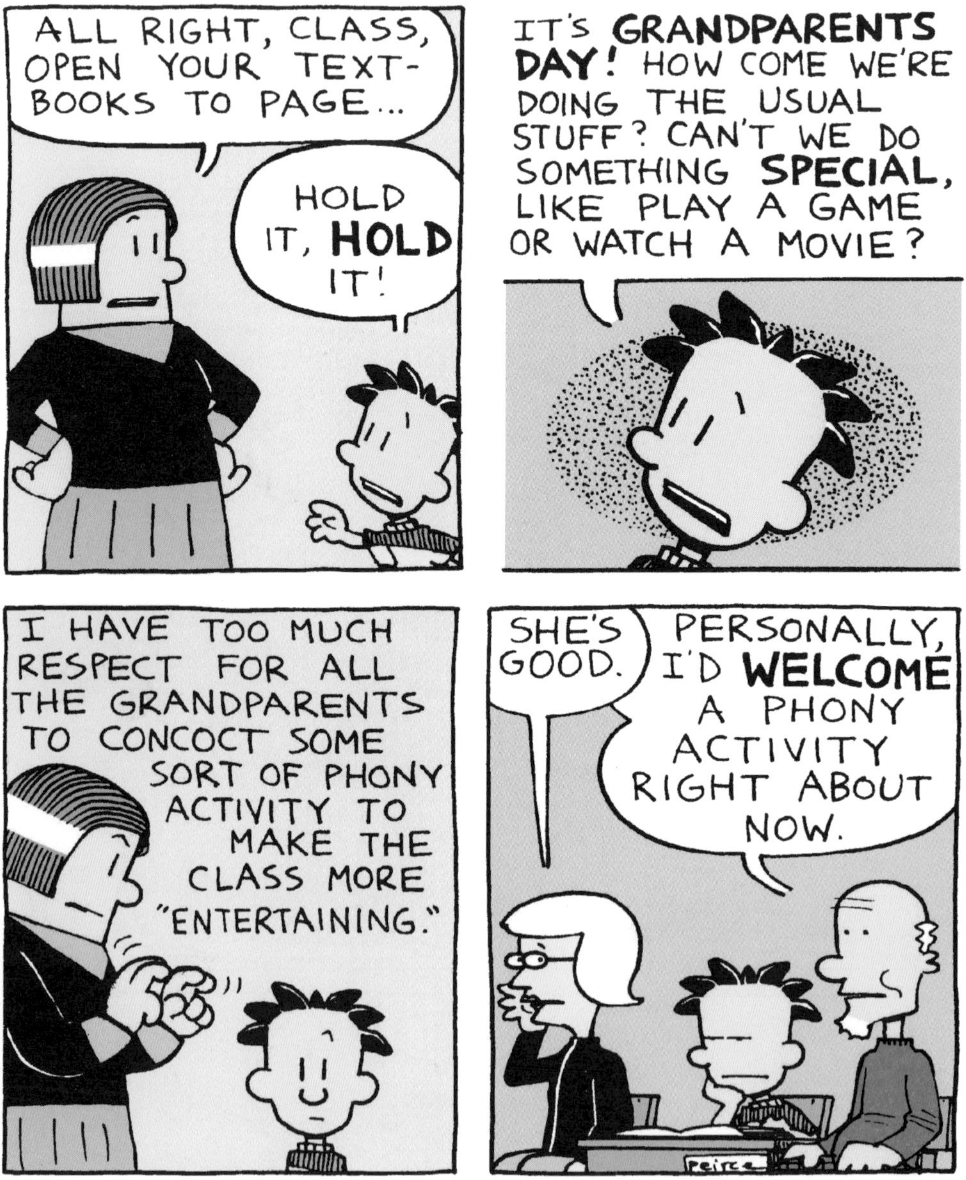
ALL RIGHT, CLASS, OPEN YOUR TEXT-BOOKS TO PAGE...
HOLD IT, **HOLD** IT!
IT'S **GRANDPARENTS DAY!** HOW COME WE'RE DOING THE USUAL STUFF? CAN'T WE DO SOMETHING **SPECIAL**, LIKE PLAY A GAME OR WATCH A MOVIE?
I HAVE TOO MUCH RESPECT FOR ALL THE GRANDPARENTS TO CONCOCT SOME SORT OF PHONY ACTIVITY TO MAKE THE CLASS MORE "ENTERTAINING."
SHE'S GOOD.
PERSONALLY, I'D **WELCOME** A PHONY ACTIVITY RIGHT ABOUT NOW.
PEIRCE

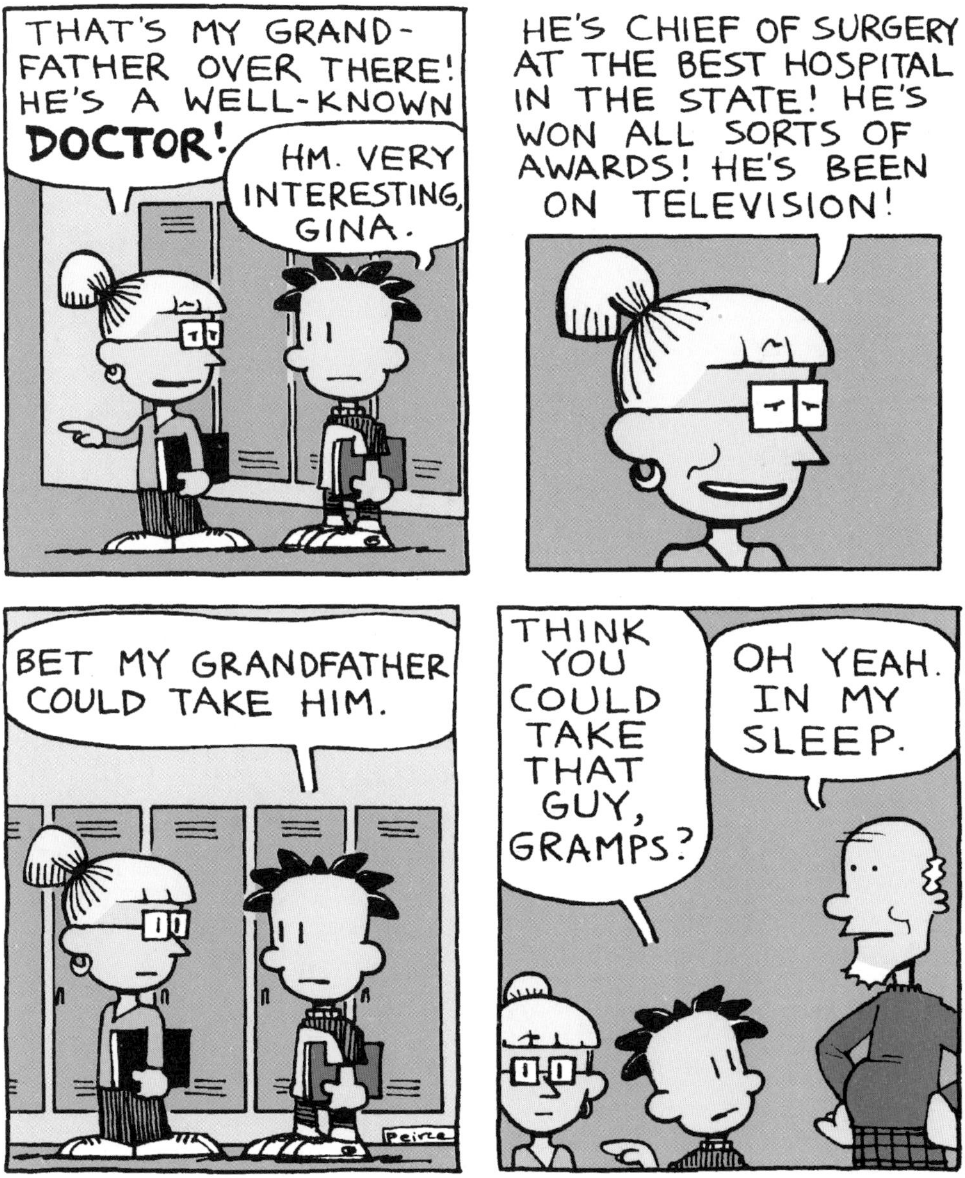
THAT'S MY GRANDFATHER OVER THERE! HE'S A WELL-KNOWN **DOCTOR**!
HM. VERY INTERESTING, GINA.
HE'S CHIEF OF SURGERY AT THE BEST HOSPITAL IN THE STATE! HE'S WON ALL SORTS OF AWARDS! HE'S BEEN ON TELEVISION!
BET MY GRANDFATHER COULD TAKE HIM.
THINK YOU COULD TAKE THAT GUY, GRAMPS?
OH YEAH. IN MY SLEEP.
Peirce

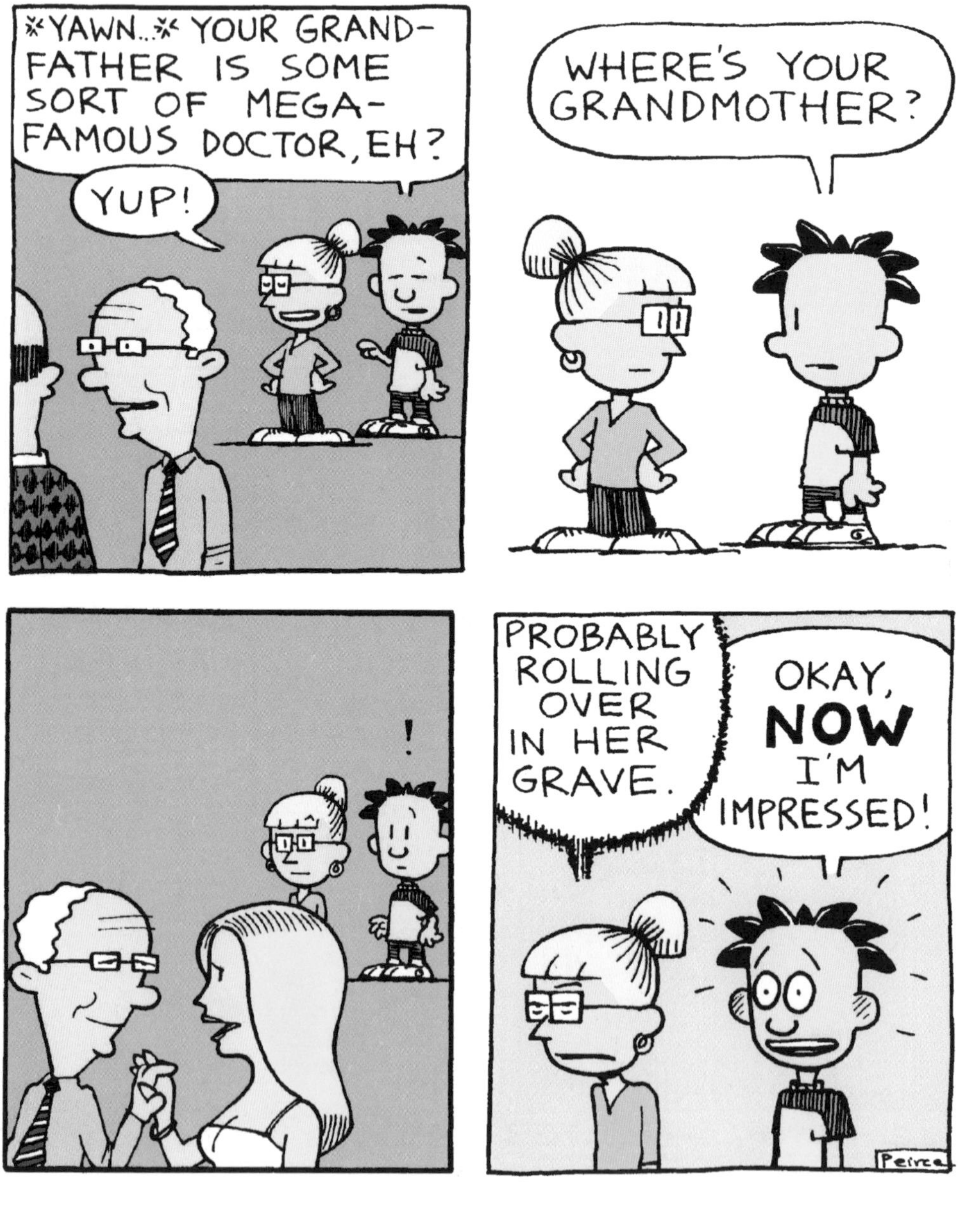
YAWN... YOUR GRAND-FATHER IS SOME SORT OF MEGA-FAMOUS DOCTOR, EH?
YUP!
WHERE'S YOUR GRANDMOTHER?
!
PROBABLY ROLLING OVER IN HER GRAVE.
OKAY, **NOW** I'M IMPRESSED!
Peirce

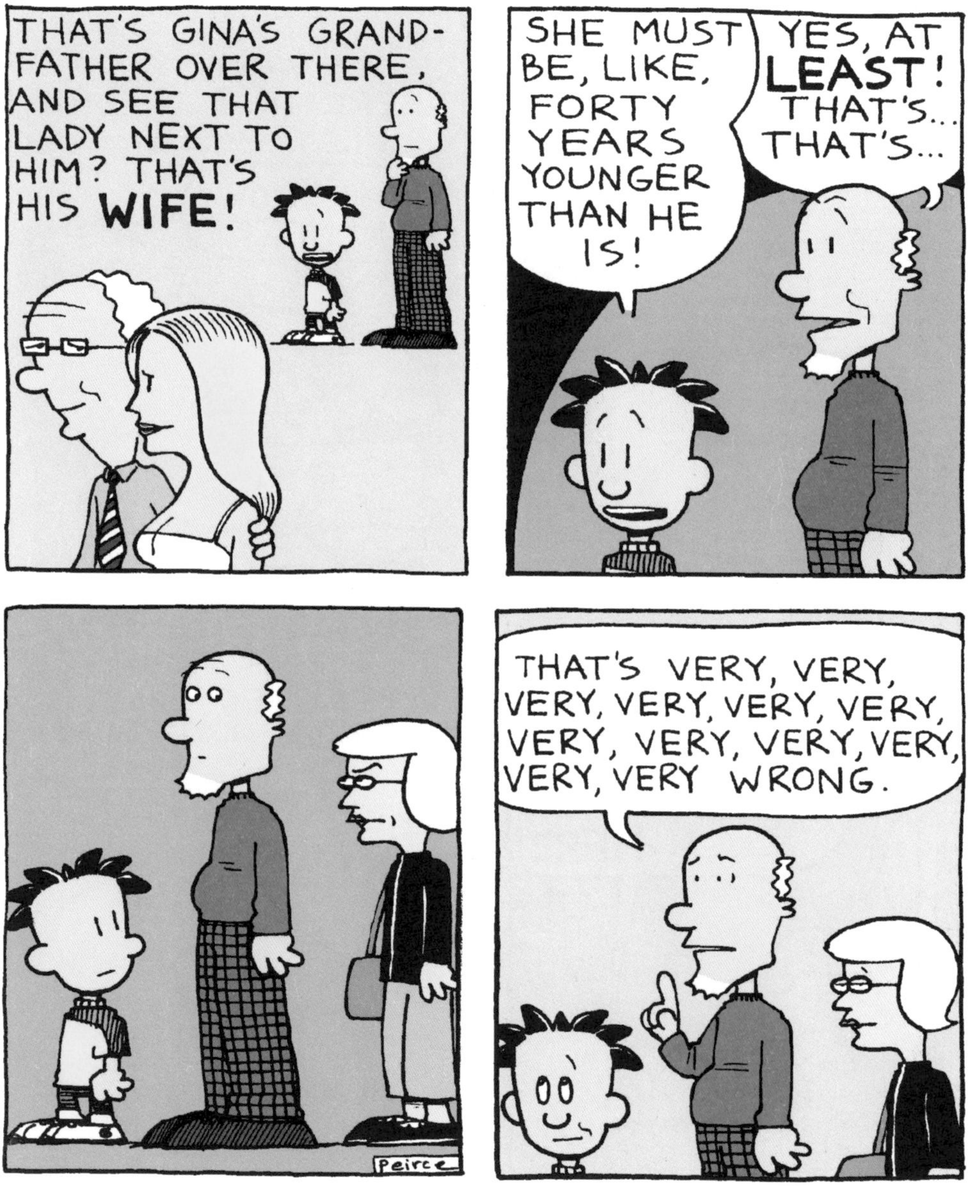
THAT'S GINA'S GRAND-FATHER OVER THERE, AND SEE THAT LADY NEXT TO HIM? THAT'S HIS **WIFE**!
SHE MUST BE, LIKE, FORTY YEARS YOUNGER THAN HE IS!
YES, AT **LEAST**! THAT'S... THAT'S...
THAT'S VERY, VERY, VERY, VERY, VERY, VERY, VERY, VERY, VERY, VERY, VERY, VERY WRONG.
Peirce

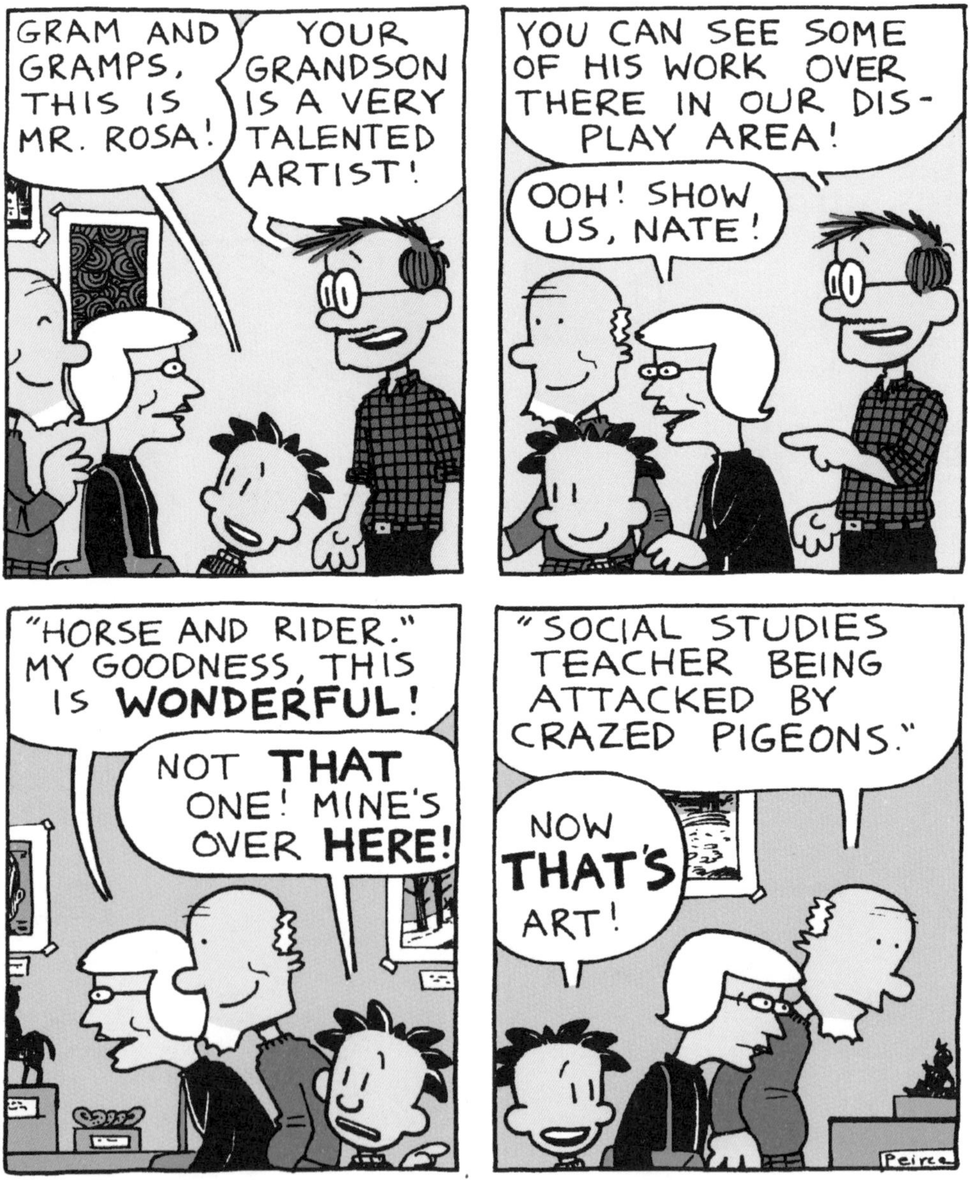
GRAM AND GRAMPS, THIS IS MR. ROSA!
YOUR GRANDSON IS A VERY TALENTED ARTIST!
YOU CAN SEE SOME OF HIS WORK OVER THERE IN OUR DIS-PLAY AREA!
OOH! SHOW US, NATE!
"HORSE AND RIDER." MY GOODNESS, THIS IS **WONDERFUL**!
NOT **THAT** ONE! MINE'S OVER **HERE**!
"SOCIAL STUDIES TEACHER BEING ATTACKED BY CRAZED PIGEONS."
NOW **THAT'S** ART!
Peirce

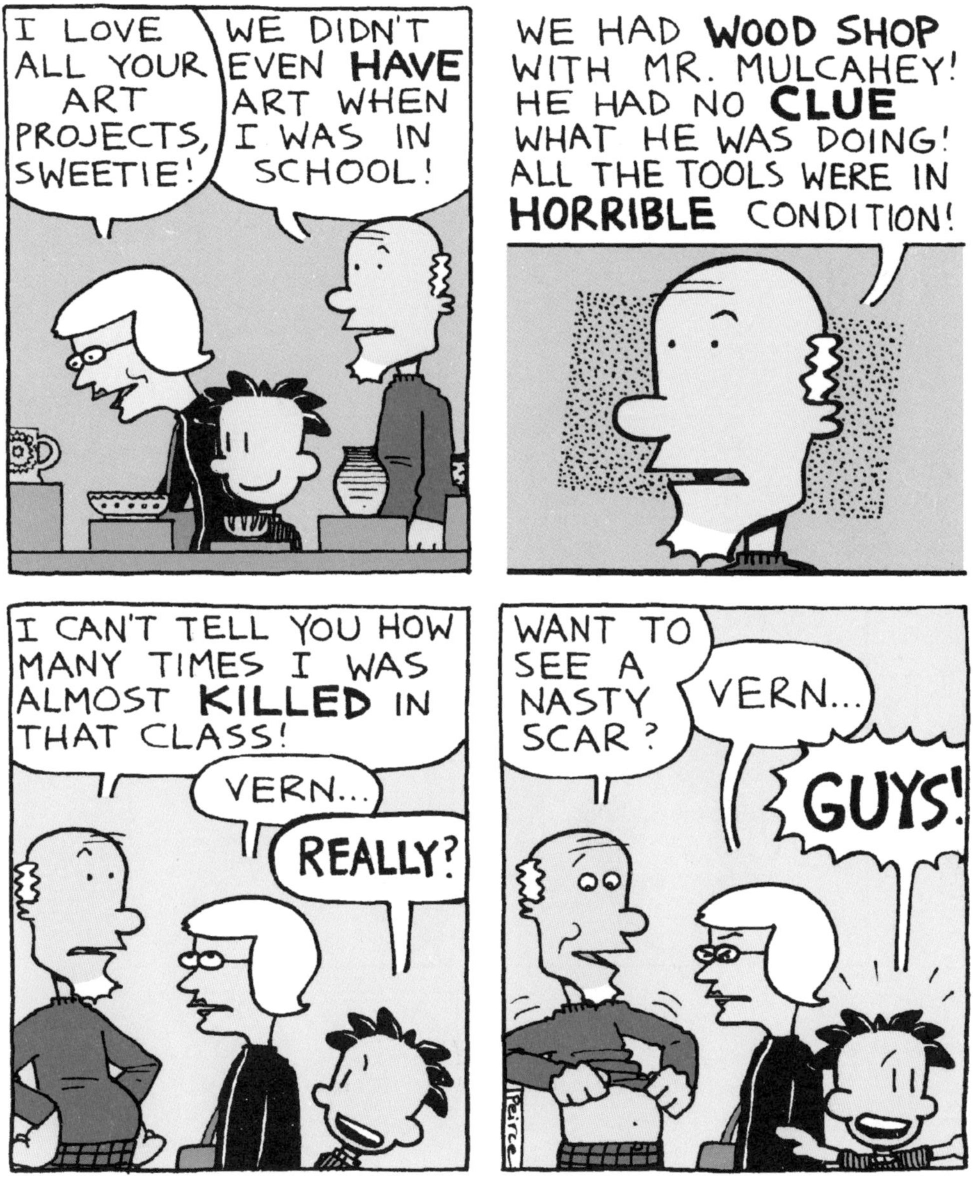
I LOVE ALL YOUR ART PROJECTS, SWEETIE!
WE DIDN'T EVEN HAVE ART WHEN I WAS IN SCHOOL!
WE HAD WOOD SHOP WITH MR. MULCAHEY! HE HAD NO CLUE WHAT HE WAS DOING! ALL THE TOOLS WERE IN HORRIBLE CONDITION!
I CAN'T TELL YOU HOW MANY TIMES I WAS ALMOST KILLED IN THAT CLASS!
VERN...
REALLY?
WANT TO SEE A NASTY SCAR?
VERN...
GUYS!
Peirce

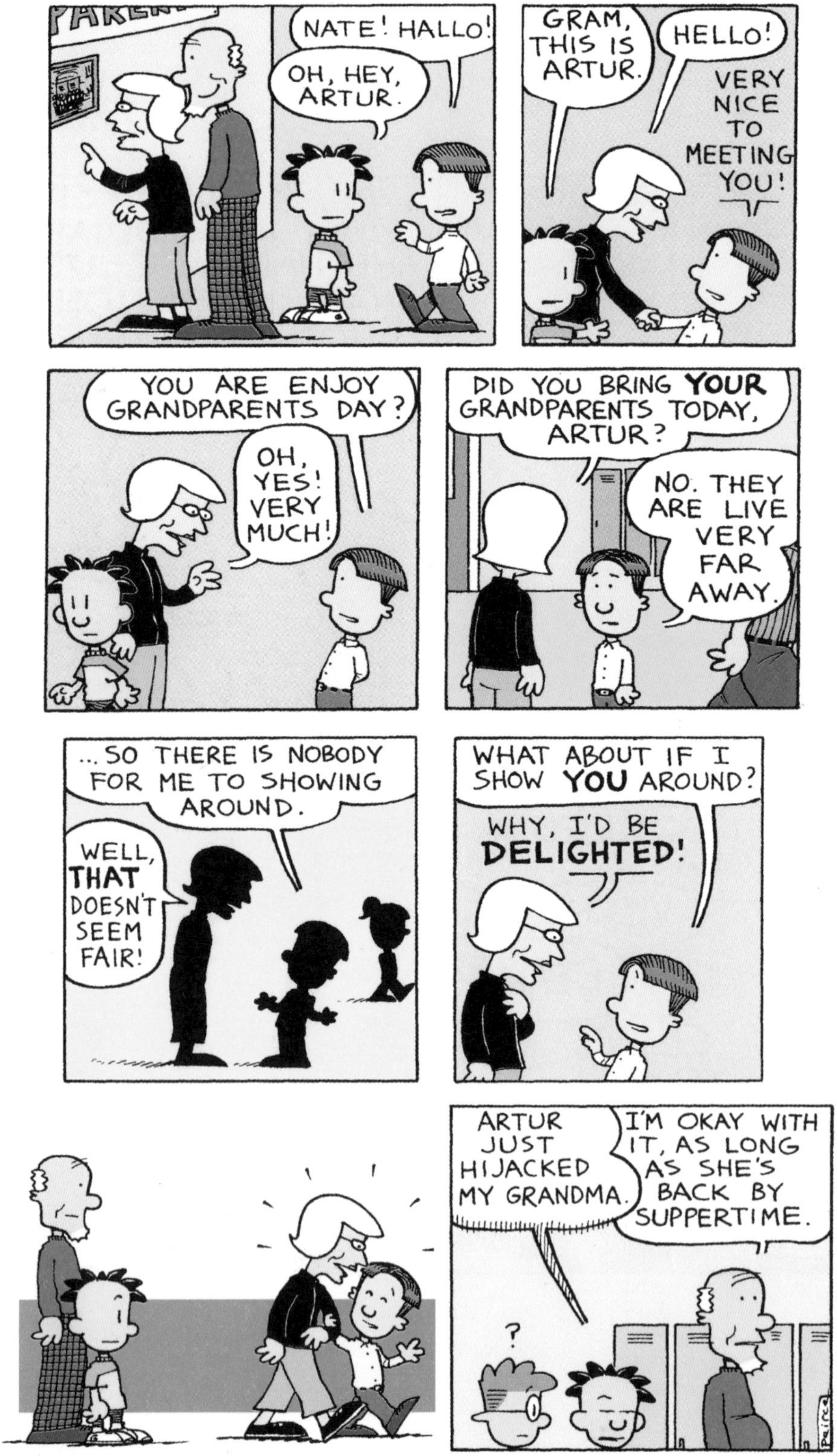
NATE! HALLO!
OH, HEY, ARTUR.
GRAM, THIS IS ARTUR.
HELLO!
VERY NICE TO MEETING YOU!
YOU ARE ENJOY GRANDPARENTS DAY?
OH, YES! VERY MUCH!
DID YOU BRING YOUR GRANDPARENTS TODAY, ARTUR?
NO. THEY ARE LIVE VERY FAR AWAY.
...SO THERE IS NOBODY FOR ME TO SHOWING AROUND.
WELL, THAT DOESN'T SEEM FAIR!
WHAT ABOUT IF I SHOW YOU AROUND?
WHY, I'D BE DELIGHTED!
ARTUR JUST HIJACKED MY GRANDMA.
I'M OKAY WITH IT, AS LONG AS SHE'S BACK BY SUPPERTIME.
?
PEIRCE

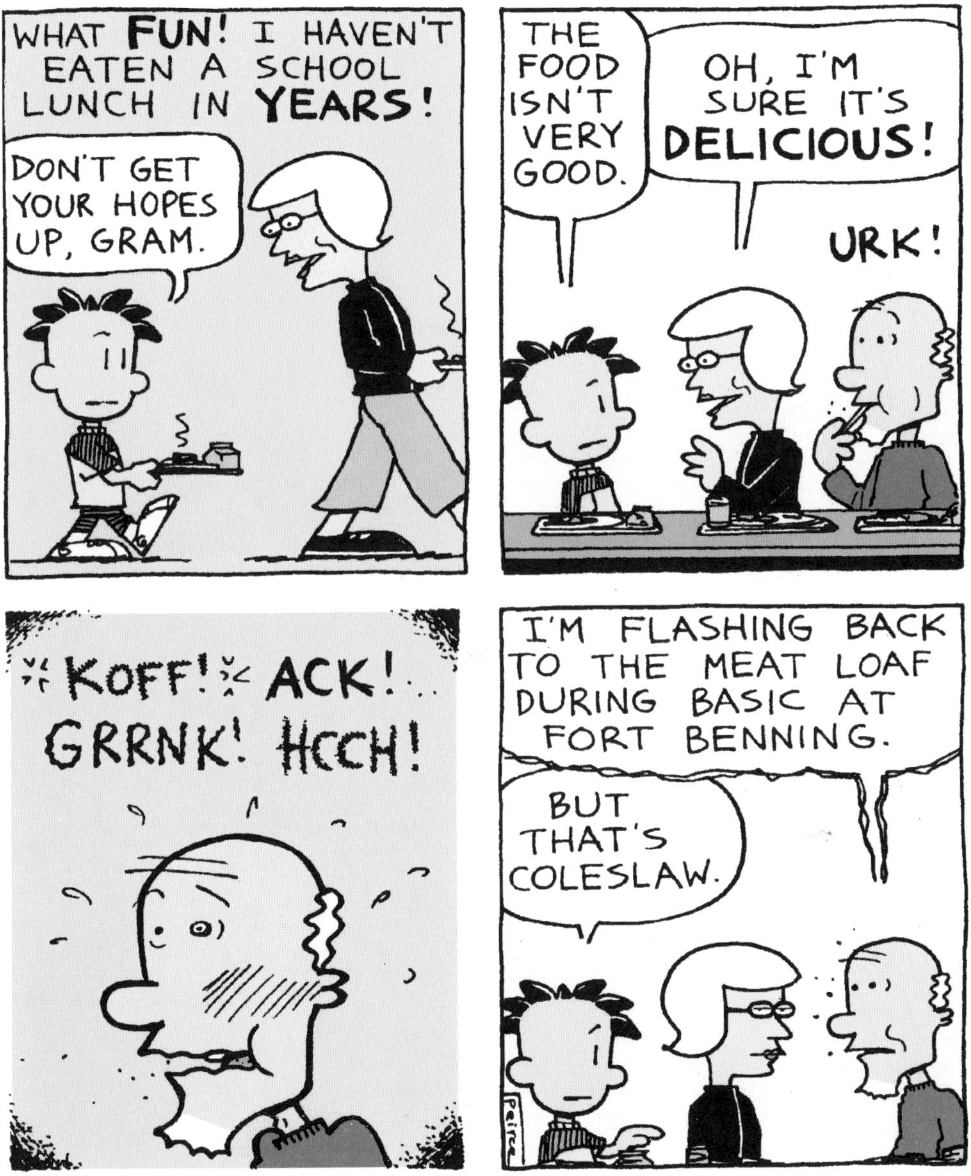
WHAT FUN! I HAVEN'T EATEN A SCHOOL LUNCH IN YEARS!
DON'T GET YOUR HOPES UP, GRAM.
THE FOOD ISN'T VERY GOOD.
OH, I'M SURE IT'S DELICIOUS!
URK!
KOFF! ACK!
GRRNK! HCCH!
I'M FLASHING BACK TO THE MEAT LOAF DURING BASIC AT FORT BENNING.
BUT THAT'S COLESLAW.

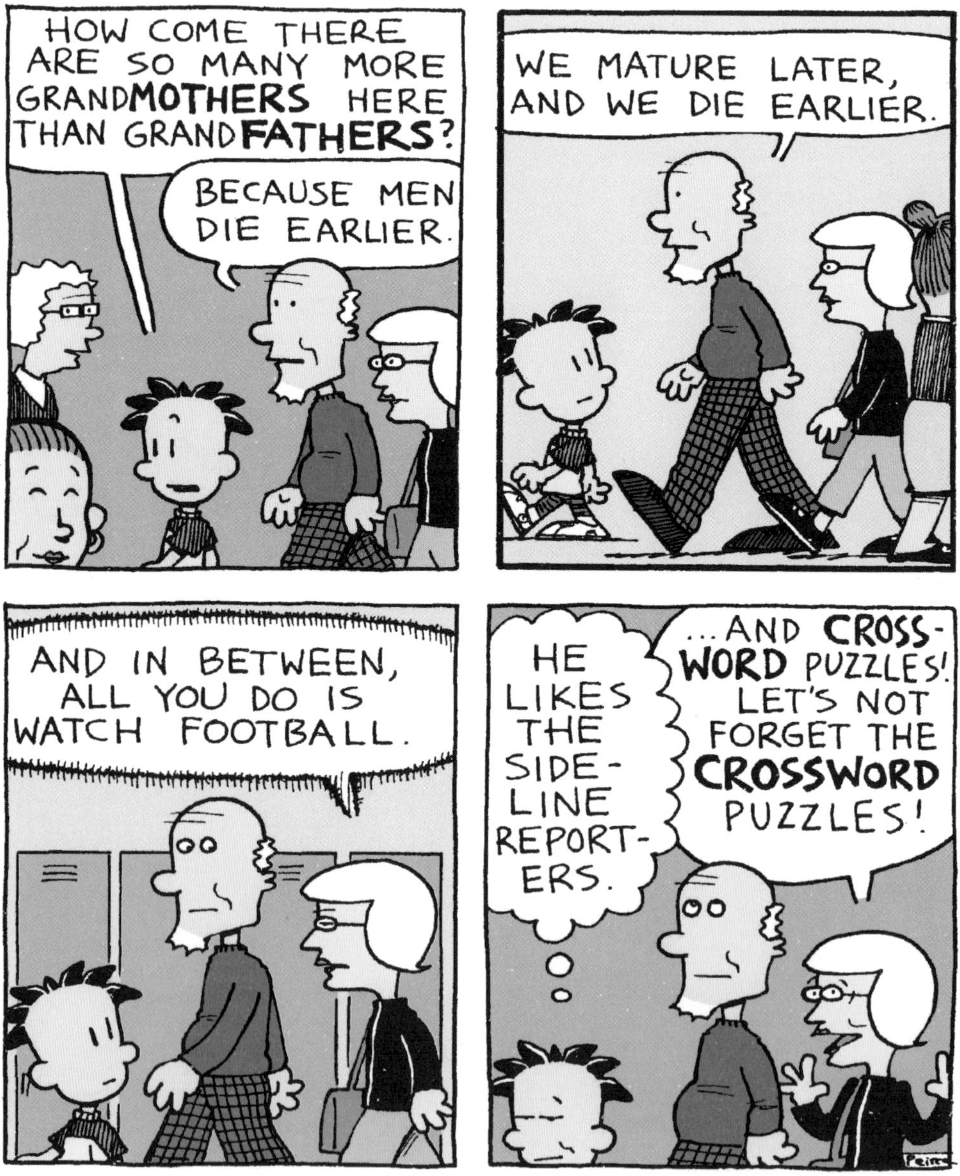

HOW COME THERE ARE SO MANY MORE GRANDMOTHERS HERE THAN GRANDFATHERS?
BECAUSE MEN DIE EARLIER.
WE MATURE LATER, AND WE DIE EARLIER.
AND IN BETWEEN, ALL YOU DO IS WATCH FOOTBALL.
HE LIKES THE SIDE-LINE REPORT-ERS.
...AND CROSS-WORD PUZZLES! LET'S NOT FORGET THE CROSSWORD PUZZLES!

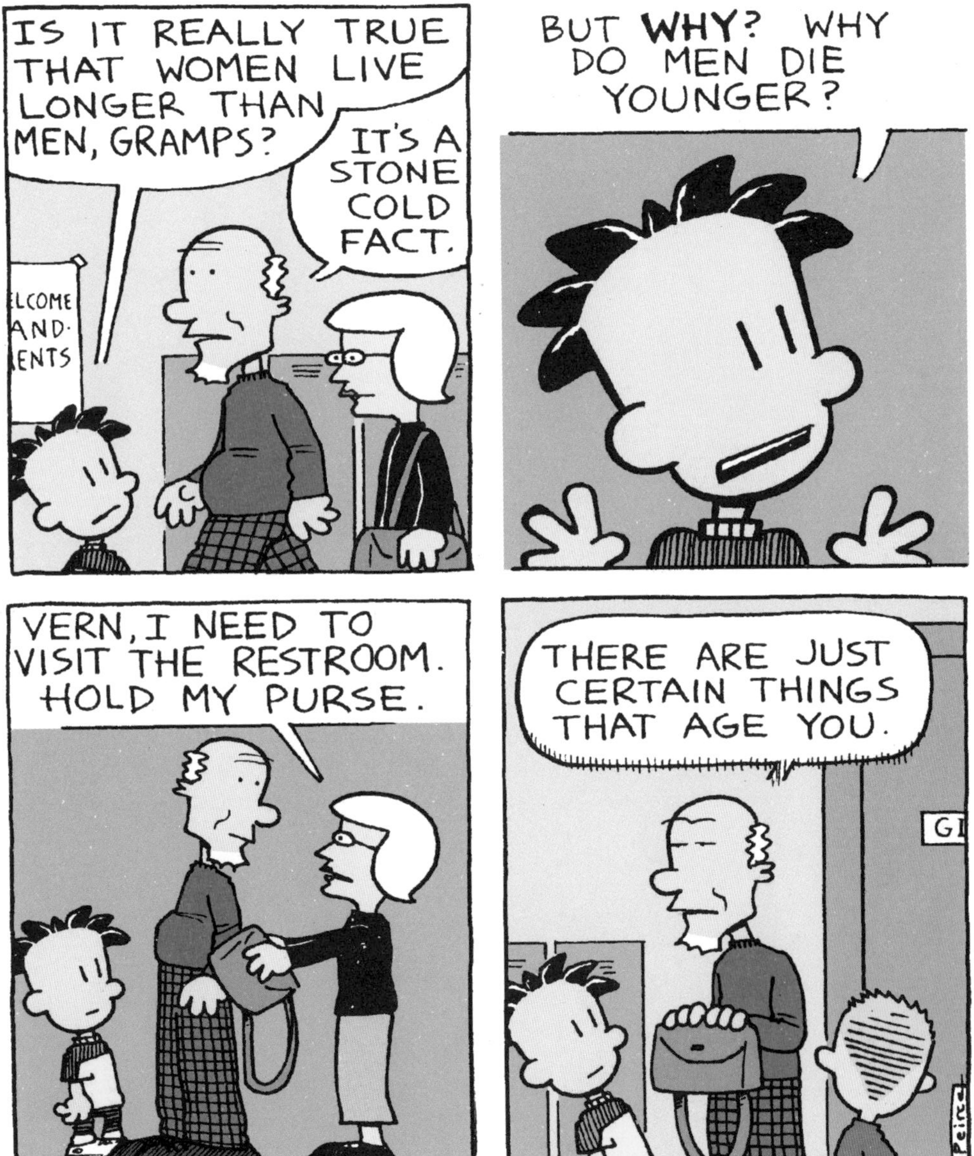
IS IT REALLY TRUE THAT WOMEN LIVE LONGER THAN MEN, GRAMPS?
IT'S A STONE COLD FACT.
BUT WHY? WHY DO MEN DIE YOUNGER?
VERN, I NEED TO VISIT THE RESTROOM. HOLD MY PURSE.
THERE ARE JUST CERTAIN THINGS THAT AGE YOU.
Peirce

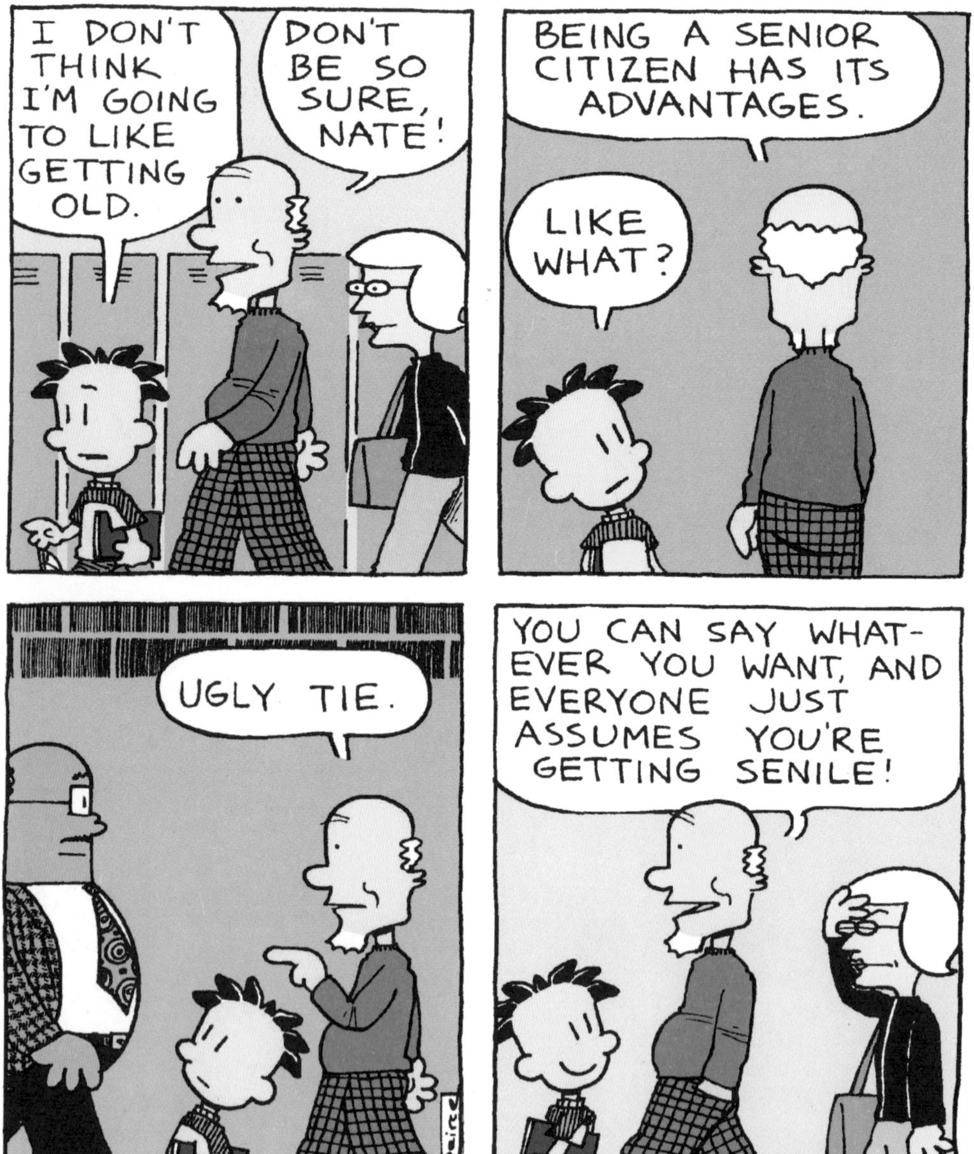
I DON'T THINK I'M GOING TO LIKE GETTING OLD.
DON'T BE SO SURE, NATE!
BEING A SENIOR CITIZEN HAS ITS ADVANTAGES.
LIKE WHAT?
UGLY TIE.
YOU CAN SAY WHAT-EVER YOU WANT, AND EVERYONE JUST ASSUMES YOU'RE GETTING SENILE!
PEIRCE

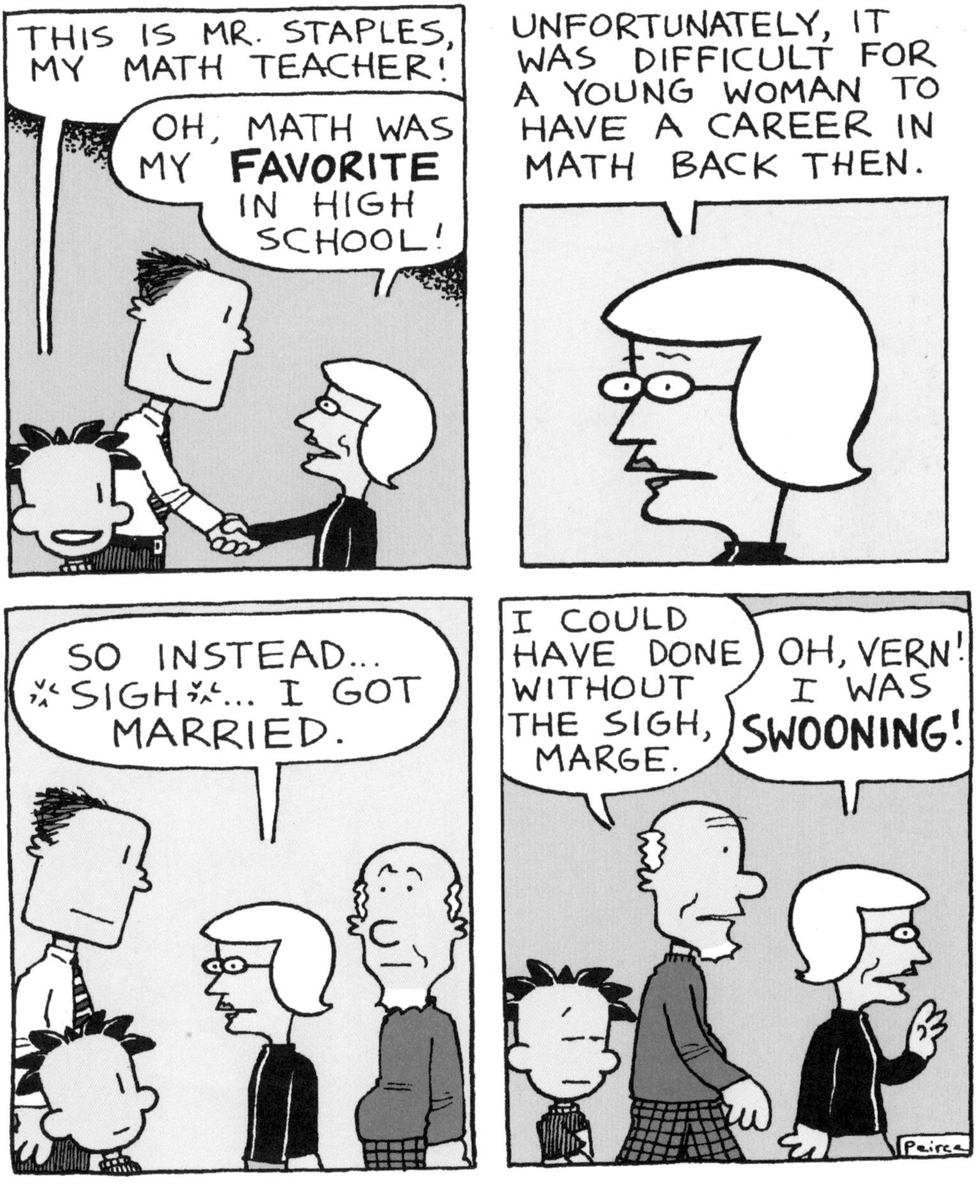
THIS IS MR. STAPLES, MY MATH TEACHER!
OH, MATH WAS MY **FAVORITE** IN HIGH SCHOOL!
UNFORTUNATELY, IT WAS DIFFICULT FOR A YOUNG WOMAN TO HAVE A CAREER IN MATH BACK THEN.
SO INSTEAD... *SIGH*... I GOT MARRIED.
I COULD HAVE DONE WITHOUT THE SIGH, MARGE.
OH, VERN! I WAS **SWOONING**!
Peirce

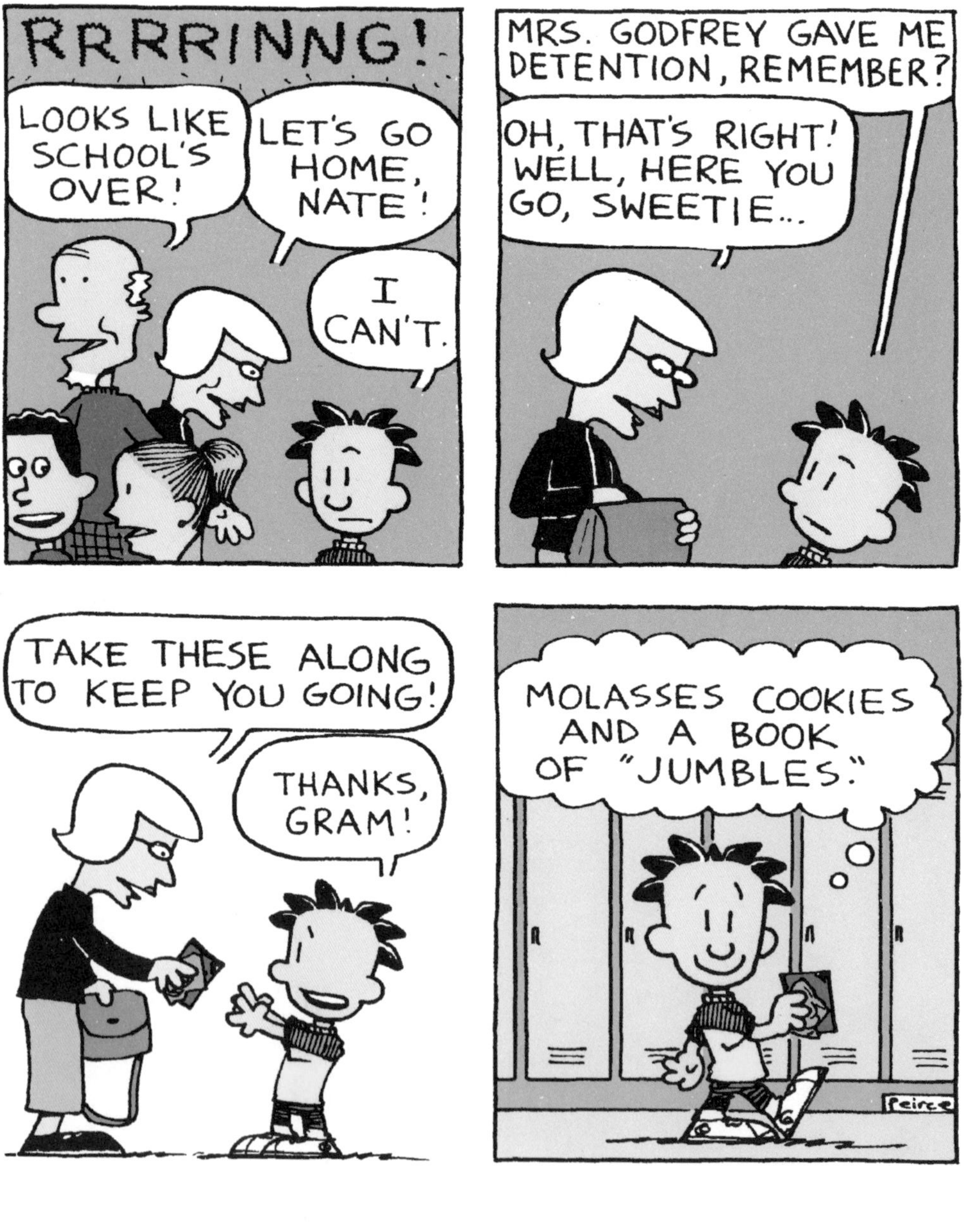
RRRRINNG!
LOOKS LIKE SCHOOL'S OVER!
LET'S GO HOME, NATE!
I CAN'T.
MRS. GODFREY GAVE ME DETENTION, REMEMBER?
OH, THAT'S RIGHT! WELL, HERE YOU GO, SWEETIE...
TAKE THESE ALONG TO KEEP YOU GOING!
THANKS, GRAM!
MOLASSES COOKIES AND A BOOK OF "JUMBLES."
Peirce

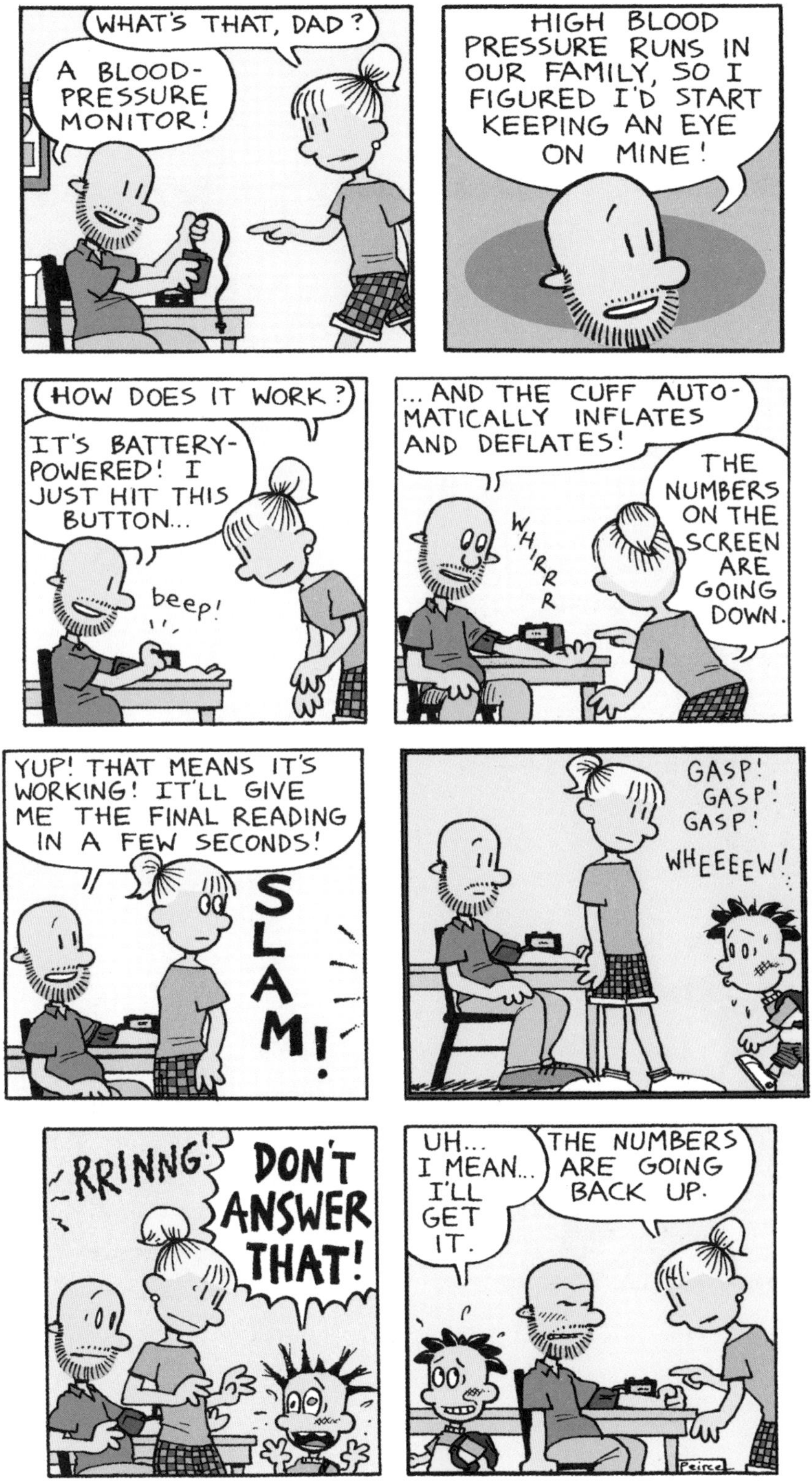
WHAT'S THAT, DAD?
A BLOOD-PRESSURE MONITOR!
HIGH BLOOD PRESSURE RUNS IN OUR FAMILY, SO I FIGURED I'D START KEEPING AN EYE ON MINE!
HOW DOES IT WORK?
IT'S BATTERY-POWERED! I JUST HIT THIS BUTTON...
beep!
...AND THE CUFF AUTO-MATICALLY INFLATES AND DEFLATES!
WHIRRR
THE NUMBERS ON THE SCREEN ARE GOING DOWN.
YUP! THAT MEANS IT'S WORKING! IT'LL GIVE ME THE FINAL READING IN A FEW SECONDS!
SLAM!
GASP! GASP! GASP!
WHEEEEW!
RRINNG!
DON'T ANSWER THAT!
UH... I MEAN... I'LL GET IT.
THE NUMBERS ARE GOING BACK UP.
Peirce

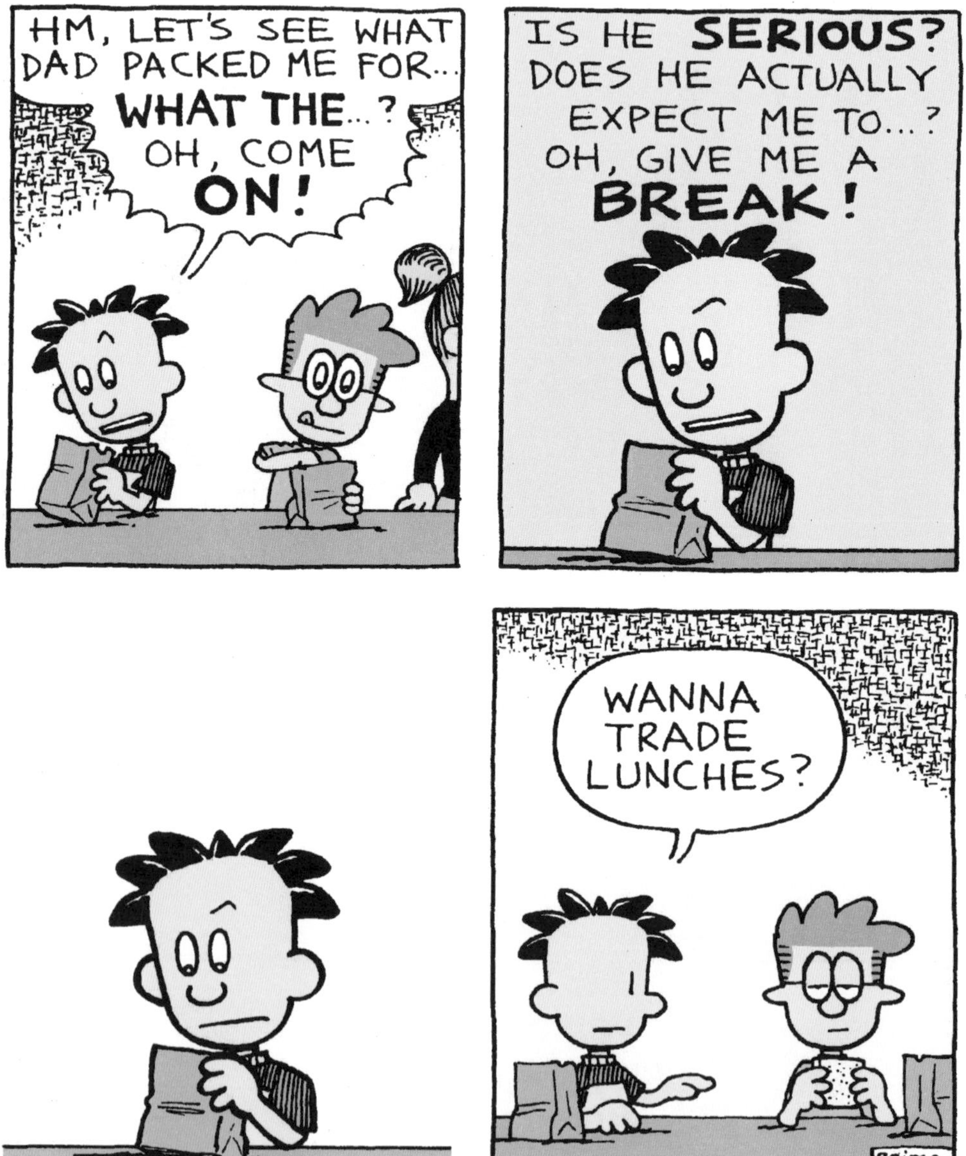
HM, LET'S SEE WHAT DAD PACKED ME FOR...
WHAT THE...? OH, COME ON!
IS HE SERIOUS? DOES HE ACTUALLY EXPECT ME TO...? OH, GIVE ME A BREAK!
WANNA TRADE LUNCHES?
peirce

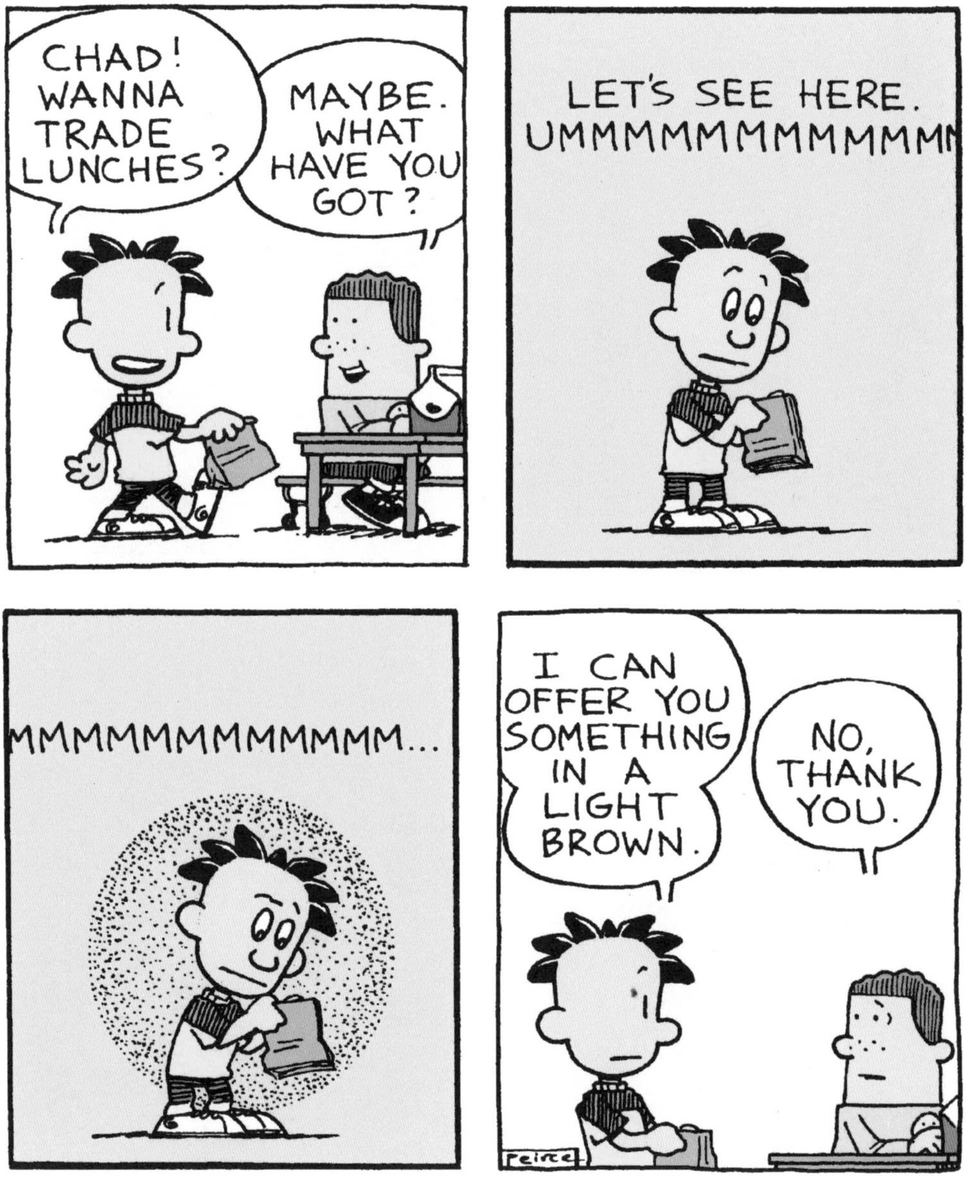
CHAD! WANNA TRADE LUNCHES?
MAYBE. WHAT HAVE YOU GOT?
LET'S SEE HERE. UMMMMMMMMMMMM
MMMMMMMMMMMM...
I CAN OFFER YOU SOMETHING IN A LIGHT BROWN.
NO, THANK YOU.
peirce

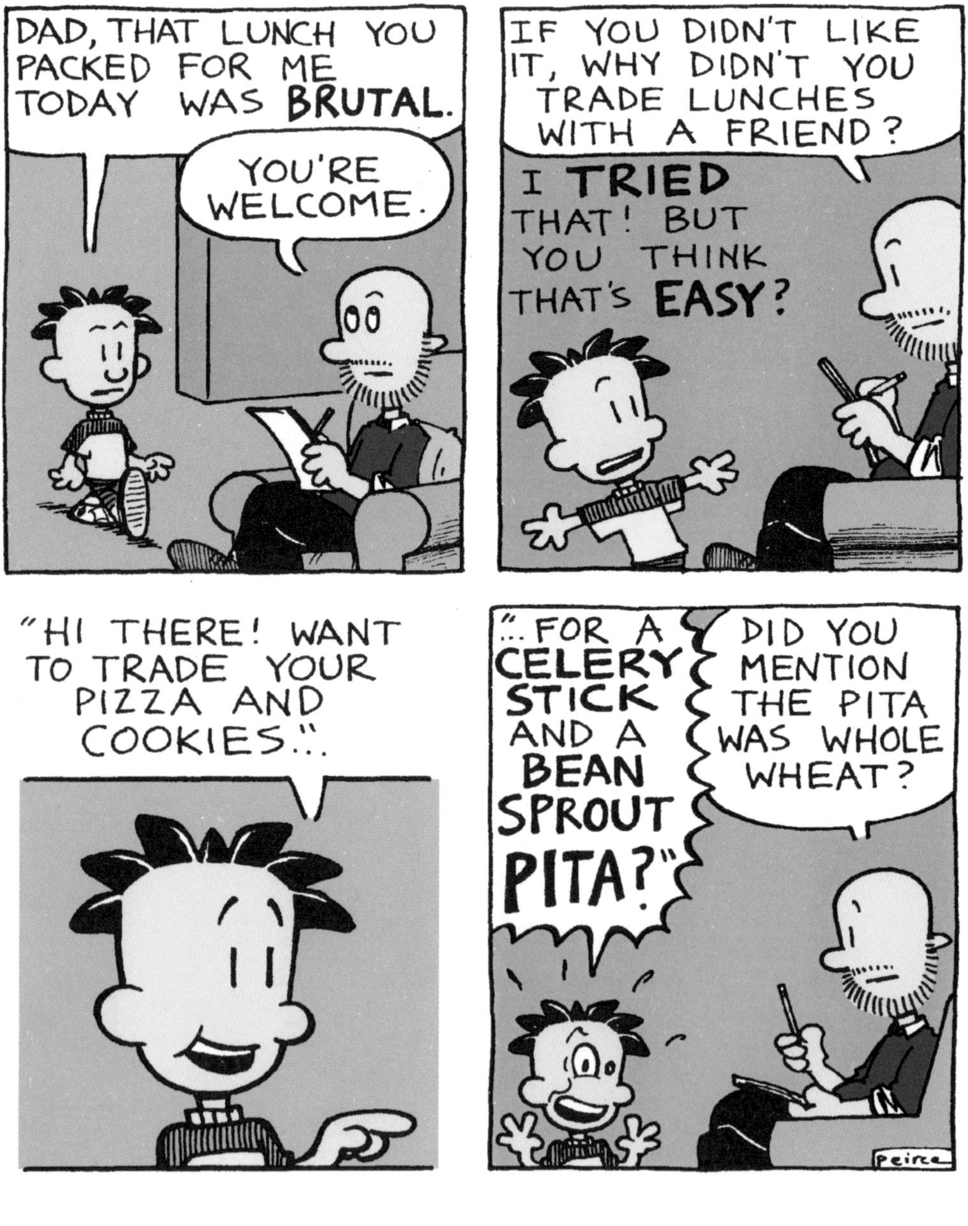

DAD, THAT LUNCH YOU PACKED FOR ME TODAY WAS **BRUTAL**.
YOU'RE WELCOME.
IF YOU DIDN'T LIKE IT, WHY DIDN'T YOU TRADE LUNCHES WITH A FRIEND?
I **TRIED** THAT! BUT YOU THINK THAT'S **EASY**?
"HI THERE! WANT TO TRADE YOUR PIZZA AND COOKIES..."
"...FOR A **CELERY STICK** AND A **BEAN SPROUT PITA?**"
DID YOU MENTION THE PITA WAS WHOLE WHEAT?
peirce

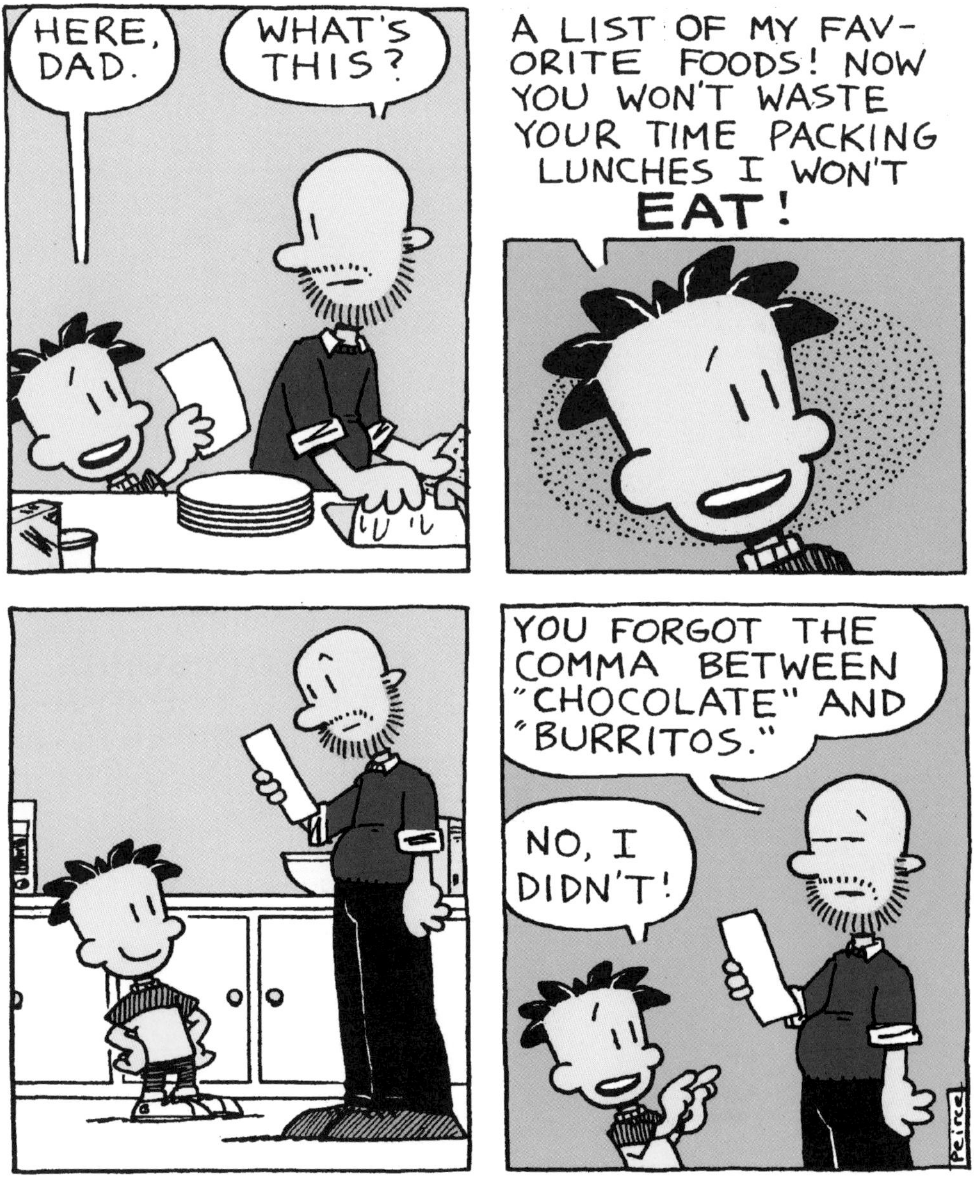
HERE, DAD.
WHAT'S THIS?
A LIST OF MY FAVORITE FOODS! NOW YOU WON'T WASTE YOUR TIME PACKING LUNCHES I WON'T **EAT**!
YOU FORGOT THE COMMA BETWEEN "CHOCOLATE" AND "BURRITOS."
NO, I DIDN'T!
Peirce

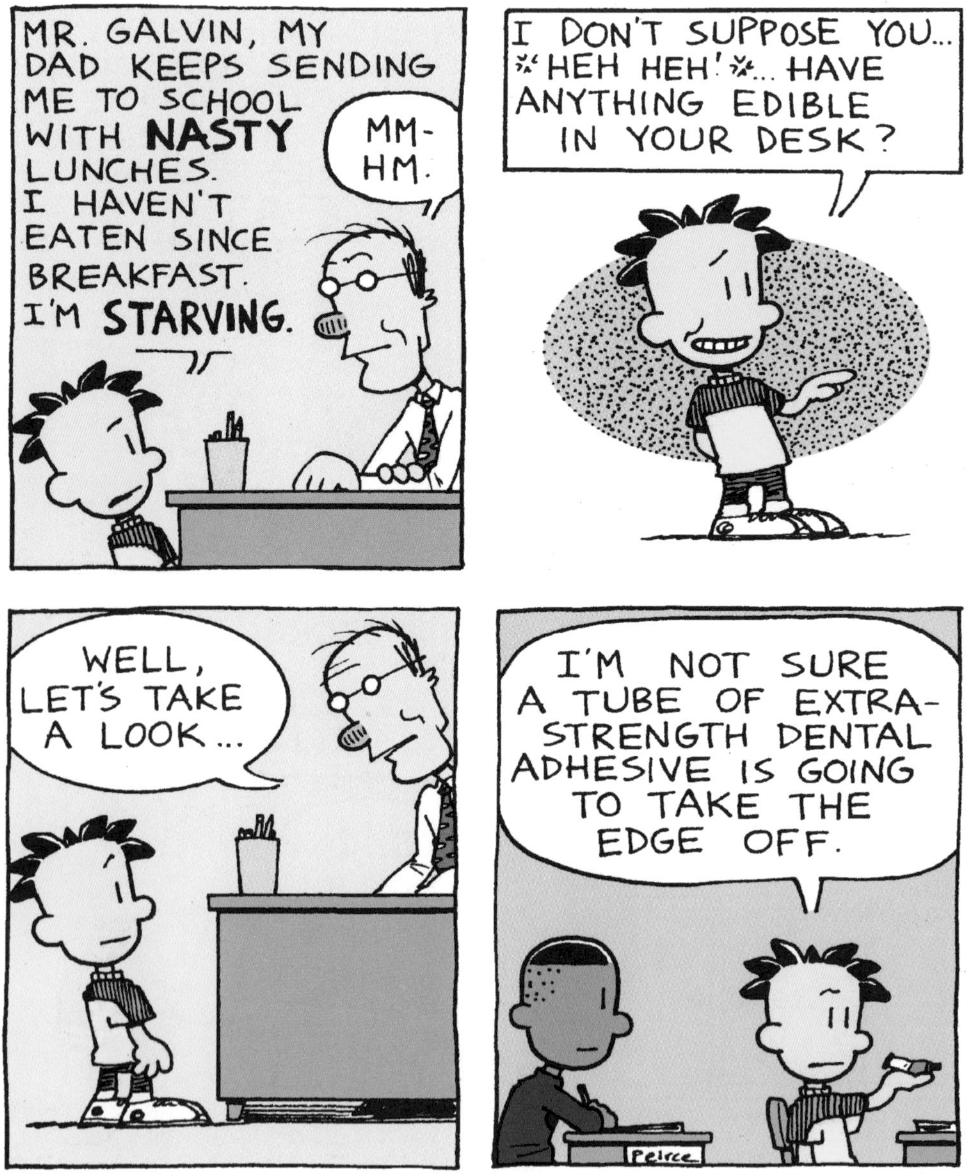
MR. GALVIN, MY DAD KEEPS SENDING ME TO SCHOOL WITH **NASTY** LUNCHES. I HAVEN'T EATEN SINCE BREAKFAST. I'M **STARVING**.
MM-HM.
I DON'T SUPPOSE YOU... *HEH HEH!*... HAVE ANYTHING EDIBLE IN YOUR DESK?
WELL, LET'S TAKE A LOOK...
I'M NOT SURE A TUBE OF EXTRA-STRENGTH DENTAL ADHESIVE IS GOING TO TAKE THE EDGE OFF.
Peirce

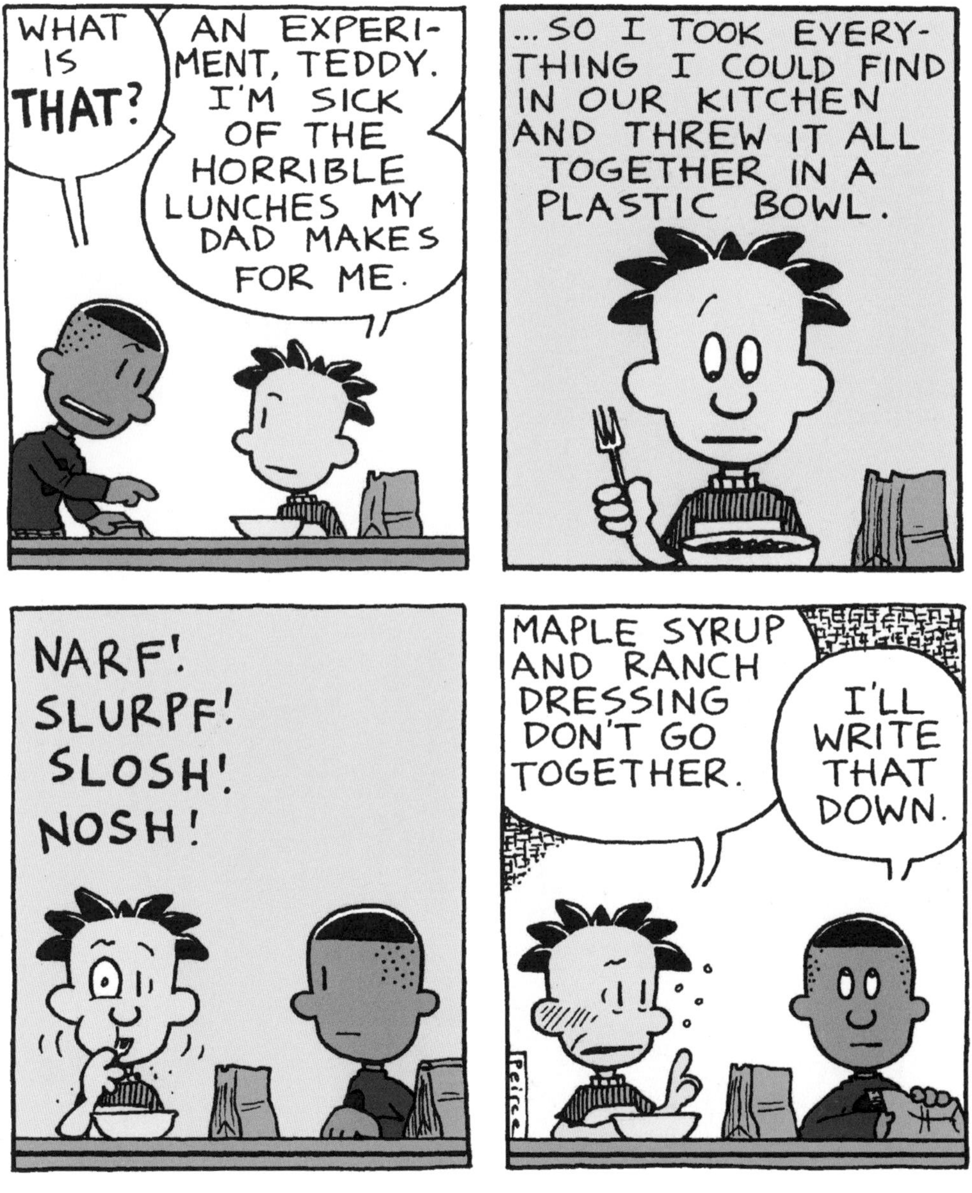
WHAT IS THAT?
AN EXPERIMENT, TEDDY. I'M SICK OF THE HORRIBLE LUNCHES MY DAD MAKES FOR ME.
...SO I TOOK EVERYTHING I COULD FIND IN OUR KITCHEN AND THREW IT ALL TOGETHER IN A PLASTIC BOWL.
NARF! SLURPF! SLOSH! NOSH!
MAPLE SYRUP AND RANCH DRESSING DON'T GO TOGETHER.
I'LL WRITE THAT DOWN.
Peirce

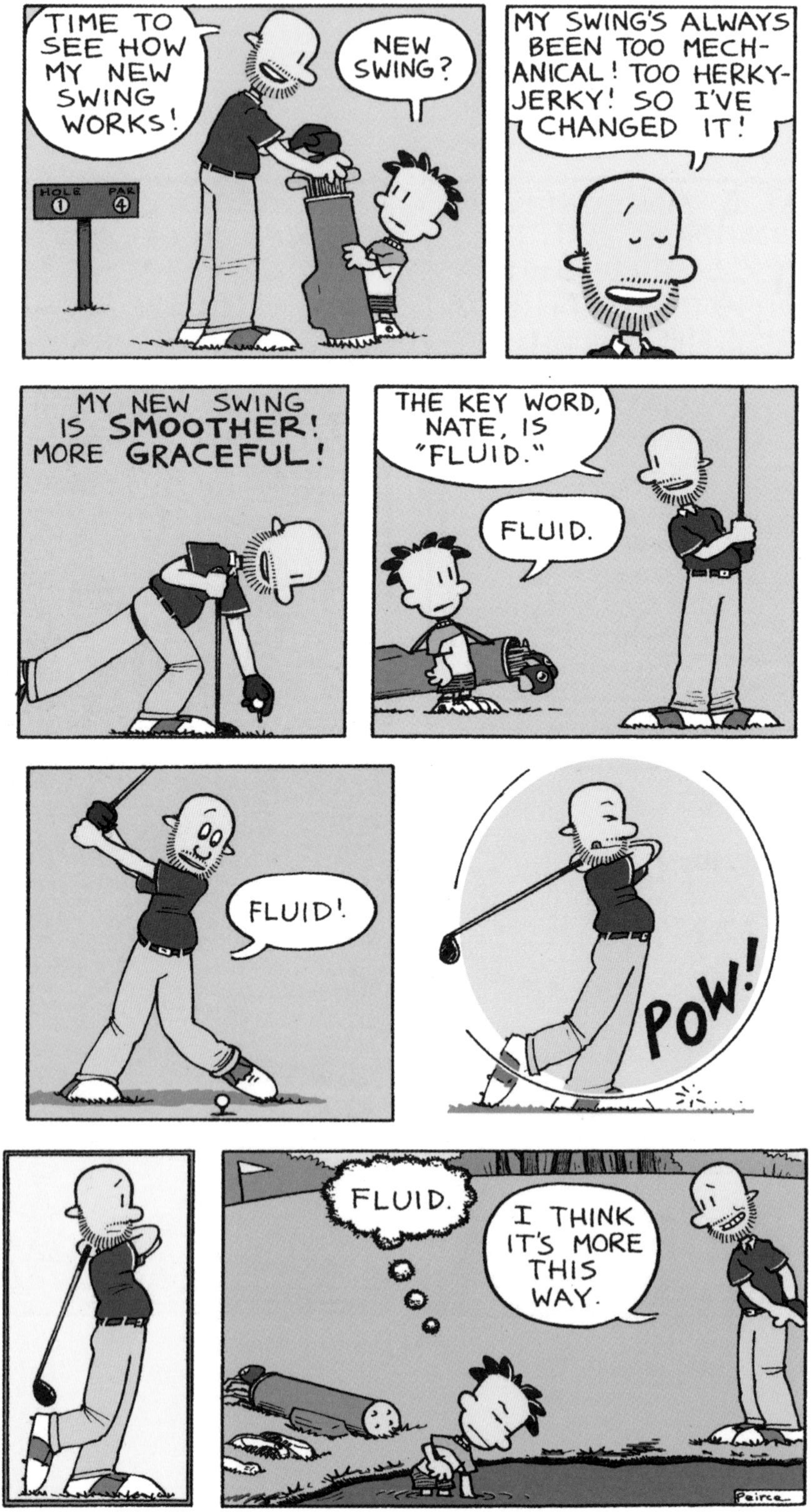
HOLE 1 PAR 4
TIME TO SEE HOW MY NEW SWING WORKS!
NEW SWING?
MY SWING'S ALWAYS BEEN TOO MECHANICAL! TOO HERKY-JERKY! SO I'VE CHANGED IT!
MY NEW SWING IS SMOOTHER! MORE GRACEFUL!
THE KEY WORD, NATE, IS "FLUID."
FLUID.
FLUID!
POW!
FLUID.
I THINK IT'S MORE THIS WAY.
Peirce

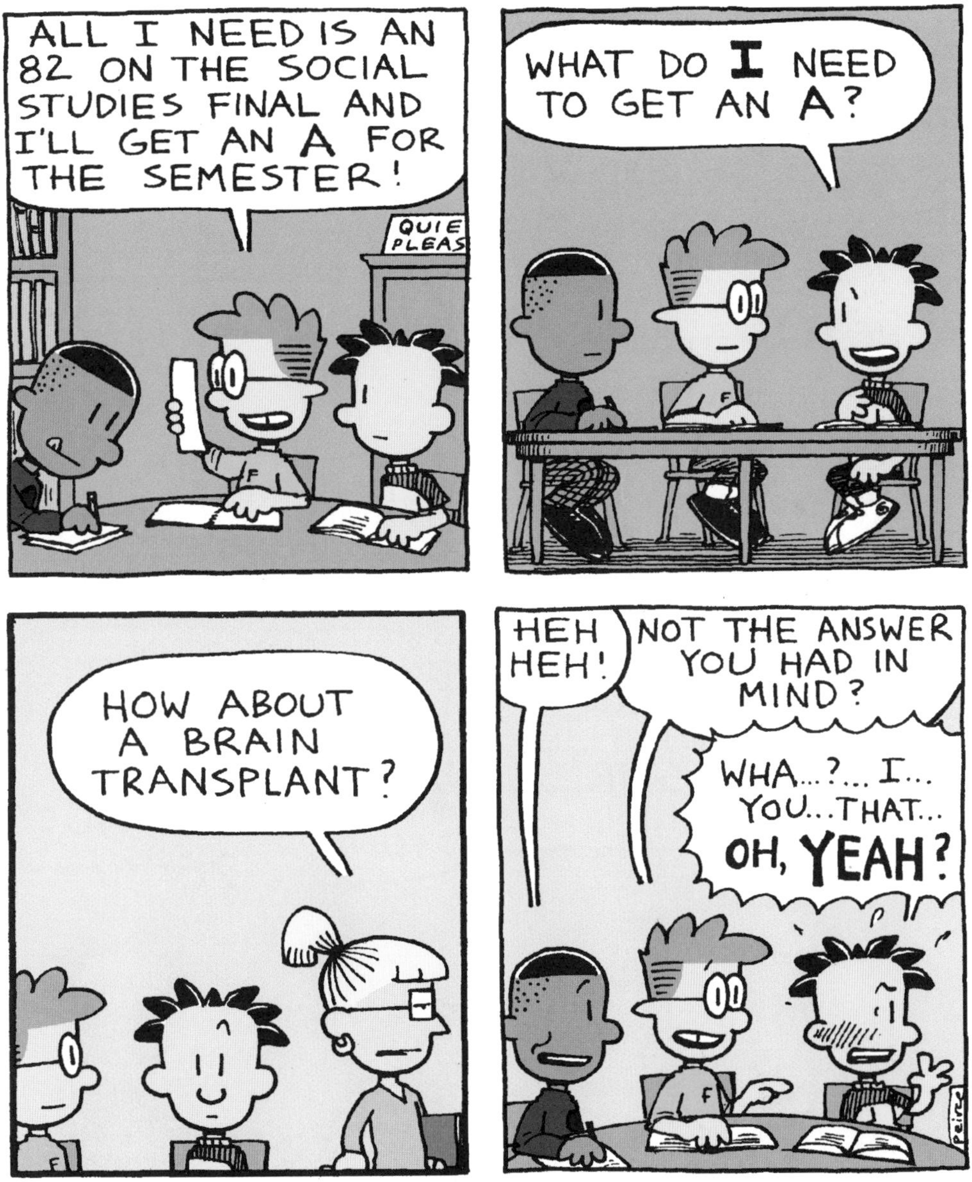
ALL I NEED IS AN 82 ON THE SOCIAL STUDIES FINAL AND I'LL GET AN A FOR THE SEMESTER!
QUIE PLEAS
WHAT DO I NEED TO GET AN A?
HOW ABOUT A BRAIN TRANSPLANT?
HEH HEH!
NOT THE ANSWER YOU HAD IN MIND?
WHA...?... I... YOU...THAT... OH, YEAH?
PEIRCE

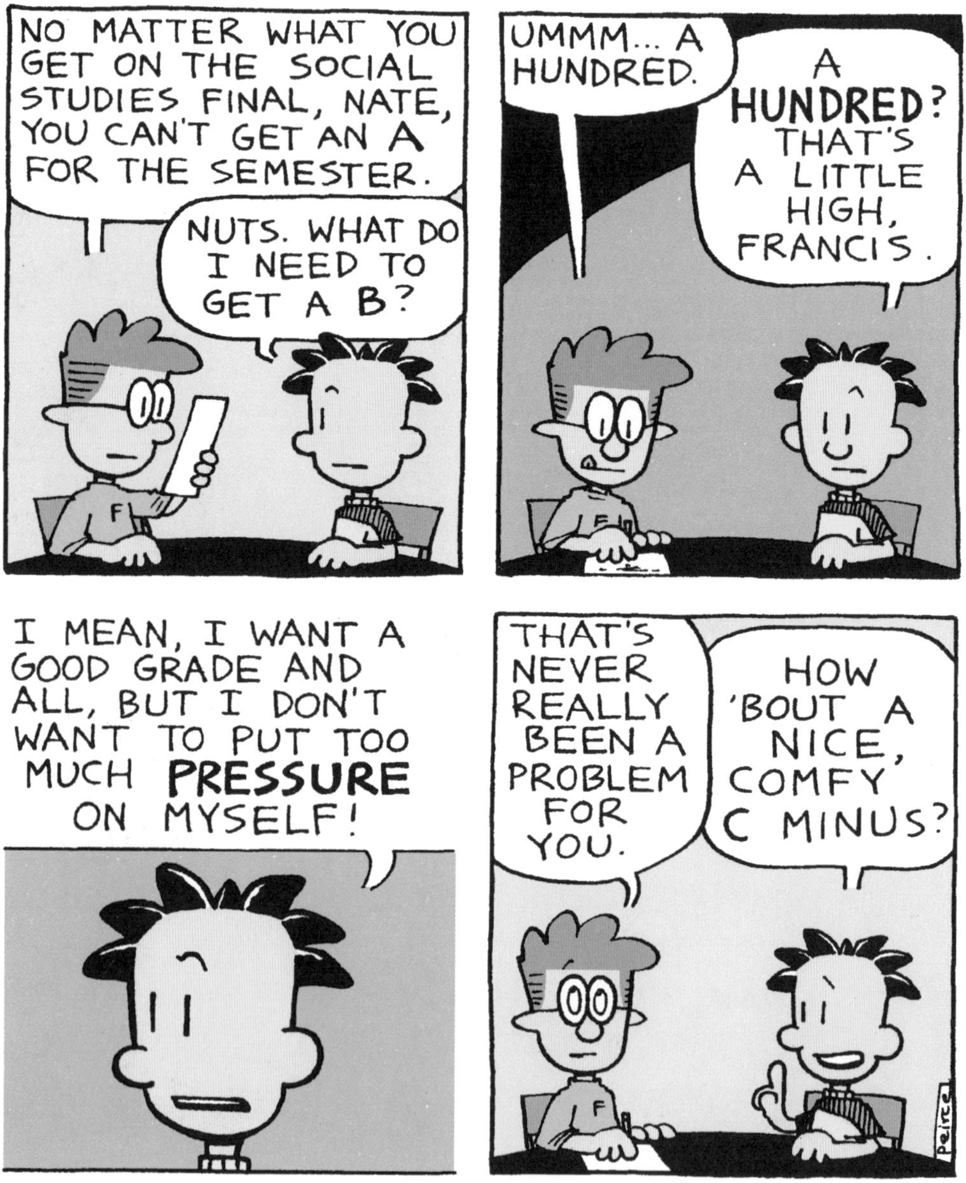
NO MATTER WHAT YOU GET ON THE SOCIAL STUDIES FINAL, NATE, YOU CAN'T GET AN A FOR THE SEMESTER.
NUTS. WHAT DO I NEED TO GET A B?
UMMM... A HUNDRED.
A HUNDRED? THAT'S A LITTLE HIGH, FRANCIS.
I MEAN, I WANT A GOOD GRADE AND ALL, BUT I DON'T WANT TO PUT TOO MUCH PRESSURE ON MYSELF!
THAT'S NEVER REALLY BEEN A PROBLEM FOR YOU.
HOW 'BOUT A NICE, COMFY C MINUS?
Peirce

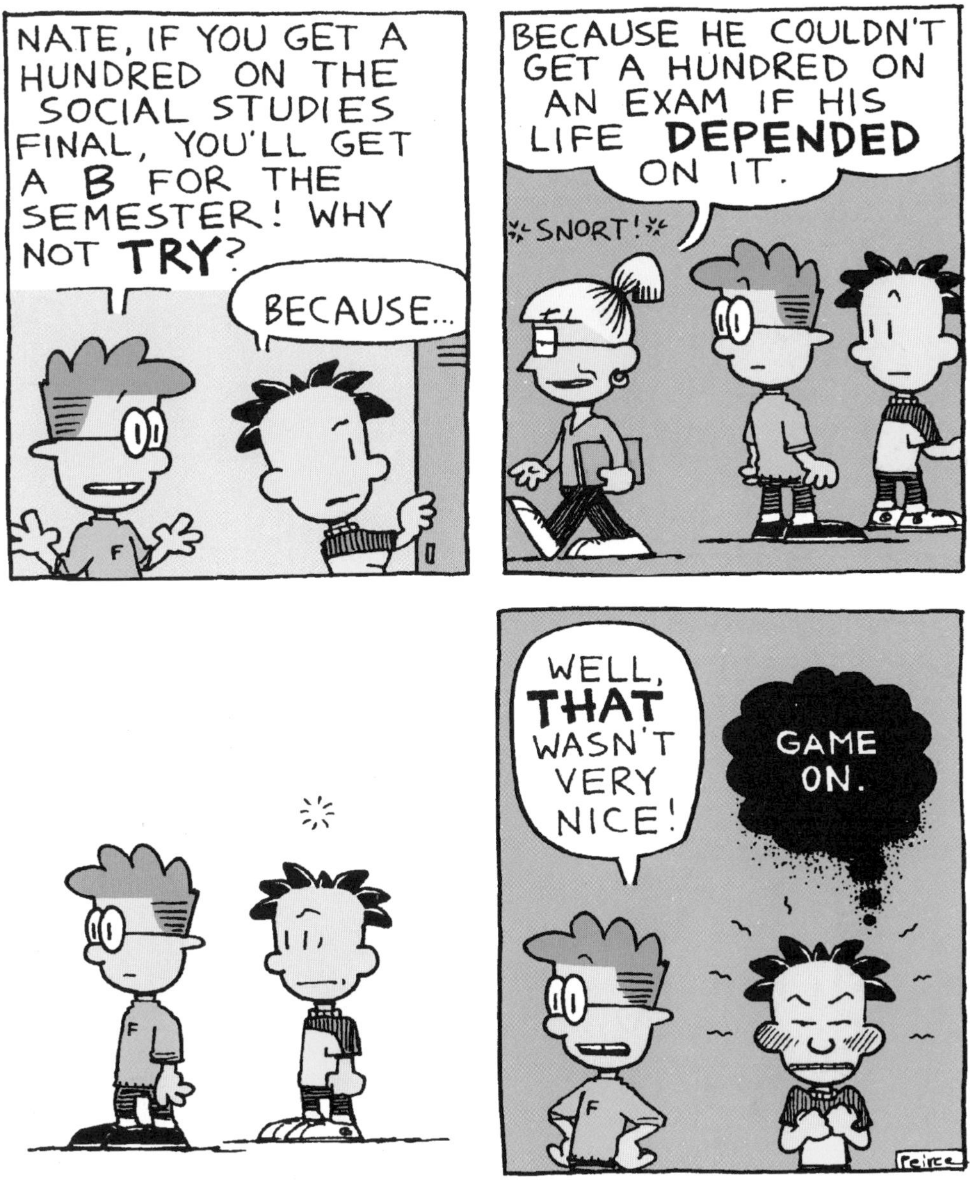
NATE, IF YOU GET A HUNDRED ON THE SOCIAL STUDIES FINAL, YOU'LL GET A B FOR THE SEMESTER! WHY NOT TRY?
BECAUSE...
BECAUSE HE COULDN'T GET A HUNDRED ON AN EXAM IF HIS LIFE DEPENDED ON IT.
SNORT!
WELL, THAT WASN'T VERY NICE!
GAME ON.
Peirce

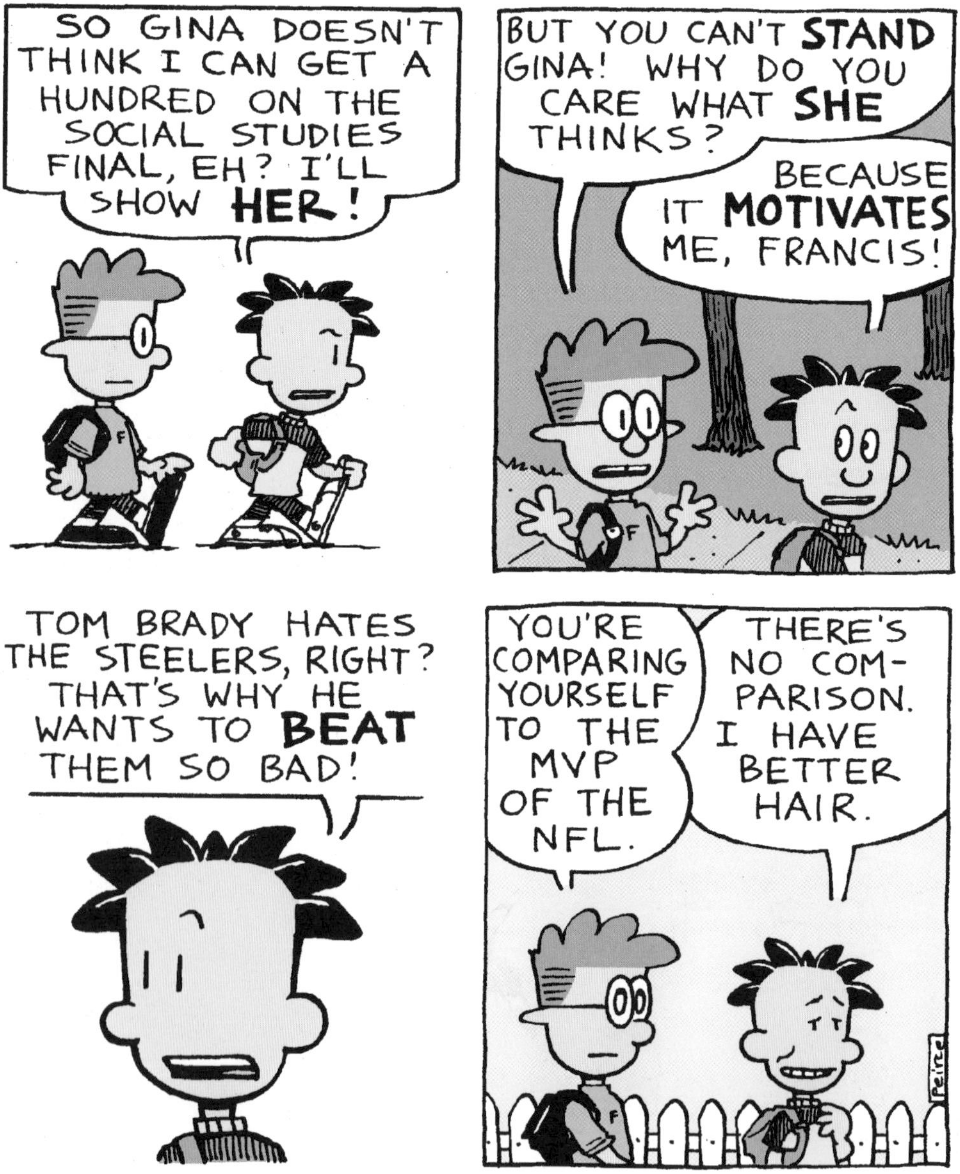
SO GINA DOESN'T THINK I CAN GET A HUNDRED ON THE SOCIAL STUDIES FINAL, EH? I'LL SHOW **HER**!
BUT YOU CAN'T **STAND** GINA! WHY DO YOU CARE WHAT **SHE** THINKS?
BECAUSE IT **MOTIVATES** ME, FRANCIS!
TOM BRADY HATES THE STEELERS, RIGHT? THAT'S WHY HE WANTS TO **BEAT** THEM SO BAD!
YOU'RE COMPARING YOURSELF TO THE MVP OF THE NFL.
THERE'S NO COMPARISON. I HAVE BETTER HAIR.
PEIRCE

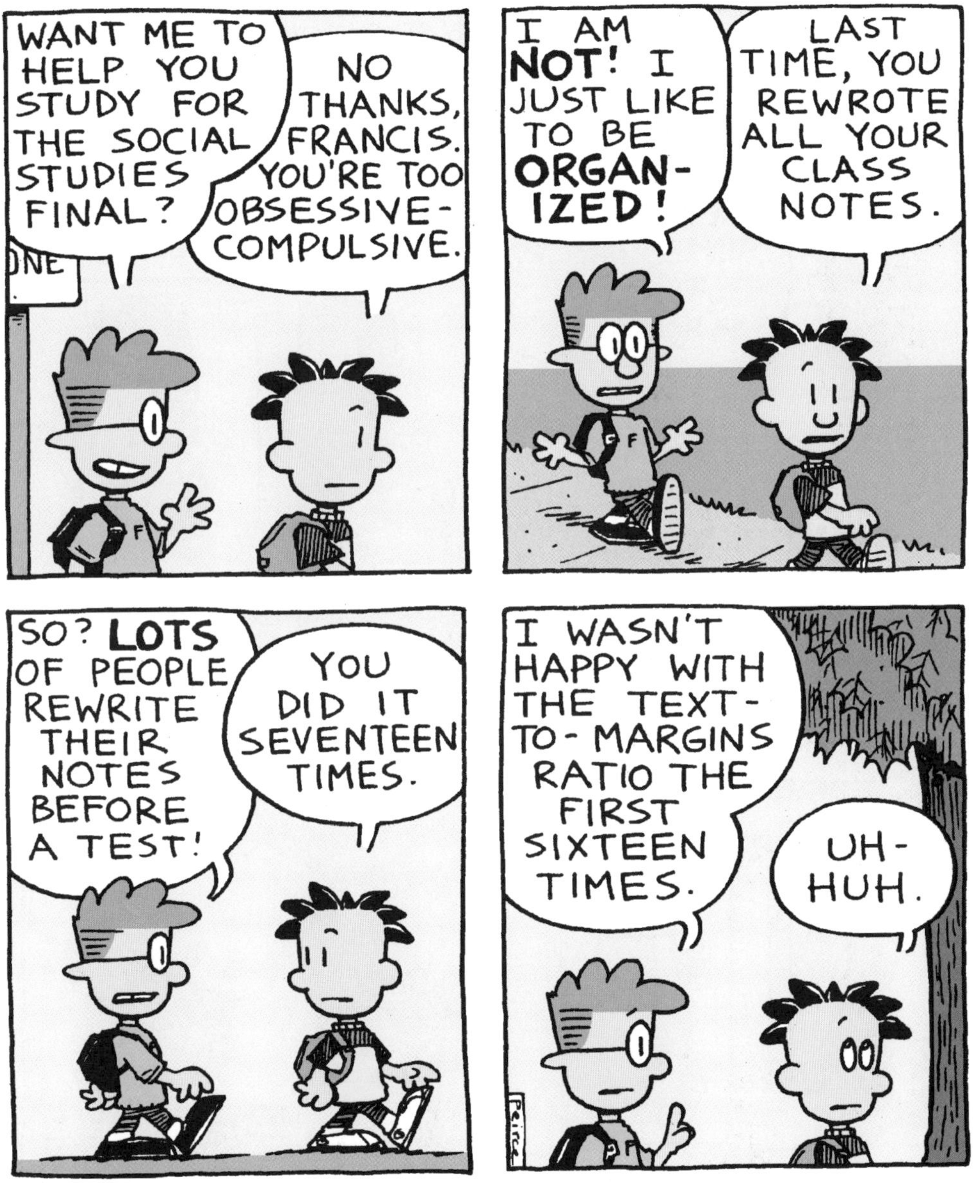
WANT ME TO HELP YOU STUDY FOR THE SOCIAL STUDIES FINAL?
NO THANKS, FRANCIS. YOU'RE TOO OBSESSIVE-COMPULSIVE.
I AM **NOT**! I JUST LIKE TO BE **ORGAN-IZED**!
LAST TIME, YOU REWROTE ALL YOUR CLASS NOTES.
SO? **LOTS** OF PEOPLE REWRITE THEIR NOTES BEFORE A TEST!
YOU DID IT SEVENTEEN TIMES.
I WASN'T HAPPY WITH THE TEXT-TO-MARGINS RATIO THE FIRST SIXTEEN TIMES.
UH-HUH.
Peirce

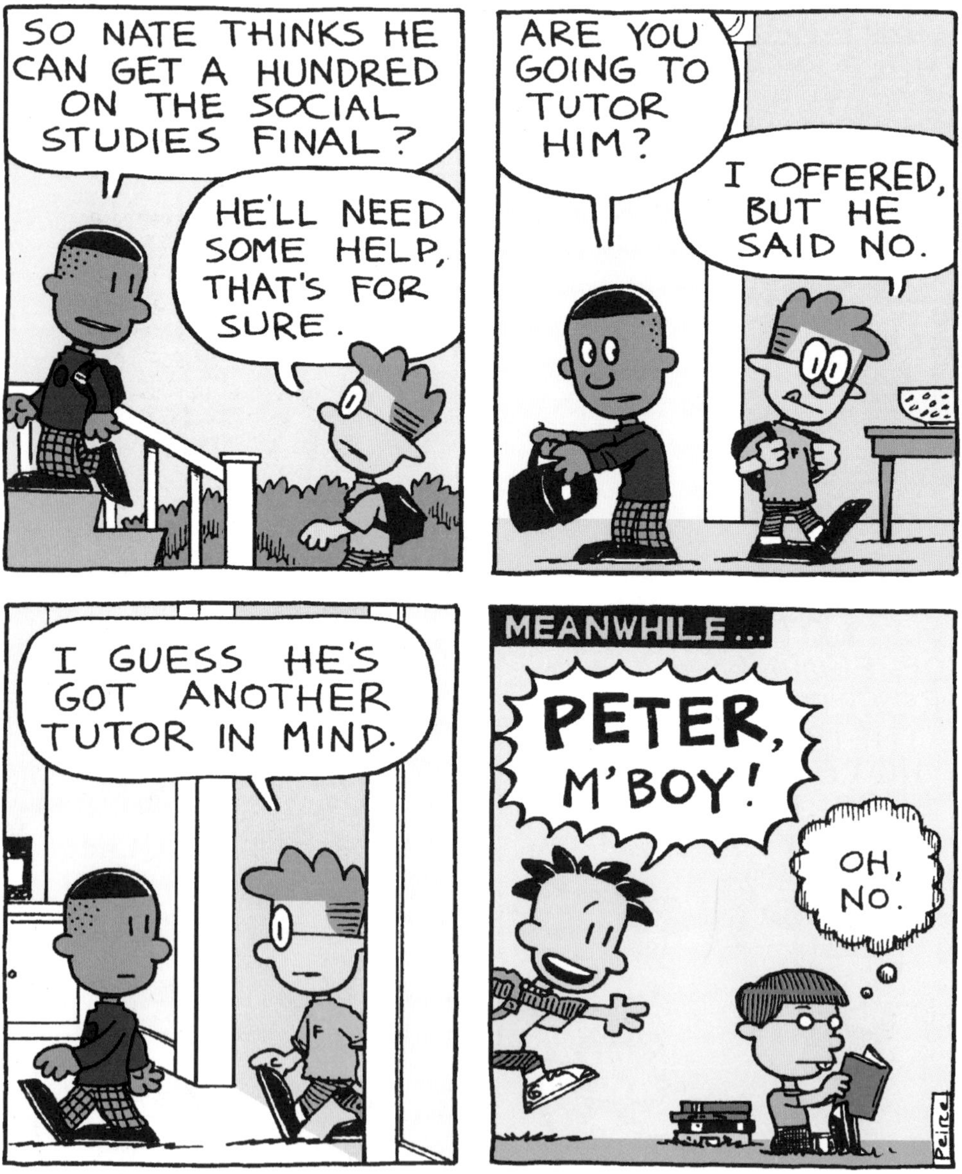
SO NATE THINKS HE CAN GET A HUNDRED ON THE SOCIAL STUDIES FINAL?
HE'LL NEED SOME HELP, THAT'S FOR SURE.
ARE YOU GOING TO TUTOR HIM?
I OFFERED, BUT HE SAID NO.
I GUESS HE'S GOT ANOTHER TUTOR IN MIND.
MEANWHILE...
PETER, M'BOY!
OH, NO.
Peirce

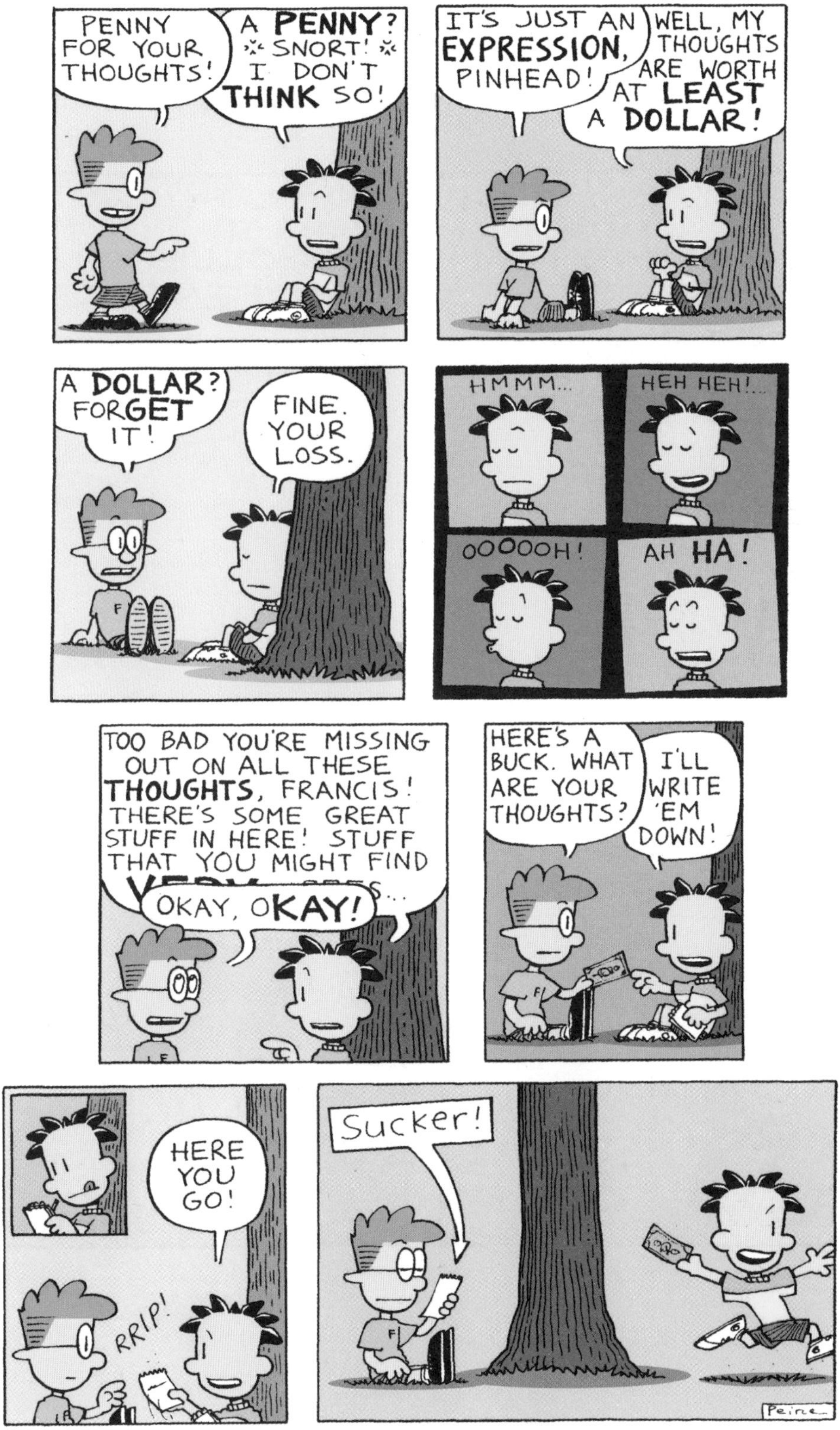
PENNY FOR YOUR THOUGHTS!
A PENNY? SNORT! I DON'T THINK SO!
IT'S JUST AN EXPRESSION, PINHEAD!
WELL, MY THOUGHTS ARE WORTH AT LEAST A DOLLAR!
A DOLLAR? FORGET IT!
FINE. YOUR LOSS.
HMMM...
HEH HEH!...
OOOOOH!
AH HA!
TOO BAD YOU'RE MISSING OUT ON ALL THESE THOUGHTS, FRANCIS! THERE'S SOME GREAT STUFF IN HERE! STUFF THAT YOU MIGHT FIND
OKAY, OKAY!
HERE'S A BUCK. WHAT ARE YOUR THOUGHTS?
I'LL WRITE 'EM DOWN!
HERE YOU GO!
RRIP!
Sucker!
Peirce

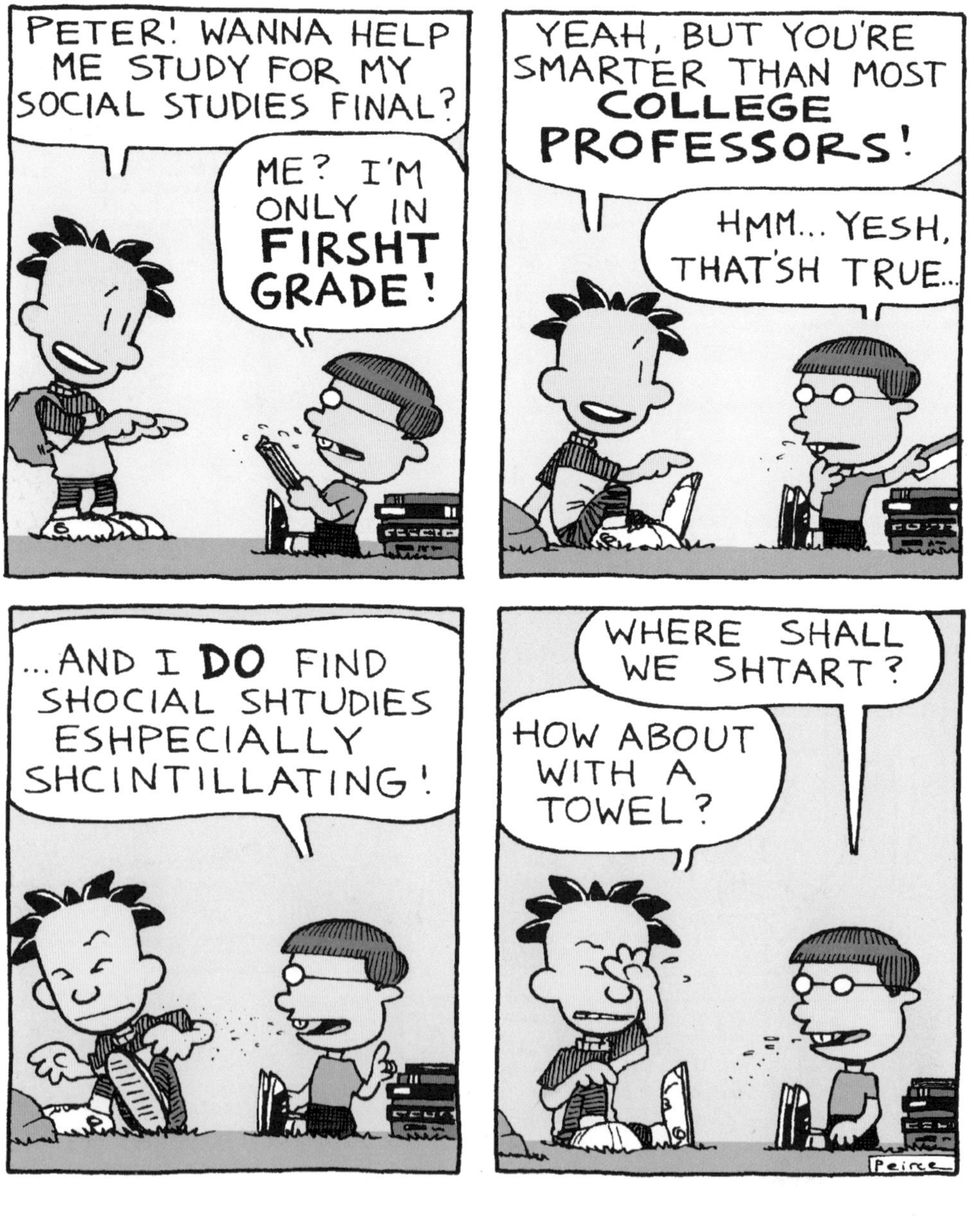
PETER! WANNA HELP ME STUDY FOR MY SOCIAL STUDIES FINAL?
ME? I'M ONLY IN FIRSHT GRADE!
YEAH, BUT YOU'RE SMARTER THAN MOST COLLEGE PROFESSORS!
HMM... YESH, THAT'SH TRUE...
...AND I DO FIND SHOCIAL SHTUDIES ESHPECIALLY SHCINTILLATING!
WHERE SHALL WE SHTART?
HOW ABOUT WITH A TOWEL?
Peirce

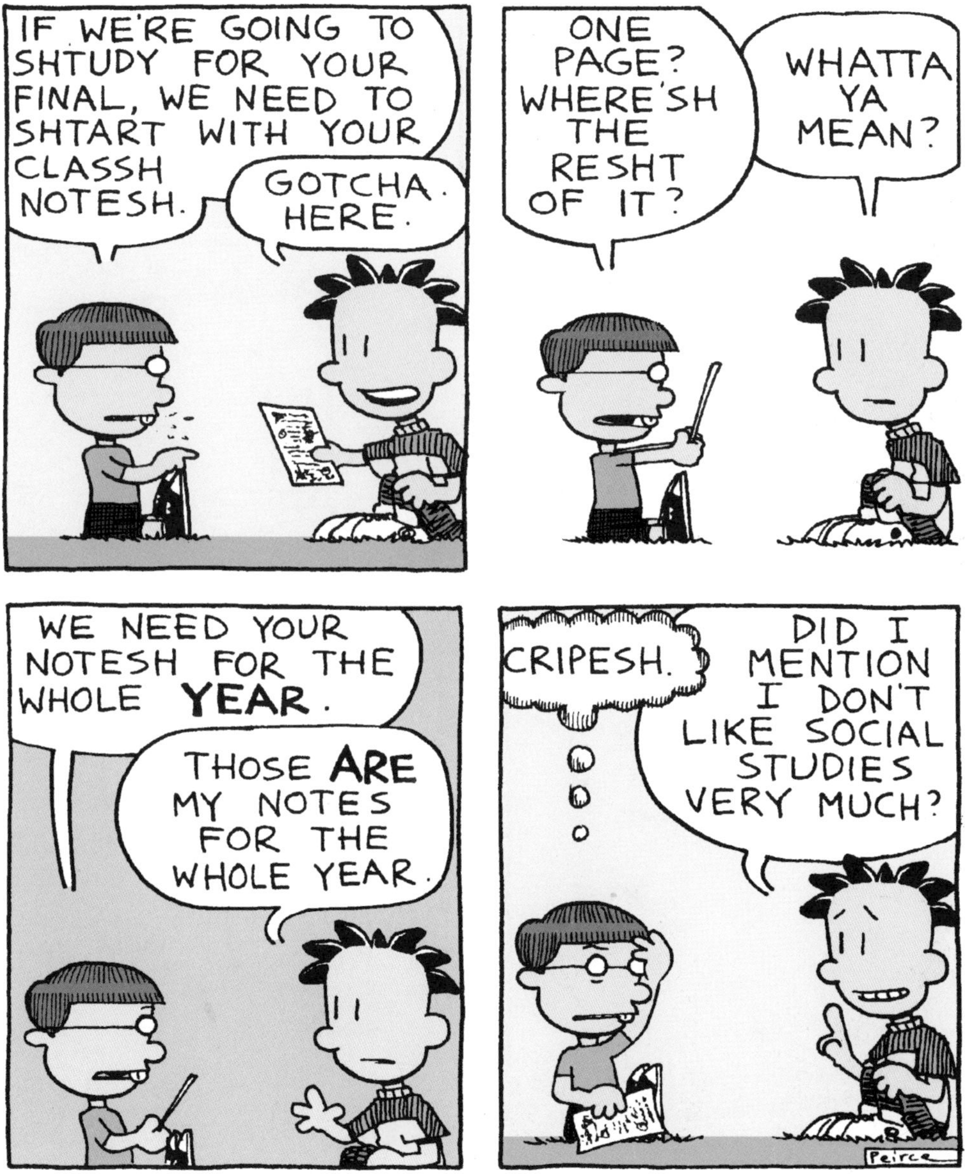
IF WE'RE GOING TO SHTUDY FOR YOUR FINAL, WE NEED TO SHTART WITH YOUR CLASSH NOTESH.
GOTCHA. HERE.
ONE PAGE? WHERE'SH THE RESHT OF IT?
WHATTA YA MEAN?
WE NEED YOUR NOTESH FOR THE WHOLE YEAR.
THOSE ARE MY NOTES FOR THE WHOLE YEAR.
CRIPESH.
DID I MENTION I DON'T LIKE SOCIAL STUDIES VERY MUCH?
Peirce

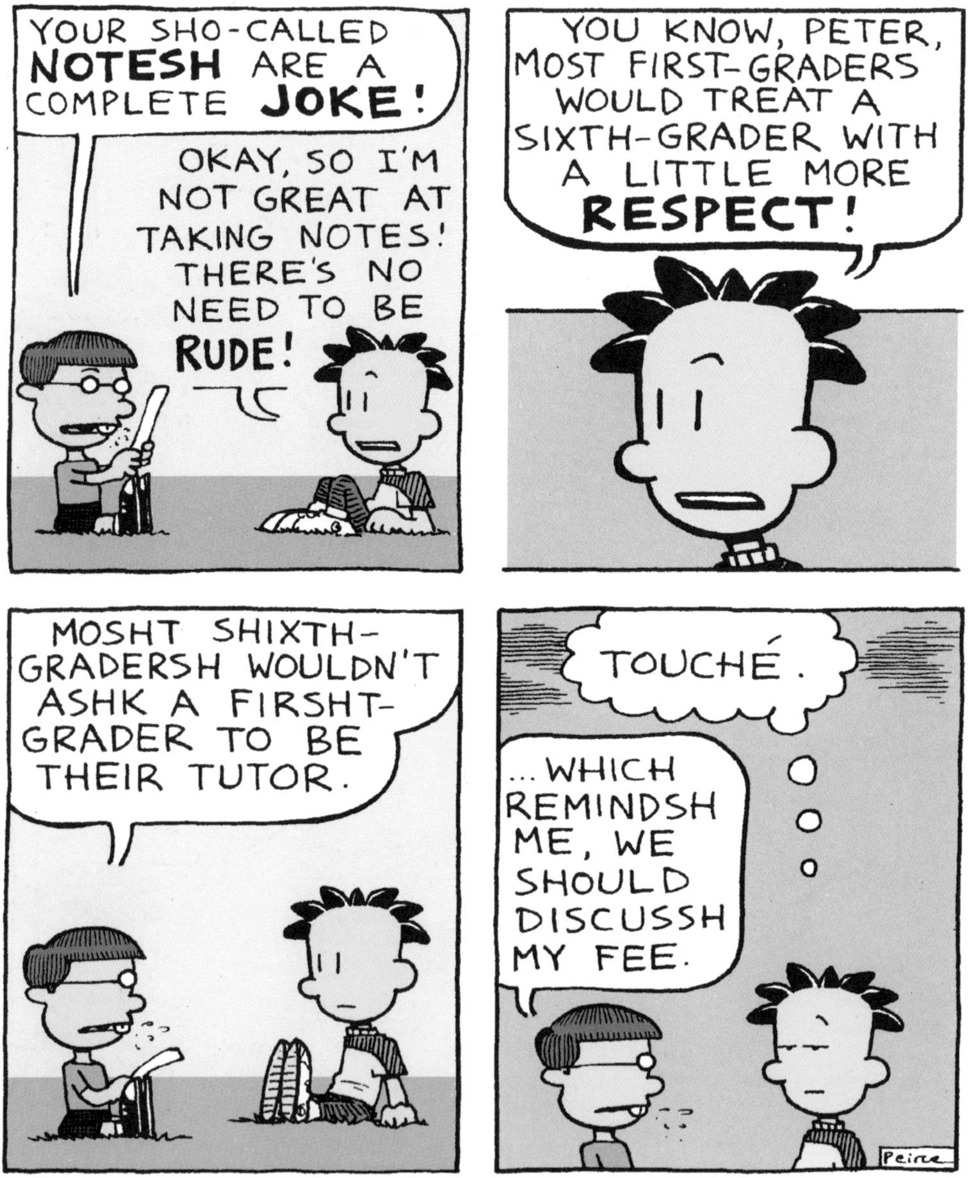
YOUR SHO-CALLED NOTESH ARE A COMPLETE JOKE!
OKAY, SO I'M NOT GREAT AT TAKING NOTES! THERE'S NO NEED TO BE RUDE!
YOU KNOW, PETER, MOST FIRST-GRADERS WOULD TREAT A SIXTH-GRADER WITH A LITTLE MORE RESPECT!
MOSHT SHIXTH-GRADERSH WOULDN'T ASHK A FIRSHT-GRADER TO BE THEIR TUTOR.
TOUCHÉ.
...WHICH REMINDSH ME, WE SHOULD DISCUSSH MY FEE.
Peirce

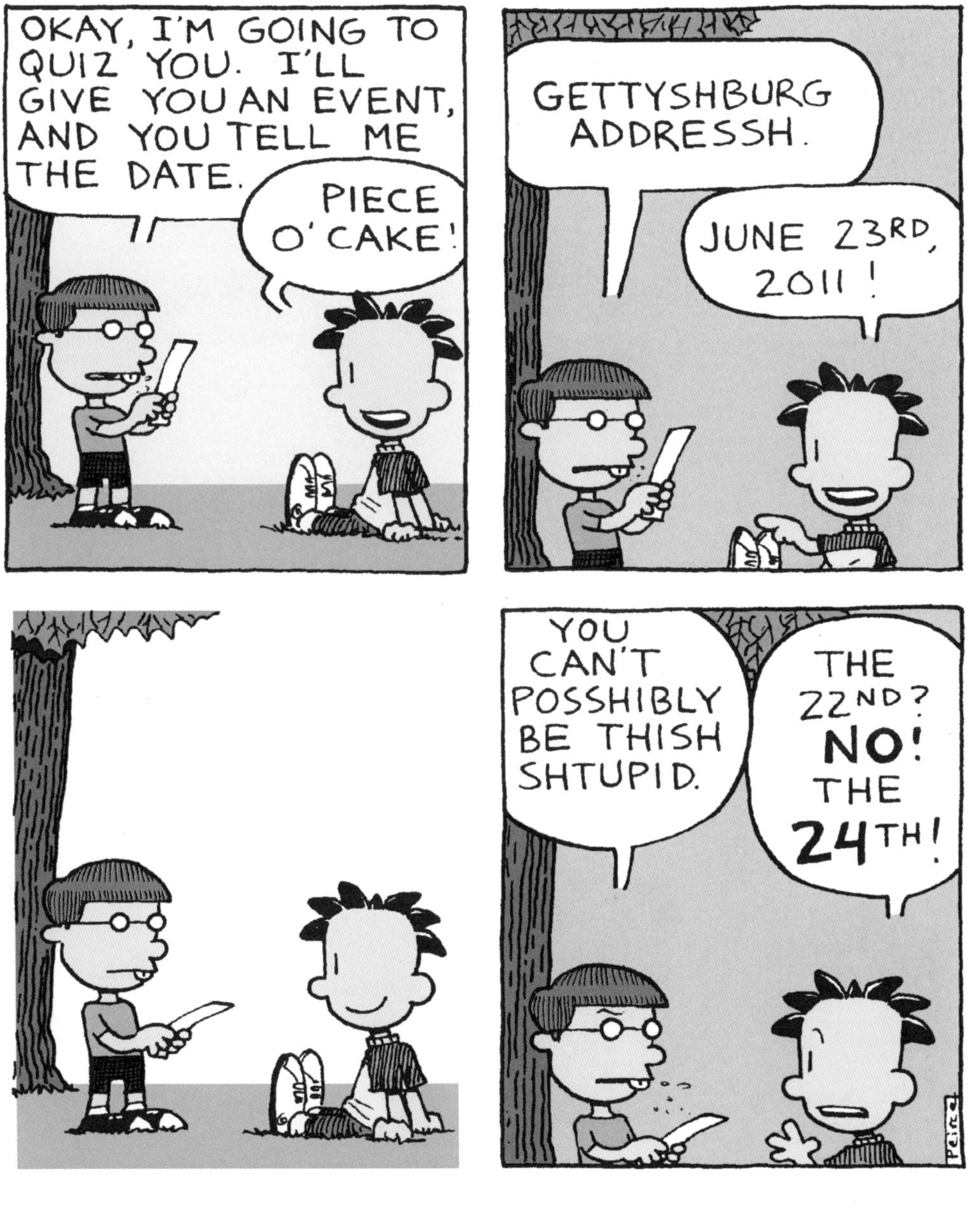

OKAY, I'M GOING TO QUIZ YOU. I'LL GIVE YOU AN EVENT, AND YOU TELL ME THE DATE.
PIECE O' CAKE!
GETTYSHBURG ADDRESSH.
JUNE 23RD, 2011!
YOU CAN'T POSSHIBLY BE THISH SHTUPID.
THE 22ND? NO! THE 24TH!
Peirce

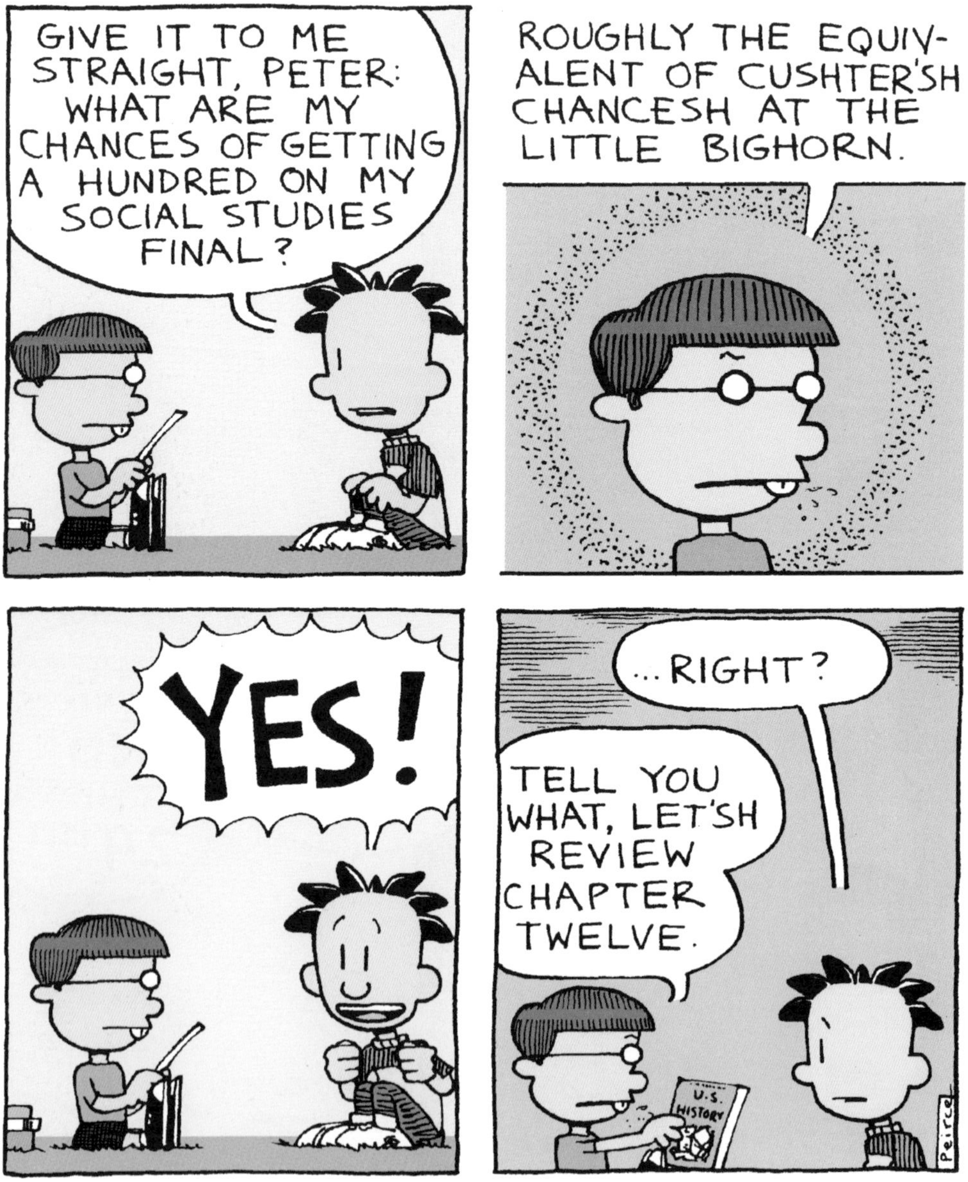
GIVE IT TO ME STRAIGHT, PETER: WHAT ARE MY CHANCES OF GETTING A HUNDRED ON MY SOCIAL STUDIES FINAL?
ROUGHLY THE EQUIV-ALENT OF CUSHTER'SH CHANCESH AT THE LITTLE BIGHORN.
YES!
...RIGHT?
TELL YOU WHAT, LET'SH REVIEW CHAPTER TWELVE.
U.S. HISTORY
Peirce

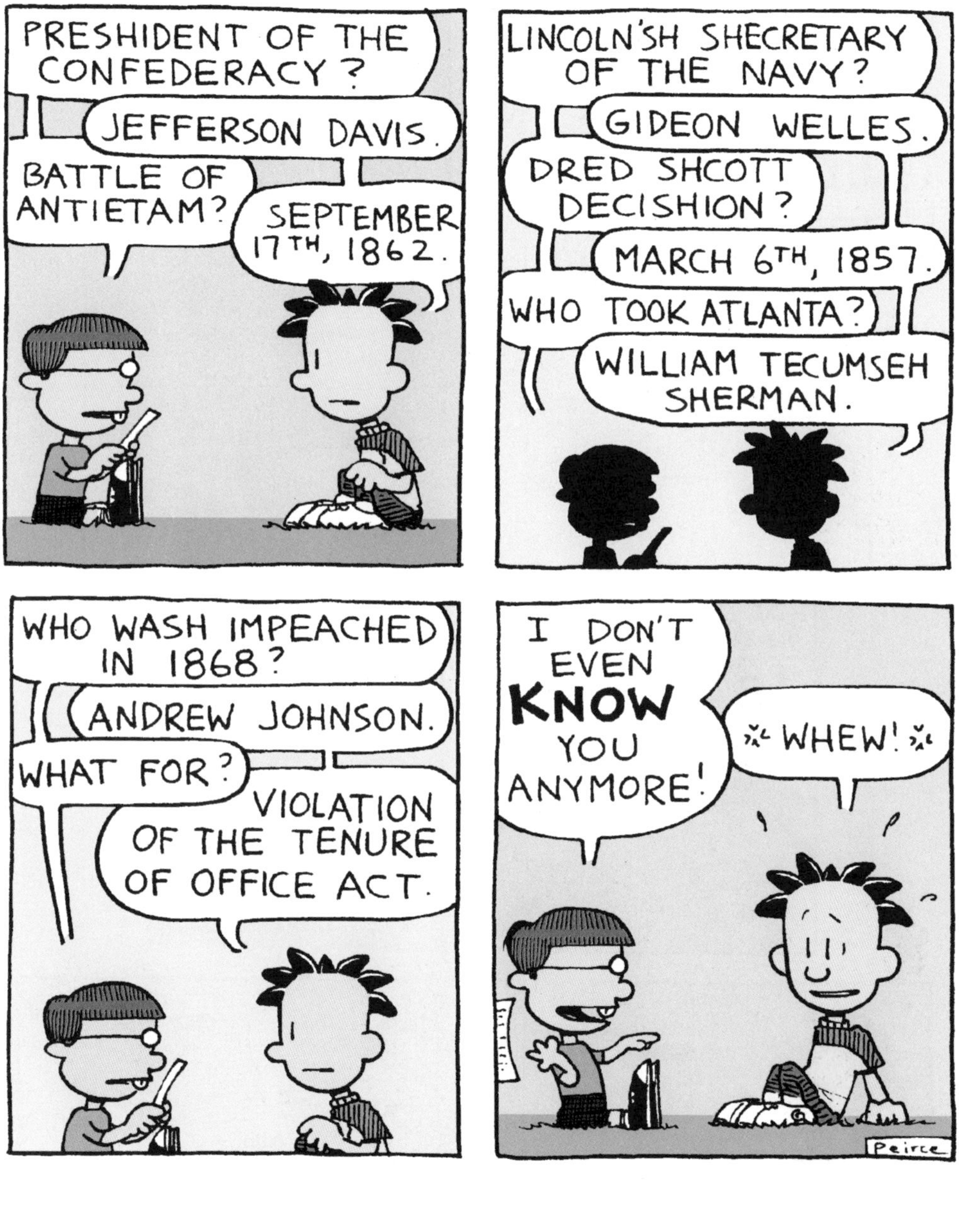
PRESHIDENT OF THE CONFEDERACY?
JEFFERSON DAVIS.
BATTLE OF ANTIETAM?
SEPTEMBER 17TH, 1862.
LINCOLN'SH SHECRETARY OF THE NAVY?
GIDEON WELLES.
DRED SHCOTT DECISHION?
MARCH 6TH, 1857.
WHO TOOK ATLANTA?
WILLIAM TECUMSEH SHERMAN.
WHO WASH IMPEACHED IN 1868?
ANDREW JOHNSON.
WHAT FOR?
VIOLATION OF THE TENURE OF OFFICE ACT.
I DON'T EVEN **KNOW** YOU ANYMORE!
WHEW!
Peirce

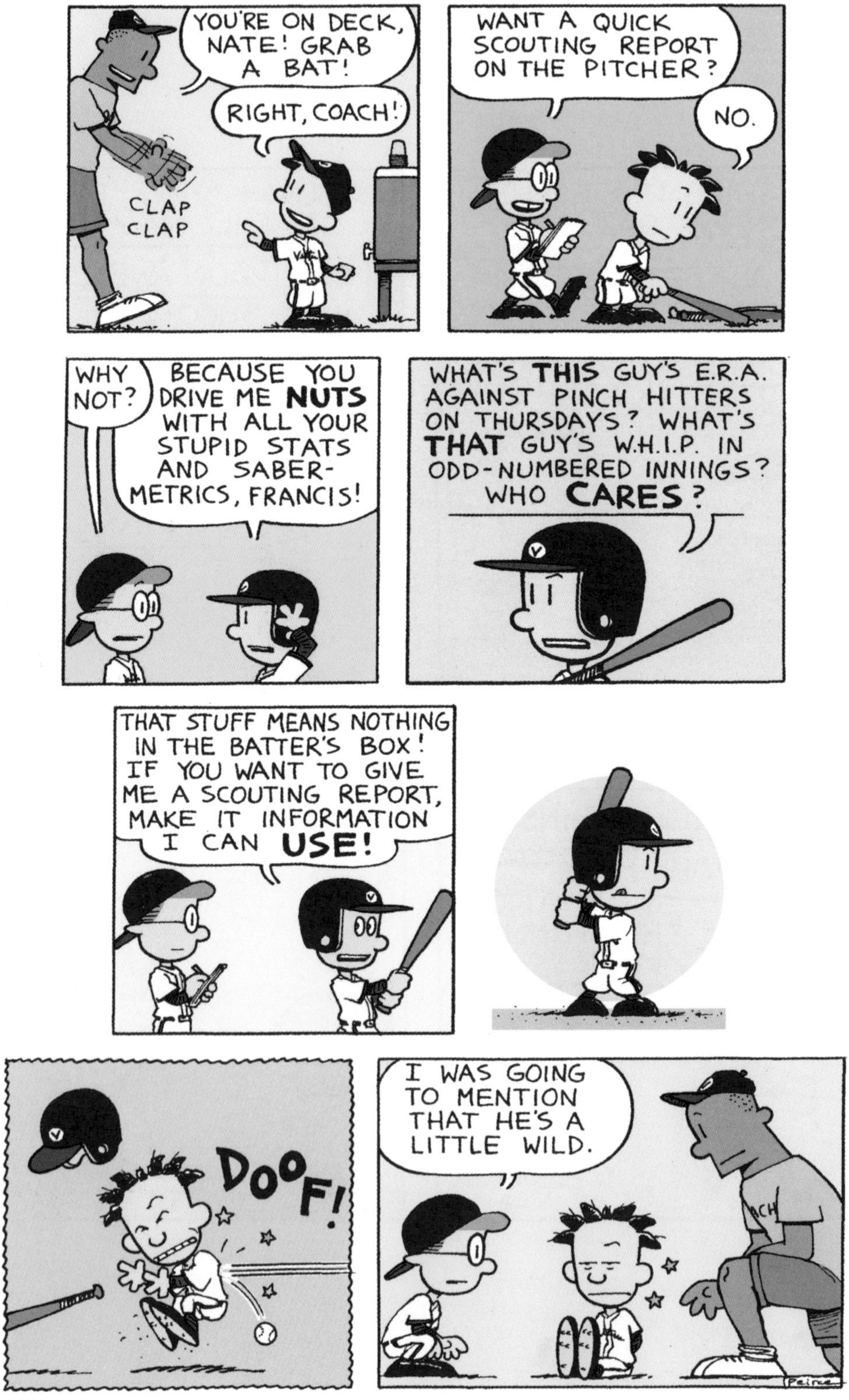
YOU'RE ON DECK, NATE! GRAB A BAT!
RIGHT, COACH!
CLAP CLAP
WANT A QUICK SCOUTING REPORT ON THE PITCHER?
NO.
WHY NOT?
BECAUSE YOU DRIVE ME NUTS WITH ALL YOUR STUPID STATS AND SABER-METRICS, FRANCIS!
WHAT'S THIS GUY'S E.R.A. AGAINST PINCH HITTERS ON THURSDAYS? WHAT'S THAT GUY'S W.H.I.P. IN ODD-NUMBERED INNINGS? WHO CARES?
THAT STUFF MEANS NOTHING IN THE BATTER'S BOX! IF YOU WANT TO GIVE ME A SCOUTING REPORT, MAKE IT INFORMATION I CAN USE!
DOOF!
I WAS GOING TO MENTION THAT HE'S A LITTLE WILD.
Peirce

READY FOR THE SOCIAL STUDIES FINAL?

YUP! READY TO GET A **HUNDRED**!

OH, **PLEASE**!

YOU'LL BE LUCKY TO **PASS**!

PASS? OH, I'LL PASS, GINA...

...JUST LIKE THE SHERMAN ANTITRUST ACT, WHICH PASSED ON JULY 2ND, 1890, MARKING THE BEGINNING OF THE GOVERNMENT'S EFFORT TO RESTRICT MONOPOLIES.

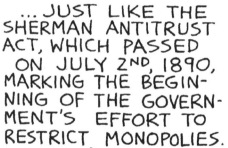

WHA...?

SO SHUT UP.

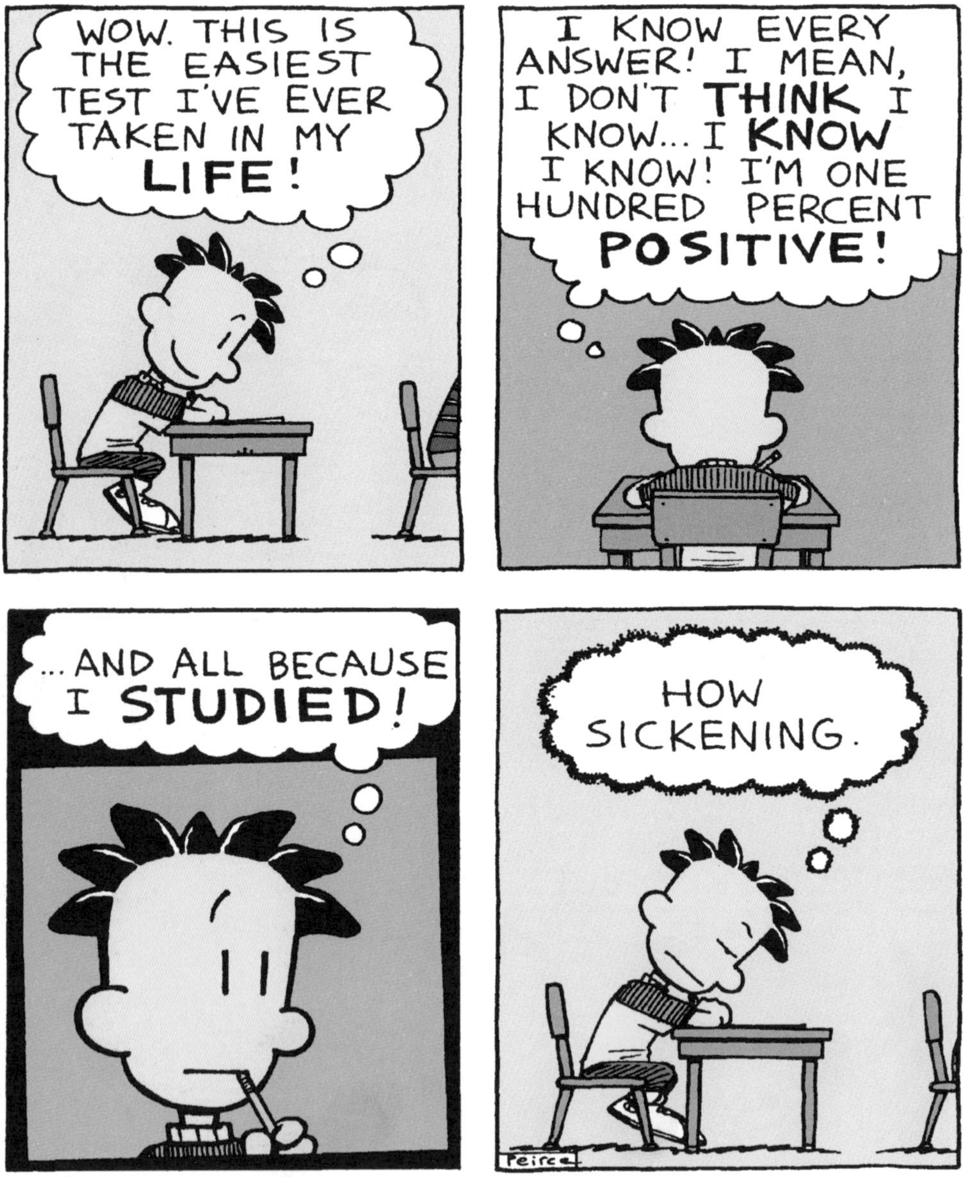
WOW. THIS IS THE EASIEST TEST I'VE EVER TAKEN IN MY LIFE!
I KNOW EVERY ANSWER! I MEAN, I DON'T THINK I KNOW... I KNOW I KNOW! I'M ONE HUNDRED PERCENT POSITIVE!
...AND ALL BECAUSE I STUDIED!
HOW SICKENING.
Peirce

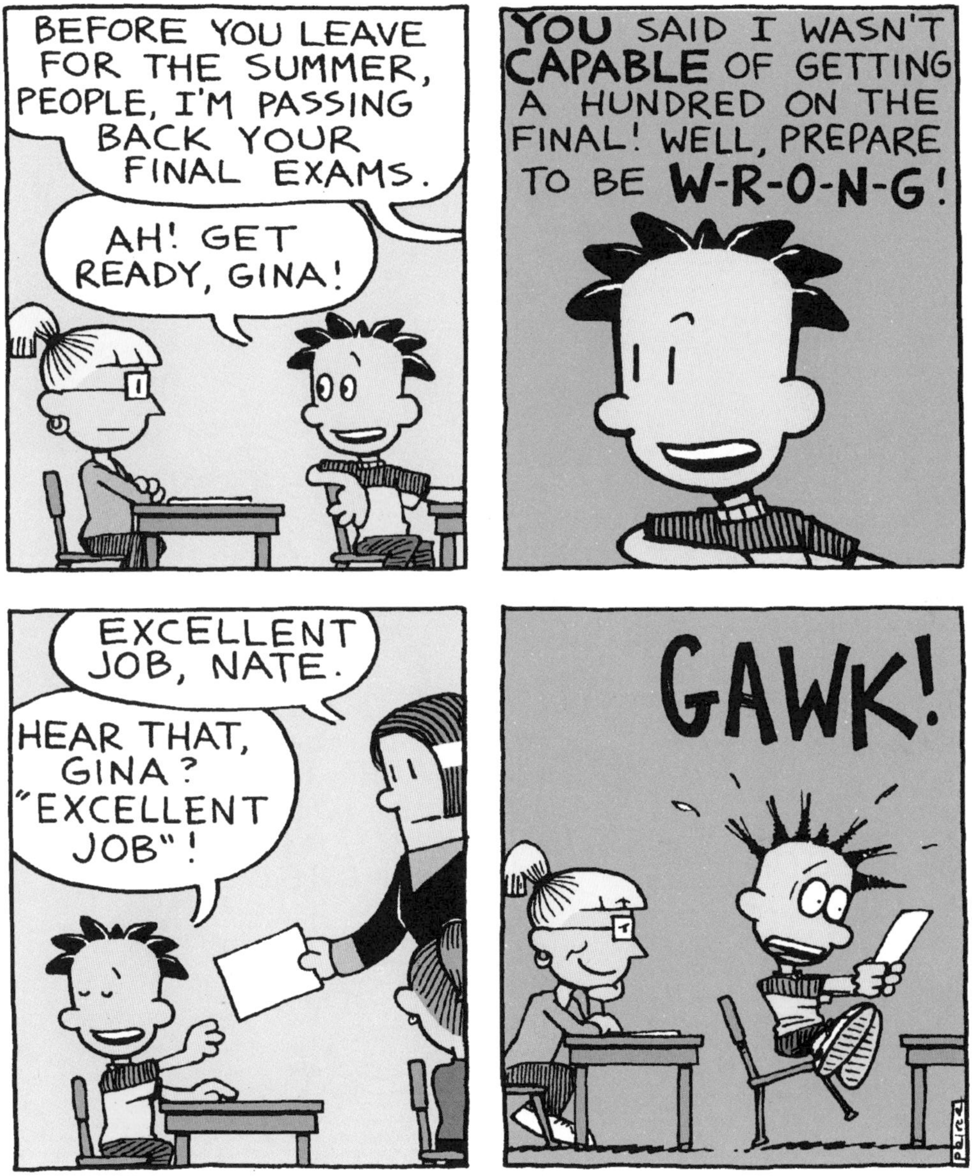
BEFORE YOU LEAVE FOR THE SUMMER, PEOPLE, I'M PASSING BACK YOUR FINAL EXAMS.
AH! GET READY, GINA!
YOU SAID I WASN'T CAPABLE OF GETTING A HUNDRED ON THE FINAL! WELL, PREPARE TO BE W-R-O-N-G!
EXCELLENT JOB, NATE.
HEAR THAT, GINA? "EXCELLENT JOB"!
GAWK!
PEIRCE

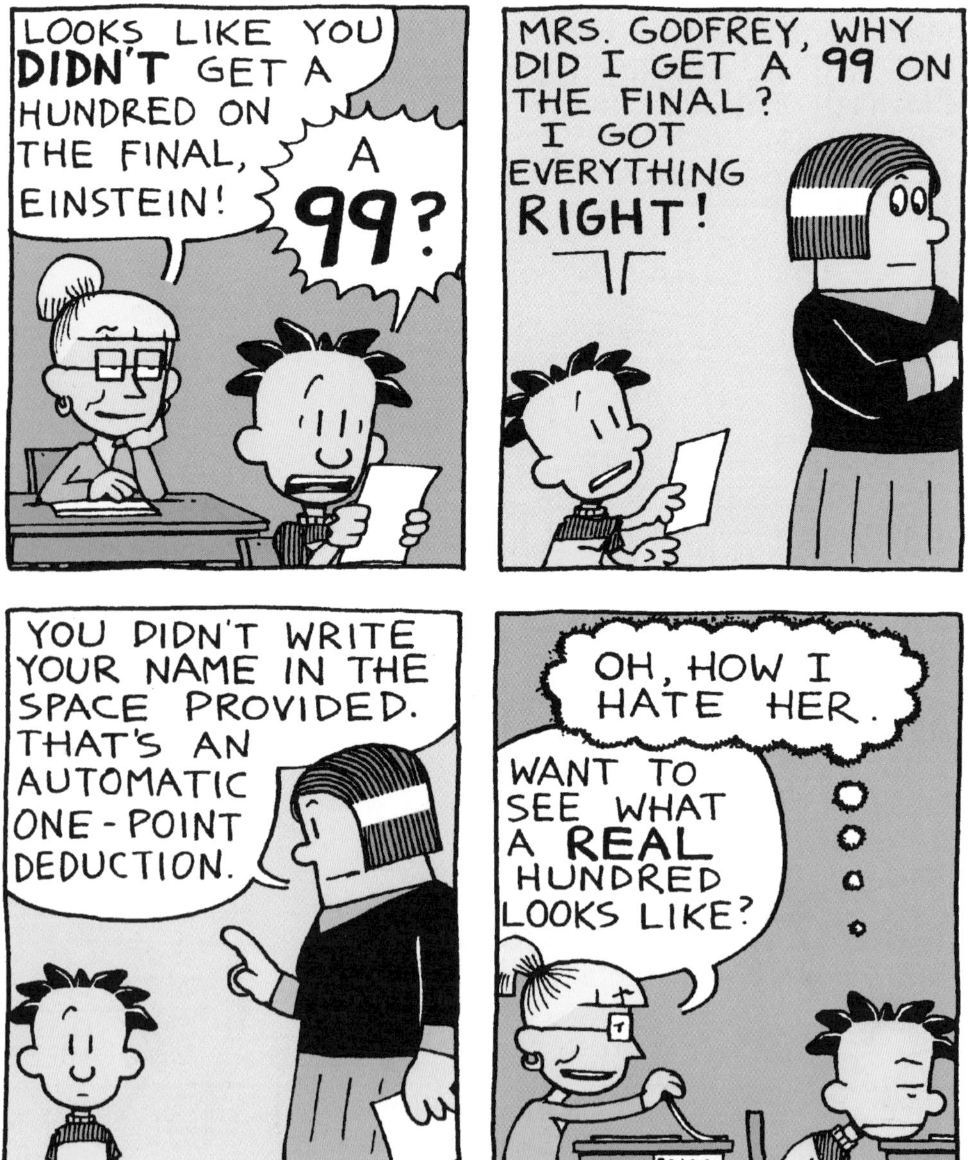
LOOKS LIKE YOU **DIDN'T** GET A HUNDRED ON THE FINAL, EINSTEIN!
A **99?**
MRS. GODFREY, WHY DID I GET A **99** ON THE FINAL? I GOT EVERYTHING **RIGHT!**
YOU DIDN'T WRITE YOUR NAME IN THE SPACE PROVIDED. THAT'S AN AUTOMATIC ONE-POINT DEDUCTION.
OH, HOW I HATE HER.
WANT TO SEE WHAT A **REAL** HUNDRED LOOKS LIKE?

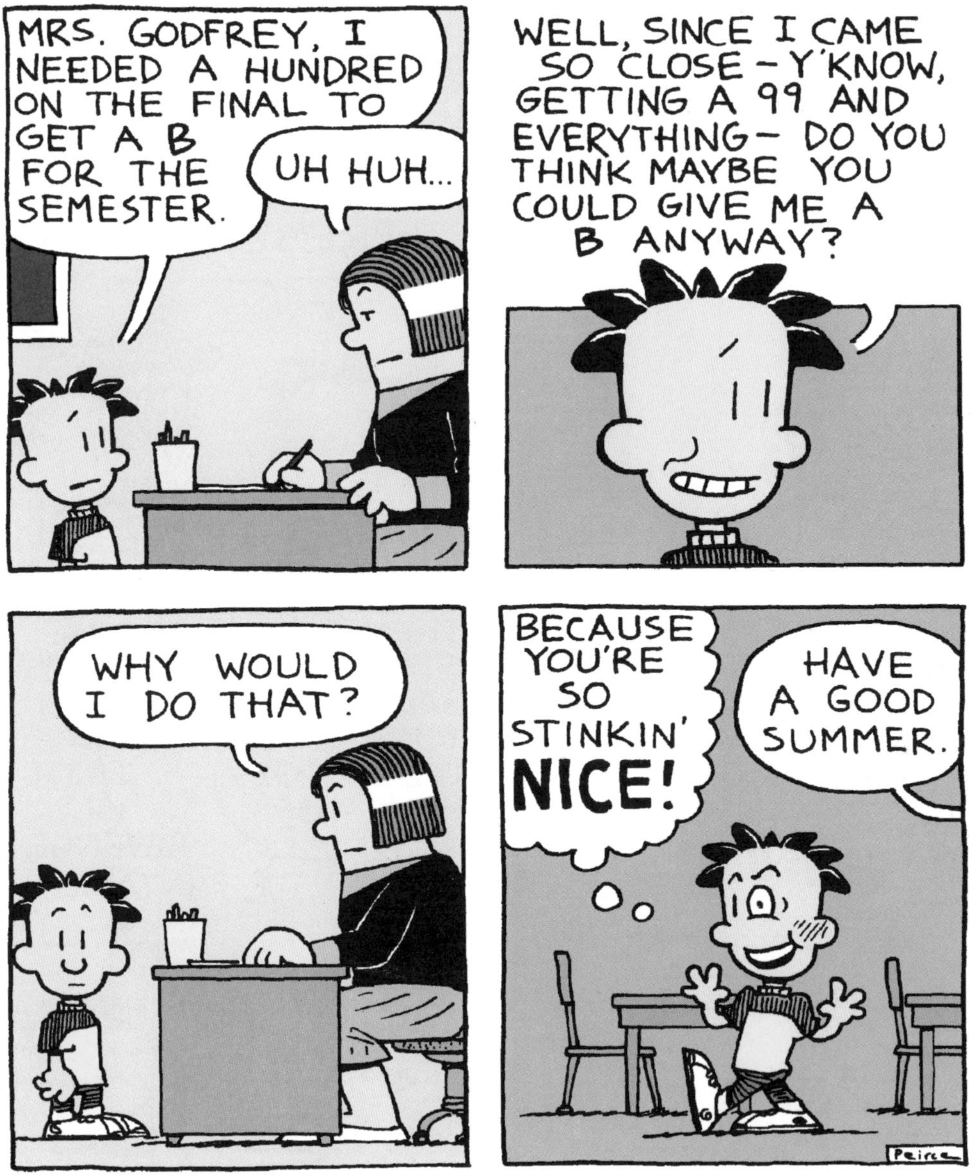
MRS. GODFREY, I NEEDED A HUNDRED ON THE FINAL TO GET A B FOR THE SEMESTER.
UH HUH...
WELL, SINCE I CAME SO CLOSE – Y'KNOW, GETTING A 99 AND EVERYTHING – DO YOU THINK MAYBE YOU COULD GIVE ME A B ANYWAY?
WHY WOULD I DO THAT?
BECAUSE YOU'RE SO STINKIN' NICE!
HAVE A GOOD SUMMER.
Peirce

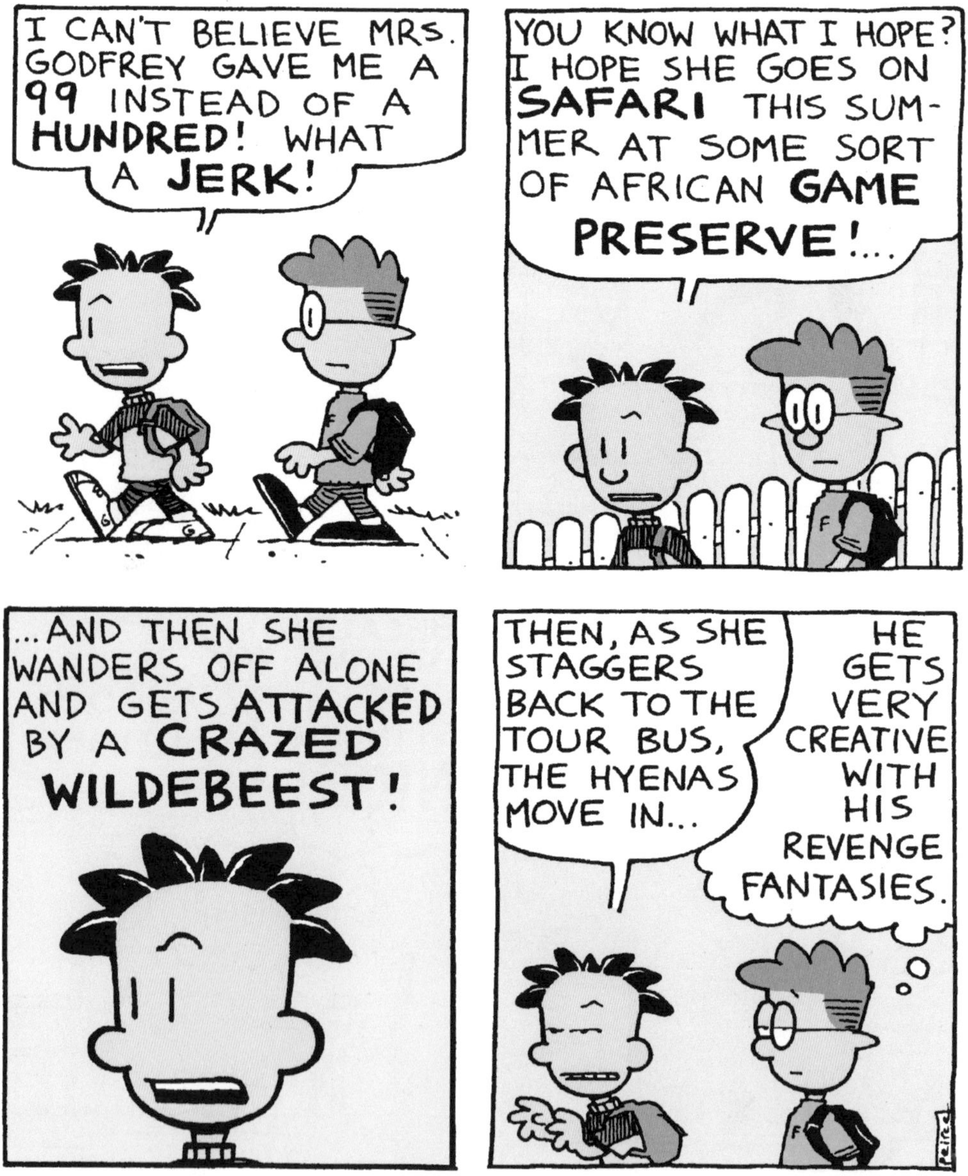
I CAN'T BELIEVE MRS. GODFREY GAVE ME A 99 INSTEAD OF A HUNDRED! WHAT A JERK!
YOU KNOW WHAT I HOPE? I HOPE SHE GOES ON SAFARI THIS SUMMER AT SOME SORT OF AFRICAN GAME PRESERVE!...
...AND THEN SHE WANDERS OFF ALONE AND GETS ATTACKED BY A CRAZED WILDEBEEST!
THEN, AS SHE STAGGERS BACK TO THE TOUR BUS, THE HYENAS MOVE IN...
HE GETS VERY CREATIVE WITH HIS REVENGE FANTASIES.

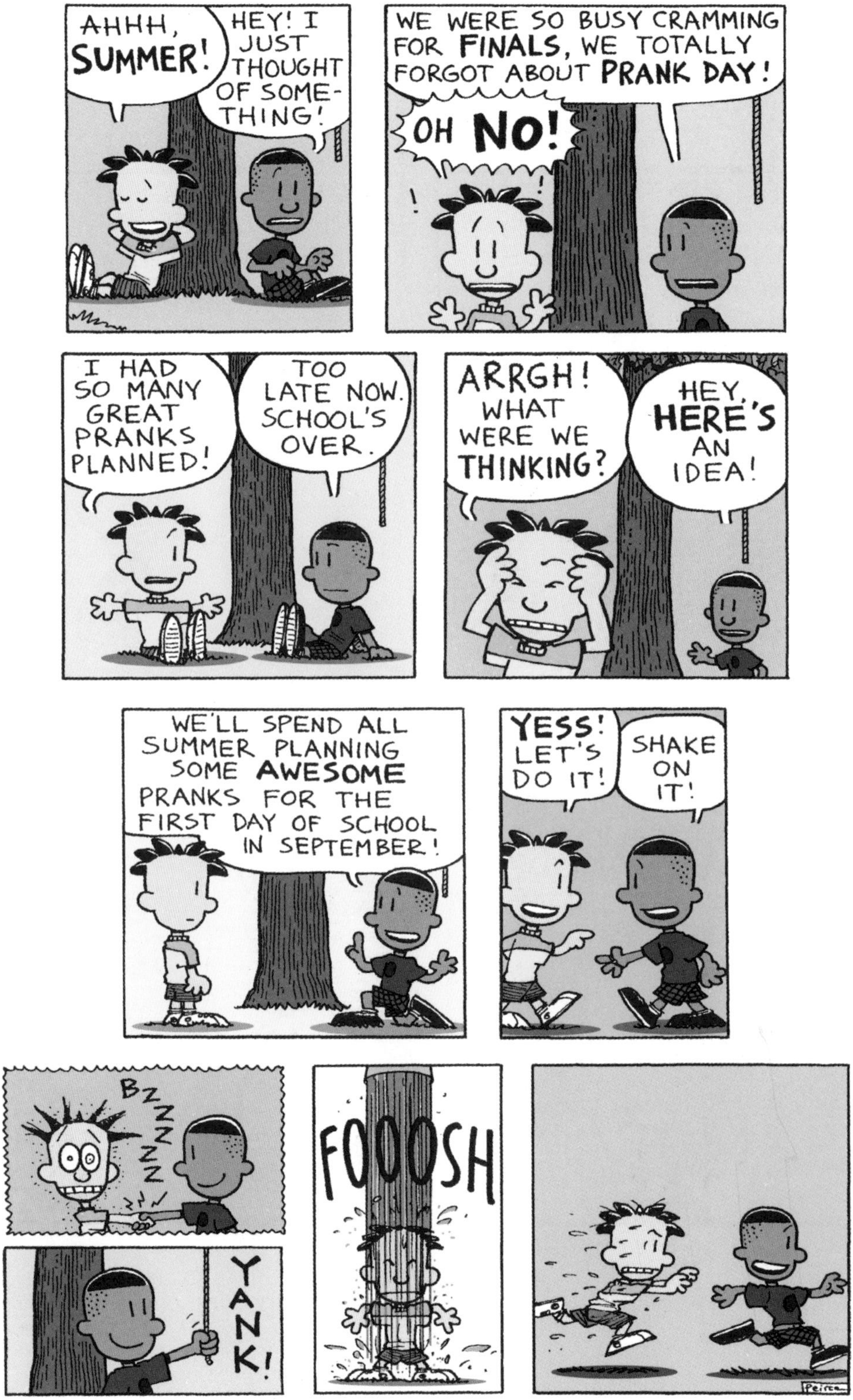
AHHH, SUMMER!
HEY! I JUST THOUGHT OF SOME-THING!
WE WERE SO BUSY CRAMMING FOR FINALS, WE TOTALLY FORGOT ABOUT PRANK DAY!
OH NO!
I HAD SO MANY GREAT PRANKS PLANNED!
TOO LATE NOW. SCHOOL'S OVER.
ARRGH! WHAT WERE WE THINKING?
HEY, HERE'S AN IDEA!
WE'LL SPEND ALL SUMMER PLANNING SOME AWESOME PRANKS FOR THE FIRST DAY OF SCHOOL IN SEPTEMBER!
YESS! LET'S DO IT!
SHAKE ON IT!
BZZZZZ
YANK!
FOOOSH

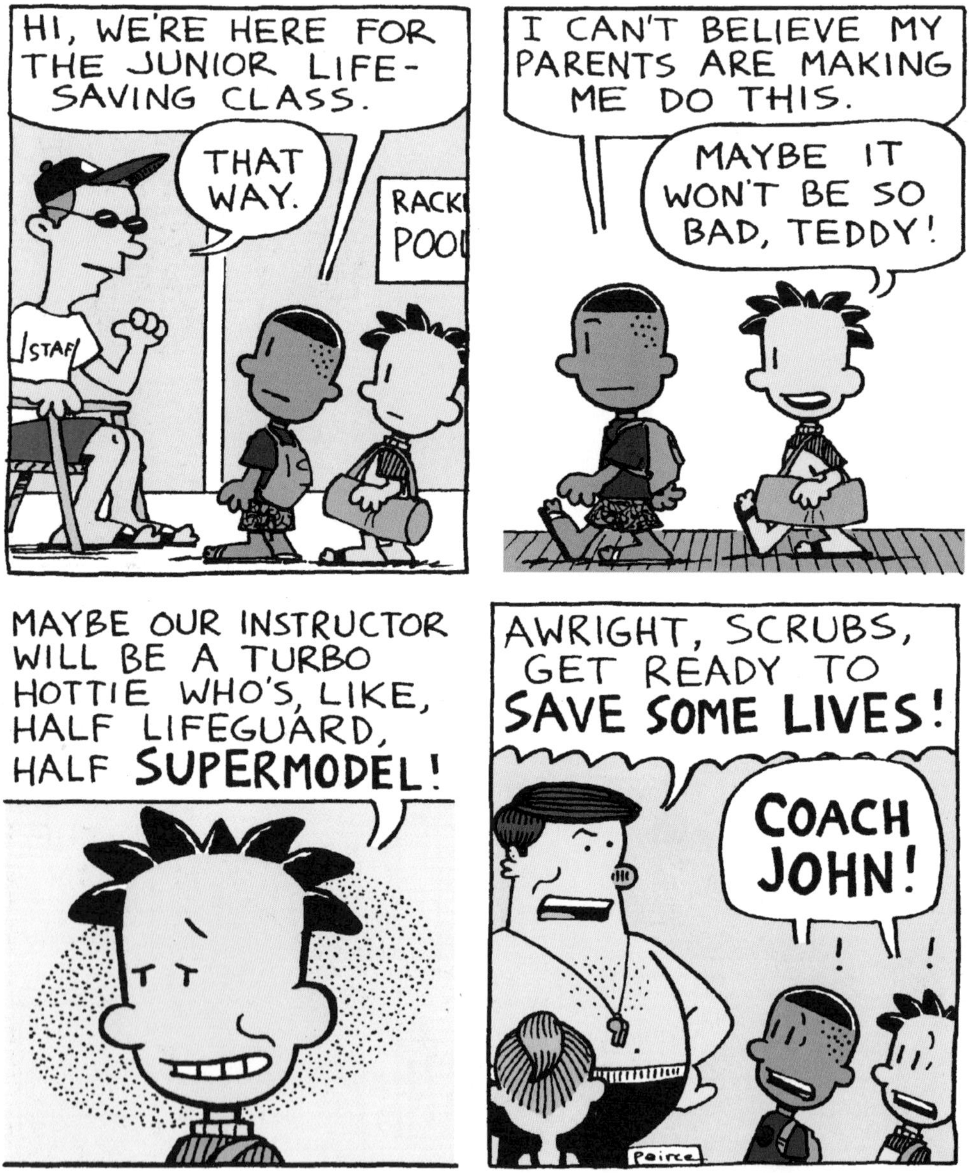
HI, WE'RE HERE FOR THE JUNIOR LIFE-SAVING CLASS.
THAT WAY.
I CAN'T BELIEVE MY PARENTS ARE MAKING ME DO THIS.
MAYBE IT WON'T BE SO BAD, TEDDY!
MAYBE OUR INSTRUCTOR WILL BE A TURBO HOTTIE WHO'S, LIKE, HALF LIFEGUARD, HALF **SUPERMODEL**!
AWRIGHT, SCRUBS, GET READY TO **SAVE SOME LIVES**!
COACH JOHN!
!
!

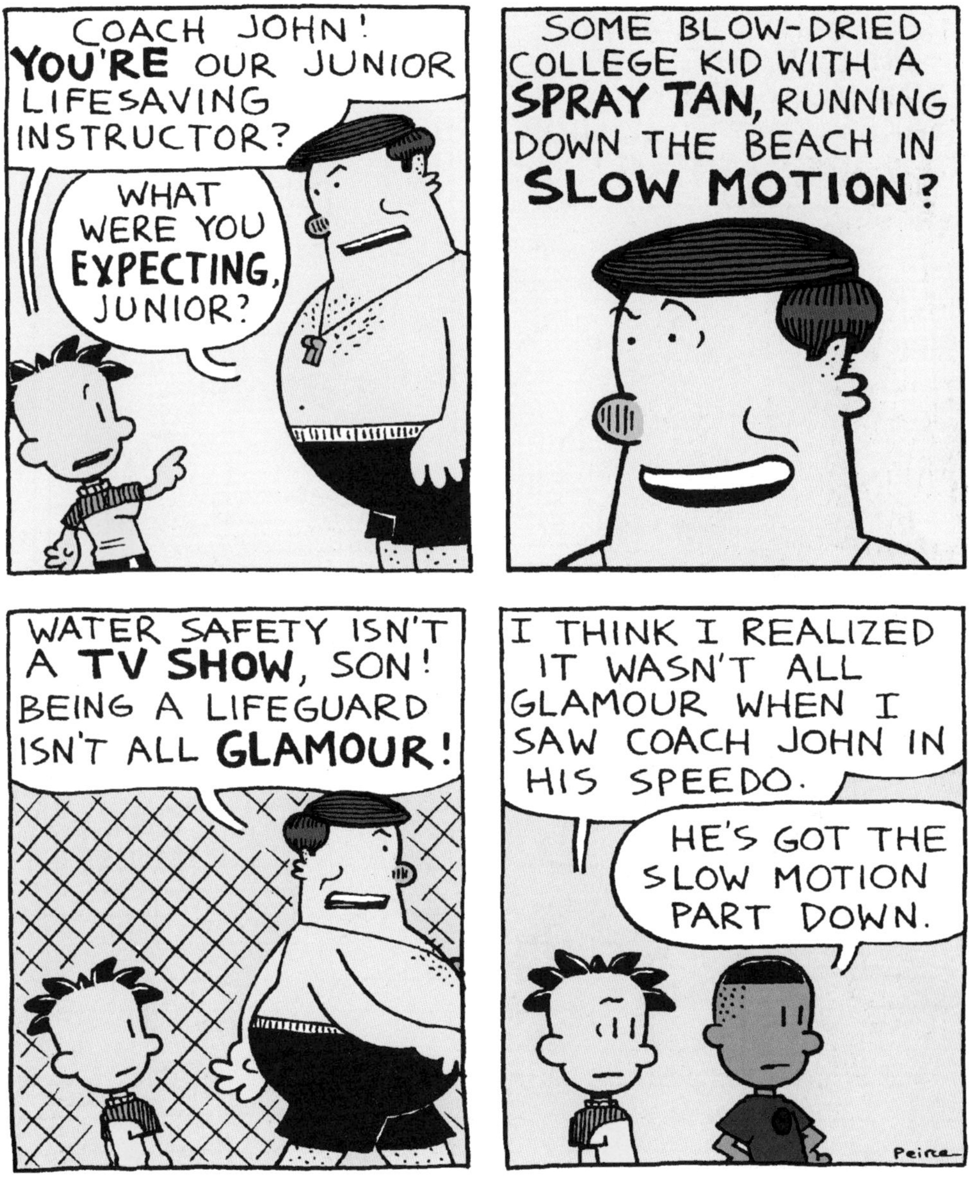
COACH JOHN! **YOU'RE** OUR JUNIOR LIFESAVING INSTRUCTOR?
WHAT WERE YOU **EXPECTING**, JUNIOR?
SOME BLOW-DRIED COLLEGE KID WITH A **SPRAY TAN**, RUNNING DOWN THE BEACH IN **SLOW MOTION**?
WATER SAFETY ISN'T A **TV SHOW**, SON! BEING A LIFEGUARD ISN'T ALL **GLAMOUR**!
I THINK I REALIZED IT WASN'T ALL GLAMOUR WHEN I SAW COACH JOHN IN HIS SPEEDO.
HE'S GOT THE SLOW MOTION PART DOWN.
Peirce

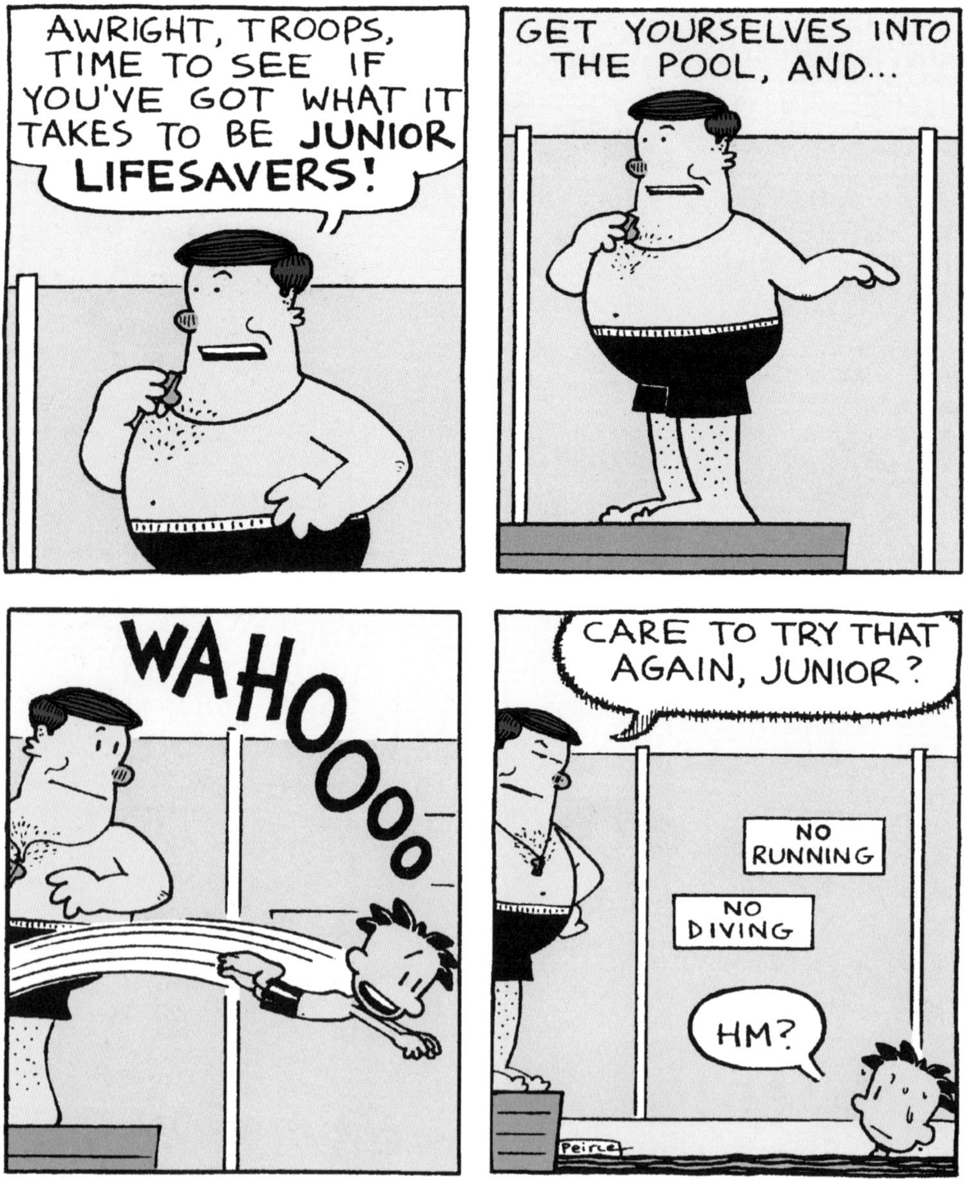
AWRIGHT, TROOPS, TIME TO SEE IF YOU'VE GOT WHAT IT TAKES TO BE **JUNIOR LIFESAVERS!**
GET YOURSELVES INTO THE POOL, AND...
WAHOOOOO
CARE TO TRY THAT AGAIN, JUNIOR?
NO RUNNING
NO DIVING
HM?
Peirce

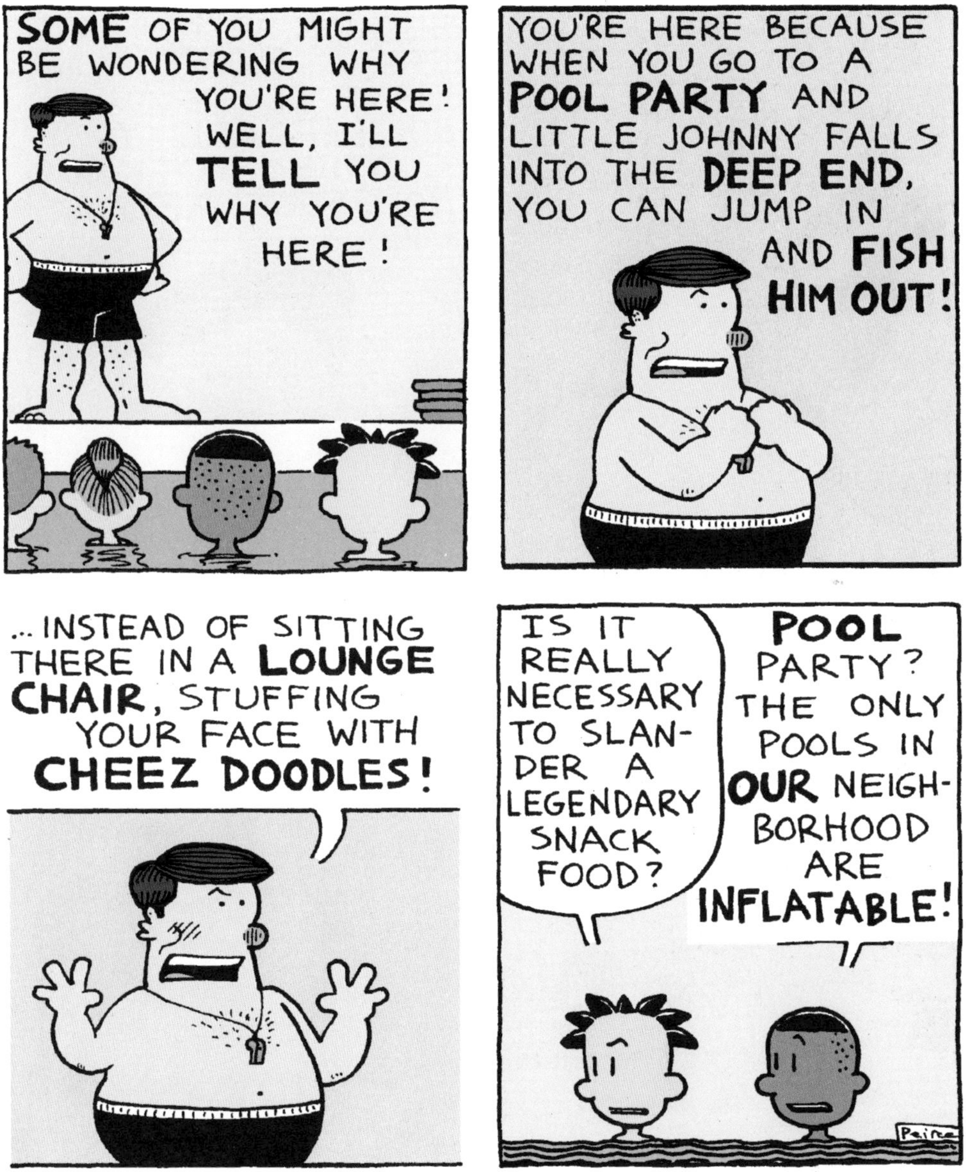
SOME OF YOU MIGHT BE WONDERING WHY YOU'RE HERE! WELL, I'LL TELL YOU WHY YOU'RE HERE!
YOU'RE HERE BECAUSE WHEN YOU GO TO A POOL PARTY AND LITTLE JOHNNY FALLS INTO THE DEEP END, YOU CAN JUMP IN AND FISH HIM OUT!
...INSTEAD OF SITTING THERE IN A LOUNGE CHAIR, STUFFING YOUR FACE WITH CHEEZ DOODLES!
IS IT REALLY NECESSARY TO SLANDER A LEGENDARY SNACK FOOD?
POOL PARTY? THE ONLY POOLS IN OUR NEIGHBORHOOD ARE INFLATABLE!

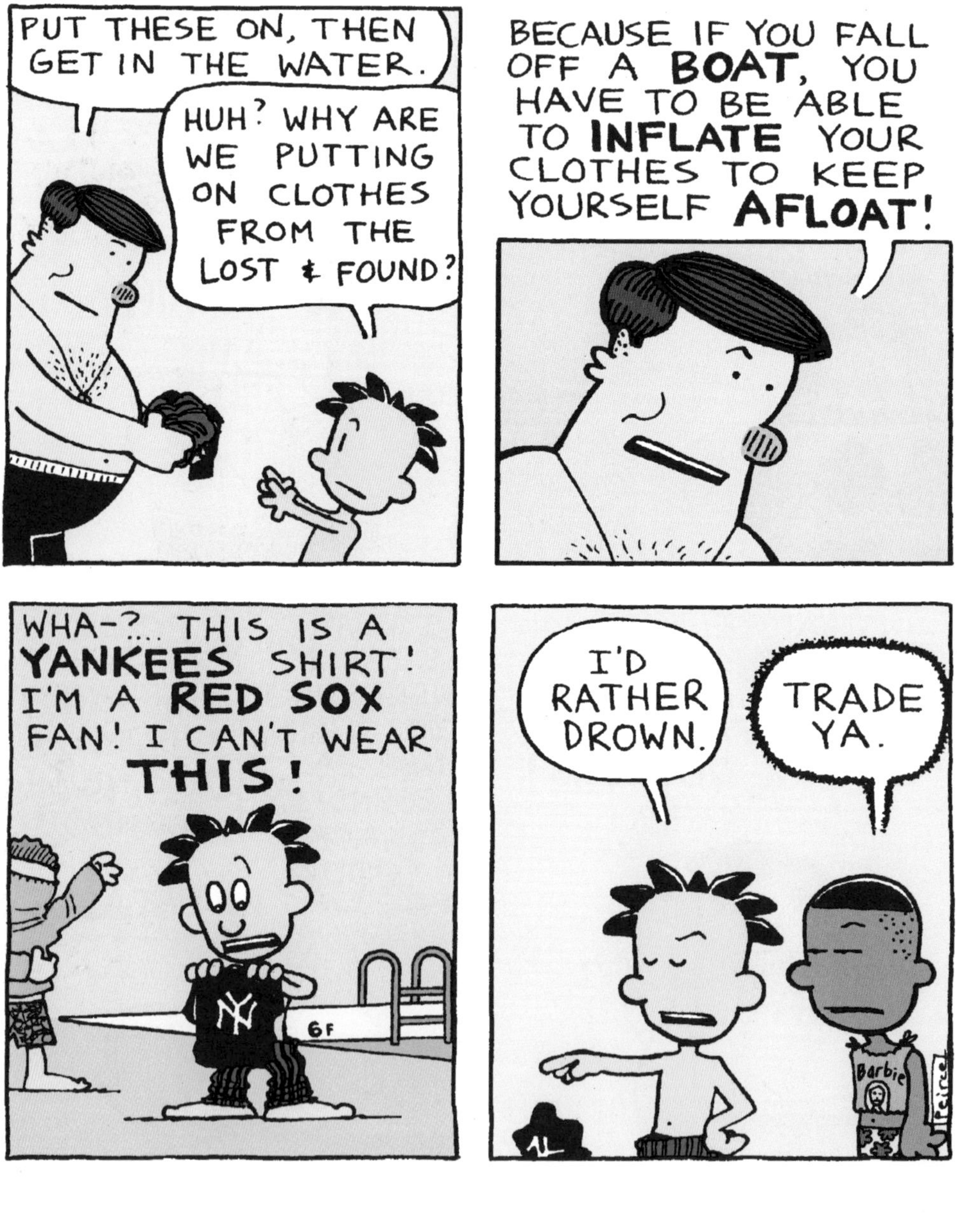
PUT THESE ON, THEN GET IN THE WATER.
HUH? WHY ARE WE PUTTING ON CLOTHES FROM THE LOST & FOUND?
BECAUSE IF YOU FALL OFF A BOAT, YOU HAVE TO BE ABLE TO INFLATE YOUR CLOTHES TO KEEP YOURSELF AFLOAT!
WHA-?... THIS IS A YANKEES SHIRT! I'M A RED SOX FAN! I CAN'T WEAR THIS!
I'D RATHER DROWN.
TRADE YA.

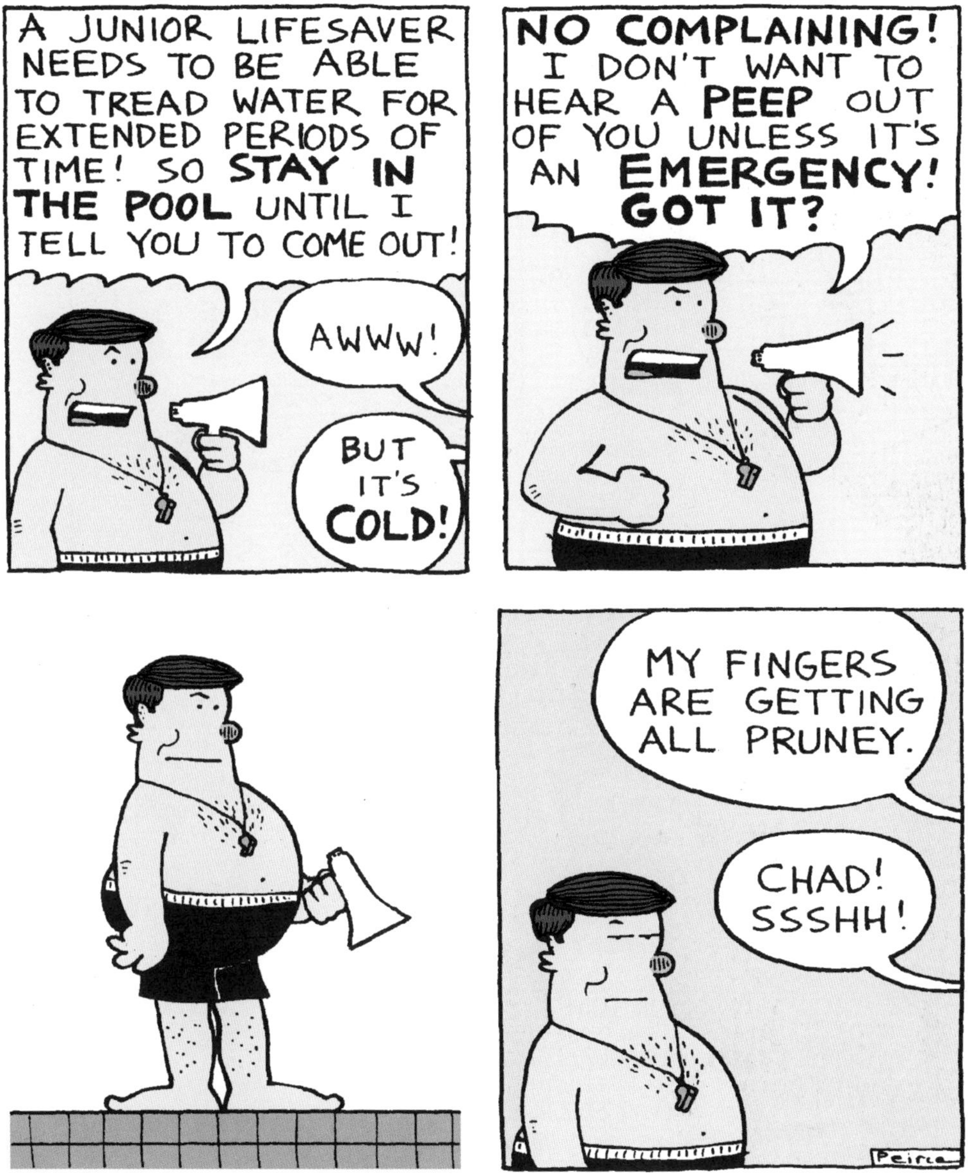
A JUNIOR LIFESAVER NEEDS TO BE ABLE TO TREAD WATER FOR EXTENDED PERIODS OF TIME! SO STAY IN THE POOL UNTIL I TELL YOU TO COME OUT!
AWWW!
BUT IT'S COLD!
NO COMPLAINING! I DON'T WANT TO HEAR A PEEP OUT OF YOU UNLESS IT'S AN EMERGENCY! GOT IT?
MY FINGERS ARE GETTING ALL PRUNEY.
CHAD! SSSHH!
Peirce

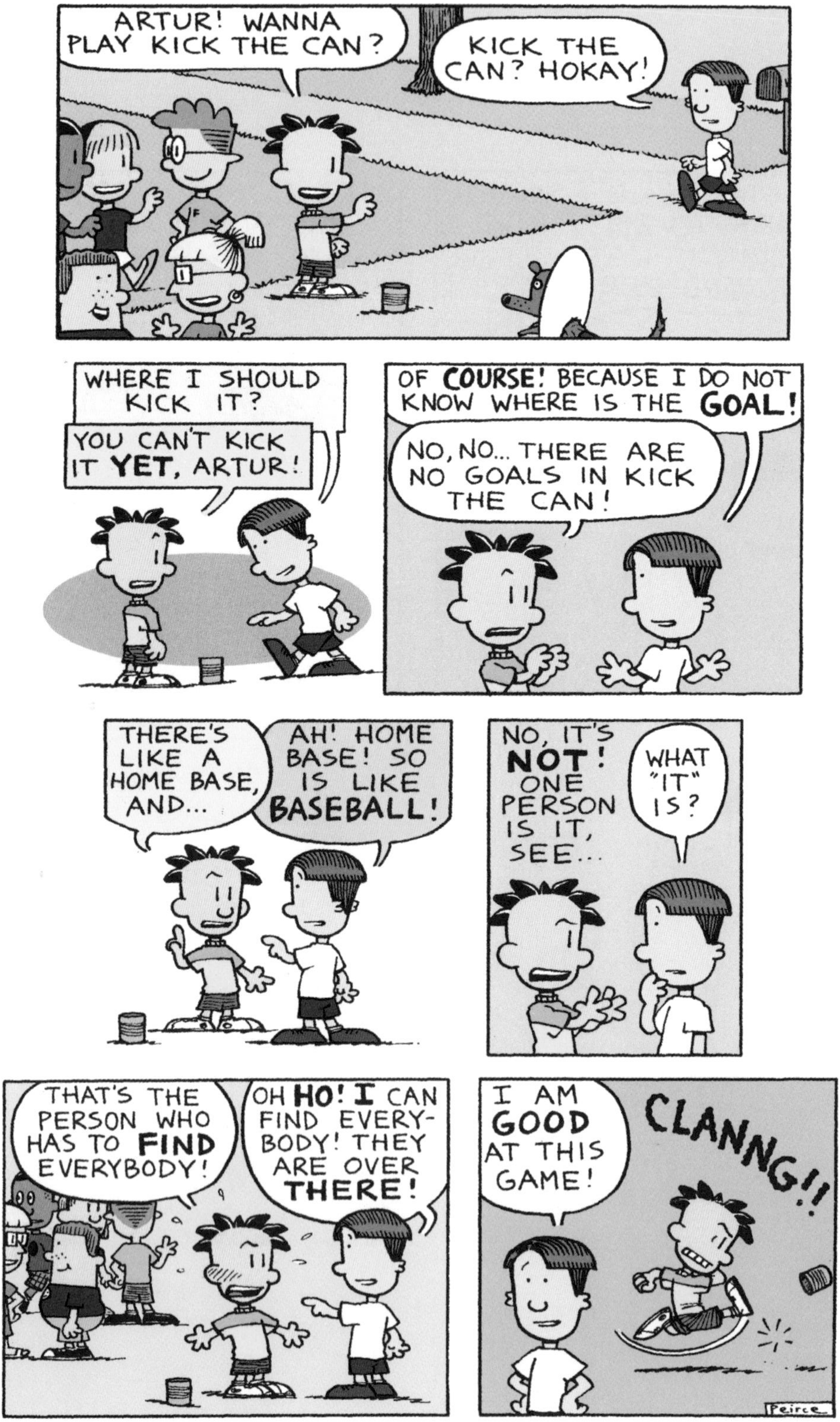
ARTUR! WANNA PLAY KICK THE CAN?
KICK THE CAN? HOKAY!
WHERE I SHOULD KICK IT?
YOU CAN'T KICK IT **YET**, ARTUR!
OF **COURSE**! BECAUSE I DO NOT KNOW WHERE IS THE **GOAL**!
NO, NO... THERE ARE NO GOALS IN KICK THE CAN!
THERE'S LIKE A HOME BASE, AND...
AH! HOME BASE! SO IS LIKE **BASEBALL**!
NO, IT'S **NOT**! ONE PERSON IS IT, SEE...
WHAT "IT" IS?
THAT'S THE PERSON WHO HAS TO **FIND** EVERYBODY!
OH **HO**! **I** CAN FIND EVERY-BODY! THEY ARE OVER **THERE**!
I AM **GOOD** AT THIS GAME!
CLANNG!!
Peirce

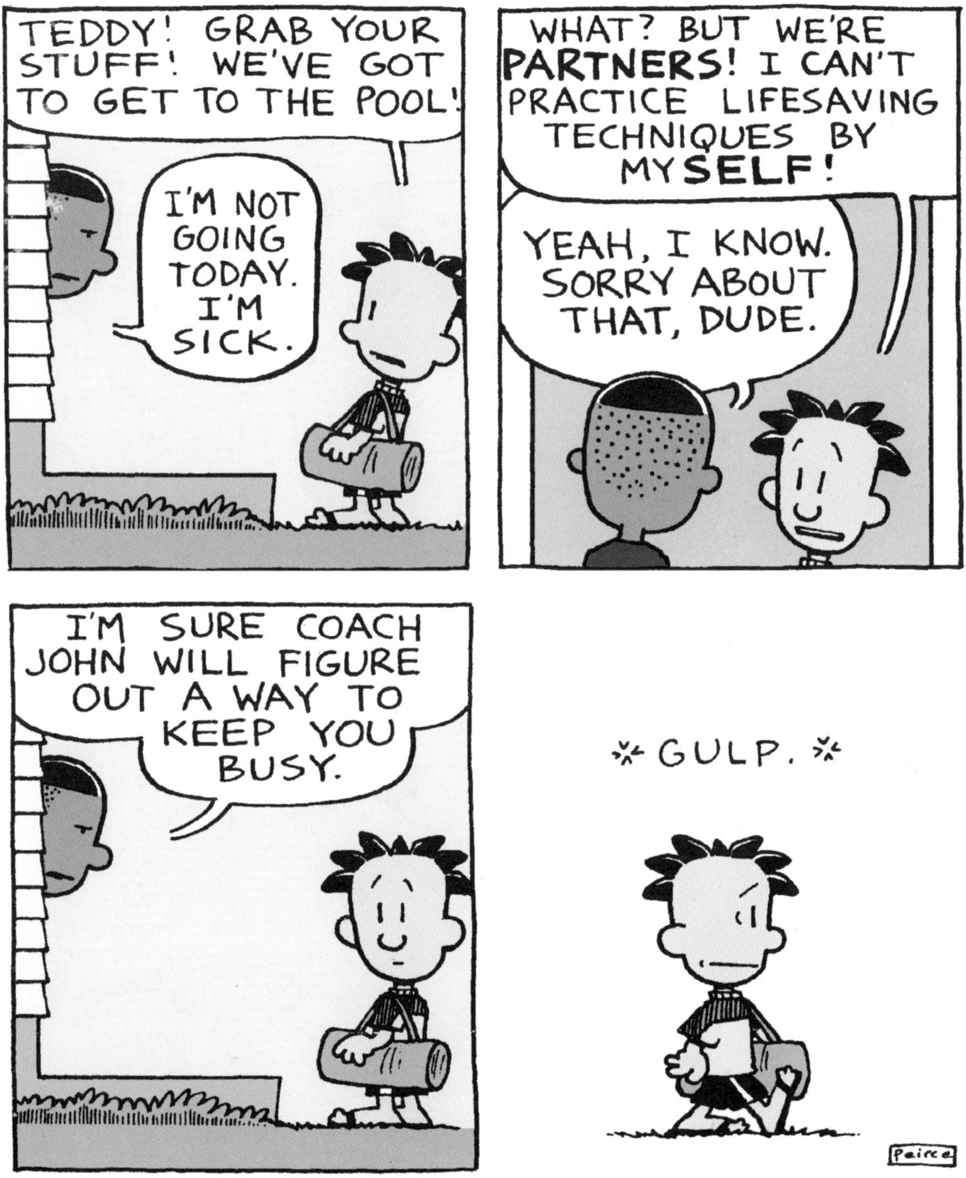
TEDDY! GRAB YOUR STUFF! WE'VE GOT TO GET TO THE POOL!
I'M NOT GOING TODAY. I'M SICK.
WHAT? BUT WE'RE PARTNERS! I CAN'T PRACTICE LIFESAVING TECHNIQUES BY MYSELF!
YEAH, I KNOW. SORRY ABOUT THAT, DUDE.
I'M SURE COACH JOHN WILL FIGURE OUT A WAY TO KEEP YOU BUSY.
GULP.
Peirce

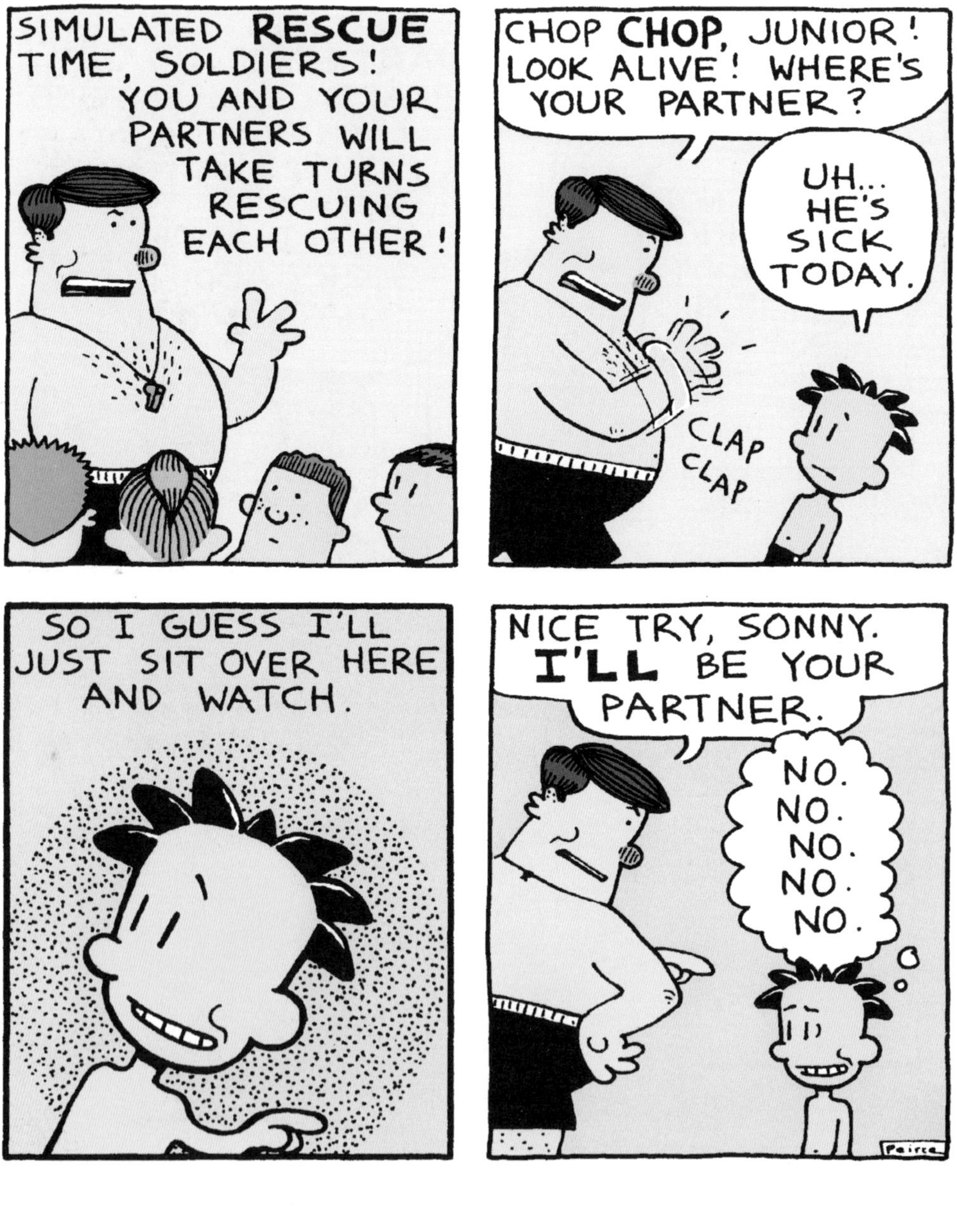
SIMULATED RESCUE TIME, SOLDIERS! YOU AND YOUR PARTNERS WILL TAKE TURNS RESCUING EACH OTHER!
CHOP CHOP, JUNIOR! LOOK ALIVE! WHERE'S YOUR PARTNER?
UH... HE'S SICK TODAY.
CLAP CLAP
SO I GUESS I'LL JUST SIT OVER HERE AND WATCH.
NICE TRY, SONNY. I'LL BE YOUR PARTNER.
NO. NO. NO. NO. NO.
Peirce

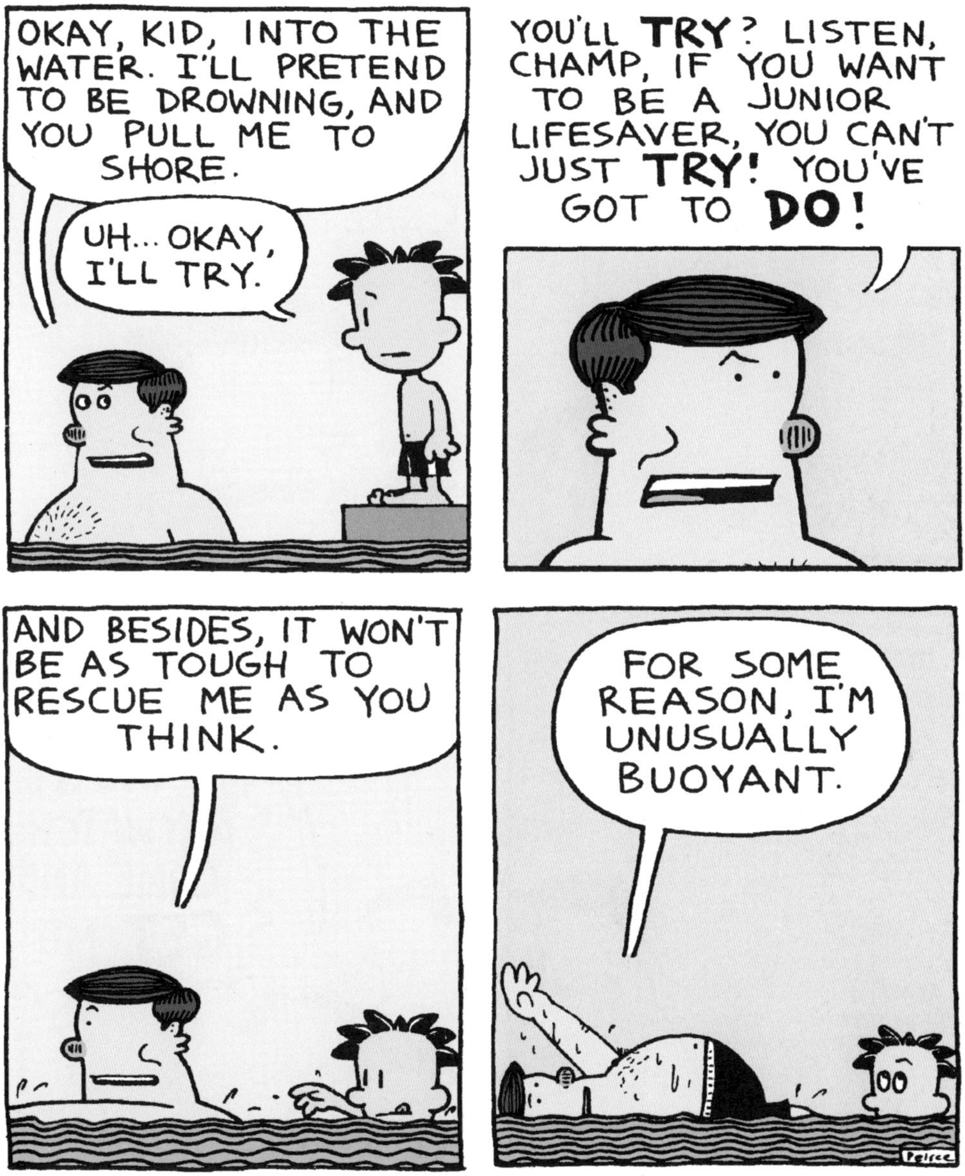
OKAY, KID, INTO THE WATER. I'LL PRETEND TO BE DROWNING, AND YOU PULL ME TO SHORE.
UH... OKAY, I'LL TRY.
YOU'LL **TRY**? LISTEN, CHAMP, IF YOU WANT TO BE A JUNIOR LIFESAVER, YOU CAN'T JUST **TRY**! YOU'VE GOT TO **DO**!
AND BESIDES, IT WON'T BE AS TOUGH TO RESCUE ME AS YOU THINK.
FOR SOME REASON, I'M UNUSUALLY BUOYANT.
Peirce

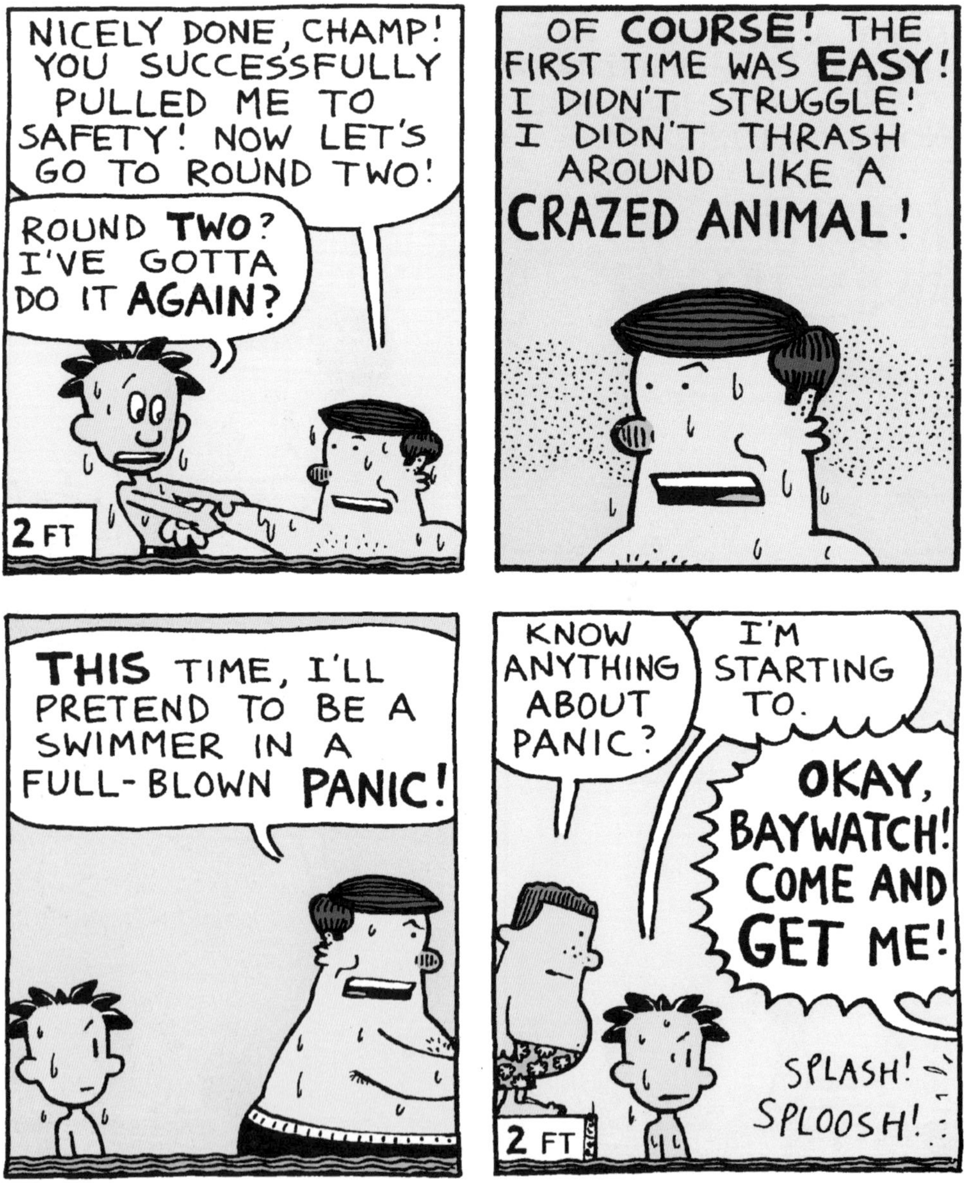
NICELY DONE, CHAMP! YOU SUCCESSFULLY PULLED ME TO SAFETY! NOW LET'S GO TO ROUND TWO!
ROUND TWO? I'VE GOTTA DO IT AGAIN?
2 FT
OF COURSE! THE FIRST TIME WAS EASY! I DIDN'T STRUGGLE! I DIDN'T THRASH AROUND LIKE A CRAZED ANIMAL!
THIS TIME, I'LL PRETEND TO BE A SWIMMER IN A FULL-BLOWN PANIC!
KNOW ANYTHING ABOUT PANIC?
I'M STARTING TO.
OKAY, BAYWATCH! COME AND GET ME!
SPLASH!
SPLOOSH!
2 FT

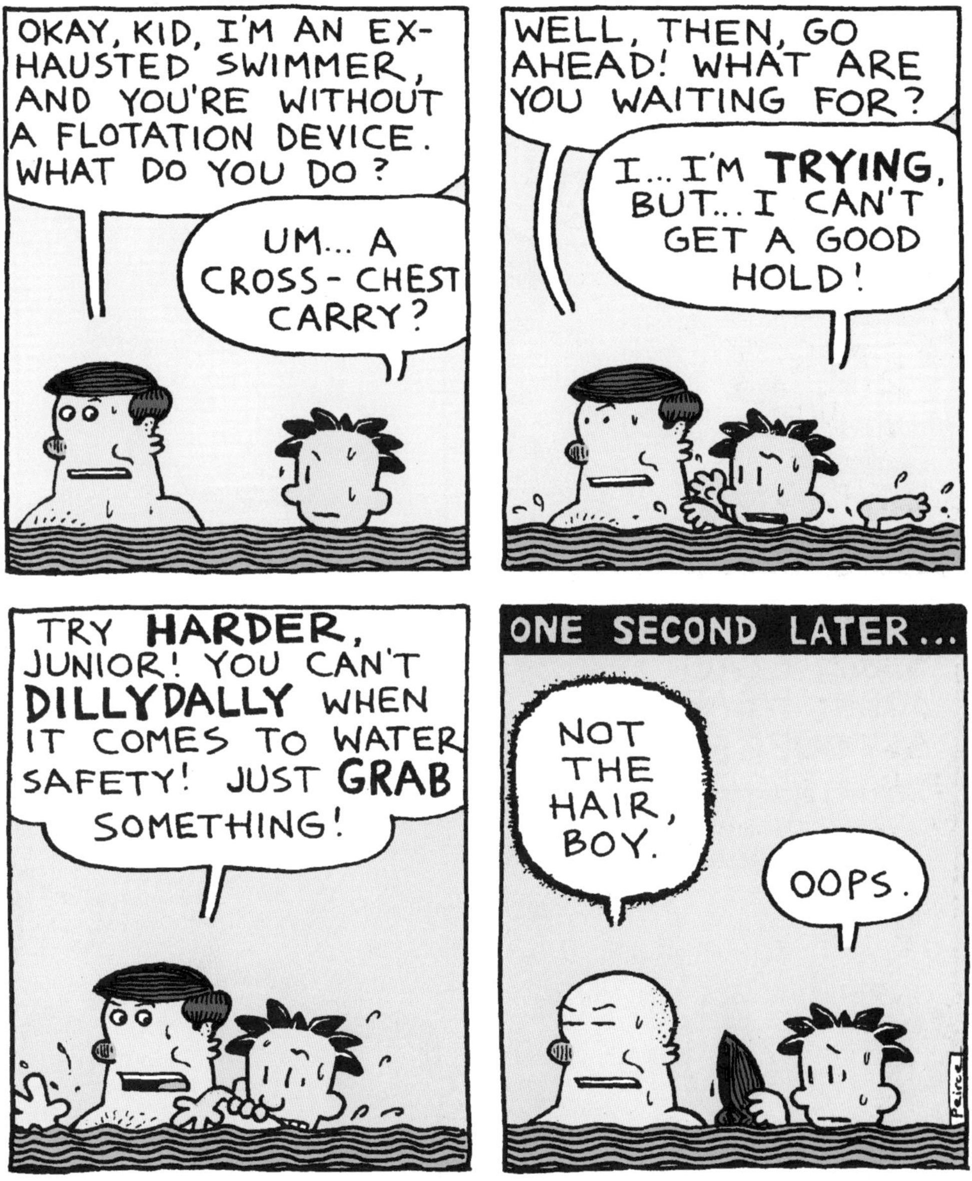
OKAY, KID, I'M AN EX-HAUSTED SWIMMER, AND YOU'RE WITHOUT A FLOTATION DEVICE. WHAT DO YOU DO?
UM... A CROSS-CHEST CARRY?
WELL, THEN, GO AHEAD! WHAT ARE YOU WAITING FOR?
I... I'M TRYING, BUT... I CAN'T GET A GOOD HOLD!
TRY HARDER, JUNIOR! YOU CAN'T DILLYDALLY WHEN IT COMES TO WATER SAFETY! JUST GRAB SOMETHING!
ONE SECOND LATER...
NOT THE HAIR, BOY.
OOPS.
Peirce

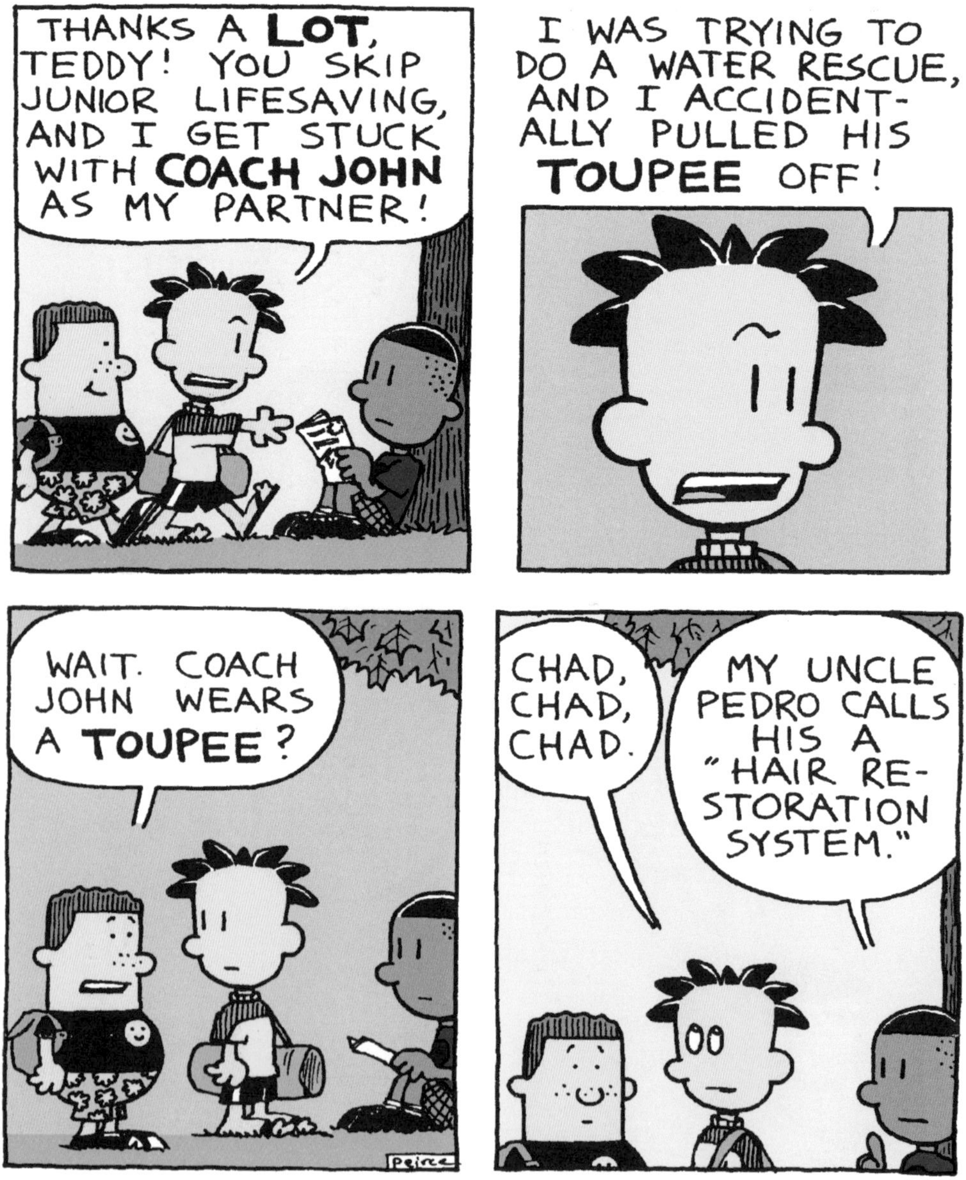
THANKS A LOT, TEDDY! YOU SKIP JUNIOR LIFESAVING, AND I GET STUCK WITH COACH JOHN AS MY PARTNER!
I WAS TRYING TO DO A WATER RESCUE, AND I ACCIDENTALLY PULLED HIS TOUPEE OFF!
WAIT. COACH JOHN WEARS A TOUPEE?
CHAD, CHAD, CHAD.
MY UNCLE PEDRO CALLS HIS A "HAIR RESTORATION SYSTEM."
Peirce

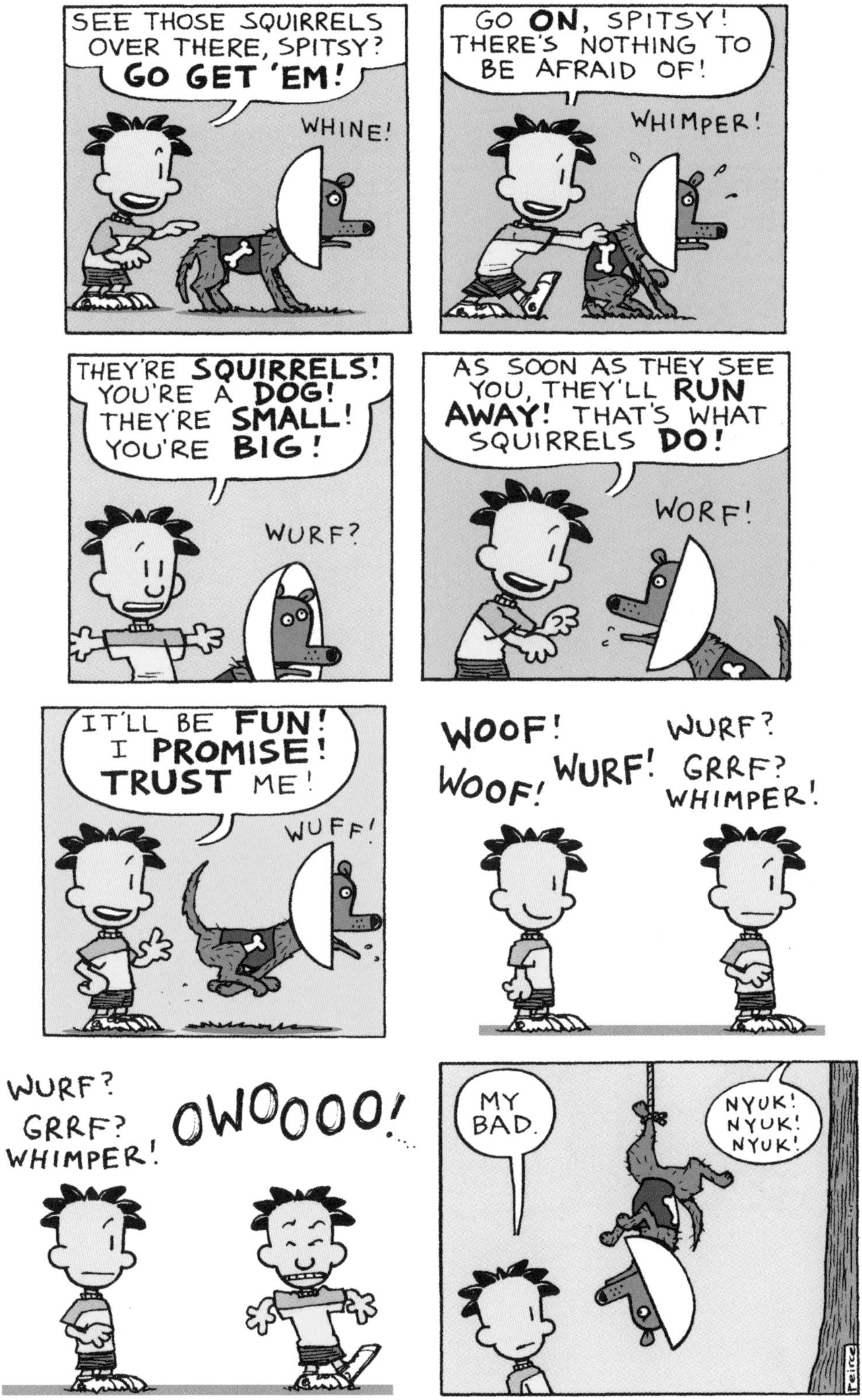
SEE THOSE SQUIRRELS OVER THERE, SPITSY? GO GET 'EM!
WHINE!
GO ON, SPITSY! THERE'S NOTHING TO BE AFRAID OF!
WHIMPER!
THEY'RE SQUIRRELS! YOU'RE A DOG! THEY'RE SMALL! YOU'RE BIG!
WURF?
AS SOON AS THEY SEE YOU, THEY'LL RUN AWAY! THAT'S WHAT SQUIRRELS DO!
WORF!
IT'LL BE FUN! I PROMISE! TRUST ME!
WUFF!
WOOF! WOOF! WURF! WURF? GRRF? WHIMPER!
WURF? GRRF? WHIMPER!
OWOOOO!...
MY BAD.
NYUK! NYUK! NYUK!

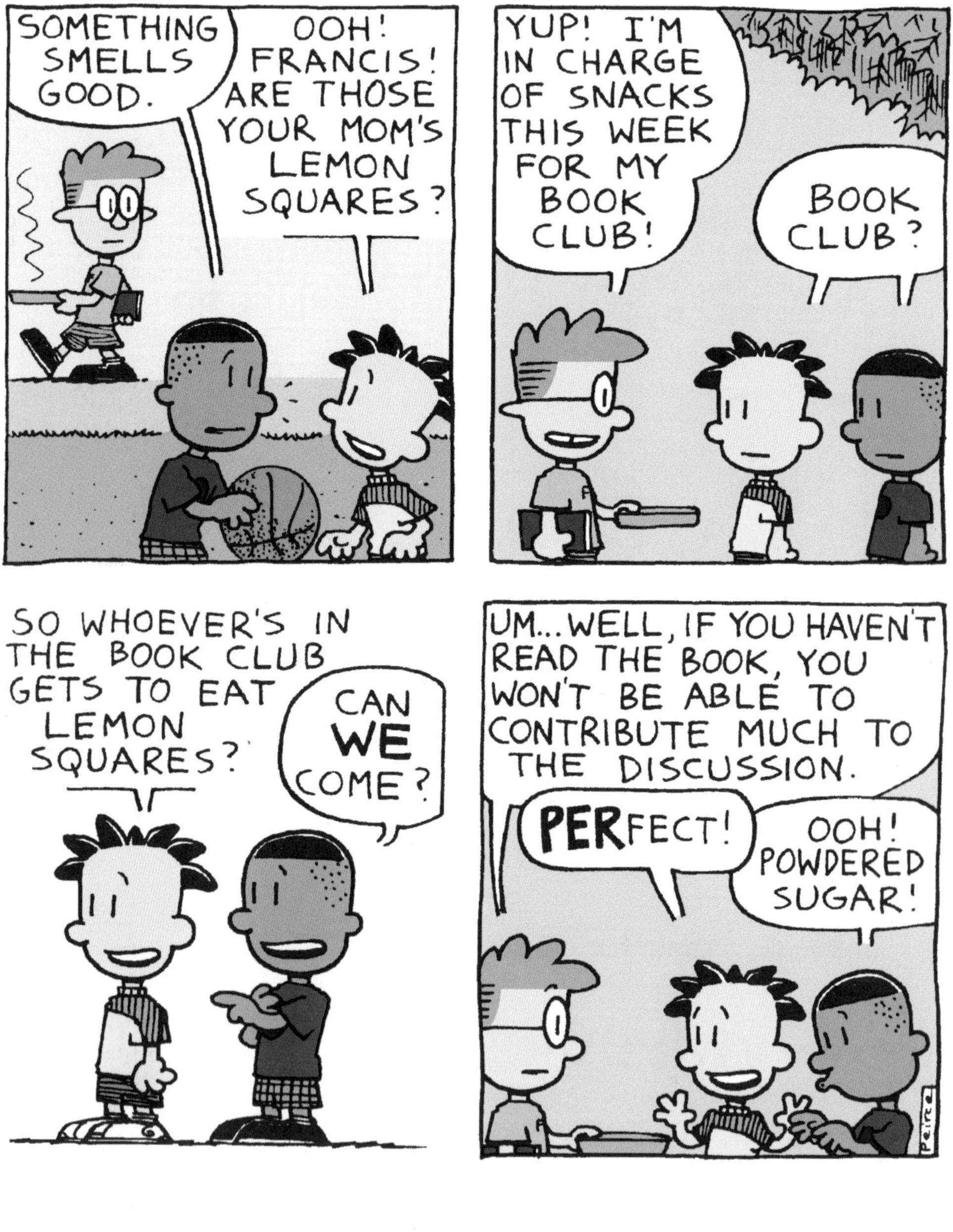
SOMETHING SMELLS GOOD.
OOH! FRANCIS! ARE THOSE YOUR MOM'S LEMON SQUARES?
YUP! I'M IN CHARGE OF SNACKS THIS WEEK FOR MY BOOK CLUB!
BOOK CLUB?
SO WHOEVER'S IN THE BOOK CLUB GETS TO EAT LEMON SQUARES?
CAN **WE** COME?
UM... WELL, IF YOU HAVEN'T READ THE BOOK, YOU WON'T BE ABLE TO CONTRIBUTE MUCH TO THE DISCUSSION.
PERFECT!
OOH! POWDERED SUGAR!
Peirce

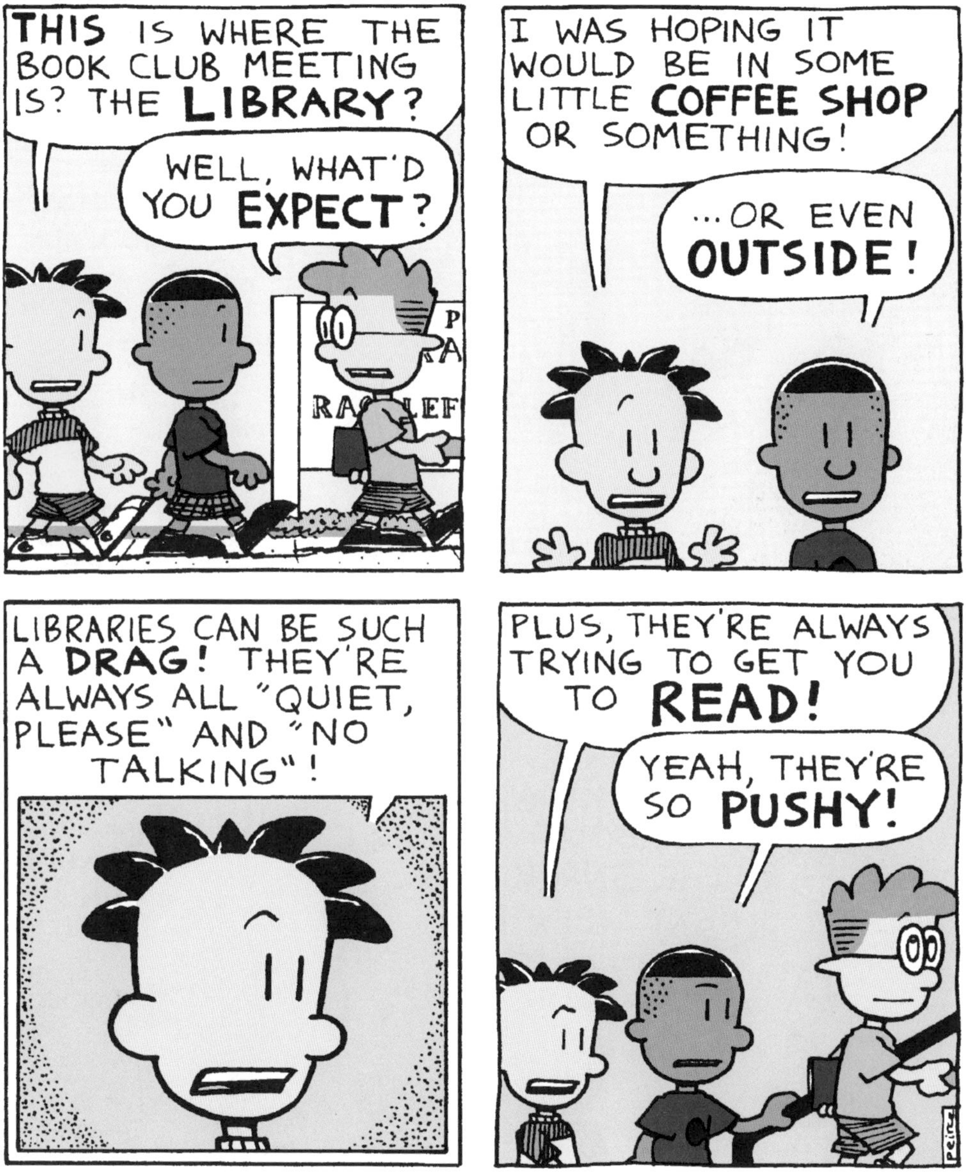
THIS IS WHERE THE BOOK CLUB MEETING IS? THE LIBRARY?
WELL, WHAT'D YOU EXPECT?
I WAS HOPING IT WOULD BE IN SOME LITTLE COFFEE SHOP OR SOMETHING!
...OR EVEN OUTSIDE!
LIBRARIES CAN BE SUCH A DRAG! THEY'RE ALWAYS ALL "QUIET, PLEASE" AND "NO TALKING"!
PLUS, THEY'RE ALWAYS TRYING TO GET YOU TO READ!
YEAH, THEY'RE SO PUSHY!
PEIRCE

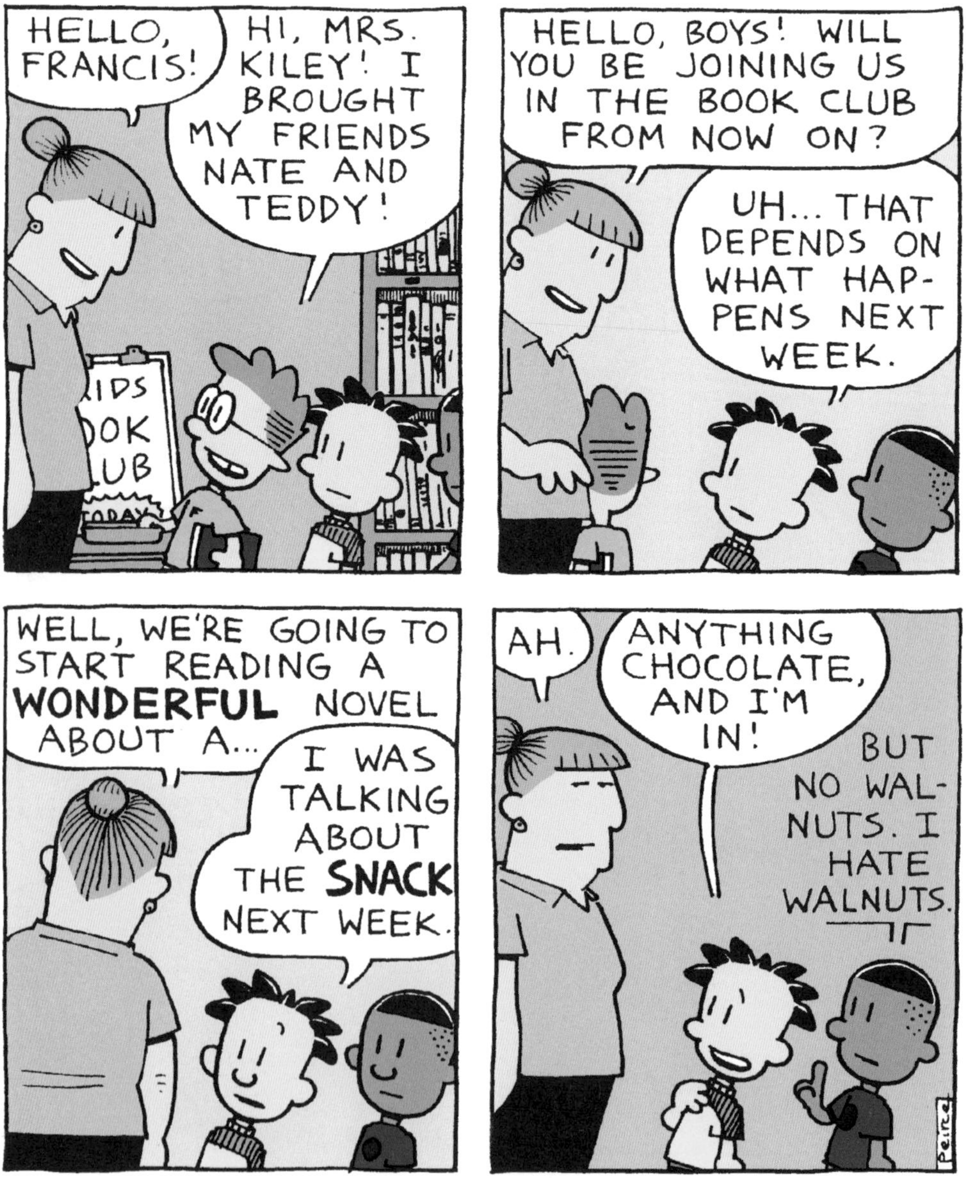
HELLO, FRANCIS!
HI, MRS. KILEY! I BROUGHT MY FRIENDS NATE AND TEDDY!
HELLO, BOYS! WILL YOU BE JOINING US IN THE BOOK CLUB FROM NOW ON?
UH... THAT DEPENDS ON WHAT HAP-PENS NEXT WEEK.
WELL, WE'RE GOING TO START READING A WONDERFUL NOVEL ABOUT A...
I WAS TALKING ABOUT THE SNACK NEXT WEEK.
AH.
ANYTHING CHOCOLATE, AND I'M IN!
BUT NO WAL-NUTS. I HATE WALNUTS.

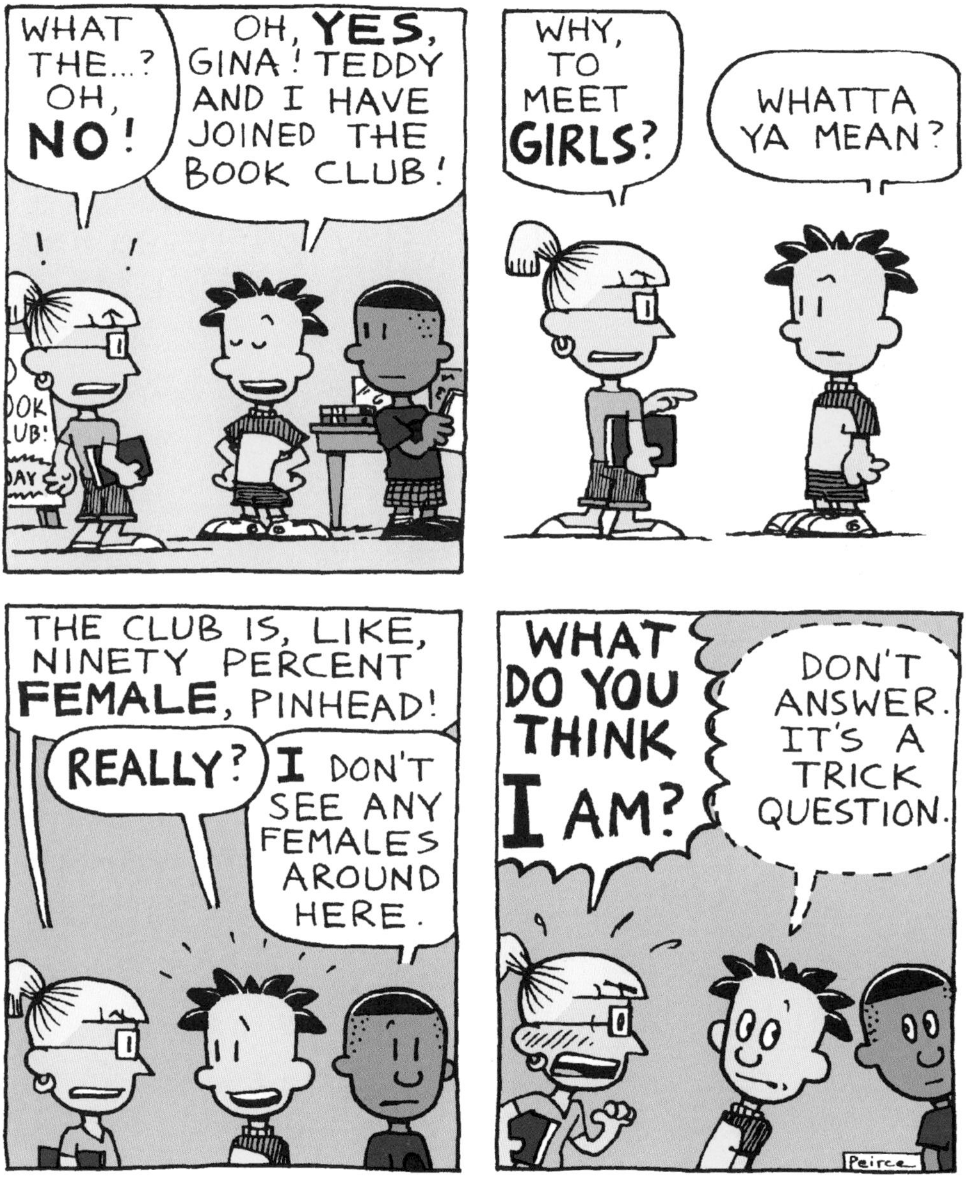
WHAT THE...? OH, NO!
OH, YES, GINA! TEDDY AND I HAVE JOINED THE BOOK CLUB!
WHY, TO MEET GIRLS?
WHATTA YA MEAN?
THE CLUB IS, LIKE, NINETY PERCENT FEMALE, PINHEAD!
REALLY?
I DON'T SEE ANY FEMALES AROUND HERE.
WHAT DO YOU THINK I AM?
DON'T ANSWER. IT'S A TRICK QUESTION.
Peirce

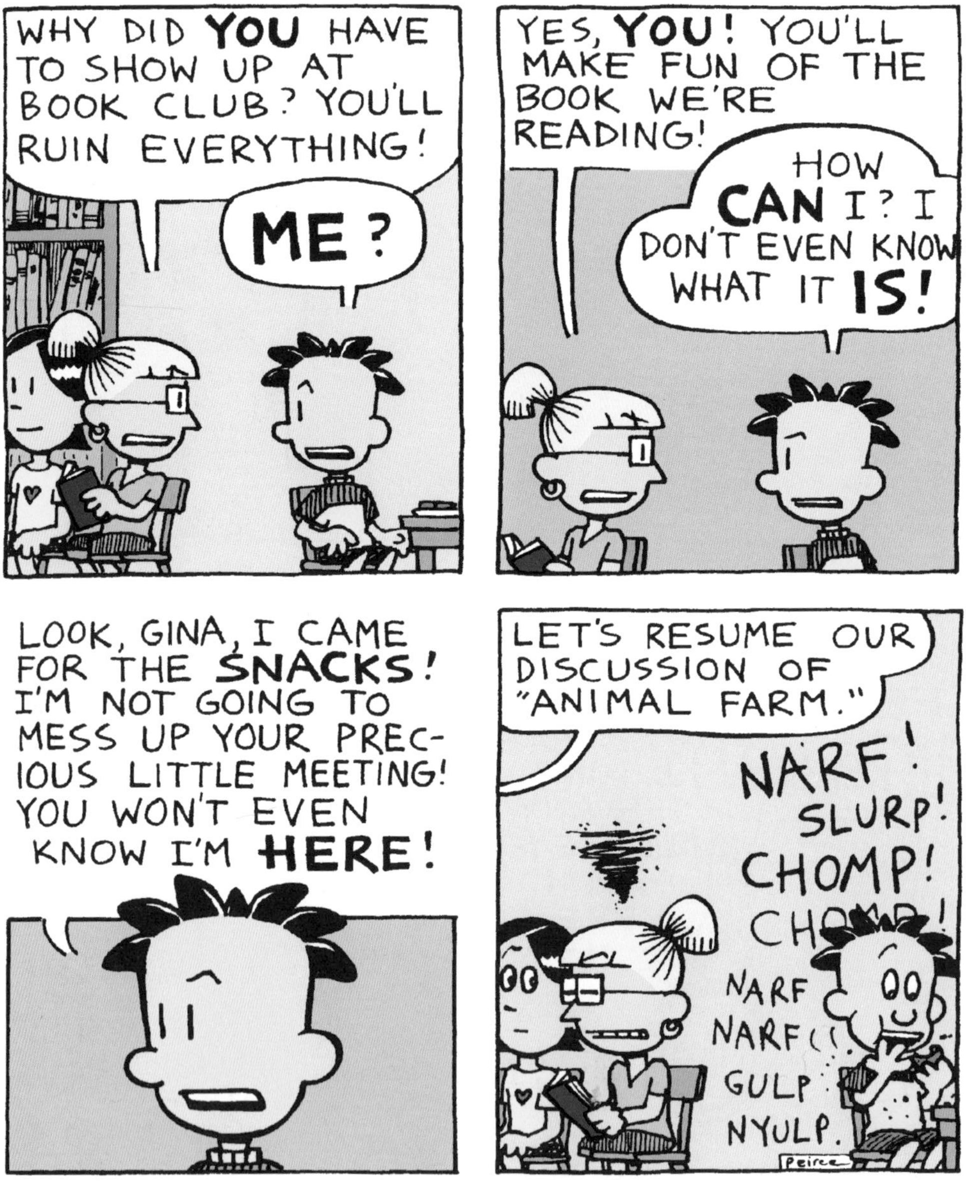
WHY DID YOU HAVE TO SHOW UP AT BOOK CLUB? YOU'LL RUIN EVERYTHING!
ME?
YES, YOU! YOU'LL MAKE FUN OF THE BOOK WE'RE READING!
HOW CAN I? I DON'T EVEN KNOW WHAT IT IS!
LOOK, GINA, I CAME FOR THE SNACKS! I'M NOT GOING TO MESS UP YOUR PRECIOUS LITTLE MEETING! YOU WON'T EVEN KNOW I'M HERE!
LET'S RESUME OUR DISCUSSION OF "ANIMAL FARM."
NARF!
SLURP!
CHOMP!
NARF
NARF
GULP
NYULP.
Peirce

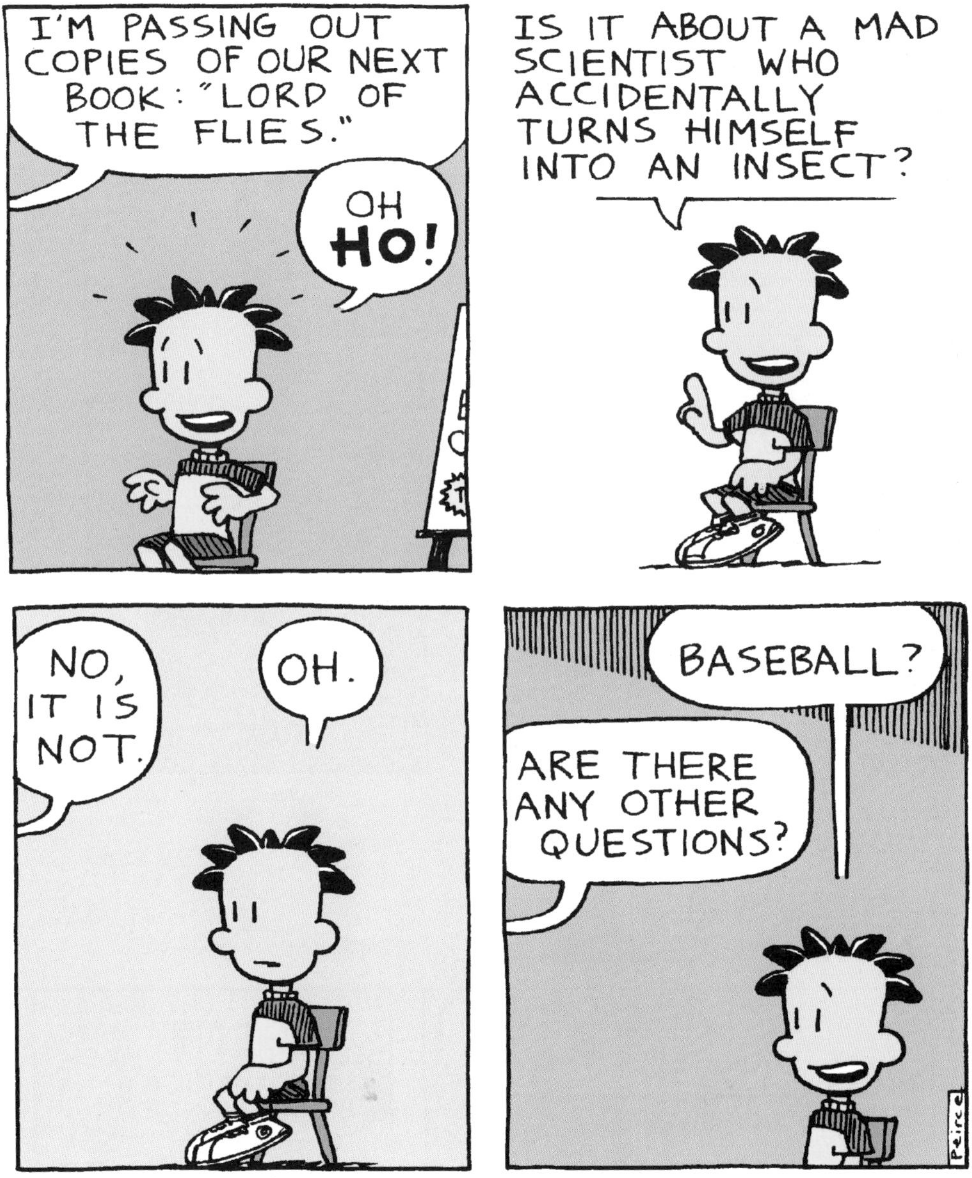
I'M PASSING OUT COPIES OF OUR NEXT BOOK: "LORD OF THE FLIES."
OH HO!
IS IT ABOUT A MAD SCIENTIST WHO ACCIDENTALLY TURNS HIMSELF INTO AN INSECT?
NO, IT IS NOT.
OH.
ARE THERE ANY OTHER QUESTIONS?
BASEBALL?
Peirce

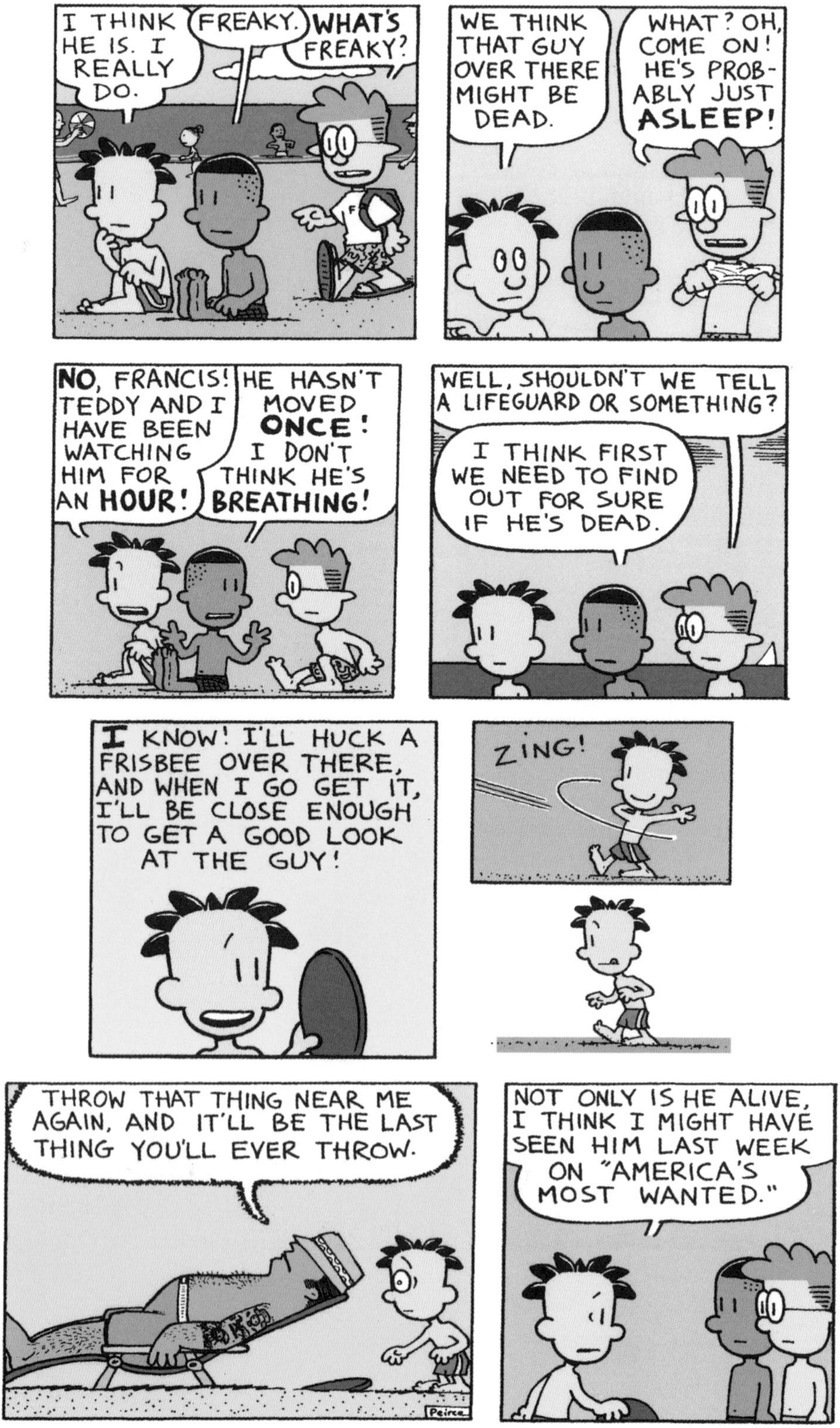
I THINK HE IS. I REALLY DO.
FREAKY.
WHAT'S FREAKY?
WE THINK THAT GUY OVER THERE MIGHT BE DEAD.
WHAT? OH, COME ON! HE'S PROBABLY JUST ASLEEP!
NO, FRANCIS! TEDDY AND I HAVE BEEN WATCHING HIM FOR AN HOUR!
HE HASN'T MOVED ONCE! I DON'T THINK HE'S BREATHING!
WELL, SHOULDN'T WE TELL A LIFEGUARD OR SOMETHING?
I THINK FIRST WE NEED TO FIND OUT FOR SURE IF HE'S DEAD.
I KNOW! I'LL HUCK A FRISBEE OVER THERE, AND WHEN I GO GET IT, I'LL BE CLOSE ENOUGH TO GET A GOOD LOOK AT THE GUY!
ZING!
THROW THAT THING NEAR ME AGAIN, AND IT'LL BE THE LAST THING YOU'LL EVER THROW.
Peirce
NOT ONLY IS HE ALIVE, I THINK I MIGHT HAVE SEEN HIM LAST WEEK ON "AMERICA'S MOST WANTED."

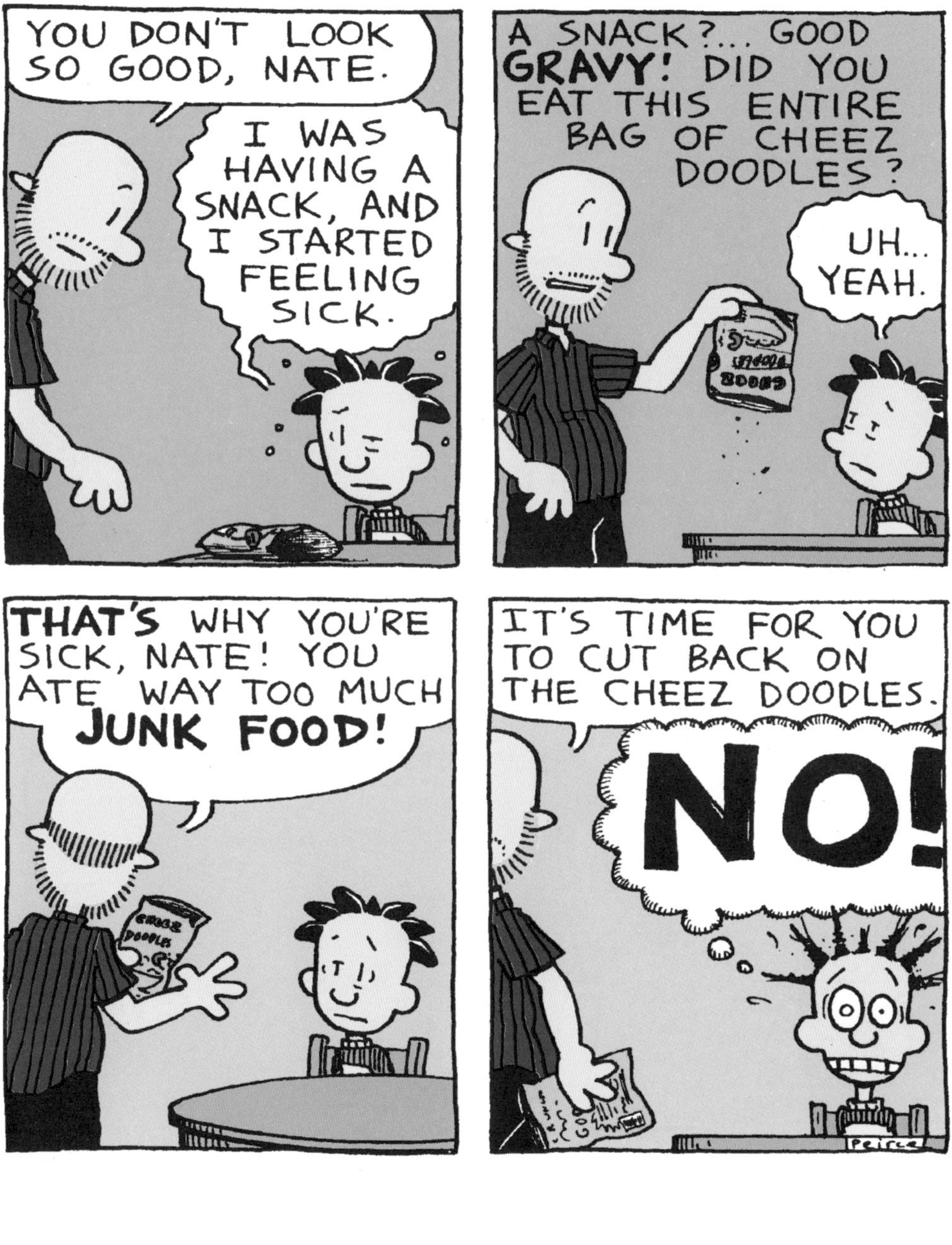
YOU DON'T LOOK SO GOOD, NATE.
I WAS HAVING A SNACK, AND I STARTED FEELING SICK.
A SNACK?... GOOD **GRAVY!** DID YOU EAT THIS ENTIRE BAG OF CHEEZ DOODLES?
UH... YEAH.
THAT'S WHY YOU'RE SICK, NATE! YOU ATE WAY TOO MUCH **JUNK FOOD!**
IT'S TIME FOR YOU TO CUT BACK ON THE CHEEZ DOODLES.
NO!
Peirce

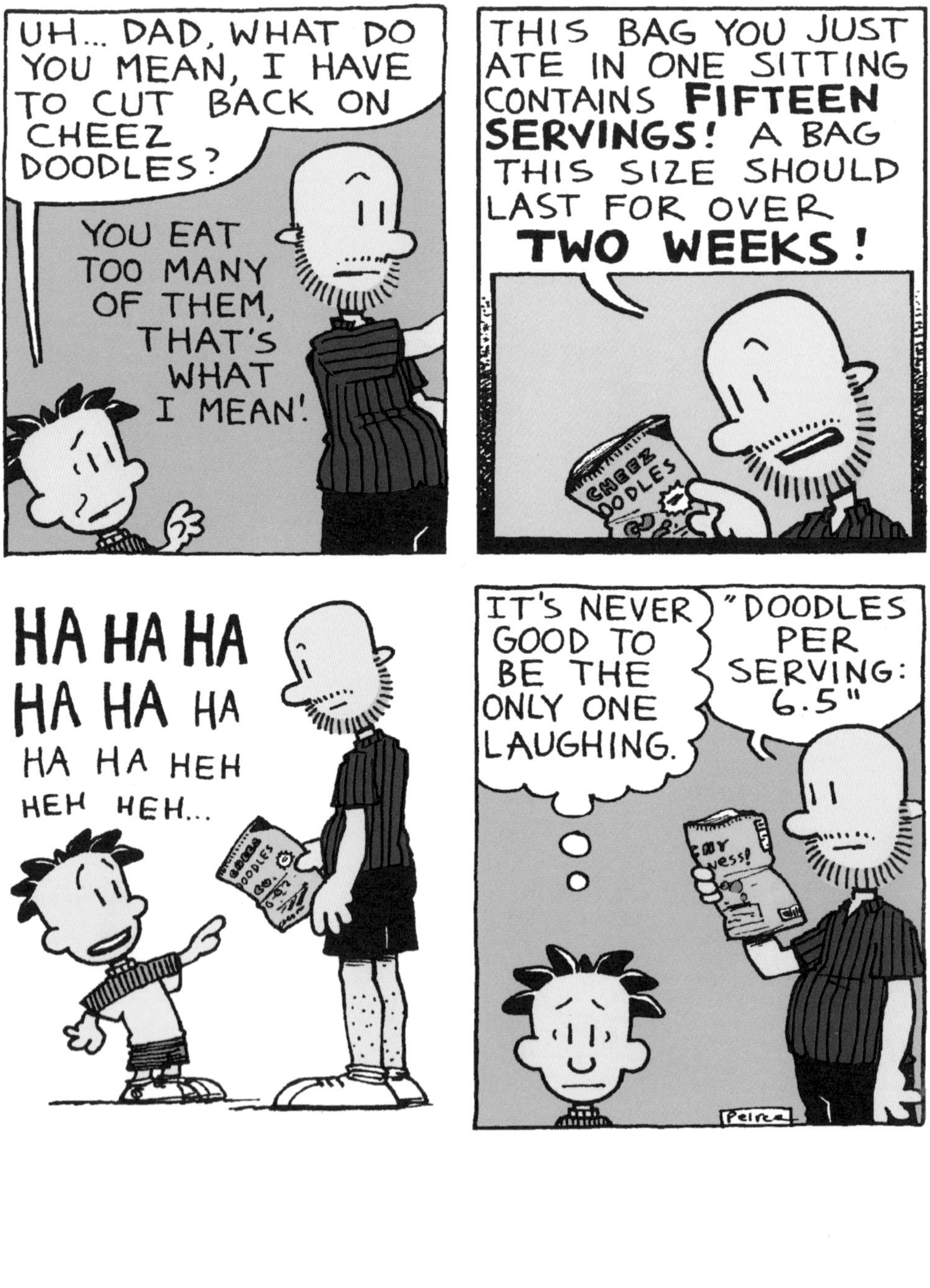
UH... DAD, WHAT DO YOU MEAN, I HAVE TO CUT BACK ON CHEEZ DOODLES?
YOU EAT TOO MANY OF THEM, THAT'S WHAT I MEAN!
THIS BAG YOU JUST ATE IN ONE SITTING CONTAINS **FIFTEEN SERVINGS!** A BAG THIS SIZE SHOULD LAST FOR OVER **TWO WEEKS!**
CHEEZ DOODLES
HA HA HA HA HA HA HA HA HEH HEH HEH...
IT'S NEVER GOOD TO BE THE ONLY ONE LAUGHING.
"DOODLES PER SERVING: 6.5"
Peirce

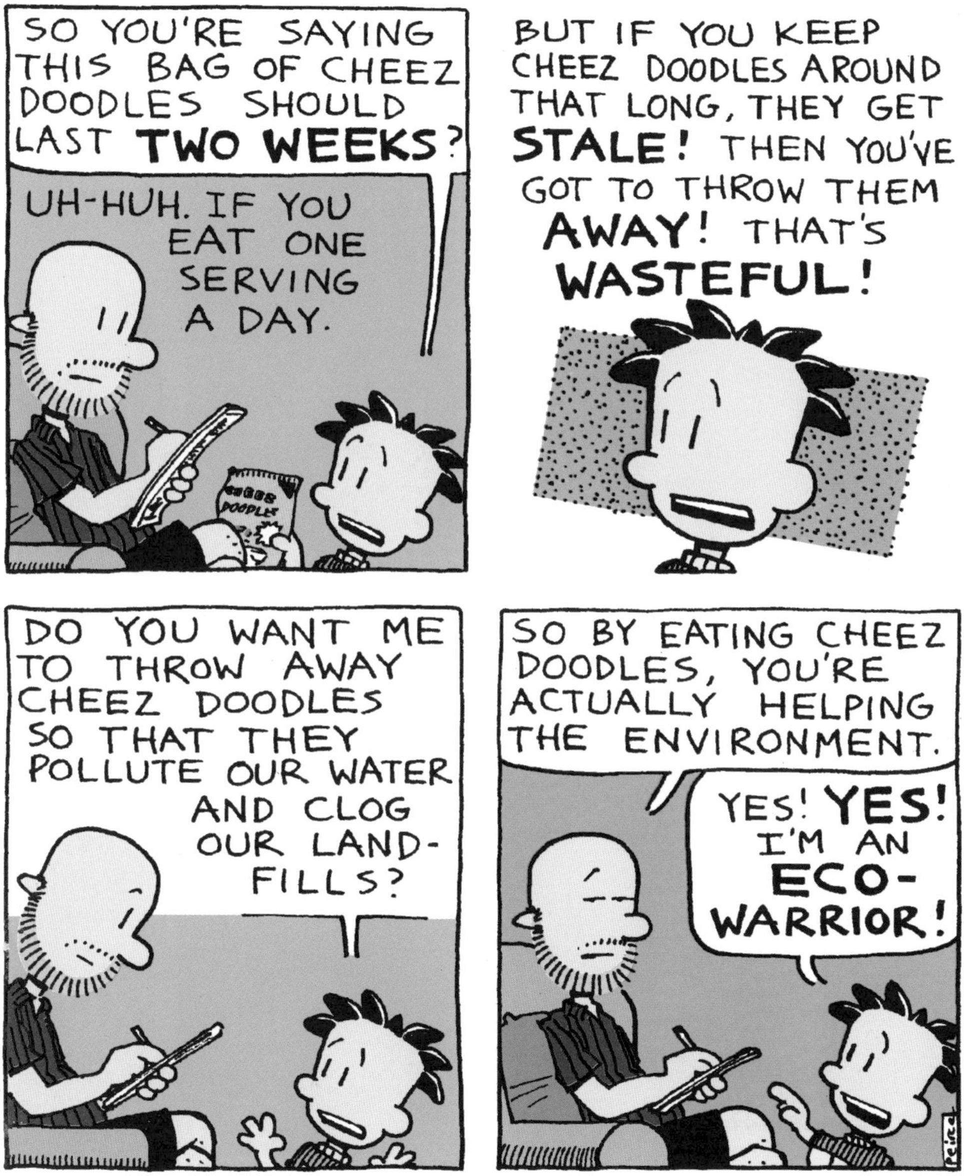
SO YOU'RE SAYING THIS BAG OF CHEEZ DOODLES SHOULD LAST TWO WEEKS?
UH-HUH. IF YOU EAT ONE SERVING A DAY.
BUT IF YOU KEEP CHEEZ DOODLES AROUND THAT LONG, THEY GET STALE! THEN YOU'VE GOT TO THROW THEM AWAY! THAT'S WASTEFUL!
DO YOU WANT ME TO THROW AWAY CHEEZ DOODLES SO THAT THEY POLLUTE OUR WATER AND CLOG OUR LAND-FILLS?
SO BY EATING CHEEZ DOODLES, YOU'RE ACTUALLY HELPING THE ENVIRONMENT.
YES! YES! I'M AN ECO-WARRIOR!

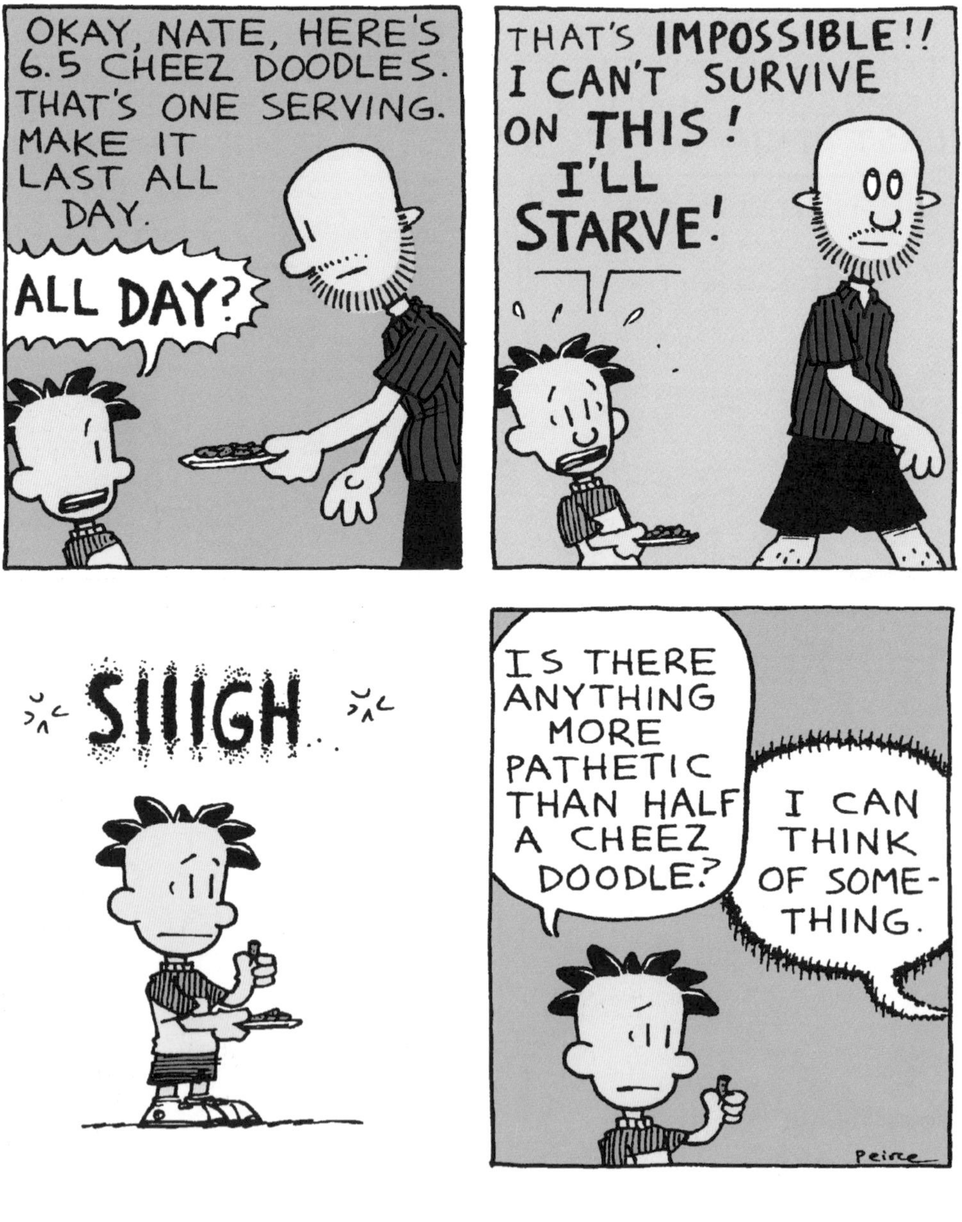
OKAY, NATE, HERE'S 6.5 CHEEZ DOODLES. THAT'S ONE SERVING. MAKE IT LAST ALL DAY.
ALL DAY?
THAT'S IMPOSSIBLE!! I CAN'T SURVIVE ON THIS! I'LL STARVE!
SIIIGH...
IS THERE ANYTHING MORE PATHETIC THAN HALF A CHEEZ DOODLE?
I CAN THINK OF SOME-THING.
Peirce

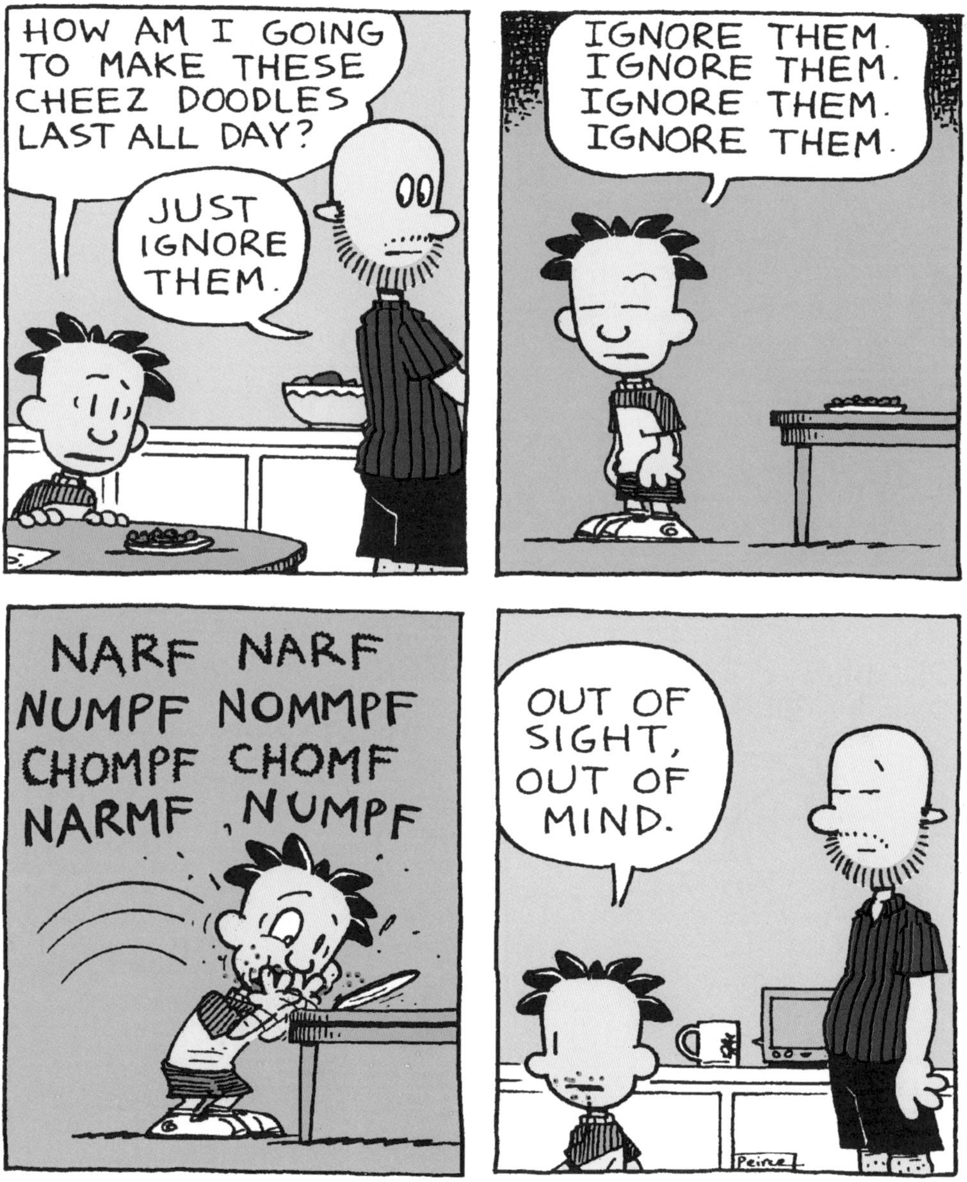

HOW AM I GOING TO MAKE THESE CHEEZ DOODLES LAST ALL DAY?
JUST IGNORE THEM.
IGNORE THEM. IGNORE THEM. IGNORE THEM. IGNORE THEM.
NARF NARF NUMPF NOMMPF CHOMPF CHOMF NARMF, NUMPF
OUT OF SIGHT, OUT OF MIND.
Peirce

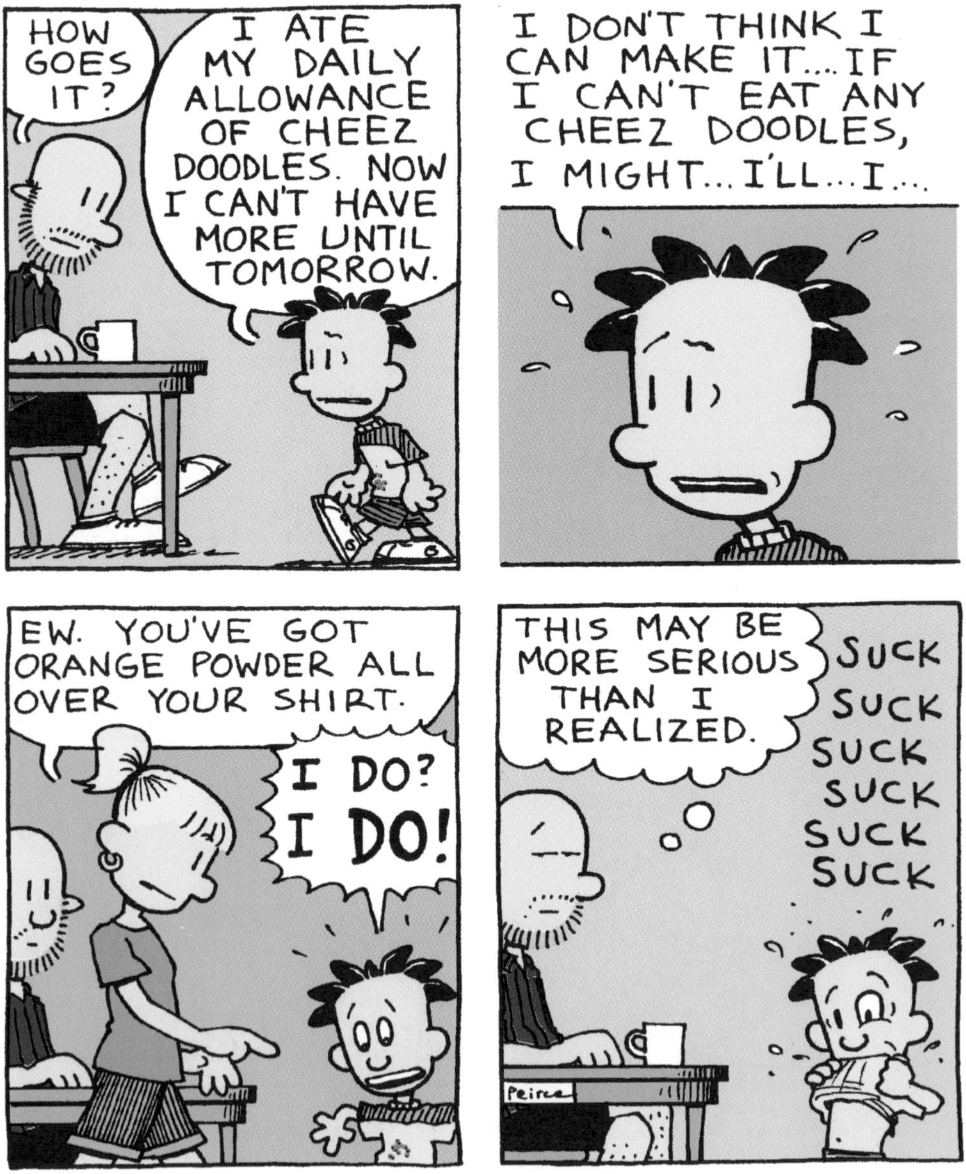
HOW GOES IT?
I ATE MY DAILY ALLOWANCE OF CHEEZ DOODLES. NOW I CAN'T HAVE MORE UNTIL TOMORROW.
I DON'T THINK I CAN MAKE IT.... IF I CAN'T EAT ANY CHEEZ DOODLES, I MIGHT... I'LL... I...
EW. YOU'VE GOT ORANGE POWDER ALL OVER YOUR SHIRT.
I DO? I DO!
THIS MAY BE MORE SERIOUS THAN I REALIZED.
SUCK SUCK SUCK SUCK SUCK SUCK
Peirce

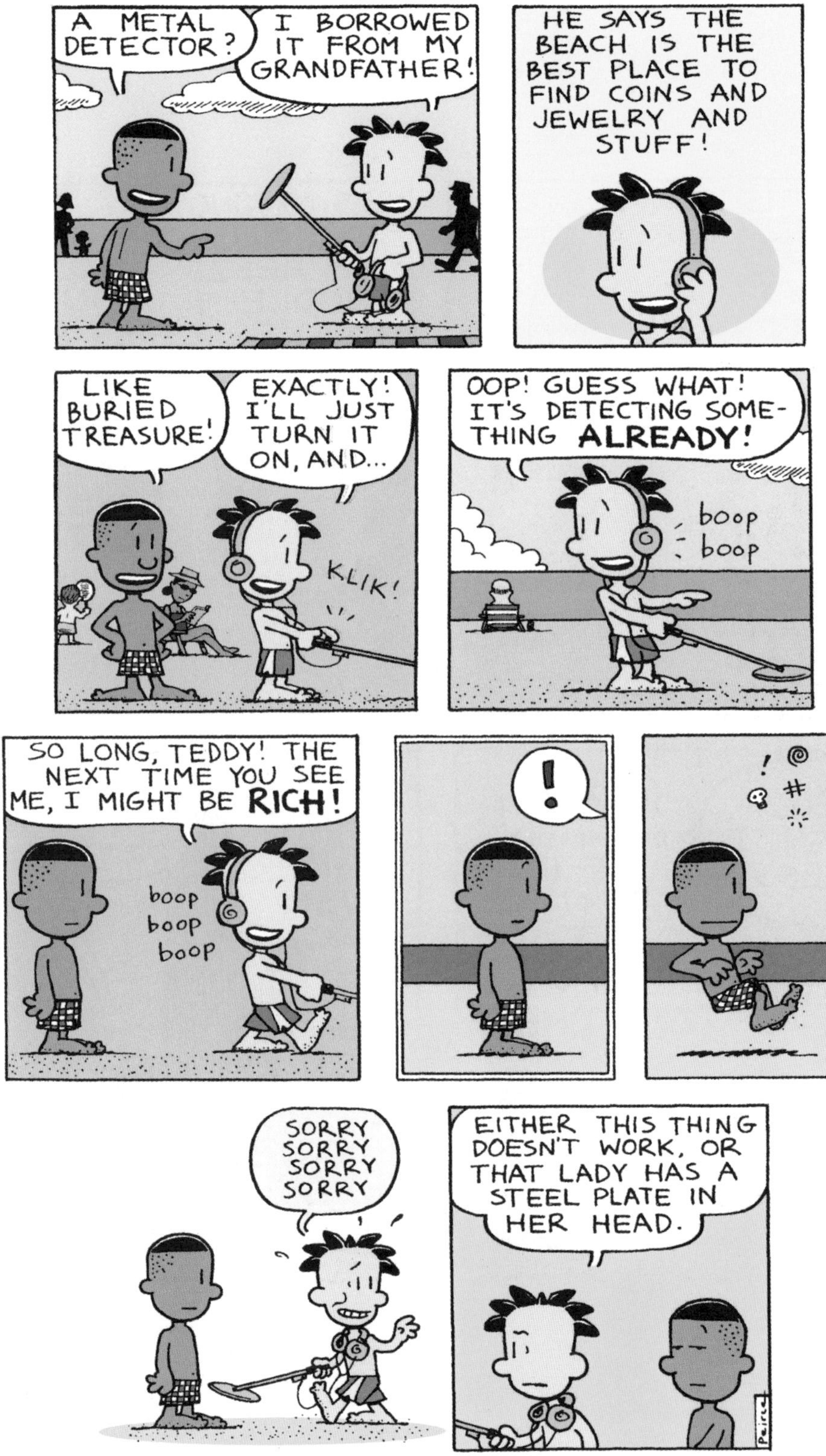
A METAL DETECTOR?
I BORROWED IT FROM MY GRANDFATHER!
HE SAYS THE BEACH IS THE BEST PLACE TO FIND COINS AND JEWELRY AND STUFF!
LIKE BURIED TREASURE!
EXACTLY! I'LL JUST TURN IT ON, AND...
KLIK!
OOP! GUESS WHAT! IT'S DETECTING SOMETHING **ALREADY**!
boop boop
SO LONG, TEDDY! THE NEXT TIME YOU SEE ME, I MIGHT BE **RICH**!
boop boop boop
!
SORRY SORRY SORRY SORRY
EITHER THIS THING DOESN'T WORK, OR THAT LADY HAS A STEEL PLATE IN HER HEAD.
Peirce

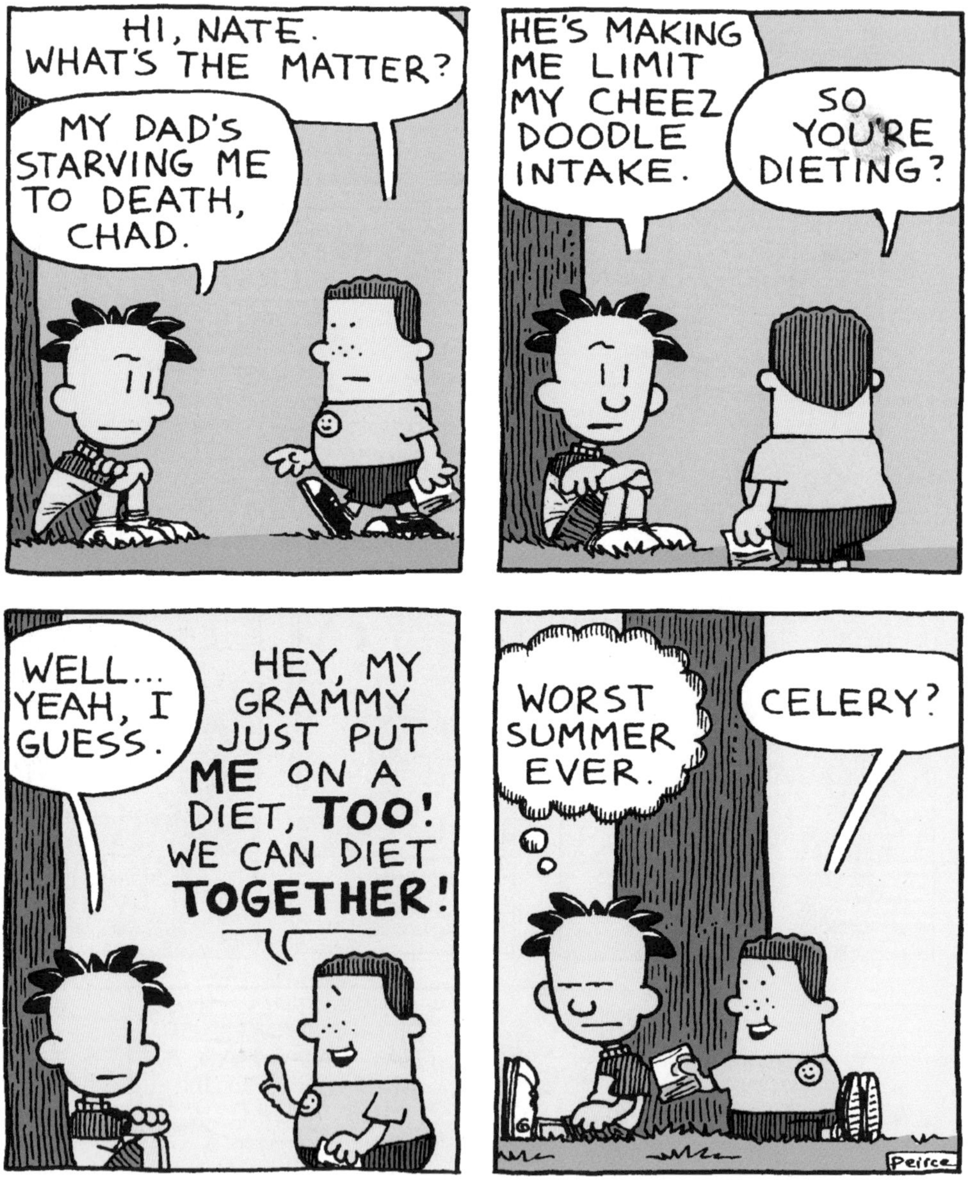
HI, NATE. WHAT'S THE MATTER?
MY DAD'S STARVING ME TO DEATH, CHAD.
HE'S MAKING ME LIMIT MY CHEEZ DOODLE INTAKE.
SO YOU'RE DIETING?
WELL... YEAH, I GUESS.
HEY, MY GRAMMY JUST PUT **ME** ON A DIET, **TOO**! WE CAN DIET **TOGETHER**!
WORST SUMMER EVER.
CELERY?
Peirce

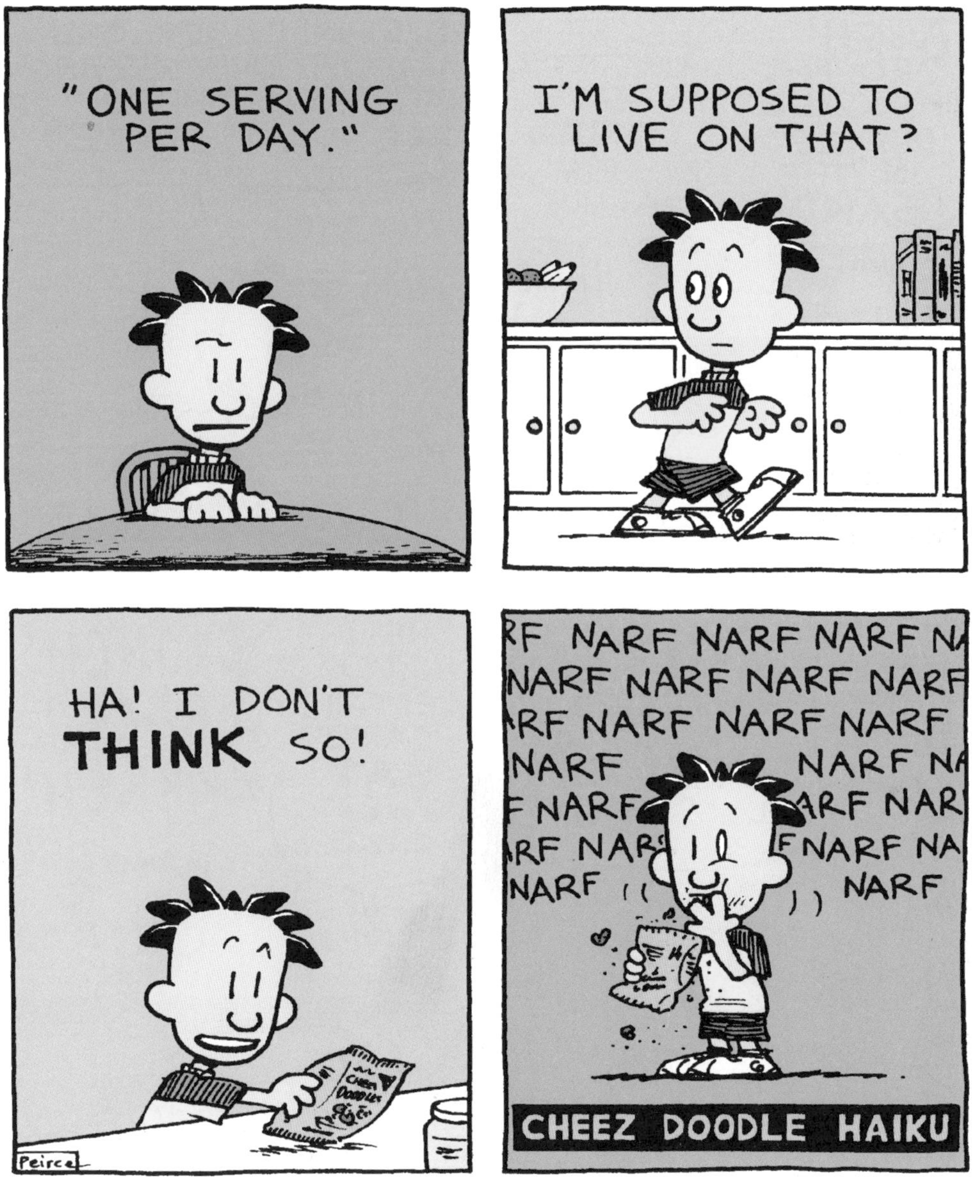

"ONE SERVING PER DAY."
I'M SUPPOSED TO LIVE ON THAT?
HA! I DON'T **THINK** SO!
RF NARF NARF NARF NA
NARF NARF NARF NARF
RF NARF NARF NARF
NARF NARF NA
F NARF ARF NAR
RF NAR NARF NA
NARF NARF
CHEEZ DOODLE HAIKU
Peirce

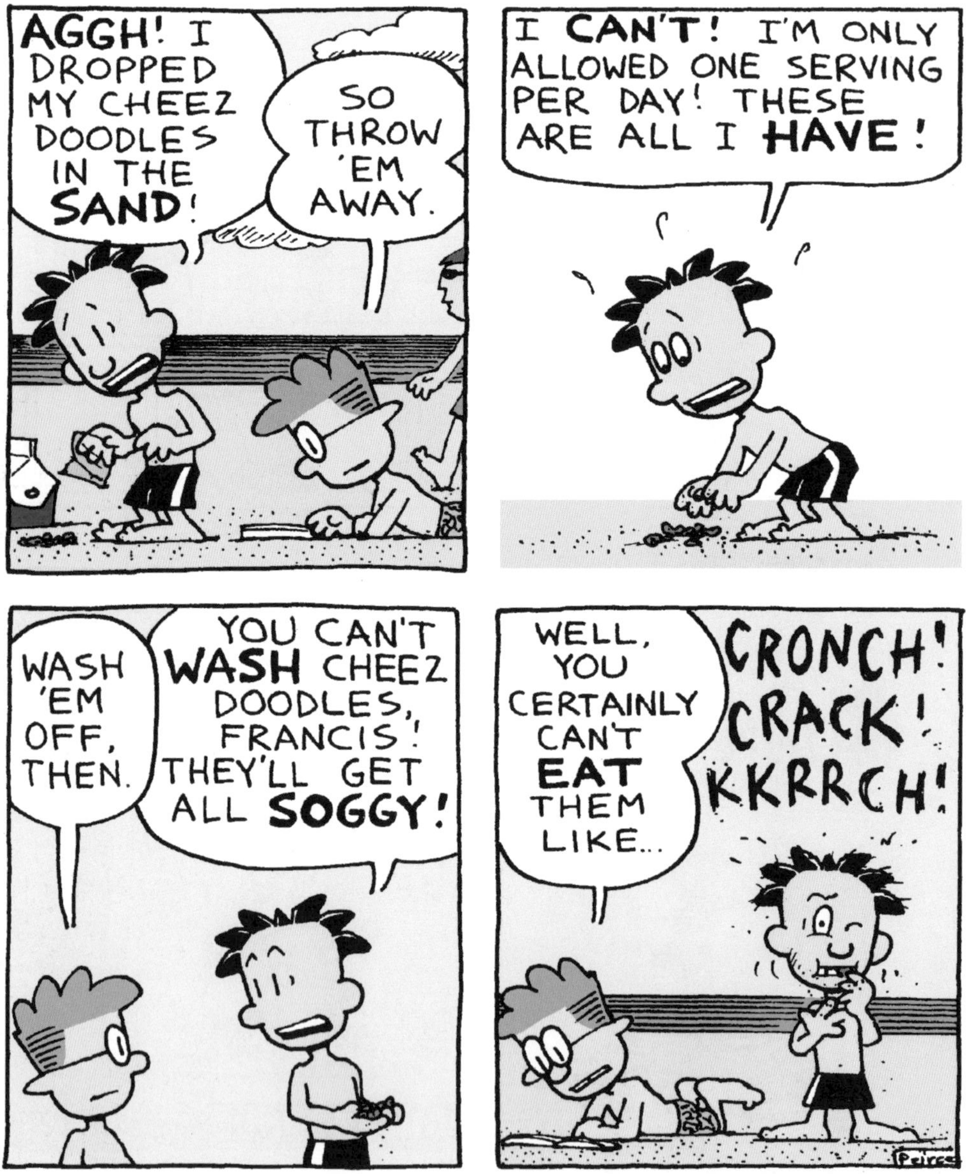
AGGH! I DROPPED MY CHEEZ DOODLES IN THE SAND!
SO THROW 'EM AWAY.
I CAN'T! I'M ONLY ALLOWED ONE SERVING PER DAY! THESE ARE ALL I HAVE!
WASH 'EM OFF, THEN.
YOU CAN'T WASH CHEEZ DOODLES, FRANCIS! THEY'LL GET ALL SOGGY!
WELL, YOU CERTAINLY CAN'T EAT THEM LIKE...
CRONCH! CRACK! KKRRCH!
Peirce

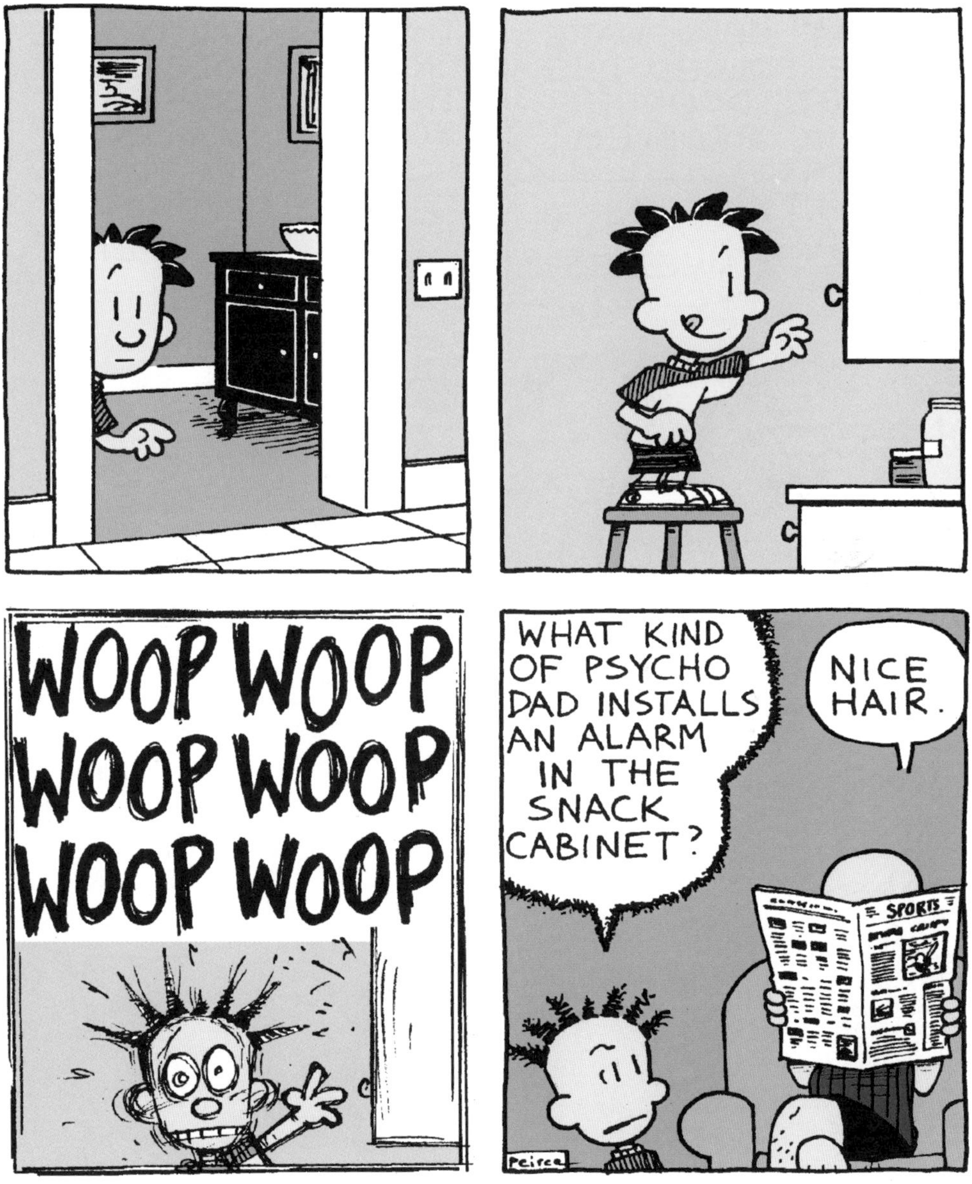
WOOP WOOP WOOP WOOP WOOP WOOP
WHAT KIND OF PSYCHO DAD INSTALLS AN ALARM IN THE SNACK CABINET?
NICE HAIR.
SPORTS
Peirce

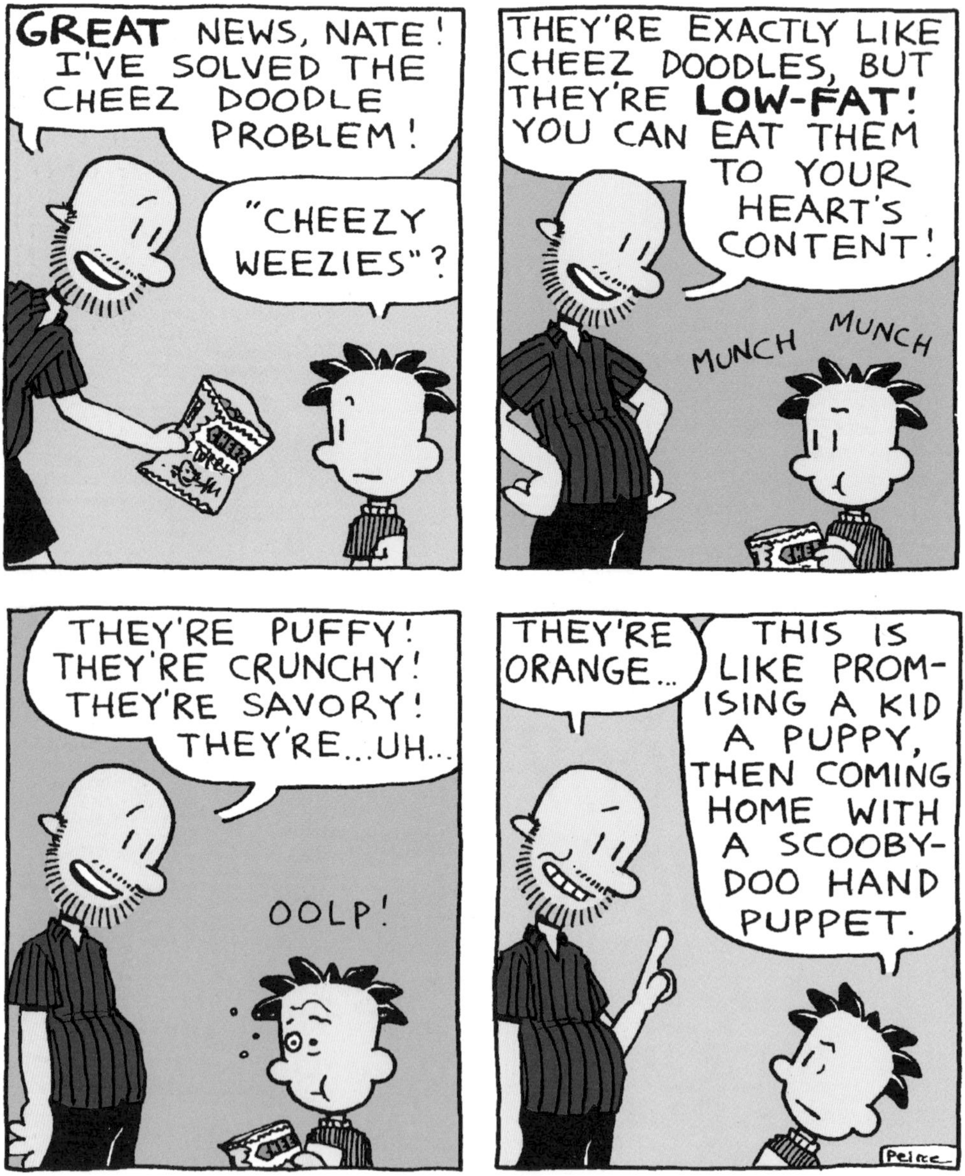
GREAT NEWS, NATE! I'VE SOLVED THE CHEEZ DOODLE PROBLEM!
"CHEEZY WEEZIES"?
THEY'RE EXACTLY LIKE CHEEZ DOODLES, BUT THEY'RE LOW-FAT! YOU CAN EAT THEM TO YOUR HEART'S CONTENT!
MUNCH MUNCH
THEY'RE PUFFY! THEY'RE CRUNCHY! THEY'RE SAVORY! THEY'RE...UH...
OOLP!
THEY'RE ORANGE...
THIS IS LIKE PROMISING A KID A PUPPY, THEN COMING HOME WITH A SCOOBY-DOO HAND PUPPET.
Peirce

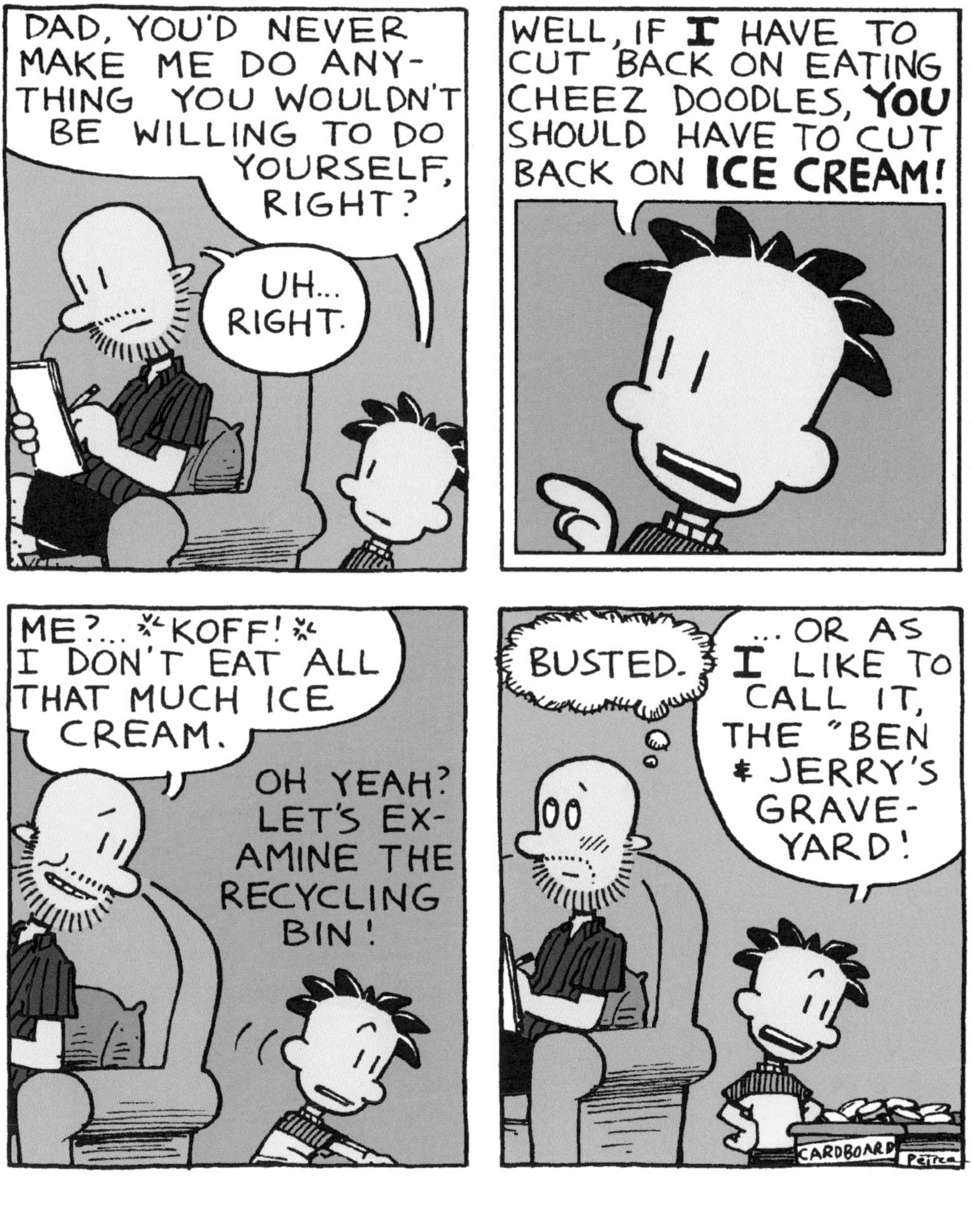
DAD, YOU'D NEVER MAKE ME DO ANYTHING YOU WOULDN'T BE WILLING TO DO YOURSELF, RIGHT?
UH... RIGHT.
WELL, IF I HAVE TO CUT BACK ON EATING CHEEZ DOODLES, YOU SHOULD HAVE TO CUT BACK ON ICE CREAM!
ME?... KOFF! I DON'T EAT ALL THAT MUCH ICE CREAM.
OH YEAH? LET'S EXAMINE THE RECYCLING BIN!
BUSTED.
...OR AS I LIKE TO CALL IT, THE "BEN & JERRY'S GRAVEYARD!
CARDBOARD
Peirce

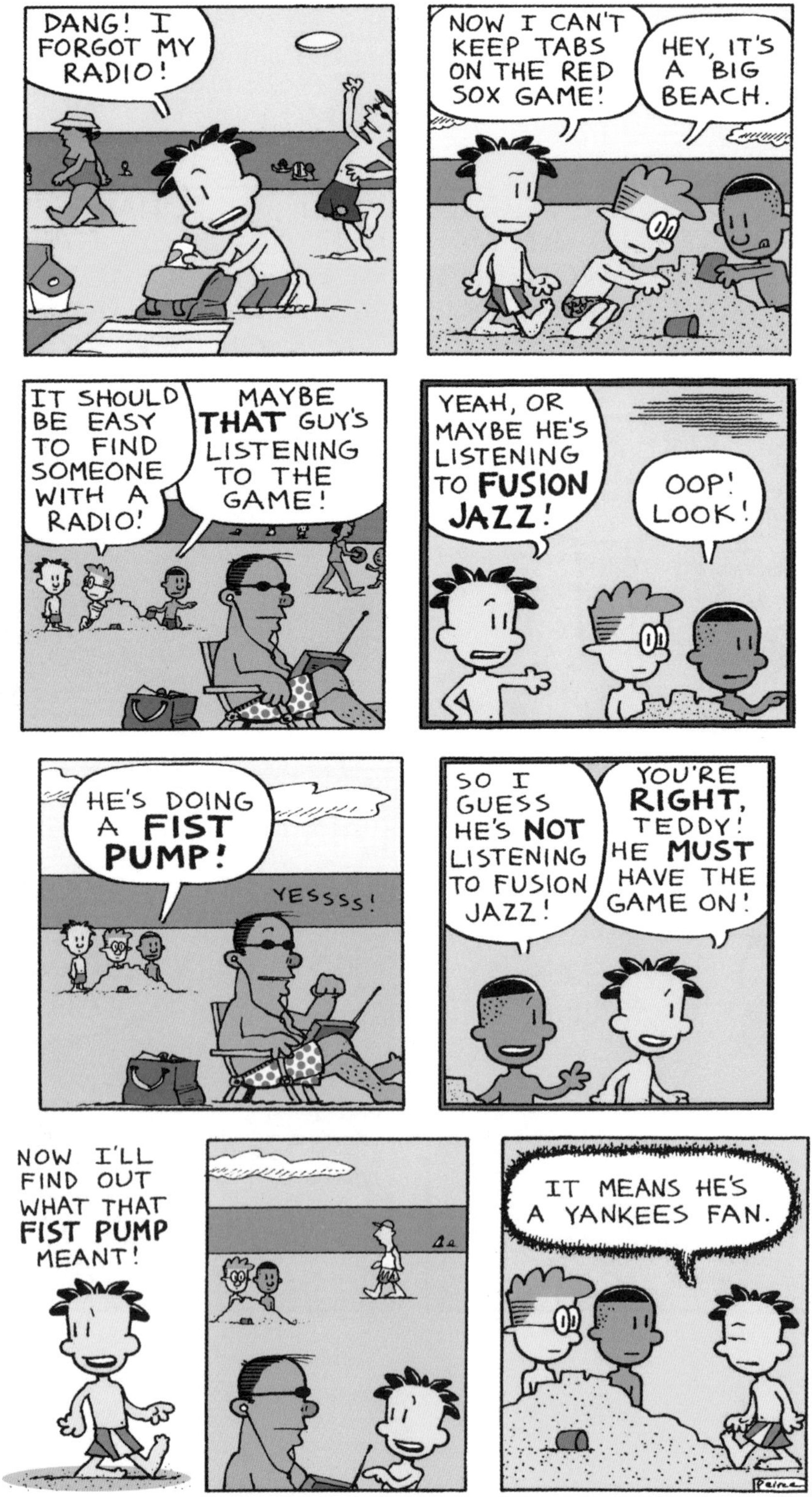

DANG! I FORGOT MY RADIO!
NOW I CAN'T KEEP TABS ON THE RED SOX GAME!
HEY, IT'S A BIG BEACH.
IT SHOULD BE EASY TO FIND SOMEONE WITH A RADIO!
MAYBE THAT GUY'S LISTENING TO THE GAME!
YEAH, OR MAYBE HE'S LISTENING TO FUSION JAZZ!
OOP! LOOK!
HE'S DOING A FIST PUMP!
YESSSS!
SO I GUESS HE'S NOT LISTENING TO FUSION JAZZ!
YOU'RE RIGHT, TEDDY! HE MUST HAVE THE GAME ON!
NOW I'LL FIND OUT WHAT THAT FIST PUMP MEANT!
IT MEANS HE'S A YANKEES FAN.

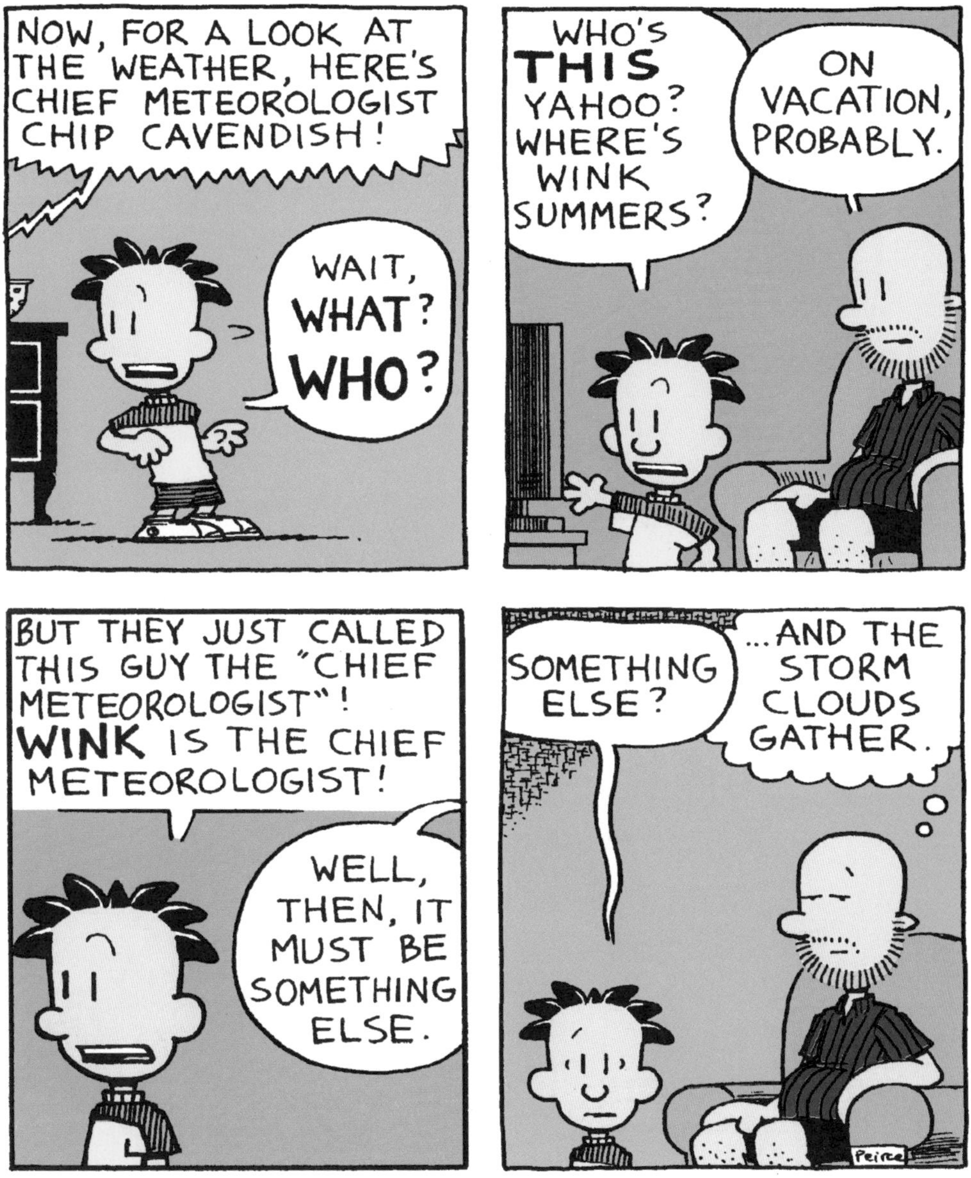
NOW, FOR A LOOK AT THE WEATHER, HERE'S CHIEF METEOROLOGIST CHIP CAVENDISH!
WAIT, WHAT? WHO?
WHO'S THIS YAHOO? WHERE'S WINK SUMMERS?
ON VACATION, PROBABLY.
BUT THEY JUST CALLED THIS GUY THE "CHIEF METEOROLOGIST"! WINK IS THE CHIEF METEOROLOGIST!
WELL, THEN, IT MUST BE SOMETHING ELSE.
SOMETHING ELSE?
...AND THE STORM CLOUDS GATHER.
Peirce

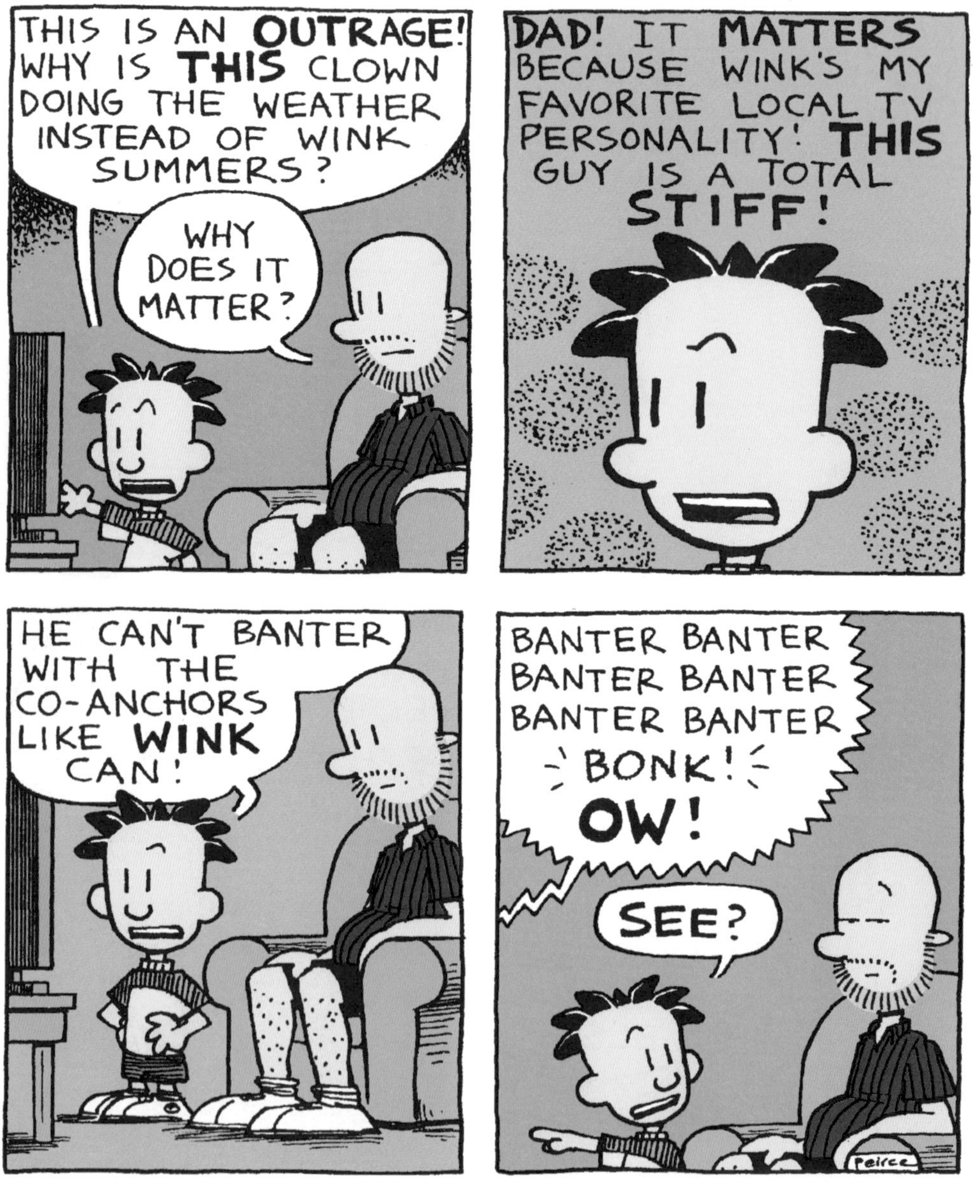
THIS IS AN OUTRAGE! WHY IS THIS CLOWN DOING THE WEATHER INSTEAD OF WINK SUMMERS?
WHY DOES IT MATTER?
DAD! IT MATTERS BECAUSE WINK'S MY FAVORITE LOCAL TV PERSONALITY! THIS GUY IS A TOTAL STIFF!
HE CAN'T BANTER WITH THE CO-ANCHORS LIKE WINK CAN!
BANTER BANTER BANTER BANTER BANTER BANTER
BONK!
OW!
SEE?
peirce

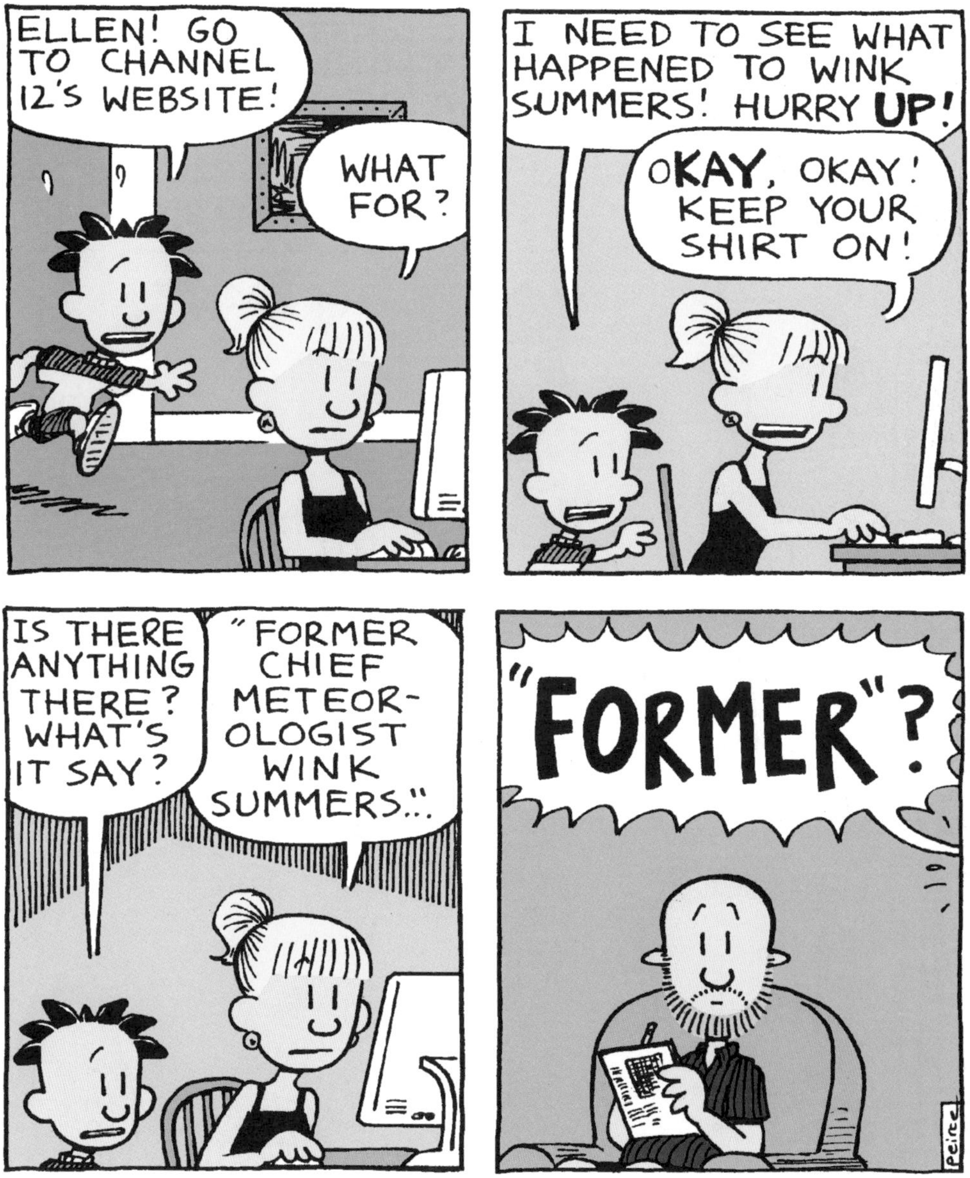
ELLEN! GO TO CHANNEL 12'S WEBSITE!
WHAT FOR?
I NEED TO SEE WHAT HAPPENED TO WINK SUMMERS! HURRY **UP**!
O**KAY**, OKAY! KEEP YOUR SHIRT ON!
IS THERE ANYTHING THERE? WHAT'S IT SAY?
"FORMER CHIEF METEOR-OLOGIST WINK SUMMERS."
"FORMER"?
peirce

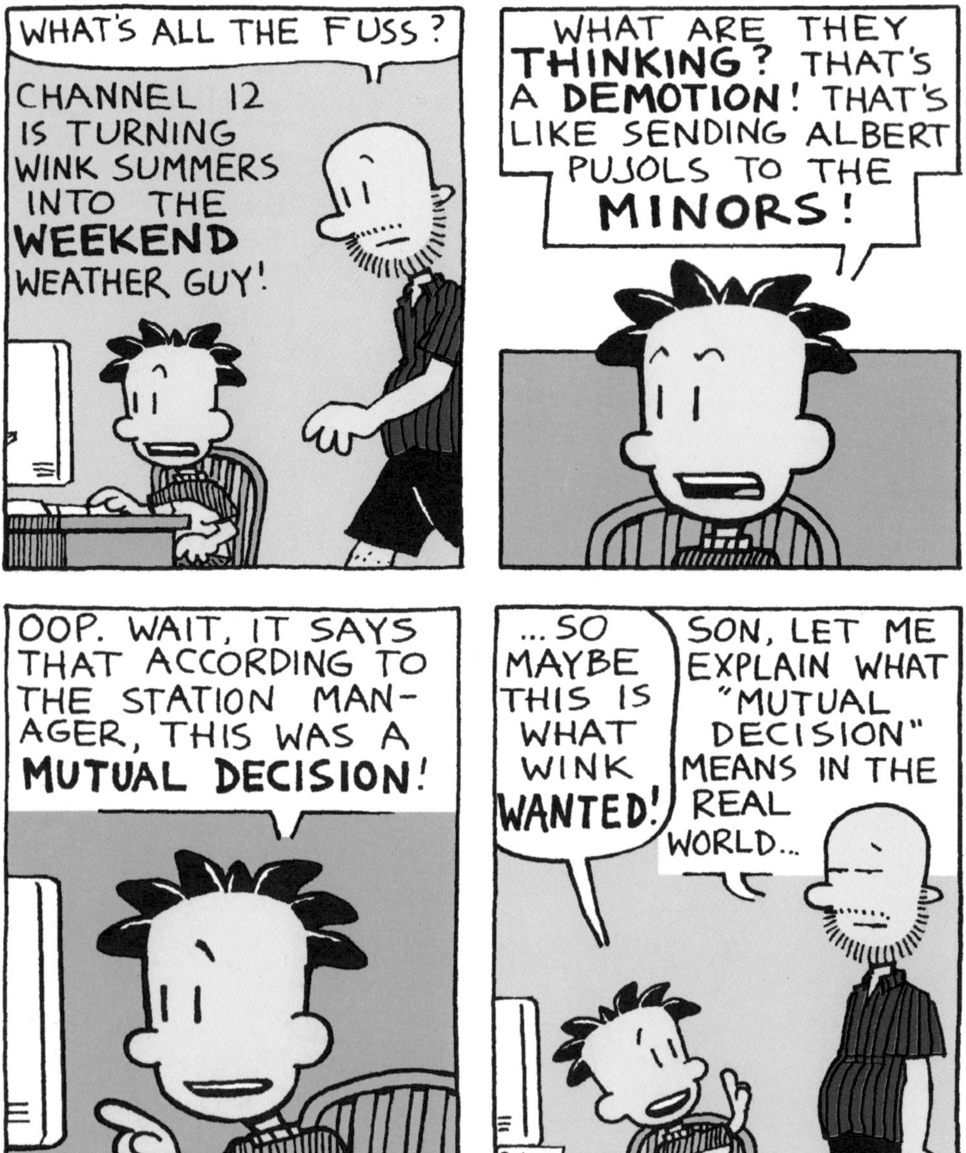
WHAT'S ALL THE FUSS?
CHANNEL 12 IS TURNING WINK SUMMERS INTO THE **WEEKEND** WEATHER GUY!
WHAT ARE THEY **THINKING?** THAT'S A **DEMOTION!** THAT'S LIKE SENDING ALBERT PUJOLS TO THE **MINORS!**
OOP. WAIT, IT SAYS THAT ACCORDING TO THE STATION MANAGER, THIS WAS A **MUTUAL DECISION!**
...SO MAYBE THIS IS WHAT WINK **WANTED!**
SON, LET ME EXPLAIN WHAT "MUTUAL DECISION" MEANS IN THE REAL WORLD...
Peirce

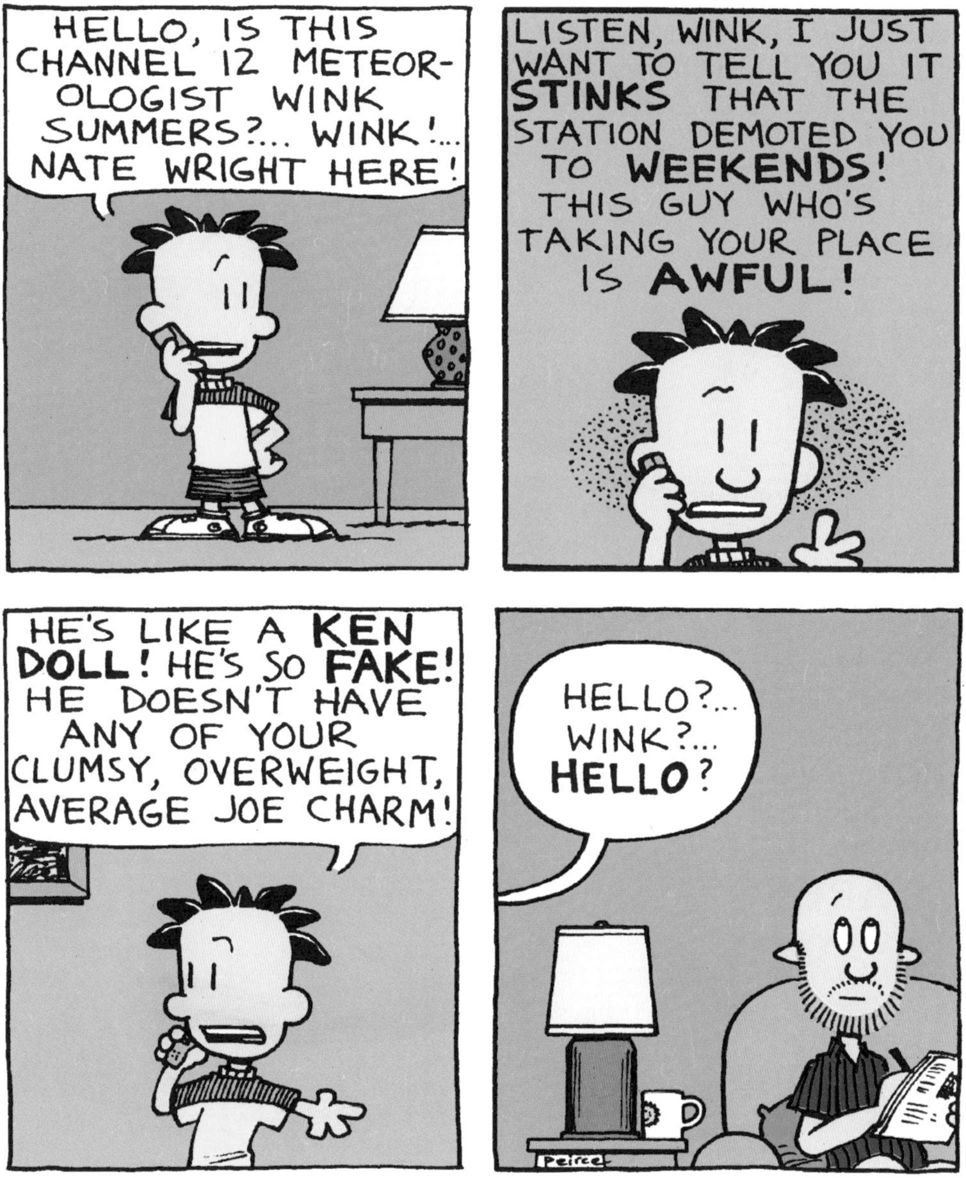
HELLO, IS THIS CHANNEL 12 METEOROLOGIST WINK SUMMERS?... WINK!... NATE WRIGHT HERE!
LISTEN, WINK, I JUST WANT TO TELL YOU IT **STINKS** THAT THE STATION DEMOTED YOU TO **WEEKENDS!** THIS GUY WHO'S TAKING YOUR PLACE IS **AWFUL!**
HE'S LIKE A **KEN DOLL!** HE'S SO **FAKE!** HE DOESN'T HAVE ANY OF YOUR CLUMSY, OVERWEIGHT, AVERAGE JOE CHARM!
HELLO?... WINK?... **HELLO**?
Peirce

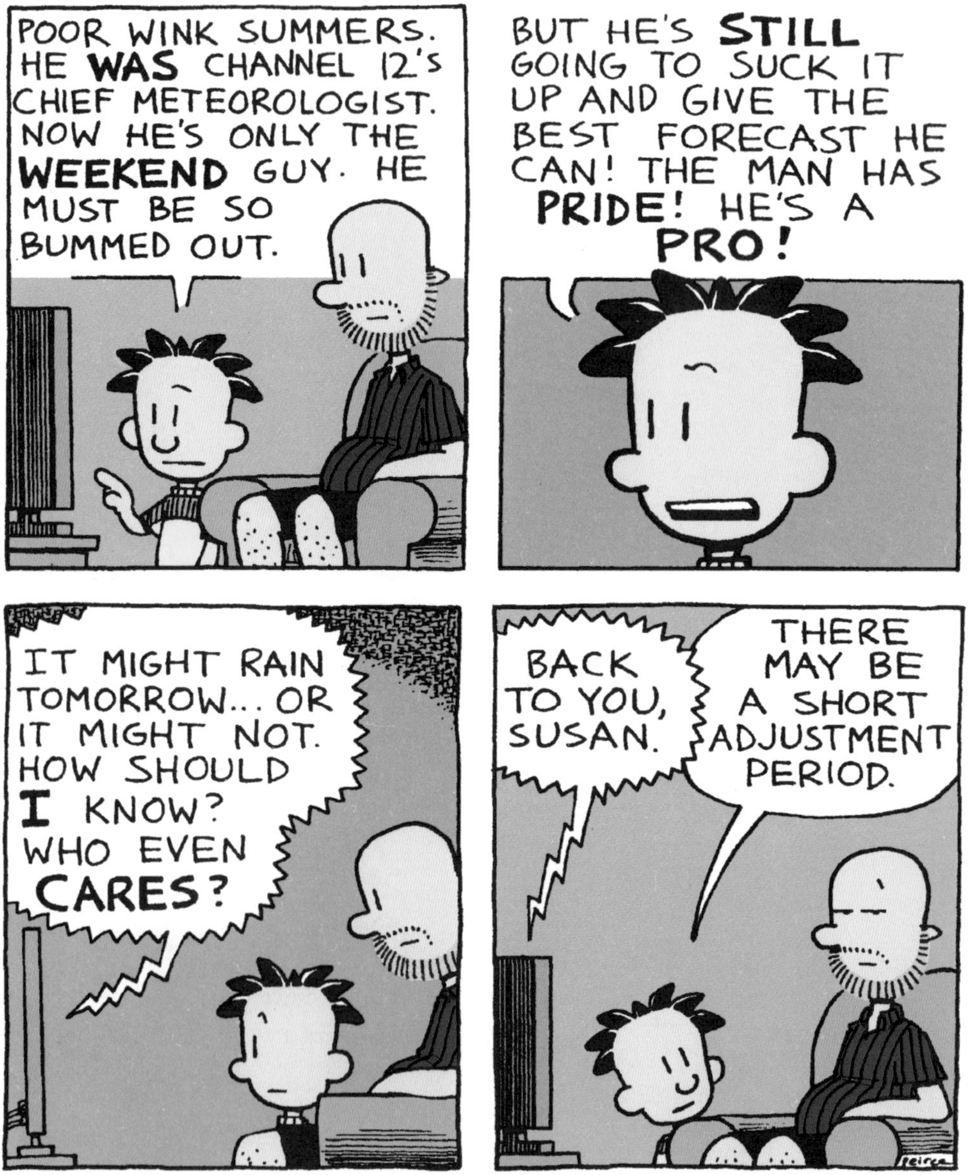
POOR WINK SUMMERS. HE **WAS** CHANNEL 12'S CHIEF METEOROLOGIST. NOW HE'S ONLY THE **WEEKEND** GUY. HE MUST BE SO BUMMED OUT.
BUT HE'S **STILL** GOING TO SUCK IT UP AND GIVE THE BEST FORECAST HE CAN! THE MAN HAS **PRIDE**! HE'S A **PRO**!
IT MIGHT RAIN TOMORROW... OR IT MIGHT NOT. HOW SHOULD **I** KNOW? WHO EVEN **CARES**?
BACK TO YOU, SUSAN.
THERE MAY BE A SHORT ADJUSTMENT PERIOD.

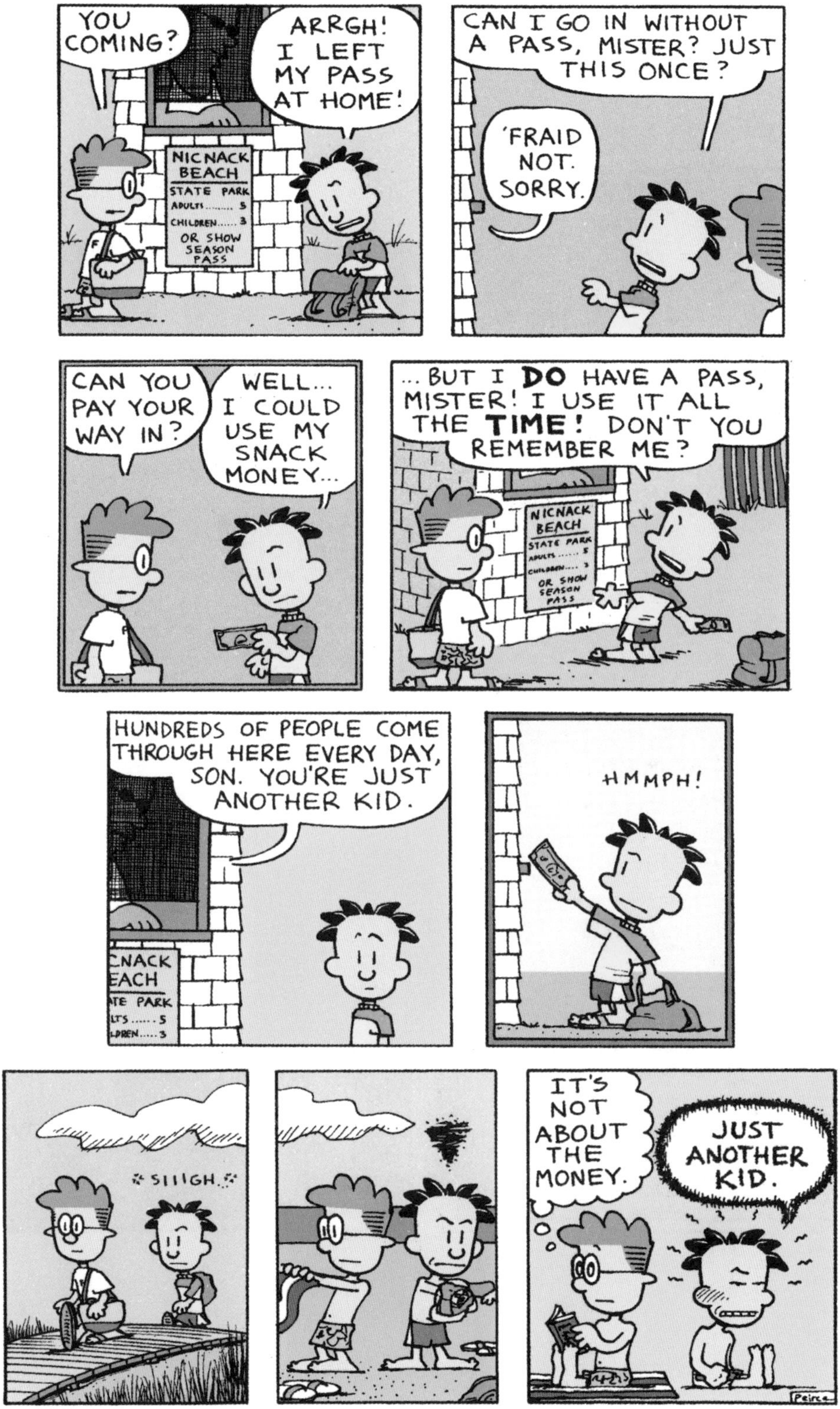
YOU COMING?
ARRGH! I LEFT MY PASS AT HOME!
NICNACK BEACH
STATE PARK
ADULTS......... 5
CHILDREN...... 3
OR SHOW SEASON PASS
CAN I GO IN WITHOUT A PASS, MISTER? JUST THIS ONCE?
'FRAID NOT. SORRY.
CAN YOU PAY YOUR WAY IN?
WELL... I COULD USE MY SNACK MONEY...
... BUT I **DO** HAVE A PASS, MISTER! I USE IT ALL THE **TIME**! DON'T YOU REMEMBER ME?
NICNACK BEACH
STATE PARK
OR SHOW SEASON PASS
HUNDREDS OF PEOPLE COME THROUGH HERE EVERY DAY, SON. YOU'RE JUST ANOTHER KID.
HMMPH!
SIIIGH
IT'S NOT ABOUT THE MONEY.
JUST ANOTHER KID.
Peirce

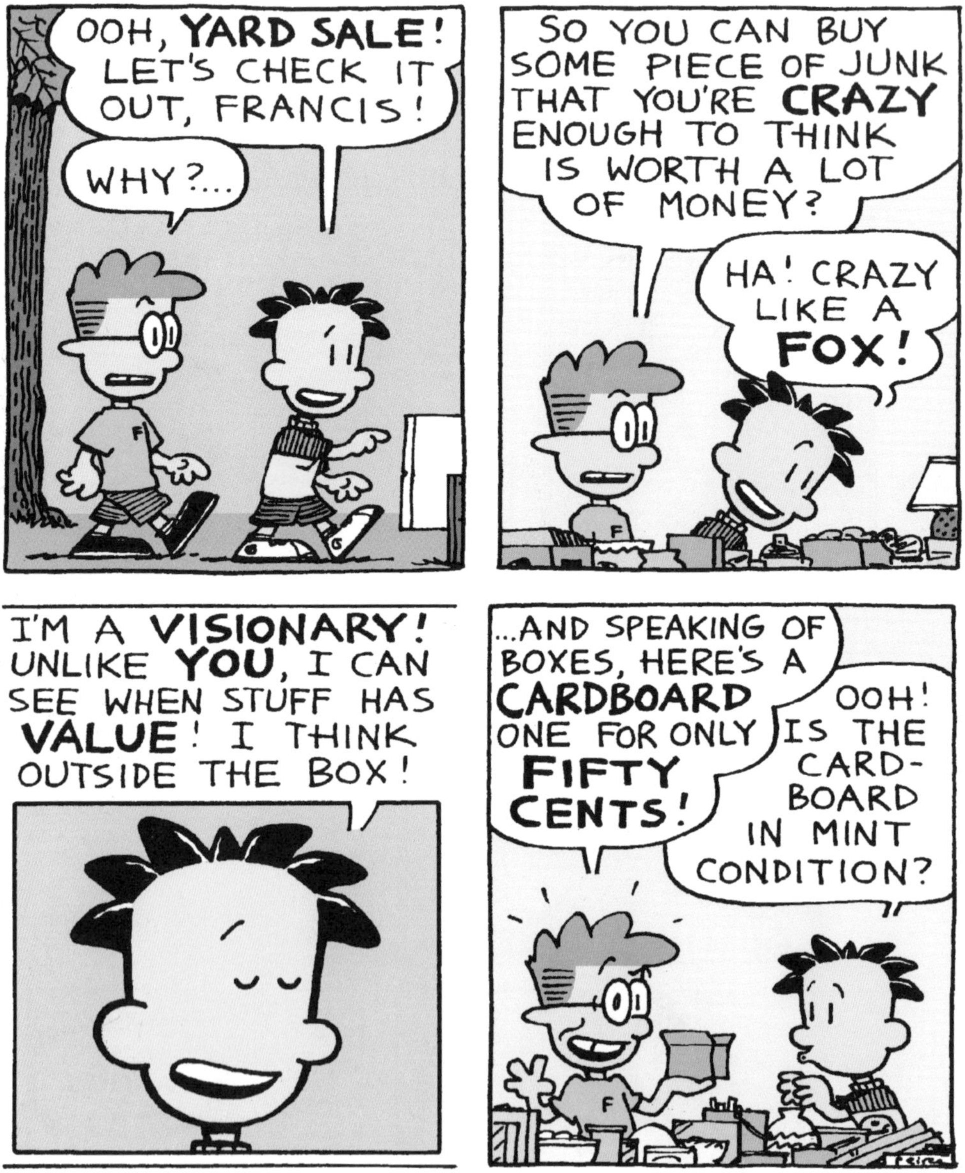
OOH, **YARD SALE**! LET'S CHECK IT OUT, FRANCIS!
WHY?...
SO YOU CAN BUY SOME PIECE OF JUNK THAT YOU'RE **CRAZY** ENOUGH TO THINK IS WORTH A LOT OF MONEY?
HA! CRAZY LIKE A **FOX**!
I'M A **VISIONARY**! UNLIKE **YOU**, I CAN SEE WHEN STUFF HAS **VALUE**! I THINK OUTSIDE THE BOX!
...AND SPEAKING OF BOXES, HERE'S A **CARDBOARD** ONE FOR ONLY **FIFTY CENTS**!
OOH! IS THE CARDBOARD IN MINT CONDITION?

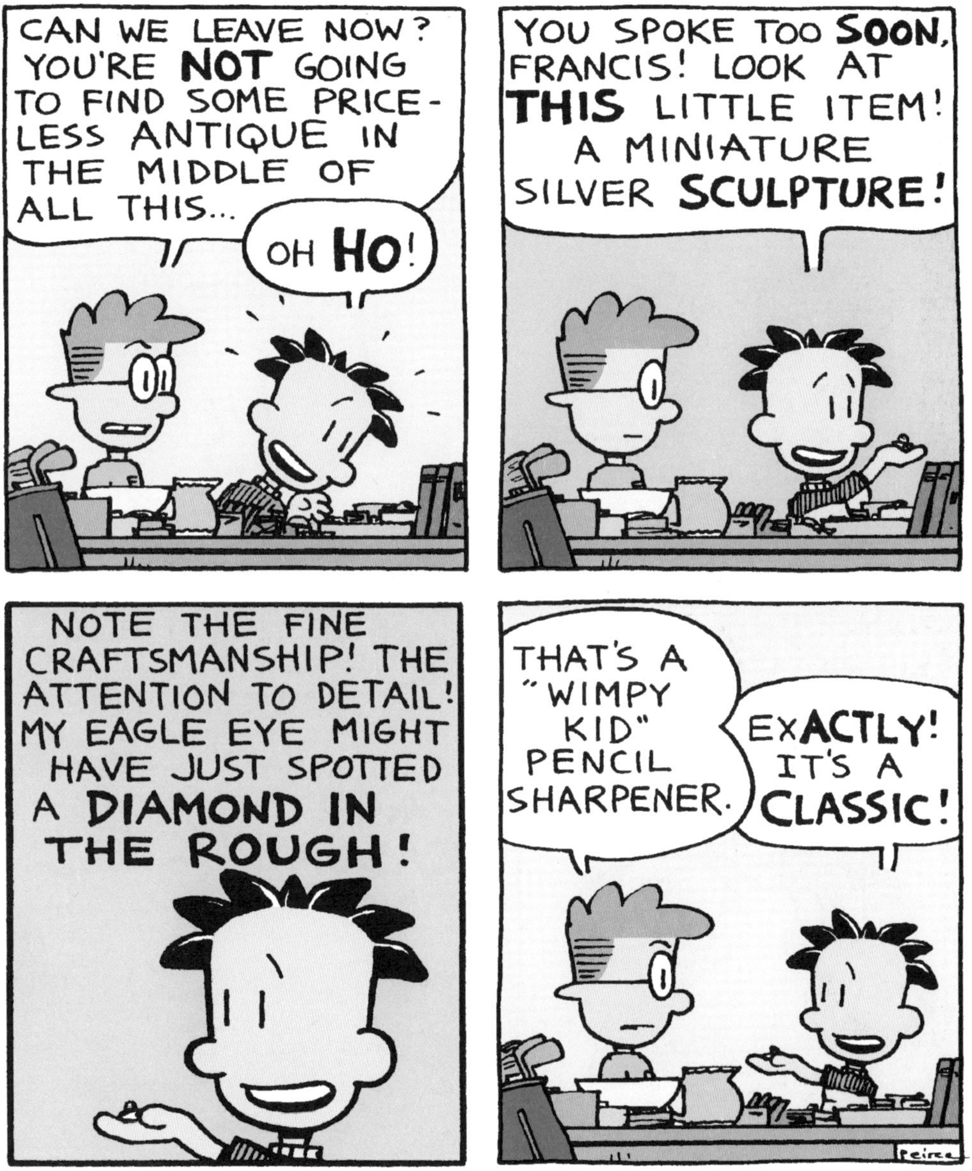
CAN WE LEAVE NOW? YOU'RE NOT GOING TO FIND SOME PRICELESS ANTIQUE IN THE MIDDLE OF ALL THIS...
OH HO!
YOU SPOKE TOO SOON, FRANCIS! LOOK AT THIS LITTLE ITEM! A MINIATURE SILVER SCULPTURE!
NOTE THE FINE CRAFTSMANSHIP! THE ATTENTION TO DETAIL! MY EAGLE EYE MIGHT HAVE JUST SPOTTED A DIAMOND IN THE ROUGH!
THAT'S A "WIMPY KID" PENCIL SHARPENER.
EXACTLY! IT'S A CLASSIC!
Peirce

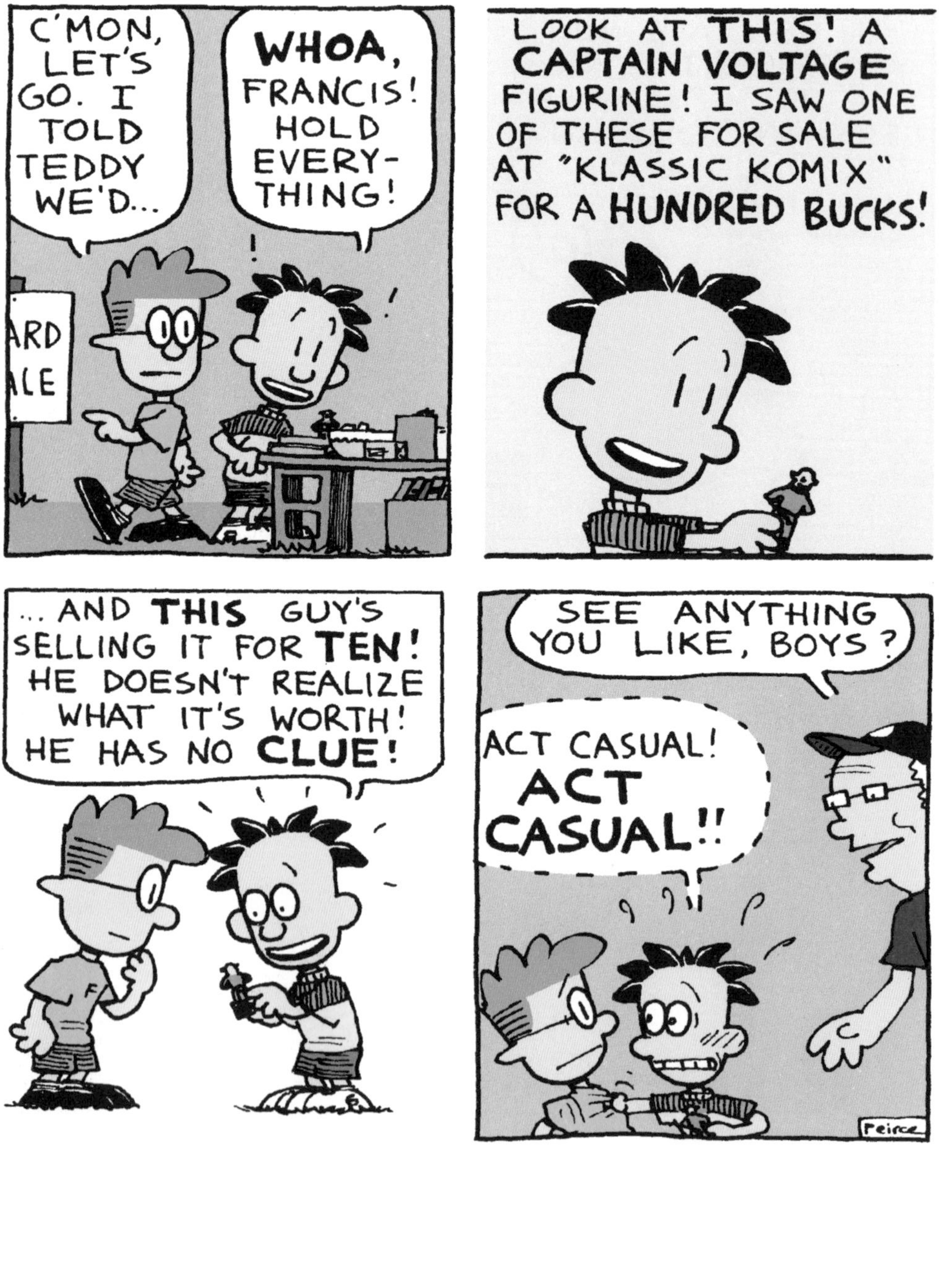
C'MON, LET'S GO. I TOLD TEDDY WE'D...
WHOA, FRANCIS! HOLD EVERYTHING!
ARD
LE
LOOK AT THIS! A CAPTAIN VOLTAGE FIGURINE! I SAW ONE OF THESE FOR SALE AT "KLASSIC KOMIX" FOR A HUNDRED BUCKS!
... AND THIS GUY'S SELLING IT FOR TEN! HE DOESN'T REALIZE WHAT IT'S WORTH! HE HAS NO CLUE!
SEE ANYTHING YOU LIKE, BOYS?
ACT CASUAL! ACT CASUAL!!
Peirce

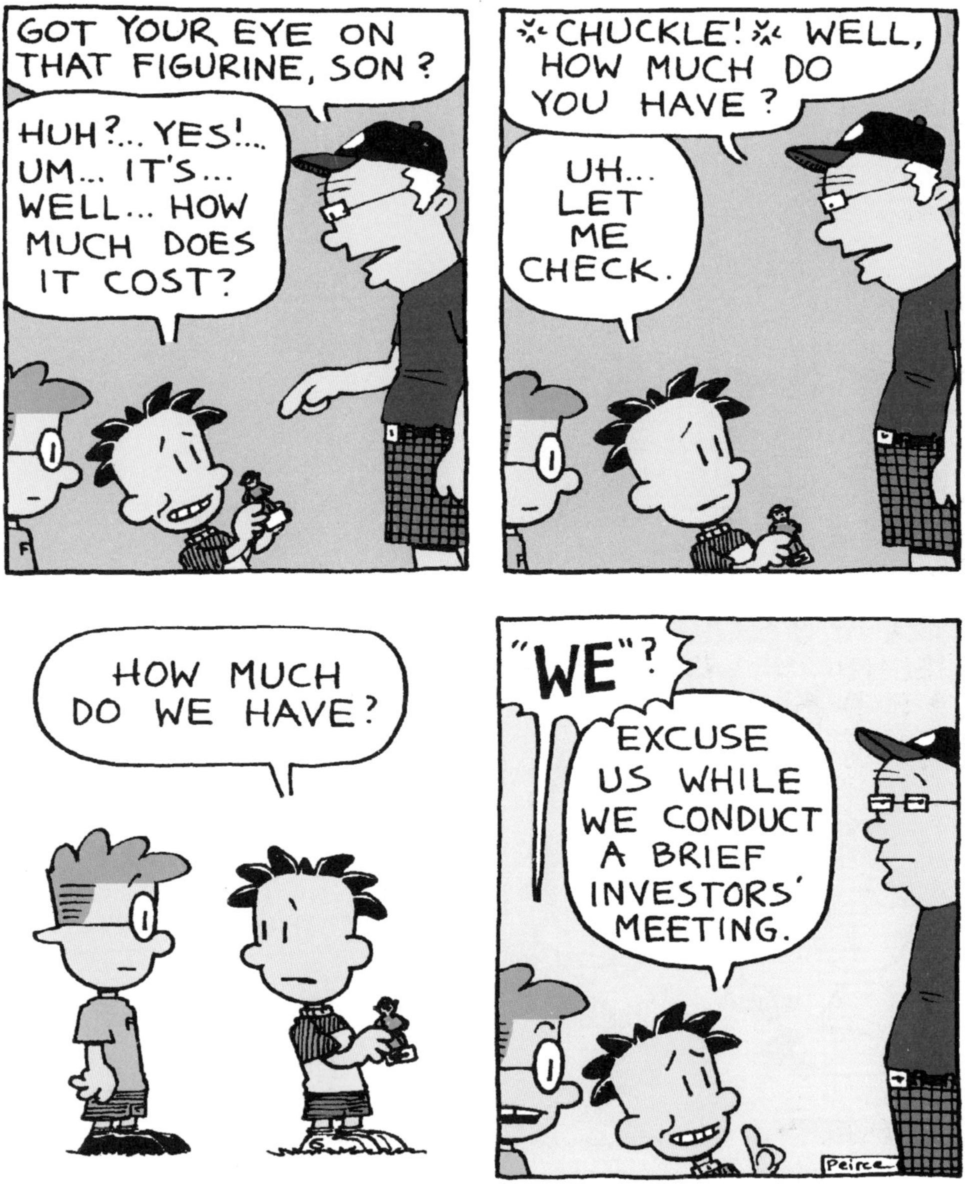
GOT YOUR EYE ON THAT FIGURINE, SON?
HUH?... YES!... UM... IT'S... WELL... HOW MUCH DOES IT COST?
CHUCKLE! WELL, HOW MUCH DO YOU HAVE?
UH... LET ME CHECK.
HOW MUCH DO WE HAVE?
"WE"?
EXCUSE US WHILE WE CONDUCT A BRIEF INVESTORS' MEETING.
Peirce

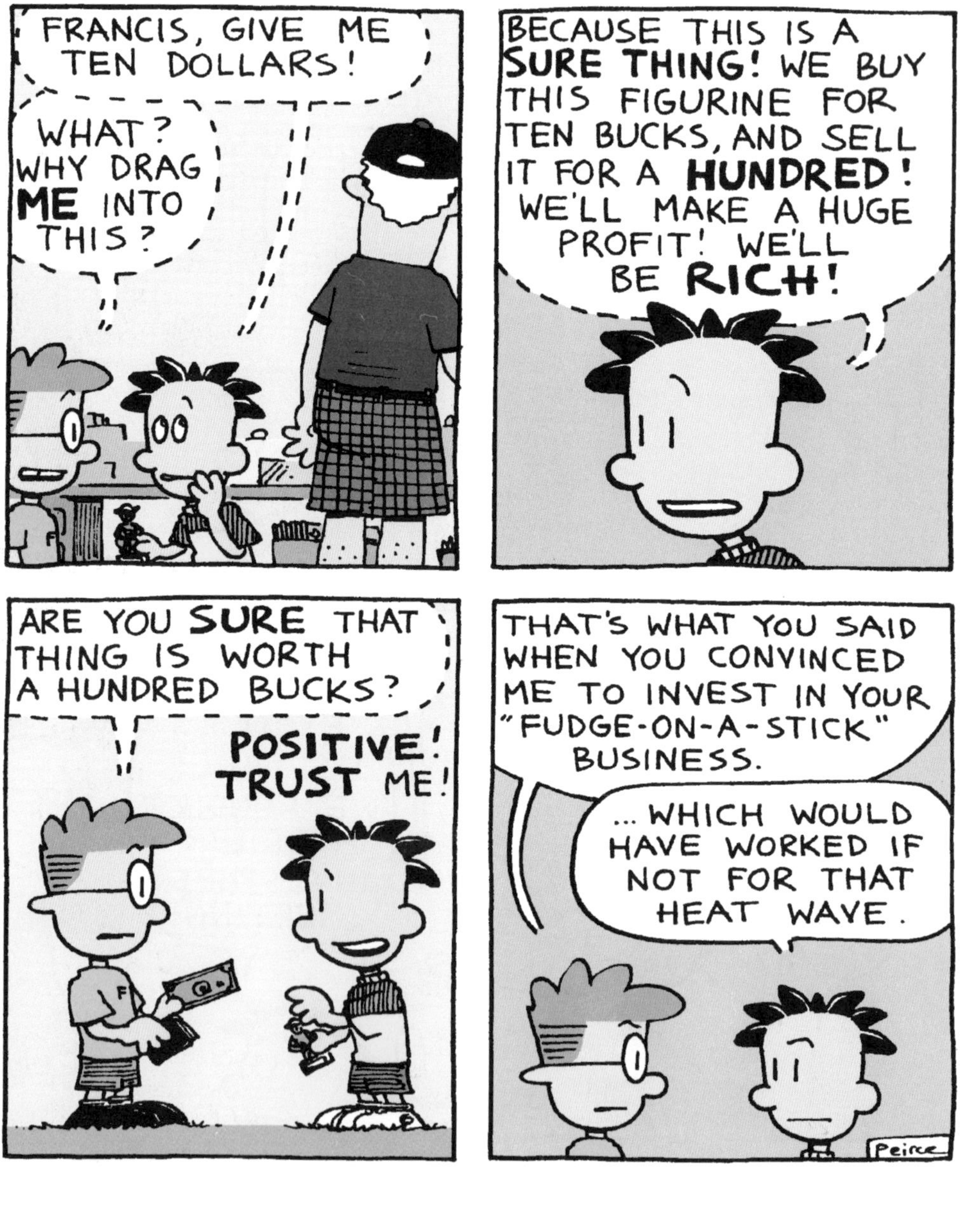
FRANCIS, GIVE ME TEN DOLLARS!
WHAT? WHY DRAG **ME** INTO THIS?
BECAUSE THIS IS A **SURE THING!** WE BUY THIS FIGURINE FOR TEN BUCKS, AND SELL IT FOR A **HUNDRED!** WE'LL MAKE A HUGE PROFIT! WE'LL BE **RICH!**
ARE YOU **SURE** THAT THING IS WORTH A HUNDRED BUCKS?
POSITIVE! TRUST ME!
THAT'S WHAT YOU SAID WHEN YOU CONVINCED ME TO INVEST IN YOUR "FUDGE-ON-A-STICK" BUSINESS.
...WHICH WOULD HAVE WORKED IF NOT FOR THAT HEAT WAVE.
Peirce

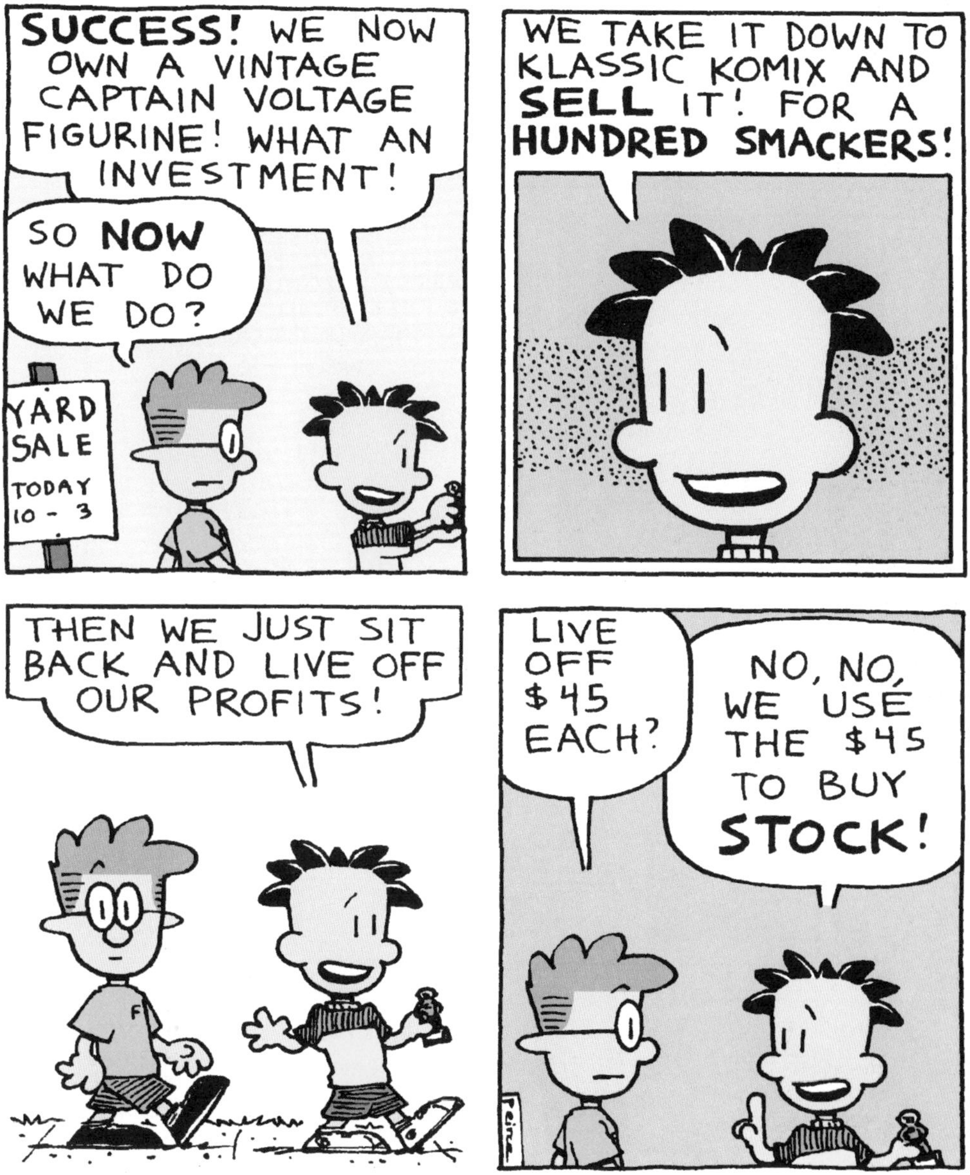
SUCCESS! WE NOW OWN A VINTAGE CAPTAIN VOLTAGE FIGURINE! WHAT AN INVESTMENT!
SO NOW WHAT DO WE DO?
YARD SALE
TODAY 10 - 3
WE TAKE IT DOWN TO KLASSIC KOMIX AND SELL IT! FOR A HUNDRED SMACKERS!
THEN WE JUST SIT BACK AND LIVE OFF OUR PROFITS!
LIVE OFF $45 EACH?
NO, NO, WE USE THE $45 TO BUY STOCK!

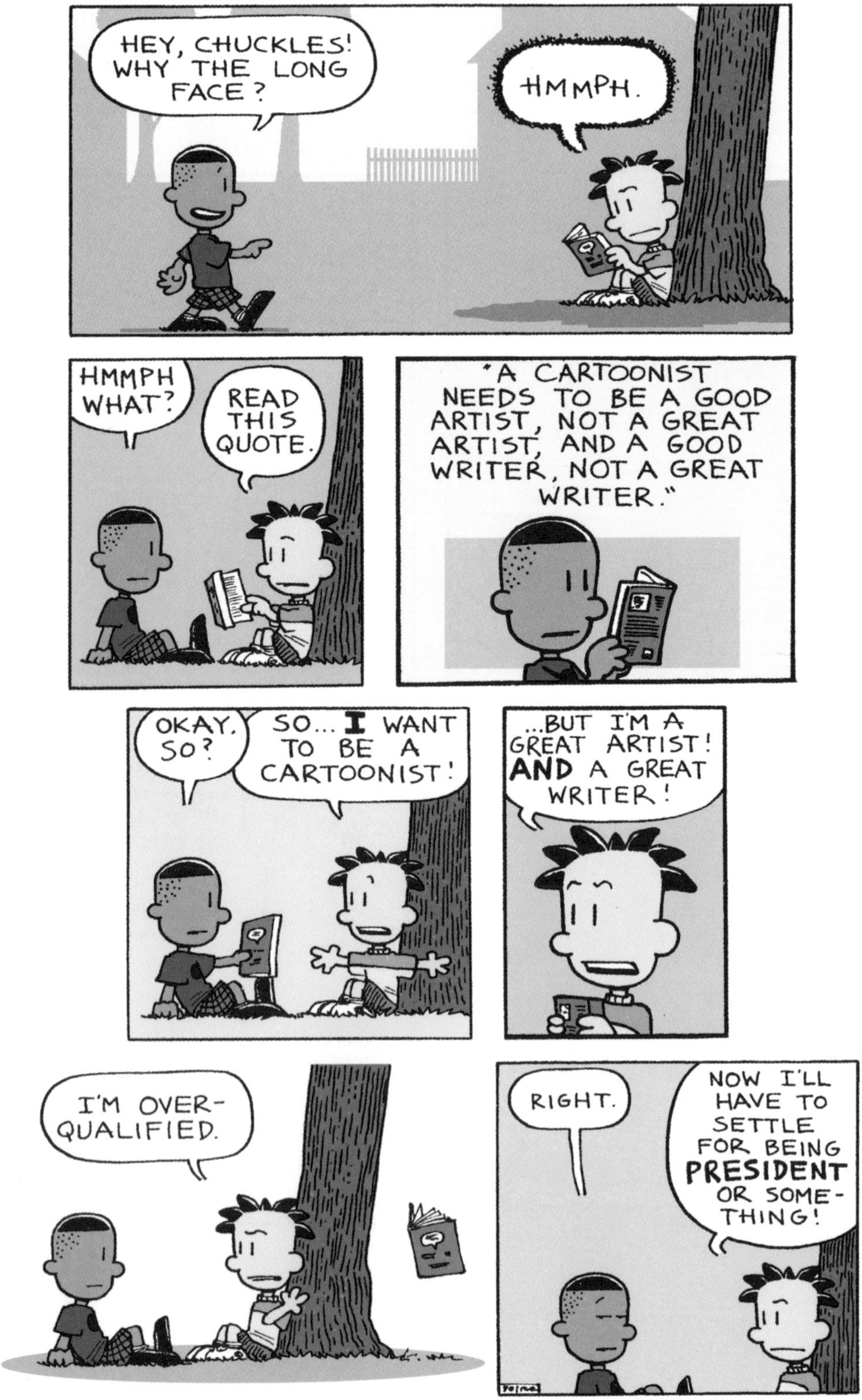
HEY, CHUCKLES! WHY THE LONG FACE?
HMMPH.
HMMPH WHAT?
READ THIS QUOTE.
"A CARTOONIST NEEDS TO BE A GOOD ARTIST, NOT A GREAT ARTIST, AND A GOOD WRITER, NOT A GREAT WRITER."
OKAY. SO?
SO... I WANT TO BE A CARTOONIST!
...BUT I'M A GREAT ARTIST! AND A GREAT WRITER!
I'M OVER-QUALIFIED.
RIGHT.
NOW I'LL HAVE TO SETTLE FOR BEING PRESIDENT OR SOME-THING!

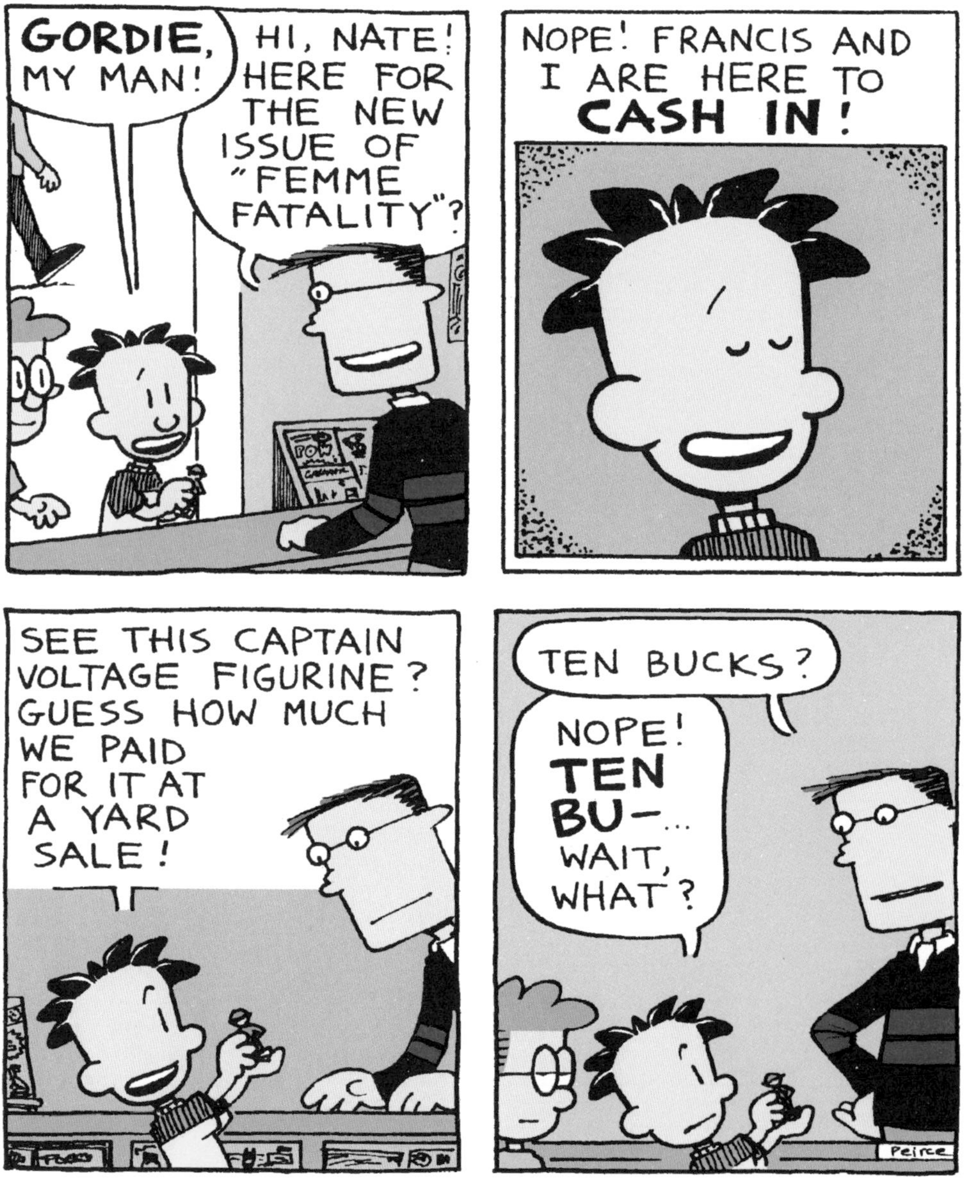
GORDIE, MY MAN!
HI, NATE! HERE FOR THE NEW ISSUE OF "FEMME FATALITY"?
NOPE! FRANCIS AND I ARE HERE TO CASH IN!
SEE THIS CAPTAIN VOLTAGE FIGURINE? GUESS HOW MUCH WE PAID FOR IT AT A YARD SALE!
TEN BUCKS?
NOPE! TEN BU-... WAIT, WHAT?
Peirce

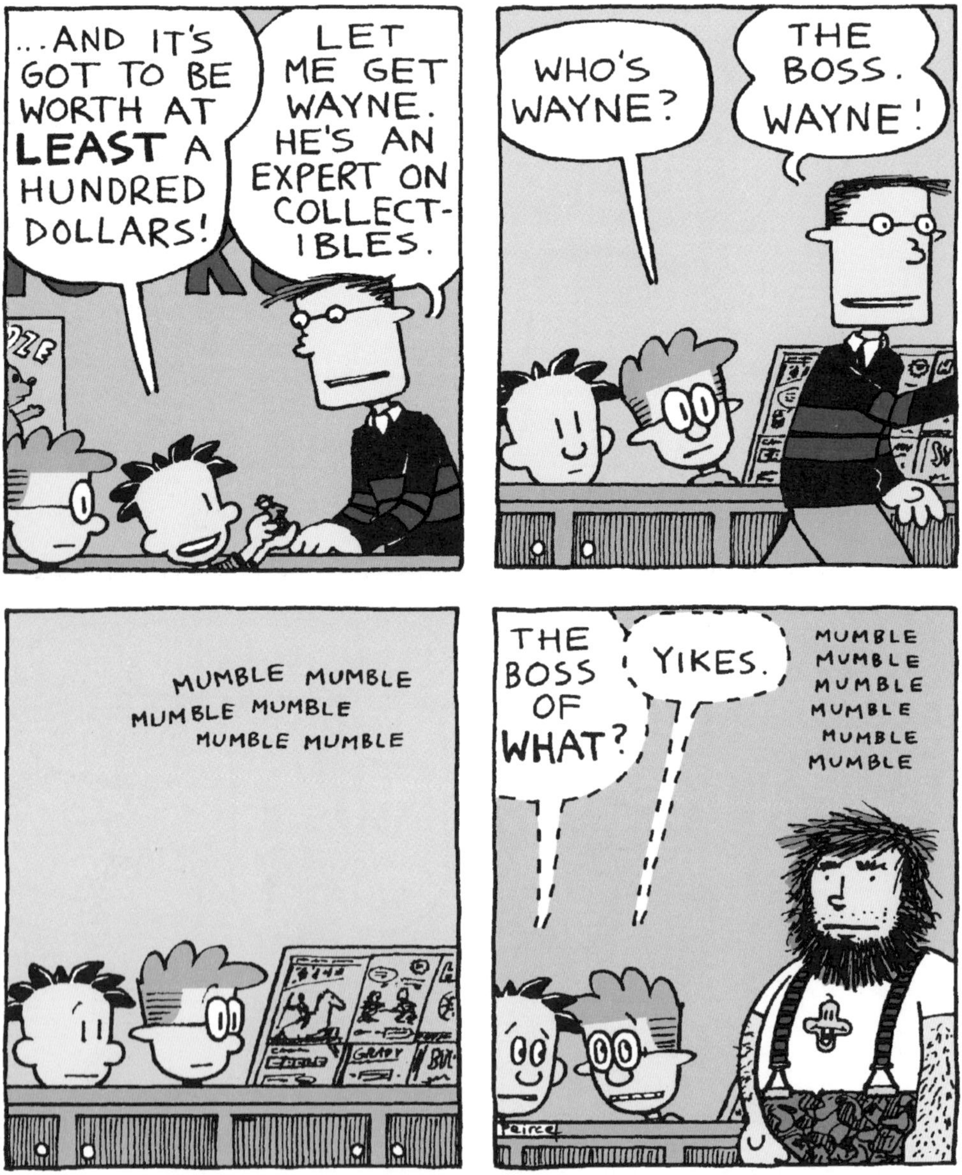
...AND IT'S GOT TO BE WORTH AT LEAST A HUNDRED DOLLARS!
LET ME GET WAYNE. HE'S AN EXPERT ON COLLECT-IBLES.
WHO'S WAYNE?
THE BOSS. WAYNE!
MUMBLE MUMBLE MUMBLE MUMBLE MUMBLE MUMBLE
THE BOSS OF WHAT?
YIKES.
MUMBLE MUMBLE MUMBLE MUMBLE MUMBLE MUMBLE

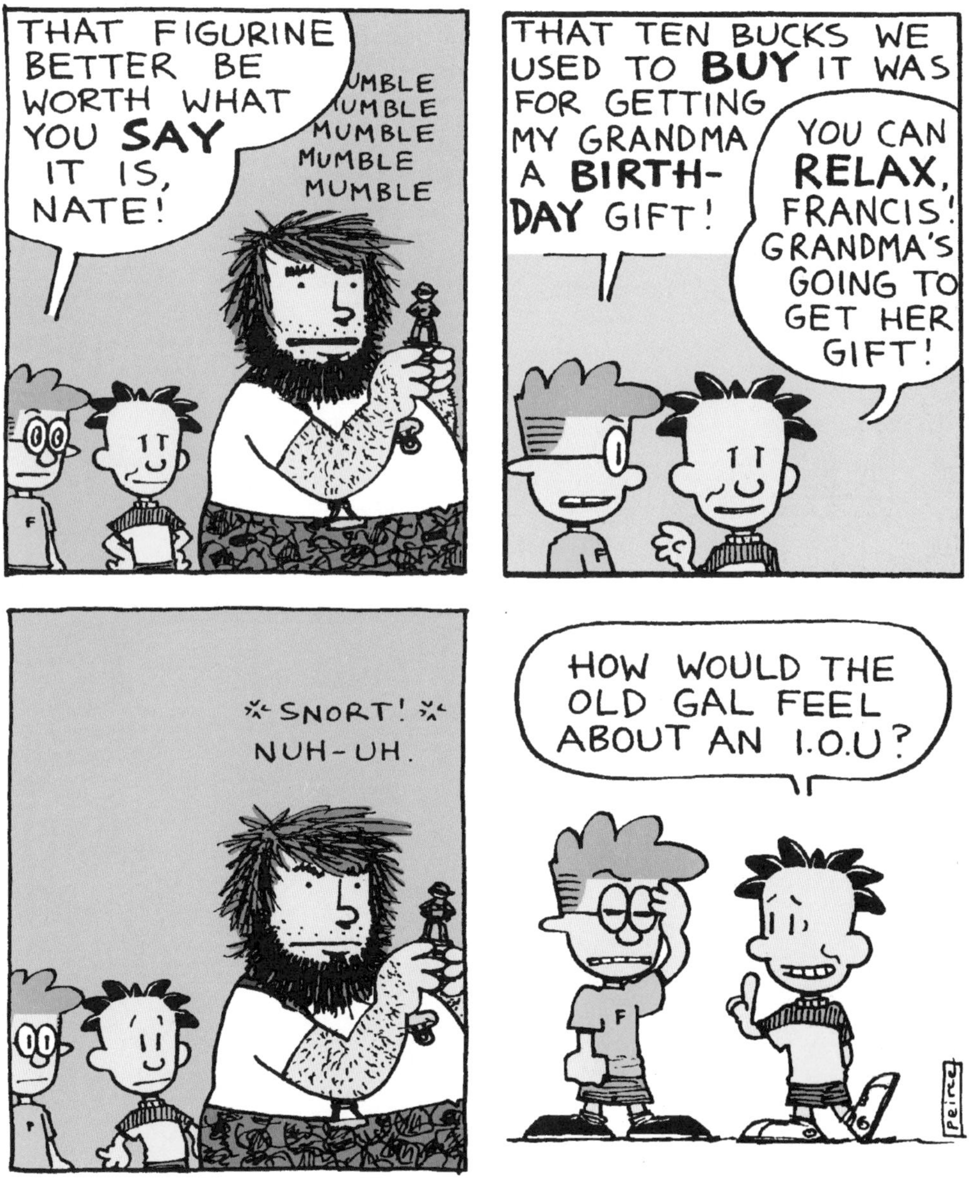
THAT FIGURINE BETTER BE WORTH WHAT YOU **SAY** IT IS, NATE!
MUMBLE MUMBLE MUMBLE
THAT TEN BUCKS WE USED TO **BUY** IT WAS FOR GETTING MY GRANDMA A **BIRTH-DAY** GIFT!
YOU CAN **RELAX**, FRANCIS! GRANDMA'S GOING TO GET HER GIFT!
SNORT!
NUH-UH.
HOW WOULD THE OLD GAL FEEL ABOUT AN I.O.U?
peirce

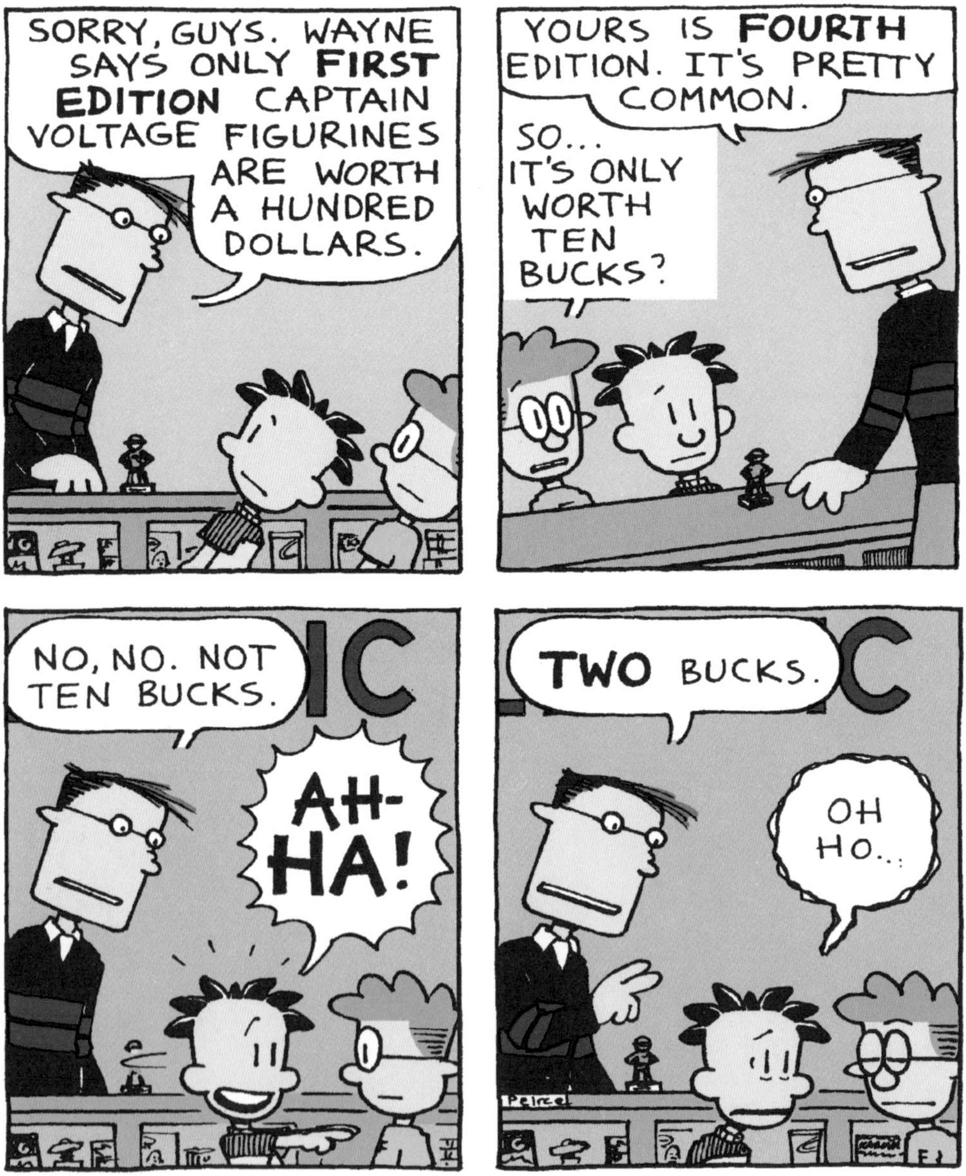
SORRY, GUYS. WAYNE SAYS ONLY **FIRST EDITION** CAPTAIN VOLTAGE FIGURINES ARE WORTH A HUNDRED DOLLARS.
YOURS IS **FOURTH** EDITION. IT'S PRETTY COMMON.
SO... IT'S ONLY WORTH TEN BUCKS?
NO, NO. NOT TEN BUCKS.
AH-HA!
TWO BUCKS.
OH HO...
Peirce

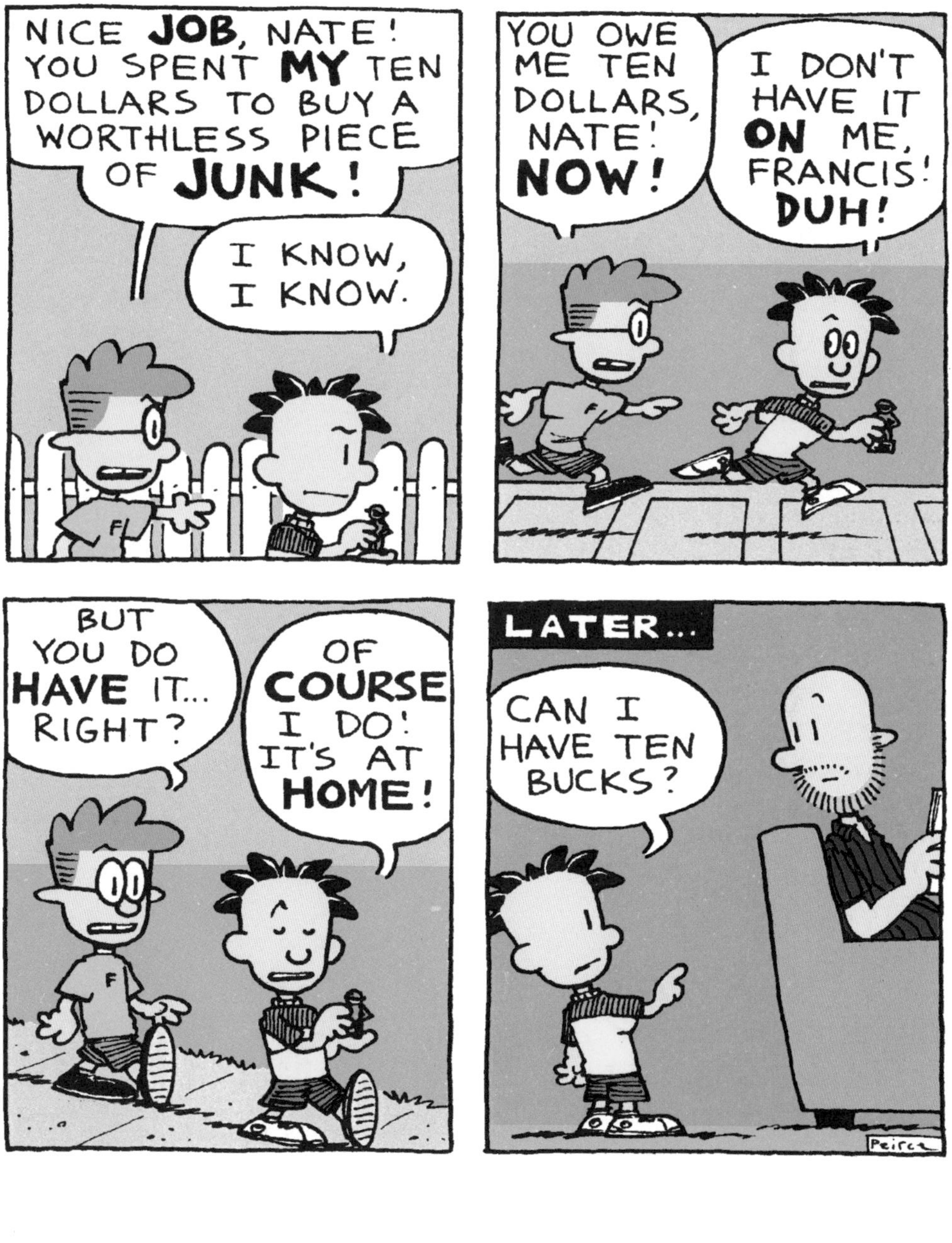
NICE JOB, NATE! YOU SPENT MY TEN DOLLARS TO BUY A WORTHLESS PIECE OF JUNK!
I KNOW, I KNOW.
YOU OWE ME TEN DOLLARS, NATE! NOW!
I DON'T HAVE IT ON ME, FRANCIS! DUH!
BUT YOU DO HAVE IT... RIGHT?
OF COURSE I DO! IT'S AT HOME!
LATER...
CAN I HAVE TEN BUCKS?
Peirce

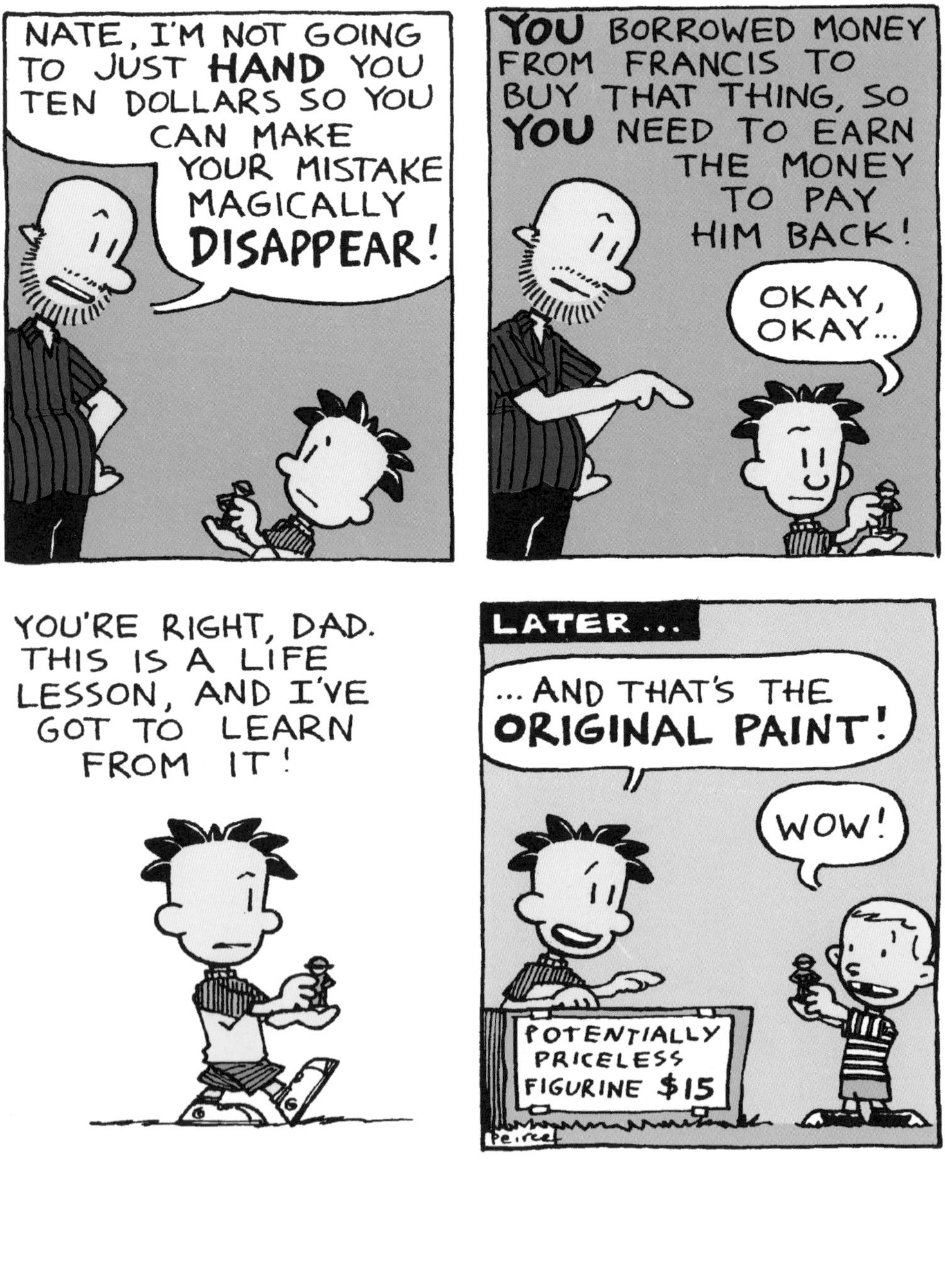
NATE, I'M NOT GOING TO JUST **HAND** YOU TEN DOLLARS SO YOU CAN MAKE YOUR MISTAKE MAGICALLY **DISAPPEAR**!
YOU BORROWED MONEY FROM FRANCIS TO BUY THAT THING, SO **YOU** NEED TO EARN THE MONEY TO PAY HIM BACK!
OKAY, OKAY...
YOU'RE RIGHT, DAD. THIS IS A LIFE LESSON, AND I'VE GOT TO LEARN FROM IT!
LATER...
...AND THAT'S THE **ORIGINAL PAINT**!
WOW!
POTENTIALLY PRICELESS FIGURINE $15
Peirce

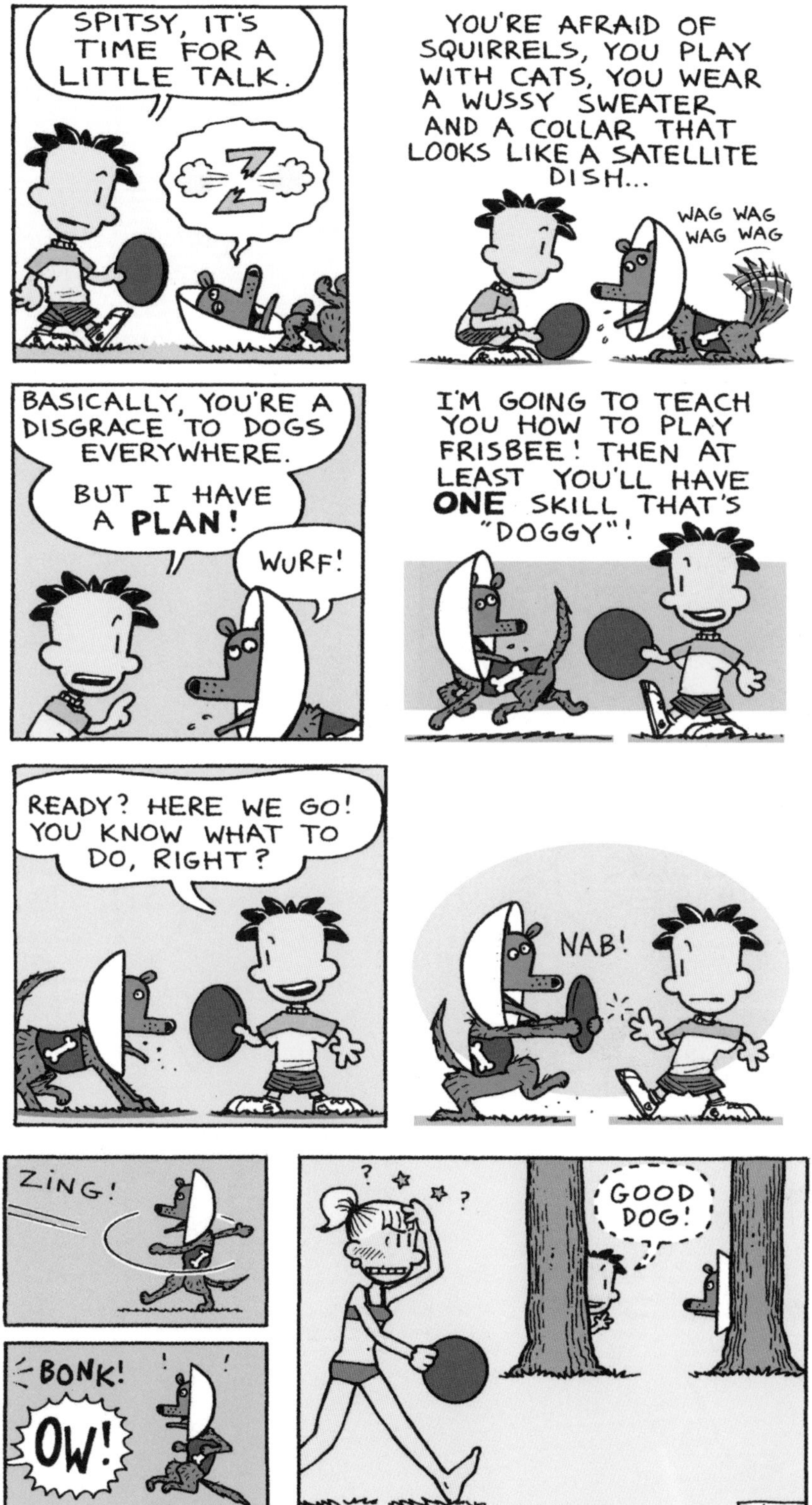
SPITSY, IT'S TIME FOR A LITTLE TALK.
YOU'RE AFRAID OF SQUIRRELS, YOU PLAY WITH CATS, YOU WEAR A WUSSY SWEATER AND A COLLAR THAT LOOKS LIKE A SATELLITE DISH...
WAG WAG WAG WAG
BASICALLY, YOU'RE A DISGRACE TO DOGS EVERYWHERE.
BUT I HAVE A PLAN!
WURF!
I'M GOING TO TEACH YOU HOW TO PLAY FRISBEE! THEN AT LEAST YOU'LL HAVE ONE SKILL THAT'S "DOGGY"!
READY? HERE WE GO! YOU KNOW WHAT TO DO, RIGHT?
NAB!
ZING!
BONK!
OW!
GOOD DOG!
Peirce

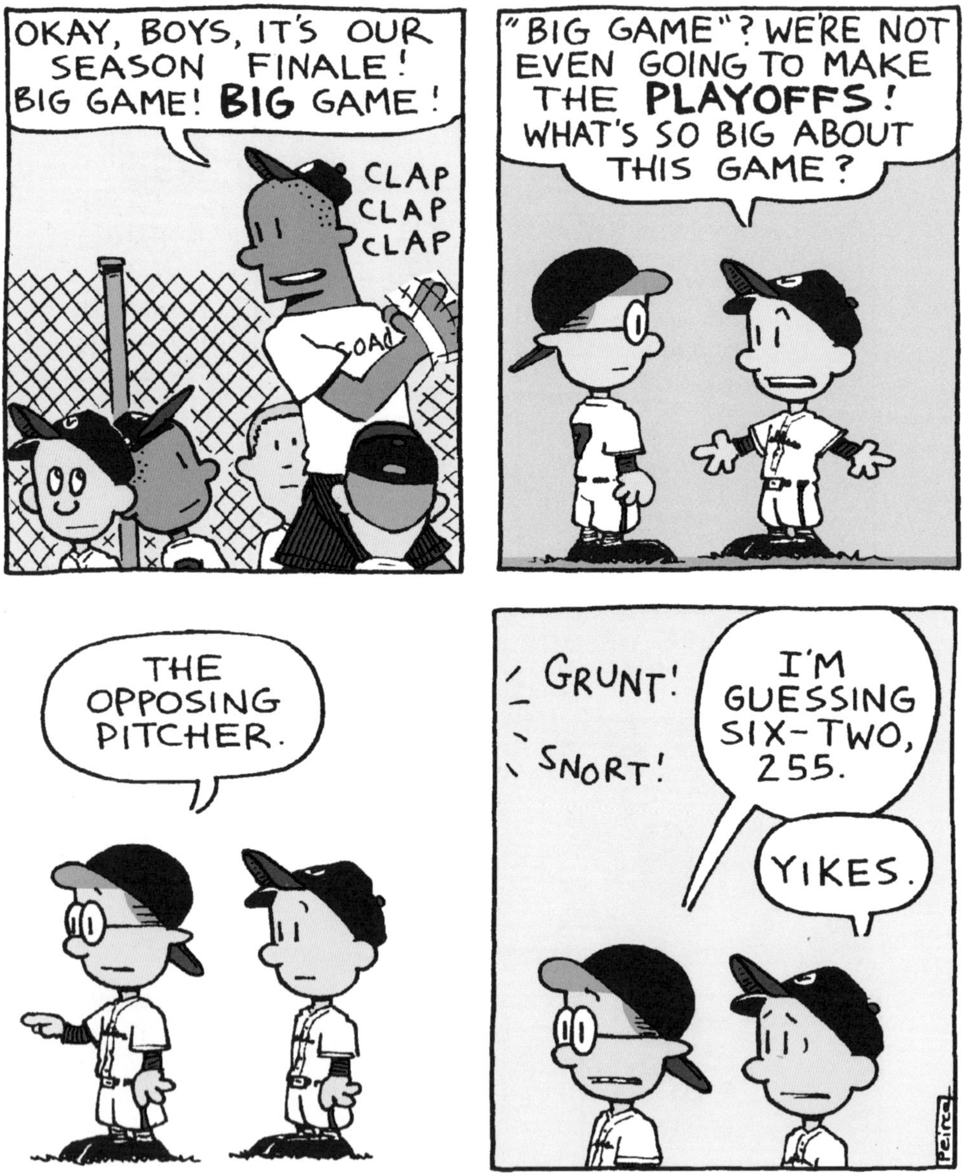
OKAY, BOYS, IT'S OUR SEASON FINALE! BIG GAME! **BIG** GAME!
CLAP CLAP CLAP
COACH
"BIG GAME"? WE'RE NOT EVEN GOING TO MAKE THE **PLAYOFFS**! WHAT'S SO BIG ABOUT THIS GAME?
THE OPPOSING PITCHER.
GRUNT!
SNORT!
I'M GUESSING SIX-TWO, 255.
YIKES.
Peirce

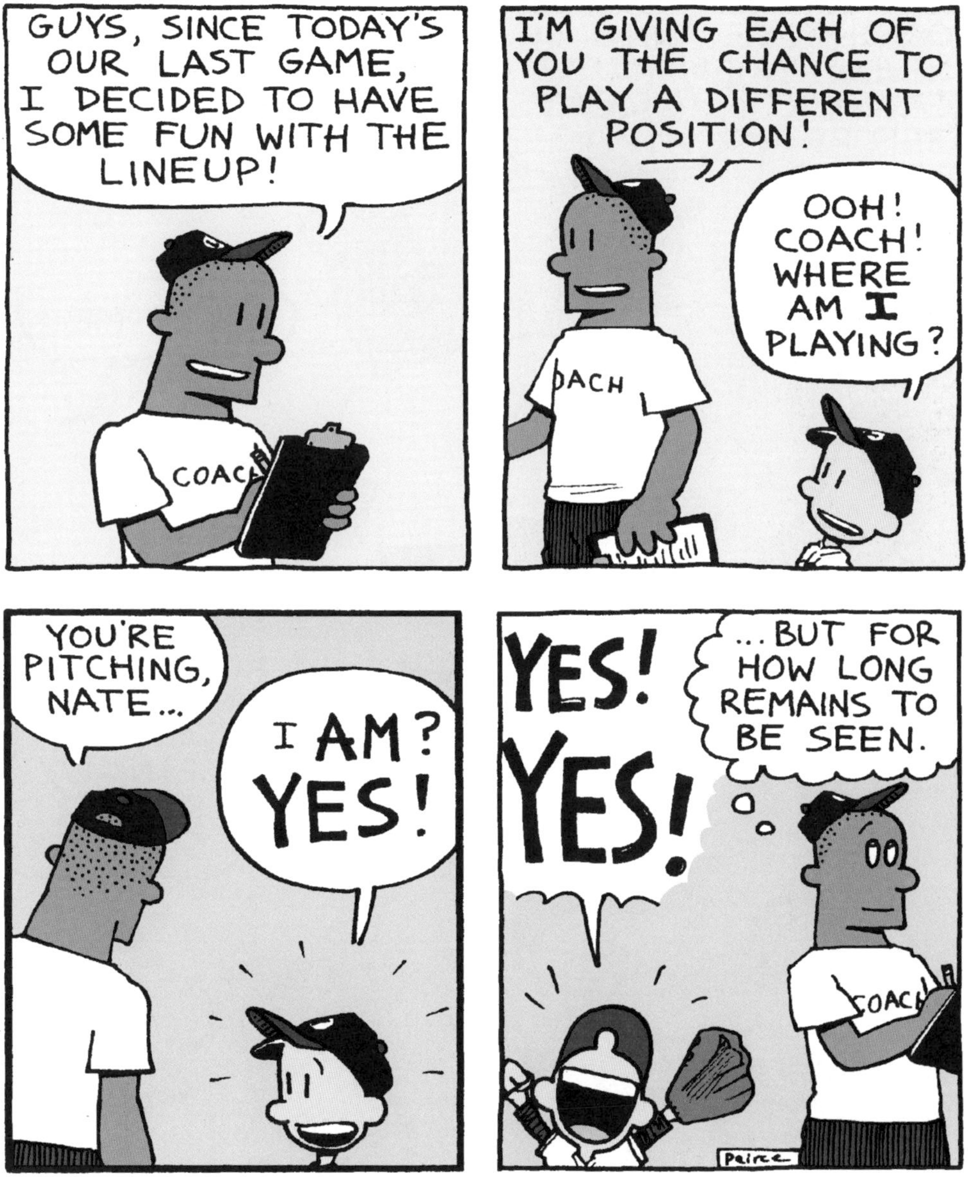
GUYS, SINCE TODAY'S OUR LAST GAME, I DECIDED TO HAVE SOME FUN WITH THE LINEUP!
COACH
I'M GIVING EACH OF YOU THE CHANCE TO PLAY A DIFFERENT POSITION!
OOH! COACH! WHERE AM I PLAYING?
YOU'RE PITCHING, NATE...
I AM? YES!
YES! YES!
...BUT FOR HOW LONG REMAINS TO BE SEEN.
COACH
Peirce

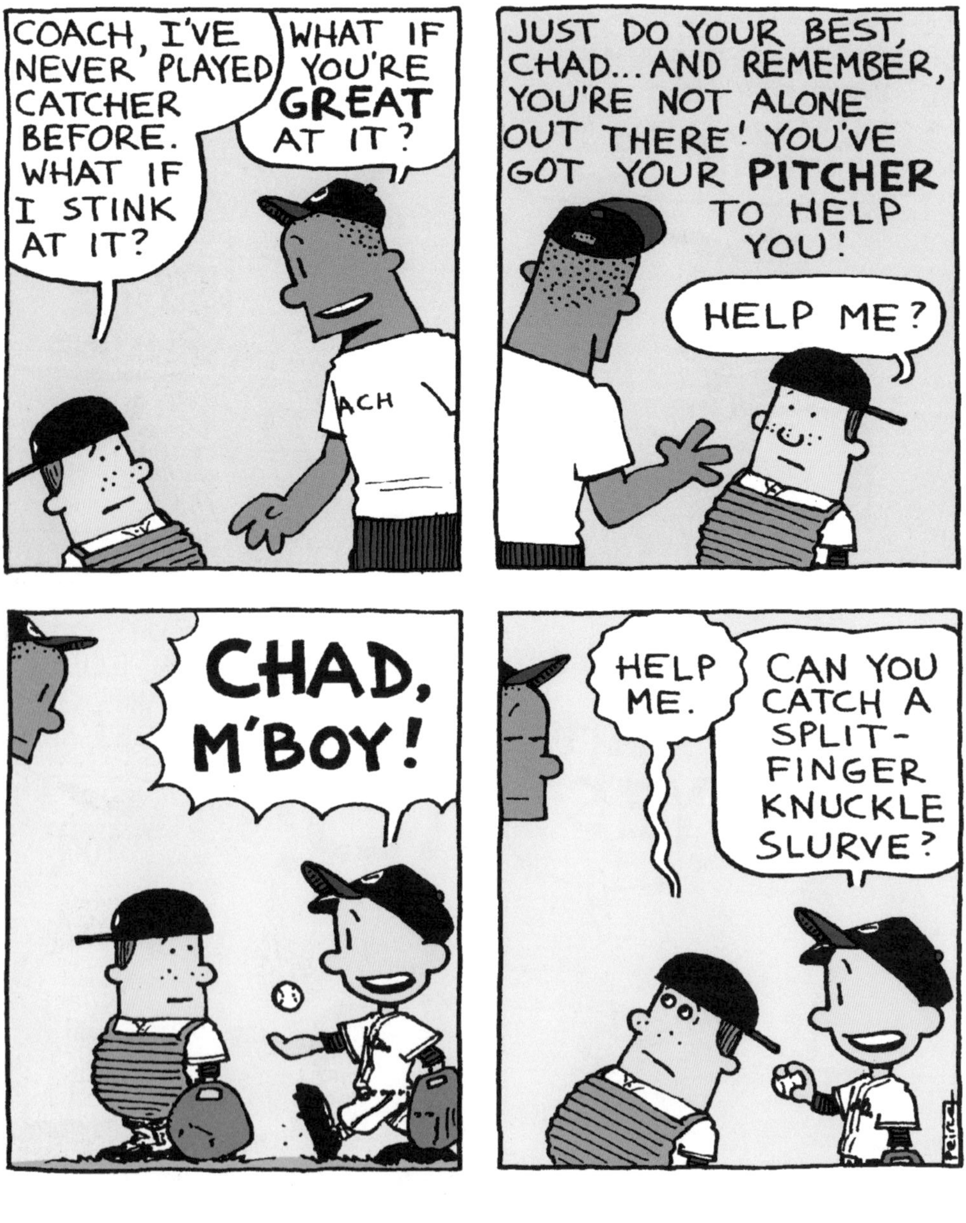
COACH, I'VE NEVER PLAYED CATCHER BEFORE. WHAT IF I STINK AT IT?
WHAT IF YOU'RE **GREAT** AT IT?
ACH
JUST DO YOUR BEST, CHAD... AND REMEMBER, YOU'RE NOT ALONE OUT THERE! YOU'VE GOT YOUR **PITCHER** TO HELP YOU!
HELP ME?
CHAD, M'BOY!
HELP ME.
CAN YOU CATCH A SPLIT-FINGER KNUCKLE SLURVE?
PEIRCE

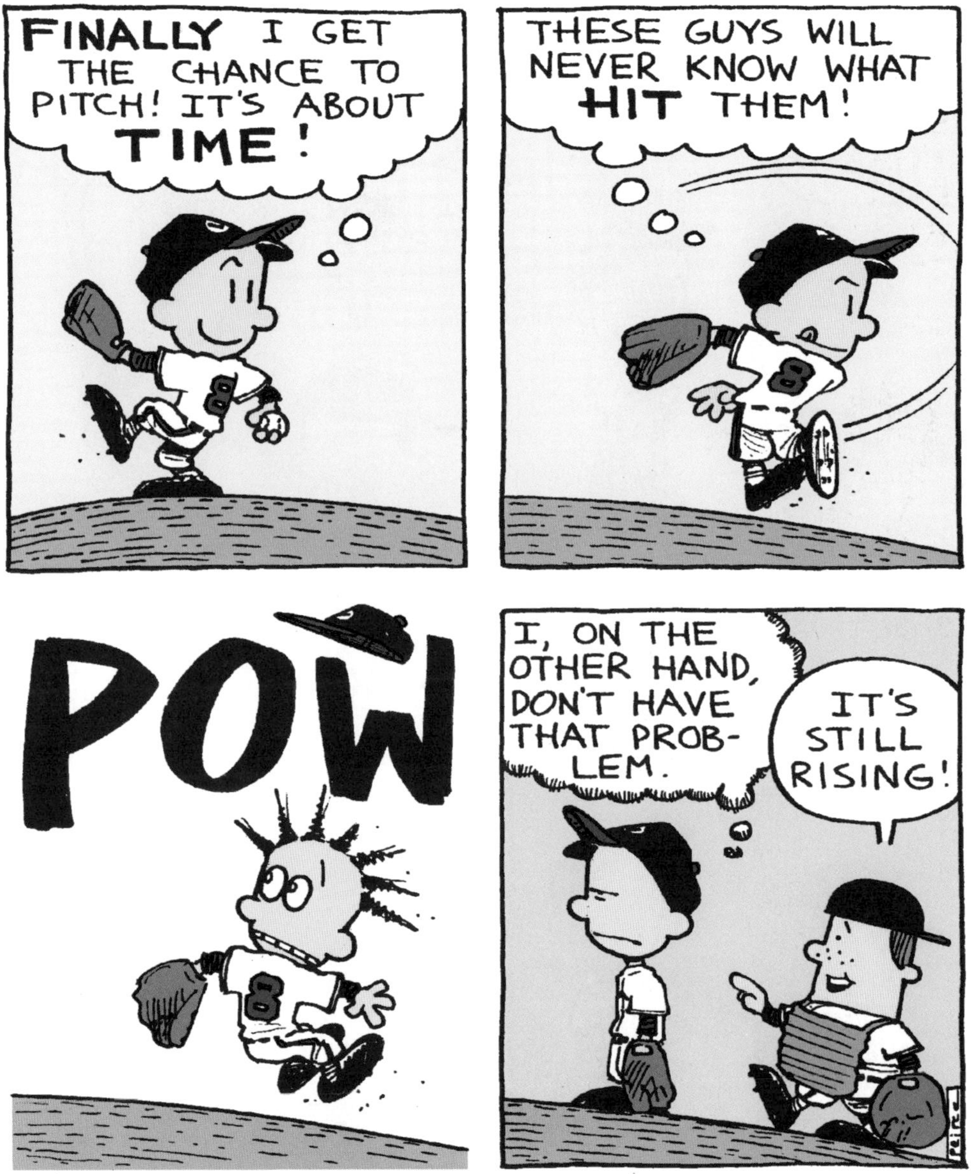
FINALLY I GET THE CHANCE TO PITCH! IT'S ABOUT TIME!
THESE GUYS WILL NEVER KNOW WHAT HIT THEM!
POW
I, ON THE OTHER HAND, DON'T HAVE THAT PROB-LEM.
IT'S STILL RISING!

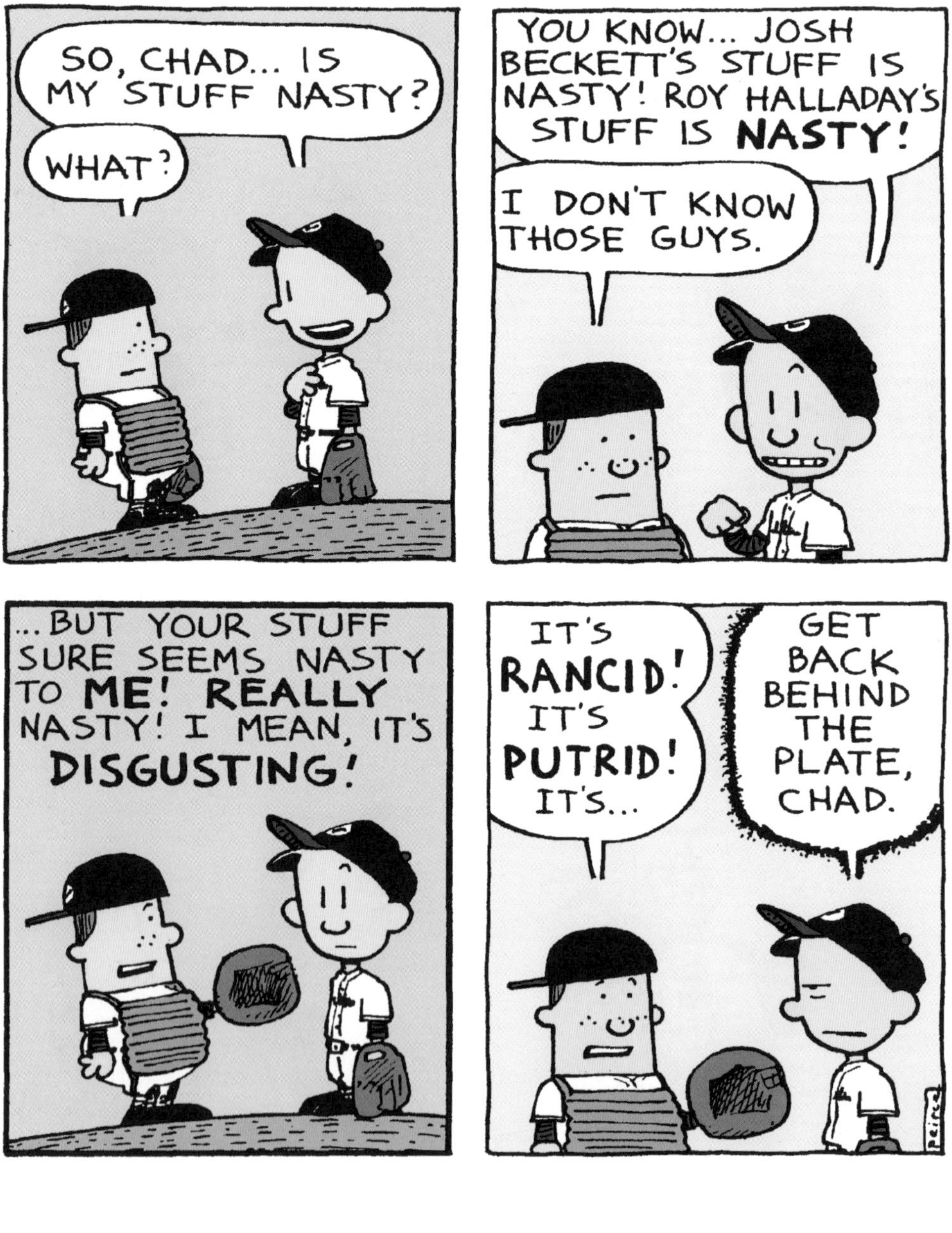
SO, CHAD... IS MY STUFF NASTY?
WHAT?
YOU KNOW... JOSH BECKETT'S STUFF IS NASTY! ROY HALLADAY'S STUFF IS **NASTY!**
I DON'T KNOW THOSE GUYS.
...BUT YOUR STUFF SURE SEEMS NASTY TO **ME! REALLY** NASTY! I MEAN, IT'S **DISGUSTING!**
IT'S **RANCID!** IT'S **PUTRID!** IT'S...
GET BACK BEHIND THE PLATE, CHAD.
PEIRCE

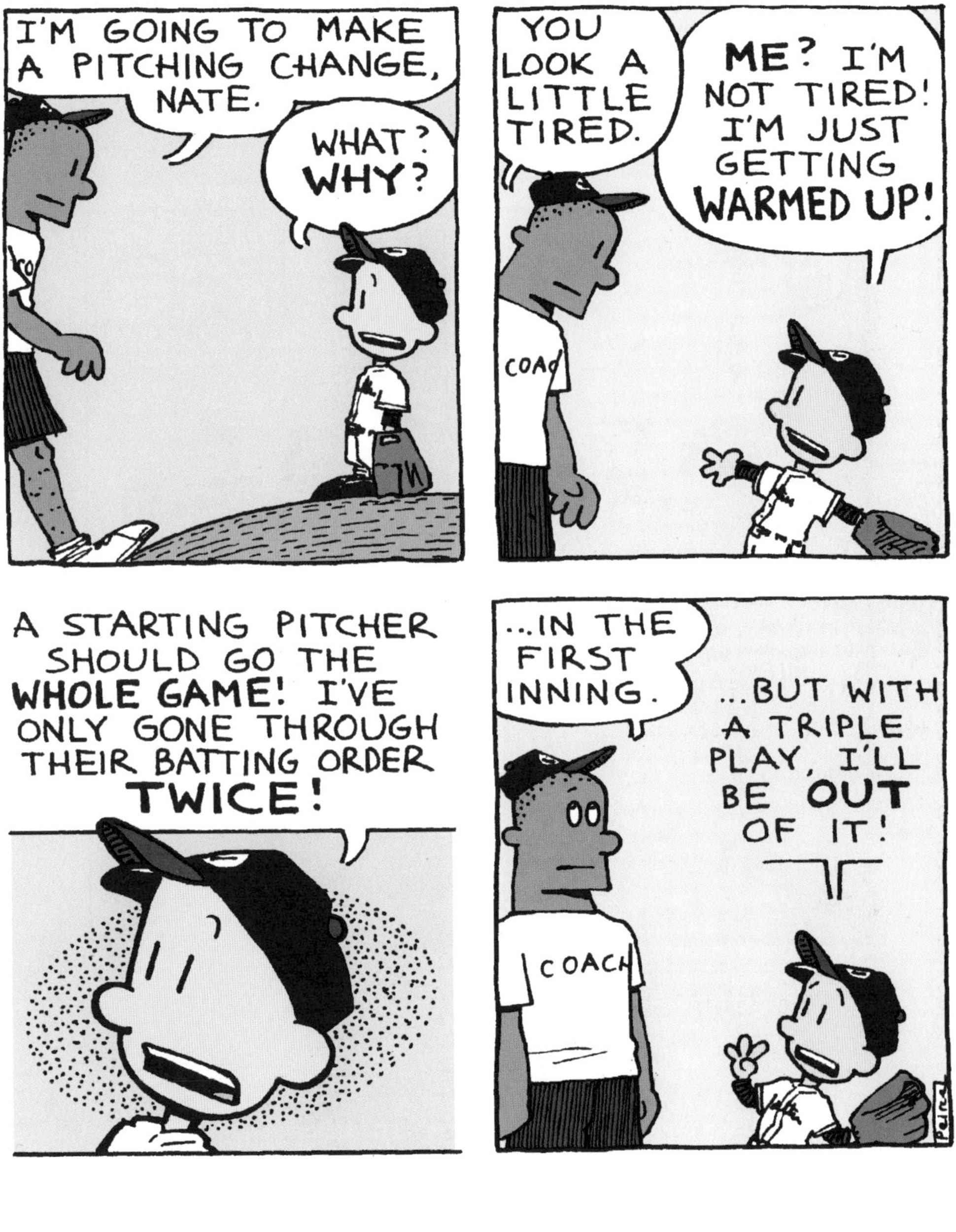
I'M GOING TO MAKE A PITCHING CHANGE, NATE.
WHAT? **WHY?**
YOU LOOK A LITTLE TIRED.
ME? I'M NOT TIRED! I'M JUST GETTING **WARMED UP!**
A STARTING PITCHER SHOULD GO THE **WHOLE GAME!** I'VE ONLY GONE THROUGH THEIR BATTING ORDER **TWICE!**
...IN THE FIRST INNING.
...BUT WITH A TRIPLE PLAY, I'LL BE **OUT** OF IT!

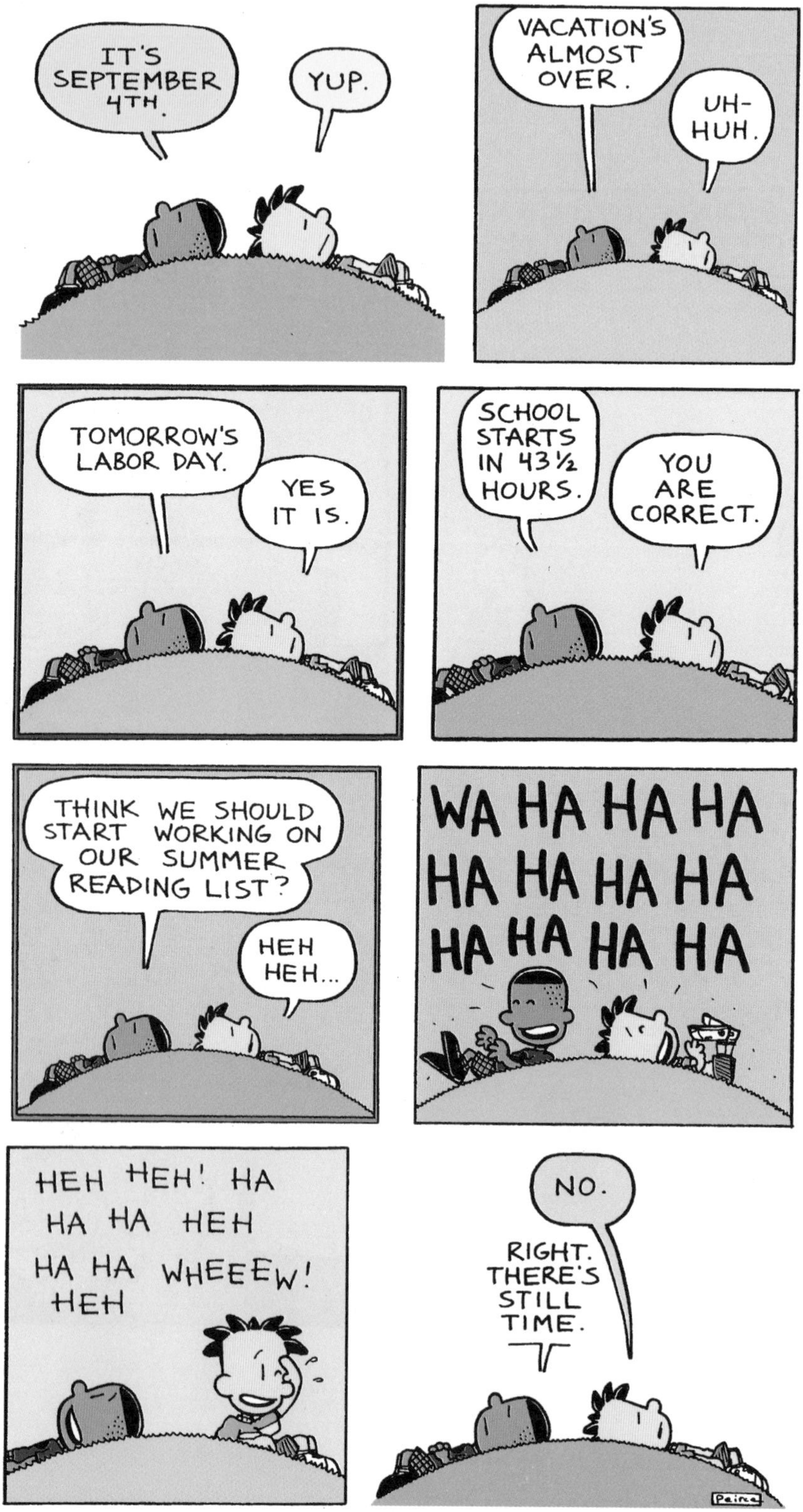
IT'S SEPTEMBER 4TH.
YUP.
VACATION'S ALMOST OVER.
UH-HUH.
TOMORROW'S LABOR DAY.
YES IT IS.
SCHOOL STARTS IN 43½ HOURS.
YOU ARE CORRECT.
THINK WE SHOULD START WORKING ON OUR SUMMER READING LIST?
HEH HEH...
WA HA HA HA HA HA HA HA HA HA HA HA
HEH HEH! HA HA HA HEH HA HA WHEEEW! HEH
NO.
RIGHT. THERE'S STILL TIME.
Peirce

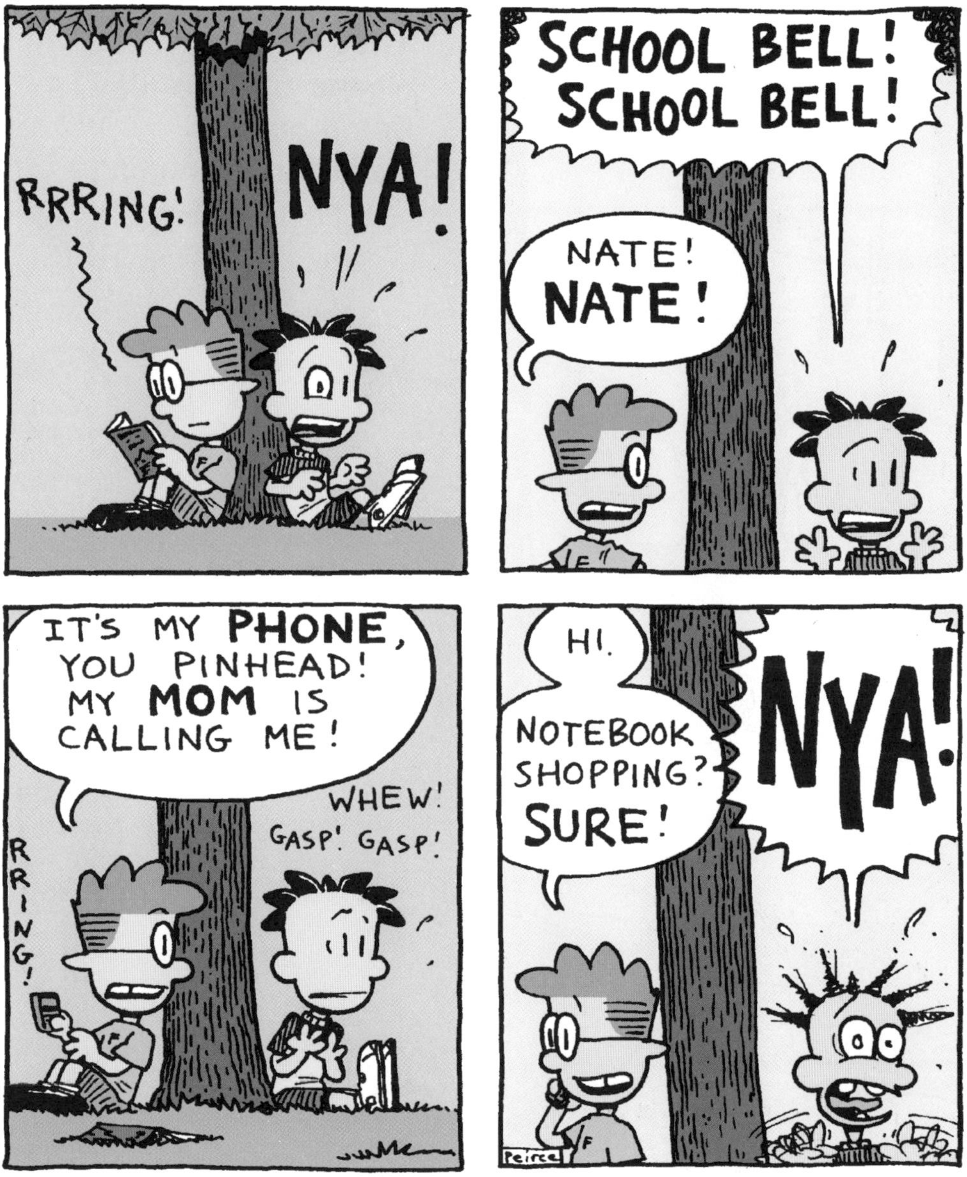
RRRING!
NYA!
SCHOOL BELL! SCHOOL BELL!
NATE! NATE!
IT'S MY PHONE, YOU PINHEAD! MY MOM IS CALLING ME!
WHEW!
GASP! GASP!
RRING!
HI.
NOTEBOOK SHOPPING? SURE!
NYA!
Peirce

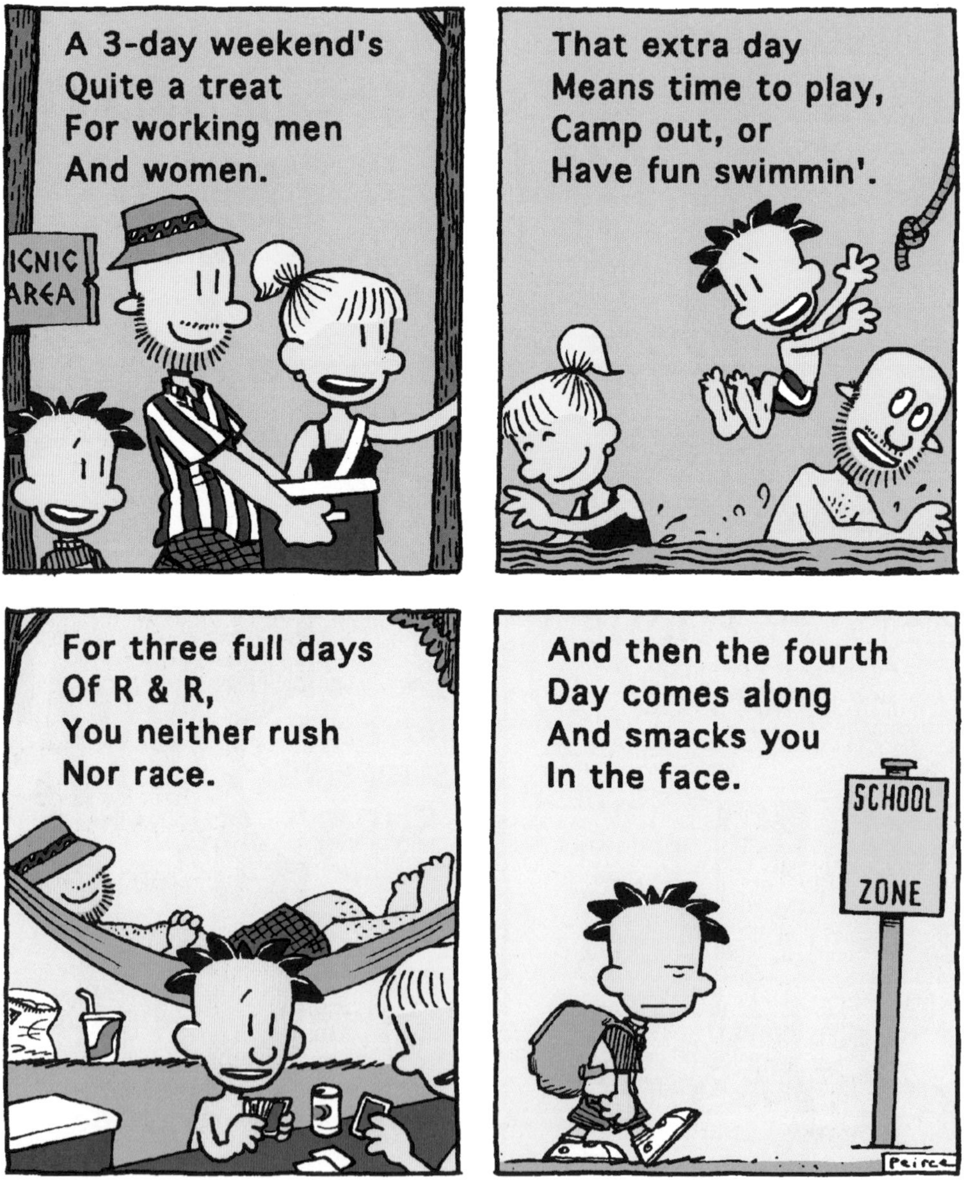
A 3-day weekend's
Quite a treat
For working men
And women.
ICNIC
AREA
That extra day
Means time to play,
Camp out, or
Have fun swimmin'.
For three full days
Of R & R,
You neither rush
Nor race.
And then the fourth
Day comes along
And smacks you
In the face.
SCHOOL
ZONE
Peirce

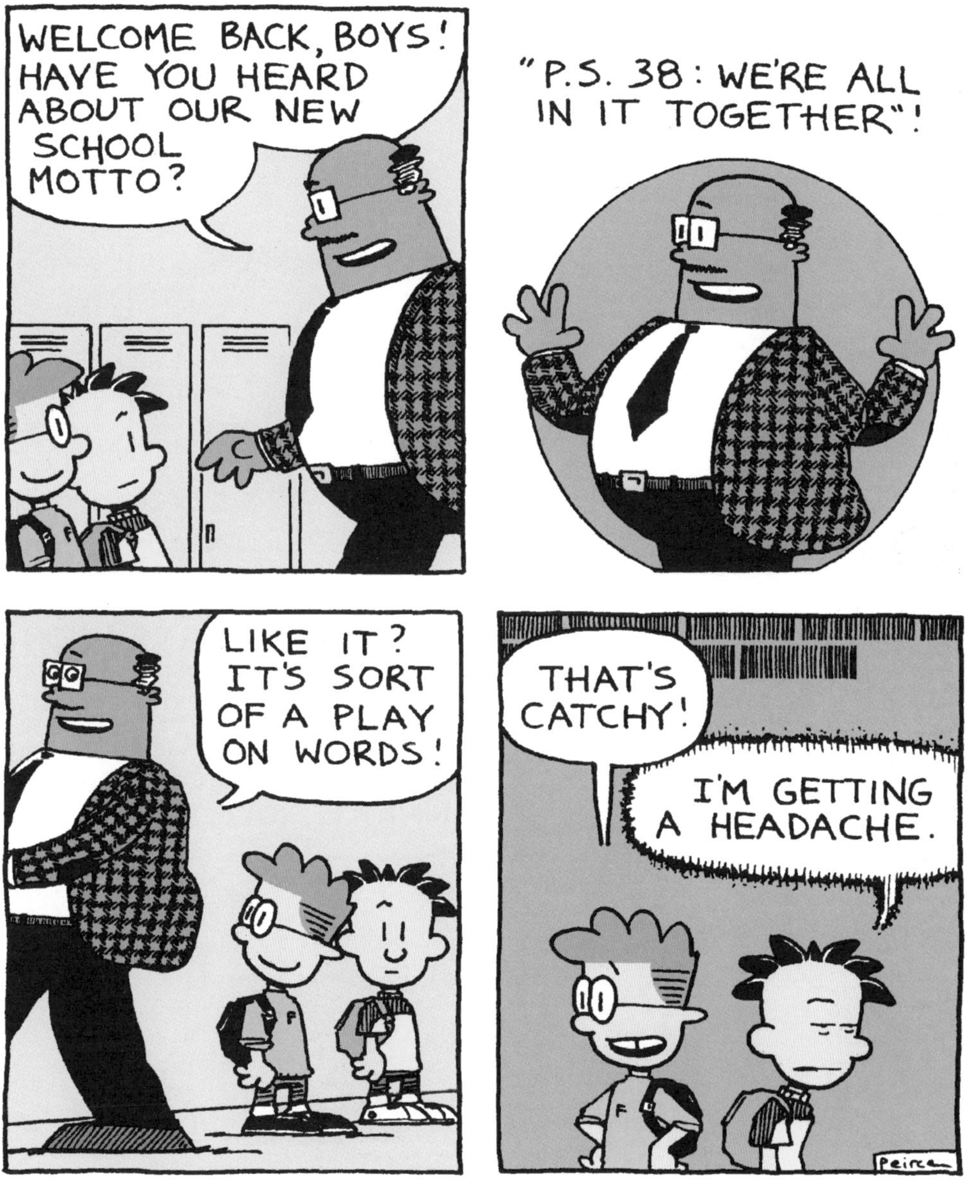
WELCOME BACK, BOYS! HAVE YOU HEARD ABOUT OUR NEW SCHOOL MOTTO?
"P.S. 38: WE'RE ALL IN IT TOGETHER"!
LIKE IT? IT'S SORT OF A PLAY ON WORDS!
THAT'S CATCHY!
I'M GETTING A HEADACHE.
Peirce

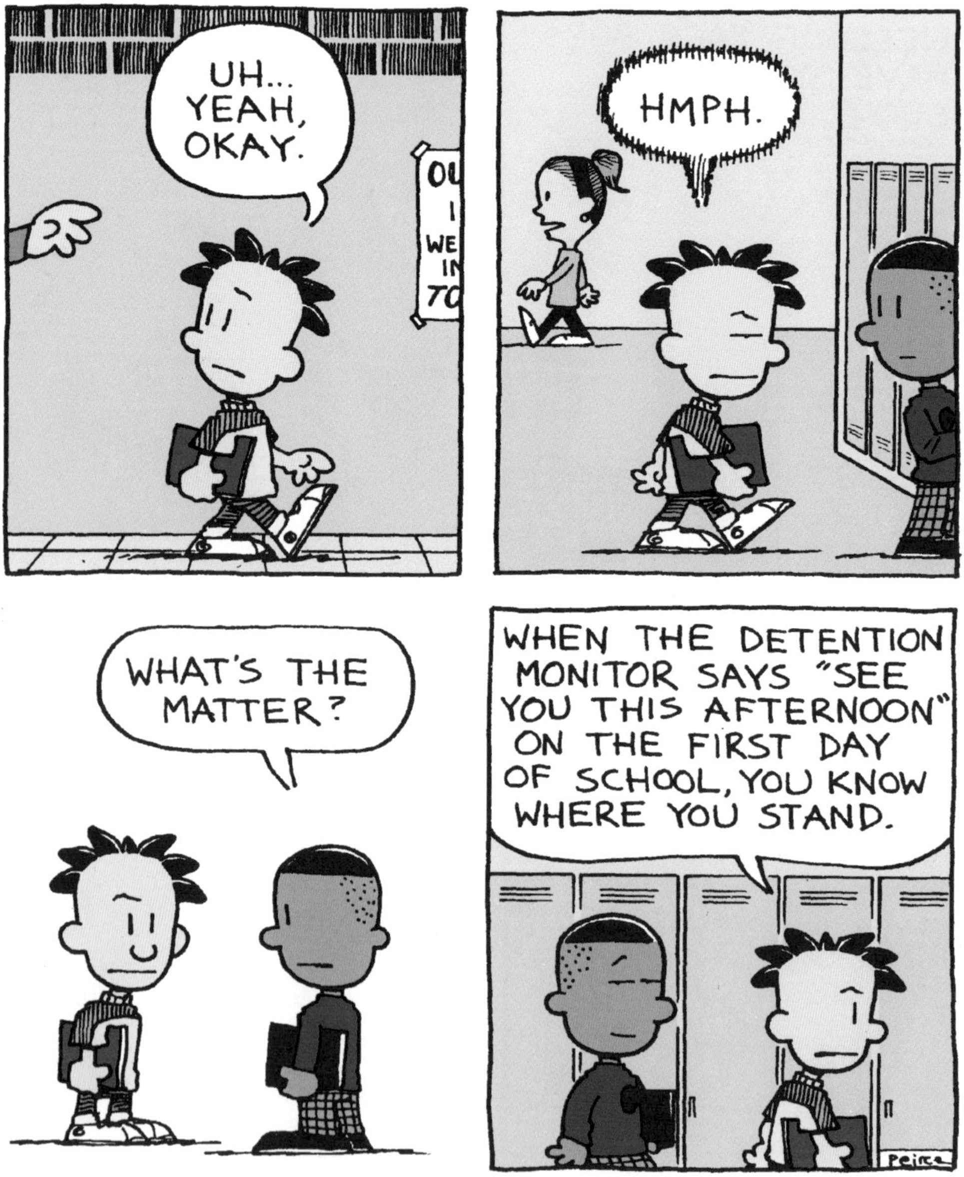
UH... YEAH, OKAY.
HMPH.
WHAT'S THE MATTER?
WHEN THE DETENTION MONITOR SAYS "SEE YOU THIS AFTERNOON" ON THE FIRST DAY OF SCHOOL, YOU KNOW WHERE YOU STAND.

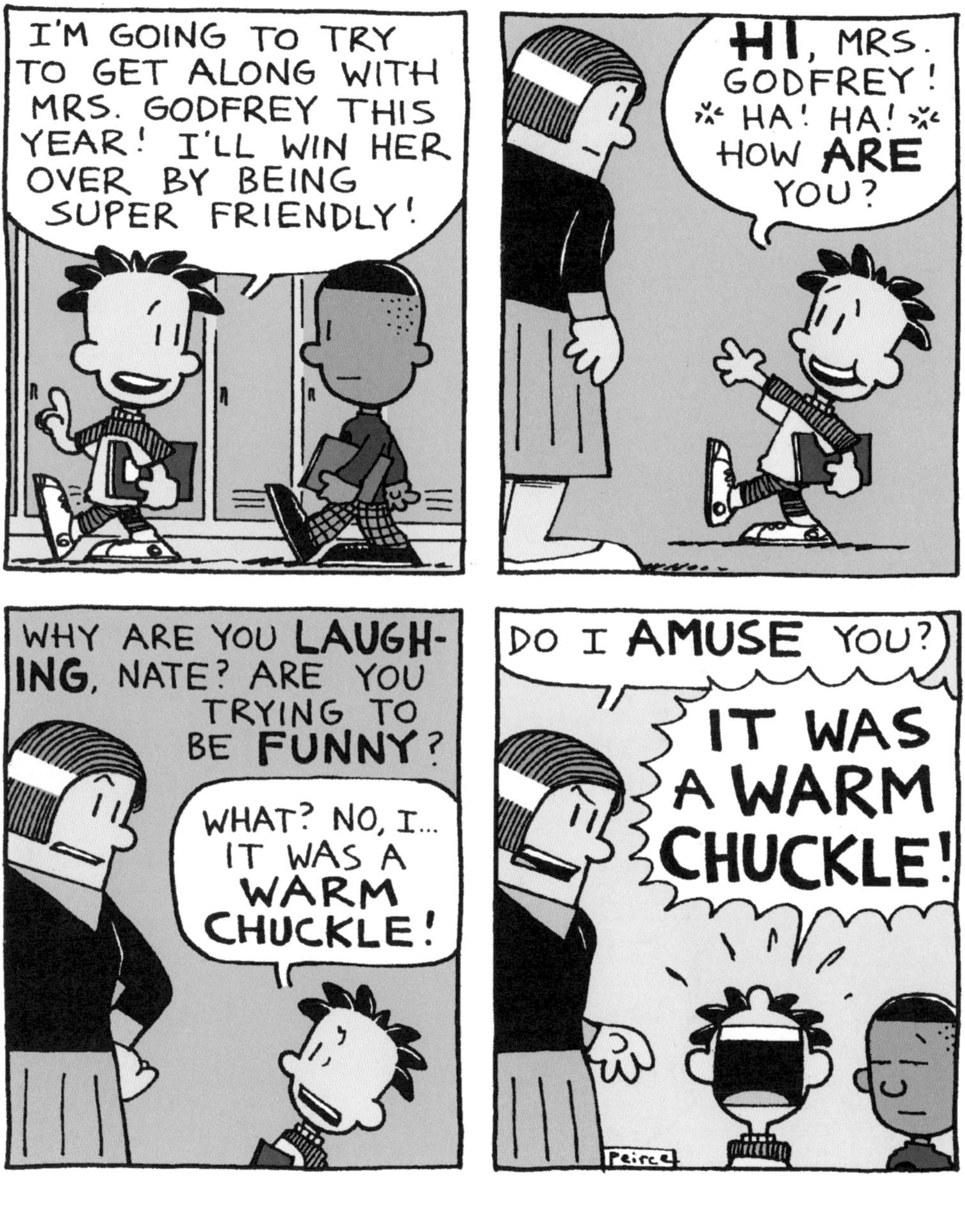
I'M GOING TO TRY TO GET ALONG WITH MRS. GODFREY THIS YEAR! I'LL WIN HER OVER BY BEING SUPER FRIENDLY!
HI, MRS. GODFREY! HA! HA! HOW ARE YOU?
WHY ARE YOU LAUGHING, NATE? ARE YOU TRYING TO BE FUNNY?
WHAT? NO, I... IT WAS A WARM CHUCKLE!
DO I AMUSE YOU?
IT WAS A WARM CHUCKLE!
Peirce

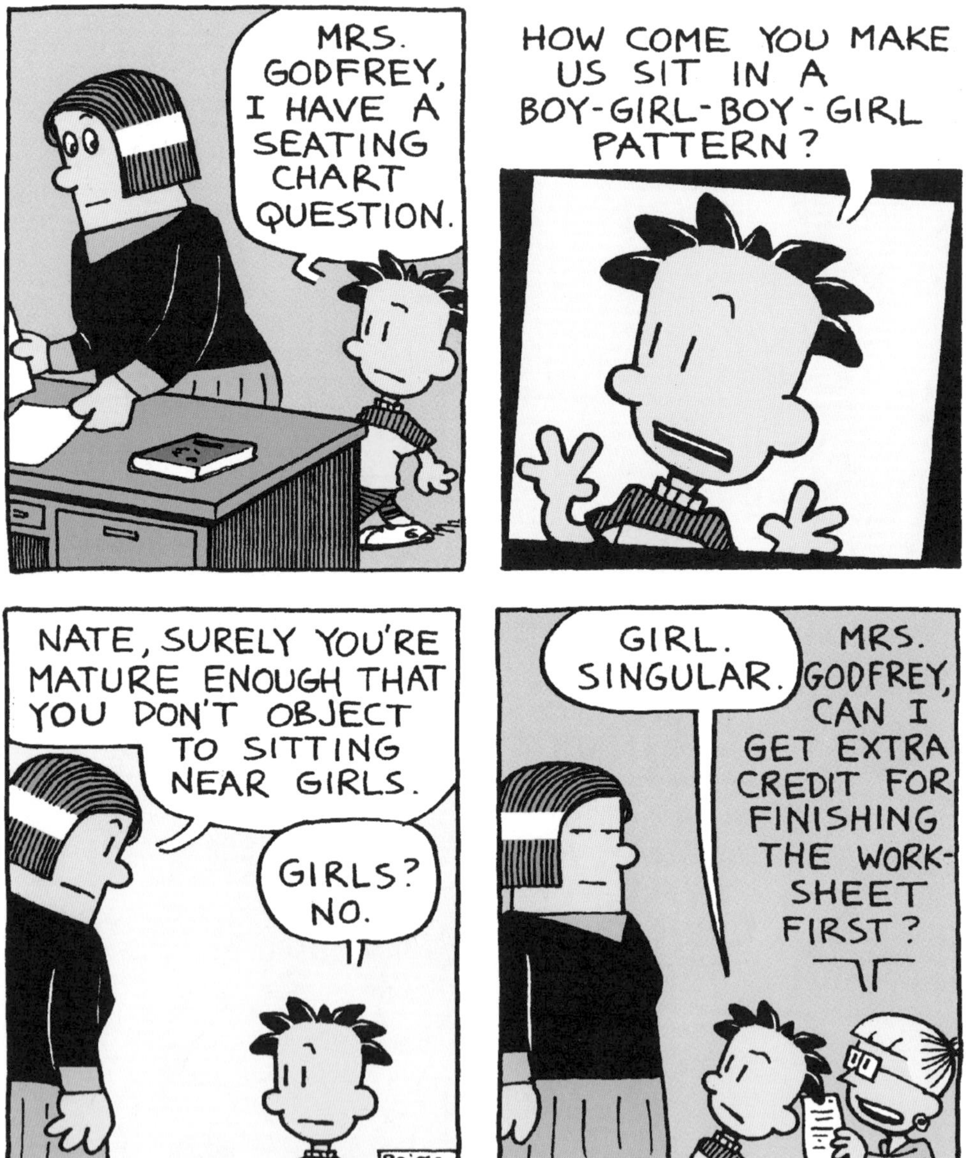
MRS. GODFREY, I HAVE A SEATING CHART QUESTION.
HOW COME YOU MAKE US SIT IN A BOY-GIRL-BOY-GIRL PATTERN?
NATE, SURELY YOU'RE MATURE ENOUGH THAT YOU DON'T OBJECT TO SITTING NEAR GIRLS.
GIRLS? NO.
GIRL. SINGULAR.
MRS. GODFREY, CAN I GET EXTRA CREDIT FOR FINISHING THE WORK-SHEET FIRST?
Peirce

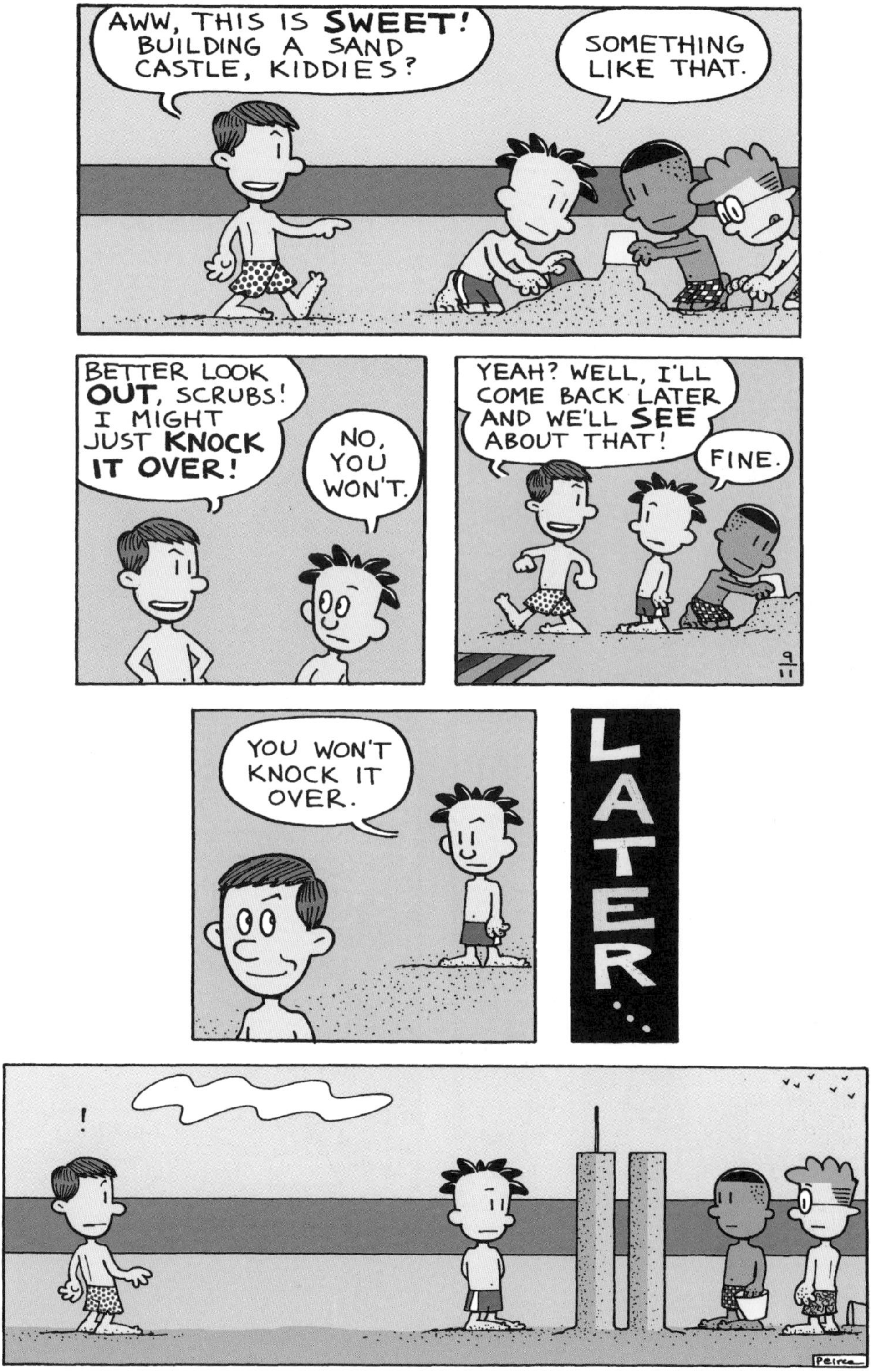
AWW, THIS IS SWEET! BUILDING A SAND CASTLE, KIDDIES?
SOMETHING LIKE THAT.
BETTER LOOK OUT, SCRUBS! I MIGHT JUST KNOCK IT OVER!
NO, YOU WON'T.
YEAH? WELL, I'LL COME BACK LATER AND WE'LL SEE ABOUT THAT!
FINE.
9/11
YOU WON'T KNOCK IT OVER.
LATER...
!
Peirce

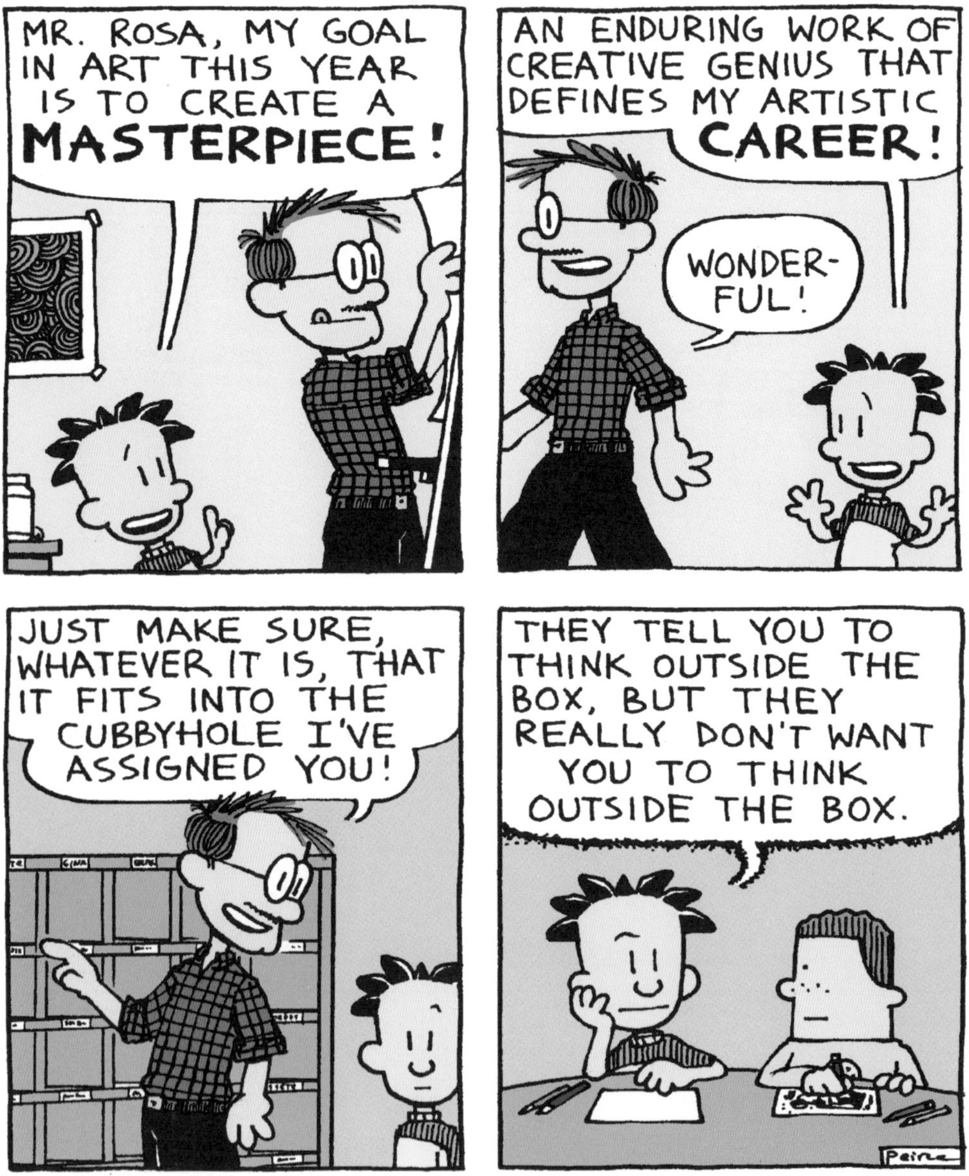
MR. ROSA, MY GOAL IN ART THIS YEAR IS TO CREATE A **MASTERPIECE**!
AN ENDURING WORK OF CREATIVE GENIUS THAT DEFINES MY ARTISTIC **CAREER**!
WONDER-FUL!
JUST MAKE SURE, WHATEVER IT IS, THAT IT FITS INTO THE CUBBYHOLE I'VE ASSIGNED YOU!
THEY TELL YOU TO THINK OUTSIDE THE BOX, BUT THEY REALLY DON'T WANT YOU TO THINK OUTSIDE THE BOX.
Peirce

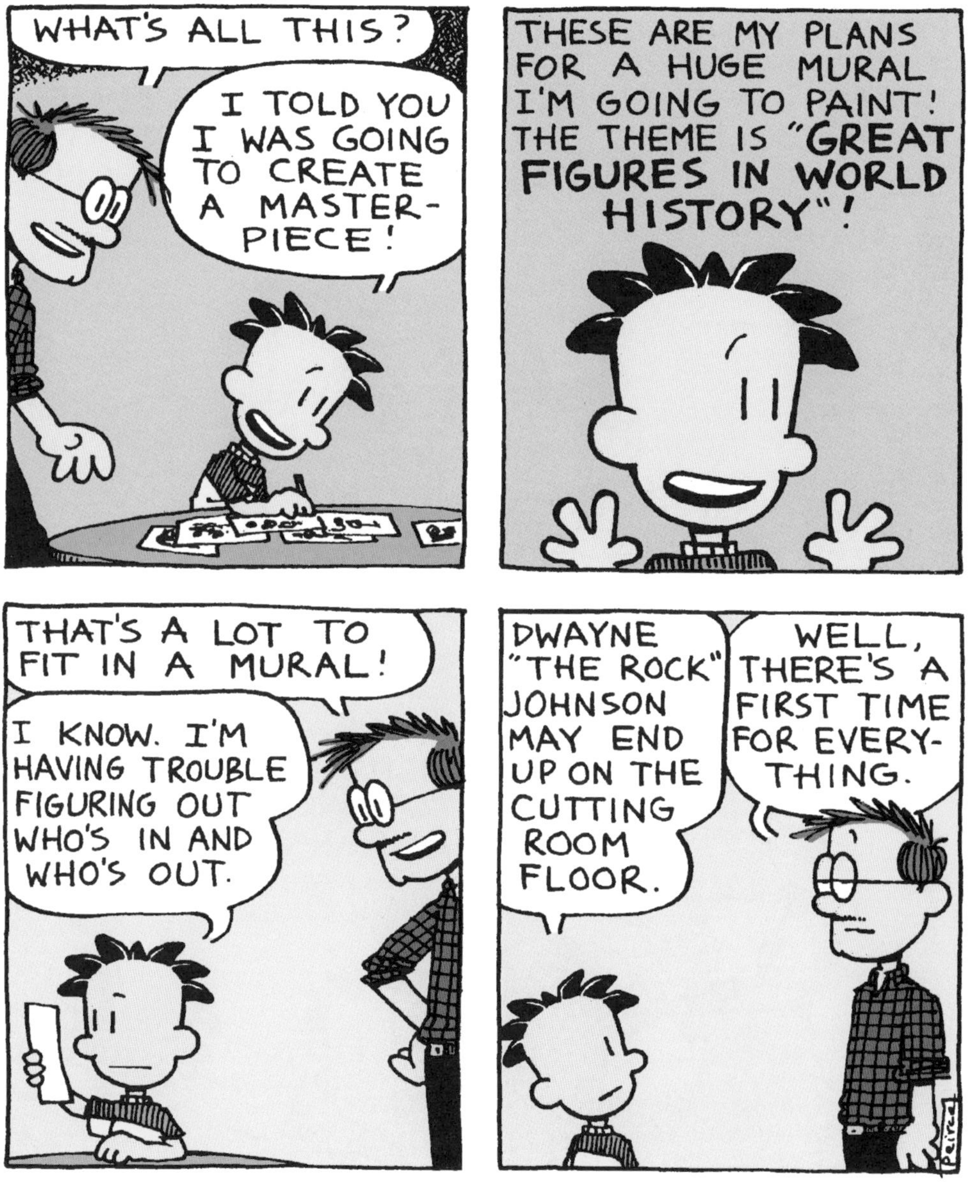
WHAT'S ALL THIS?
I TOLD YOU I WAS GOING TO CREATE A MASTER-PIECE!
THESE ARE MY PLANS FOR A HUGE MURAL I'M GOING TO PAINT! THE THEME IS "GREAT FIGURES IN WORLD HISTORY"!
THAT'S A LOT TO FIT IN A MURAL!
I KNOW. I'M HAVING TROUBLE FIGURING OUT WHO'S IN AND WHO'S OUT.
DWAYNE "THE ROCK" JOHNSON MAY END UP ON THE CUTTING ROOM FLOOR.
WELL, THERE'S A FIRST TIME FOR EVERY-THING.
Peirce

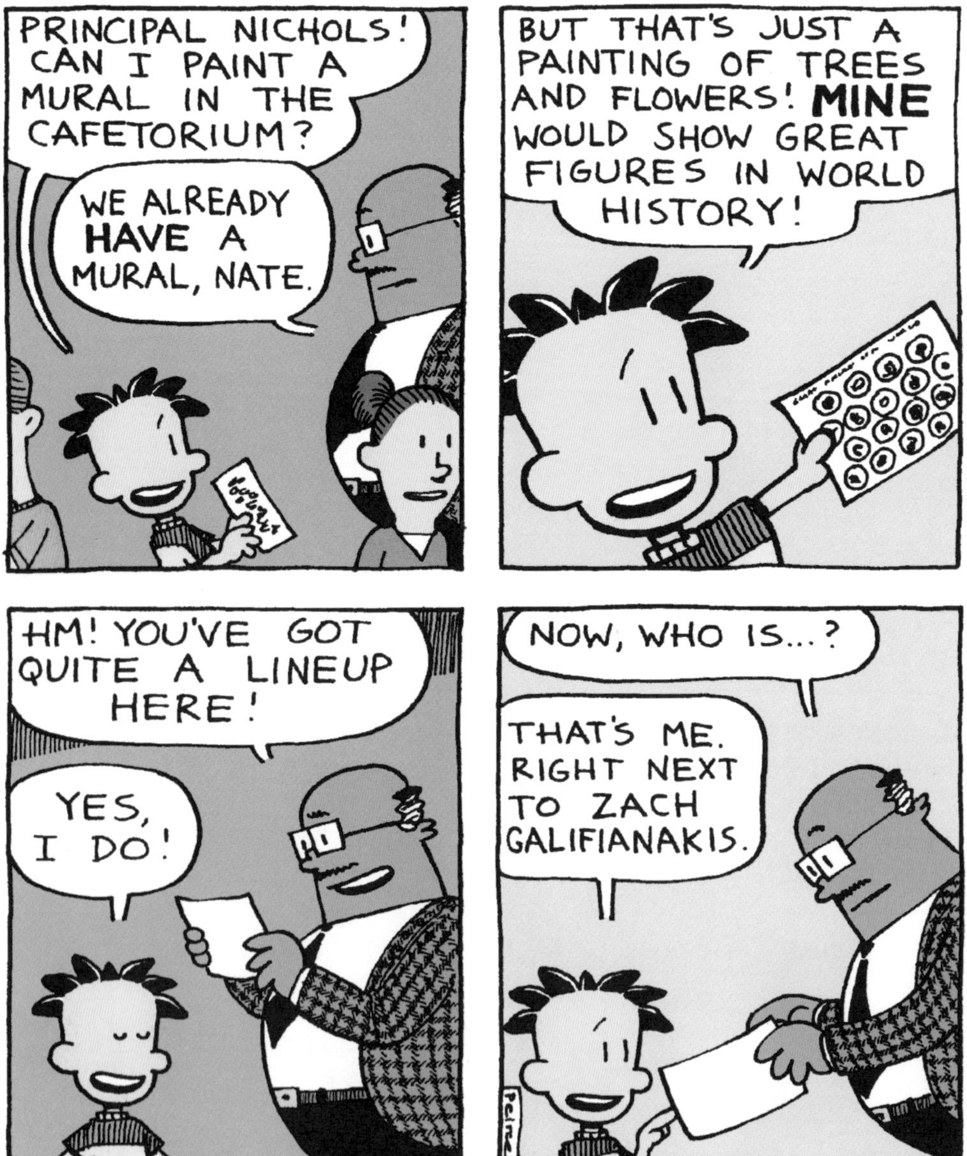
PRINCIPAL NICHOLS! CAN I PAINT A MURAL IN THE CAFETORIUM?
WE ALREADY **HAVE** A MURAL, NATE.
BUT THAT'S JUST A PAINTING OF TREES AND FLOWERS! **MINE** WOULD SHOW GREAT FIGURES IN WORLD HISTORY!
HM! YOU'VE GOT QUITE A LINEUP HERE!
YES, I DO!
NOW, WHO IS...?
THAT'S ME. RIGHT NEXT TO ZACH GALIFIANAKIS.
PEIRCE

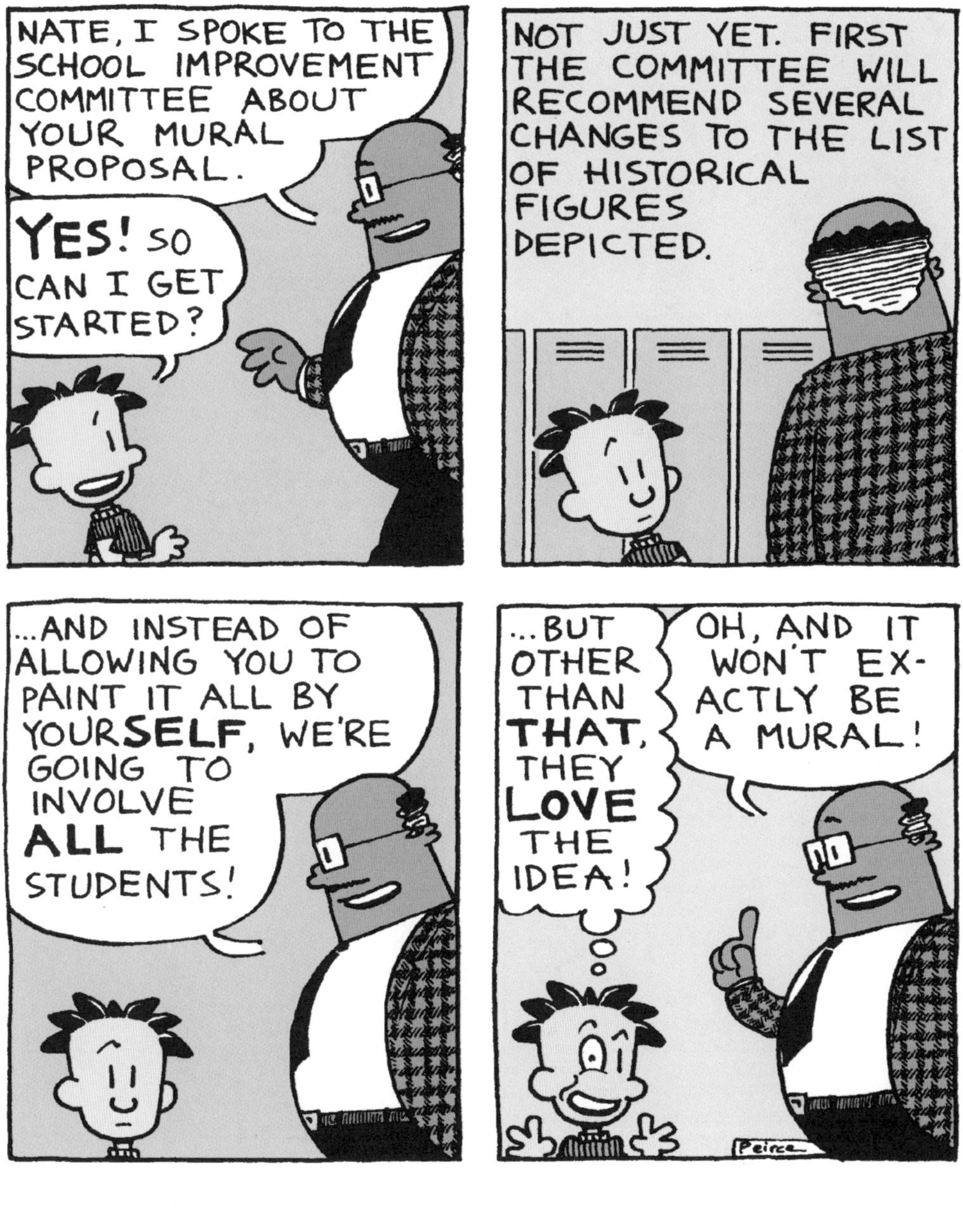

NATE, I SPOKE TO THE SCHOOL IMPROVEMENT COMMITTEE ABOUT YOUR MURAL PROPOSAL.
YES! SO CAN I GET STARTED?
NOT JUST YET. FIRST THE COMMITTEE WILL RECOMMEND SEVERAL CHANGES TO THE LIST OF HISTORICAL FIGURES DEPICTED.
...AND INSTEAD OF ALLOWING YOU TO PAINT IT ALL BY YOURSELF, WE'RE GOING TO INVOLVE ALL THE STUDENTS!
...BUT OTHER THAN THAT, THEY LOVE THE IDEA!
OH, AND IT WON'T EXACTLY BE A MURAL!
Peirce

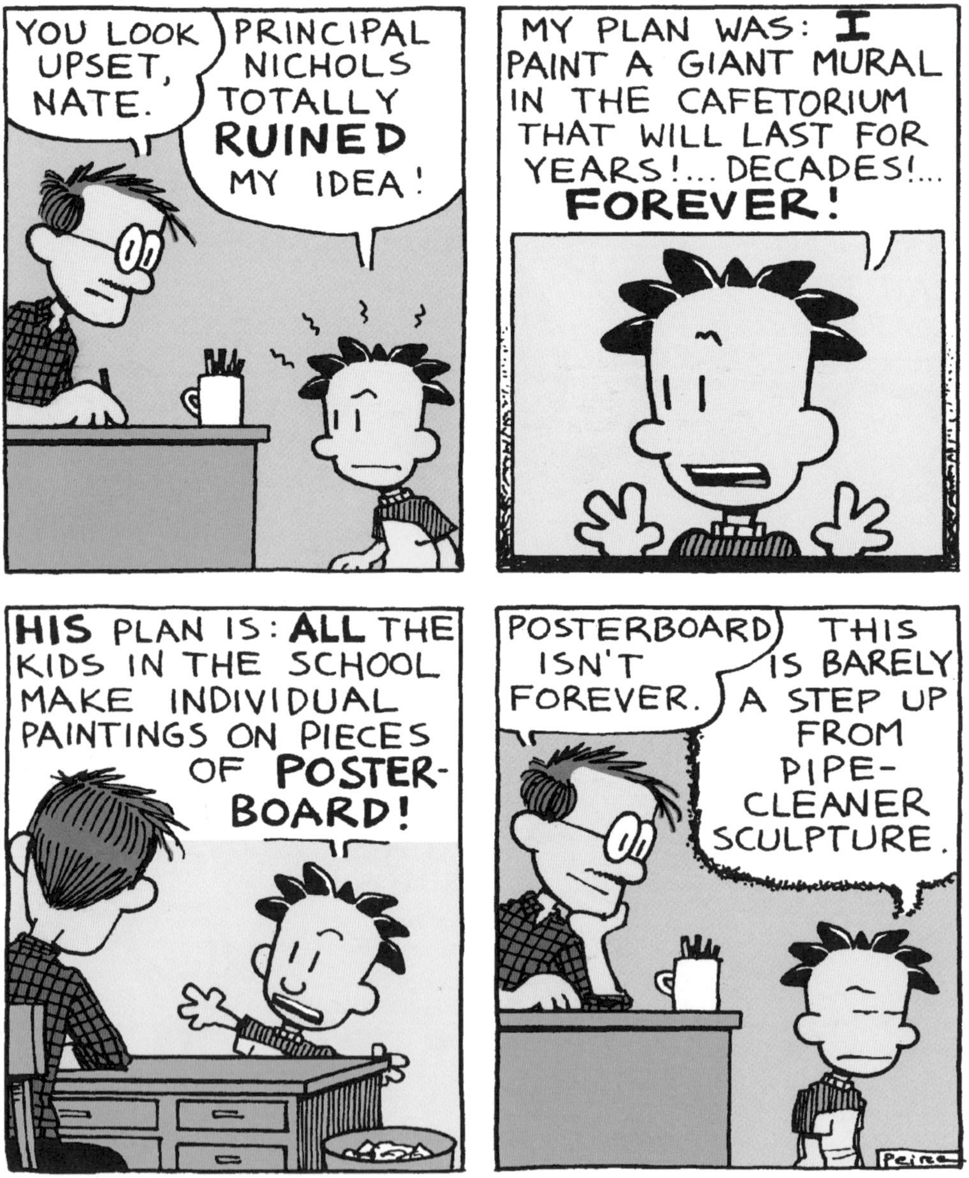
YOU LOOK UPSET, NATE.
PRINCIPAL NICHOLS TOTALLY **RUINED** MY IDEA!
MY PLAN WAS: **I** PAINT A GIANT MURAL IN THE CAFETORIUM THAT WILL LAST FOR YEARS!... DECADES!... **FOREVER!**
HIS PLAN IS: **ALL** THE KIDS IN THE SCHOOL MAKE INDIVIDUAL PAINTINGS ON PIECES OF **POSTER-BOARD!**
POSTERBOARD ISN'T FOREVER.
THIS IS BARELY A STEP UP FROM PIPE-CLEANER SCULPTURE.
Peirce

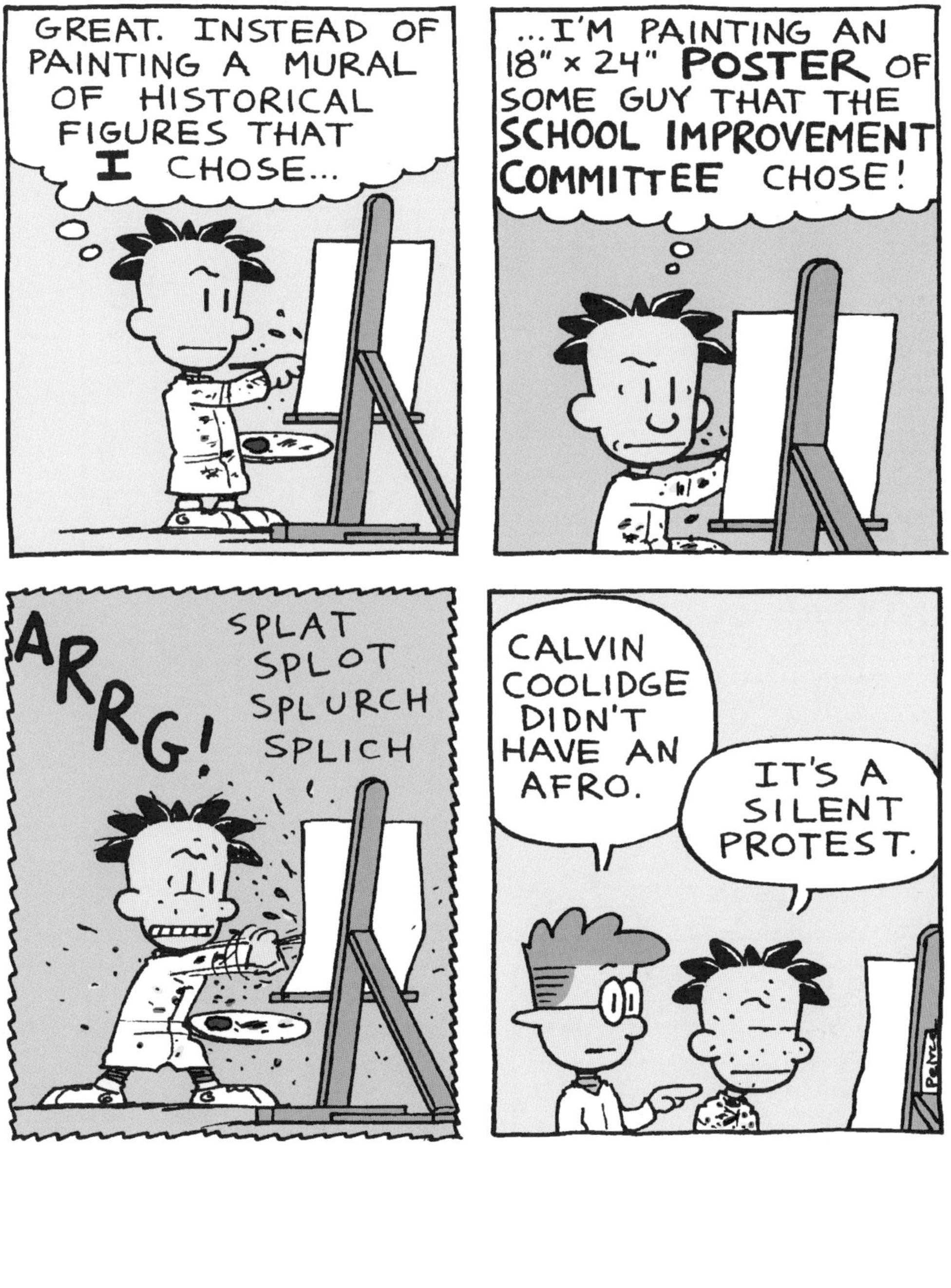
GREAT. INSTEAD OF PAINTING A MURAL OF HISTORICAL FIGURES THAT I CHOSE...
...I'M PAINTING AN 18" x 24" POSTER OF SOME GUY THAT THE SCHOOL IMPROVEMENT COMMITTEE CHOSE!
ARRG!
SPLAT
SPLOT
SPLURCH
SPLICH
CALVIN COOLIDGE DIDN'T HAVE AN AFRO.
IT'S A SILENT PROTEST.

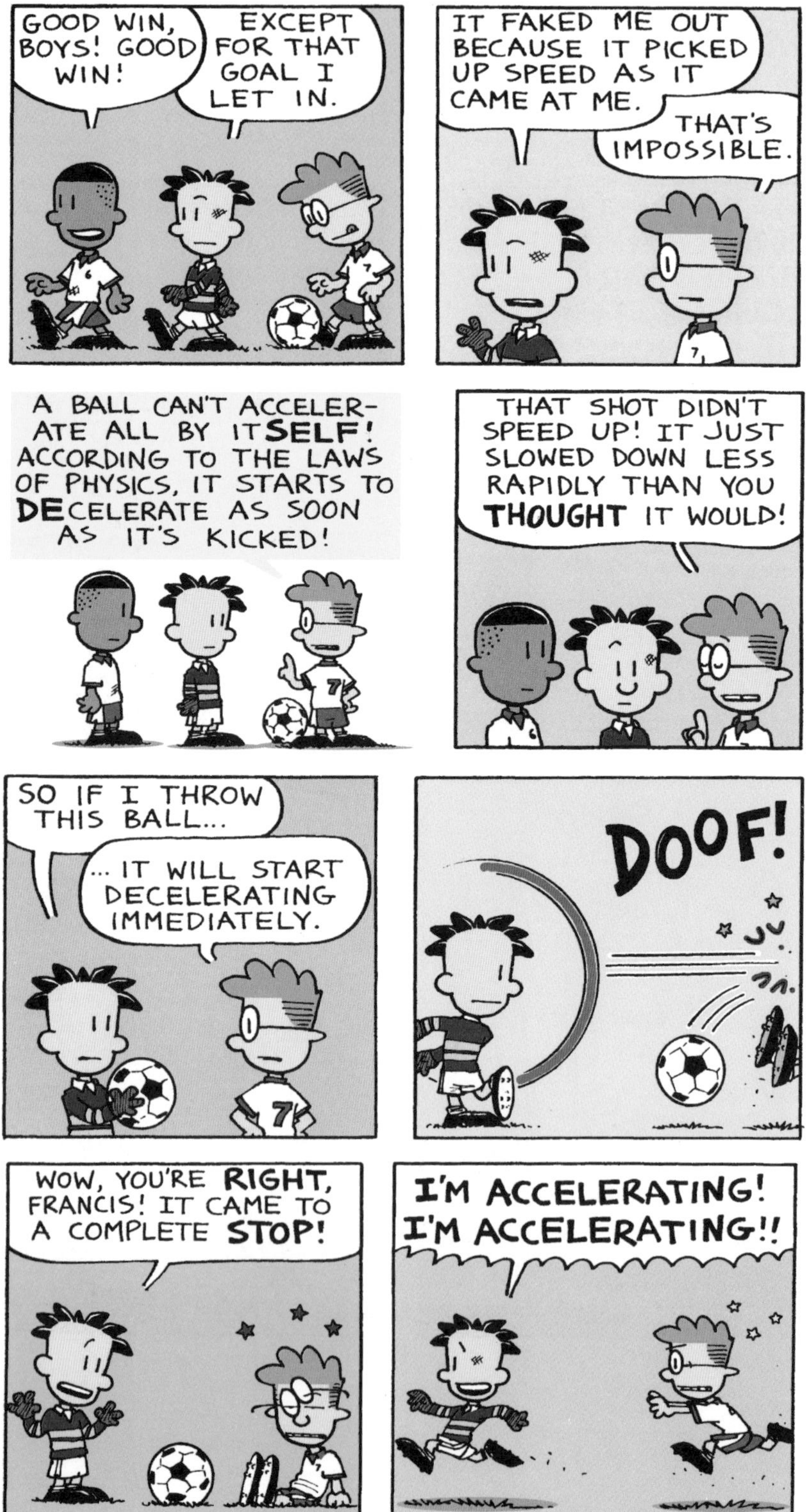
GOOD WIN, BOYS! GOOD WIN!
EXCEPT FOR THAT GOAL I LET IN.
IT FAKED ME OUT BECAUSE IT PICKED UP SPEED AS IT CAME AT ME.
THAT'S IMPOSSIBLE.
A BALL CAN'T ACCELERATE ALL BY ITSELF! ACCORDING TO THE LAWS OF PHYSICS, IT STARTS TO DECELERATE AS SOON AS IT'S KICKED!
THAT SHOT DIDN'T SPEED UP! IT JUST SLOWED DOWN LESS RAPIDLY THAN YOU THOUGHT IT WOULD!
SO IF I THROW THIS BALL...
... IT WILL START DECELERATING IMMEDIATELY.
DOOF!
WOW, YOU'RE RIGHT, FRANCIS! IT CAME TO A COMPLETE STOP!
I'M ACCELERATING! I'M ACCELERATING!!

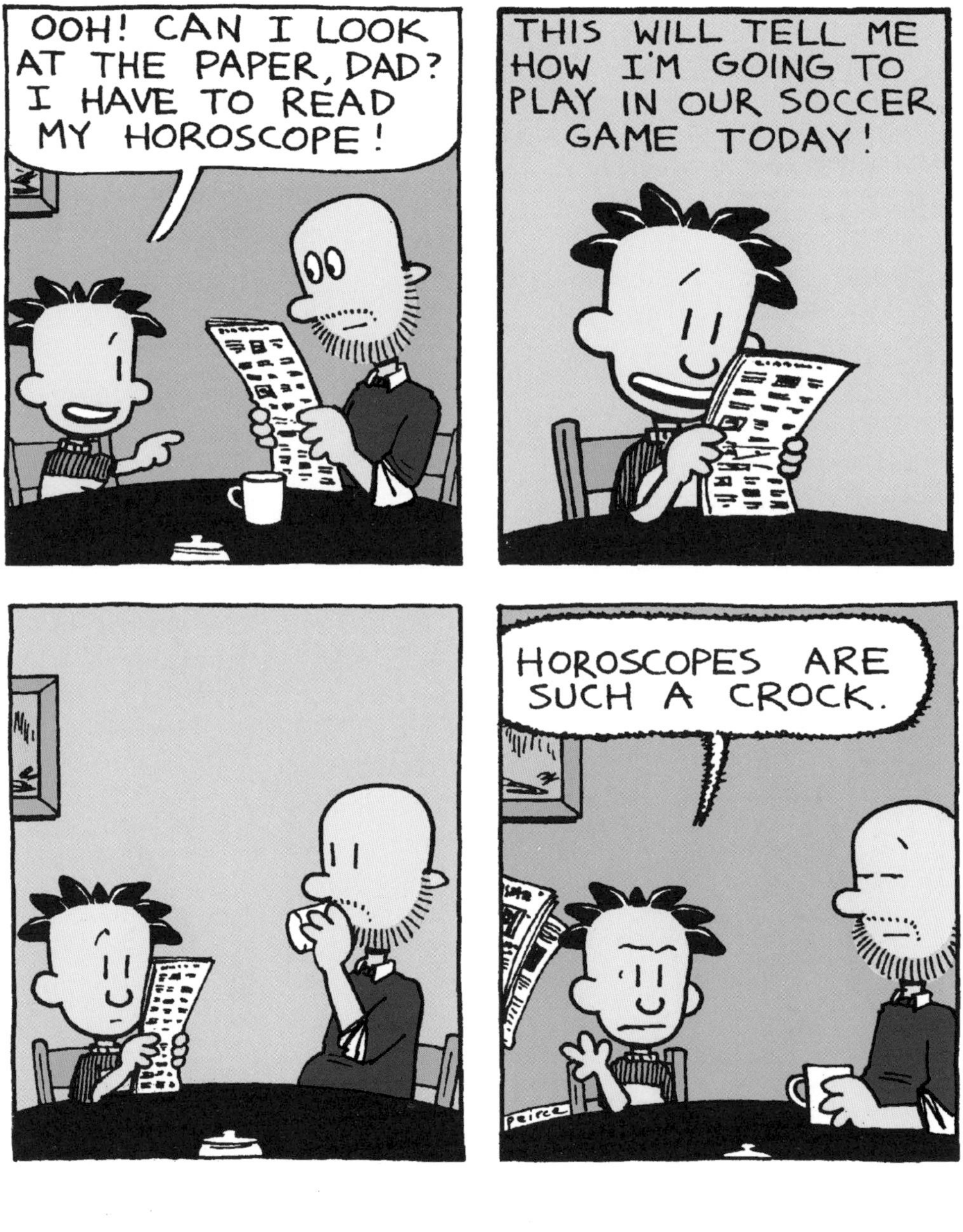
OOH! CAN I LOOK AT THE PAPER, DAD? I HAVE TO READ MY HOROSCOPE!
THIS WILL TELL ME HOW I'M GOING TO PLAY IN OUR SOCCER GAME TODAY!
HOROSCOPES ARE SUCH A CROCK.
peirce

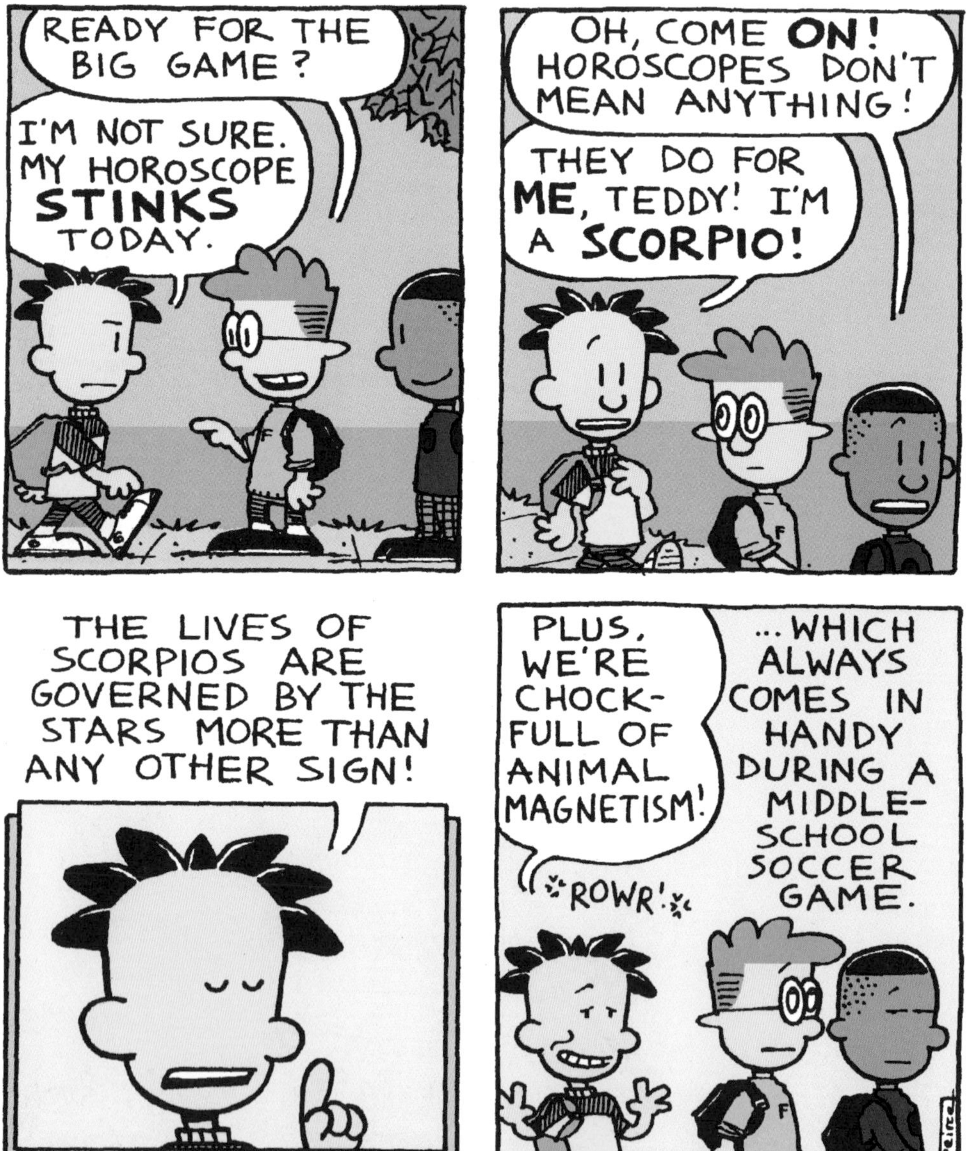
READY FOR THE BIG GAME?
I'M NOT SURE. MY HOROSCOPE **STINKS** TODAY.
OH, COME **ON**! HOROSCOPES DON'T MEAN ANYTHING!
THEY DO FOR **ME**, TEDDY! I'M A **SCORPIO**!
THE LIVES OF SCORPIOS ARE GOVERNED BY THE STARS MORE THAN ANY OTHER SIGN!
PLUS, WE'RE CHOCK-FULL OF ANIMAL MAGNETISM!
ROWR!
...WHICH ALWAYS COMES IN HANDY DURING A MIDDLE-SCHOOL SOCCER GAME.
PEIRCE

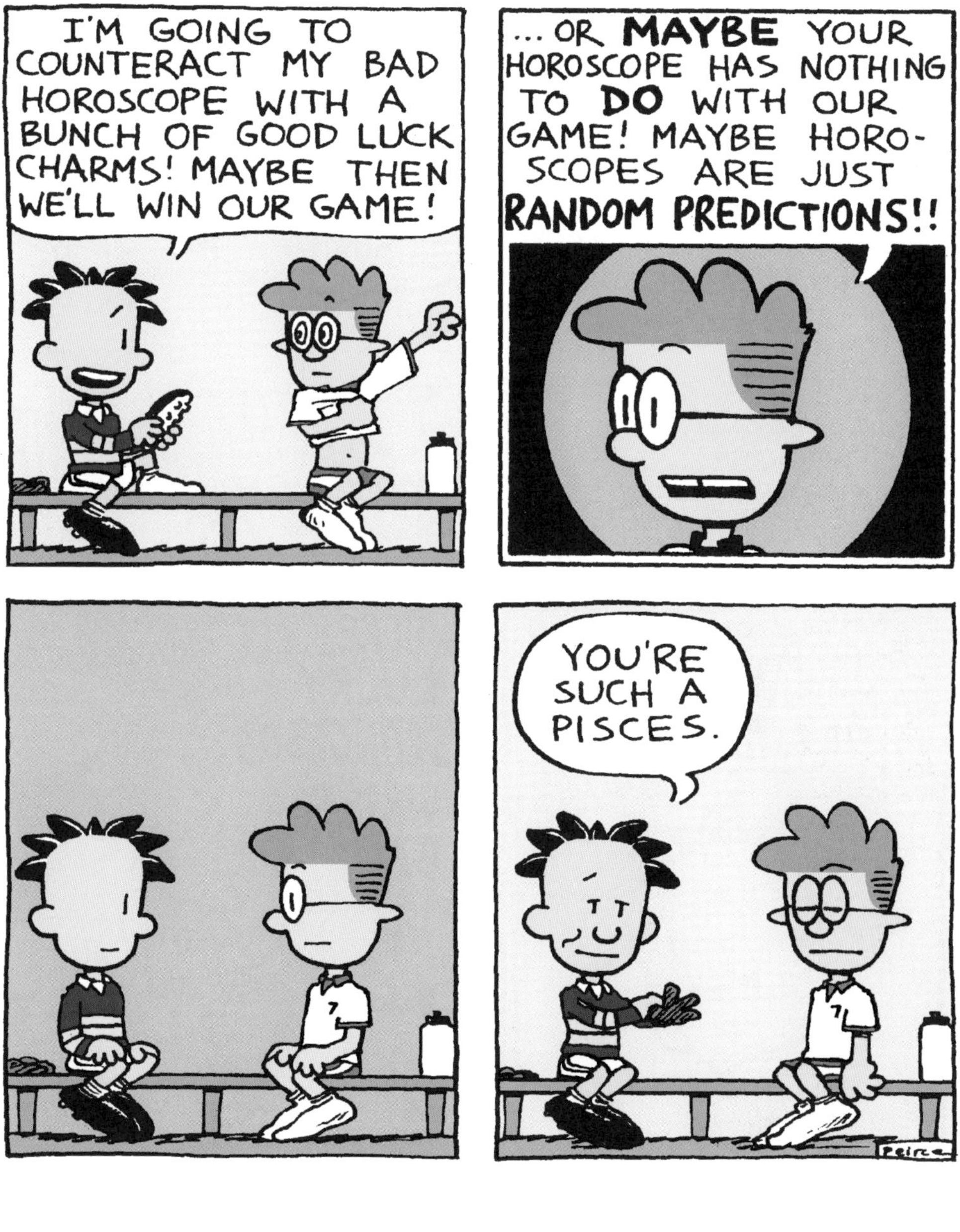
I'M GOING TO COUNTERACT MY BAD HOROSCOPE WITH A BUNCH OF GOOD LUCK CHARMS! MAYBE THEN WE'LL WIN OUR GAME!
...OR **MAYBE** YOUR HOROSCOPE HAS NOTHING TO **DO** WITH OUR GAME! MAYBE HORO-SCOPES ARE JUST **RANDOM PREDICTIONS!!**
YOU'RE SUCH A PISCES.
PEIRCE

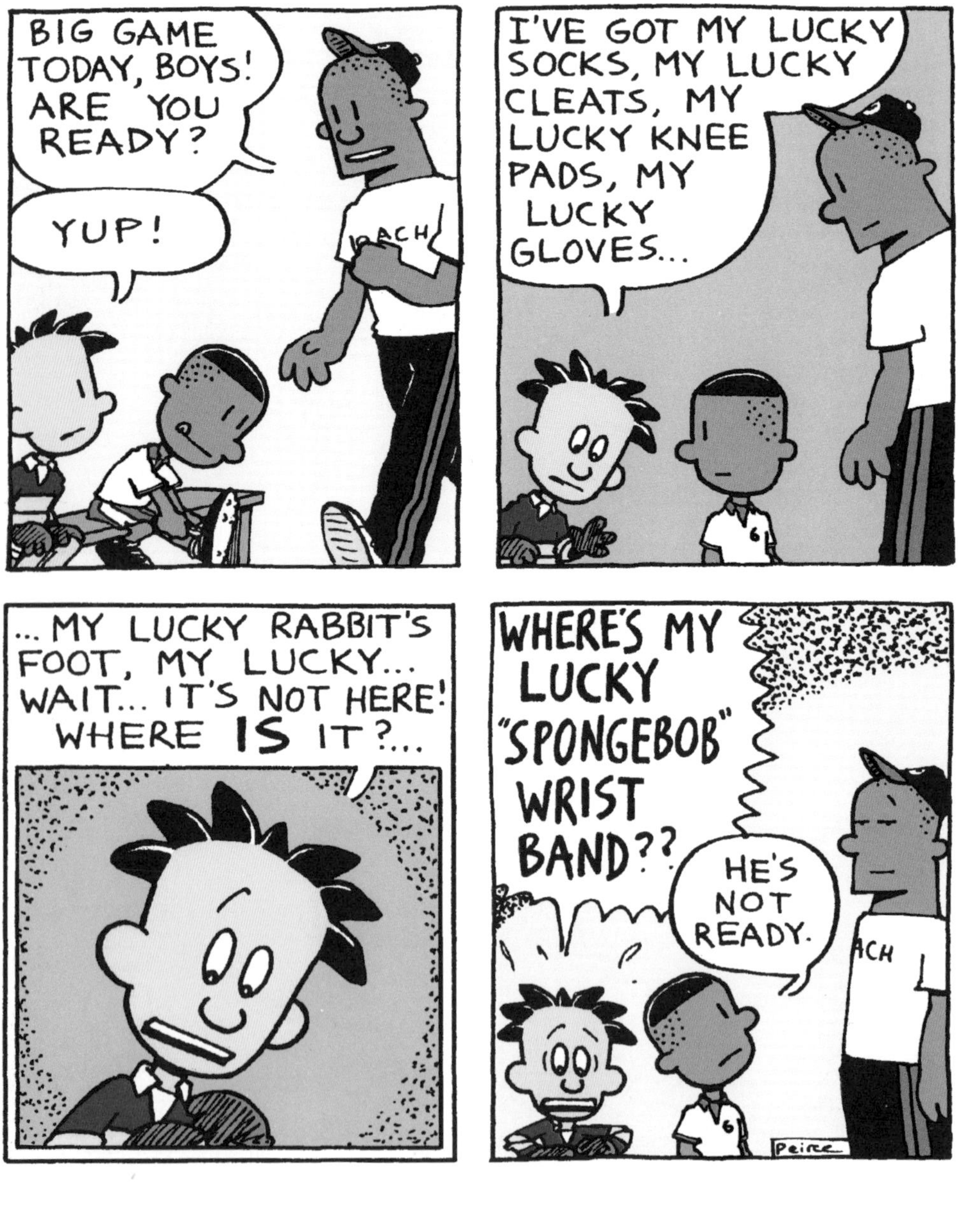
BIG GAME TODAY, BOYS! ARE YOU READY?
YUP!
I'VE GOT MY LUCKY SOCKS, MY LUCKY CLEATS, MY LUCKY KNEE PADS, MY LUCKY GLOVES...
... MY LUCKY RABBIT'S FOOT, MY LUCKY... WAIT... IT'S NOT HERE! WHERE IS IT?...
WHERE'S MY LUCKY "SPONGEBOB" WRIST BAND??
HE'S NOT READY.
Peirce

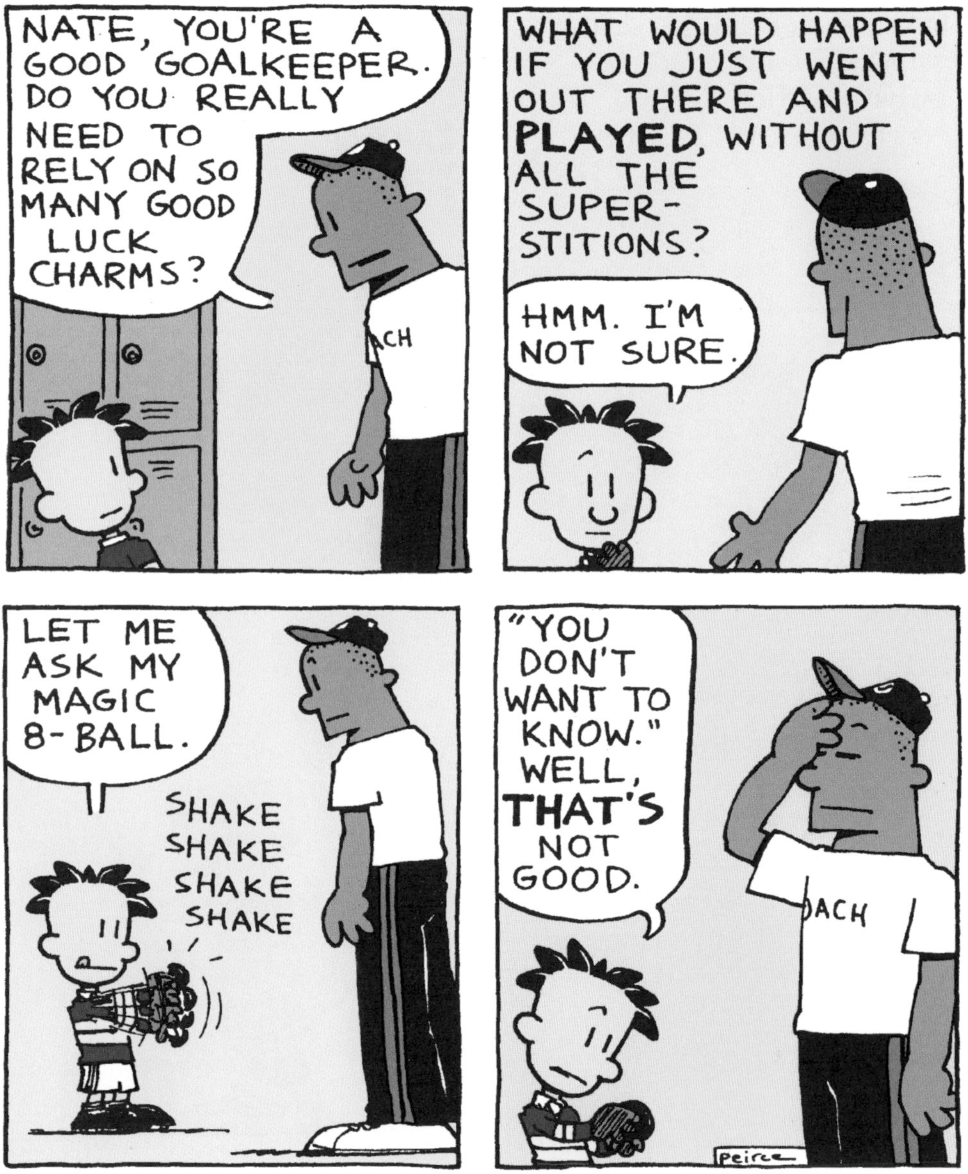
NATE, YOU'RE A GOOD GOALKEEPER. DO YOU REALLY NEED TO RELY ON SO MANY GOOD LUCK CHARMS?
WHAT WOULD HAPPEN IF YOU JUST WENT OUT THERE AND **PLAYED**, WITHOUT ALL THE SUPER-STITIONS?
HMM. I'M NOT SURE.
LET ME ASK MY MAGIC 8-BALL.
SHAKE
SHAKE
SHAKE
SHAKE
"YOU DON'T WANT TO KNOW." WELL, **THAT'S** NOT GOOD.
peirce

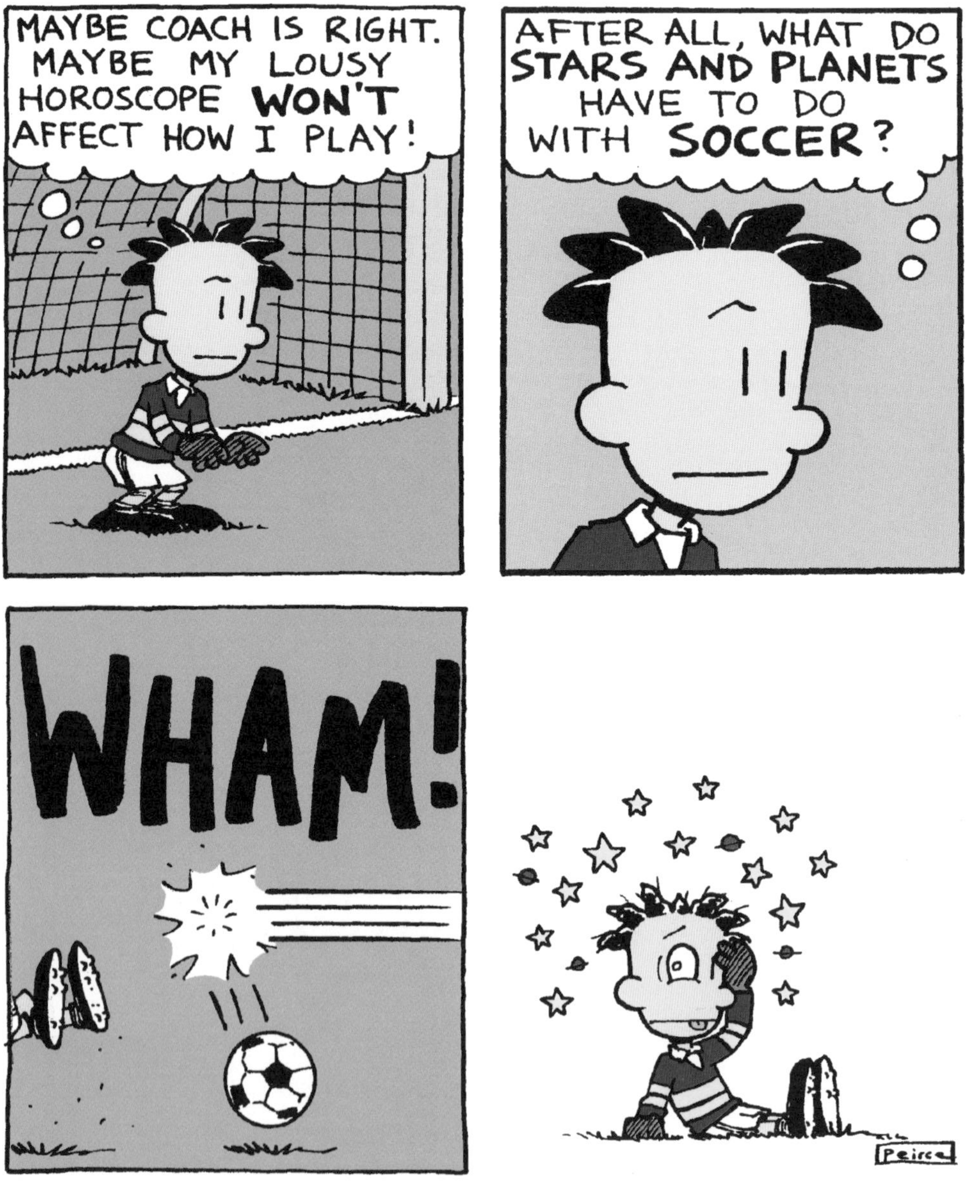
MAYBE COACH IS RIGHT. MAYBE MY LOUSY HOROSCOPE WON'T AFFECT HOW I PLAY!
AFTER ALL, WHAT DO STARS AND PLANETS HAVE TO DO WITH SOCCER?
WHAM!
Peirce

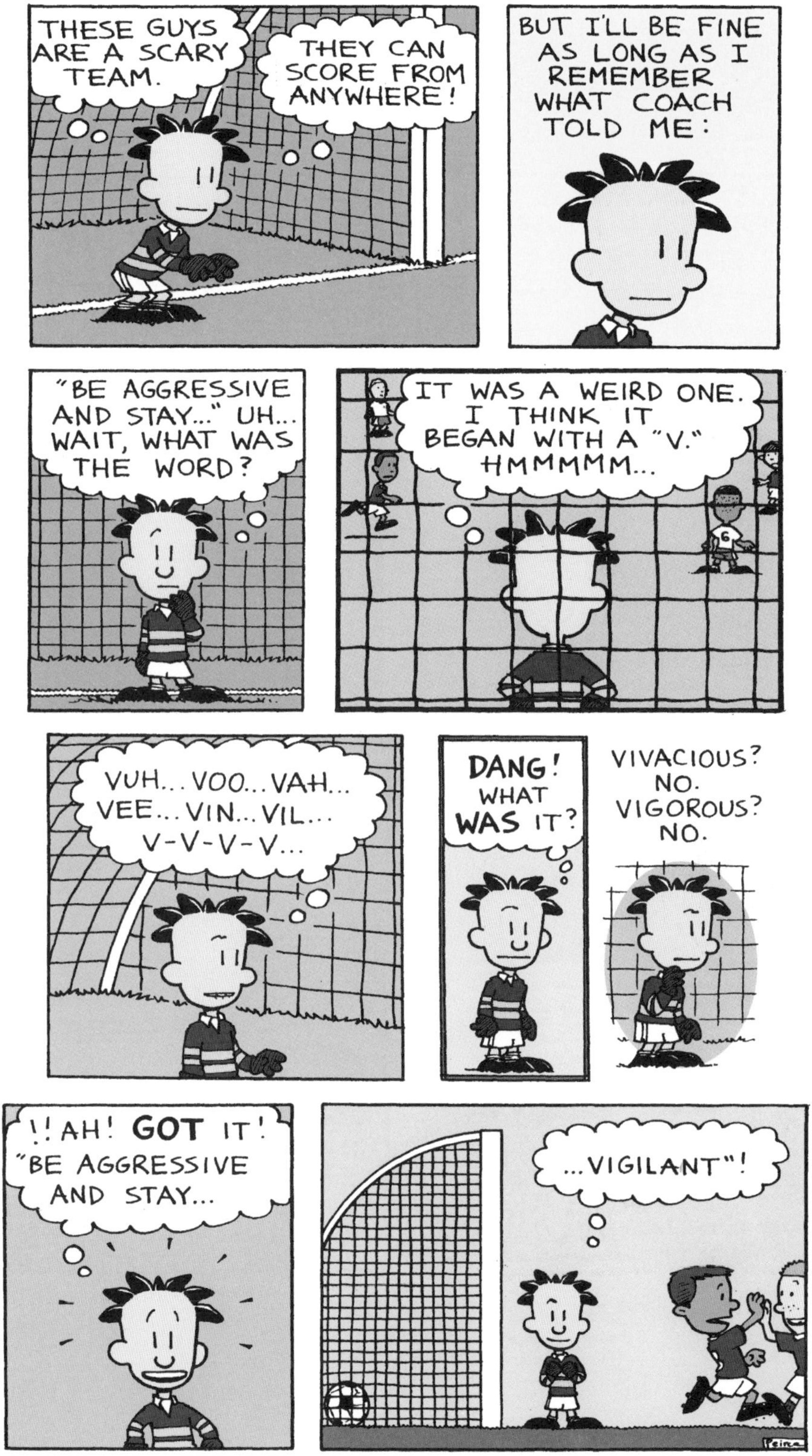
THESE GUYS ARE A SCARY TEAM.
THEY CAN SCORE FROM ANYWHERE!
BUT I'LL BE FINE AS LONG AS I REMEMBER WHAT COACH TOLD ME:
"BE AGGRESSIVE AND STAY..." UH... WAIT, WHAT WAS THE WORD?
IT WAS A WEIRD ONE. I THINK IT BEGAN WITH A "V." HMMMMM...
VUH...VOO...VAH... VEE...VIN...VIL... V-V-V-V...
DANG! WHAT WAS IT?
VIVACIOUS? NO. VIGOROUS? NO.
!! AH! GOT IT! "BE AGGRESSIVE AND STAY...
...VIGILANT"!

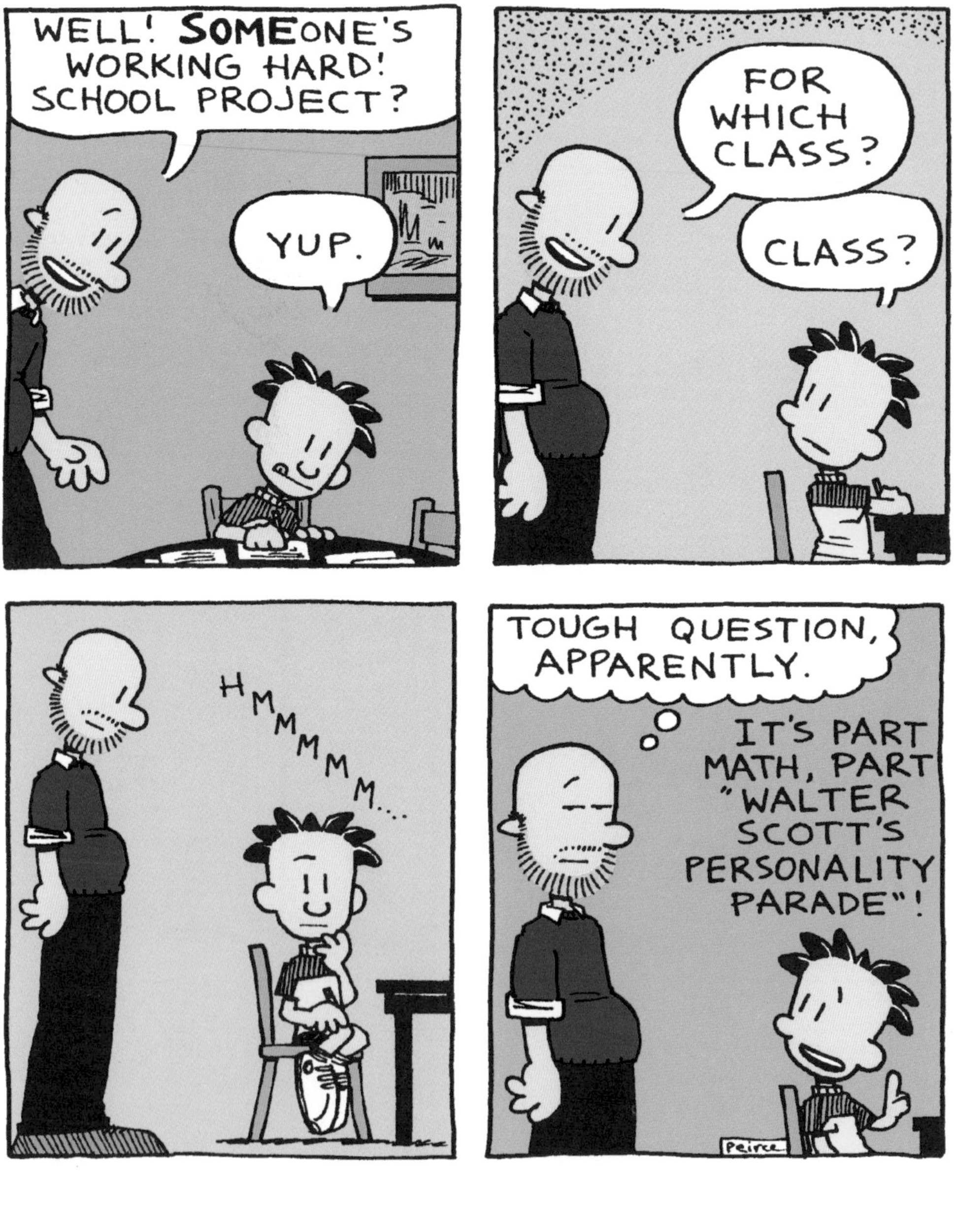

WELL! SOMEONE'S WORKING HARD! SCHOOL PROJECT?
YUP.
FOR WHICH CLASS?
CLASS?
HMMMMM...
TOUGH QUESTION, APPARENTLY.
IT'S PART MATH, PART "WALTER SCOTT'S PERSONALITY PARADE"!
Peirce

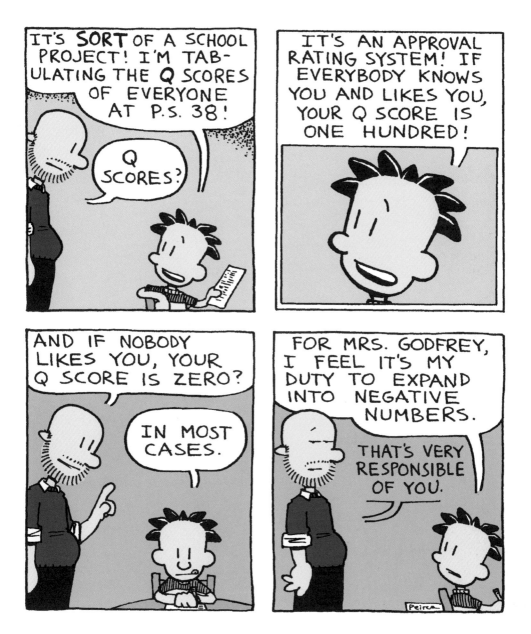

IT'S **SORT** OF A SCHOOL PROJECT! I'M TAB-ULATING THE **Q** SCORES OF EVERYONE AT P.S. 38!

Q SCORES?

IT'S AN APPROVAL RATING SYSTEM! IF EVERYBODY KNOWS YOU AND LIKES YOU, YOUR Q SCORE IS ONE HUNDRED!

AND IF NOBODY LIKES YOU, YOUR Q SCORE IS ZERO?

IN MOST CASES.

FOR MRS. GODFREY, I FEEL IT'S MY DUTY TO EXPAND INTO NEGATIVE NUMBERS.

THAT'S VERY RESPONSIBLE OF YOU.

Peirce

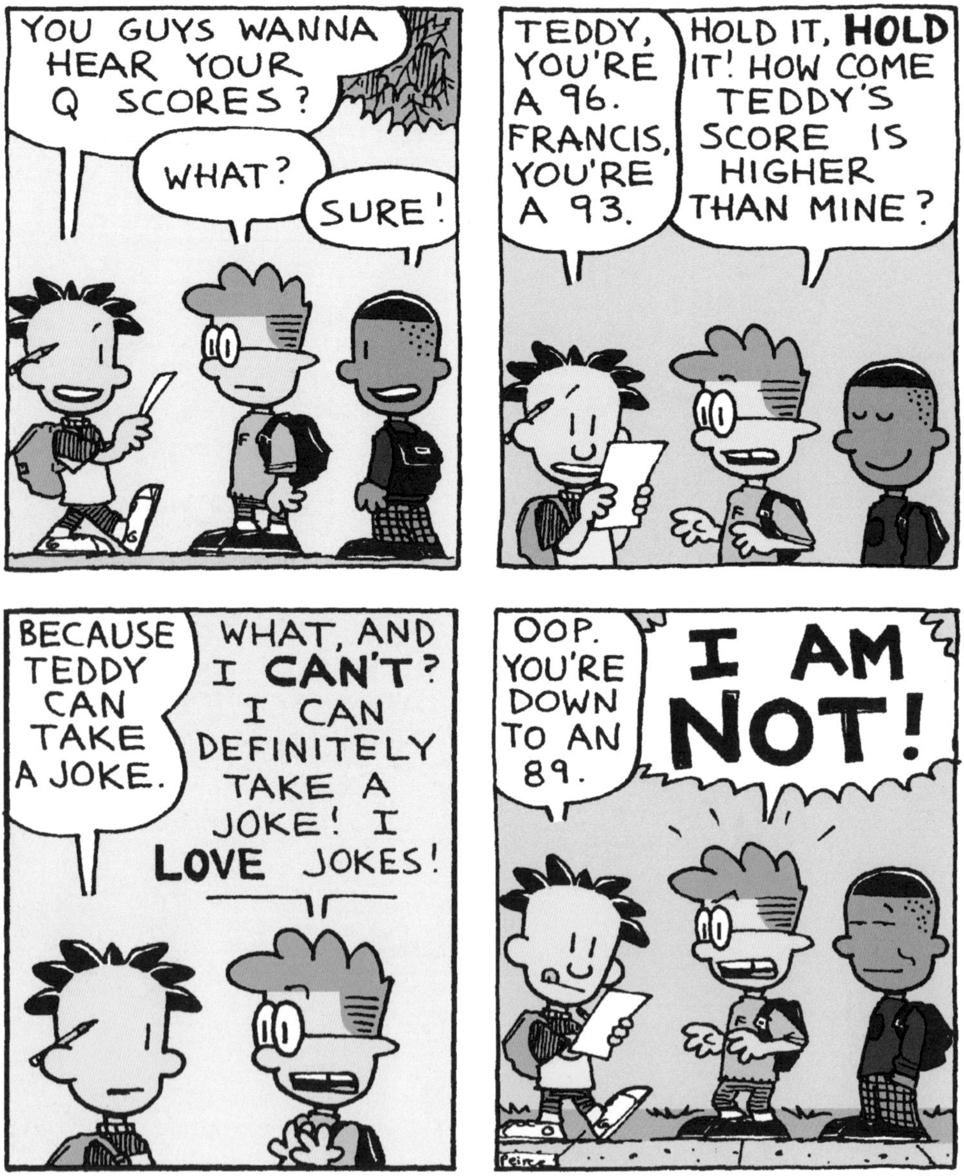
YOU GUYS WANNA HEAR YOUR Q SCORES?
WHAT?
SURE!
TEDDY, YOU'RE A 96. FRANCIS, YOU'RE A 93.
HOLD IT, HOLD IT! HOW COME TEDDY'S SCORE IS HIGHER THAN MINE?
BECAUSE TEDDY CAN TAKE A JOKE.
WHAT, AND I CAN'T? I CAN DEFINITELY TAKE A JOKE! I LOVE JOKES!
OOP. YOU'RE DOWN TO AN 89.
I AM NOT!
Peirce

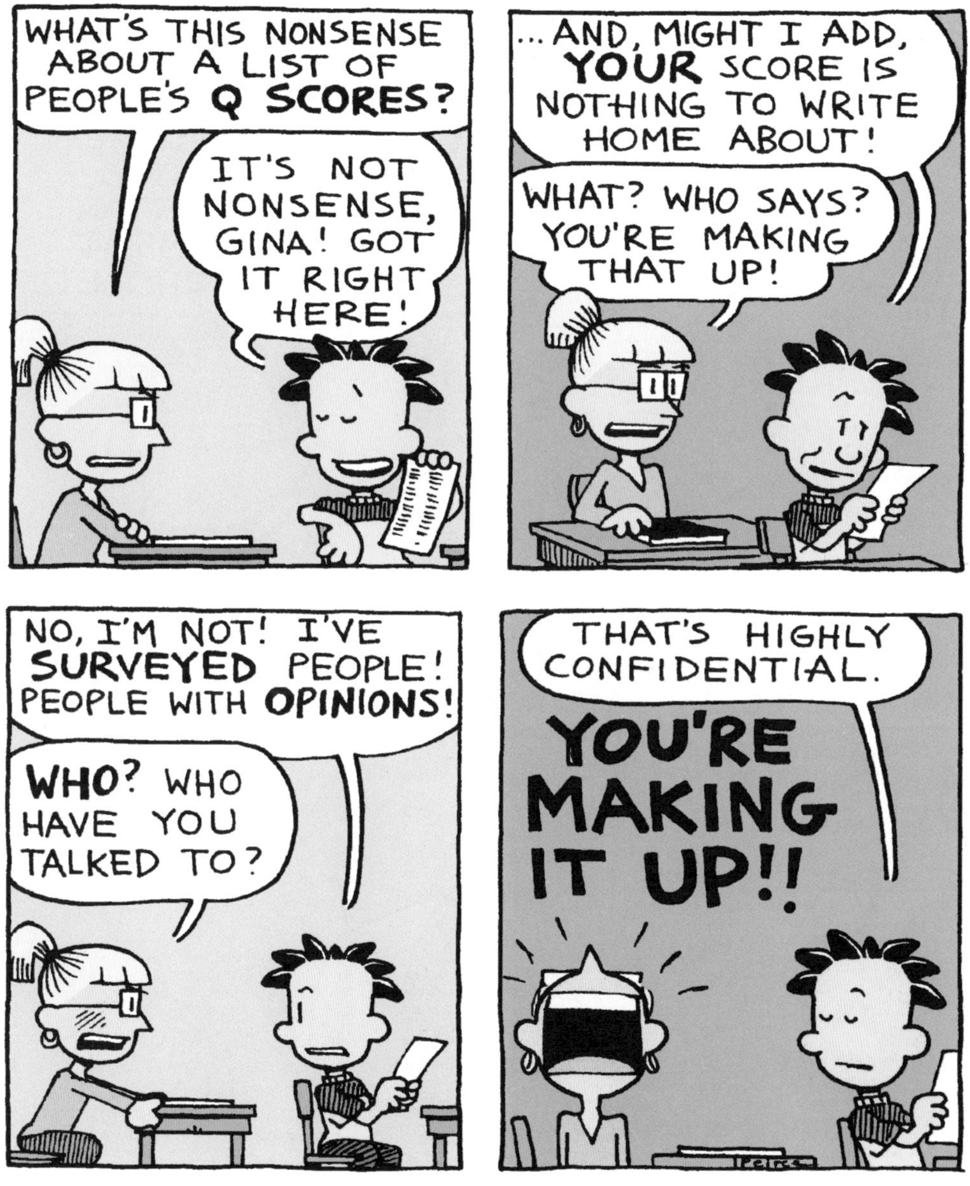
WHAT'S THIS NONSENSE ABOUT A LIST OF PEOPLE'S Q SCORES?
IT'S NOT NONSENSE, GINA! GOT IT RIGHT HERE!
...AND, MIGHT I ADD, YOUR SCORE IS NOTHING TO WRITE HOME ABOUT!
WHAT? WHO SAYS? YOU'RE MAKING THAT UP!
NO, I'M NOT! I'VE SURVEYED PEOPLE! PEOPLE WITH OPINIONS!
WHO? WHO HAVE YOU TALKED TO?
THAT'S HIGHLY CONFIDENTIAL.
YOU'RE MAKING IT UP!!

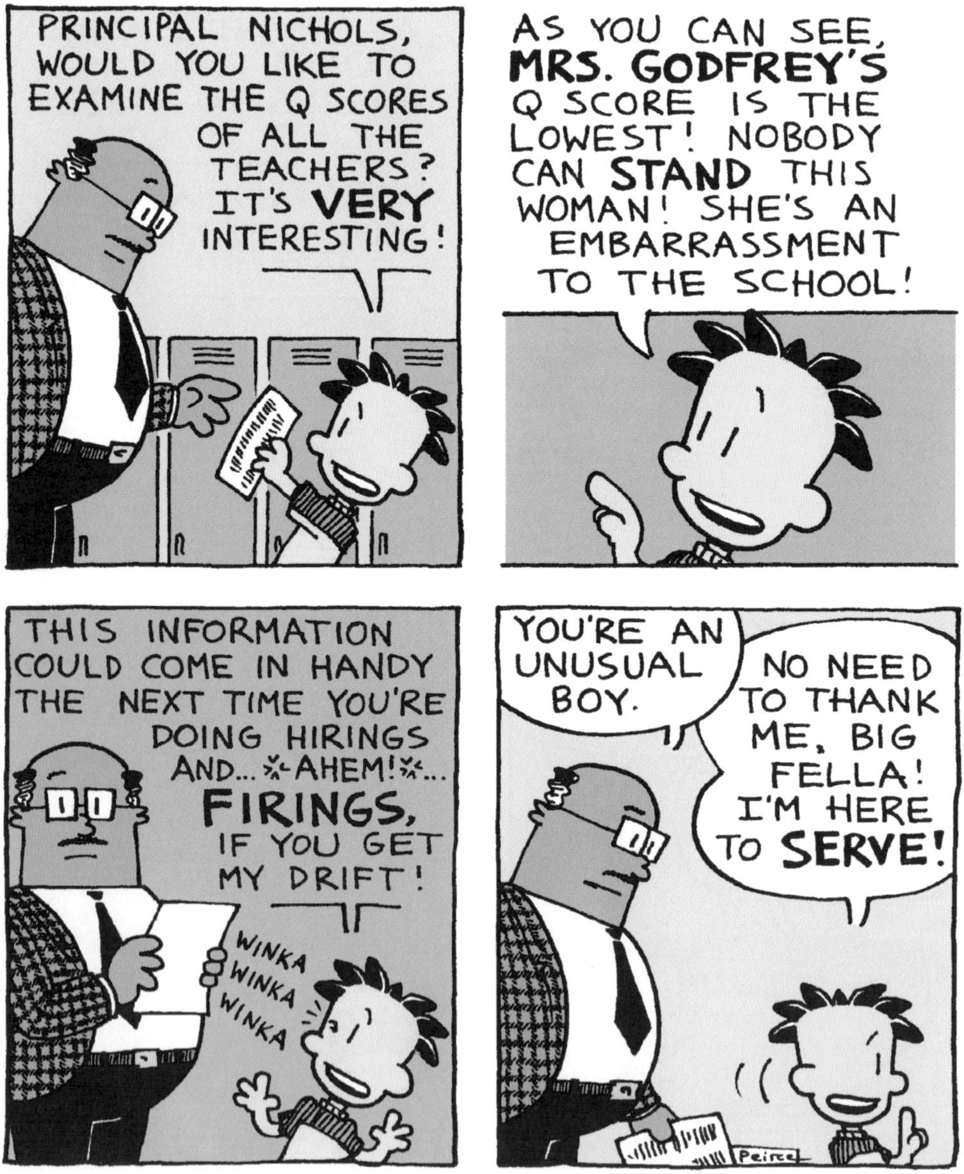
PRINCIPAL NICHOLS, WOULD YOU LIKE TO EXAMINE THE Q SCORES OF ALL THE TEACHERS? IT'S VERY INTERESTING!
AS YOU CAN SEE, MRS. GODFREY'S Q SCORE IS THE LOWEST! NOBODY CAN STAND THIS WOMAN! SHE'S AN EMBARRASSMENT TO THE SCHOOL!
THIS INFORMATION COULD COME IN HANDY THE NEXT TIME YOU'RE DOING HIRINGS AND... *AHEM!*... FIRINGS, IF YOU GET MY DRIFT!
WINKA WINKA WINKA
YOU'RE AN UNUSUAL BOY.
NO NEED TO THANK ME, BIG FELLA! I'M HERE TO SERVE!
Peirce

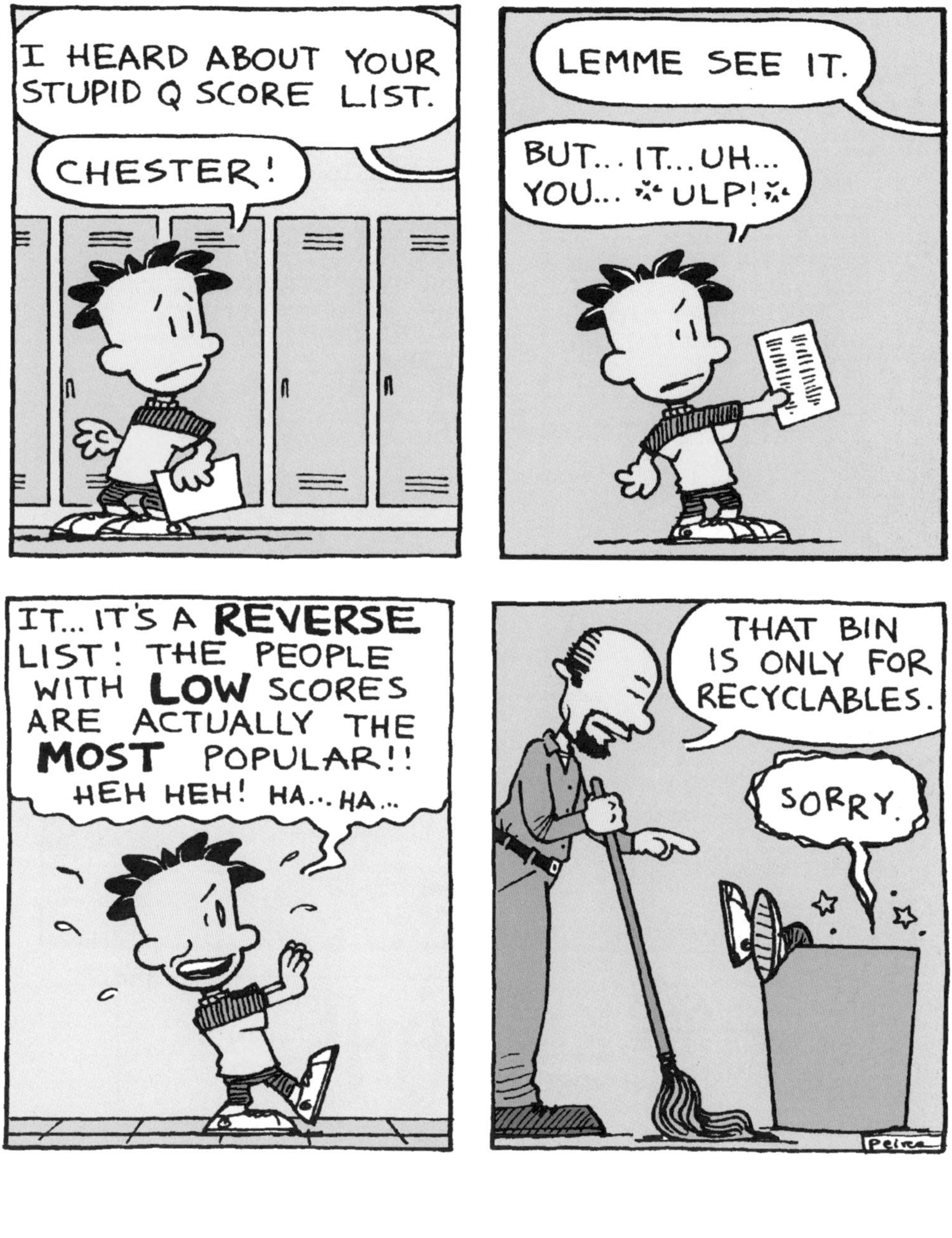
CHESTER!
I HEARD ABOUT YOUR STUPID Q SCORE LIST.
LEMME SEE IT.
BUT... IT... UH... YOU... ULP!
IT... IT'S A REVERSE LIST! THE PEOPLE WITH LOW SCORES ARE ACTUALLY THE MOST POPULAR!! HEH HEH! HA... HA...
THAT BIN IS ONLY FOR RECYCLABLES.
SORRY.
Peirce

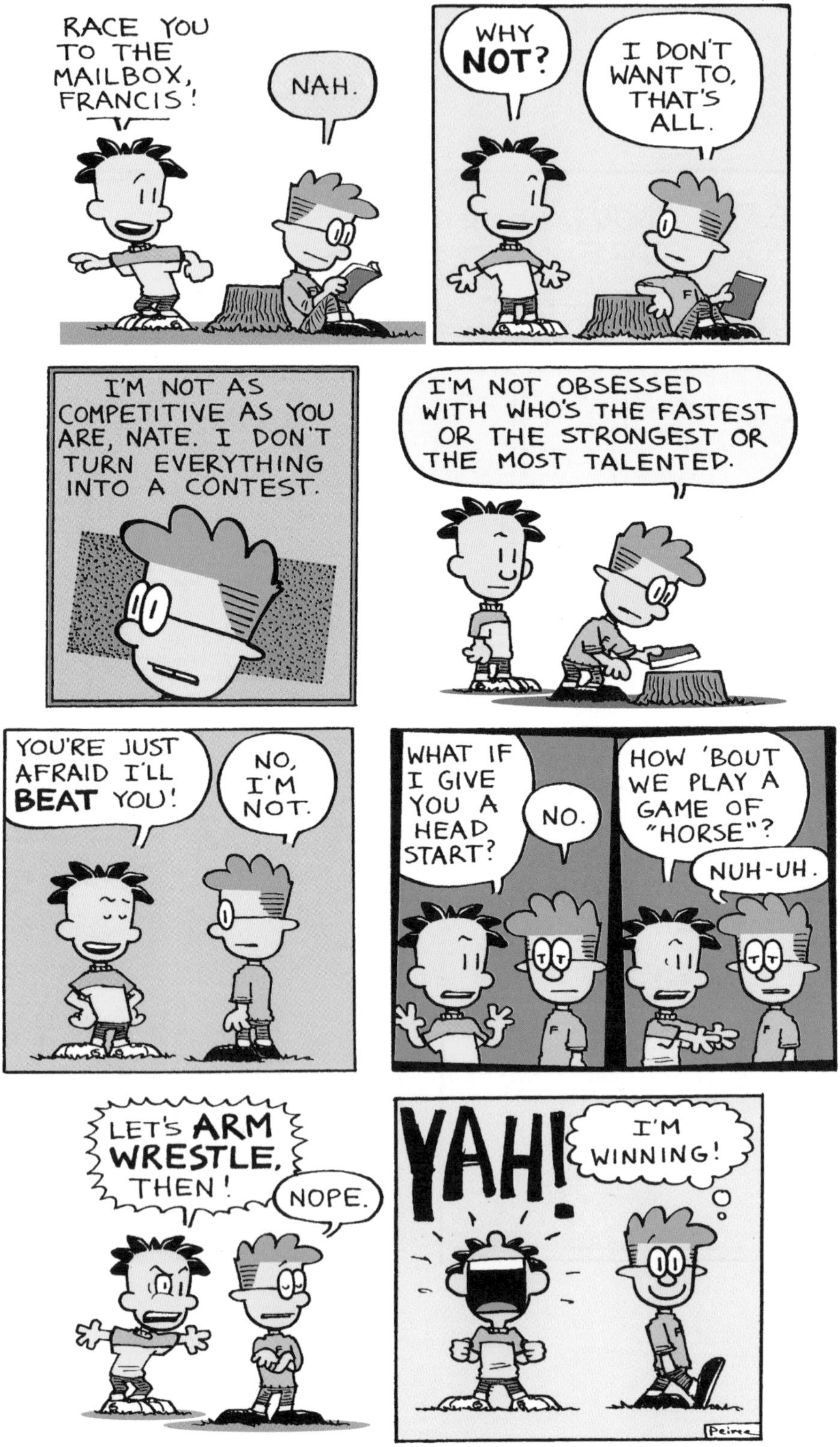
RACE YOU TO THE MAILBOX, FRANCIS!
NAH.
WHY NOT?
I DON'T WANT TO, THAT'S ALL.
I'M NOT AS COMPETITIVE AS YOU ARE, NATE. I DON'T TURN EVERYTHING INTO A CONTEST.
I'M NOT OBSESSED WITH WHO'S THE FASTEST OR THE STRONGEST OR THE MOST TALENTED.
YOU'RE JUST AFRAID I'LL BEAT YOU!
NO, I'M NOT.
WHAT IF I GIVE YOU A HEAD START?
NO.
HOW 'BOUT WE PLAY A GAME OF "HORSE"?
NUH-UH.
LET'S ARM WRESTLE, THEN!
NOPE.
YAH!
I'M WINNING!
Peirce

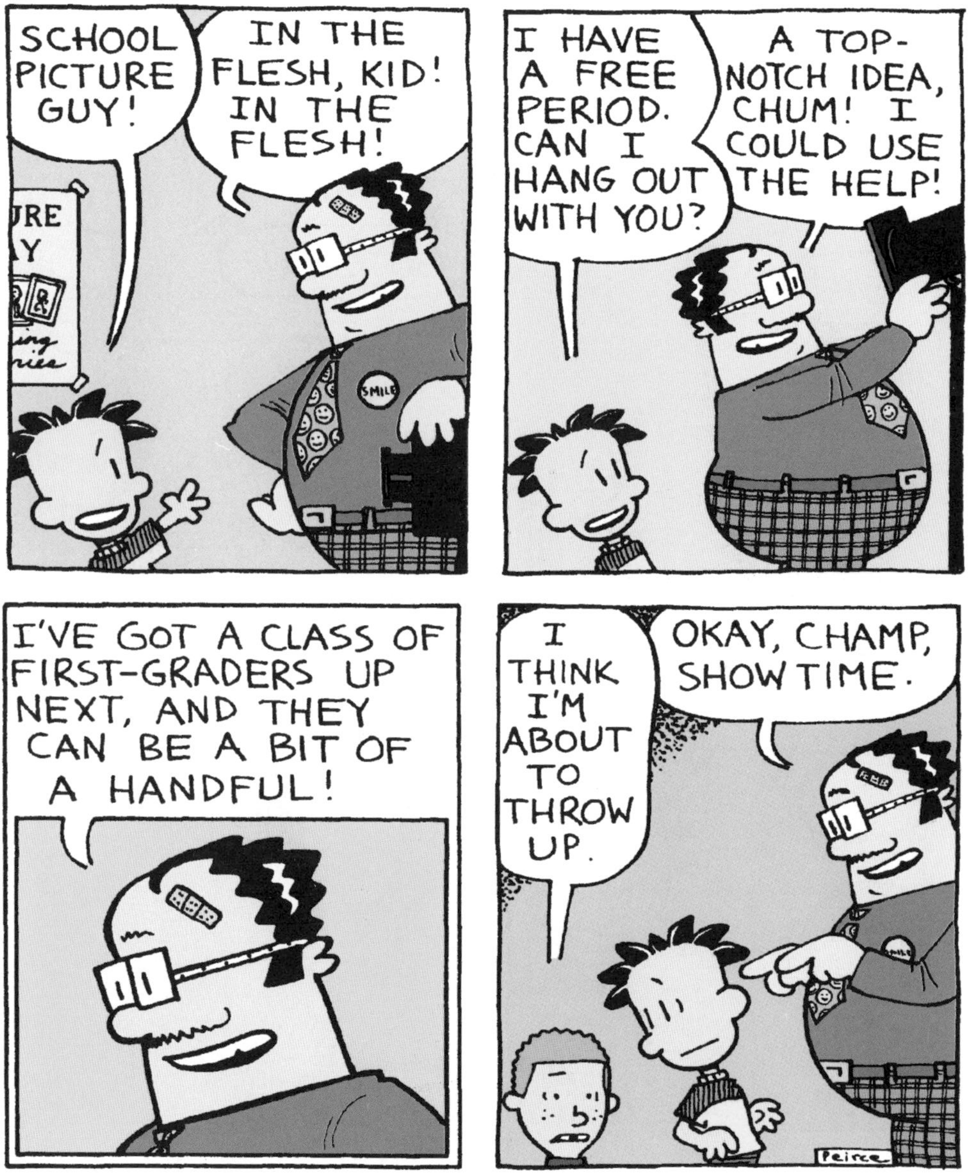

SCHOOL PICTURE GUY!
IN THE FLESH, KID! IN THE FLESH!
I HAVE A FREE PERIOD. CAN I HANG OUT WITH YOU?
A TOP-NOTCH IDEA, CHUM! I COULD USE THE HELP!
I'VE GOT A CLASS OF FIRST-GRADERS UP NEXT, AND THEY CAN BE A BIT OF A HANDFUL!
I THINK I'M ABOUT TO THROW UP.
OKAY, CHAMP, SHOWTIME.
Peirce

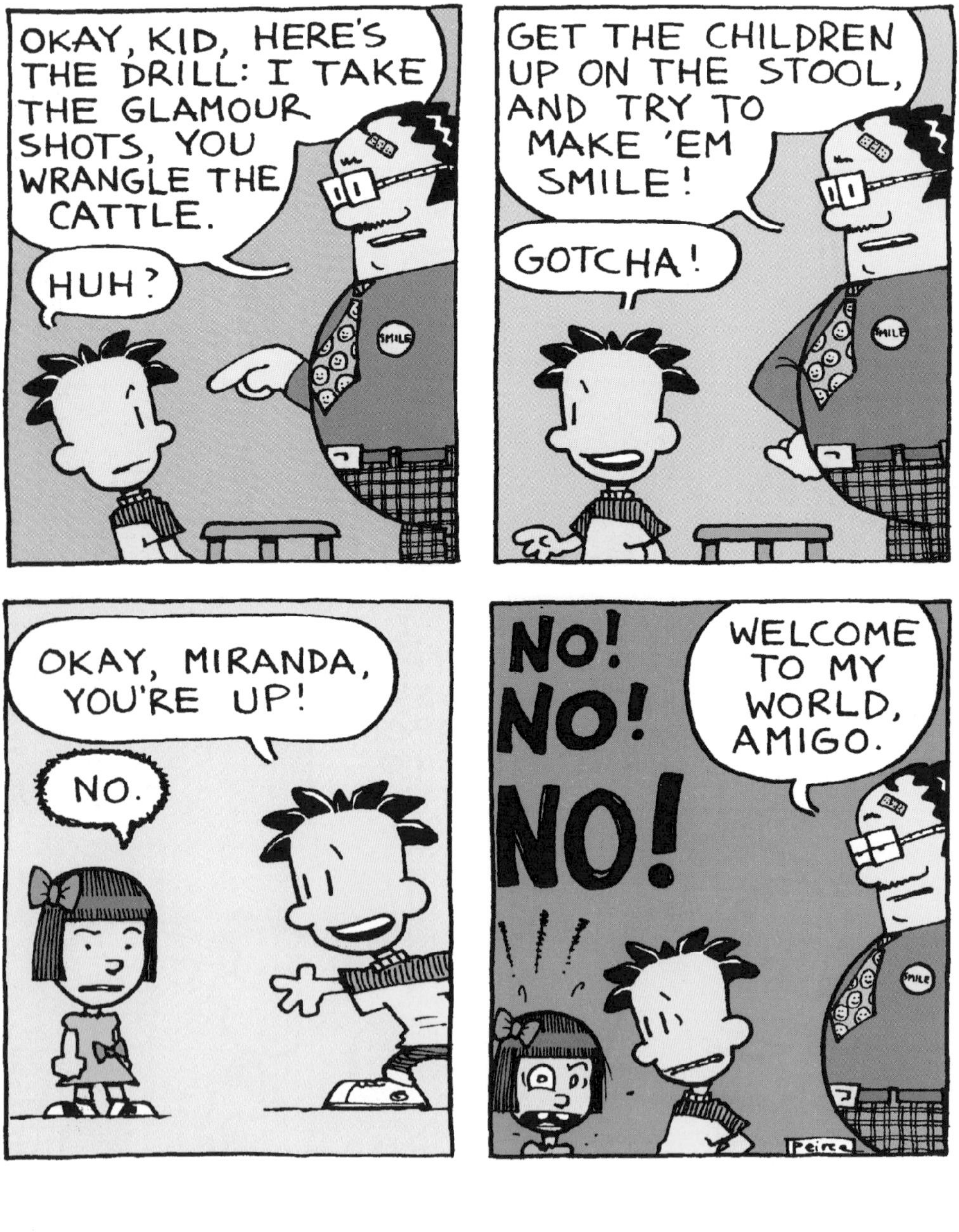
OKAY, KID, HERE'S THE DRILL: I TAKE THE GLAMOUR SHOTS, YOU WRANGLE THE CATTLE.
HUH?
SMILE
GET THE CHILDREN UP ON THE STOOL, AND TRY TO MAKE 'EM SMILE!
GOTCHA!
SMILE
OKAY, MIRANDA, YOU'RE UP!
NO.
NO! NO! NO!
WELCOME TO MY WORLD, AMIGO.
SMILE
Peirce

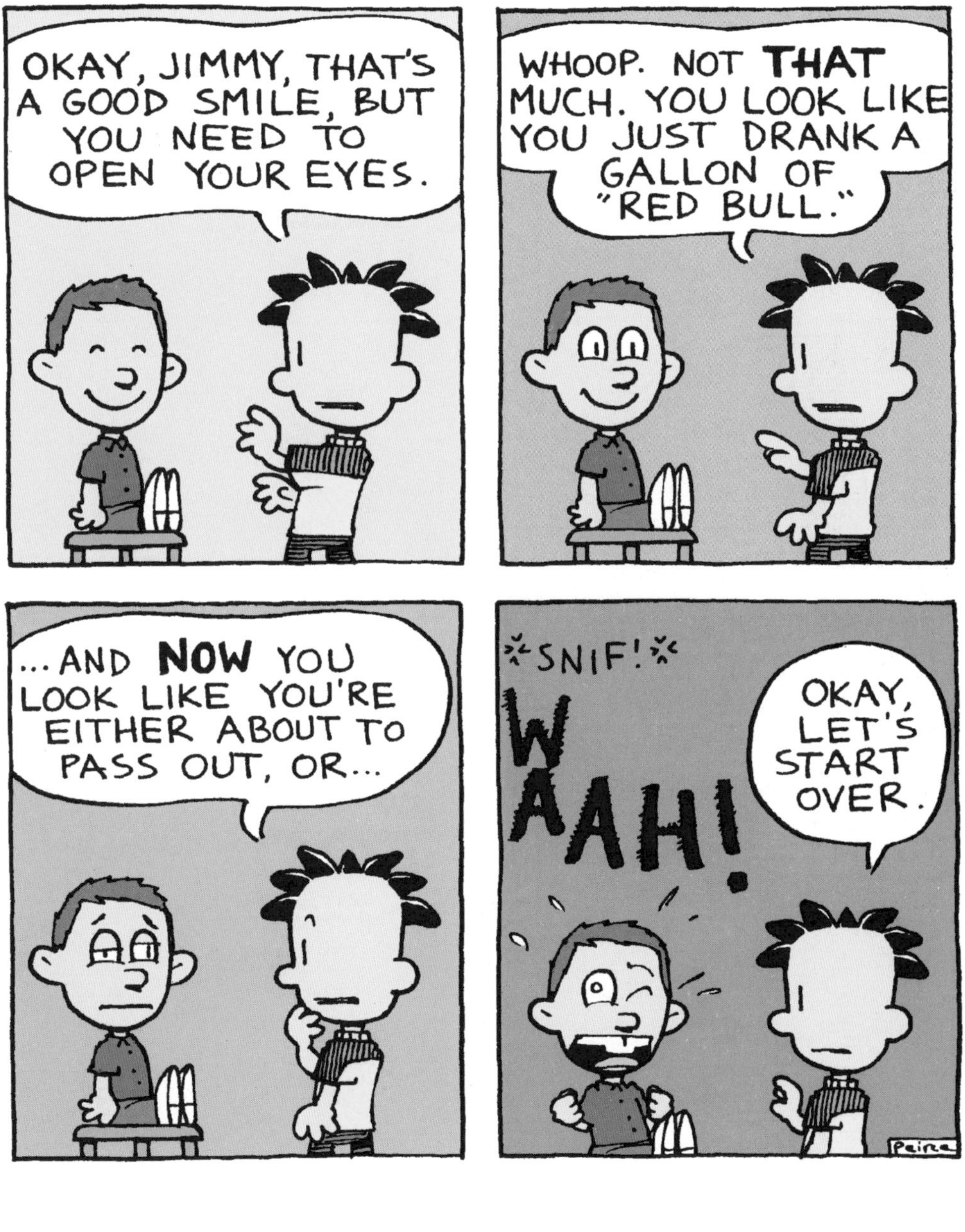
OKAY, JIMMY, THAT'S A GOOD SMILE, BUT YOU NEED TO OPEN YOUR EYES.
WHOOP. NOT **THAT** MUCH. YOU LOOK LIKE YOU JUST DRANK A GALLON OF "RED BULL."
...AND **NOW** YOU LOOK LIKE YOU'RE EITHER ABOUT TO PASS OUT, OR...
SNIF!
WAAH!
OKAY, LET'S START OVER.
Peirce

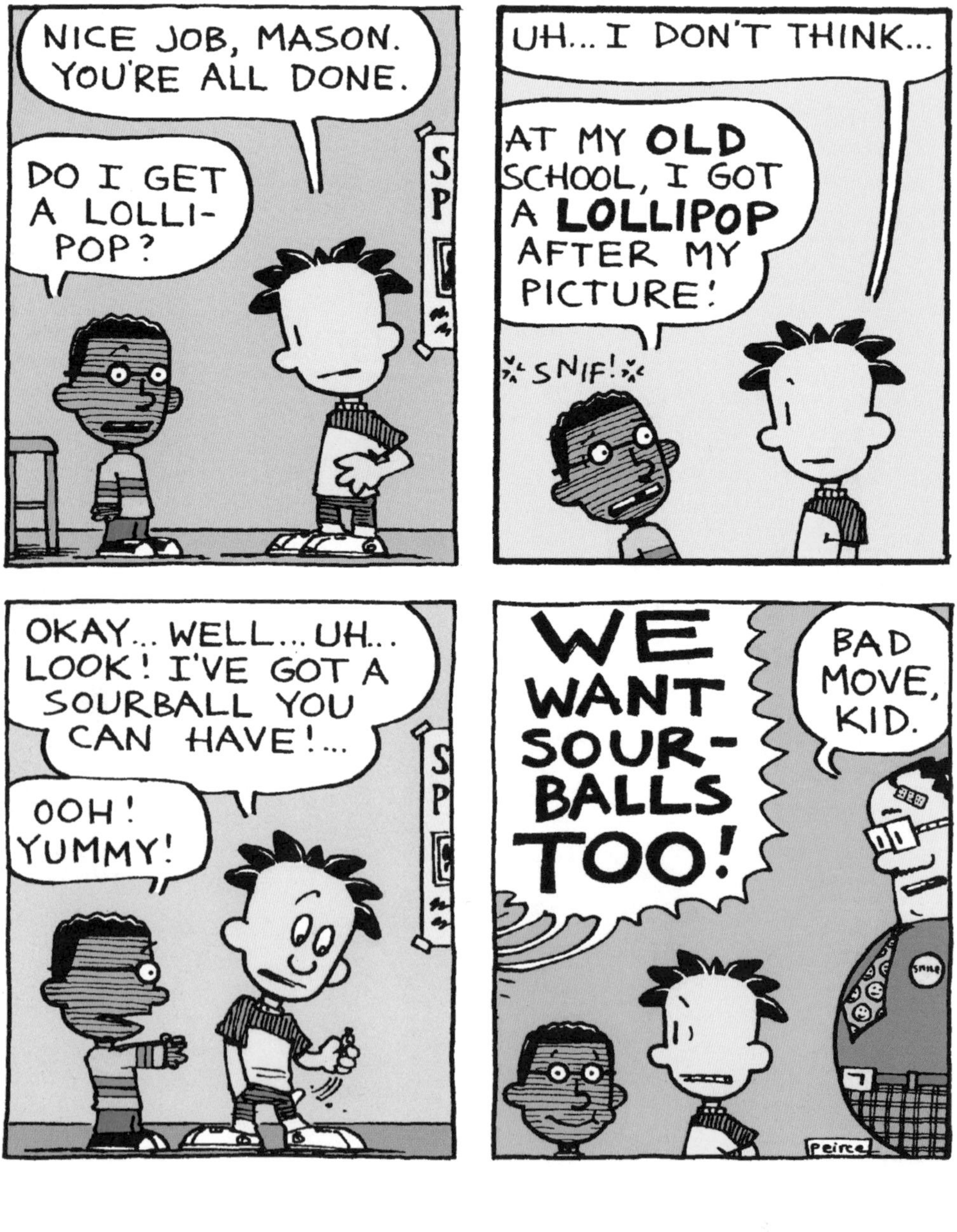
NICE JOB, MASON. YOU'RE ALL DONE.
DO I GET A LOLLI-POP?
UH... I DON'T THINK...
AT MY **OLD** SCHOOL, I GOT A **LOLLIPOP** AFTER MY PICTURE!
SNIF!
OKAY... WELL... UH... LOOK! I'VE GOT A SOURBALL YOU CAN HAVE!...
OOH! YUMMY!
WE WANT SOUR-BALLS TOO!
BAD MOVE, KID.
Peirce

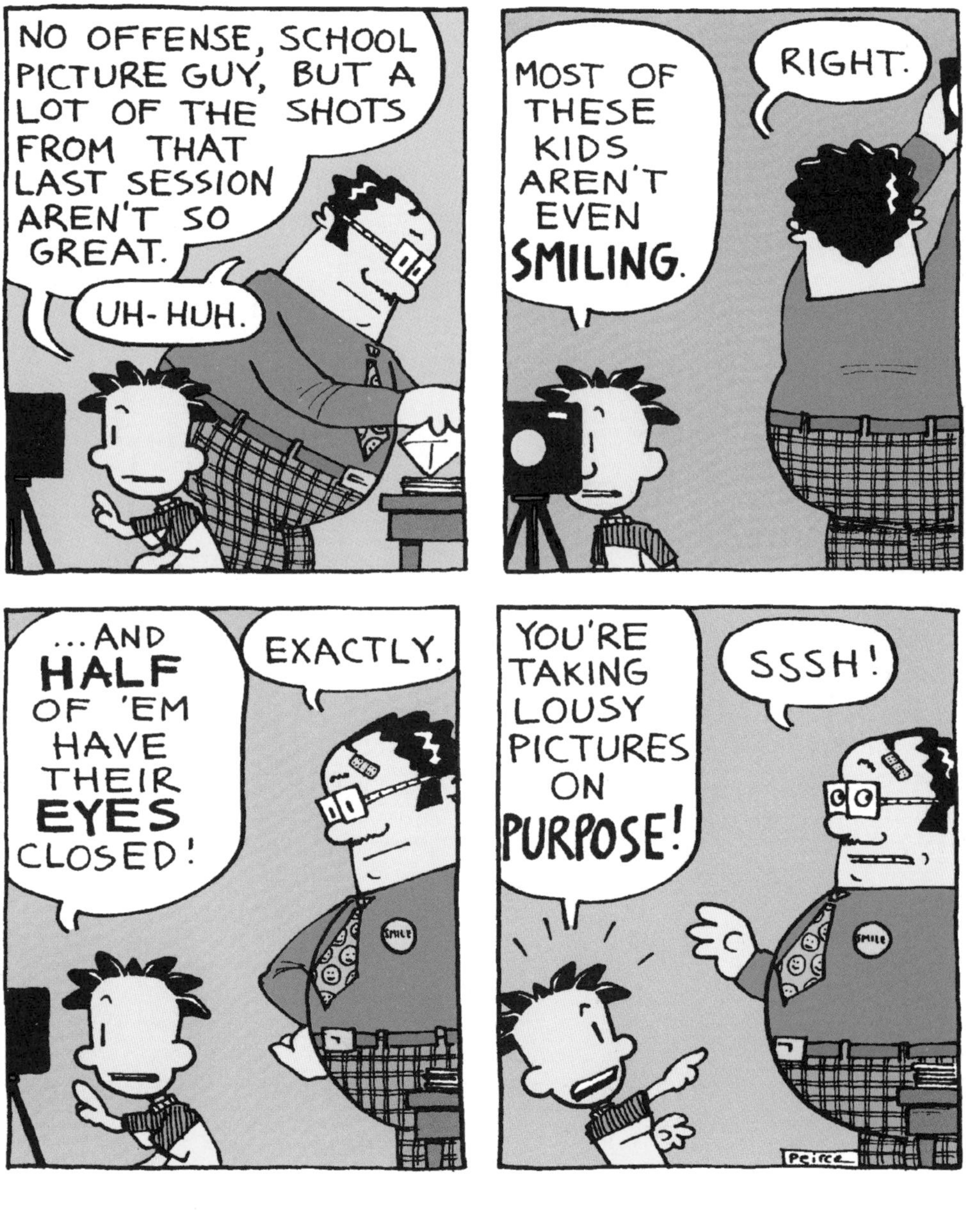
NO OFFENSE, SCHOOL PICTURE GUY, BUT A LOT OF THE SHOTS FROM THAT LAST SESSION AREN'T SO GREAT.
UH-HUH.
MOST OF THESE KIDS AREN'T EVEN SMILING.
RIGHT.
...AND HALF OF 'EM HAVE THEIR EYES CLOSED!
EXACTLY.
YOU'RE TAKING LOUSY PICTURES ON PURPOSE!
SSSH!
SMILE
Peirce

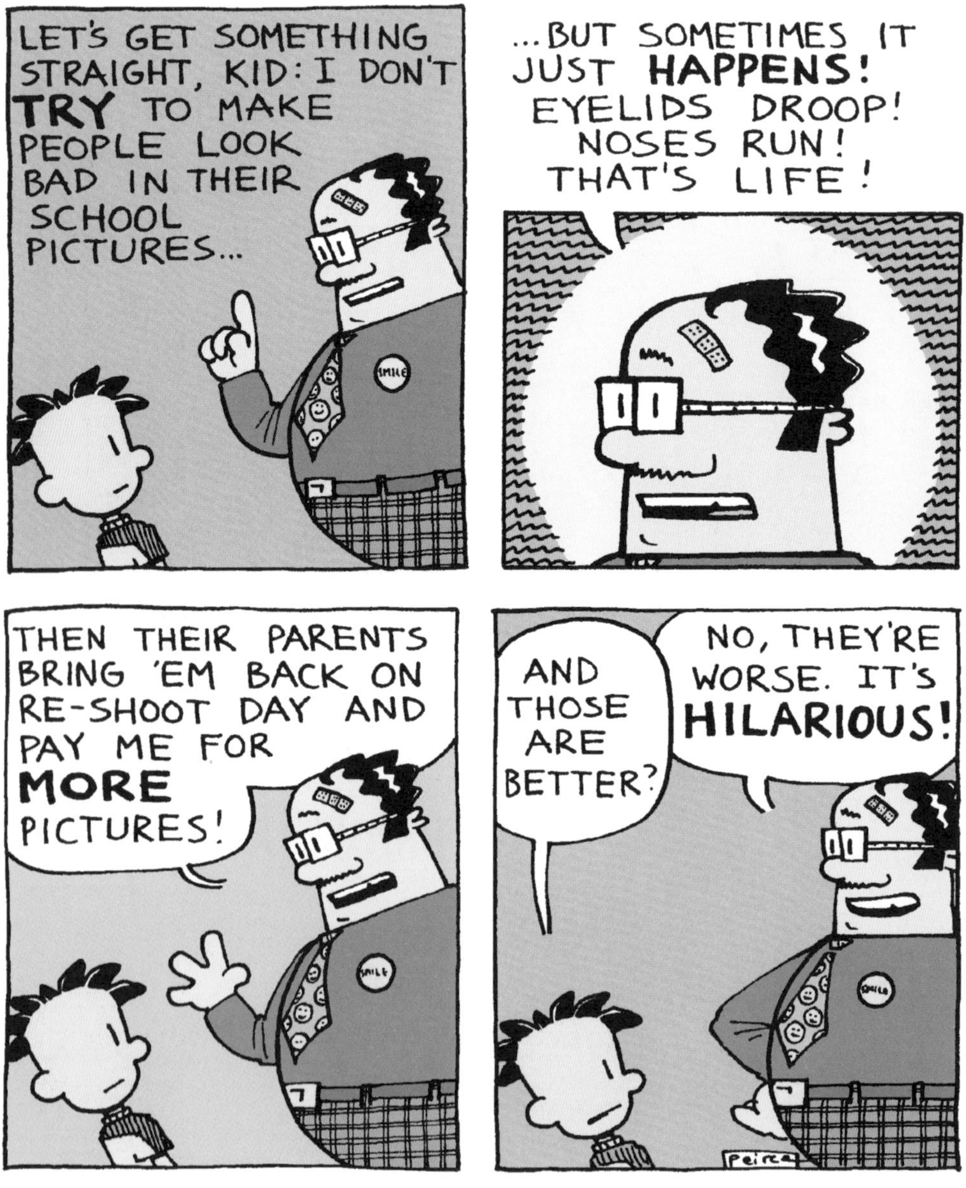
LET'S GET SOMETHING STRAIGHT, KID: I DON'T **TRY** TO MAKE PEOPLE LOOK BAD IN THEIR SCHOOL PICTURES...
SMILE
...BUT SOMETIMES IT JUST **HAPPENS!** EYELIDS DROOP! NOSES RUN! THAT'S LIFE!
THEN THEIR PARENTS BRING 'EM BACK ON RE-SHOOT DAY AND PAY ME FOR **MORE** PICTURES!
SMILE
AND THOSE ARE BETTER?
NO, THEY'RE WORSE. IT'S **HILARIOUS!**
SMILE
peirce

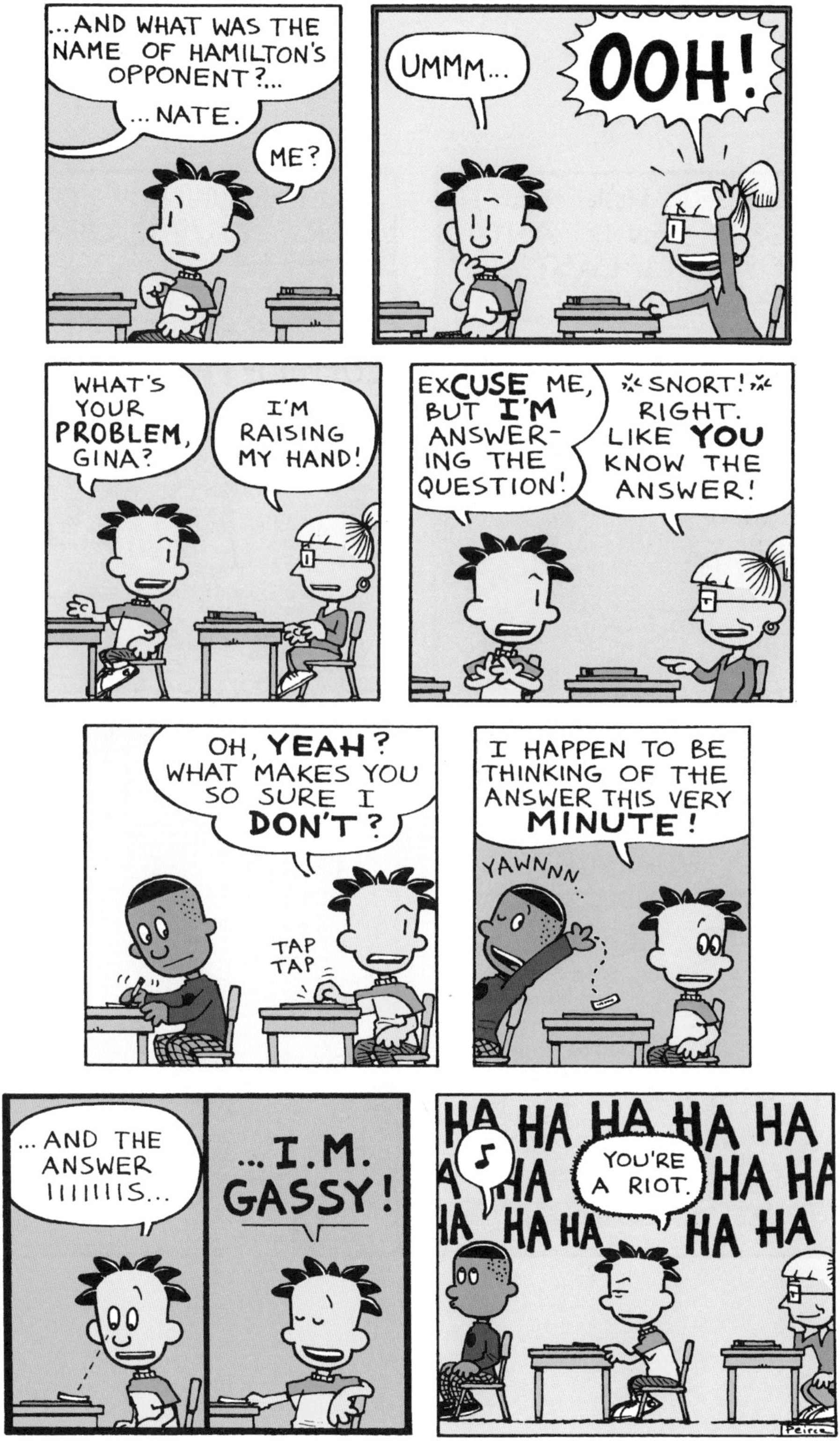

...AND WHAT WAS THE NAME OF HAMILTON'S OPPONENT?...
...NATE.
ME?
UMMM...
OOH!
WHAT'S YOUR PROBLEM, GINA?
I'M RAISING MY HAND!
EXCUSE ME, BUT I'M ANSWERING THE QUESTION!
SNORT! RIGHT. LIKE YOU KNOW THE ANSWER!
OH, YEAH? WHAT MAKES YOU SO SURE I DON'T?
TAP TAP
I HAPPEN TO BE THINKING OF THE ANSWER THIS VERY MINUTE!
YAWNNNN...
...AND THE ANSWER IIIIIIIS...
...I.M. GASSY!
HA HA HA HA HA HA HA HA HA HA HA HA HA HA HA
YOU'RE A RIOT.
Peirce

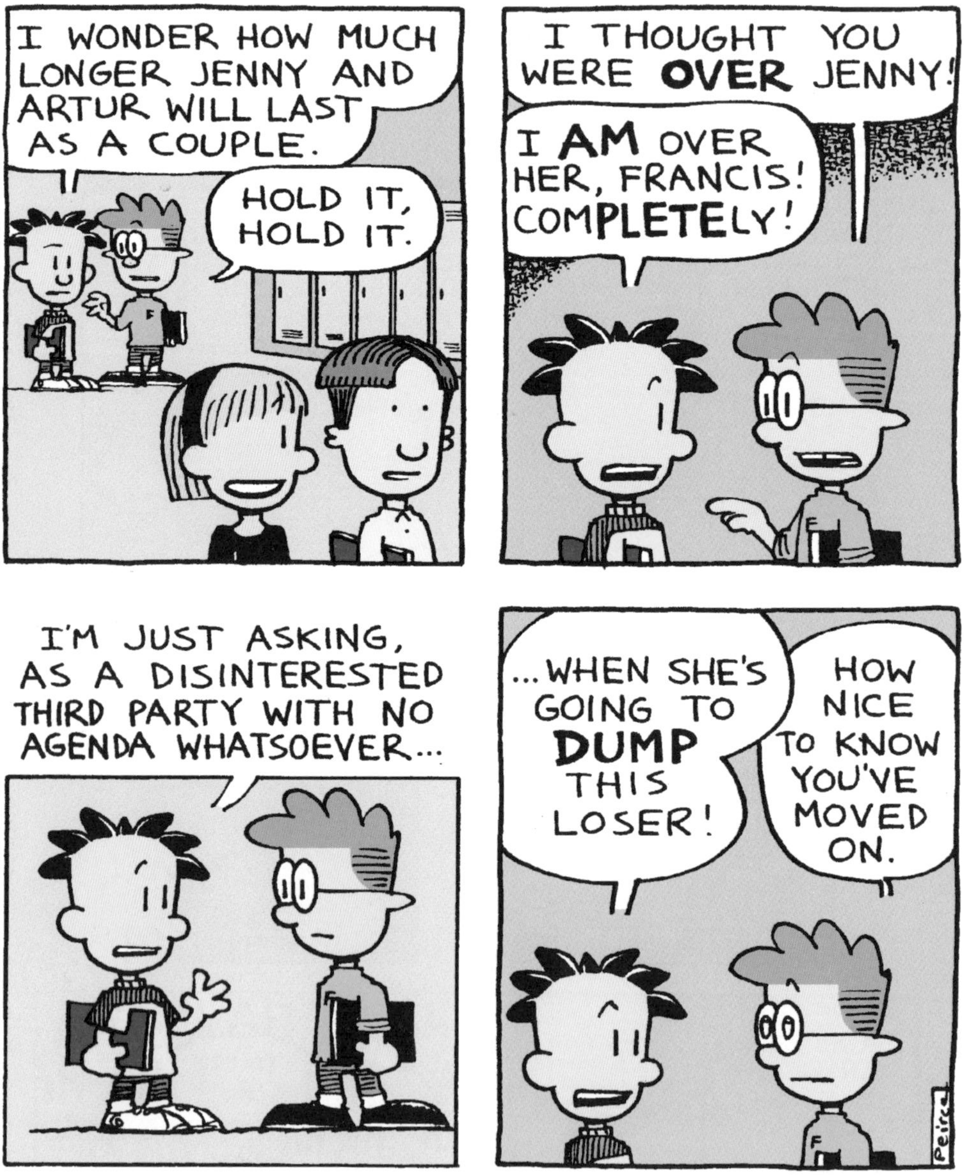
I WONDER HOW MUCH LONGER JENNY AND ARTUR WILL LAST AS A COUPLE.
HOLD IT, HOLD IT.
I THOUGHT YOU WERE OVER JENNY!
I AM OVER HER, FRANCIS! COMPLETELY!
I'M JUST ASKING, AS A DISINTERESTED THIRD PARTY WITH NO AGENDA WHATSOEVER...
...WHEN SHE'S GOING TO DUMP THIS LOSER!
HOW NICE TO KNOW YOU'VE MOVED ON.
Peirce

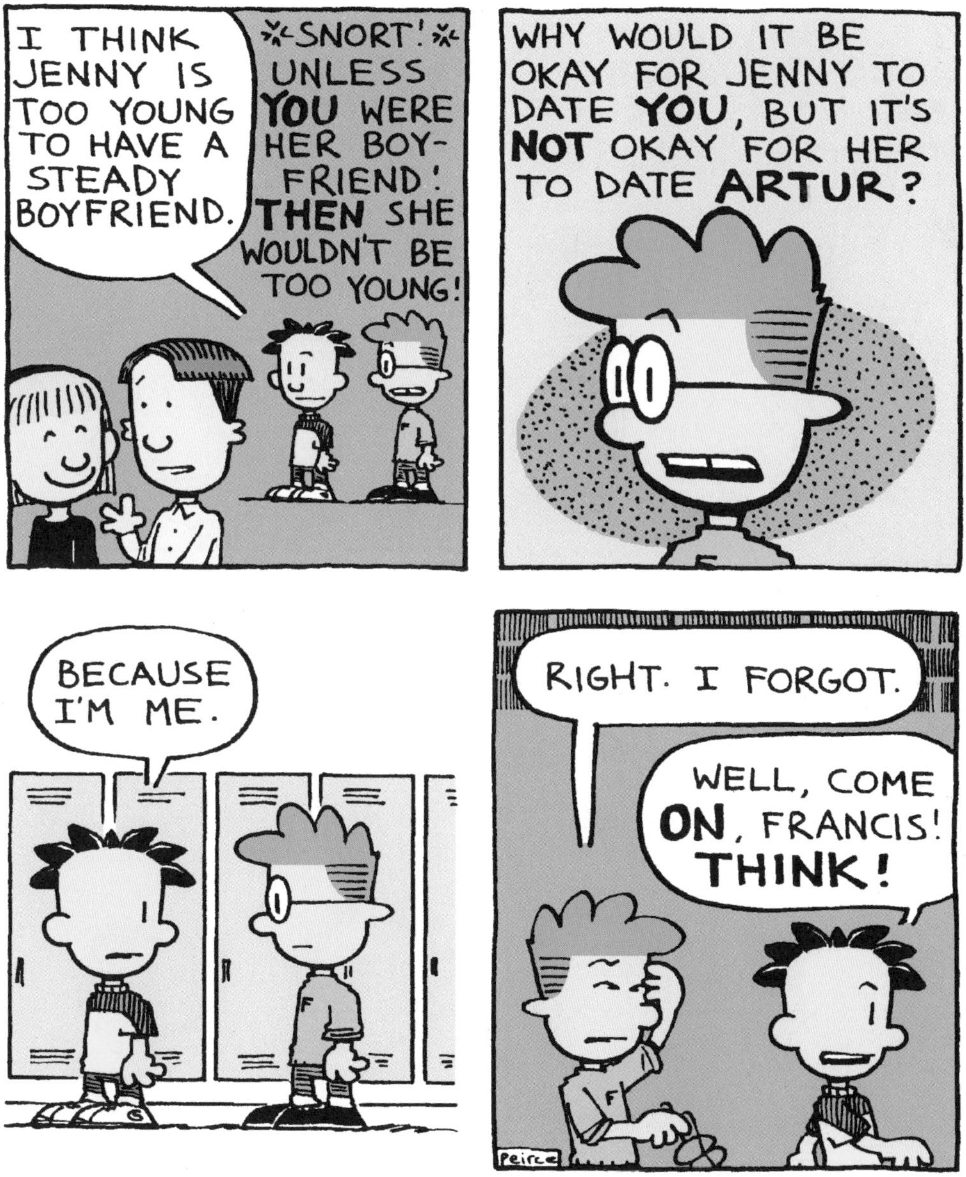
I THINK JENNY IS TOO YOUNG TO HAVE A STEADY BOYFRIEND.
SNORT! UNLESS YOU WERE HER BOY-FRIEND! THEN SHE WOULDN'T BE TOO YOUNG!
WHY WOULD IT BE OKAY FOR JENNY TO DATE YOU, BUT IT'S NOT OKAY FOR HER TO DATE ARTUR?
BECAUSE I'M ME.
RIGHT. I FORGOT.
WELL, COME ON, FRANCIS! THINK!
Peirce

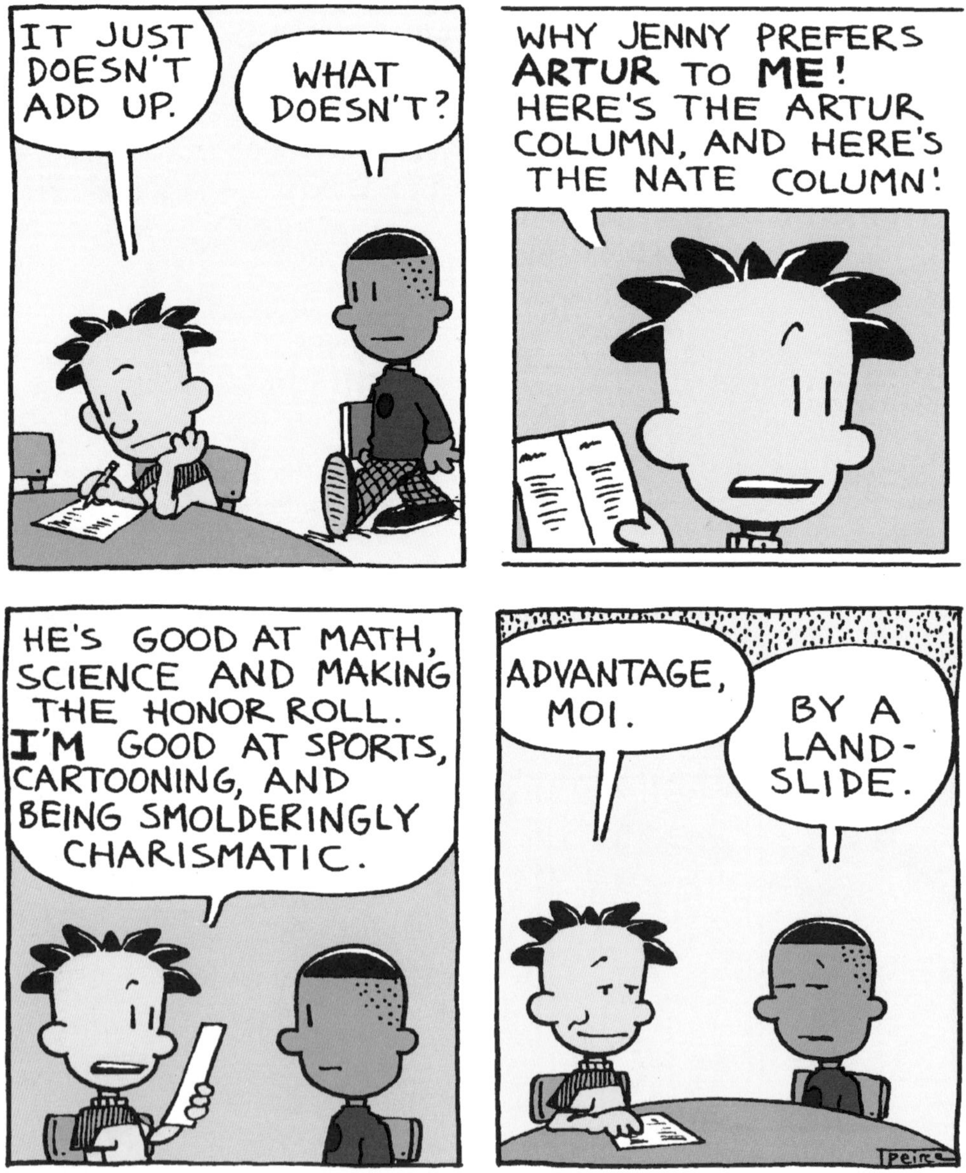
IT JUST DOESN'T ADD UP.
WHAT DOESN'T?
WHY JENNY PREFERS **ARTUR** TO **ME**! HERE'S THE ARTUR COLUMN, AND HERE'S THE NATE COLUMN!
HE'S GOOD AT MATH, SCIENCE AND MAKING THE HONOR ROLL. **I'M** GOOD AT SPORTS, CARTOONING, AND BEING SMOLDERINGLY CHARISMATIC.
ADVANTAGE, MOI.
BY A LAND-SLIDE.
PEIRCE

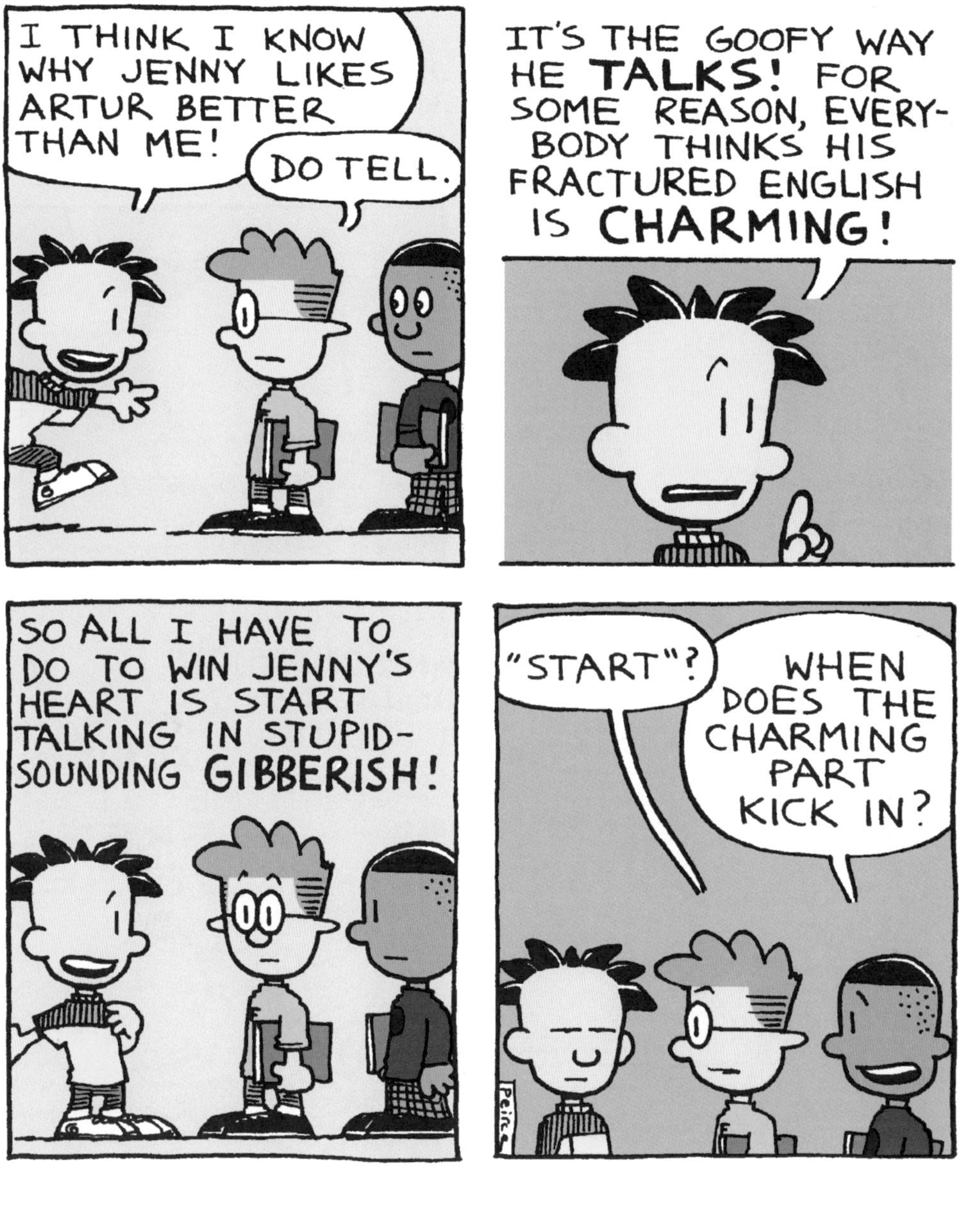
I THINK I KNOW WHY JENNY LIKES ARTUR BETTER THAN ME!
DO TELL.
IT'S THE GOOFY WAY HE **TALKS!** FOR SOME REASON, EVERY-BODY THINKS HIS FRACTURED ENGLISH IS **CHARMING!**
SO ALL I HAVE TO DO TO WIN JENNY'S HEART IS START TALKING IN STUPID-SOUNDING **GIBBERISH!**
"START"?
WHEN DOES THE CHARMING PART KICK IN?
Peirce

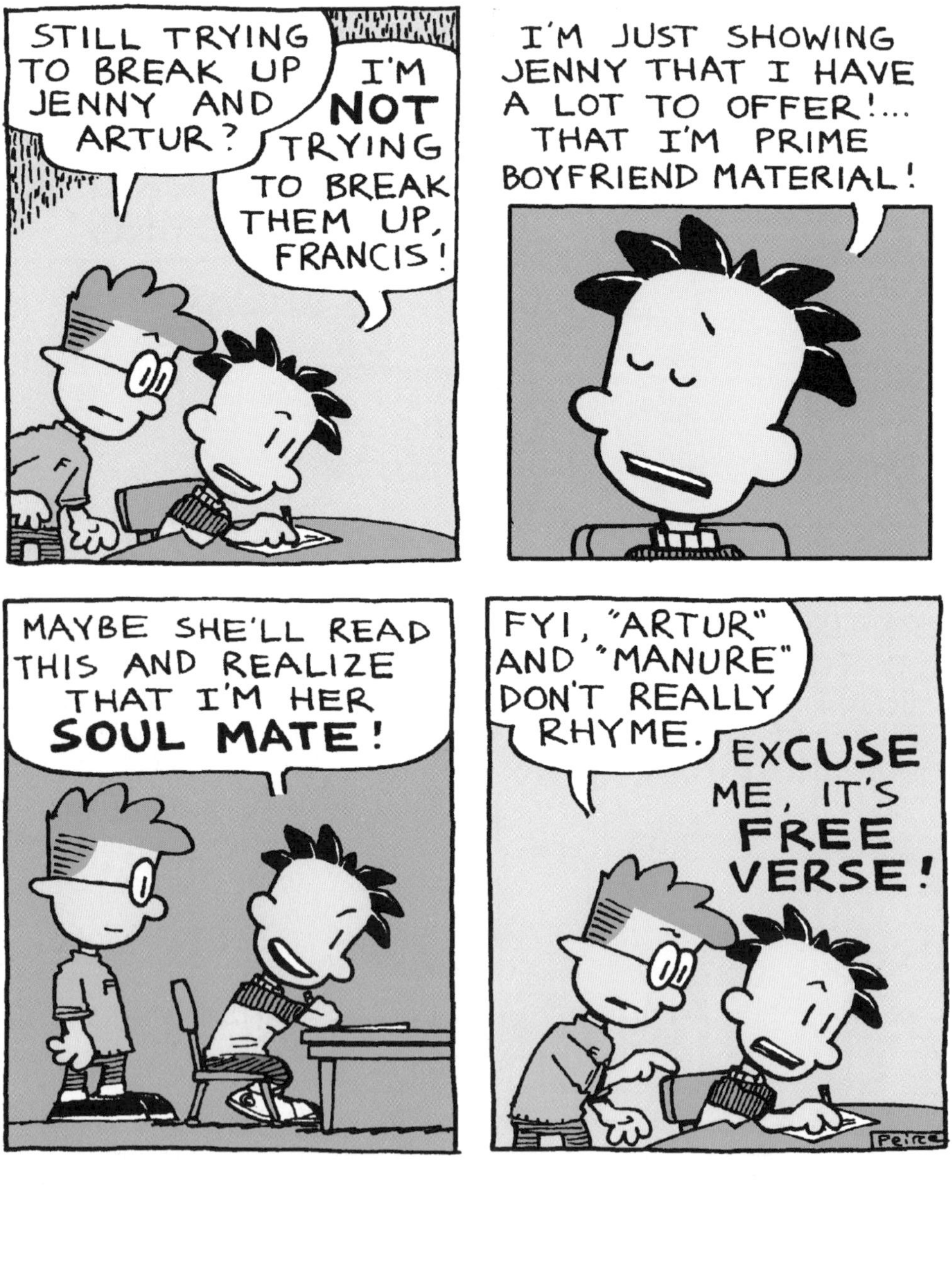
STILL TRYING TO BREAK UP JENNY AND ARTUR?
I'M **NOT** TRYING TO BREAK THEM UP, FRANCIS!
I'M JUST SHOWING JENNY THAT I HAVE A LOT TO OFFER!... THAT I'M PRIME BOYFRIEND MATERIAL!
MAYBE SHE'LL READ THIS AND REALIZE THAT I'M HER **SOUL MATE**!
FYI, "ARTUR" AND "MANURE" DON'T REALLY RHYME.
EX**CUSE** ME, IT'S **FREE VERSE**!
PEIRCE

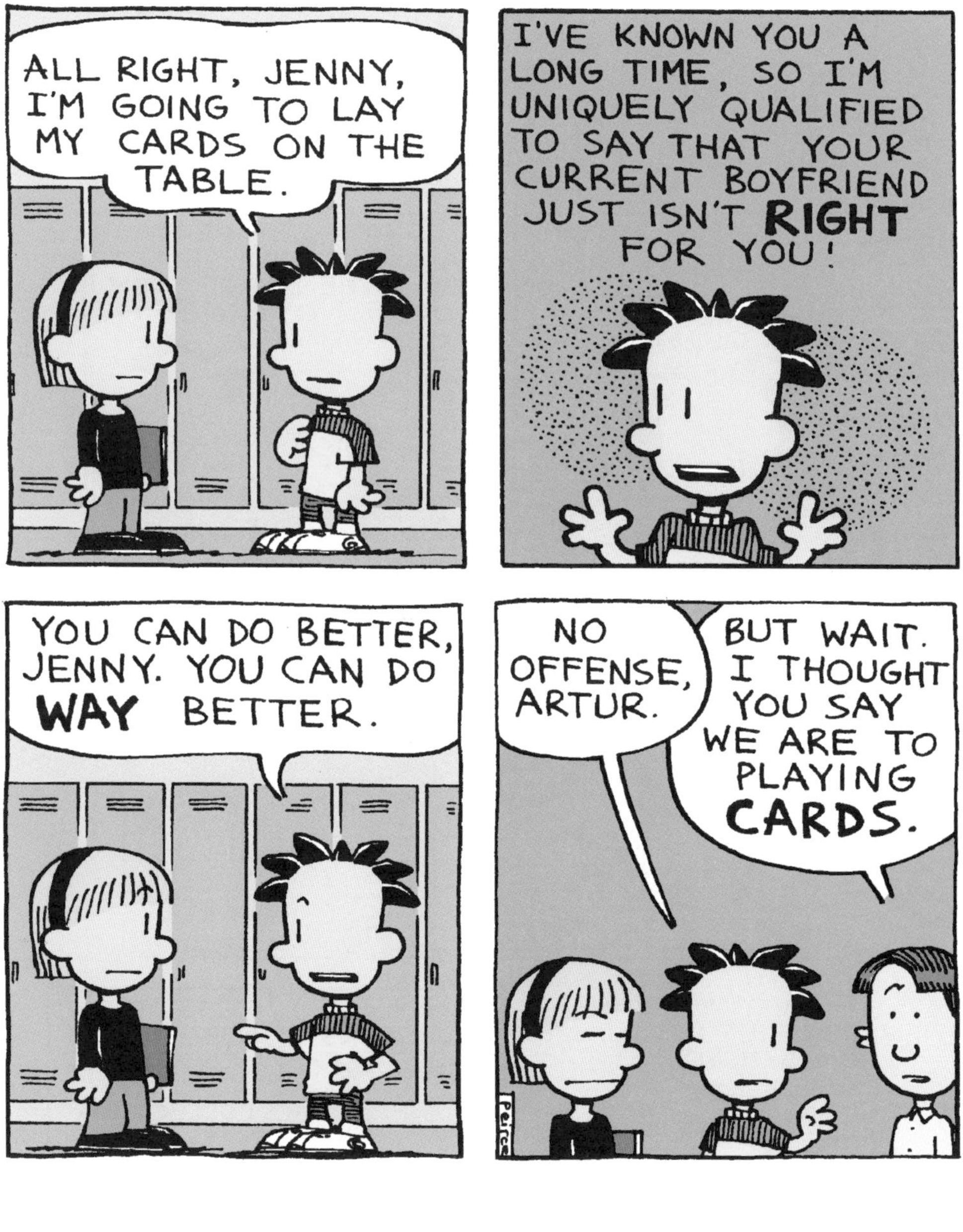

ALL RIGHT, JENNY, I'M GOING TO LAY MY CARDS ON THE TABLE.
I'VE KNOWN YOU A LONG TIME, SO I'M UNIQUELY QUALIFIED TO SAY THAT YOUR CURRENT BOYFRIEND JUST ISN'T **RIGHT** FOR YOU!
YOU CAN DO BETTER, JENNY. YOU CAN DO **WAY** BETTER.
NO OFFENSE, ARTUR.
BUT WAIT. I THOUGHT YOU SAY WE ARE TO PLAYING **CARDS**.
Peirce

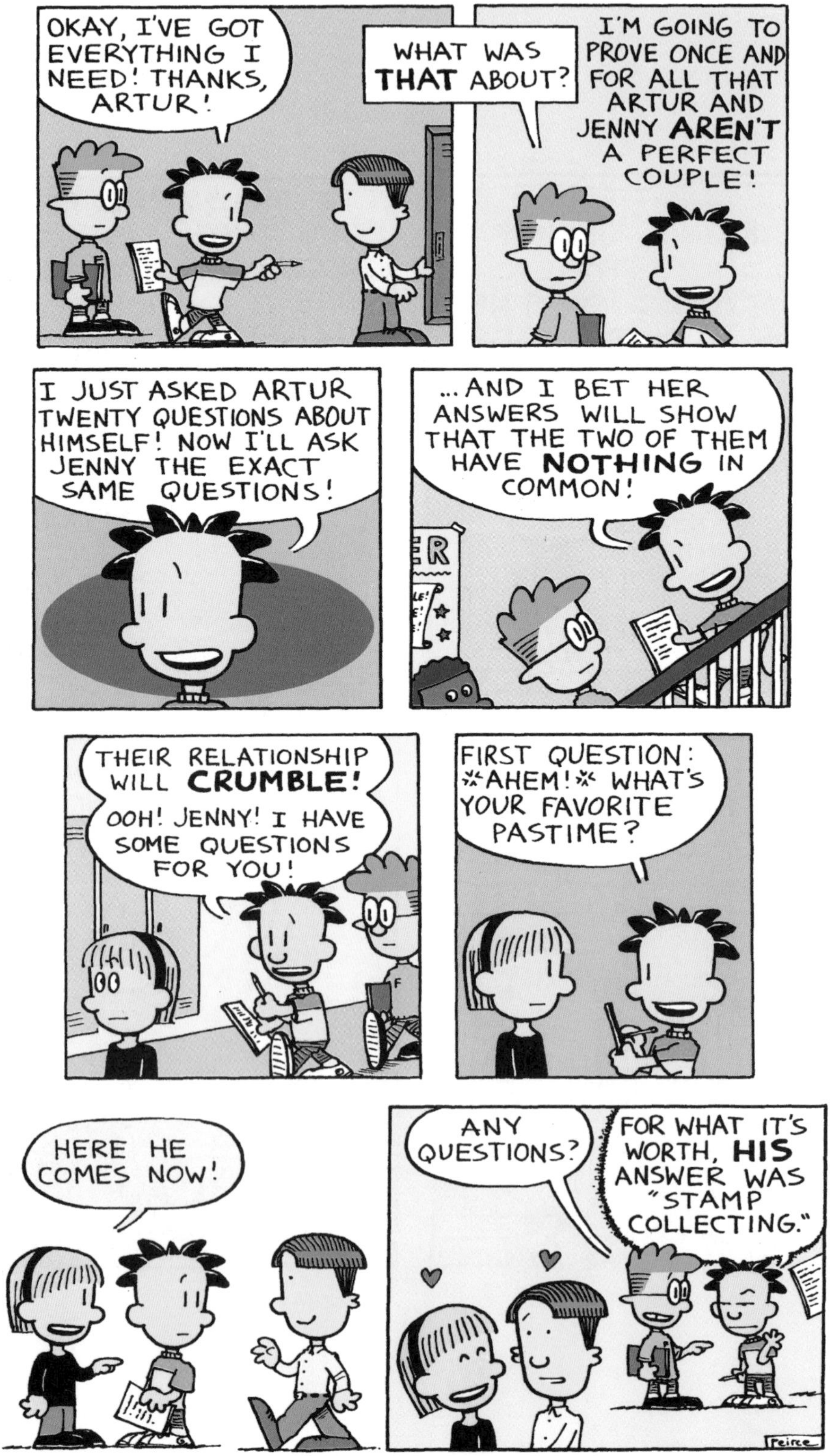

OKAY, I'VE GOT EVERYTHING I NEED! THANKS, ARTUR!
WHAT WAS THAT ABOUT?
I'M GOING TO PROVE ONCE AND FOR ALL THAT ARTUR AND JENNY AREN'T A PERFECT COUPLE!
I JUST ASKED ARTUR TWENTY QUESTIONS ABOUT HIMSELF! NOW I'LL ASK JENNY THE EXACT SAME QUESTIONS!
...AND I BET HER ANSWERS WILL SHOW THAT THE TWO OF THEM HAVE NOTHING IN COMMON!
THEIR RELATIONSHIP WILL CRUMBLE!
OOH! JENNY! I HAVE SOME QUESTIONS FOR YOU!
FIRST QUESTION: *AHEM!* WHAT'S YOUR FAVORITE PASTIME?
HERE HE COMES NOW!
ANY QUESTIONS?
FOR WHAT IT'S WORTH, HIS ANSWER WAS "STAMP COLLECTING."
Peirce

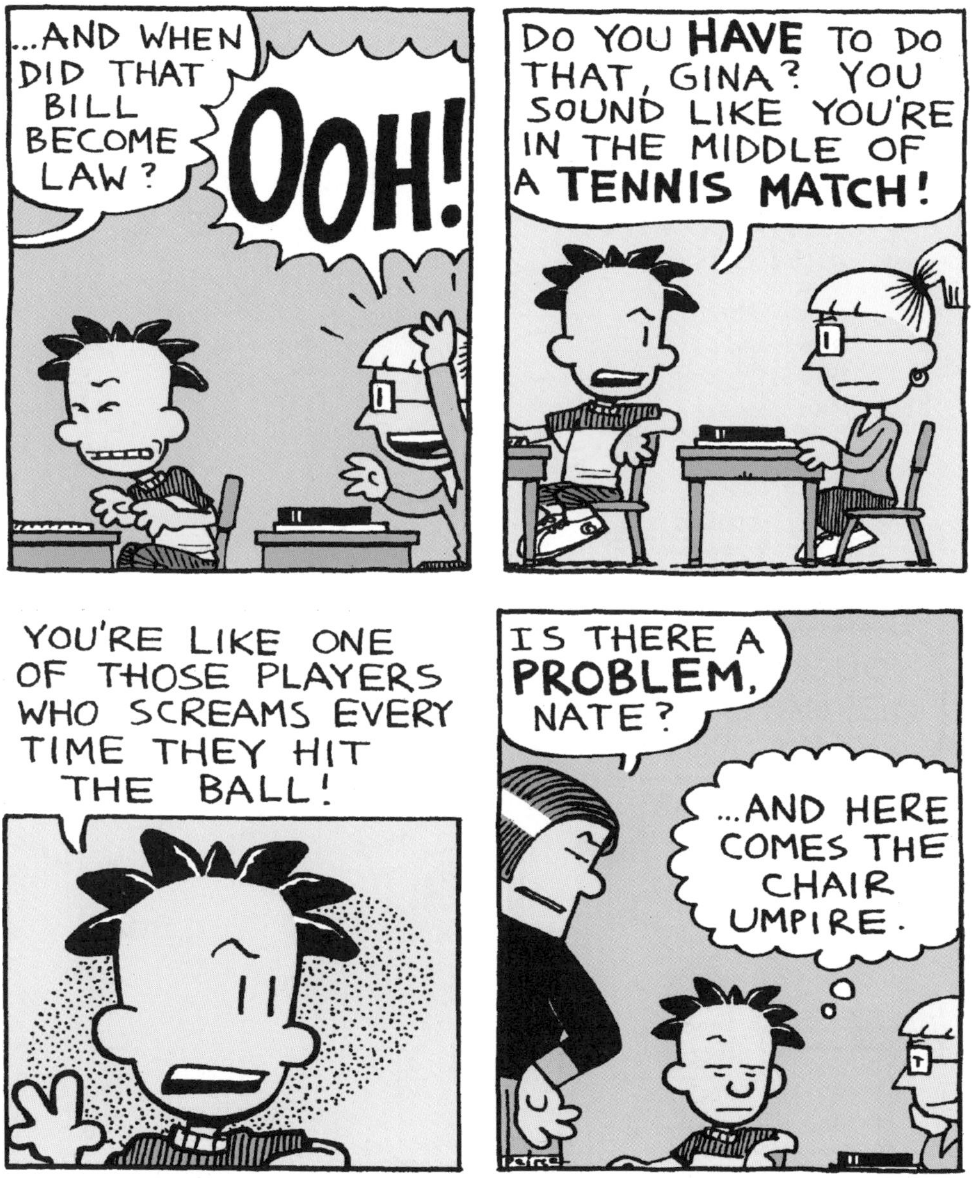
...AND WHEN DID THAT BILL BECOME LAW?
OOH!
DO YOU **HAVE** TO DO THAT, GINA? YOU SOUND LIKE YOU'RE IN THE MIDDLE OF A **TENNIS MATCH**!
YOU'RE LIKE ONE OF THOSE PLAYERS WHO SCREAMS EVERY TIME THEY HIT THE BALL!
IS THERE A **PROBLEM**, NATE?
...AND HERE COMES THE CHAIR UMPIRE.

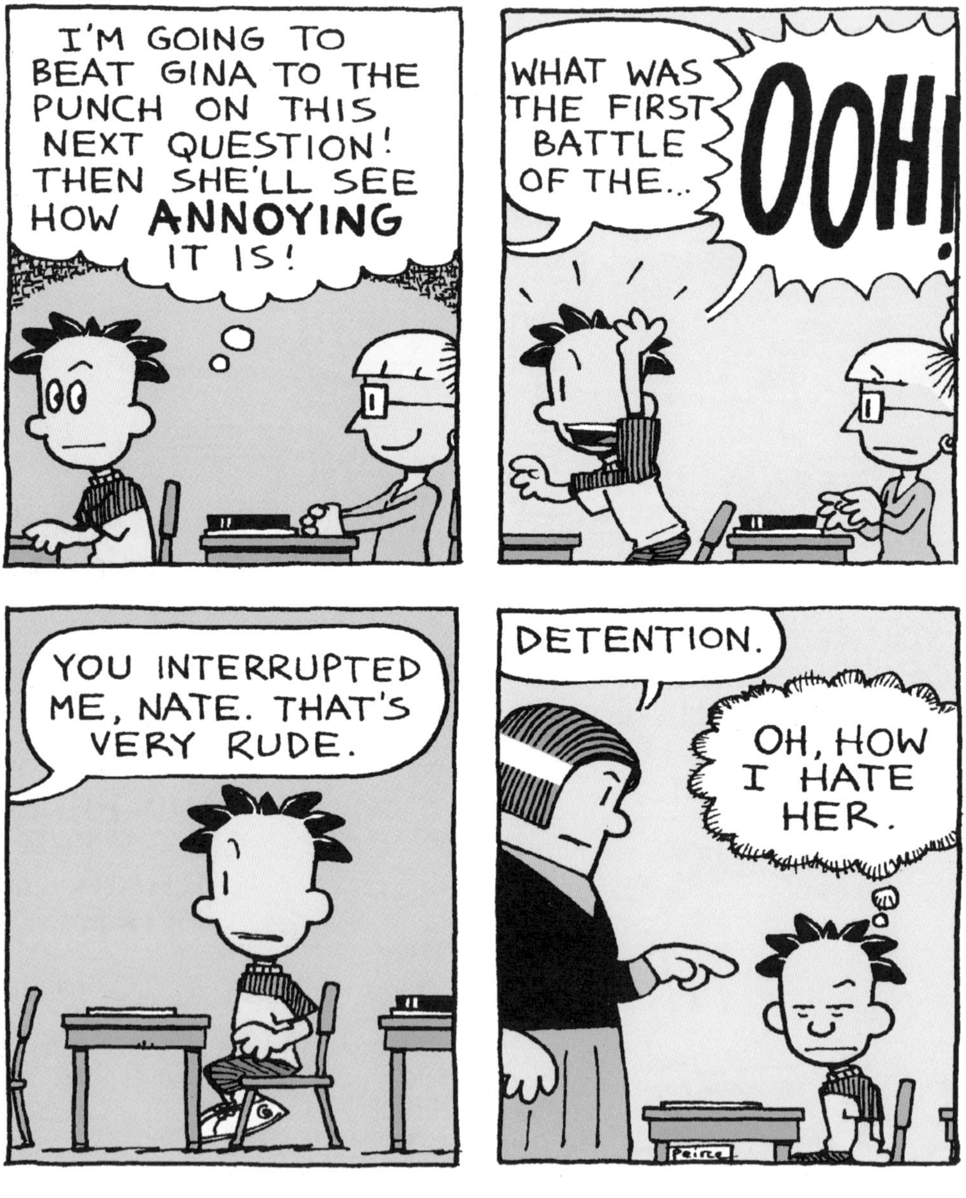
I'M GOING TO BEAT GINA TO THE PUNCH ON THIS NEXT QUESTION! THEN SHE'LL SEE HOW **ANNOYING** IT IS!
WHAT WAS THE FIRST BATTLE OF THE...
OOH!
YOU INTERRUPTED ME, NATE. THAT'S VERY RUDE.
DETENTION.
OH, HOW I HATE HER.

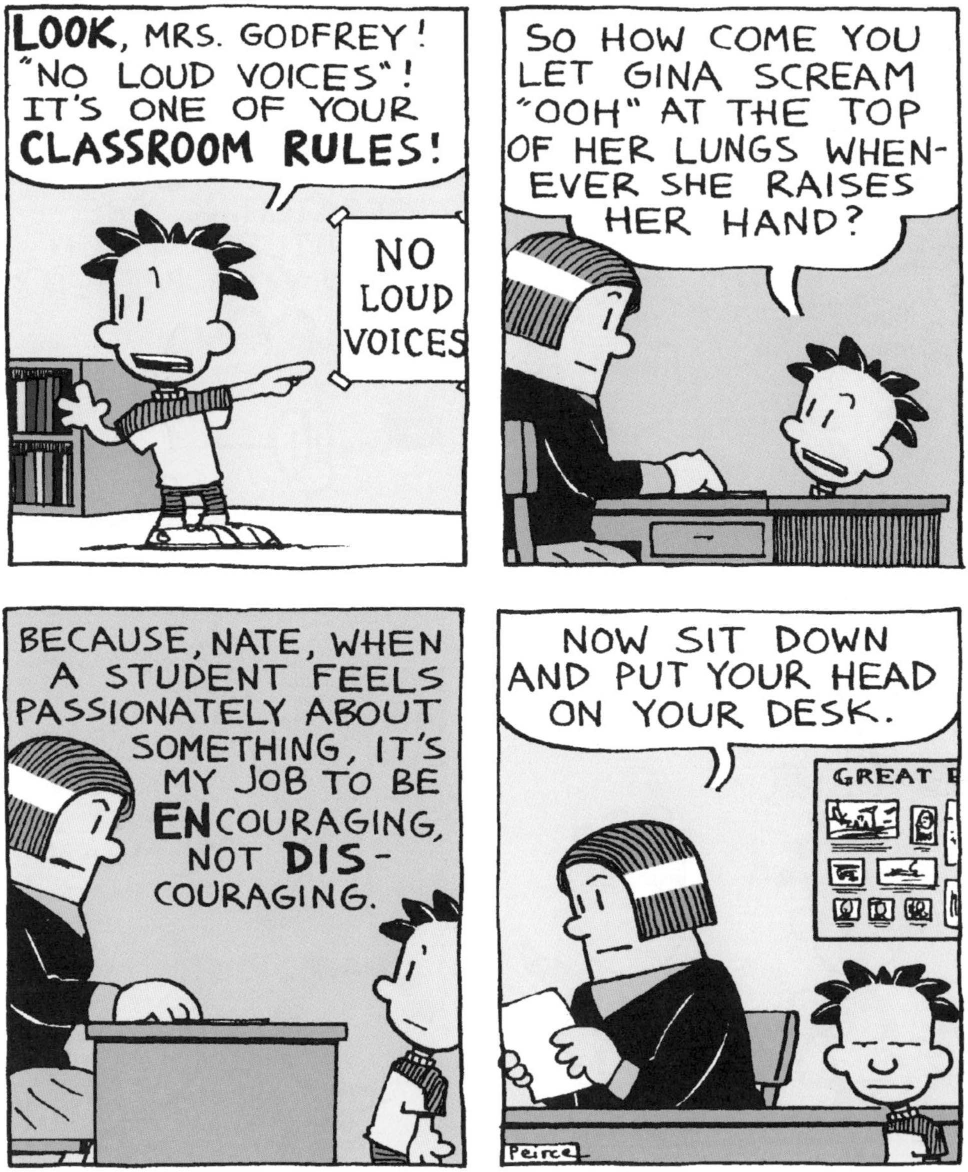
LOOK, MRS. GODFREY! "NO LOUD VOICES"! IT'S ONE OF YOUR CLASSROOM RULES!
NO LOUD VOICES
SO HOW COME YOU LET GINA SCREAM "OOH" AT THE TOP OF HER LUNGS WHEN-EVER SHE RAISES HER HAND?
BECAUSE, NATE, WHEN A STUDENT FEELS PASSIONATELY ABOUT SOMETHING, IT'S MY JOB TO BE ENCOURAGING, NOT DIS-COURAGING.
NOW SIT DOWN AND PUT YOUR HEAD ON YOUR DESK.
GREAT
Peirce

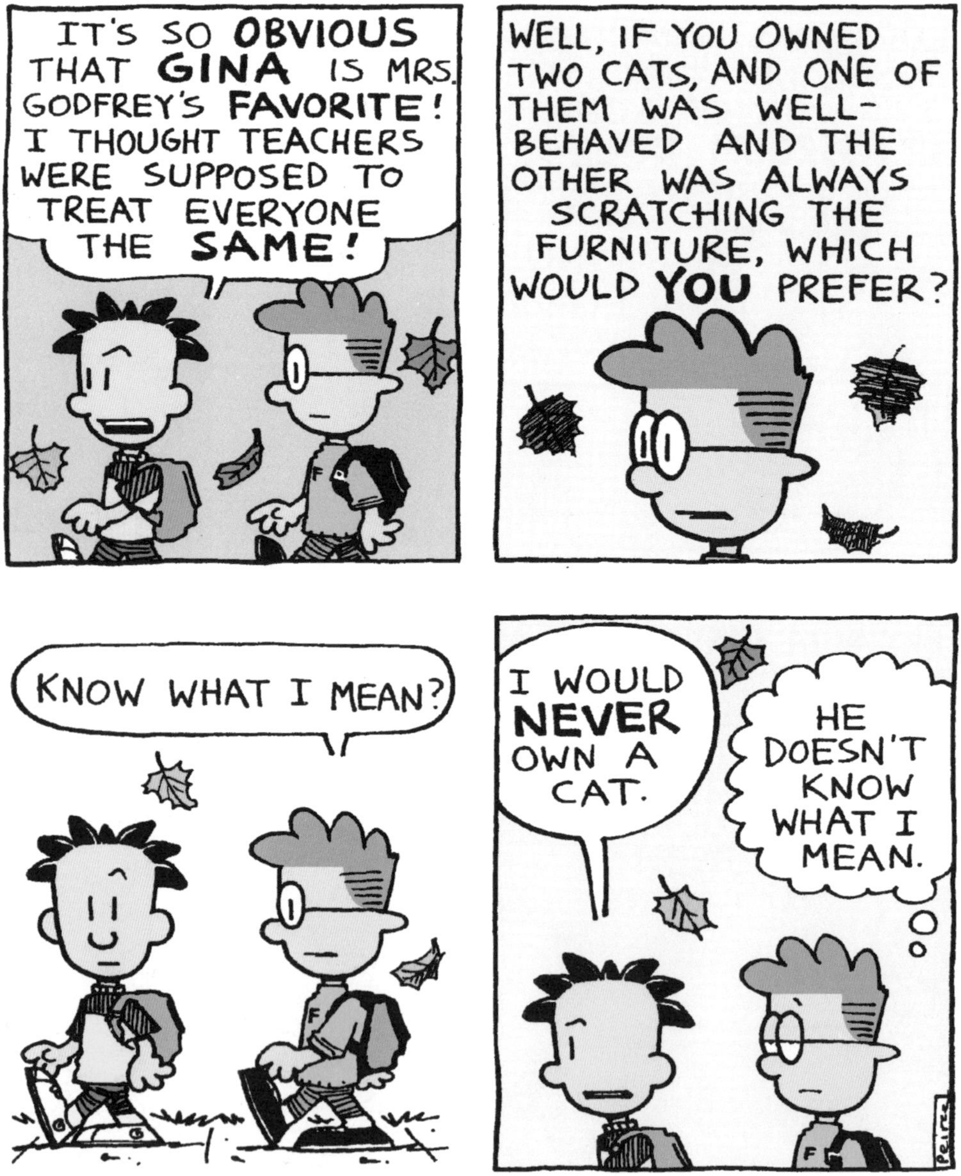
IT'S SO **OBVIOUS** THAT **GINA** IS MRS. GODFREY'S **FAVORITE**! I THOUGHT TEACHERS WERE SUPPOSED TO TREAT EVERYONE THE **SAME**!
WELL, IF YOU OWNED TWO CATS, AND ONE OF THEM WAS WELL-BEHAVED AND THE OTHER WAS ALWAYS SCRATCHING THE FURNITURE, WHICH WOULD **YOU** PREFER?
KNOW WHAT I MEAN?
I WOULD **NEVER** OWN A CAT.
HE DOESN'T KNOW WHAT I MEAN.
PEIRCE

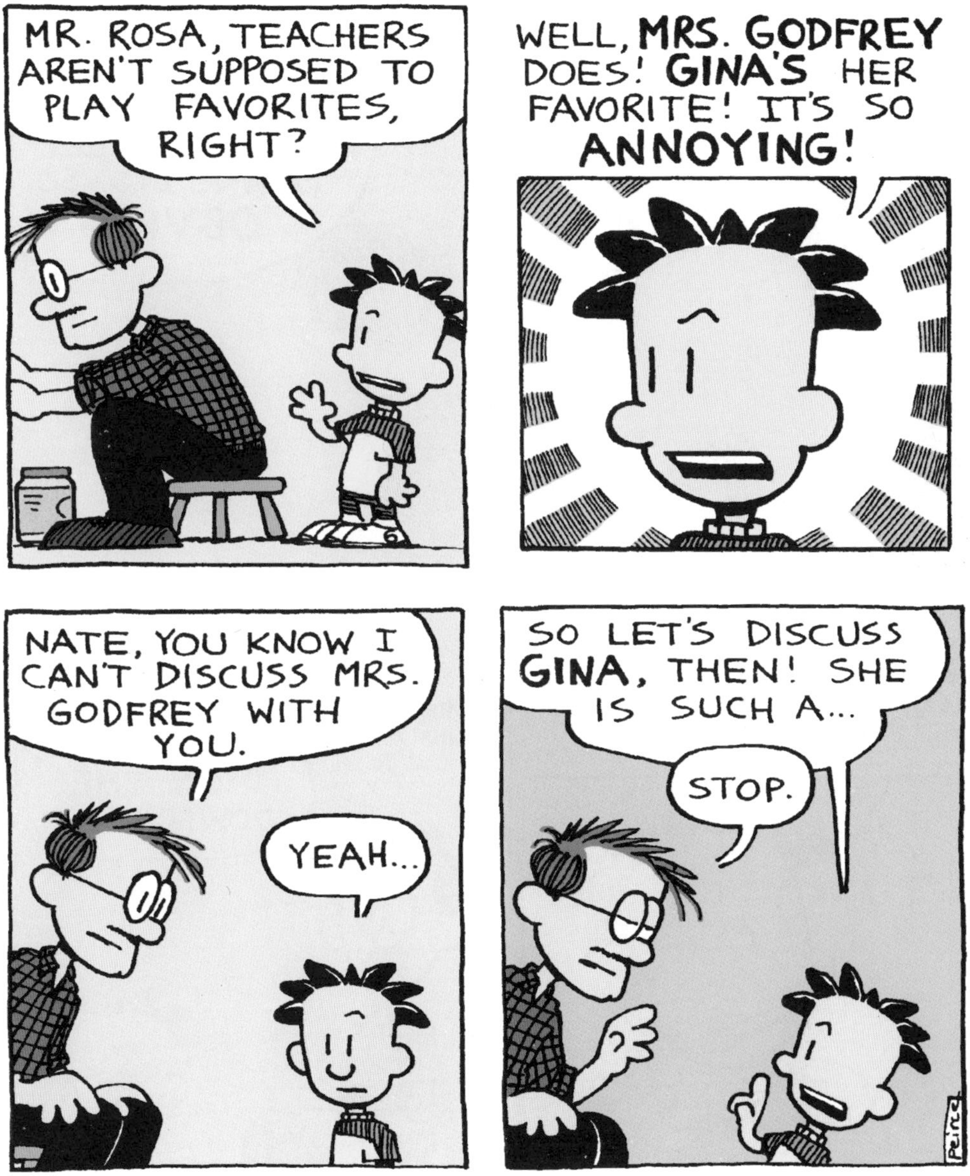
MR. ROSA, TEACHERS AREN'T SUPPOSED TO PLAY FAVORITES, RIGHT?
WELL, **MRS. GODFREY** DOES! **GINA'S** HER FAVORITE! IT'S SO **ANNOYING**!
NATE, YOU KNOW I CAN'T DISCUSS MRS. GODFREY WITH YOU.
YEAH...
SO LET'S DISCUSS **GINA**, THEN! SHE IS SUCH A...
STOP.
Peirce

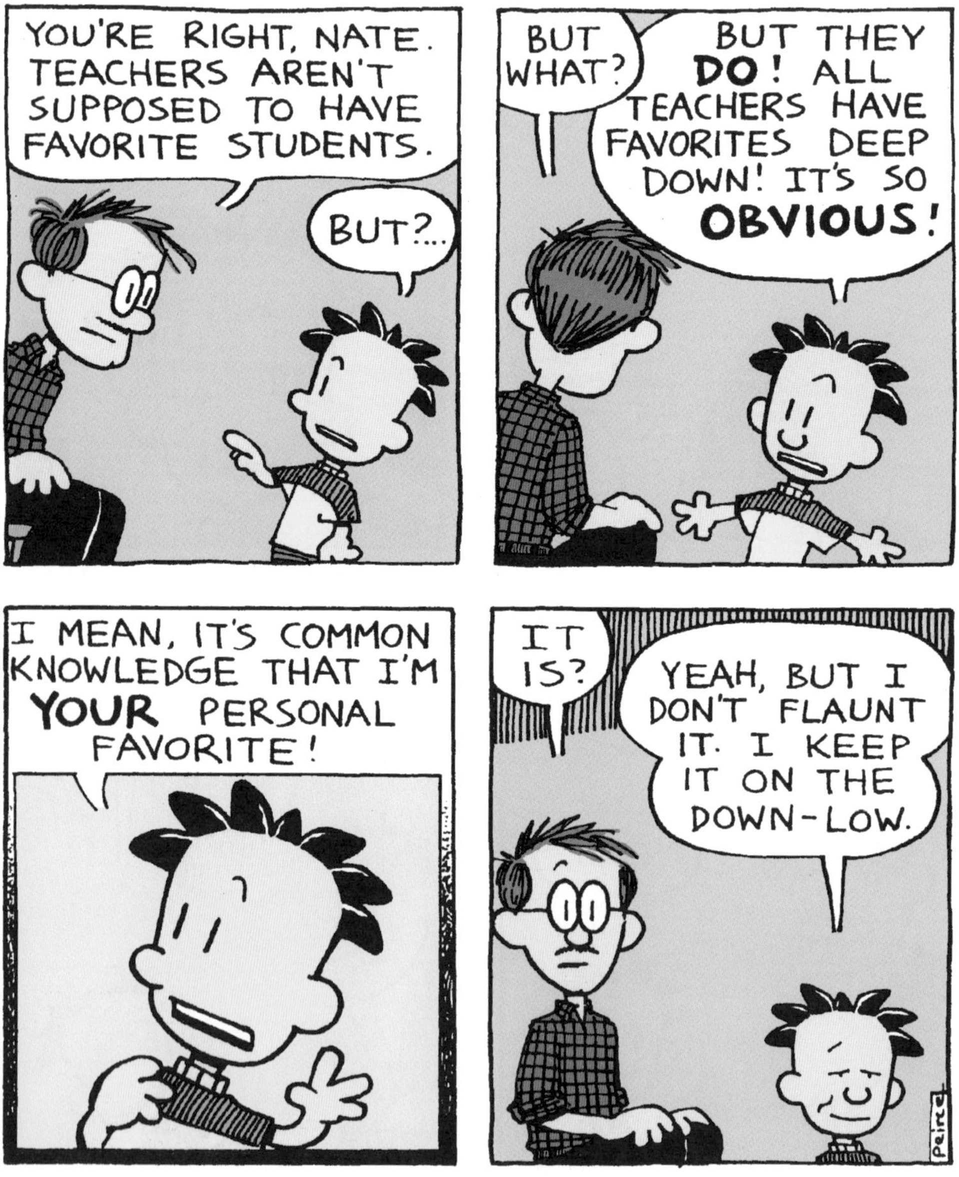
YOU'RE RIGHT, NATE. TEACHERS AREN'T SUPPOSED TO HAVE FAVORITE STUDENTS.
BUT?...
BUT WHAT?
BUT THEY DO! ALL TEACHERS HAVE FAVORITES DEEP DOWN! IT'S SO OBVIOUS!
I MEAN, IT'S COMMON KNOWLEDGE THAT I'M YOUR PERSONAL FAVORITE!
IT IS?
YEAH, BUT I DON'T FLAUNT IT. I KEEP IT ON THE DOWN-LOW.
Peirce

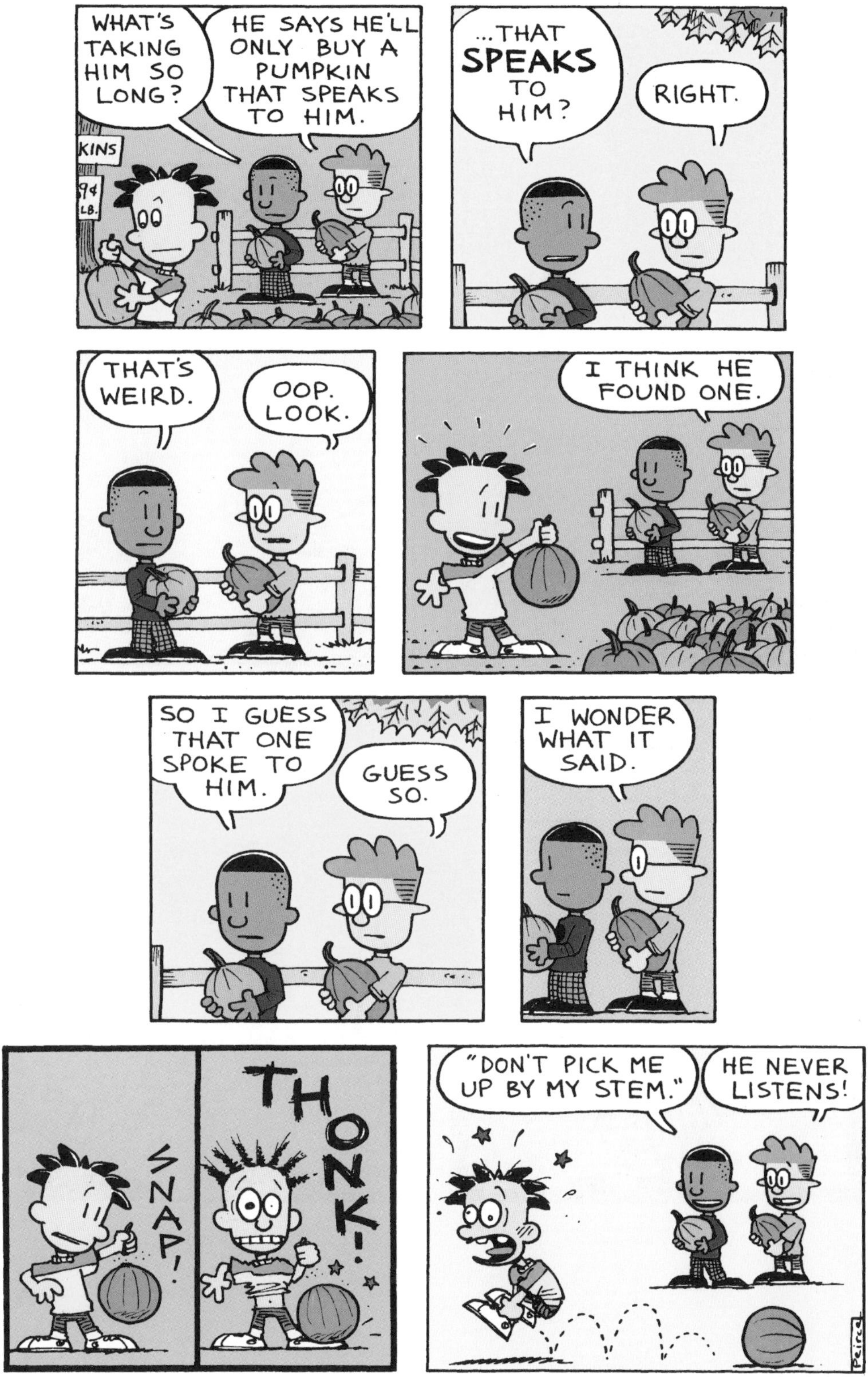
WHAT'S TAKING HIM SO LONG?
HE SAYS HE'LL ONLY BUY A PUMPKIN THAT SPEAKS TO HIM.
KINS
9¢ LB.
...THAT SPEAKS TO HIM?
RIGHT.
THAT'S WEIRD.
OOP. LOOK.
I THINK HE FOUND ONE.
SO I GUESS THAT ONE SPOKE TO HIM.
GUESS SO.
I WONDER WHAT IT SAID.
SNAP!
THONK!
"DON'T PICK ME UP BY MY STEM."
HE NEVER LISTENS!
Peirce

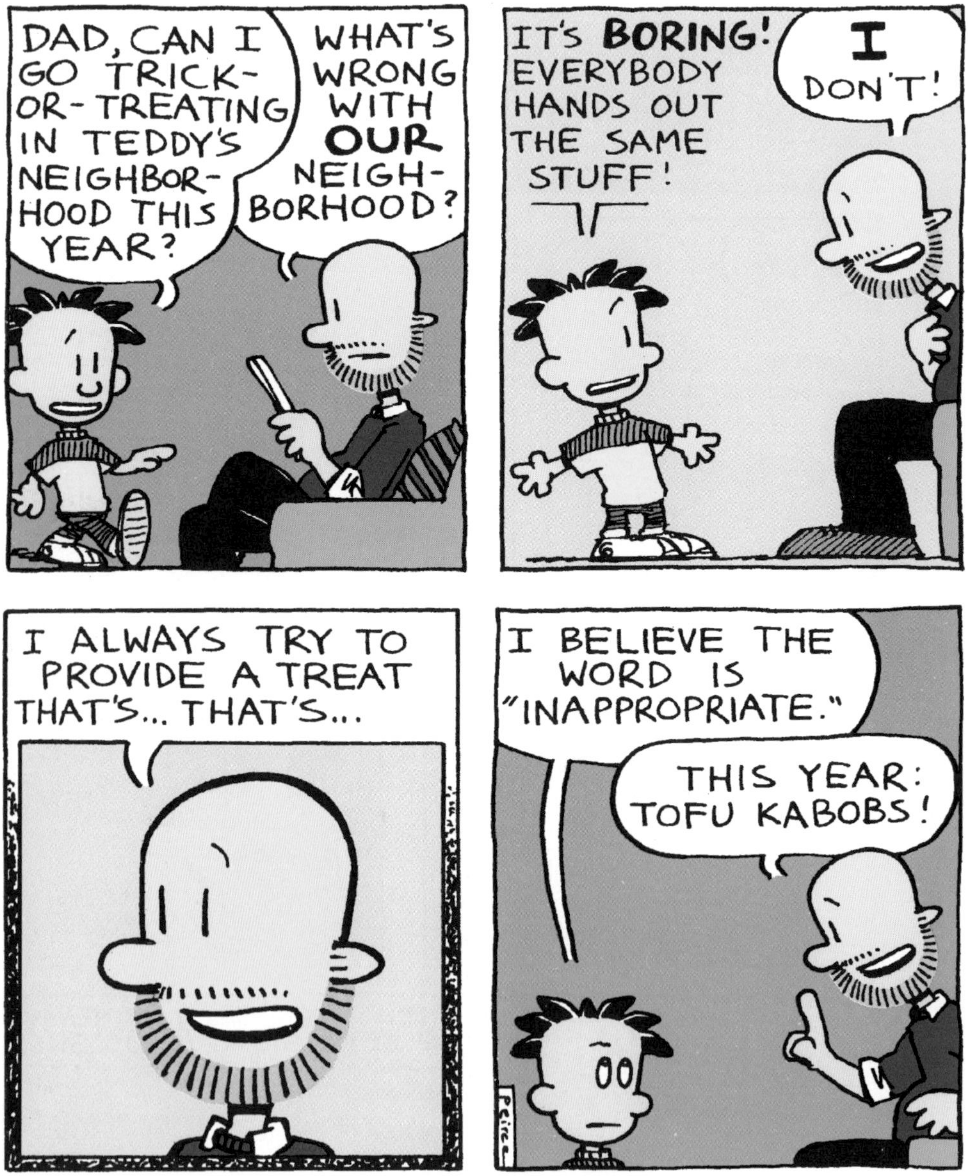
DAD, CAN I GO TRICK-OR-TREATING IN TEDDY'S NEIGHBORHOOD THIS YEAR?
WHAT'S WRONG WITH OUR NEIGHBORHOOD?
IT'S BORING! EVERYBODY HANDS OUT THE SAME STUFF!
I DON'T!
I ALWAYS TRY TO PROVIDE A TREAT THAT'S... THAT'S...
I BELIEVE THE WORD IS "INAPPROPRIATE."
THIS YEAR: TOFU KABOBS!
PEIRCE

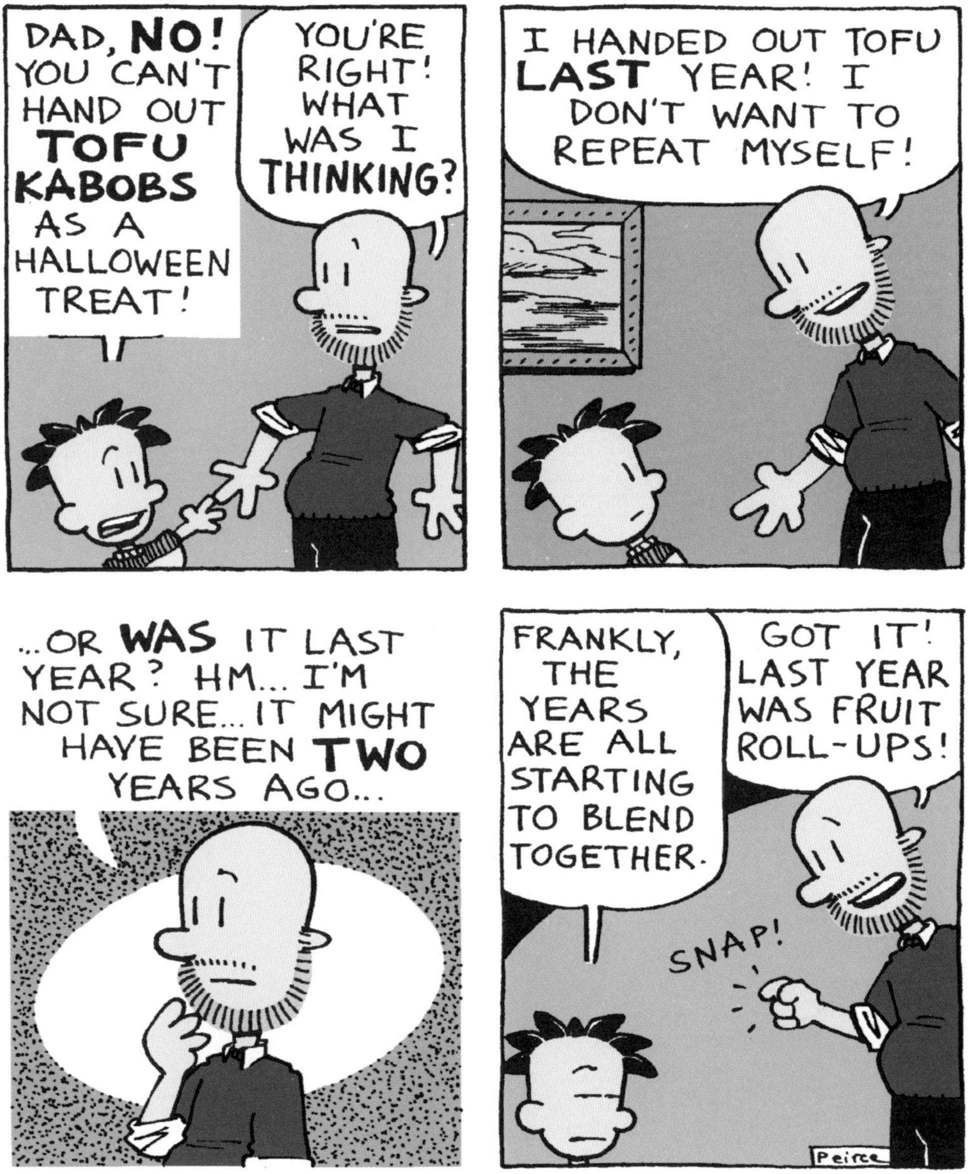
DAD, **NO!** YOU CAN'T HAND OUT **TOFU KABOBS** AS A HALLOWEEN TREAT!
YOU'RE RIGHT! WHAT WAS I **THINKING?**
I HANDED OUT TOFU **LAST** YEAR! I DON'T WANT TO REPEAT MYSELF!
...OR **WAS** IT LAST YEAR? HM... I'M NOT SURE... IT MIGHT HAVE BEEN **TWO** YEARS AGO...
FRANKLY, THE YEARS ARE ALL STARTING TO BLEND TOGETHER.
GOT IT! LAST YEAR WAS FRUIT ROLL-UPS!
SNAP!
Peirce

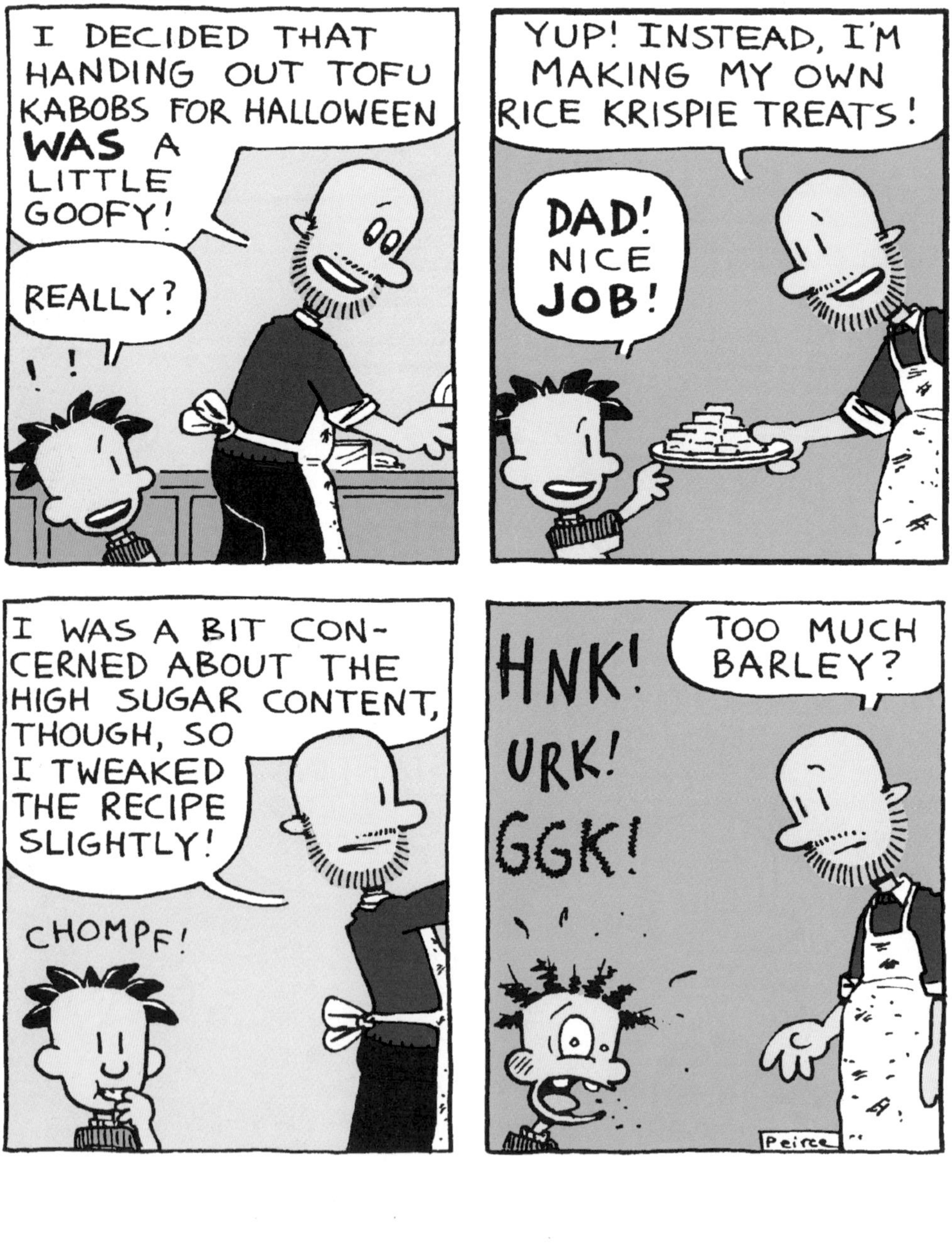
I DECIDED THAT HANDING OUT TOFU KABOBS FOR HALLOWEEN **WAS** A LITTLE GOOFY!
REALLY?
! !
YUP! INSTEAD, I'M MAKING MY OWN RICE KRISPIE TREATS!
DAD! NICE JOB!
I WAS A BIT CONCERNED ABOUT THE HIGH SUGAR CONTENT, THOUGH, SO I TWEAKED THE RECIPE SLIGHTLY!
CHOMPF!
HNK!
URK!
GGK!
TOO MUCH BARLEY?
Peirce

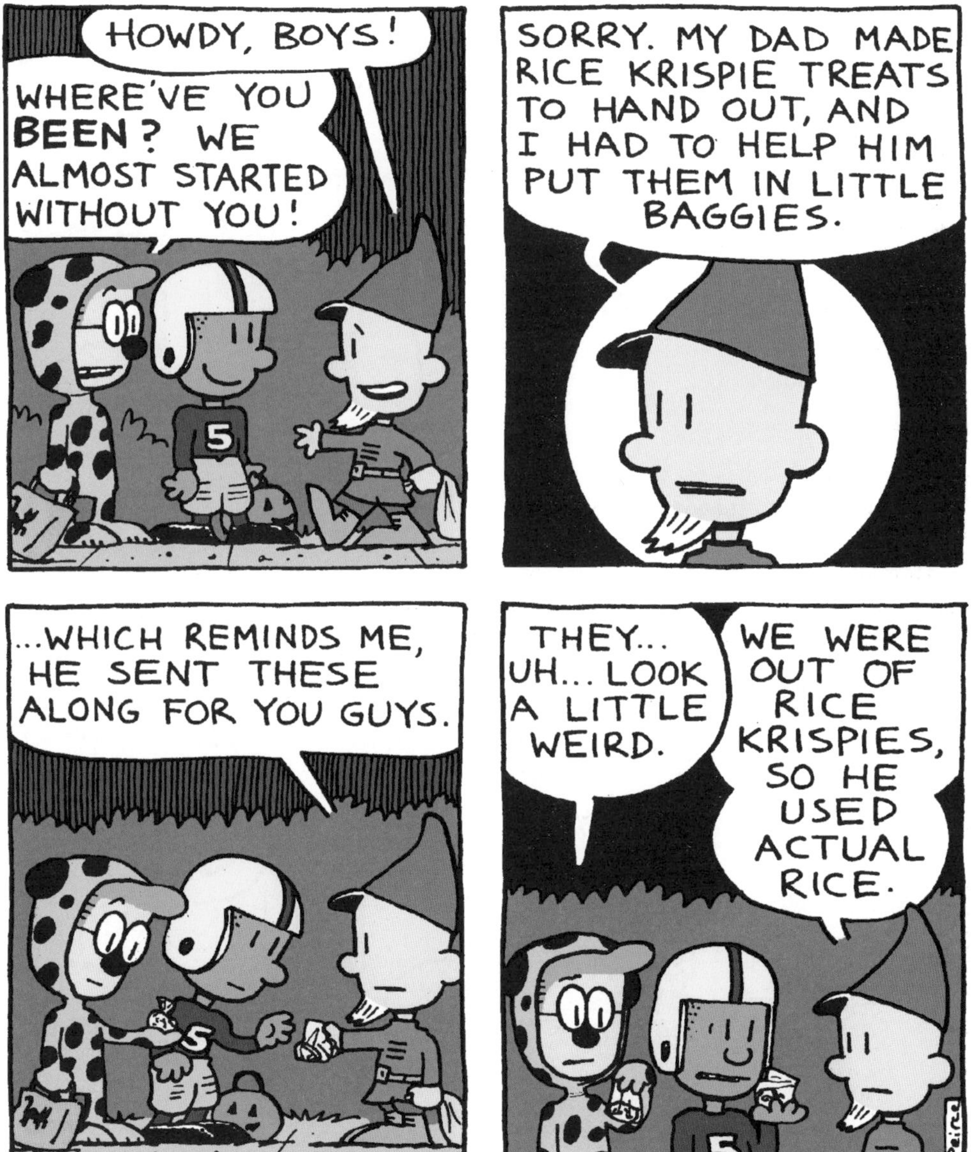
HOWDY, BOYS!
WHERE'VE YOU BEEN? WE ALMOST STARTED WITHOUT YOU!
SORRY. MY DAD MADE RICE KRISPIE TREATS TO HAND OUT, AND I HAD TO HELP HIM PUT THEM IN LITTLE BAGGIES.
...WHICH REMINDS ME, HE SENT THESE ALONG FOR YOU GUYS.
THEY... UH... LOOK A LITTLE WEIRD.
WE WERE OUT OF RICE KRISPIES, SO HE USED ACTUAL RICE.
5
5
5
Peirce

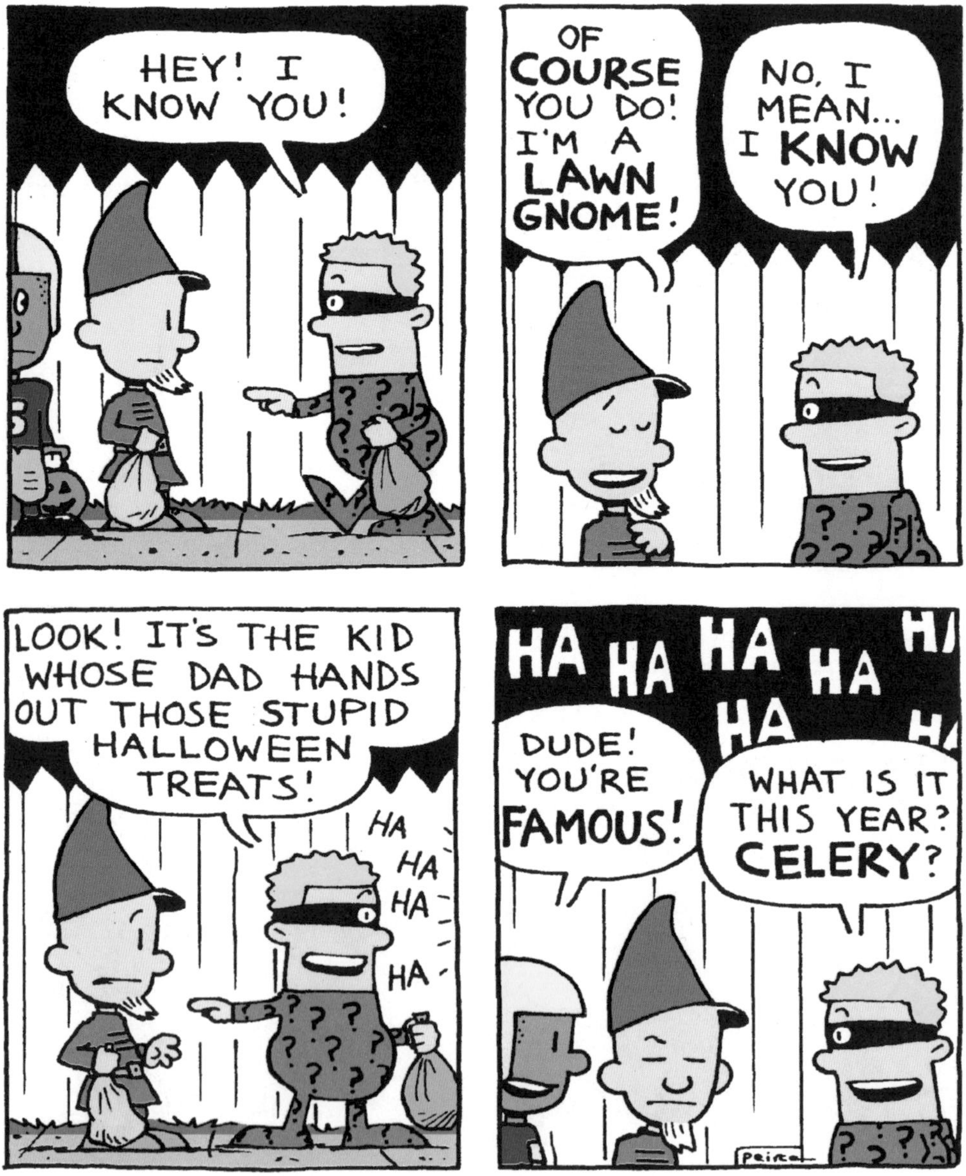
HEY! I KNOW YOU!
OF COURSE YOU DO! I'M A LAWN GNOME!
NO, I MEAN... I KNOW YOU!
LOOK! IT'S THE KID WHOSE DAD HANDS OUT THOSE STUPID HALLOWEEN TREATS!
HA HA HA HA
HA HA HA HA
HA
DUDE! YOU'RE FAMOUS!
WHAT IS IT THIS YEAR? CELERY?
PEIRCE

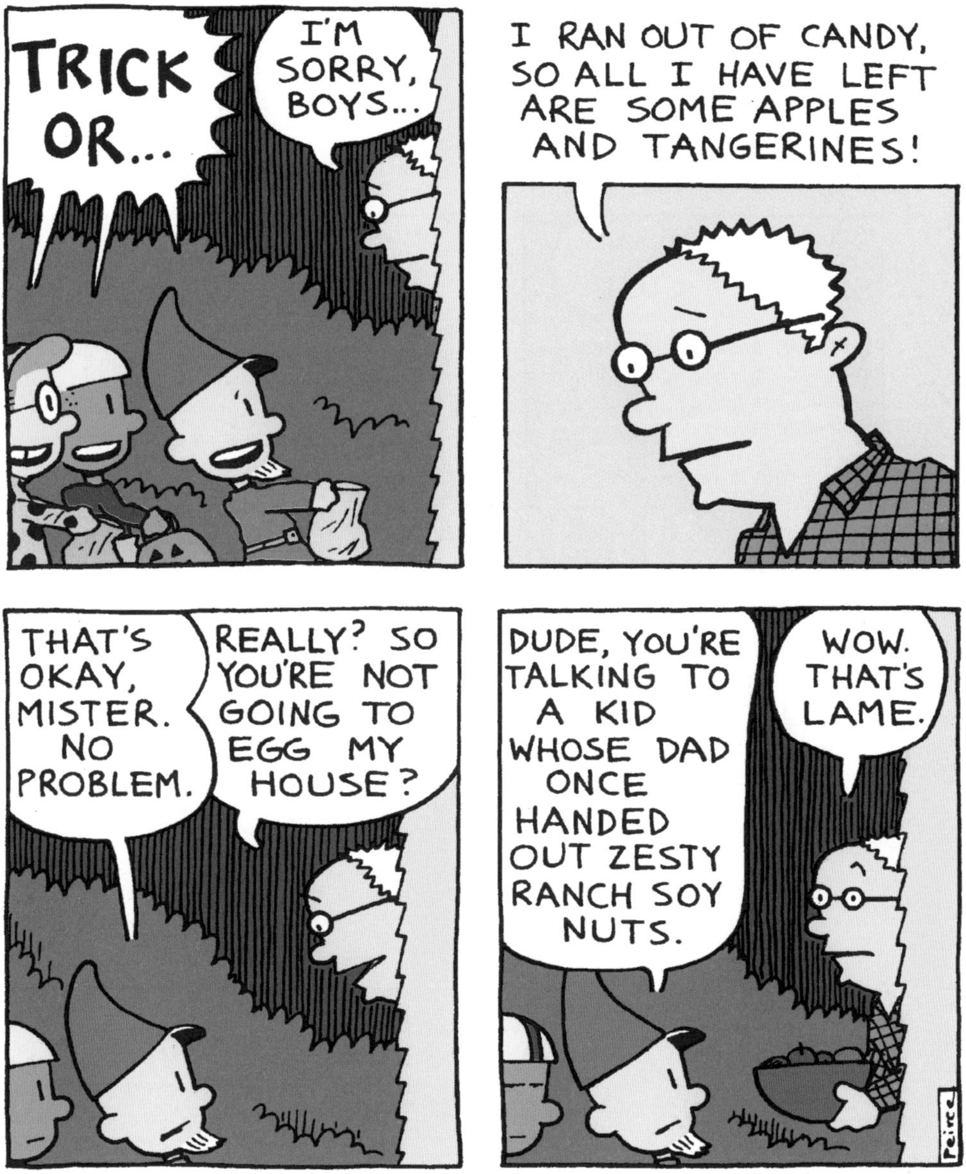
TRICK OR...
I'M SORRY, BOYS...
I RAN OUT OF CANDY, SO ALL I HAVE LEFT ARE SOME APPLES AND TANGERINES!
THAT'S OKAY, MISTER. NO PROBLEM.
REALLY? SO YOU'RE NOT GOING TO EGG MY HOUSE?
DUDE, YOU'RE TALKING TO A KID WHOSE DAD ONCE HANDED OUT ZESTY RANCH SOY NUTS.
WOW. THAT'S LAME.
Peirce

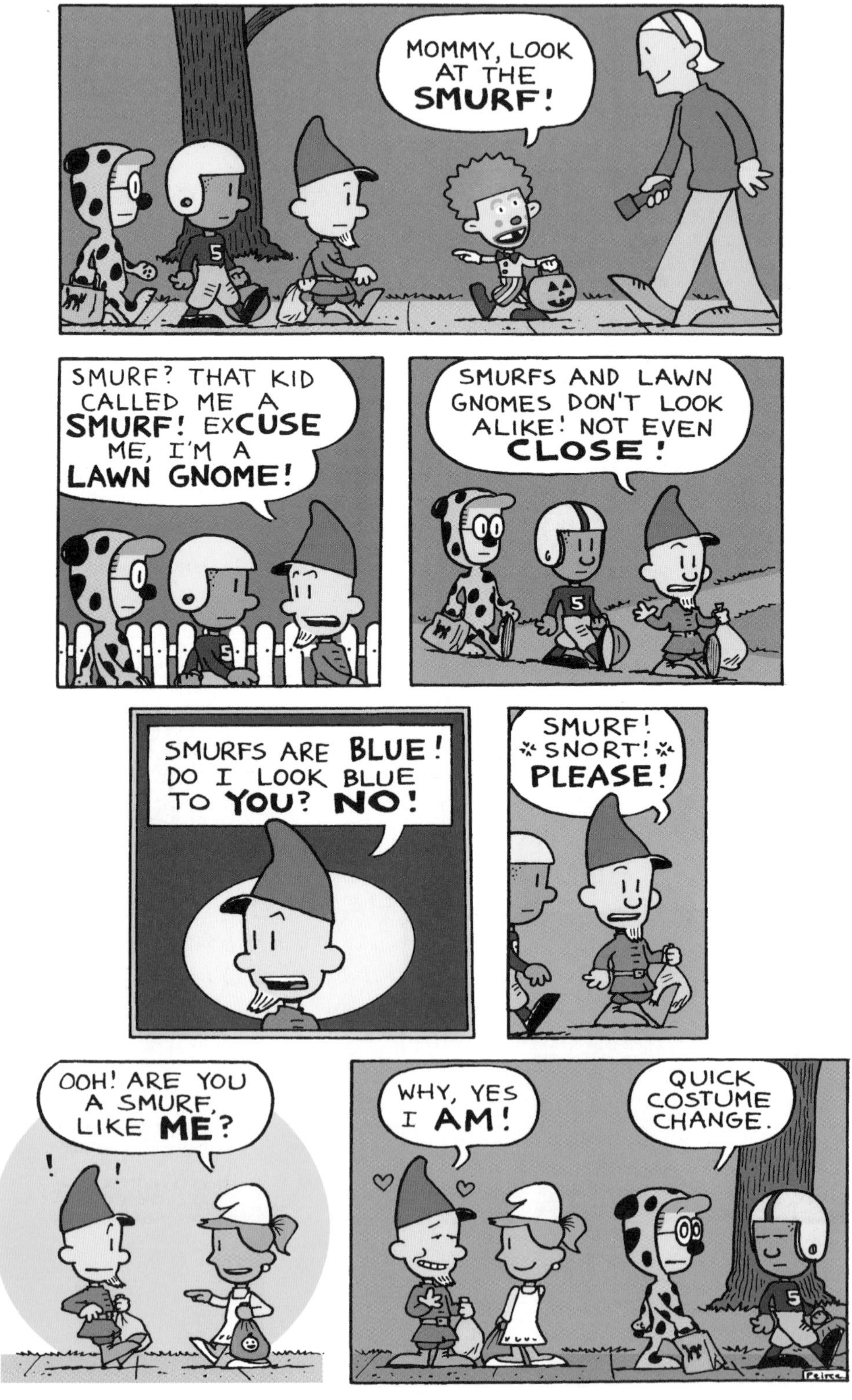
MOMMY, LOOK AT THE SMURF!
SMURF? THAT KID CALLED ME A SMURF! EXCUSE ME, I'M A LAWN GNOME!
SMURFS AND LAWN GNOMES DON'T LOOK ALIKE! NOT EVEN CLOSE!
SMURFS ARE BLUE! DO I LOOK BLUE TO YOU? NO!
SMURF! *SNORT!* PLEASE!
OOH! ARE YOU A SMURF, LIKE ME?
!
!
WHY, YES I AM!
QUICK COSTUME CHANGE.
Peirce

big
NATE
THUNKA, THUNKA, THUNKA

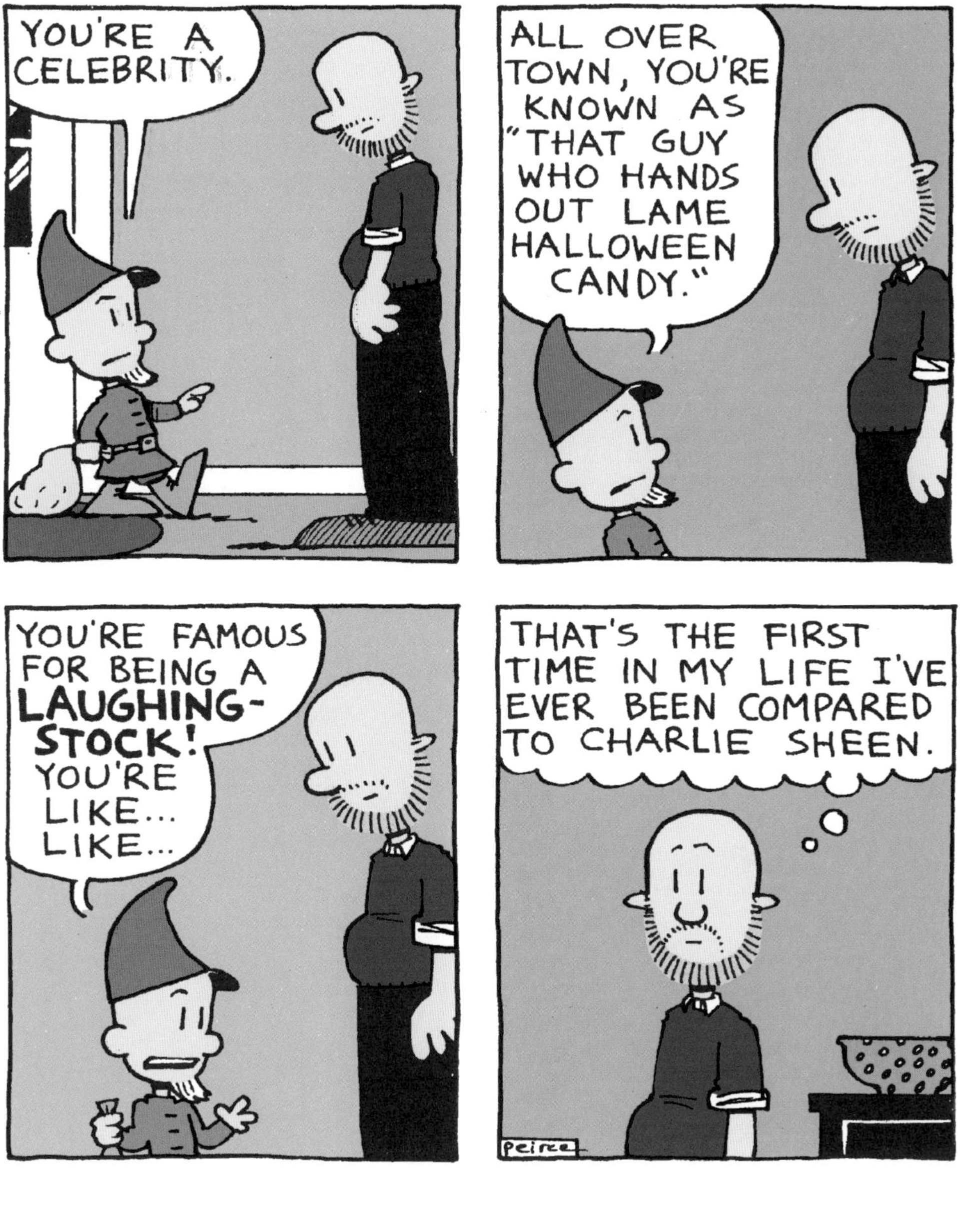
YOU'RE A CELEBRITY.
ALL OVER TOWN, YOU'RE KNOWN AS "THAT GUY WHO HANDS OUT LAME HALLOWEEN CANDY."
YOU'RE FAMOUS FOR BEING A **LAUGHING-STOCK!** YOU'RE LIKE... LIKE...
THAT'S THE FIRST TIME IN MY LIFE I'VE EVER BEEN COMPARED TO CHARLIE SHEEN.
peirce

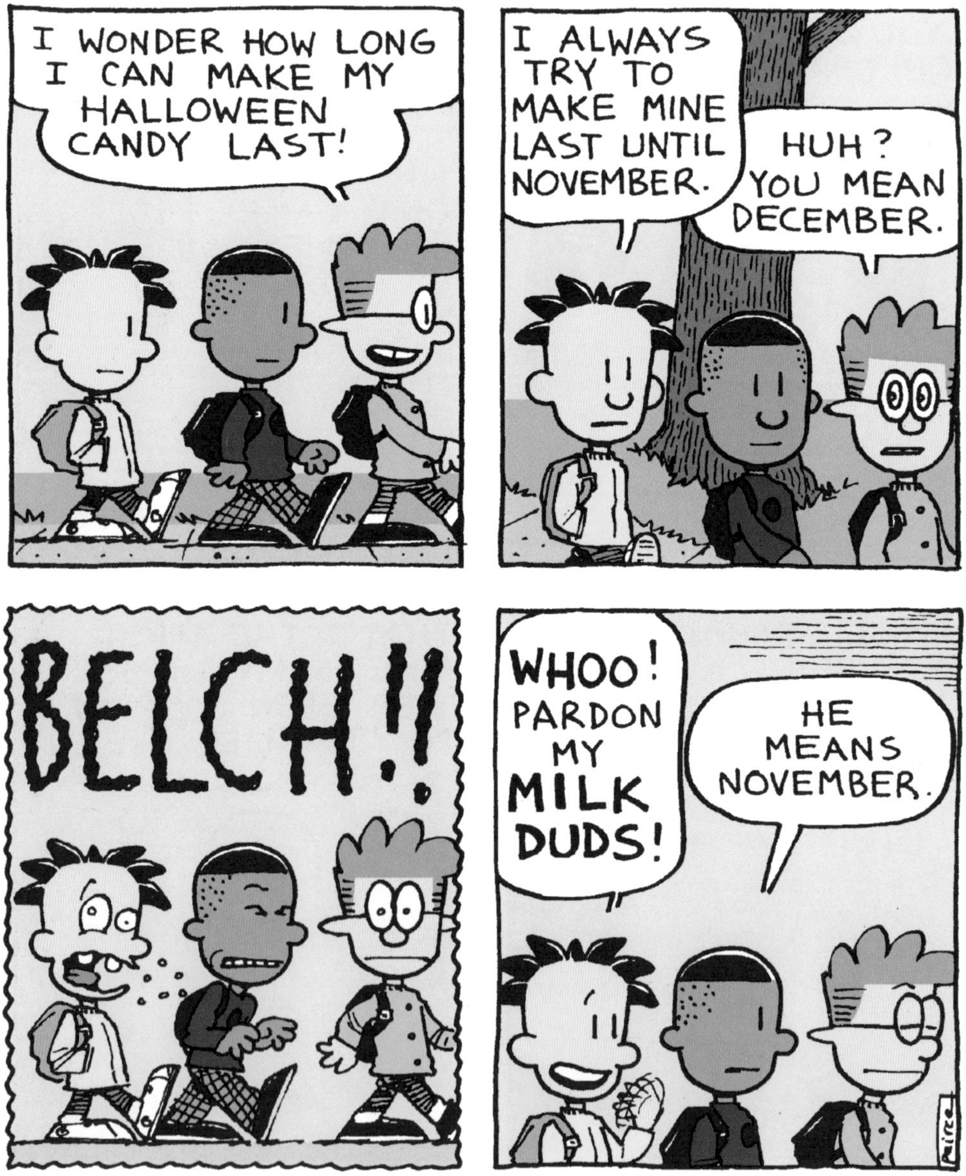
I WONDER HOW LONG I CAN MAKE MY HALLOWEEN CANDY LAST!
I ALWAYS TRY TO MAKE MINE LAST UNTIL NOVEMBER.
HUH? YOU MEAN DECEMBER.
BELCH!!
WHOO! PARDON MY MILK DUDS!
HE MEANS NOVEMBER.
PEIRCE

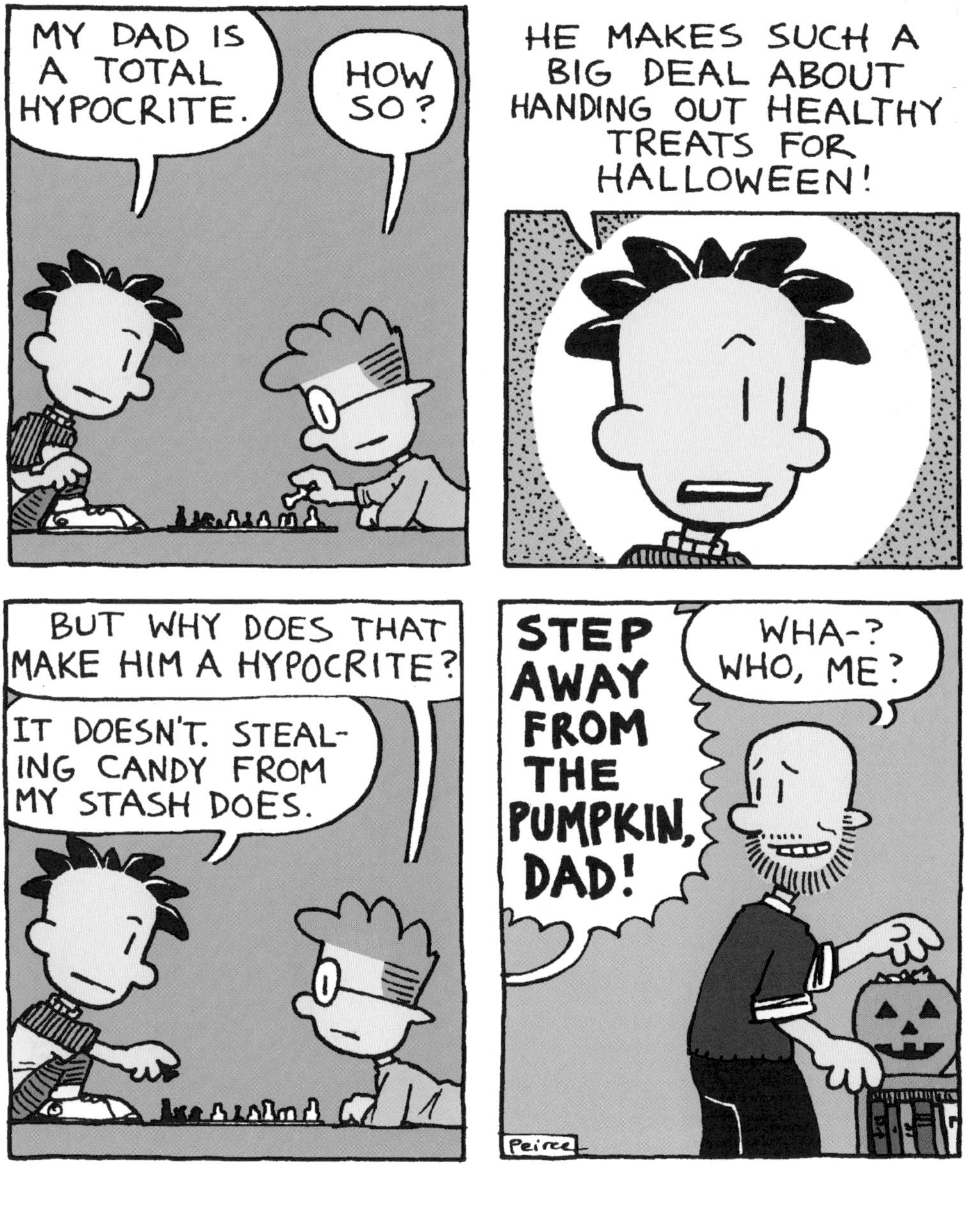
MY DAD IS A TOTAL HYPOCRITE.
HOW SO?
HE MAKES SUCH A BIG DEAL ABOUT HANDING OUT HEALTHY TREATS FOR HALLOWEEN!
BUT WHY DOES THAT MAKE HIM A HYPOCRITE?
IT DOESN'T. STEALING CANDY FROM MY STASH DOES.
STEP AWAY FROM THE PUMPKIN, DAD!
WHA-? WHO, ME?
Peirce

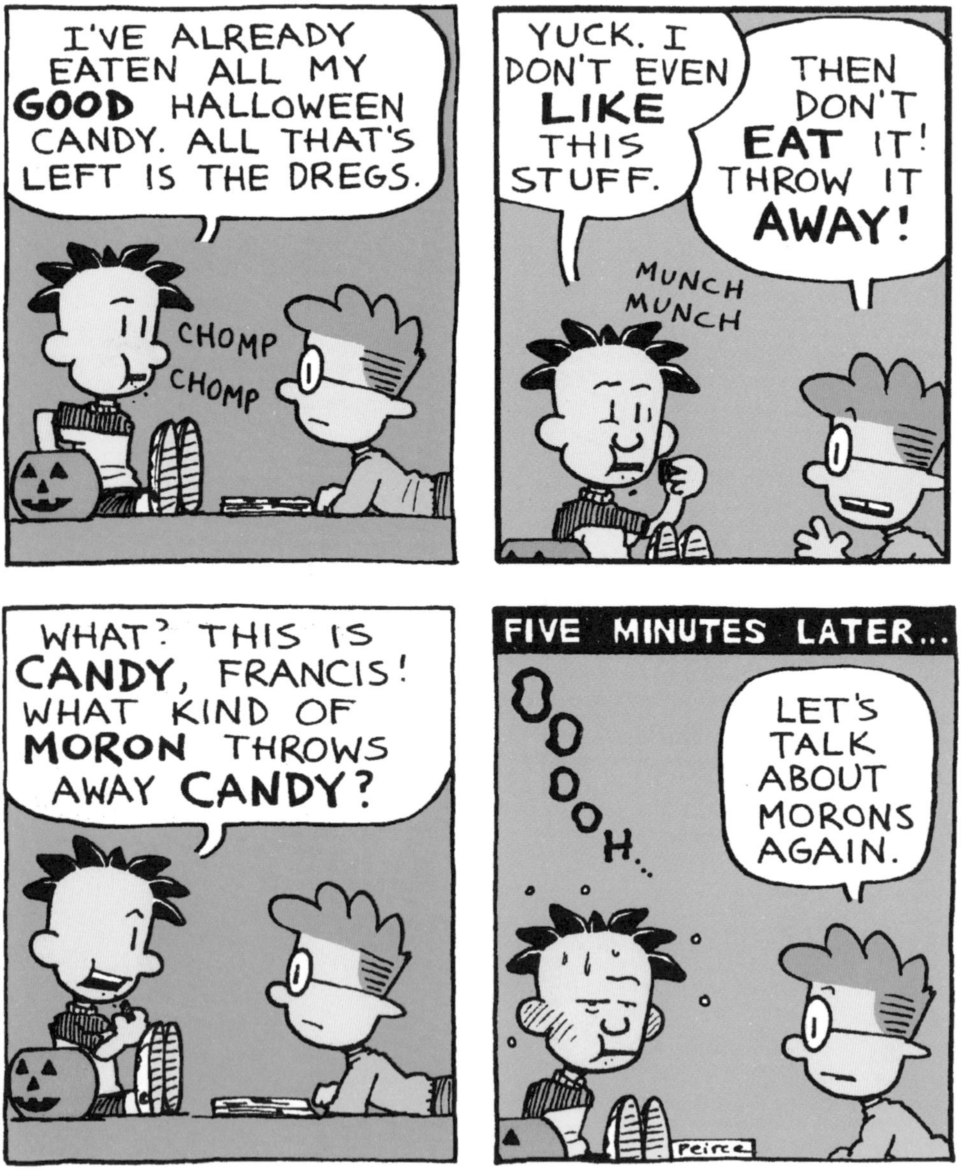
I'VE ALREADY EATEN ALL MY GOOD HALLOWEEN CANDY. ALL THAT'S LEFT IS THE DREGS.
CHOMP CHOMP
YUCK. I DON'T EVEN LIKE THIS STUFF.
THEN DON'T EAT IT! THROW IT AWAY!
MUNCH MUNCH
WHAT? THIS IS CANDY, FRANCIS! WHAT KIND OF MORON THROWS AWAY CANDY?
FIVE MINUTES LATER...
OOOOH...
LET'S TALK ABOUT MORONS AGAIN.
Peirce

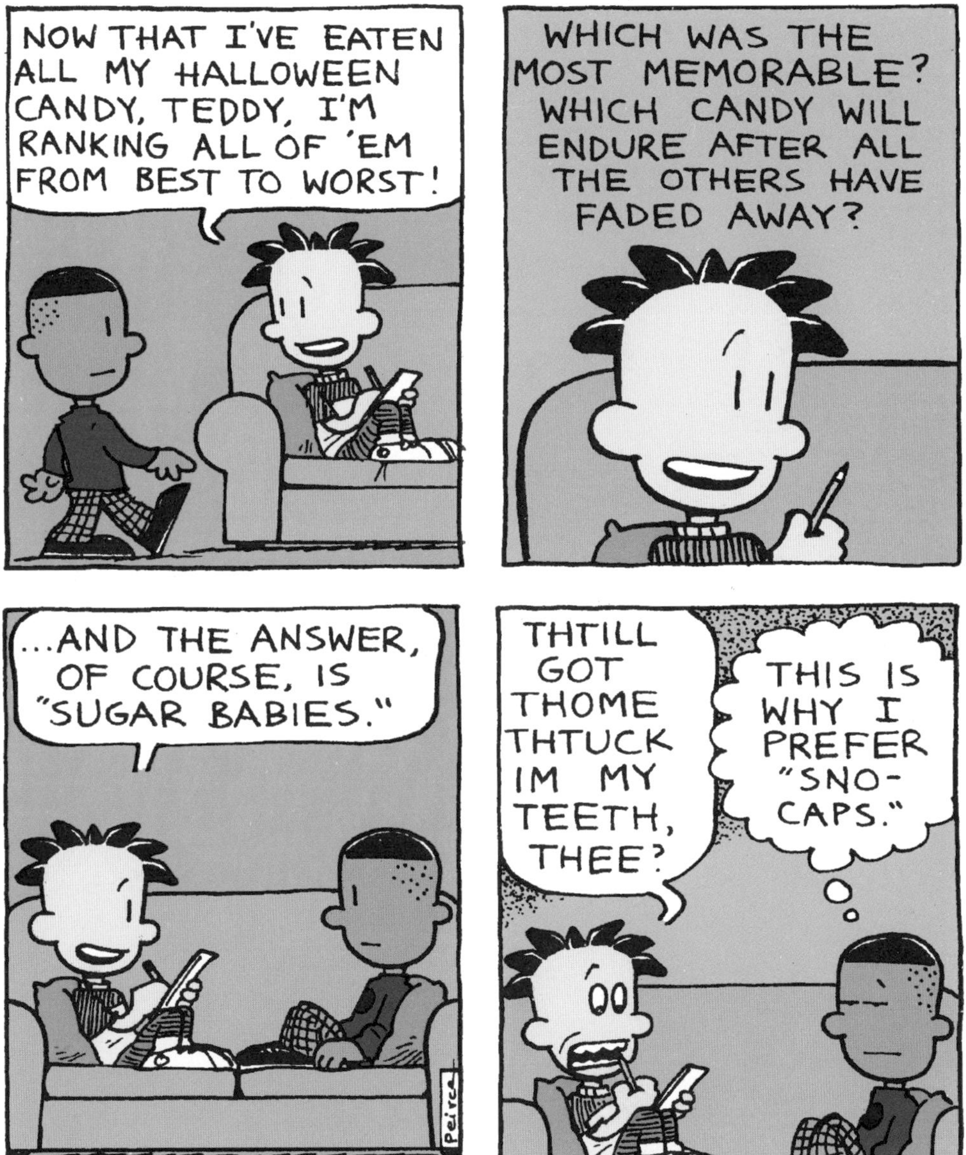
NOW THAT I'VE EATEN ALL MY HALLOWEEN CANDY, TEDDY, I'M RANKING ALL OF 'EM FROM BEST TO WORST!
WHICH WAS THE MOST MEMORABLE? WHICH CANDY WILL ENDURE AFTER ALL THE OTHERS HAVE FADED AWAY?
...AND THE ANSWER, OF COURSE, IS "SUGAR BABIES."
Peirce
THTILL GOT THOME THTUCK IM MY TEETH, THEE?
THIS IS WHY I PREFER "SNO-CAPS."

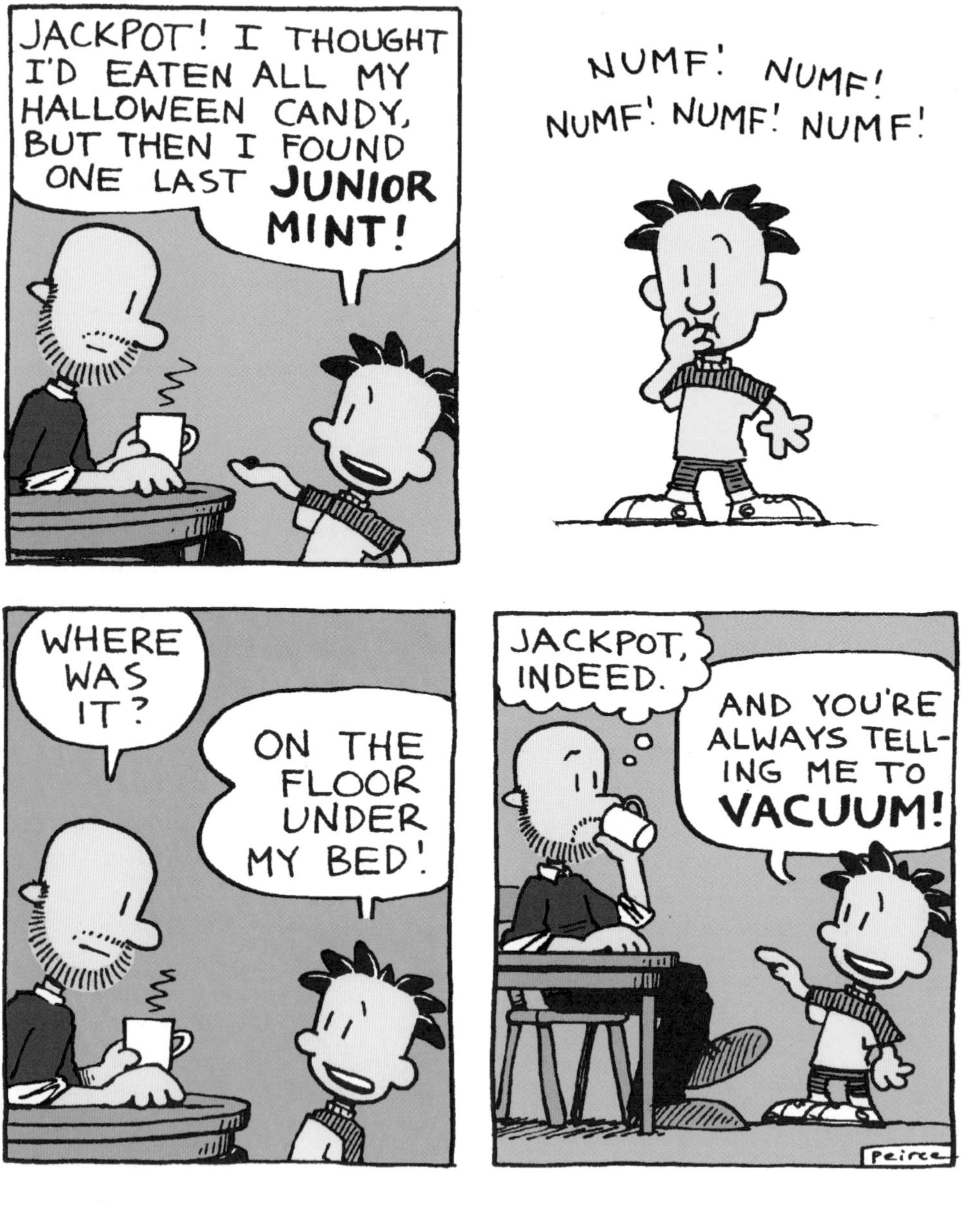
JACKPOT! I THOUGHT I'D EATEN ALL MY HALLOWEEN CANDY, BUT THEN I FOUND ONE LAST JUNIOR MINT!
NUMF! NUMF! NUMF! NUMF! NUMF!
WHERE WAS IT?
ON THE FLOOR UNDER MY BED!
JACKPOT, INDEED.
AND YOU'RE ALWAYS TELL-ING ME TO VACUUM!
Peirce

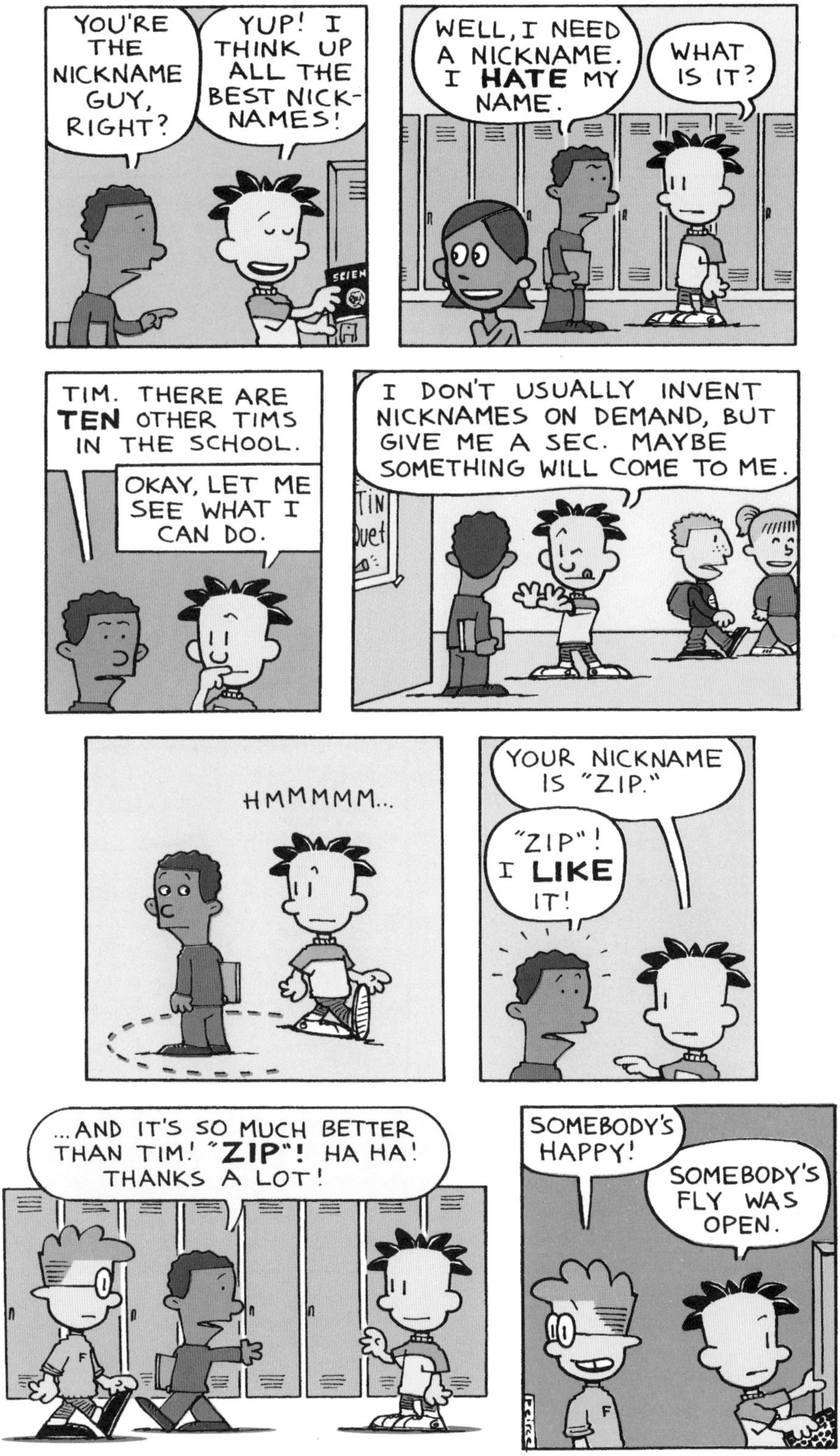
YOU'RE THE NICKNAME GUY, RIGHT?
YUP! I THINK UP ALL THE BEST NICK-NAMES!
WELL, I NEED A NICKNAME. I **HATE** MY NAME.
WHAT IS IT?
TIM. THERE ARE **TEN** OTHER TIMS IN THE SCHOOL.
OKAY, LET ME SEE WHAT I CAN DO.
I DON'T USUALLY INVENT NICKNAMES ON DEMAND, BUT GIVE ME A SEC. MAYBE SOMETHING WILL COME TO ME.
HMMMMM...
YOUR NICKNAME IS "ZIP."
"ZIP"! I **LIKE** IT!
...AND IT'S SO MUCH BETTER THAN TIM! **"ZIP"!** HA HA! THANKS A LOT!
SOMEBODY'S HAPPY!
SOMEBODY'S FLY WAS OPEN.

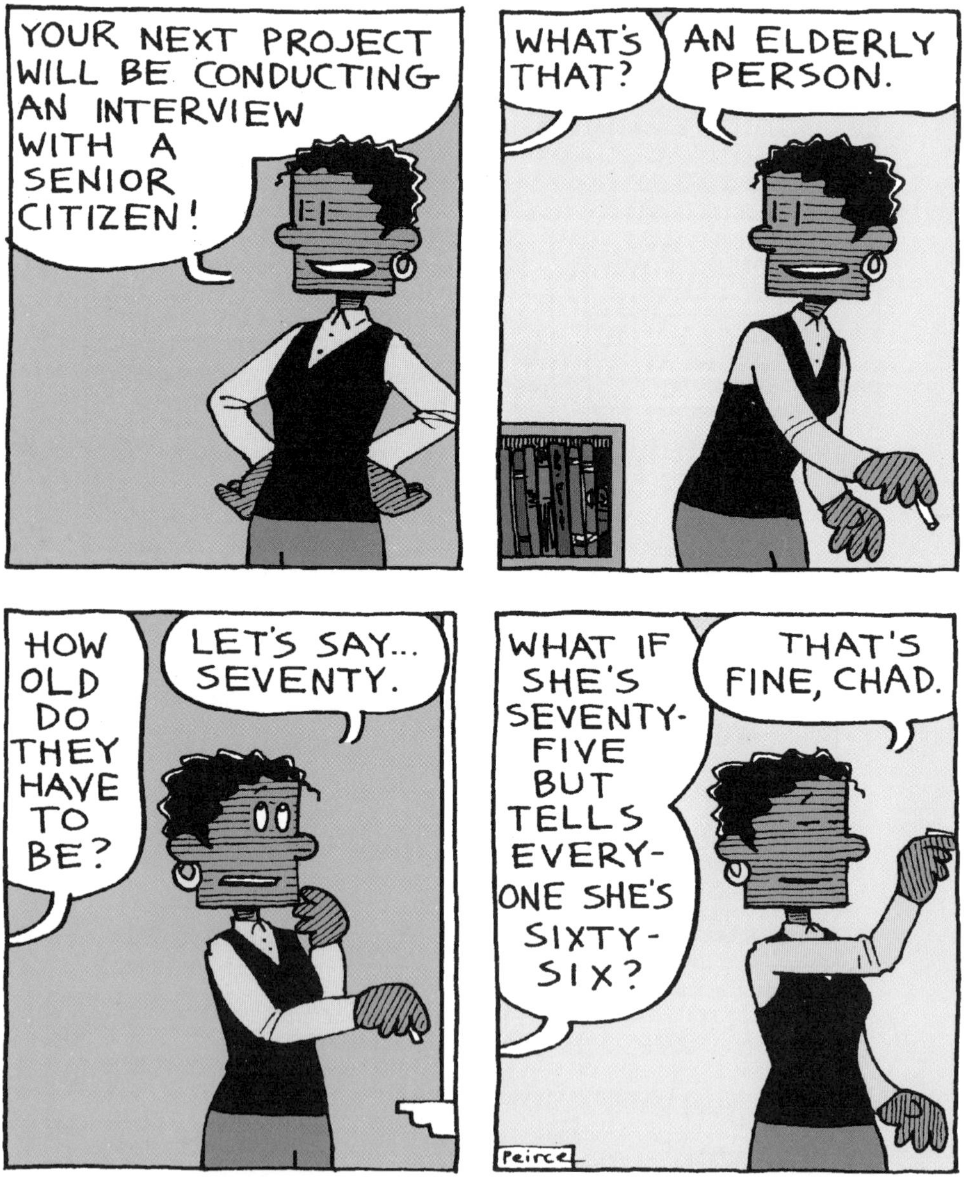
YOUR NEXT PROJECT WILL BE CONDUCTING AN INTERVIEW WITH A SENIOR CITIZEN!
WHAT'S THAT?
AN ELDERLY PERSON.
HOW OLD DO THEY HAVE TO BE?
LET'S SAY... SEVENTY.
WHAT IF SHE'S SEVENTY-FIVE BUT TELLS EVERYONE SHE'S SIXTY-SIX?
THAT'S FINE, CHAD.
Peirce

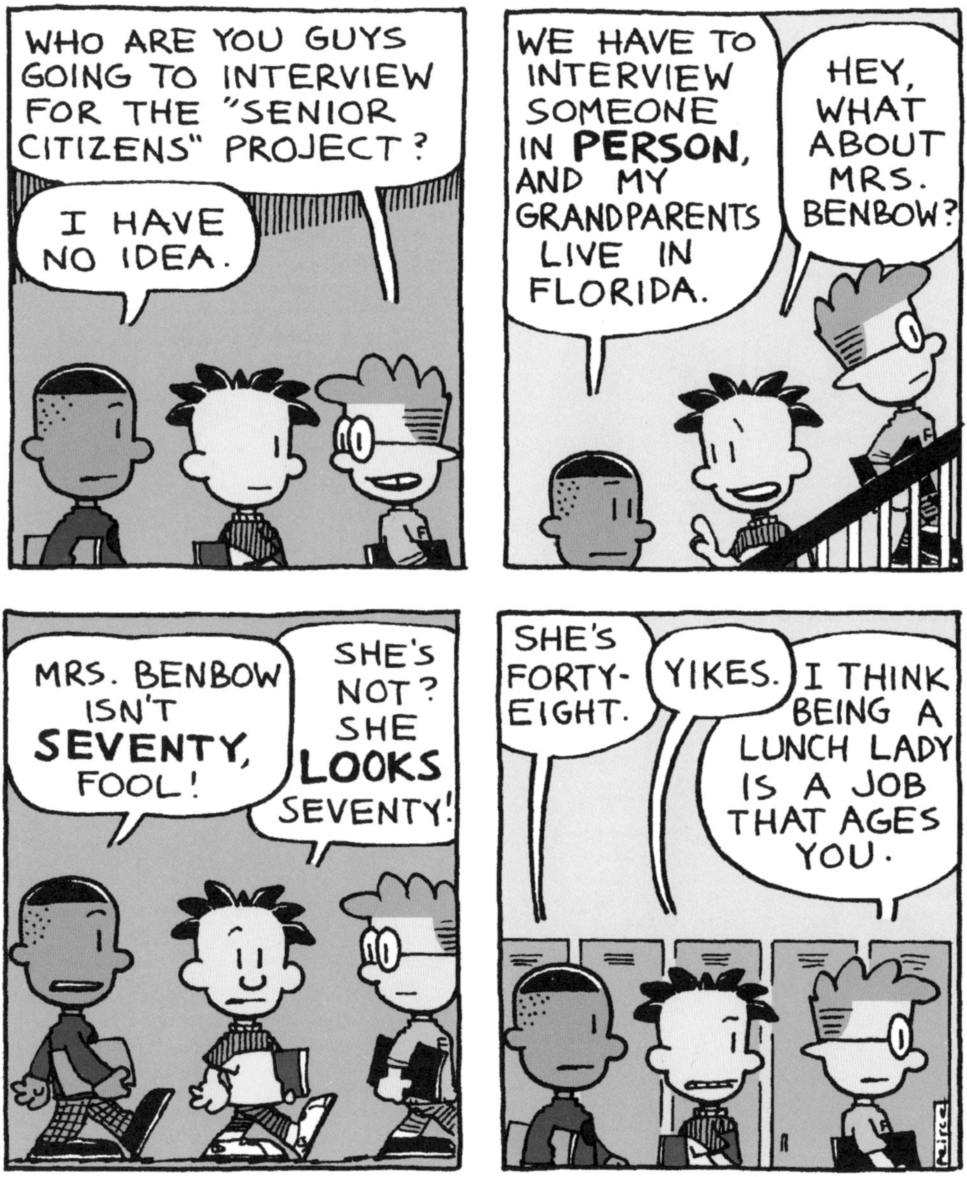
WHO ARE YOU GUYS GOING TO INTERVIEW FOR THE "SENIOR CITIZENS" PROJECT?
I HAVE NO IDEA.
WE HAVE TO INTERVIEW SOMEONE IN **PERSON**, AND MY GRANDPARENTS LIVE IN FLORIDA.
HEY, WHAT ABOUT MRS. BENBOW?
MRS. BENBOW ISN'T **SEVENTY**, FOOL!
SHE'S NOT? SHE **LOOKS** SEVENTY!
SHE'S FORTY-EIGHT.
YIKES.
I THINK BEING A LUNCH LADY IS A JOB THAT AGES YOU.

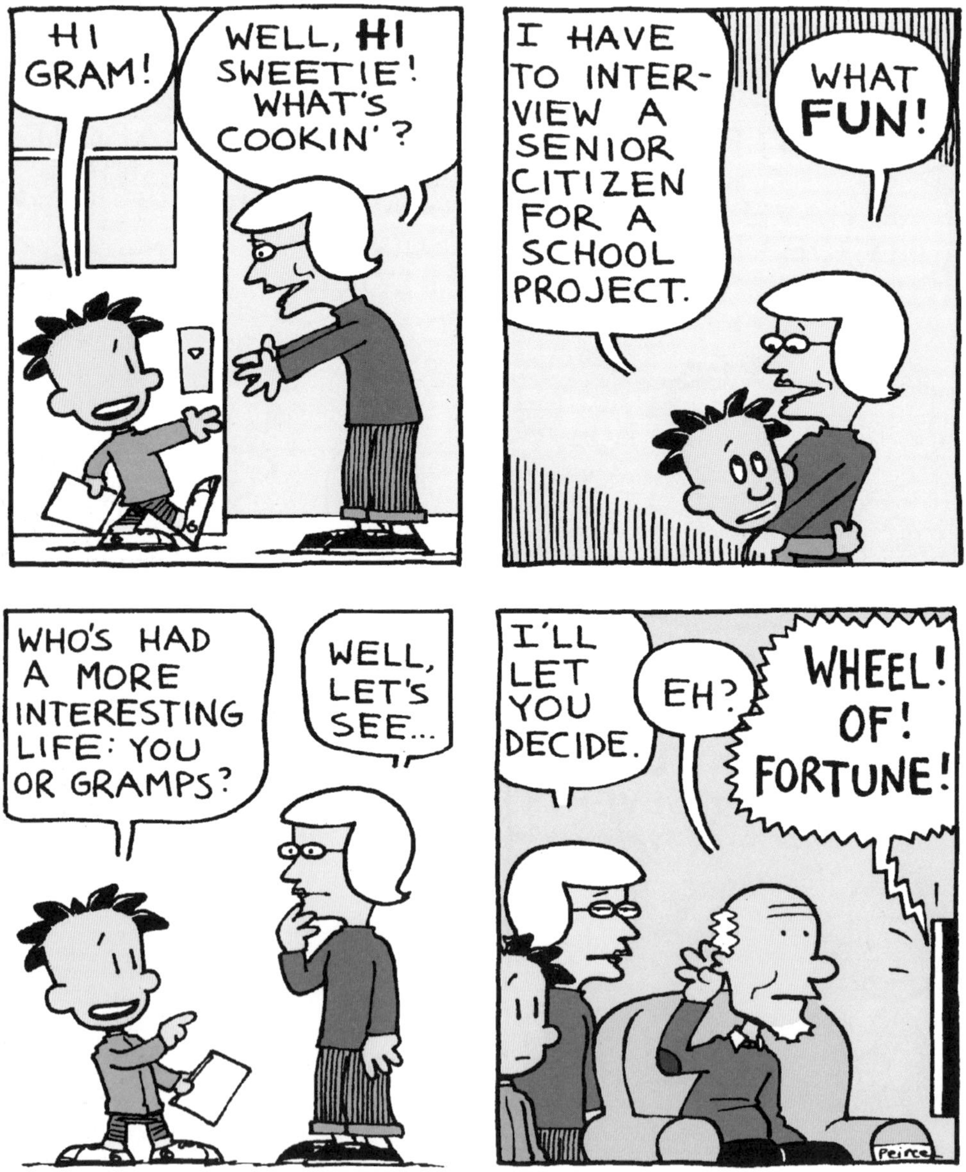
HI GRAM!
WELL, **HI** SWEETIE! WHAT'S COOKIN'?
I HAVE TO INTER-VIEW A SENIOR CITIZEN FOR A SCHOOL PROJECT.
WHAT **FUN**!
WHO'S HAD A MORE INTERESTING LIFE: YOU OR GRAMPS?
WELL, LET'S SEE...
I'LL LET YOU DECIDE.
EH?
WHEEL! OF! FORTUNE!
Peirce

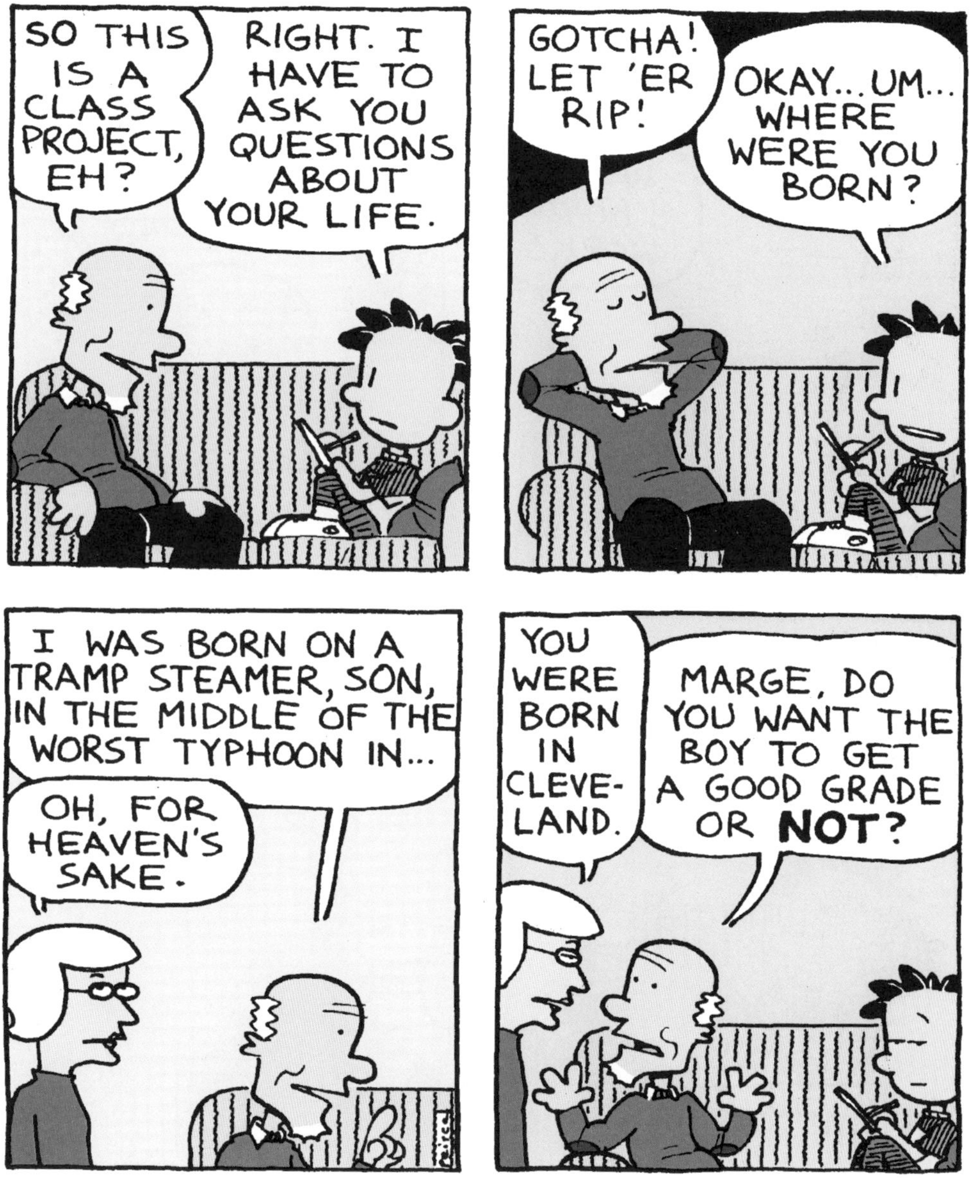
SO THIS IS A CLASS PROJECT, EH?
RIGHT. I HAVE TO ASK YOU QUESTIONS ABOUT YOUR LIFE.
GOTCHA! LET 'ER RIP!
OKAY... UM... WHERE WERE YOU BORN?
I WAS BORN ON A TRAMP STEAMER, SON, IN THE MIDDLE OF THE WORST TYPHOON IN...
OH, FOR HEAVEN'S SAKE.
YOU WERE BORN IN CLEVE-LAND.
MARGE, DO YOU WANT THE BOY TO GET A GOOD GRADE OR **NOT**?

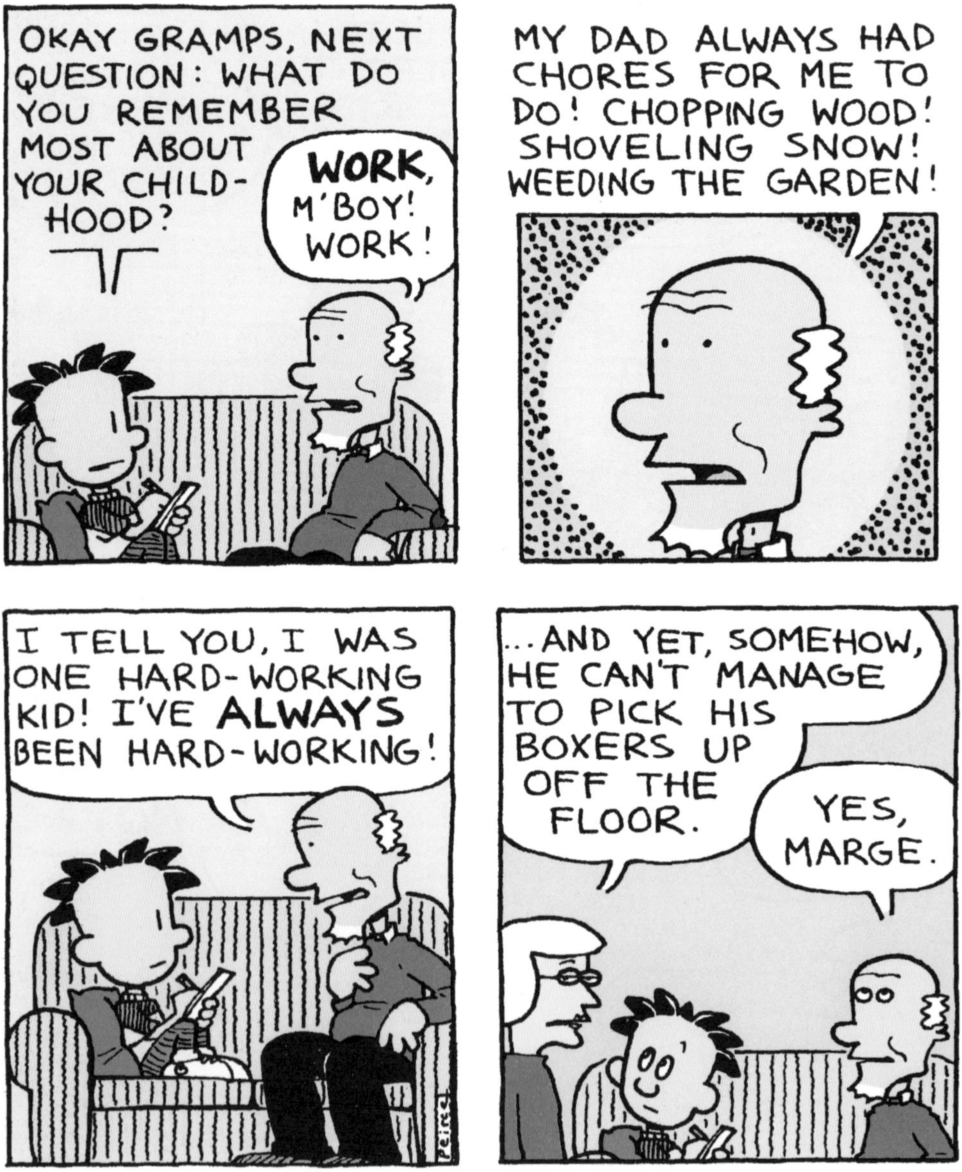
OKAY GRAMPS, NEXT QUESTION: WHAT DO YOU REMEMBER MOST ABOUT YOUR CHILD-HOOD?
WORK, M'BOY! WORK!
MY DAD ALWAYS HAD CHORES FOR ME TO DO! CHOPPING WOOD! SHOVELING SNOW! WEEDING THE GARDEN!
I TELL YOU, I WAS ONE HARD-WORKING KID! I'VE ALWAYS BEEN HARD-WORKING!
...AND YET, SOMEHOW, HE CAN'T MANAGE TO PICK HIS BOXERS UP OFF THE FLOOR.
YES, MARGE.

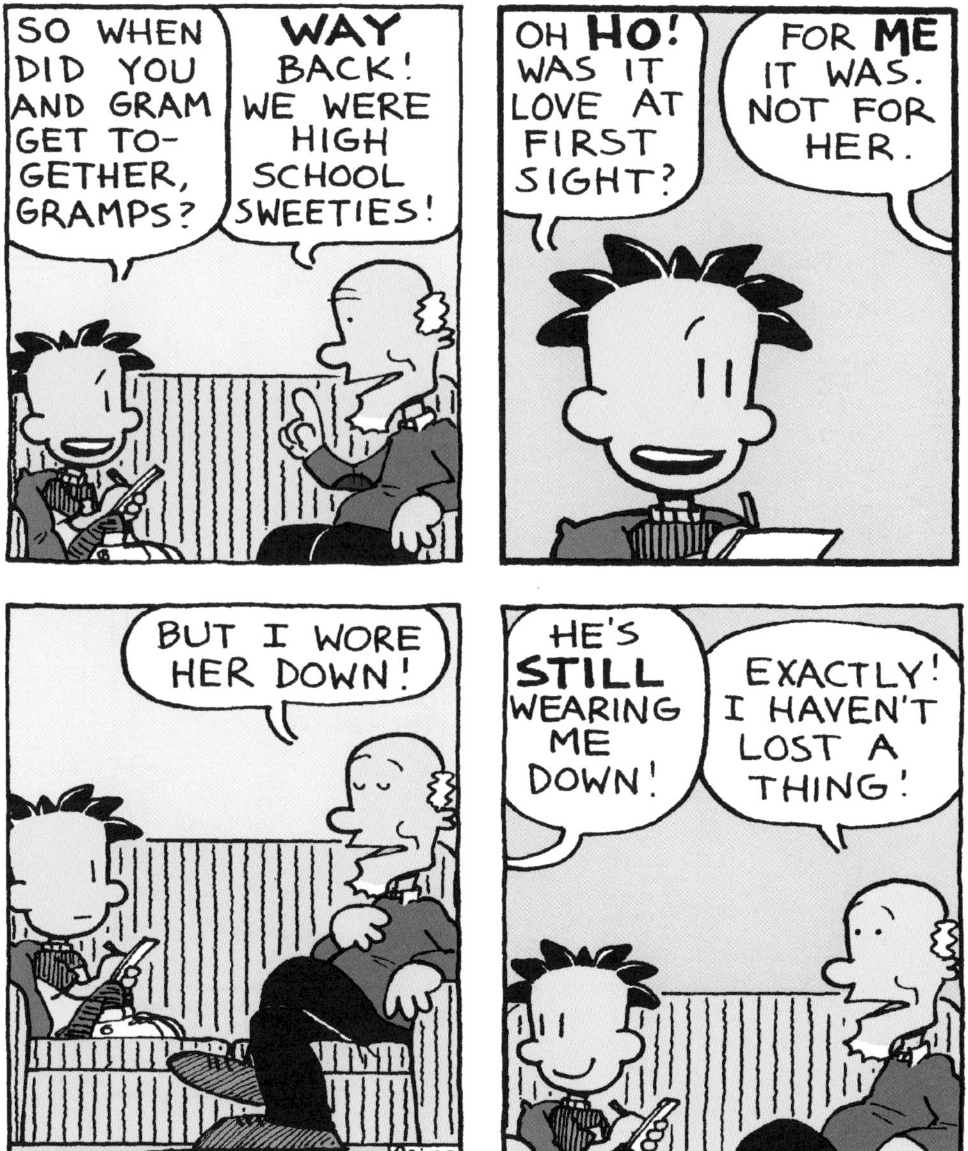
SO WHEN DID YOU AND GRAM GET TOGETHER, GRAMPS?
WAY BACK! WE WERE HIGH SCHOOL SWEETIES!
OH HO! WAS IT LOVE AT FIRST SIGHT?
FOR ME IT WAS. NOT FOR HER.
BUT I WORE HER DOWN!
HE'S STILL WEARING ME DOWN!
EXACTLY! I HAVEN'T LOST A THING!
Peirce

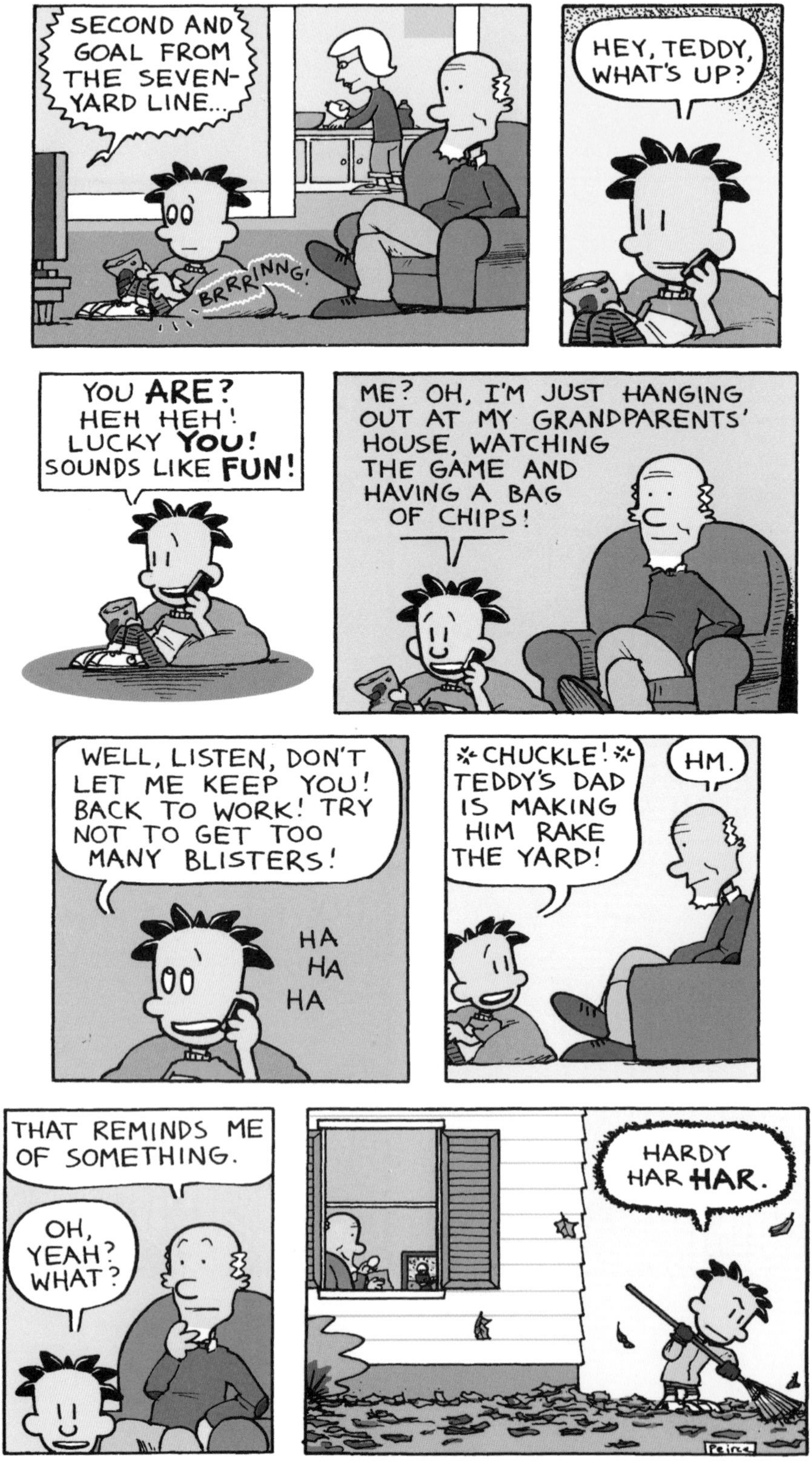
SECOND AND GOAL FROM THE SEVEN-YARD LINE...
BRRRINNG!
HEY, TEDDY, WHAT'S UP?
YOU ARE? HEH HEH! LUCKY YOU! SOUNDS LIKE FUN!
ME? OH, I'M JUST HANGING OUT AT MY GRANDPARENTS' HOUSE, WATCHING THE GAME AND HAVING A BAG OF CHIPS!
WELL, LISTEN, DON'T LET ME KEEP YOU! BACK TO WORK! TRY NOT TO GET TOO MANY BLISTERS!
HA HA HA
CHUCKLE! TEDDY'S DAD IS MAKING HIM RAKE THE YARD!
HM.
THAT REMINDS ME OF SOMETHING.
OH, YEAH? WHAT?
HARDY HAR HAR.
Peirce

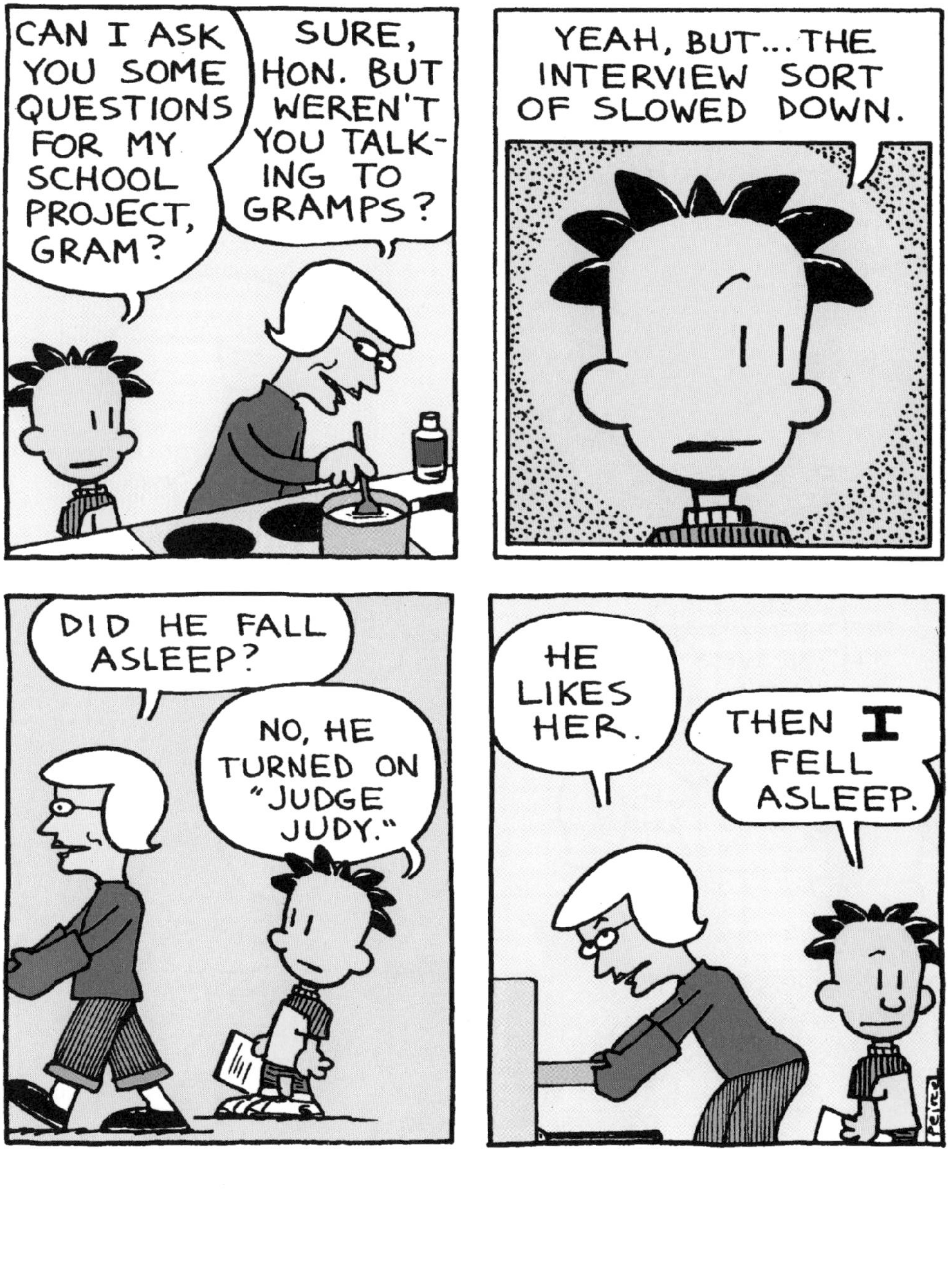
CAN I ASK YOU SOME QUESTIONS FOR MY SCHOOL PROJECT, GRAM?
SURE, HON. BUT WEREN'T YOU TALKING TO GRAMPS?
YEAH, BUT... THE INTERVIEW SORT OF SLOWED DOWN.
DID HE FALL ASLEEP?
NO, HE TURNED ON "JUDGE JUDY."
HE LIKES HER.
THEN I FELL ASLEEP.
PEIRCE

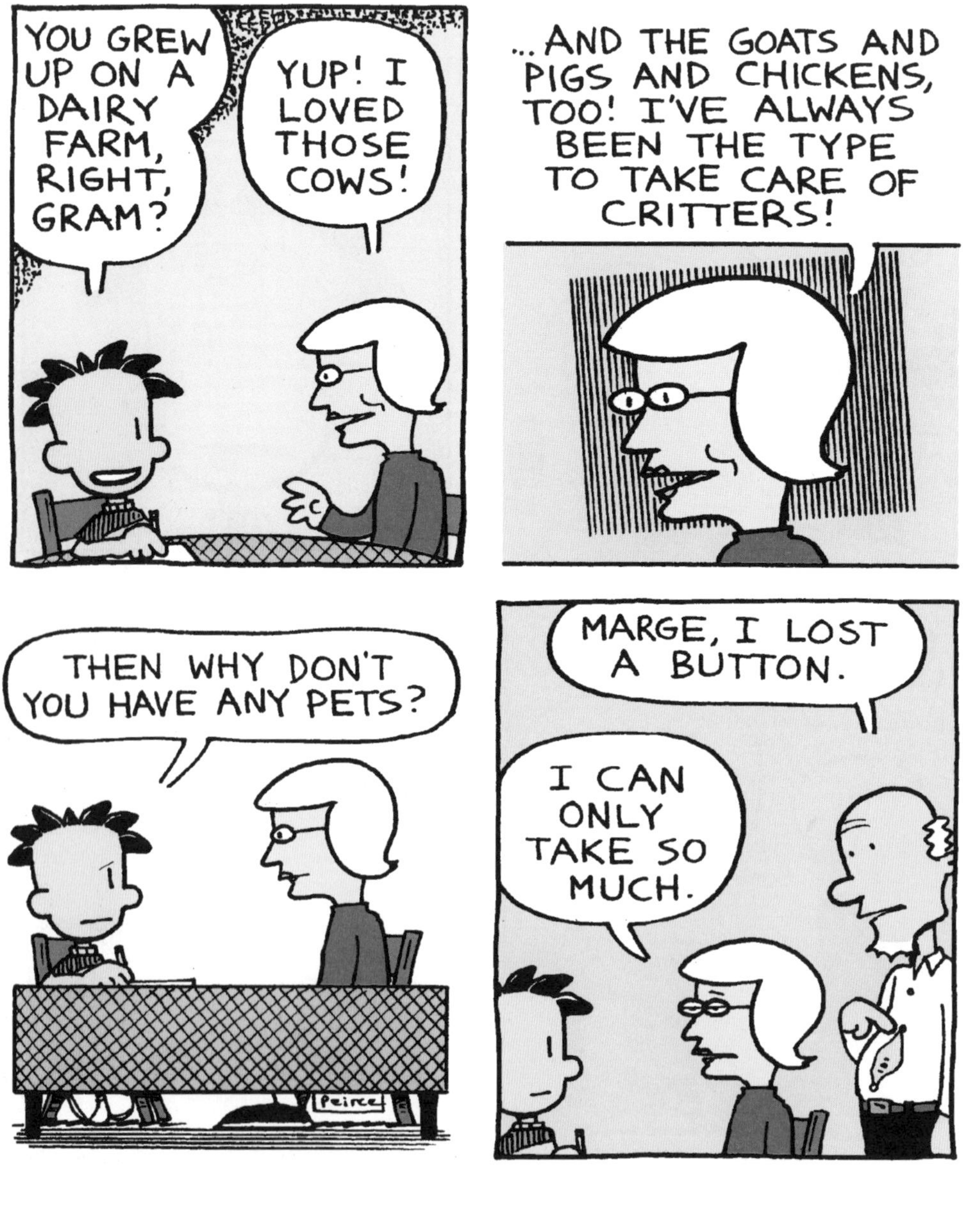
YOU GREW UP ON A DAIRY FARM, RIGHT, GRAM?
YUP! I LOVED THOSE COWS!
...AND THE GOATS AND PIGS AND CHICKENS, TOO! I'VE ALWAYS BEEN THE TYPE TO TAKE CARE OF CRITTERS!
THEN WHY DON'T YOU HAVE ANY PETS?
Peirce
MARGE, I LOST A BUTTON.
I CAN ONLY TAKE SO MUCH.

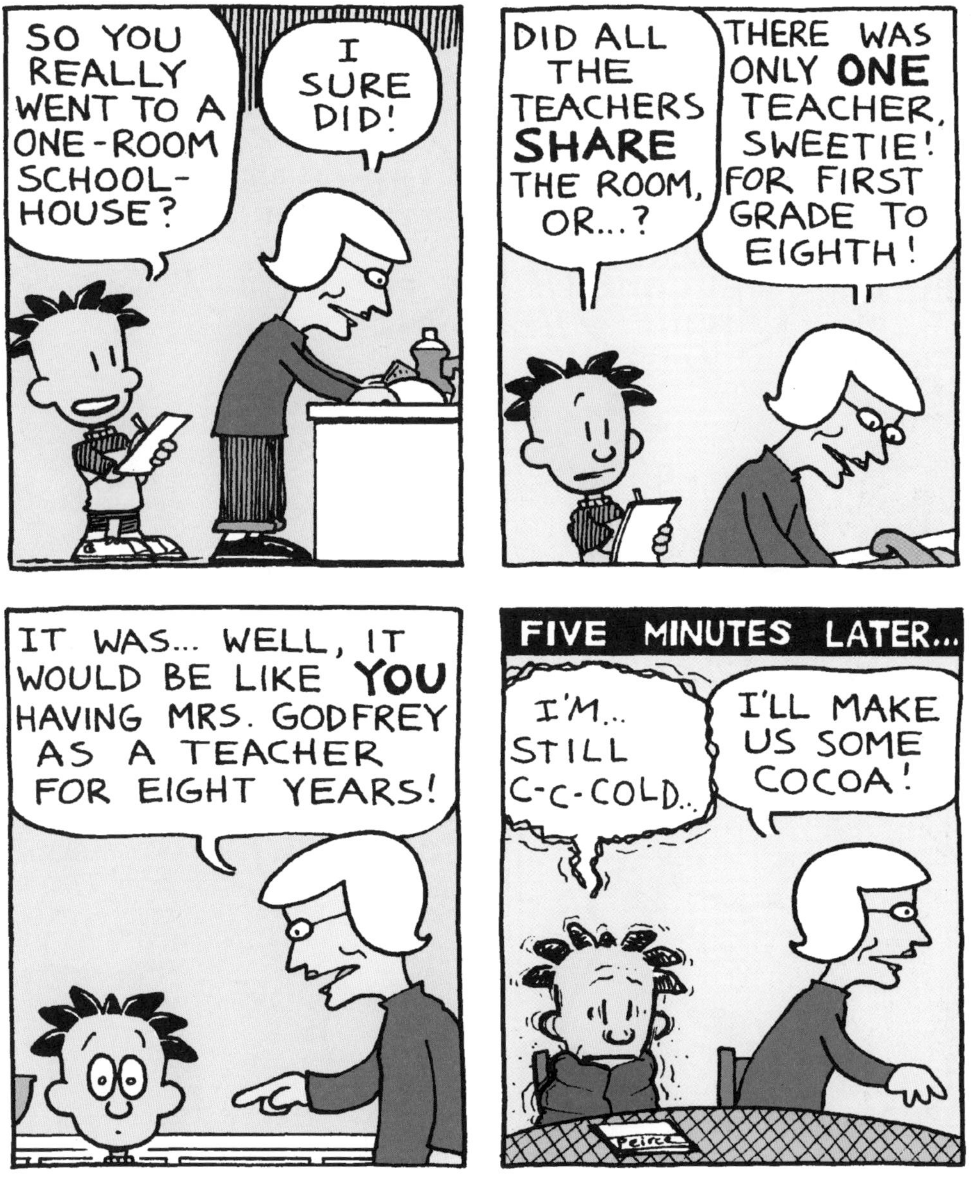
SO YOU REALLY WENT TO A ONE-ROOM SCHOOL-HOUSE?
I SURE DID!
DID ALL THE TEACHERS SHARE THE ROOM, OR...?
THERE WAS ONLY ONE TEACHER, SWEETIE! FOR FIRST GRADE TO EIGHTH!
IT WAS... WELL, IT WOULD BE LIKE YOU HAVING MRS. GODFREY AS A TEACHER FOR EIGHT YEARS!
FIVE MINUTES LATER...
I'M... STILL C-C-COLD...
I'LL MAKE US SOME COCOA!
Peirce

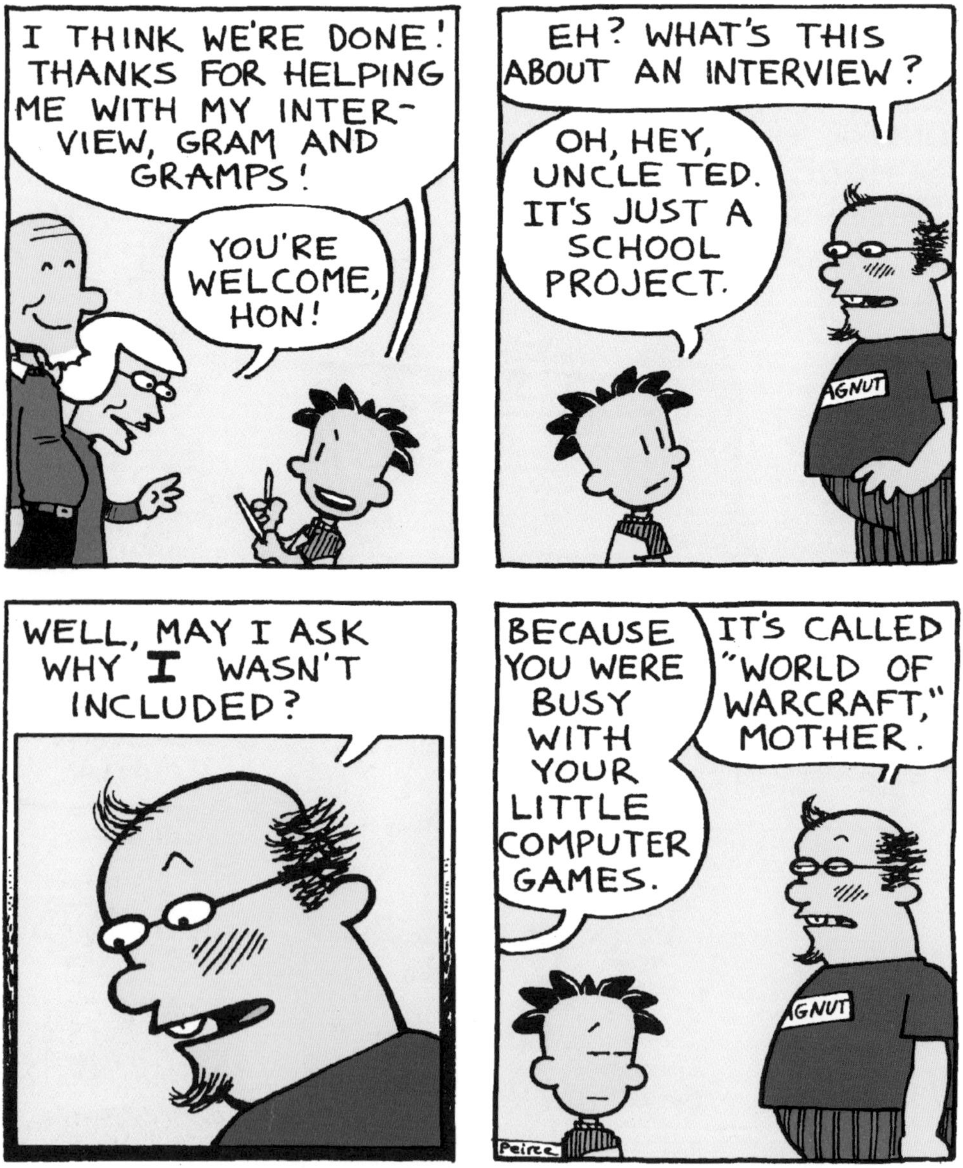
I THINK WE'RE DONE! THANKS FOR HELPING ME WITH MY INTER-VIEW, GRAM AND GRAMPS!
YOU'RE WELCOME, HON!
EH? WHAT'S THIS ABOUT AN INTERVIEW?
OH, HEY, UNCLE TED. IT'S JUST A SCHOOL PROJECT.
AGNUT
WELL, MAY I ASK WHY **I** WASN'T INCLUDED?
BECAUSE YOU WERE BUSY WITH YOUR LITTLE COMPUTER GAMES.
IT'S CALLED "WORLD OF WARCRAFT," MOTHER.
GNUT
Peirce

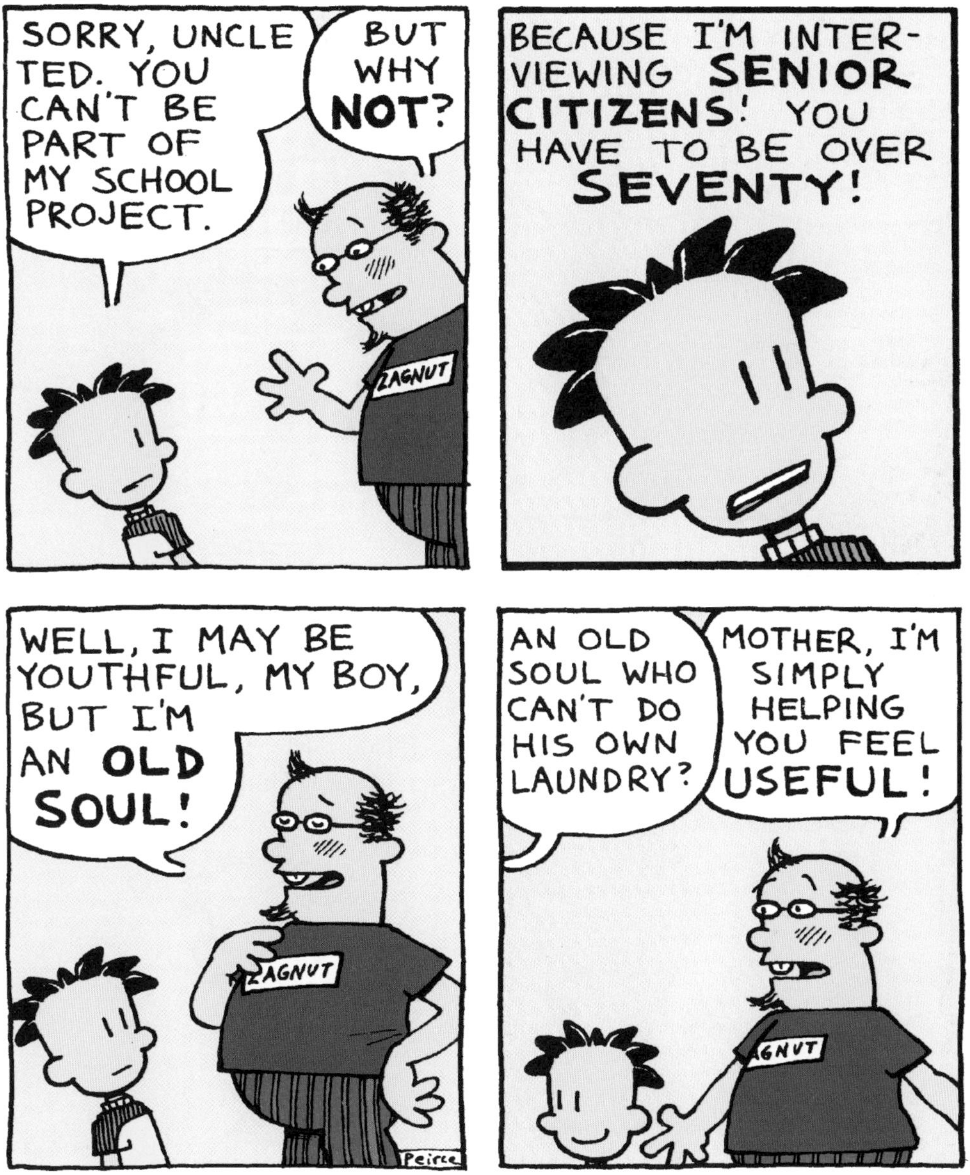
SORRY, UNCLE TED. YOU CAN'T BE PART OF MY SCHOOL PROJECT.
BUT WHY NOT?
ZAGNUT
BECAUSE I'M INTER-VIEWING SENIOR CITIZENS! YOU HAVE TO BE OVER SEVENTY!
WELL, I MAY BE YOUTHFUL, MY BOY, BUT I'M AN OLD SOUL!
ZAGNUT
Peirce
AN OLD SOUL WHO CAN'T DO HIS OWN LAUNDRY?
MOTHER, I'M SIMPLY HELPING YOU FEEL USEFUL!
AGNUT

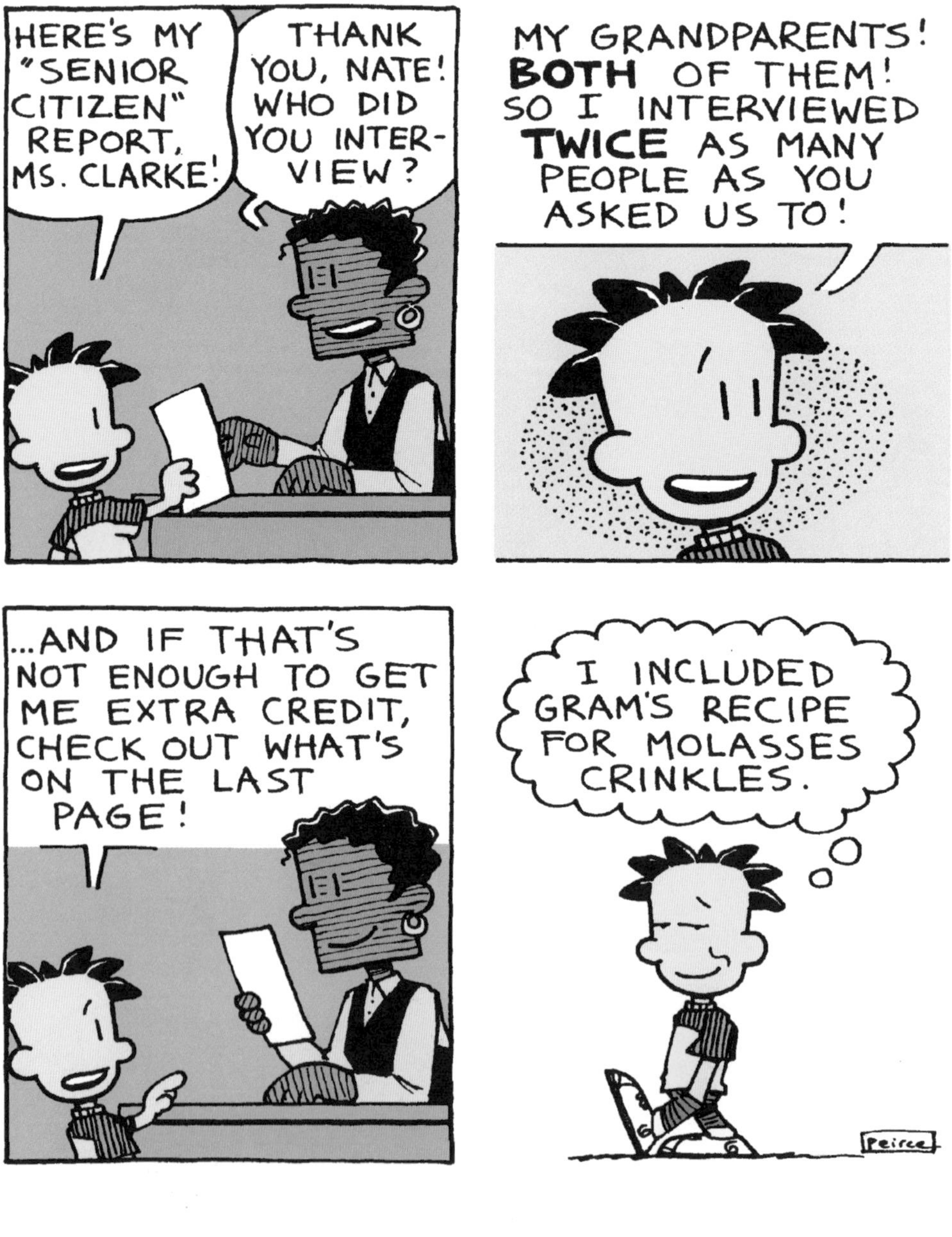
HERE'S MY "SENIOR CITIZEN" REPORT, MS. CLARKE!
THANK YOU, NATE! WHO DID YOU INTERVIEW?
MY GRANDPARENTS! BOTH OF THEM! SO I INTERVIEWED TWICE AS MANY PEOPLE AS YOU ASKED US TO!
...AND IF THAT'S NOT ENOUGH TO GET ME EXTRA CREDIT, CHECK OUT WHAT'S ON THE LAST PAGE!
I INCLUDED GRAM'S RECIPE FOR MOLASSES CRINKLES.
Peirce

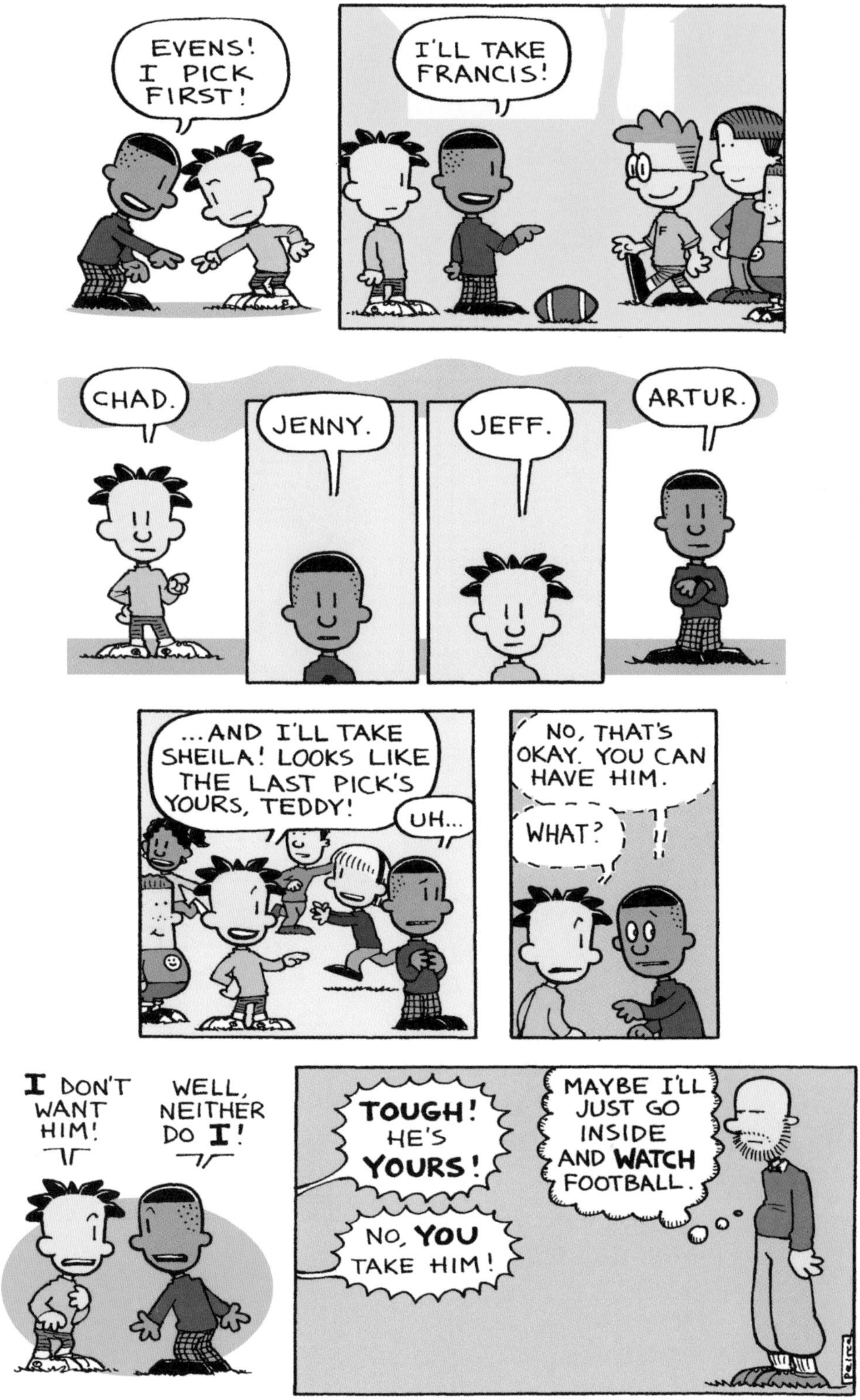
EVENS! I PICK FIRST!
I'LL TAKE FRANCIS!
CHAD.
JENNY.
JEFF.
ARTUR.
...AND I'LL TAKE SHEILA! LOOKS LIKE THE LAST PICK'S YOURS, TEDDY!
UH...
NO, THAT'S OKAY. YOU CAN HAVE HIM.
WHAT?
I DON'T WANT HIM!
WELL, NEITHER DO I!
TOUGH! HE'S YOURS!
NO, YOU TAKE HIM!
MAYBE I'LL JUST GO INSIDE AND WATCH FOOTBALL.
PEIRCE

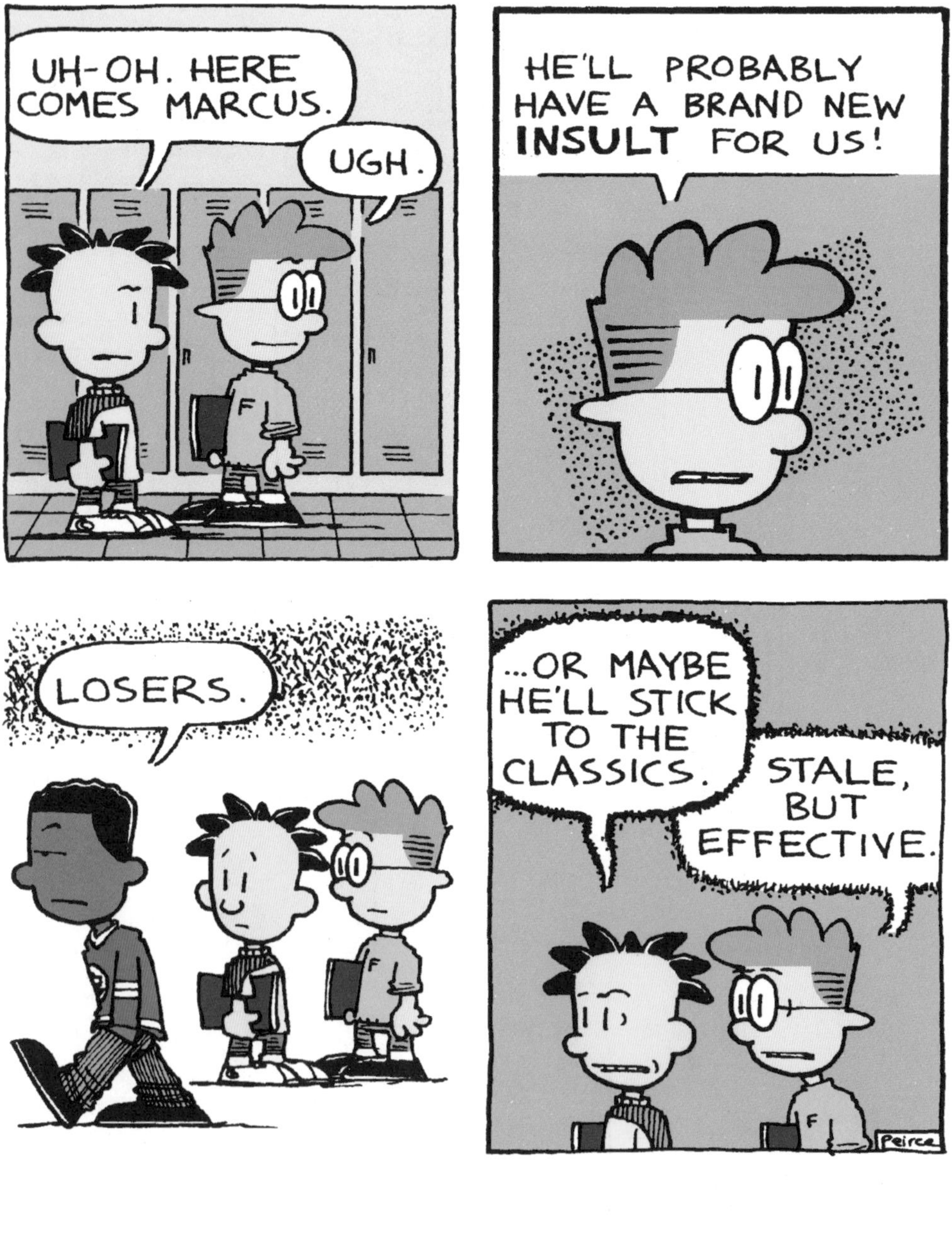
UH-OH. HERE COMES MARCUS.
UGH.
HE'LL PROBABLY HAVE A BRAND NEW **INSULT** FOR US!
LOSERS.
...OR MAYBE HE'LL STICK TO THE CLASSICS.
STALE, BUT EFFECTIVE.
Peirce

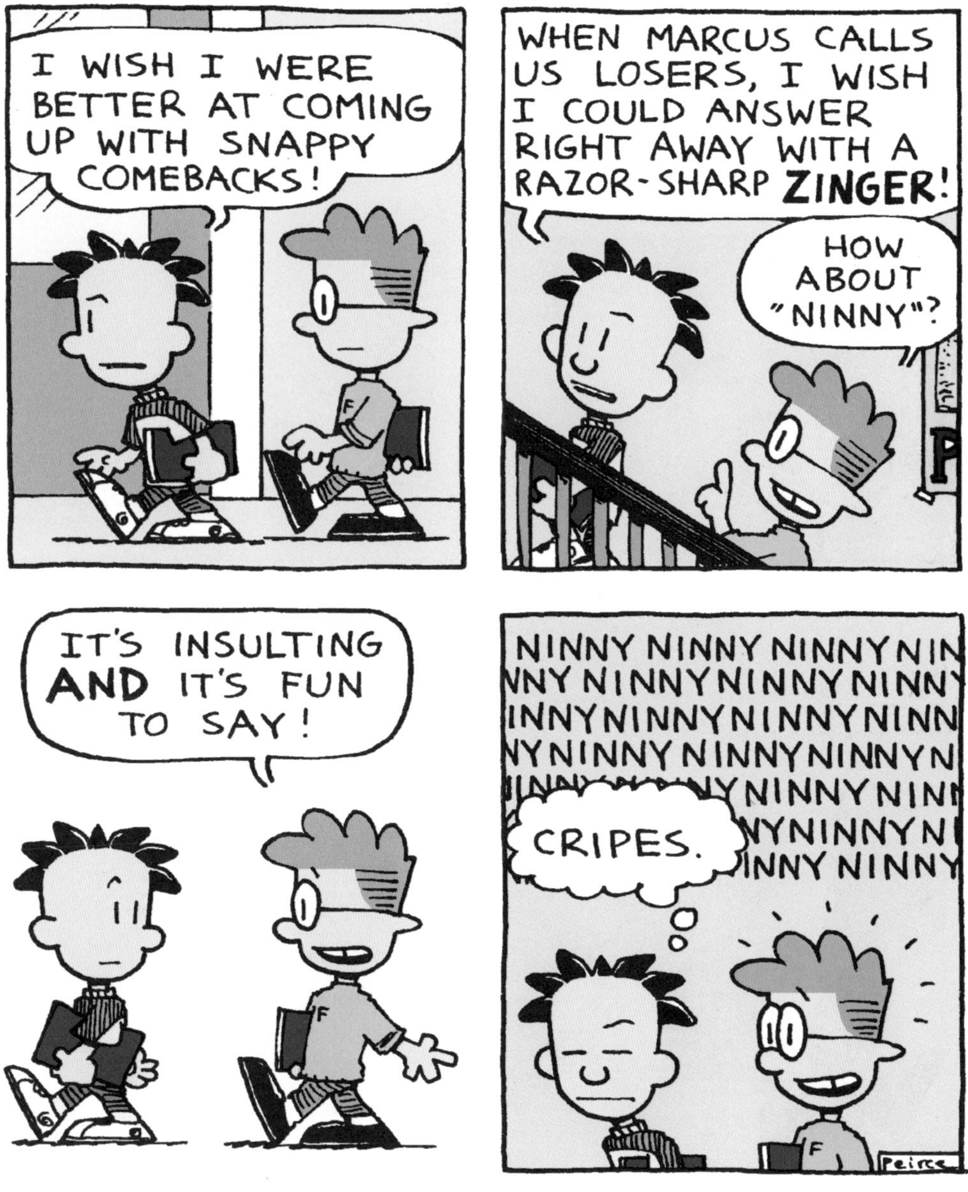
I WISH I WERE BETTER AT COMING UP WITH SNAPPY COMEBACKS!
WHEN MARCUS CALLS US LOSERS, I WISH I COULD ANSWER RIGHT AWAY WITH A RAZOR-SHARP **ZINGER**!
HOW ABOUT "NINNY"?
IT'S INSULTING **AND** IT'S FUN TO SAY!
CRIPES.
Peirce

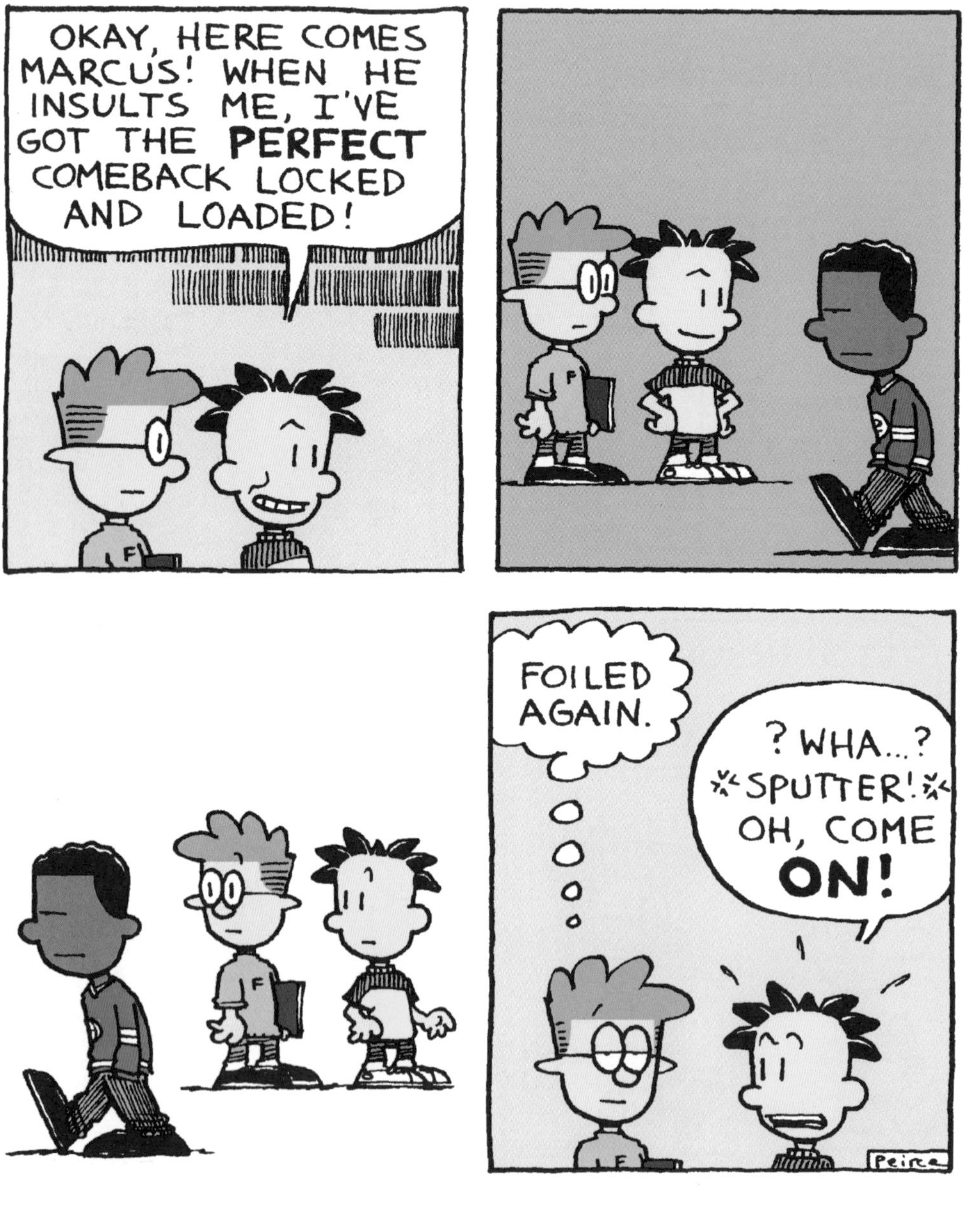
OKAY, HERE COMES MARCUS! WHEN HE INSULTS ME, I'VE GOT THE **PERFECT** COMEBACK LOCKED AND LOADED!
FOILED AGAIN.
? WHA...? SPUTTER! OH, COME **ON!**
peirce

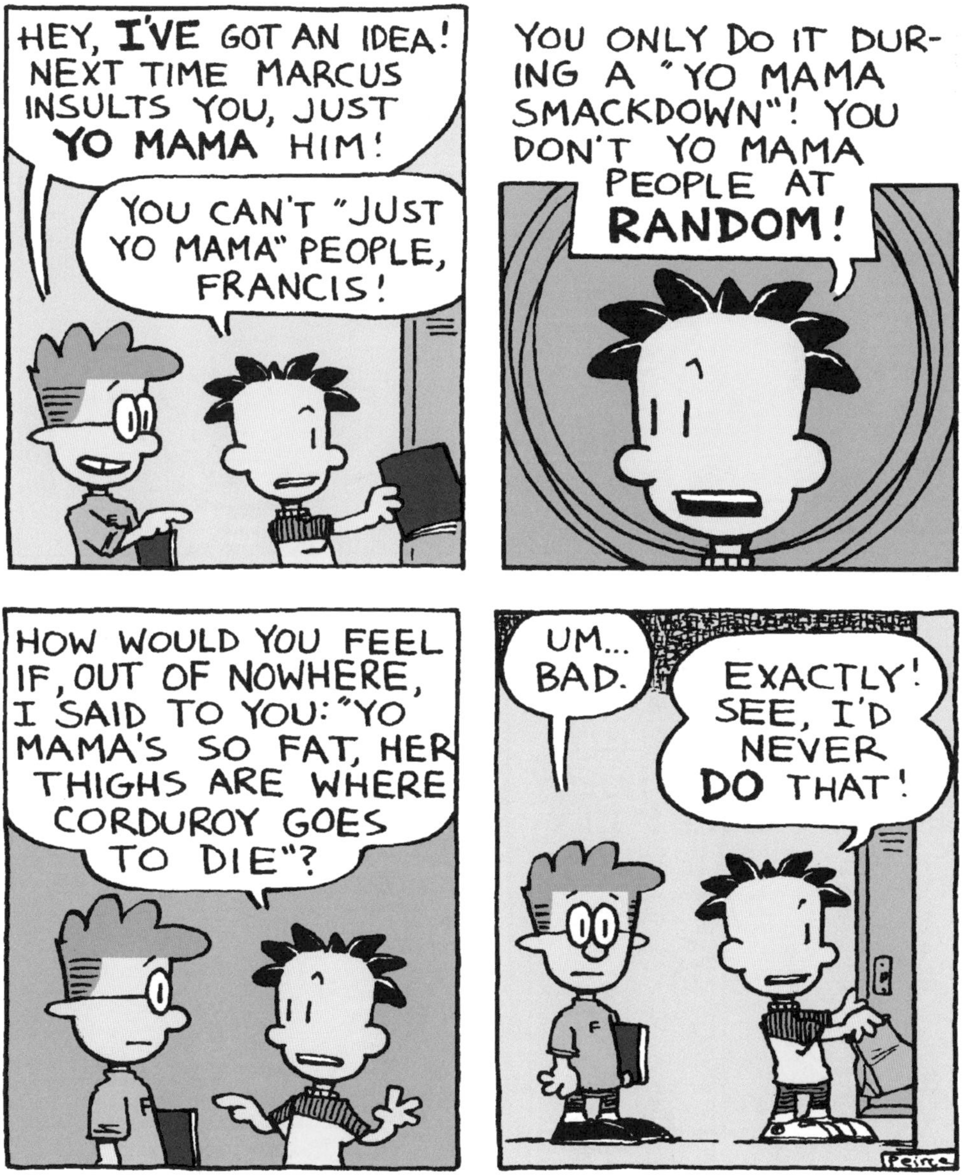
HEY, I'VE GOT AN IDEA! NEXT TIME MARCUS INSULTS YOU, JUST YO MAMA HIM!
YOU CAN'T "JUST YO MAMA" PEOPLE, FRANCIS!
YOU ONLY DO IT DURING A "YO MAMA SMACKDOWN"! YOU DON'T YO MAMA PEOPLE AT RANDOM!
HOW WOULD YOU FEEL IF, OUT OF NOWHERE, I SAID TO YOU: "YO MAMA'S SO FAT, HER THIGHS ARE WHERE CORDUROY GOES TO DIE"?
UM... BAD.
EXACTLY! SEE, I'D NEVER DO THAT!
Peirce

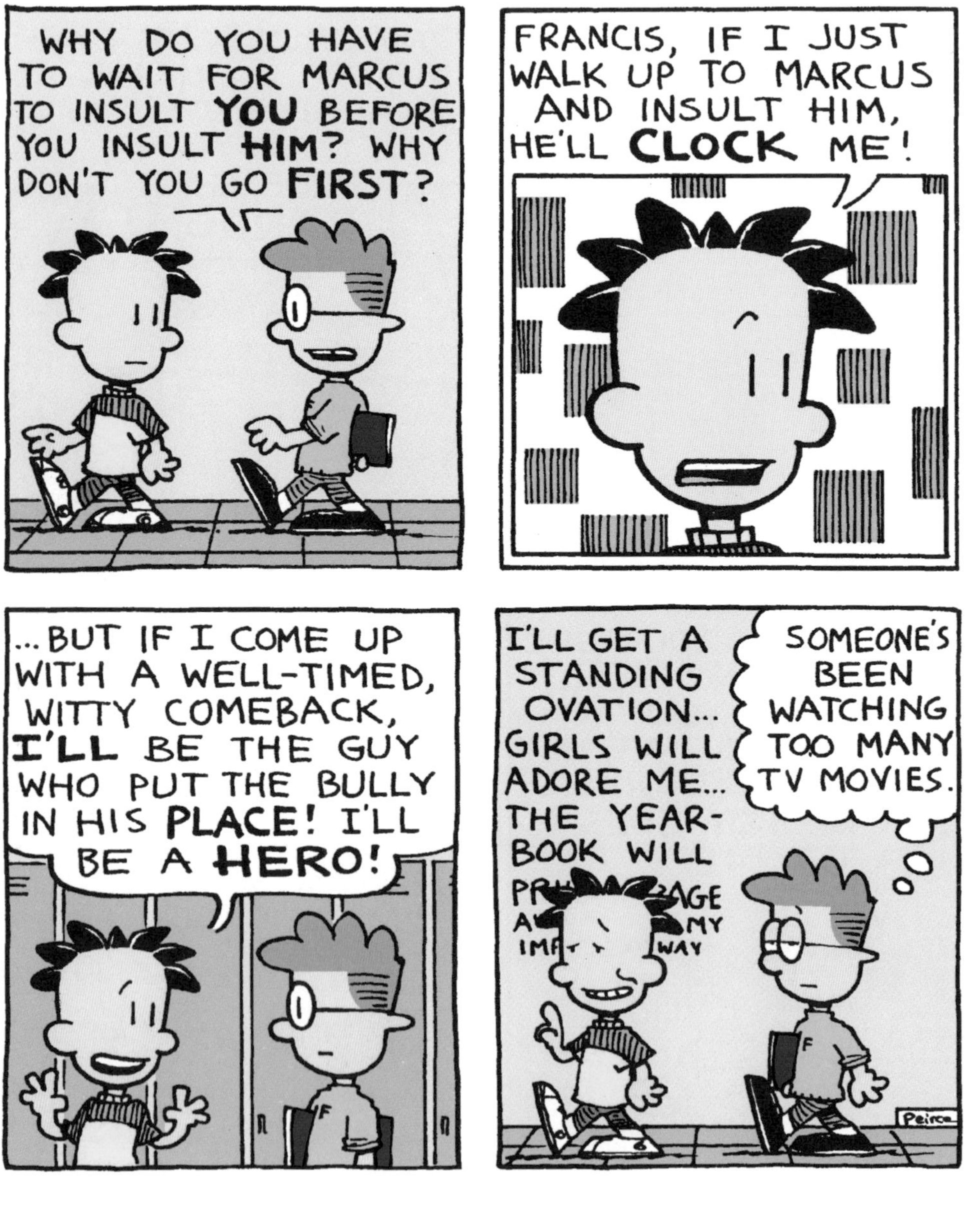
WHY DO YOU HAVE TO WAIT FOR MARCUS TO INSULT YOU BEFORE YOU INSULT HIM? WHY DON'T YOU GO FIRST?
FRANCIS, IF I JUST WALK UP TO MARCUS AND INSULT HIM, HE'LL CLOCK ME!
...BUT IF I COME UP WITH A WELL-TIMED, WITTY COMEBACK, I'LL BE THE GUY WHO PUT THE BULLY IN HIS PLACE! I'LL BE A HERO!
I'LL GET A STANDING OVATION... GIRLS WILL ADORE ME... THE YEAR-BOOK WILL
SOMEONE'S BEEN WATCHING TOO MANY TV MOVIES.
Peirce

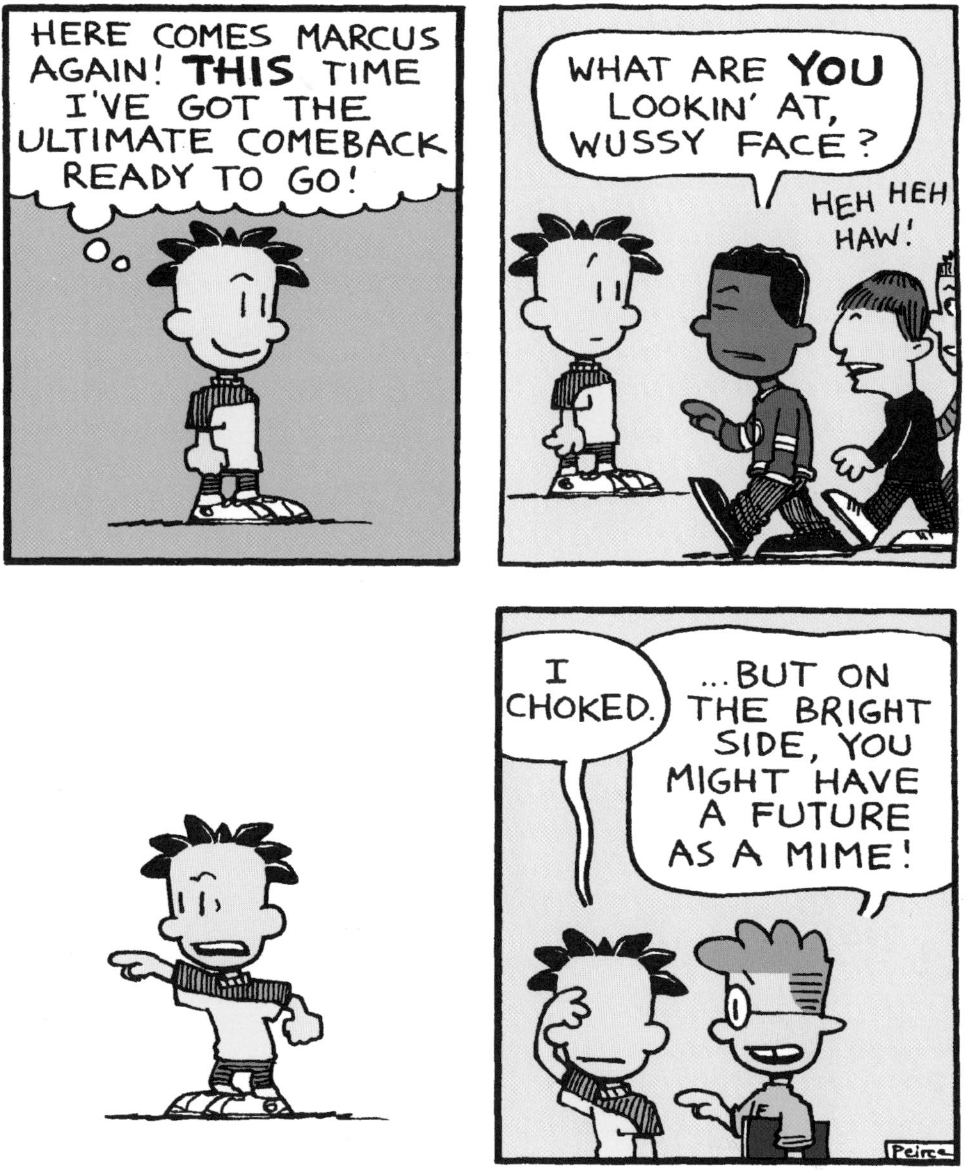
HERE COMES MARCUS AGAIN! THIS TIME I'VE GOT THE ULTIMATE COMEBACK READY TO GO!
WHAT ARE YOU LOOKIN' AT, WUSSY FACE?
HEH HEH HAW!
I CHOKED.
...BUT ON THE BRIGHT SIDE, YOU MIGHT HAVE A FUTURE AS A MIME!
Peirce

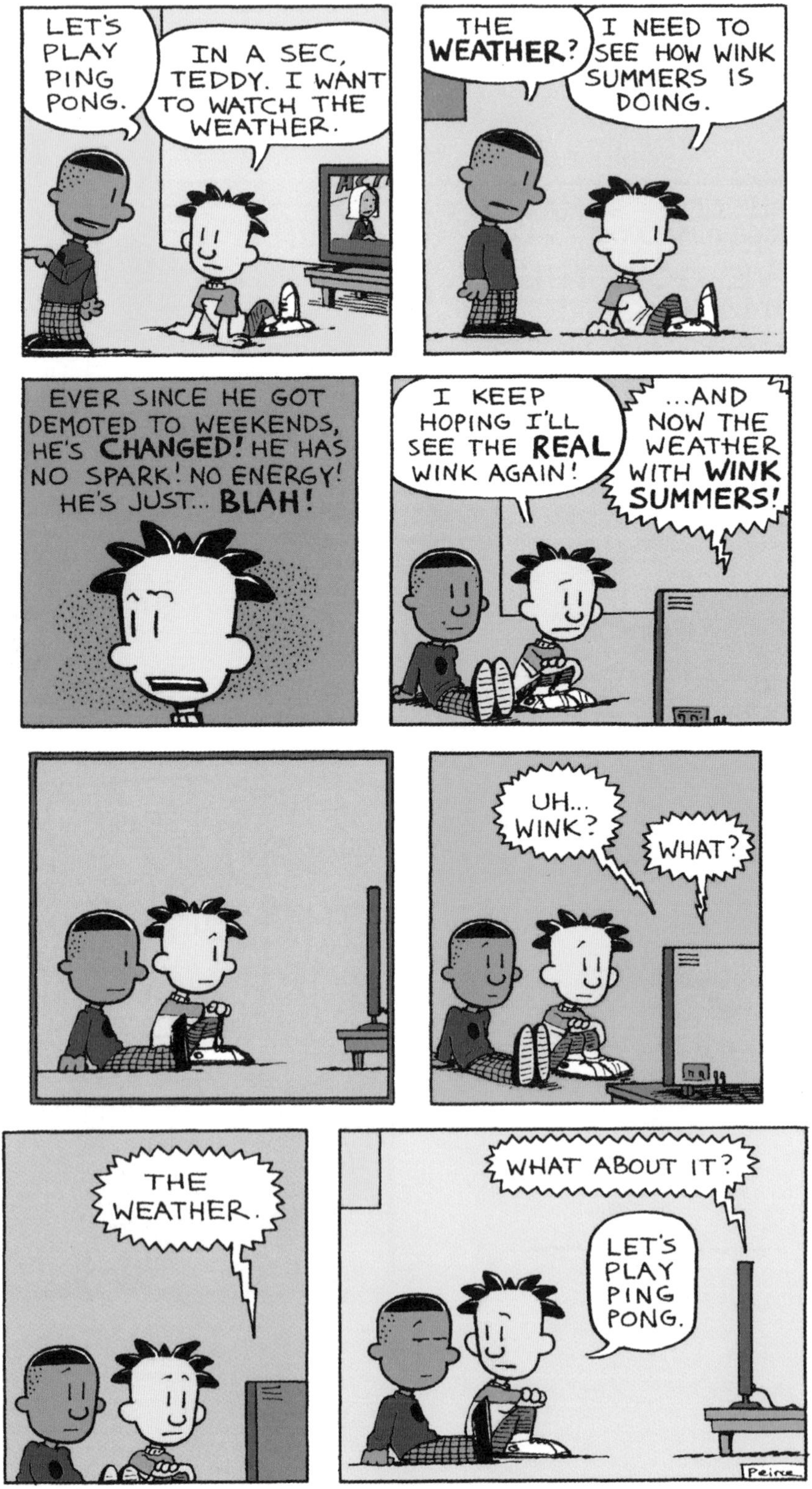
LET'S PLAY PING PONG.
IN A SEC, TEDDY. I WANT TO WATCH THE WEATHER.
THE **WEATHER**?
I NEED TO SEE HOW WINK SUMMERS IS DOING.
EVER SINCE HE GOT DEMOTED TO WEEKENDS, HE'S **CHANGED!** HE HAS NO SPARK! NO ENERGY! HE'S JUST... **BLAH!**
I KEEP HOPING I'LL SEE THE **REAL** WINK AGAIN!
...AND NOW THE WEATHER WITH **WINK SUMMERS!**
UH... WINK?
WHAT?
THE WEATHER.
WHAT ABOUT IT?
LET'S PLAY PING PONG.
Peirce

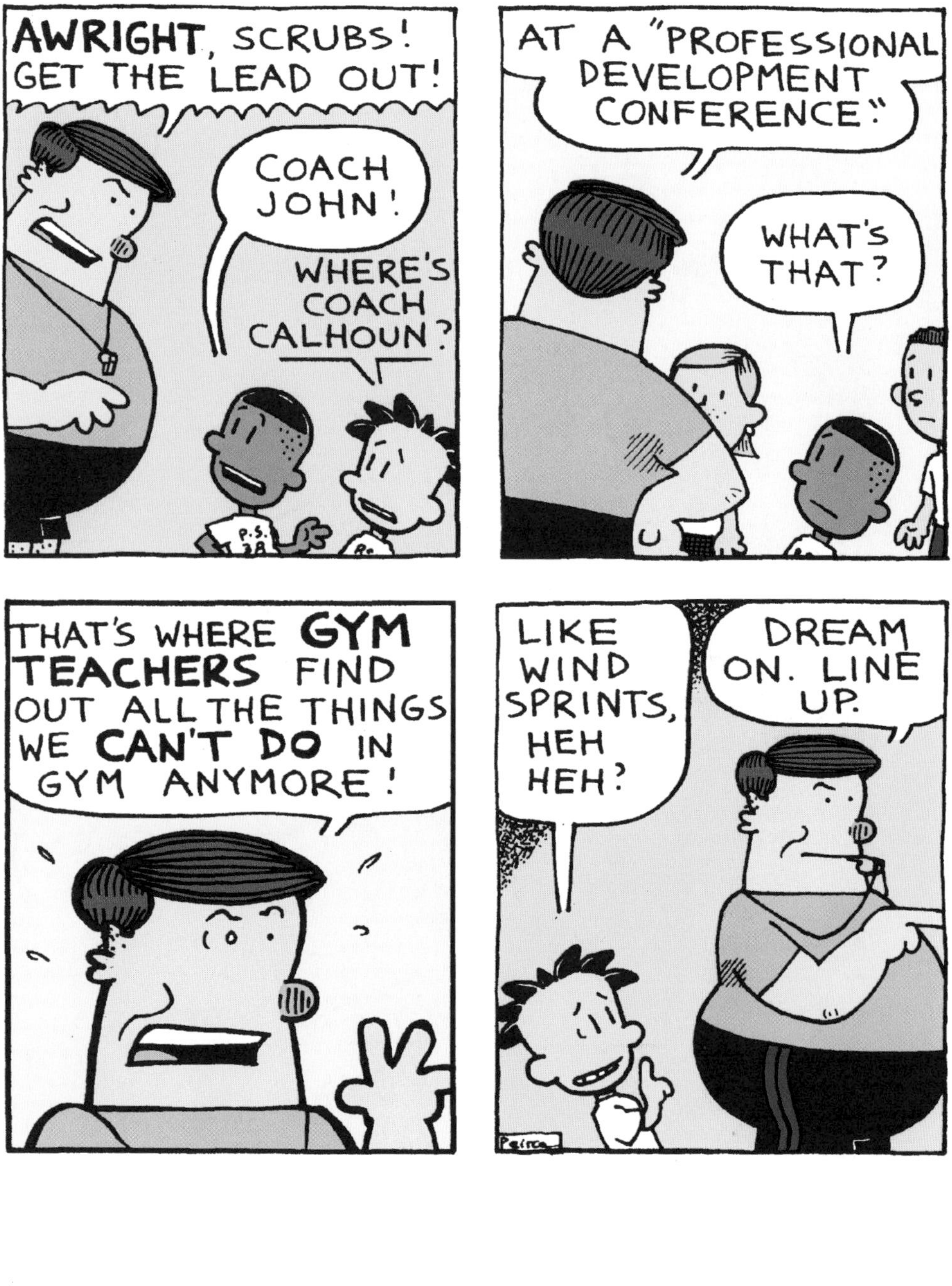
AWRIGHT, SCRUBS! GET THE LEAD OUT!
COACH JOHN!
WHERE'S COACH CALHOUN?
P.S. 38
AT A "PROFESSIONAL DEVELOPMENT CONFERENCE."
WHAT'S THAT?
THAT'S WHERE GYM TEACHERS FIND OUT ALL THE THINGS WE CAN'T DO IN GYM ANYMORE!
LIKE WIND SPRINTS, HEH HEH?
DREAM ON. LINE UP.
Peirce

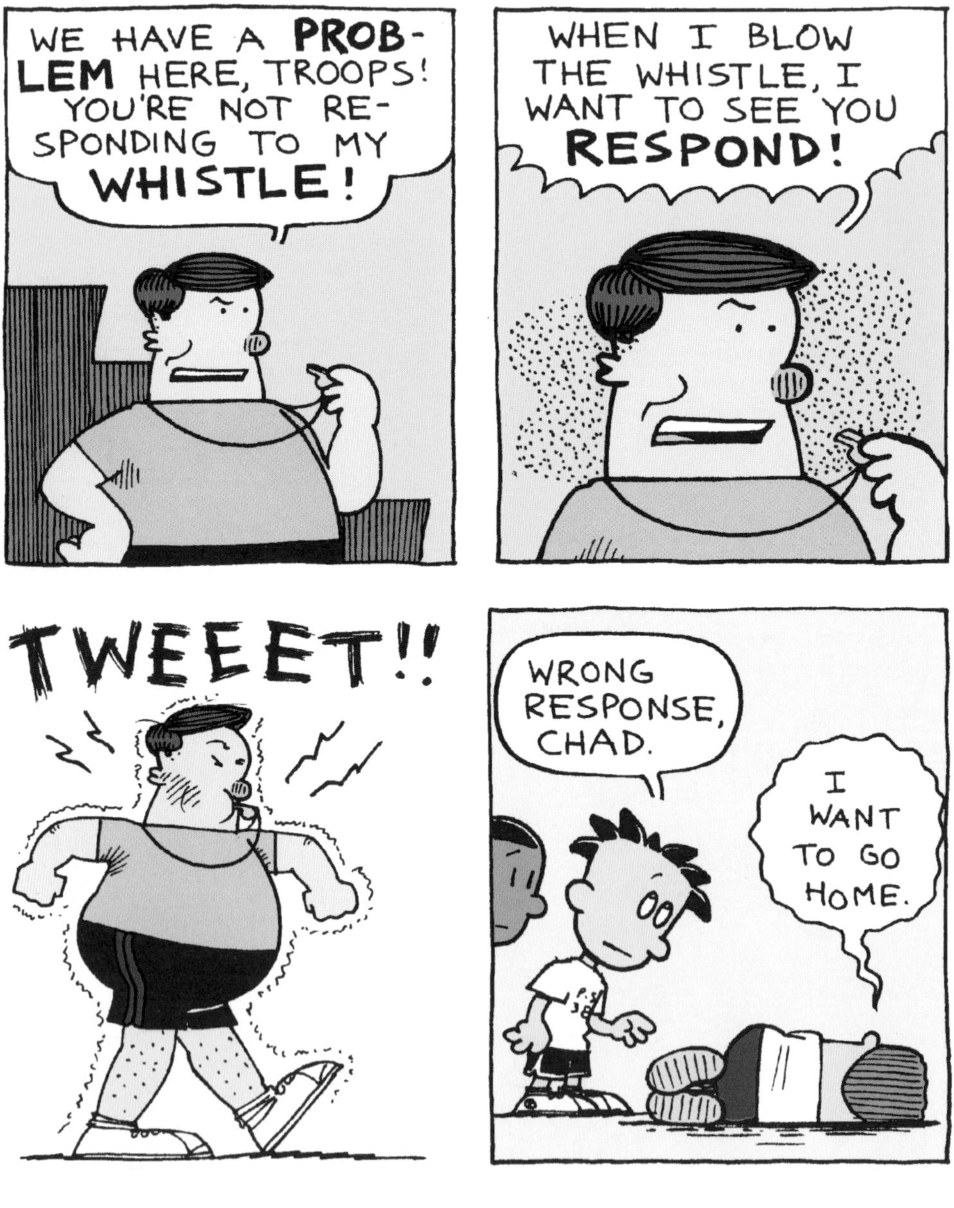
WE HAVE A **PROBLEM** HERE, TROOPS! YOU'RE NOT RESPONDING TO MY **WHISTLE**!
WHEN I BLOW THE WHISTLE, I WANT TO SEE YOU **RESPOND**!
TWEEET!!
WRONG RESPONSE, CHAD.
I WANT TO GO HOME.

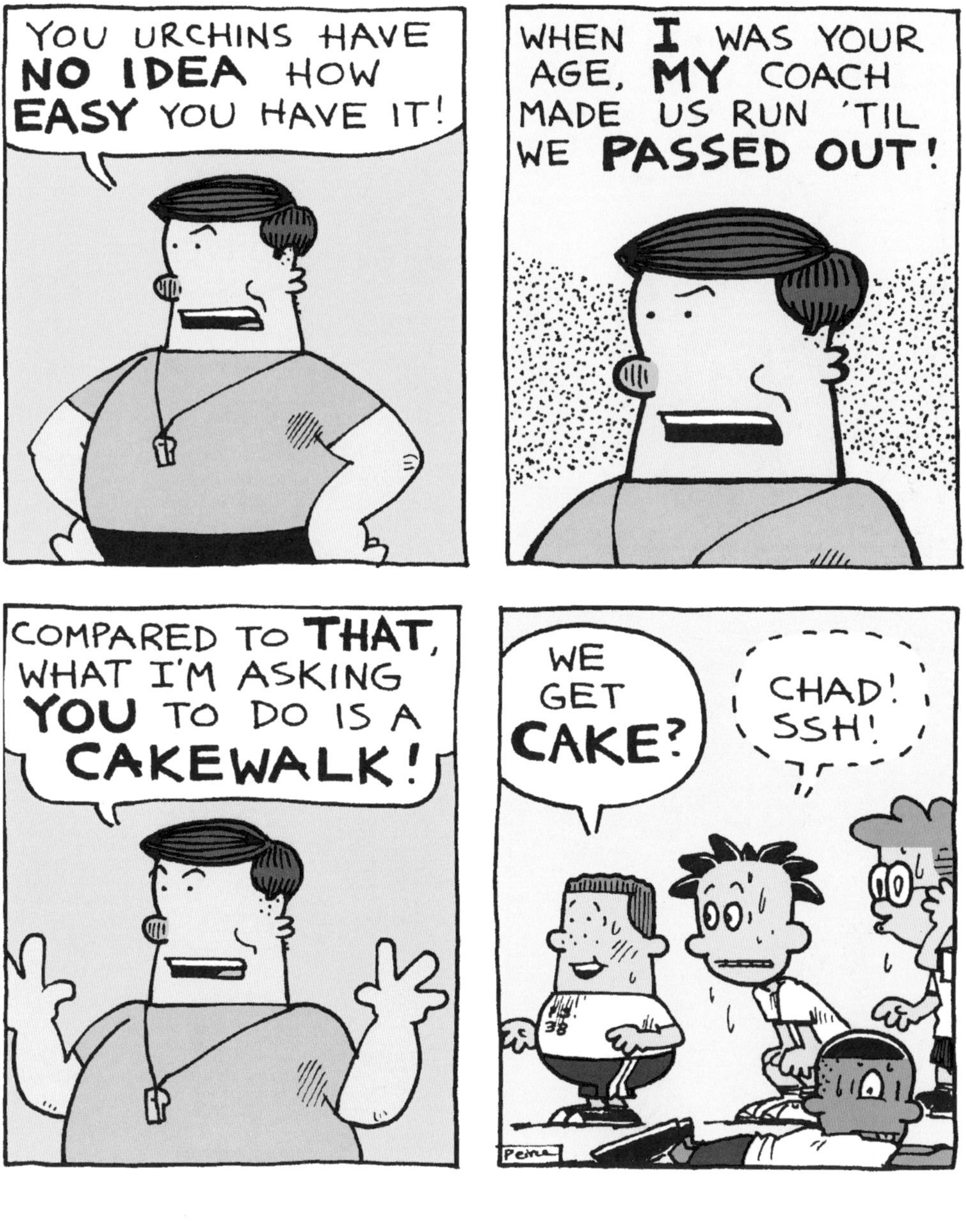
YOU URCHINS HAVE NO IDEA HOW EASY YOU HAVE IT!
WHEN I WAS YOUR AGE, MY COACH MADE US RUN 'TIL WE PASSED OUT!
COMPARED TO THAT, WHAT I'M ASKING YOU TO DO IS A CAKEWALK!
WE GET CAKE?
CHAD! SSH!

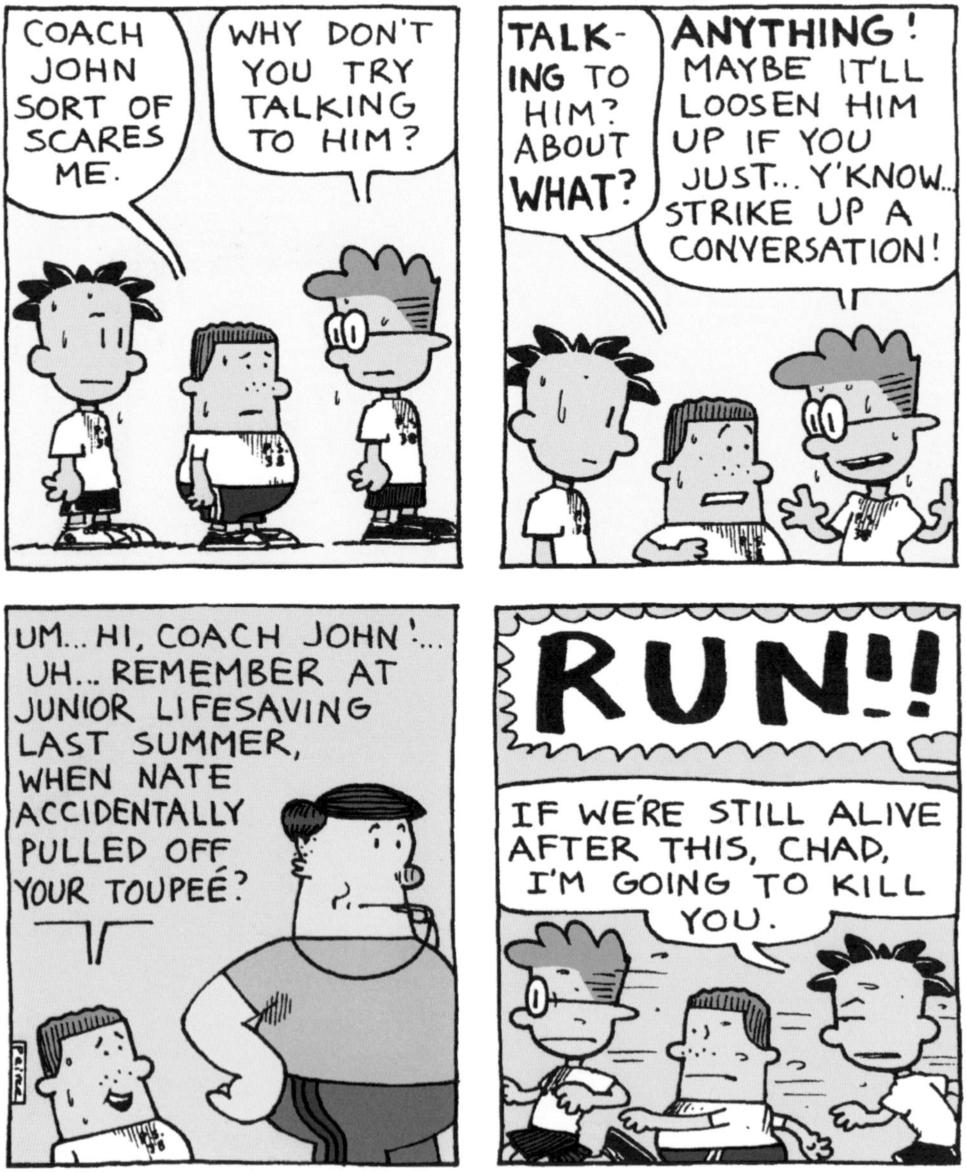
COACH JOHN SORT OF SCARES ME.
WHY DON'T YOU TRY TALKING TO HIM?
TALKING TO HIM? ABOUT WHAT?
ANYTHING! MAYBE IT'LL LOOSEN HIM UP IF YOU JUST... Y'KNOW... STRIKE UP A CONVERSATION!
UM... HI, COACH JOHN!... UH... REMEMBER AT JUNIOR LIFESAVING LAST SUMMER, WHEN NATE ACCIDENTALLY PULLED OFF YOUR TOUPEÉ?
RUN!!
IF WE'RE STILL ALIVE AFTER THIS, CHAD, I'M GOING TO KILL YOU.

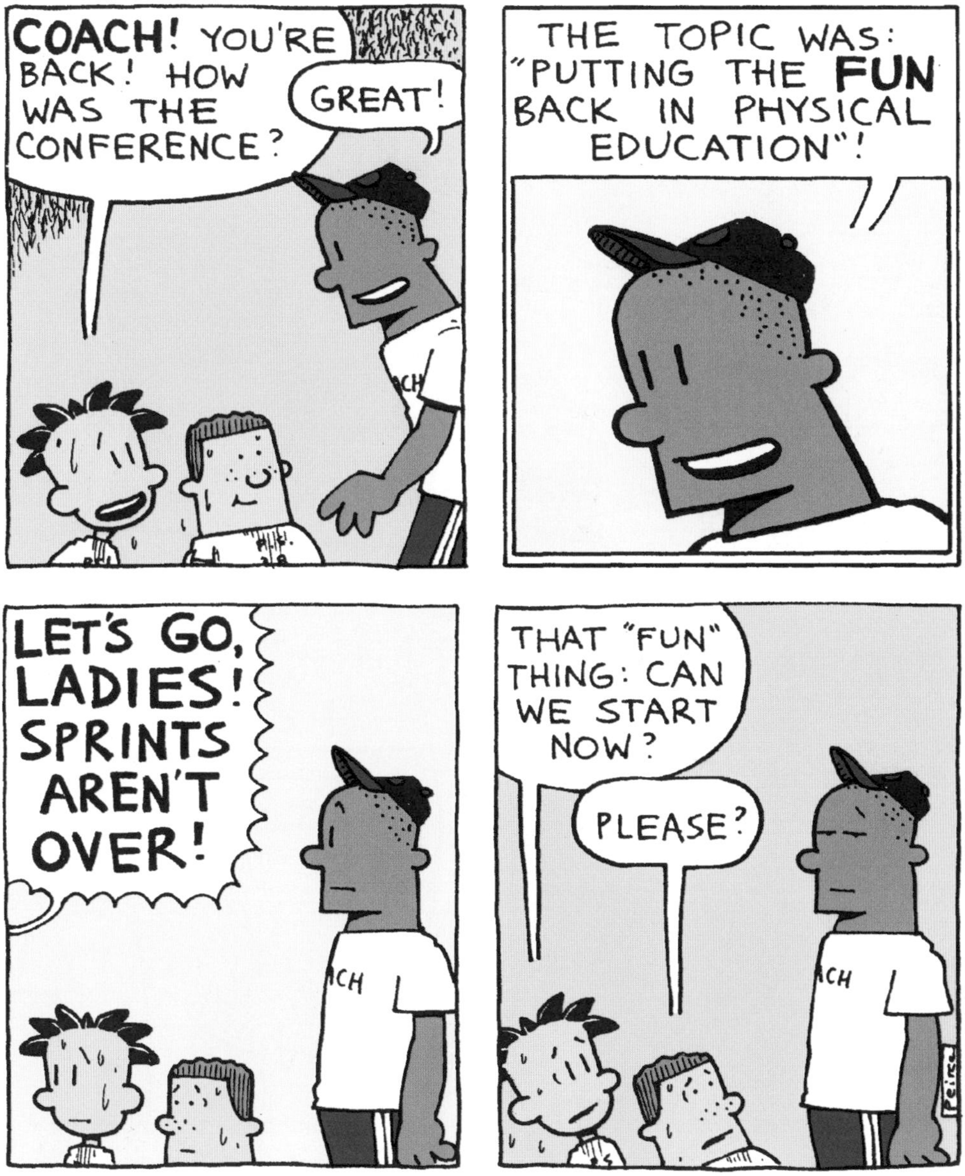
COACH! YOU'RE BACK! HOW WAS THE CONFERENCE?
GREAT!
THE TOPIC WAS: "PUTTING THE FUN BACK IN PHYSICAL EDUCATION"!
LET'S GO, LADIES! SPRINTS AREN'T OVER!
THAT "FUN" THING: CAN WE START NOW?
PLEASE?
Peirce

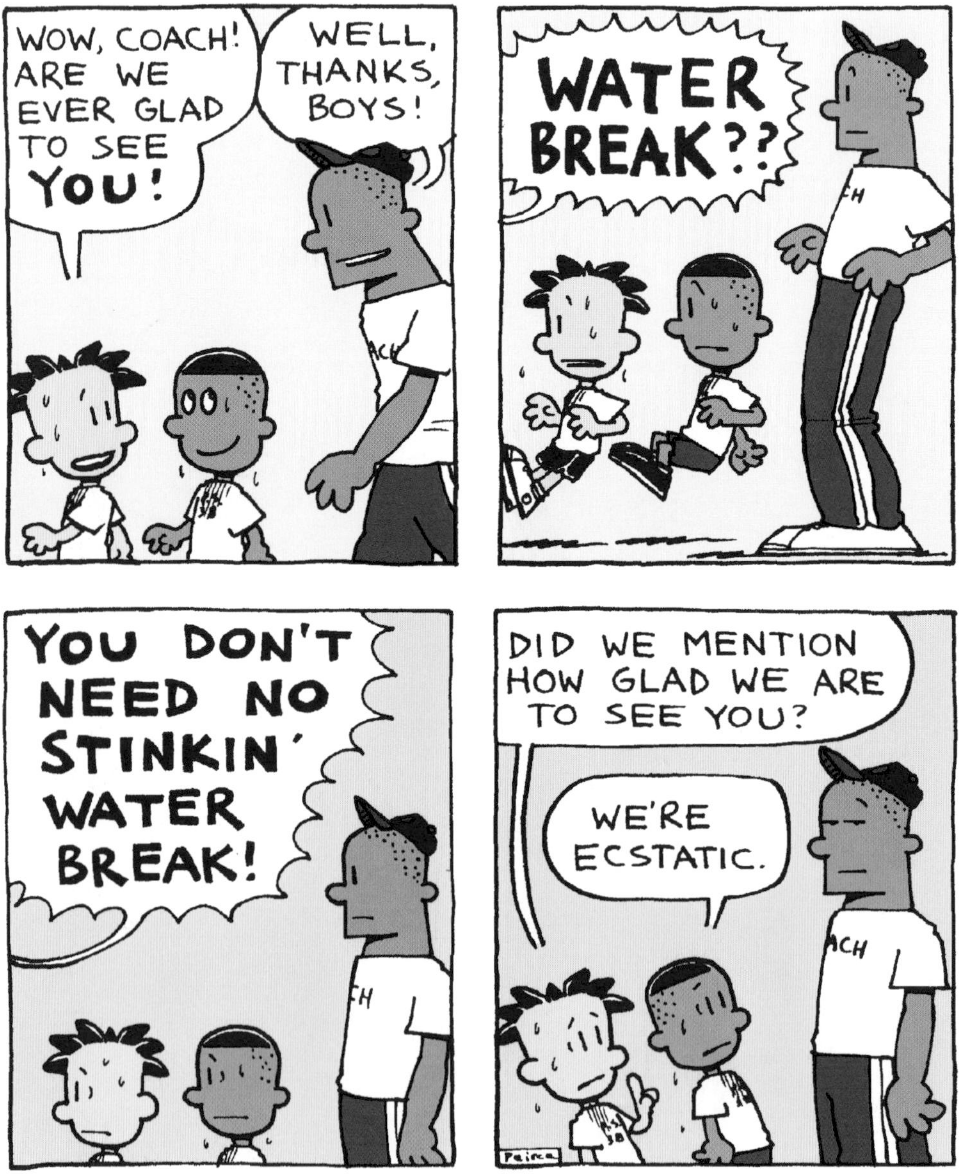
WOW, COACH! ARE WE EVER GLAD TO SEE YOU!
WELL, THANKS, BOYS!
WATER BREAK??
YOU DON'T NEED NO STINKIN' WATER BREAK!
DID WE MENTION HOW GLAD WE ARE TO SEE YOU?
WE'RE ECSTATIC.
Peirce

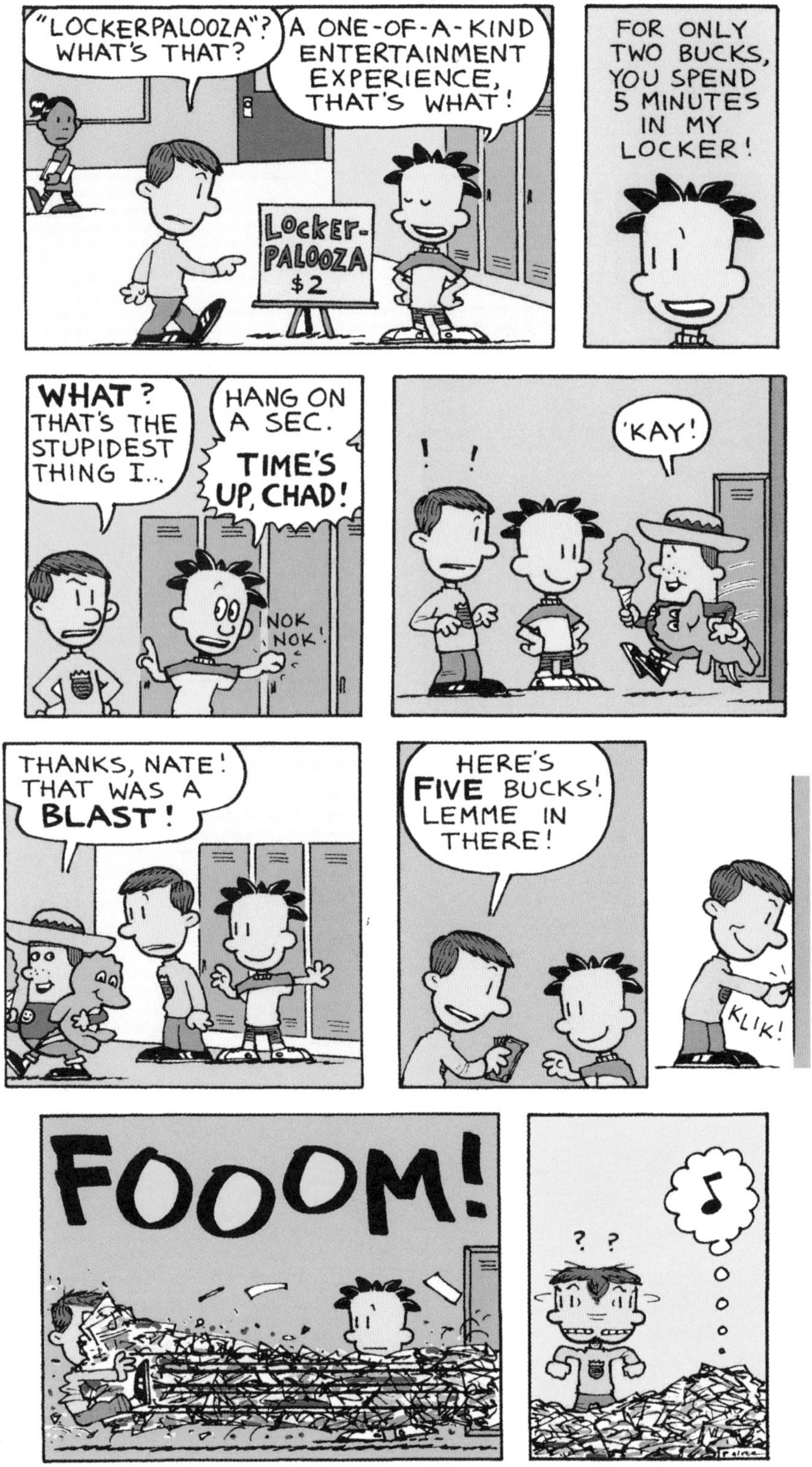
"LOCKERPALOOZA"? WHAT'S THAT?
A ONE-OF-A-KIND ENTERTAINMENT EXPERIENCE, THAT'S WHAT!
LOCKER-PALOOZA $2
FOR ONLY TWO BUCKS, YOU SPEND 5 MINUTES IN MY LOCKER!
WHAT? THAT'S THE STUPIDEST THING I...
HANG ON A SEC.
TIME'S UP, CHAD!
NOK NOK!
! !
'KAY!
THANKS, NATE! THAT WAS A BLAST!
HERE'S FIVE BUCKS! LEMME IN THERE!
KLIK!
FOOOM!
? ?

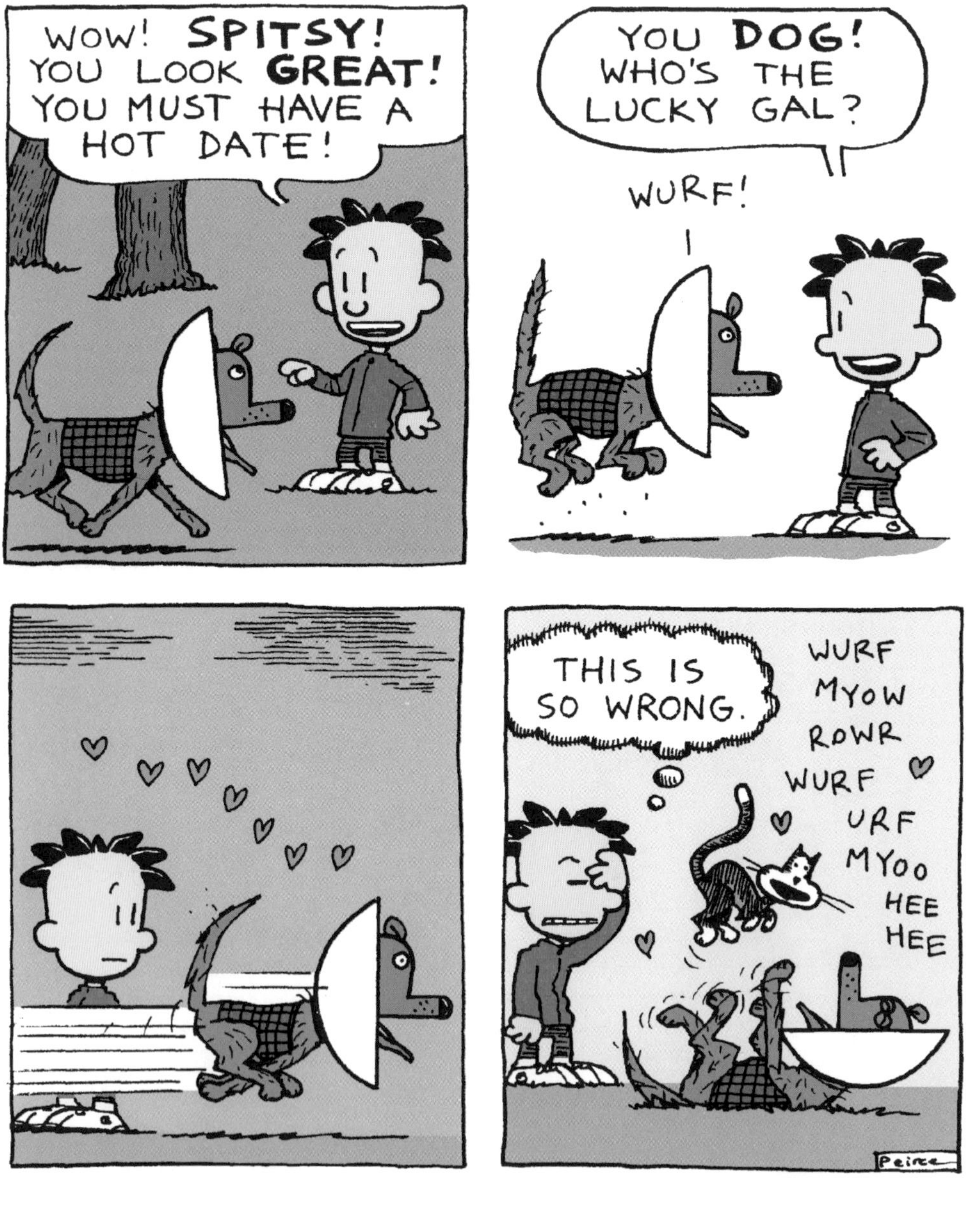
WOW! SPITSY! YOU LOOK GREAT! YOU MUST HAVE A HOT DATE!
YOU DOG! WHO'S THE LUCKY GAL?
WURF!
THIS IS SO WRONG.
WURF
MYOW
ROWR
WURF
URF
MYOO
HEE
HEE
Peirce

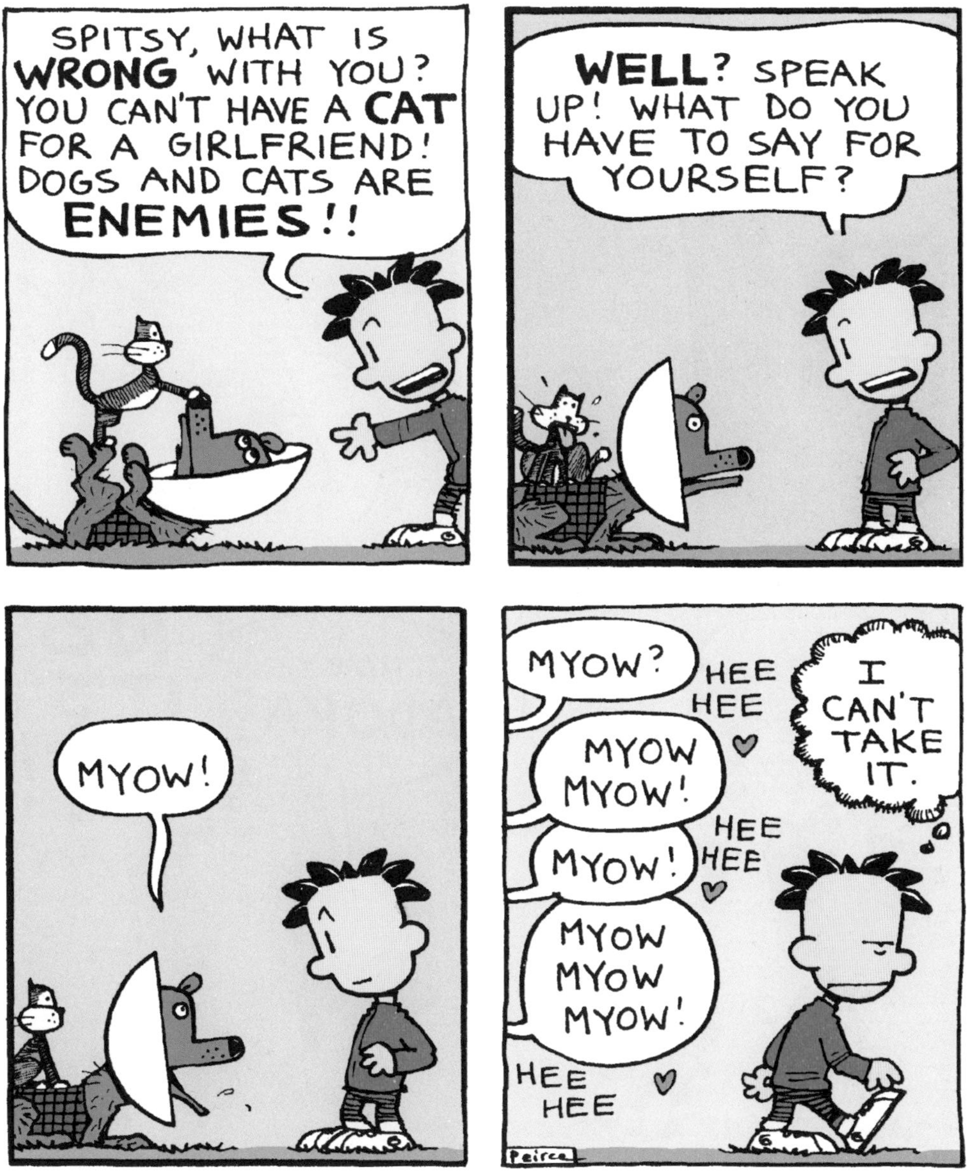
SPITSY, WHAT IS **WRONG** WITH YOU? YOU CAN'T HAVE A **CAT** FOR A GIRLFRIEND! DOGS AND CATS ARE **ENEMIES**!!
WELL? SPEAK UP! WHAT DO YOU HAVE TO SAY FOR YOURSELF?
MYOW!
MYOW?
HEE HEE
MYOW MYOW!
I CAN'T TAKE IT.
HEE HEE
MYOW!
MYOW MYOW MYOW!
HEE HEE
Peirce

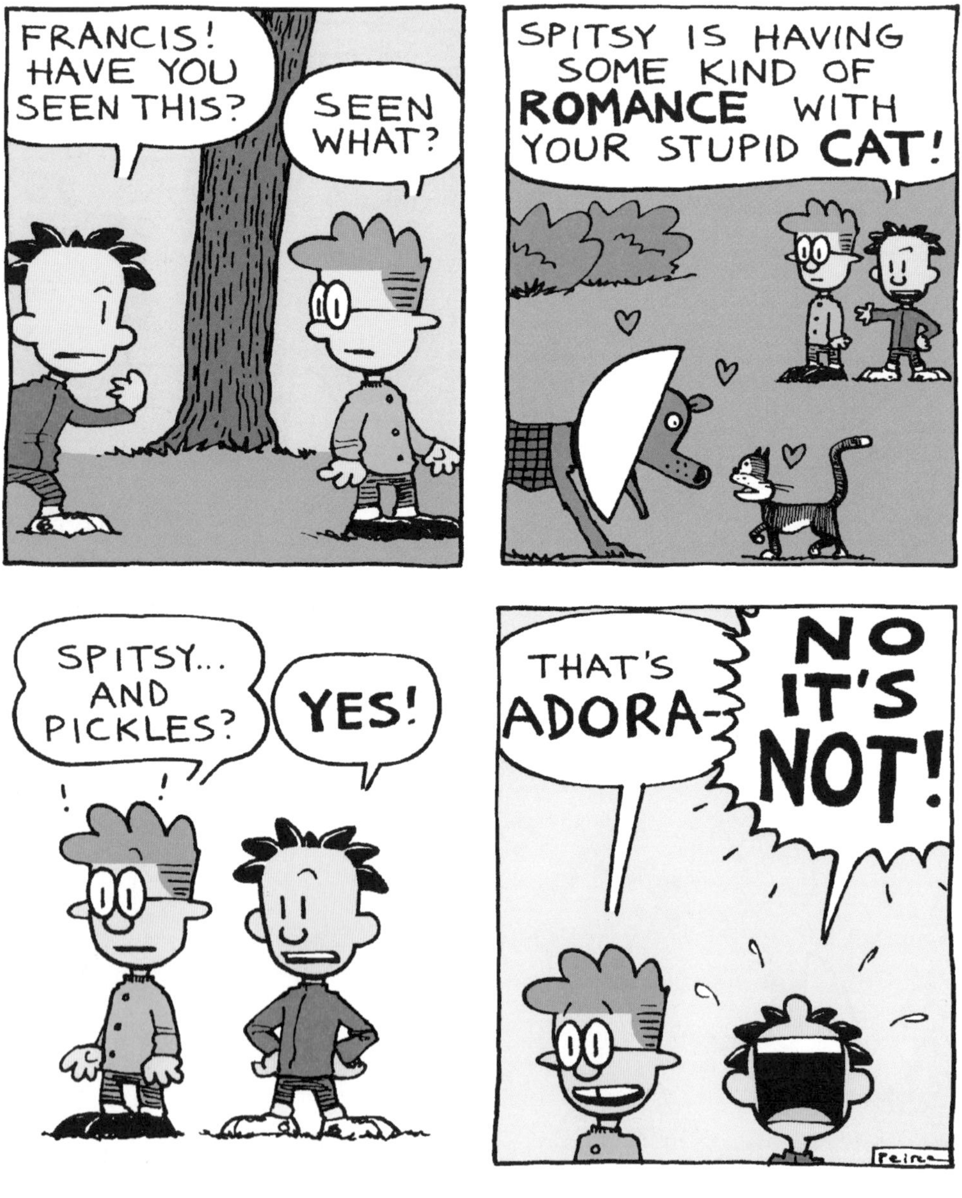
FRANCIS! HAVE YOU SEEN THIS?
SEEN WHAT?
SPITSY IS HAVING SOME KIND OF **ROMANCE** WITH YOUR STUPID **CAT**!
SPITSY... AND PICKLES?
YES!
THAT'S ADORA-
NO IT'S NOT!
Peirce

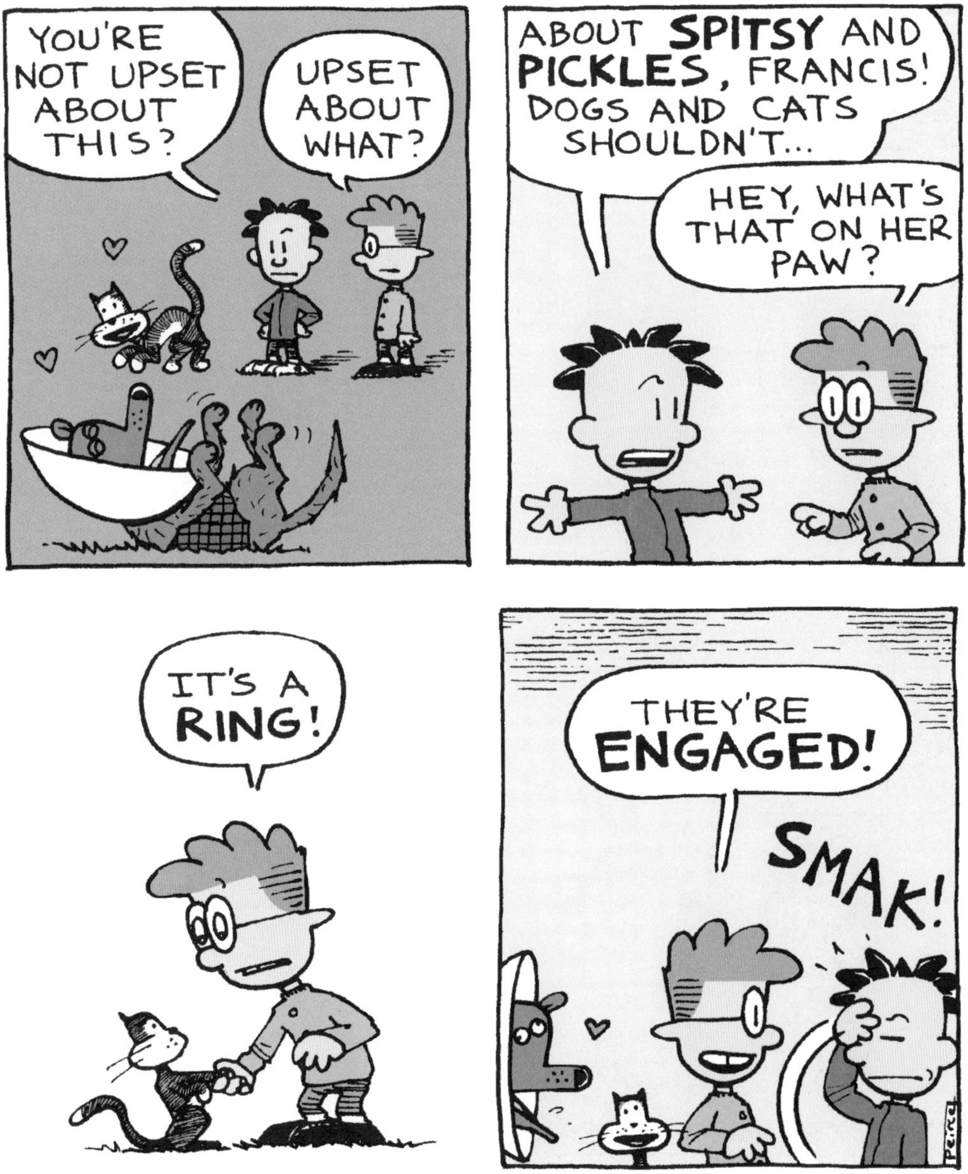
YOU'RE NOT UPSET ABOUT THIS?
UPSET ABOUT WHAT?
ABOUT **SPITSY** AND **PICKLES**, FRANCIS! DOGS AND CATS SHOULDN'T...
HEY, WHAT'S THAT ON HER PAW?
IT'S A **RING**!
THEY'RE **ENGAGED**!
SMAK!
PEIRCE

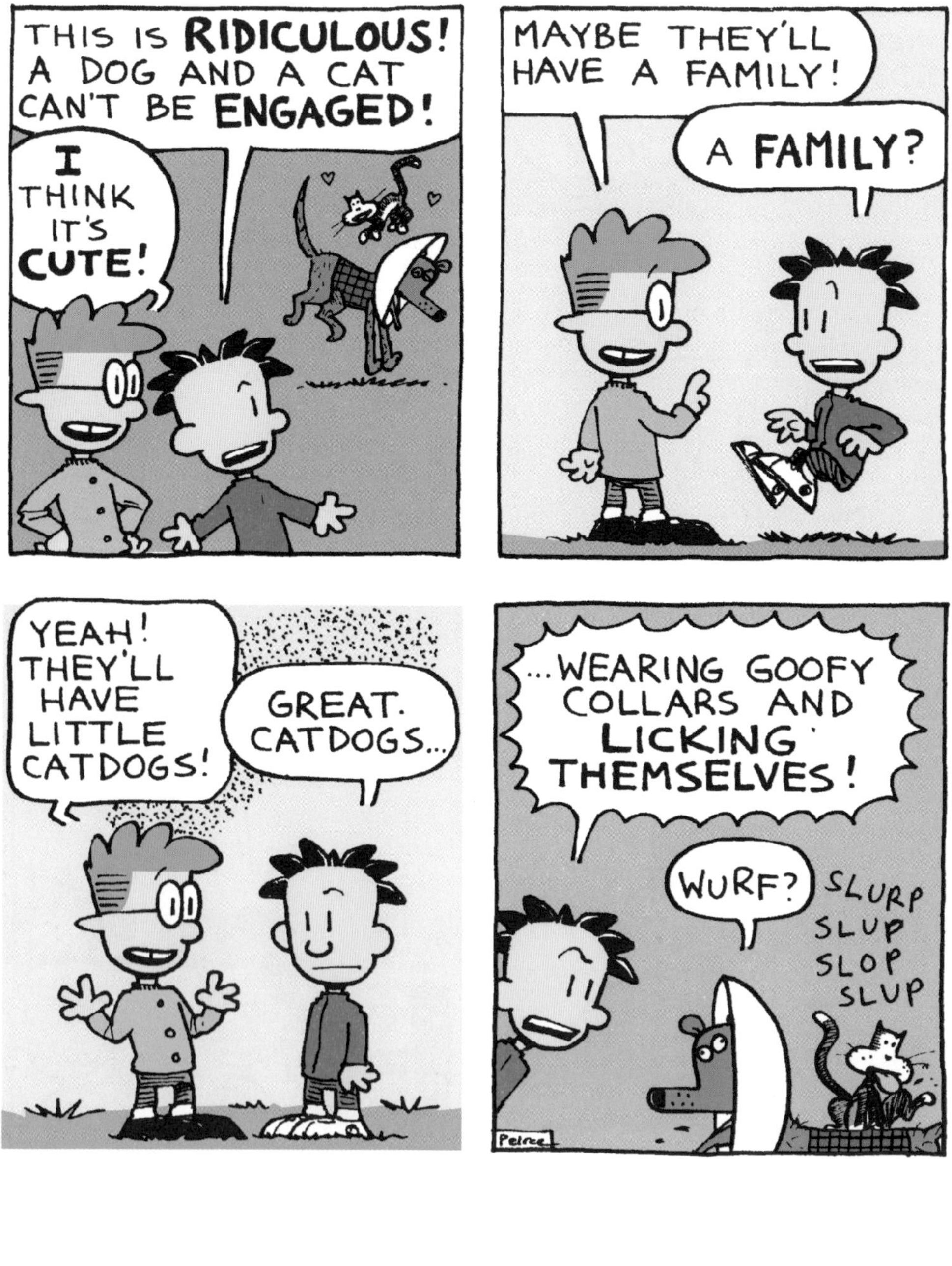
THIS IS RIDICULOUS! A DOG AND A CAT CAN'T BE ENGAGED!
I THINK IT'S CUTE!
MAYBE THEY'LL HAVE A FAMILY!
A FAMILY?
YEAH! THEY'LL HAVE LITTLE CATDOGS!
GREAT. CATDOGS...
...WEARING GOOFY COLLARS AND LICKING THEMSELVES!
WURF?
SLURP
SLUP
SLOP
SLUP
Peirce

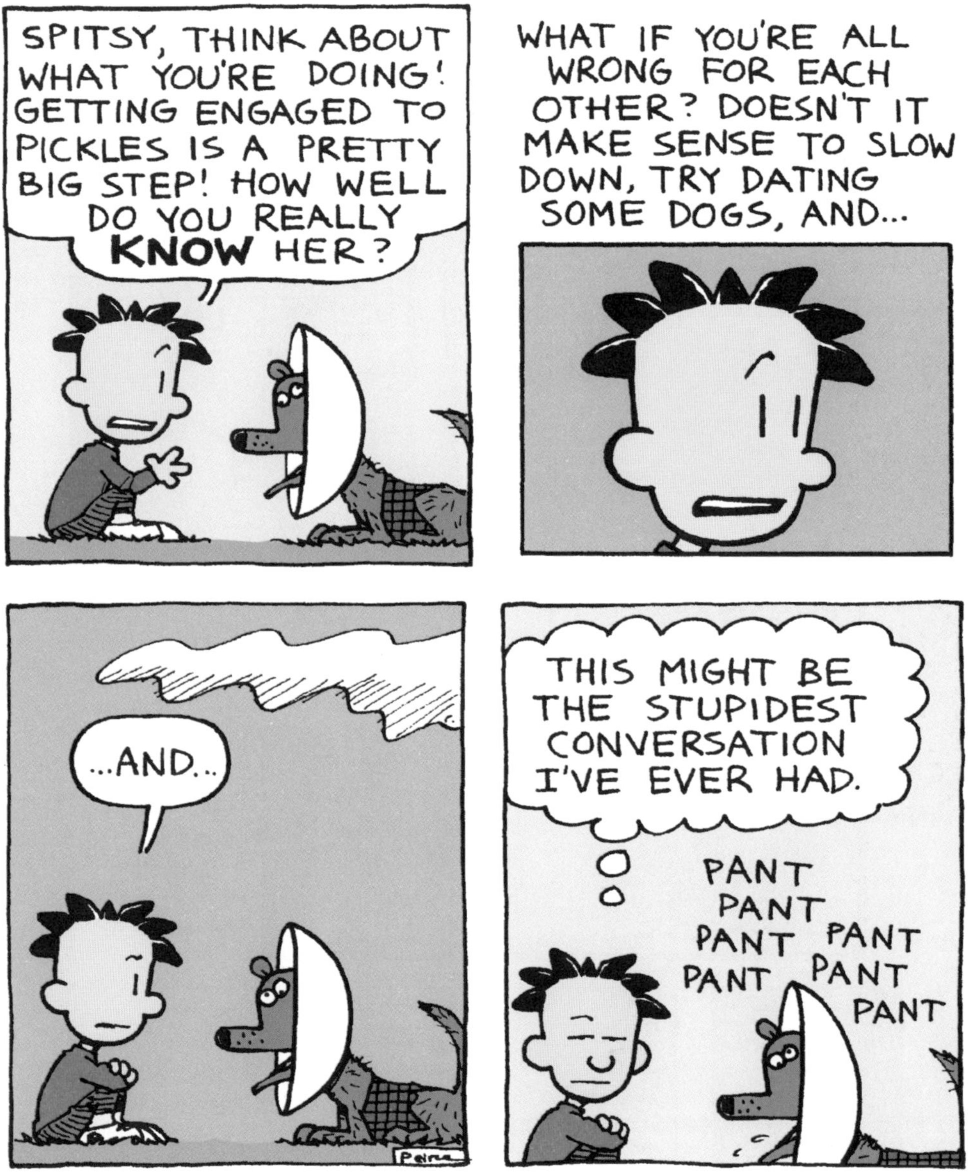
SPITSY, THINK ABOUT WHAT YOU'RE DOING! GETTING ENGAGED TO PICKLES IS A PRETTY BIG STEP! HOW WELL DO YOU REALLY **KNOW** HER?
WHAT IF YOU'RE ALL WRONG FOR EACH OTHER? DOESN'T IT MAKE SENSE TO SLOW DOWN, TRY DATING SOME DOGS, AND...
...AND...
THIS MIGHT BE THE STUPIDEST CONVERSATION I'VE EVER HAD.
PANT
PANT
PANT PANT
PANT PANT
PANT

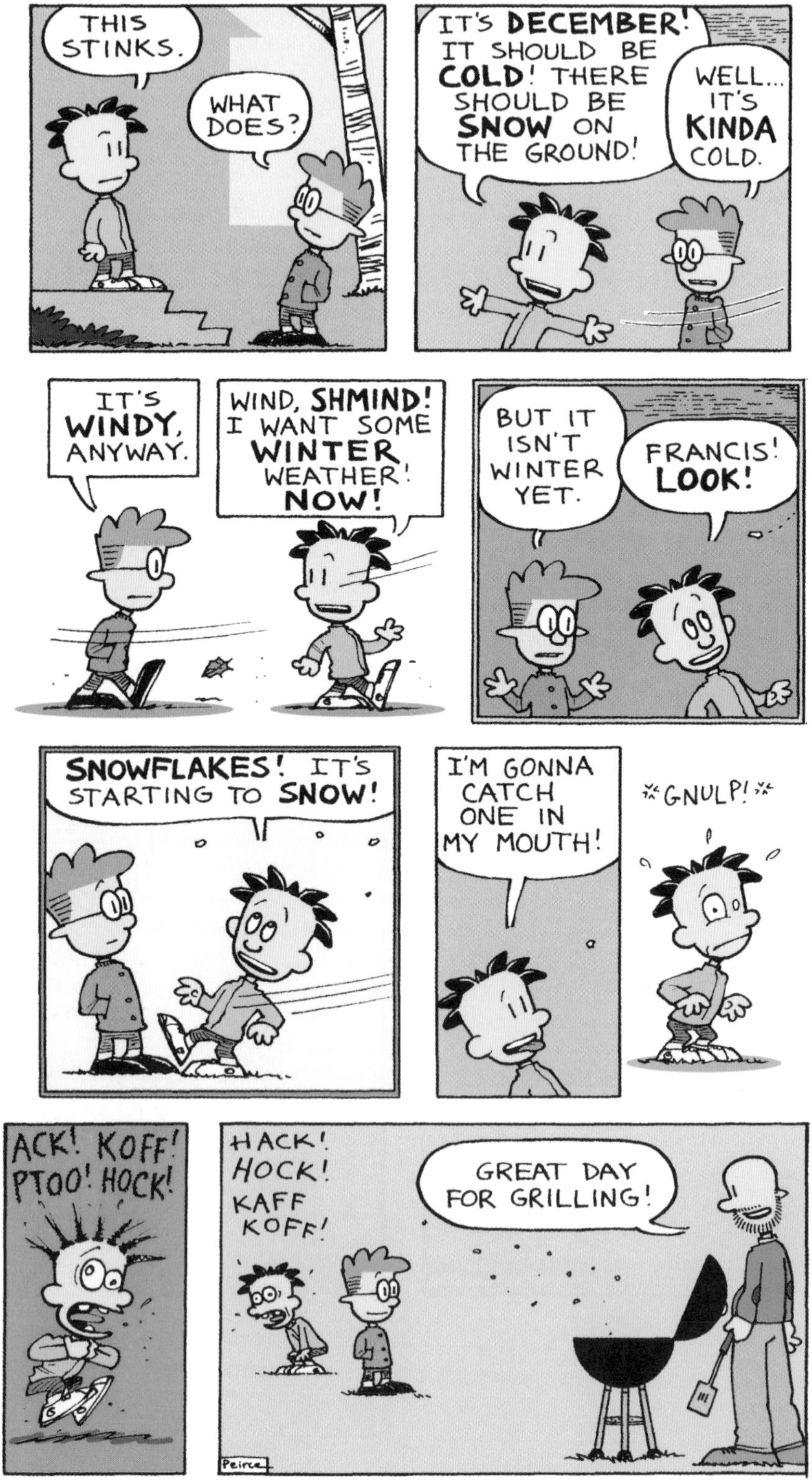
THIS STINKS.
WHAT DOES?
IT'S DECEMBER! IT SHOULD BE COLD! THERE SHOULD BE SNOW ON THE GROUND!
WELL... IT'S KINDA COLD.
IT'S WINDY, ANYWAY.
WIND, SHMIND! I WANT SOME WINTER WEATHER! NOW!
BUT IT ISN'T WINTER YET.
FRANCIS! LOOK!
SNOWFLAKES! IT'S STARTING TO SNOW!
I'M GONNA CATCH ONE IN MY MOUTH!
GNULP!
ACK! KOFF! PTOO! HOCK!
HACK! HOCK! KAFF KOFF!
GREAT DAY FOR GRILLING!
Peirce

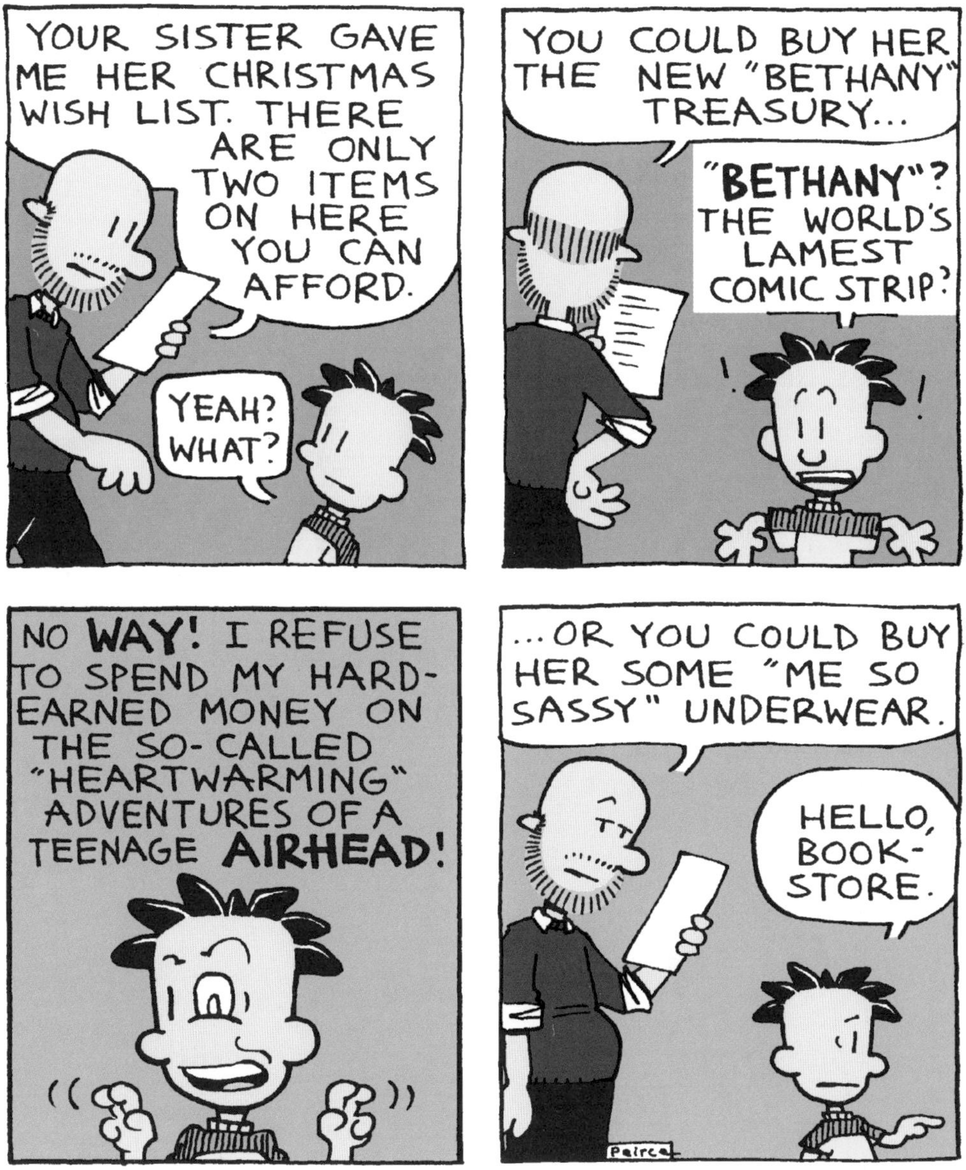
YOUR SISTER GAVE ME HER CHRISTMAS WISH LIST. THERE ARE ONLY TWO ITEMS ON HERE YOU CAN AFFORD.
YEAH? WHAT?
YOU COULD BUY HER THE NEW "BETHANY" TREASURY...
"BETHANY"? THE WORLD'S LAMEST COMIC STRIP?
NO WAY! I REFUSE TO SPEND MY HARD-EARNED MONEY ON THE SO-CALLED "HEARTWARMING" ADVENTURES OF A TEENAGE AIRHEAD!
...OR YOU COULD BUY HER SOME "ME SO SASSY" UNDERWEAR.
HELLO, BOOK-STORE.
Peirce

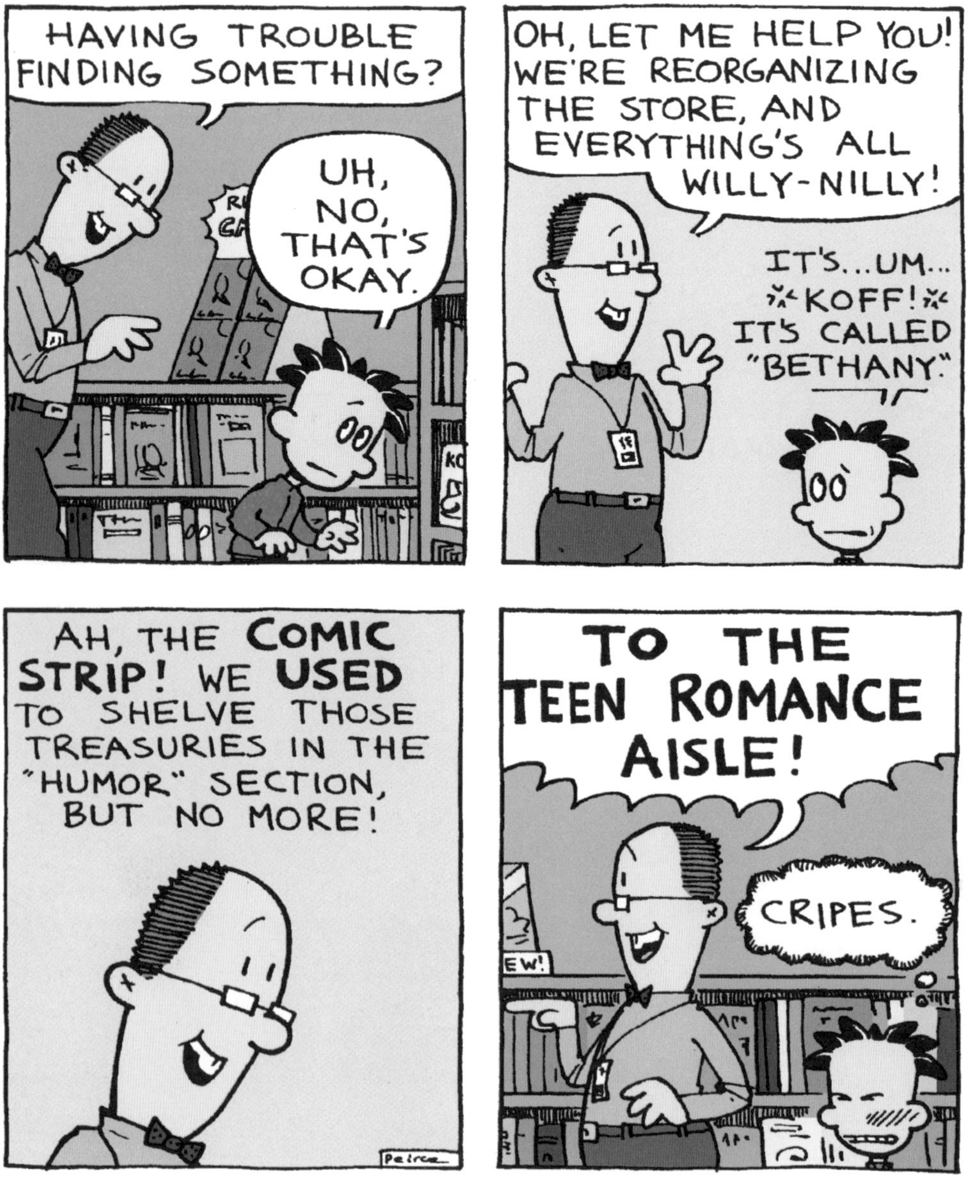
HAVING TROUBLE FINDING SOMETHING?
UH, NO, THAT'S OKAY.
OH, LET ME HELP YOU! WE'RE REORGANIZING THE STORE, AND EVERYTHING'S ALL WILLY-NILLY!
IT'S...UM... *KOFF!* IT'S CALLED "BETHANY."
AH, THE **COMIC STRIP!** WE **USED** TO SHELVE THOSE TREASURIES IN THE "HUMOR" SECTION, BUT NO MORE!
Peirce
TO THE TEEN ROMANCE AISLE!
EW!
CRIPES.

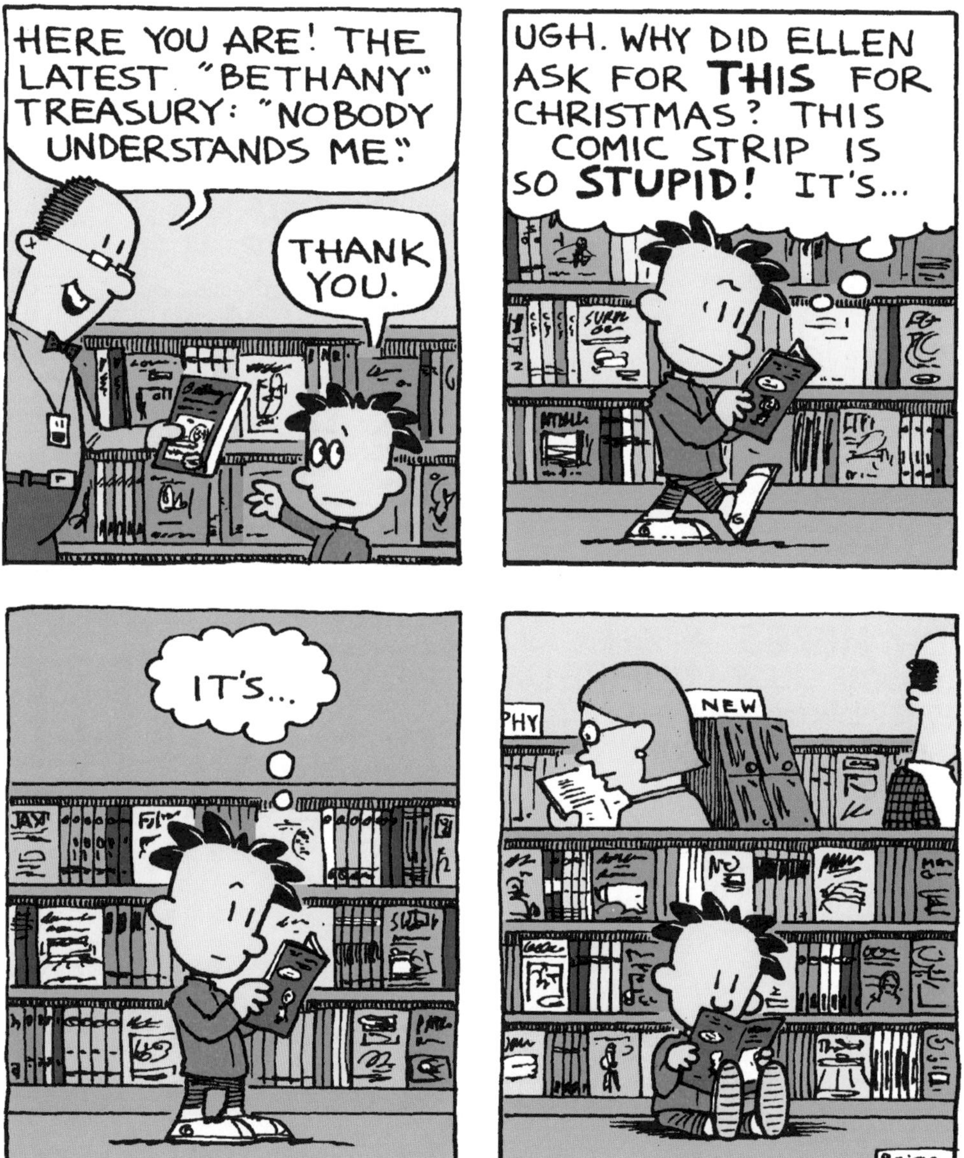
HERE YOU ARE! THE LATEST "BETHANY" TREASURY: "NOBODY UNDERSTANDS ME."
THANK YOU.
UGH. WHY DID ELLEN ASK FOR THIS FOR CHRISTMAS? THIS COMIC STRIP IS SO STUPID! IT'S...
IT'S...
PHY
NEW

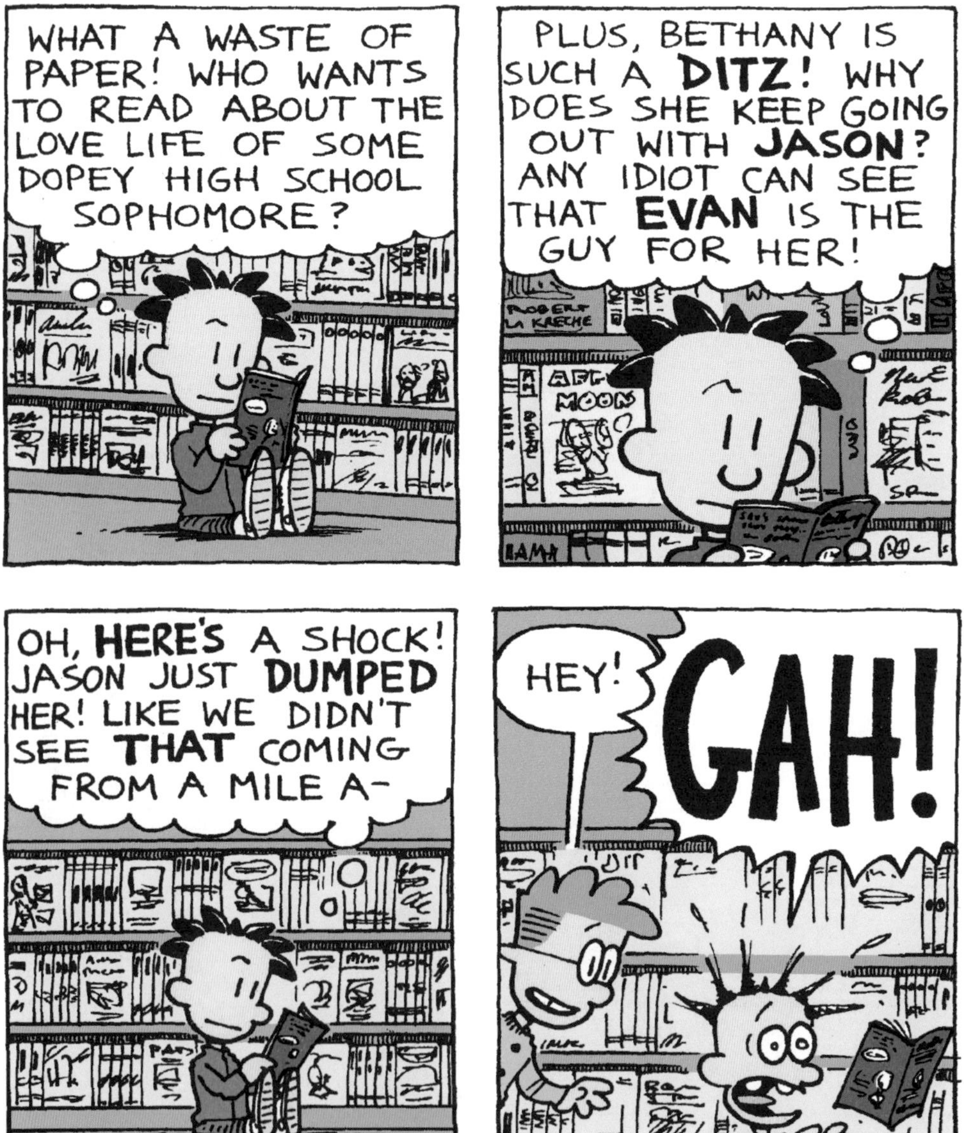
WHAT A WASTE OF PAPER! WHO WANTS TO READ ABOUT THE LOVE LIFE OF SOME DOPEY HIGH SCHOOL SOPHOMORE?
PLUS, BETHANY IS SUCH A DITZ! WHY DOES SHE KEEP GOING OUT WITH JASON? ANY IDIOT CAN SEE THAT EVAN IS THE GUY FOR HER!
OH, HERE'S A SHOCK! JASON JUST DUMPED HER! LIKE WE DIDN'T SEE THAT COMING FROM A MILE A-
HEY!
GAH!

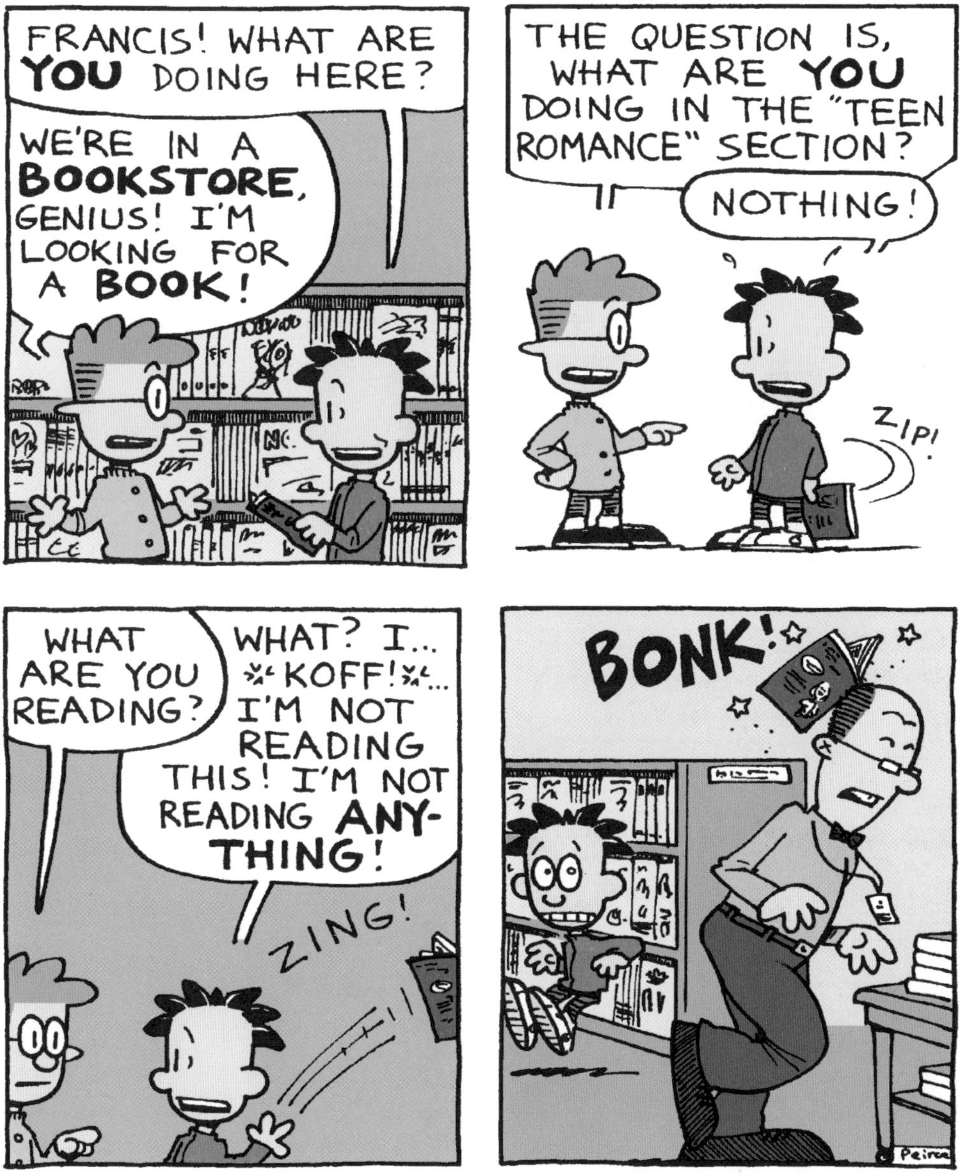
FRANCIS! WHAT ARE YOU DOING HERE?
WE'RE IN A BOOKSTORE, GENIUS! I'M LOOKING FOR A BOOK!
THE QUESTION IS, WHAT ARE YOU DOING IN THE "TEEN ROMANCE" SECTION?
NOTHING!
ZIP!
WHAT ARE YOU READING?
WHAT? I... KOFF!... I'M NOT READING THIS! I'M NOT READING ANYTHING!
ZING!
BONK!
Peirce

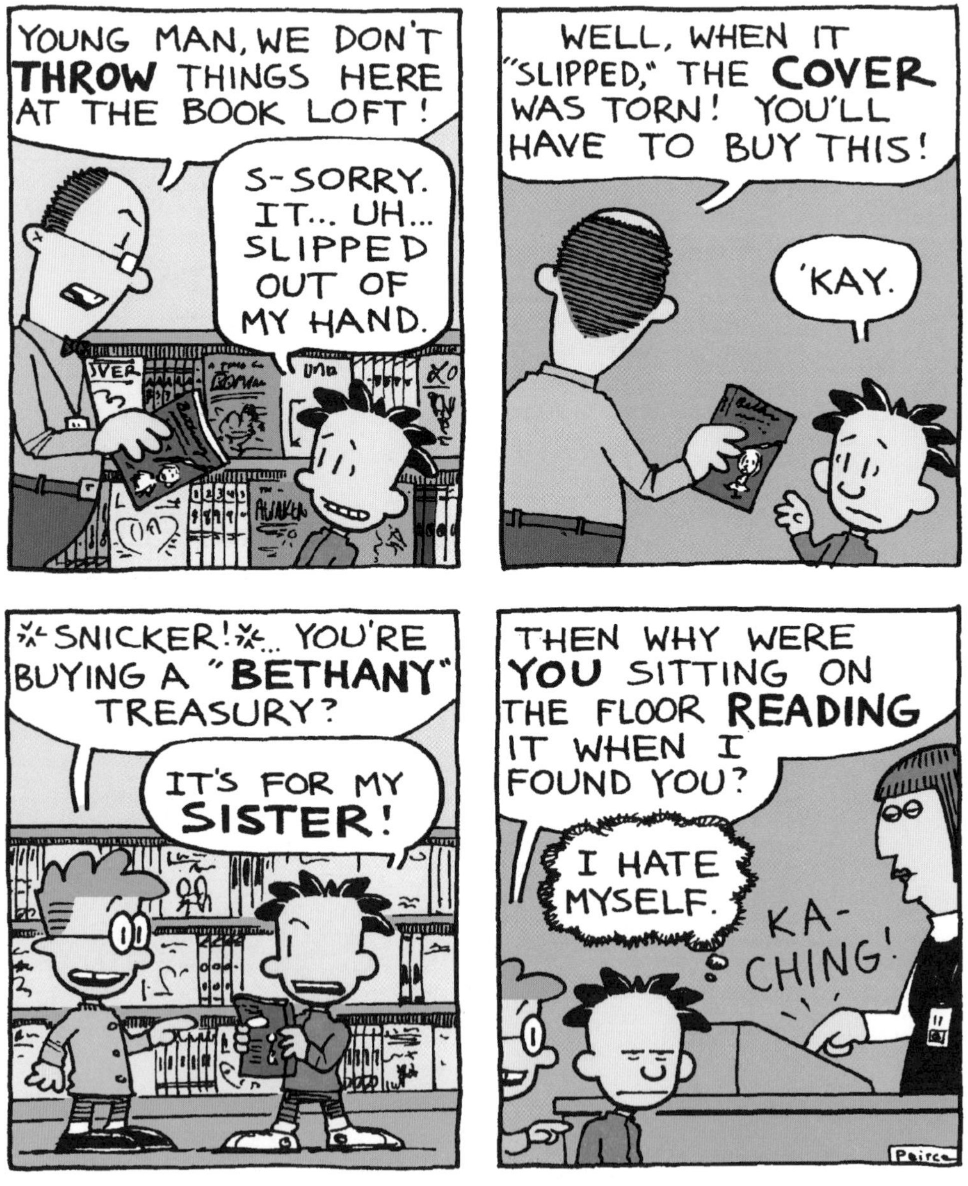
YOUNG MAN, WE DON'T THROW THINGS HERE AT THE BOOK LOFT!
S-SORRY. IT... UH... SLIPPED OUT OF MY HAND.
WELL, WHEN IT "SLIPPED," THE COVER WAS TORN! YOU'LL HAVE TO BUY THIS!
'KAY.
SNICKER! ... YOU'RE BUYING A "BETHANY" TREASURY?
IT'S FOR MY SISTER!
THEN WHY WERE YOU SITTING ON THE FLOOR READING IT WHEN I FOUND YOU?
I HATE MYSELF.
KA-CHING!
Peirce

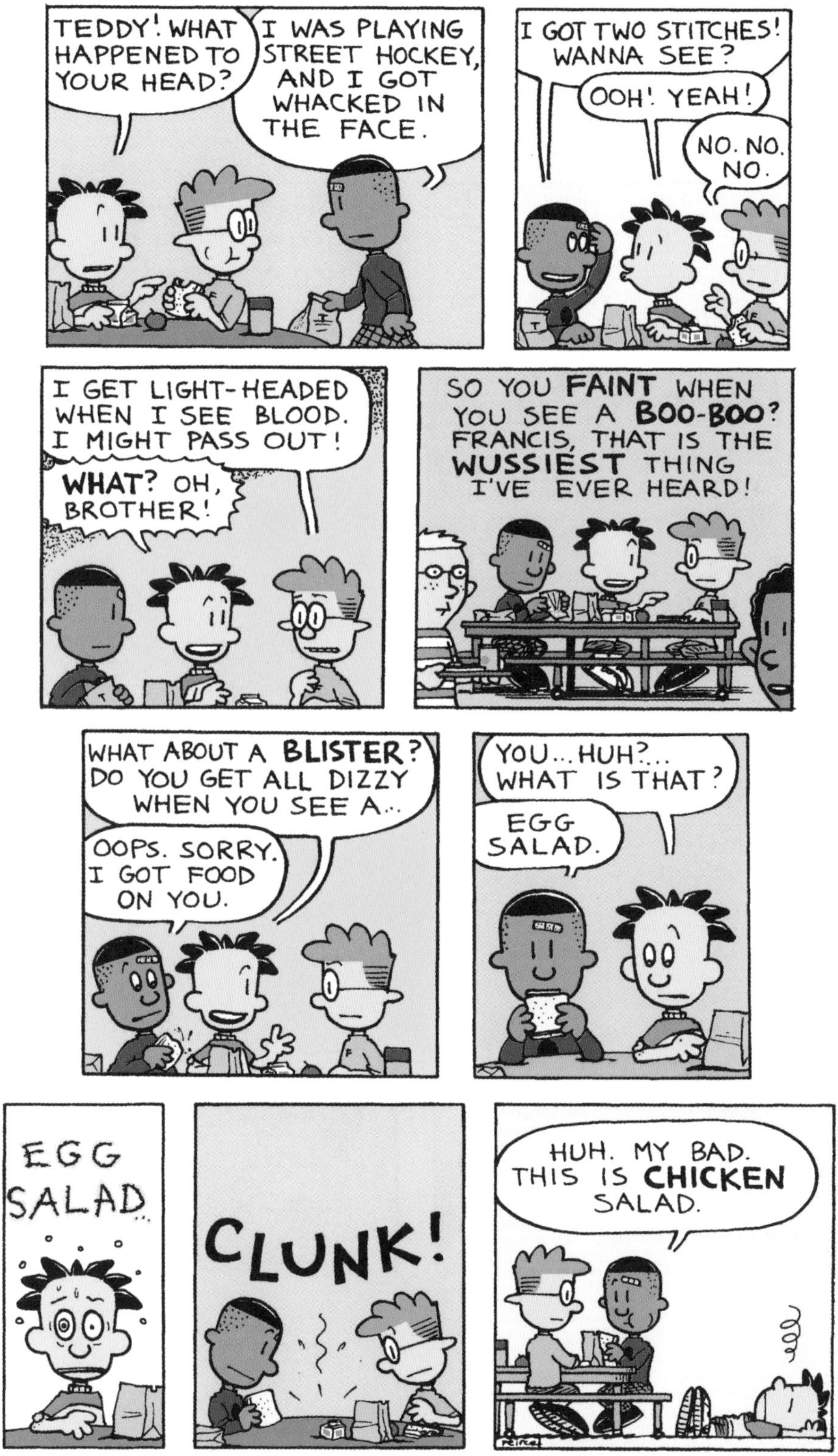
TEDDY! WHAT HAPPENED TO YOUR HEAD?
I WAS PLAYING STREET HOCKEY, AND I GOT WHACKED IN THE FACE.
I GOT TWO STITCHES! WANNA SEE?
OOH! YEAH!
NO. NO. NO.
I GET LIGHT-HEADED WHEN I SEE BLOOD. I MIGHT PASS OUT!
WHAT? OH, BROTHER!
SO YOU FAINT WHEN YOU SEE A BOO-BOO? FRANCIS, THAT IS THE WUSSIEST THING I'VE EVER HEARD!
WHAT ABOUT A BLISTER? DO YOU GET ALL DIZZY WHEN YOU SEE A...
OOPS. SORRY. I GOT FOOD ON YOU.
YOU... HUH?... WHAT IS THAT?
EGG SALAD.
EGG SALAD...
CLUNK!
HUH. MY BAD. THIS IS CHICKEN SALAD.

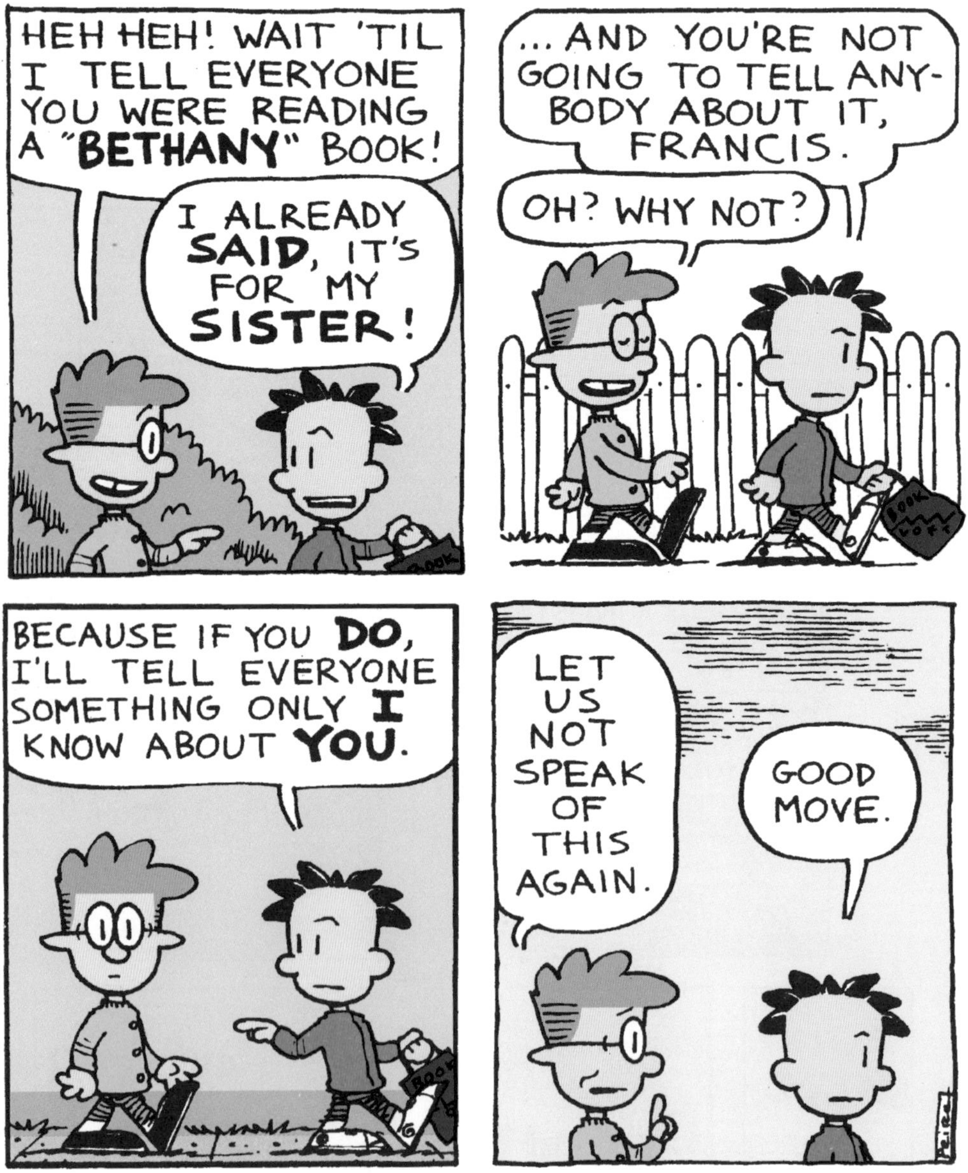
HEH HEH! WAIT 'TIL I TELL EVERYONE YOU WERE READING A "BETHANY" BOOK!
I ALREADY SAID, IT'S FOR MY SISTER!
BOOK
...AND YOU'RE NOT GOING TO TELL ANY-BODY ABOUT IT, FRANCIS.
OH? WHY NOT?
BECAUSE IF YOU DO, I'LL TELL EVERYONE SOMETHING ONLY I KNOW ABOUT YOU.
BOOK
LET US NOT SPEAK OF THIS AGAIN.
GOOD MOVE.

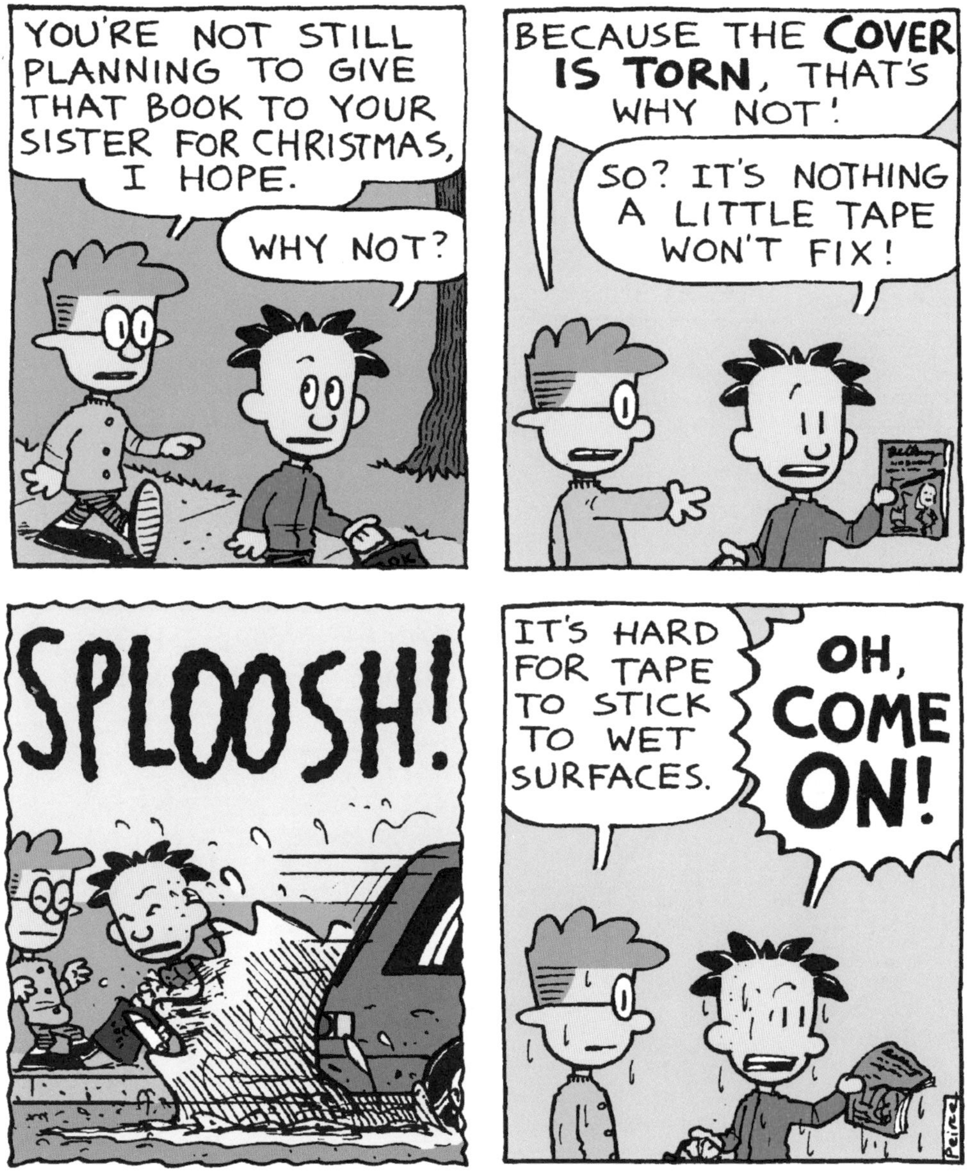
YOU'RE NOT STILL PLANNING TO GIVE THAT BOOK TO YOUR SISTER FOR CHRISTMAS, I HOPE.
WHY NOT?
BECAUSE THE **COVER IS TORN**, THAT'S WHY NOT!
SO? IT'S NOTHING A LITTLE TAPE WON'T FIX!
SPLOOSH!
IT'S HARD FOR TAPE TO STICK TO WET SURFACES.
OH, COME ON!
Peirce

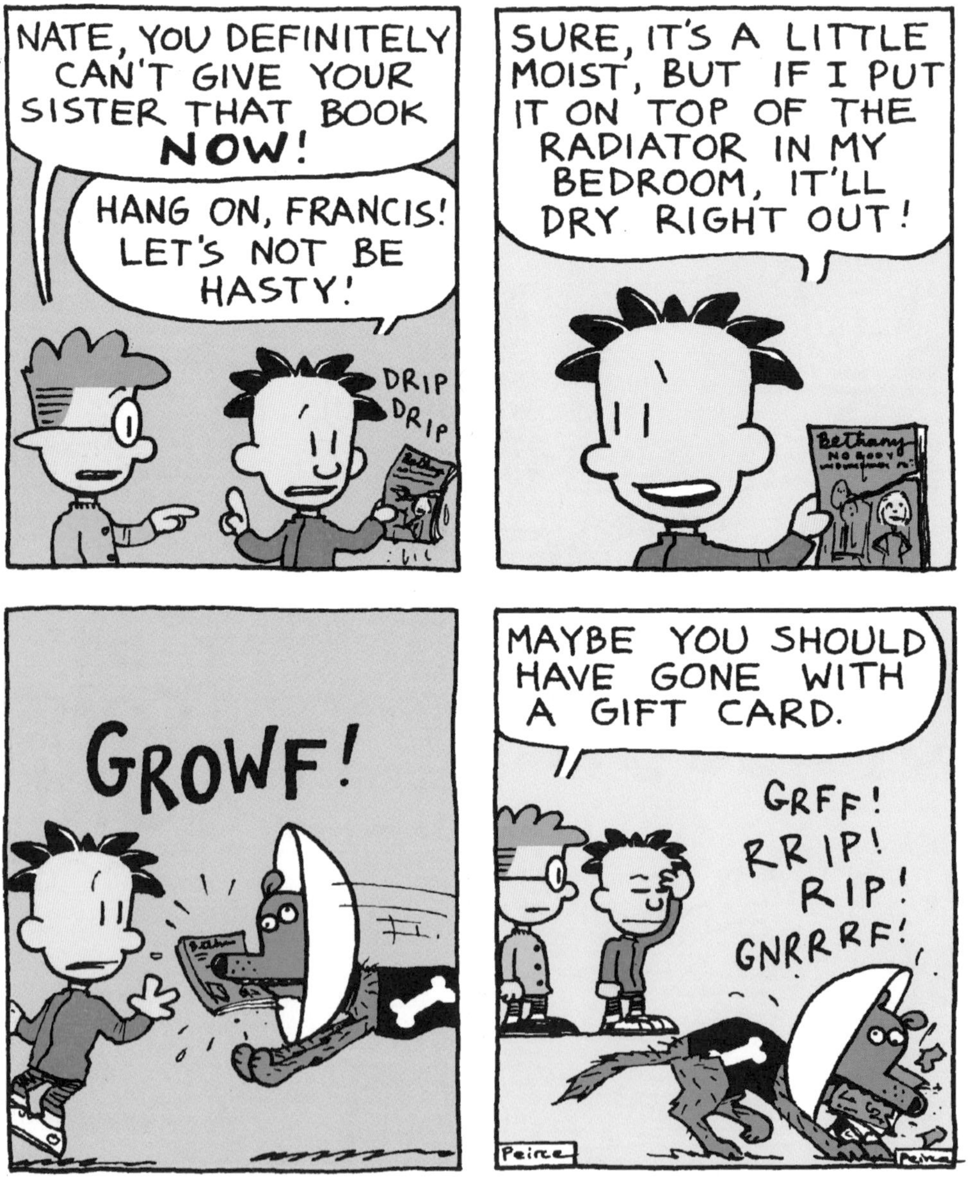
NATE, YOU DEFINITELY CAN'T GIVE YOUR SISTER THAT BOOK NOW!
HANG ON, FRANCIS! LET'S NOT BE HASTY!
DRIP DRIP
SURE, IT'S A LITTLE MOIST, BUT IF I PUT IT ON TOP OF THE RADIATOR IN MY BEDROOM, IT'LL DRY RIGHT OUT!
GROWF!
MAYBE YOU SHOULD HAVE GONE WITH A GIFT CARD.
GRFF!
RRIP!
RIP!
GNRRRF!
Peirce

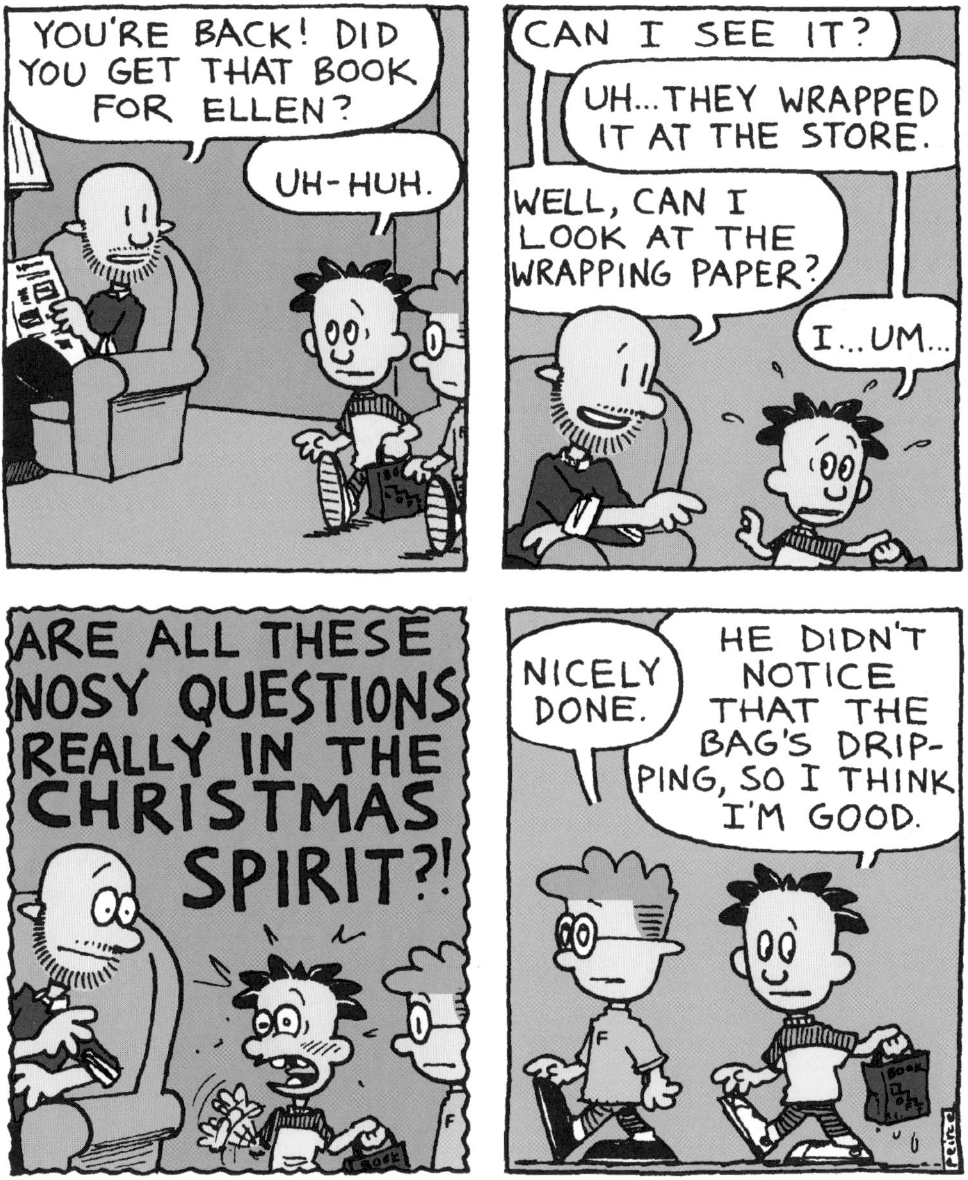
YOU'RE BACK! DID YOU GET THAT BOOK FOR ELLEN?
UH-HUH.
CAN I SEE IT?
UH...THEY WRAPPED IT AT THE STORE.
WELL, CAN I LOOK AT THE WRAPPING PAPER?
I...UM...
ARE ALL THESE NOSY QUESTIONS REALLY IN THE CHRISTMAS SPIRIT?!
NICELY DONE.
HE DIDN'T NOTICE THAT THE BAG'S DRIPPING, SO I THINK I'M GOOD.

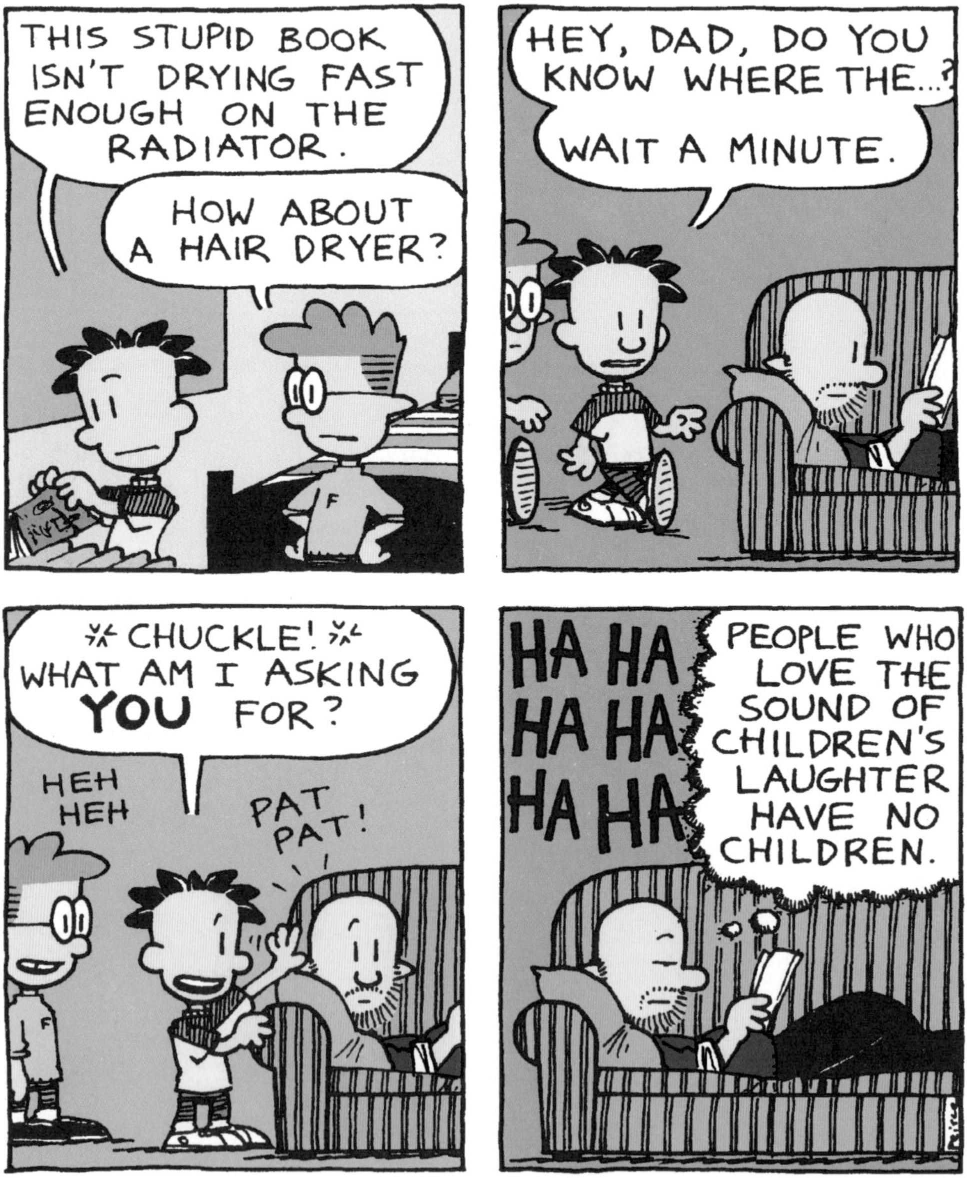

THIS STUPID BOOK ISN'T DRYING FAST ENOUGH ON THE RADIATOR.
HOW ABOUT A HAIR DRYER?
HEY, DAD, DO YOU KNOW WHERE THE...?
WAIT A MINUTE.
CHUCKLE! WHAT AM I ASKING YOU FOR?
HEH HEH
PAT PAT!
HA HA HA HA HA HA
PEOPLE WHO LOVE THE SOUND OF CHILDREN'S LAUGHTER HAVE NO CHILDREN.

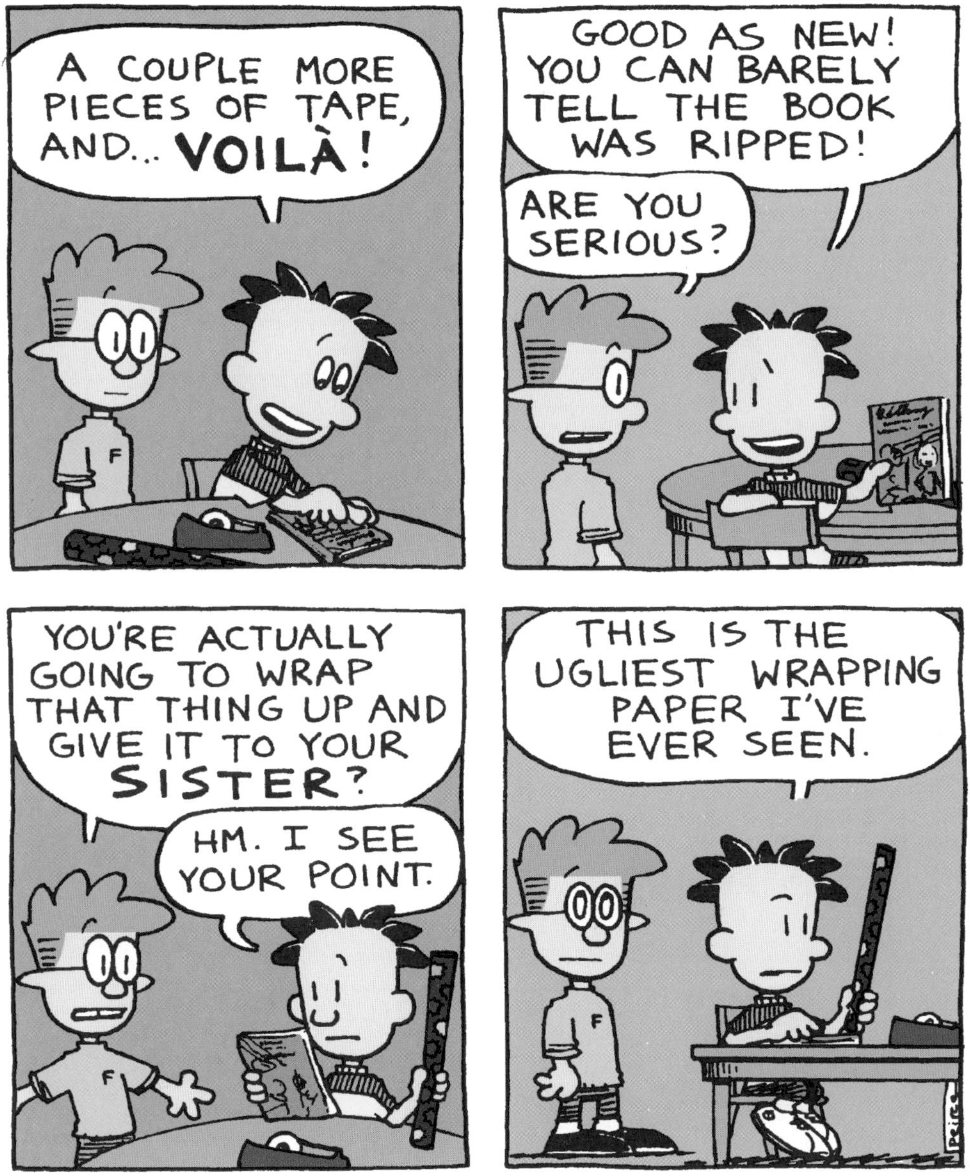
A COUPLE MORE PIECES OF TAPE, AND... VOILÀ!
GOOD AS NEW! YOU CAN BARELY TELL THE BOOK WAS RIPPED!
ARE YOU SERIOUS?
YOU'RE ACTUALLY GOING TO WRAP THAT THING UP AND GIVE IT TO YOUR SISTER?
HM. I SEE YOUR POINT.
THIS IS THE UGLIEST WRAPPING PAPER I'VE EVER SEEN.
PEIRCE

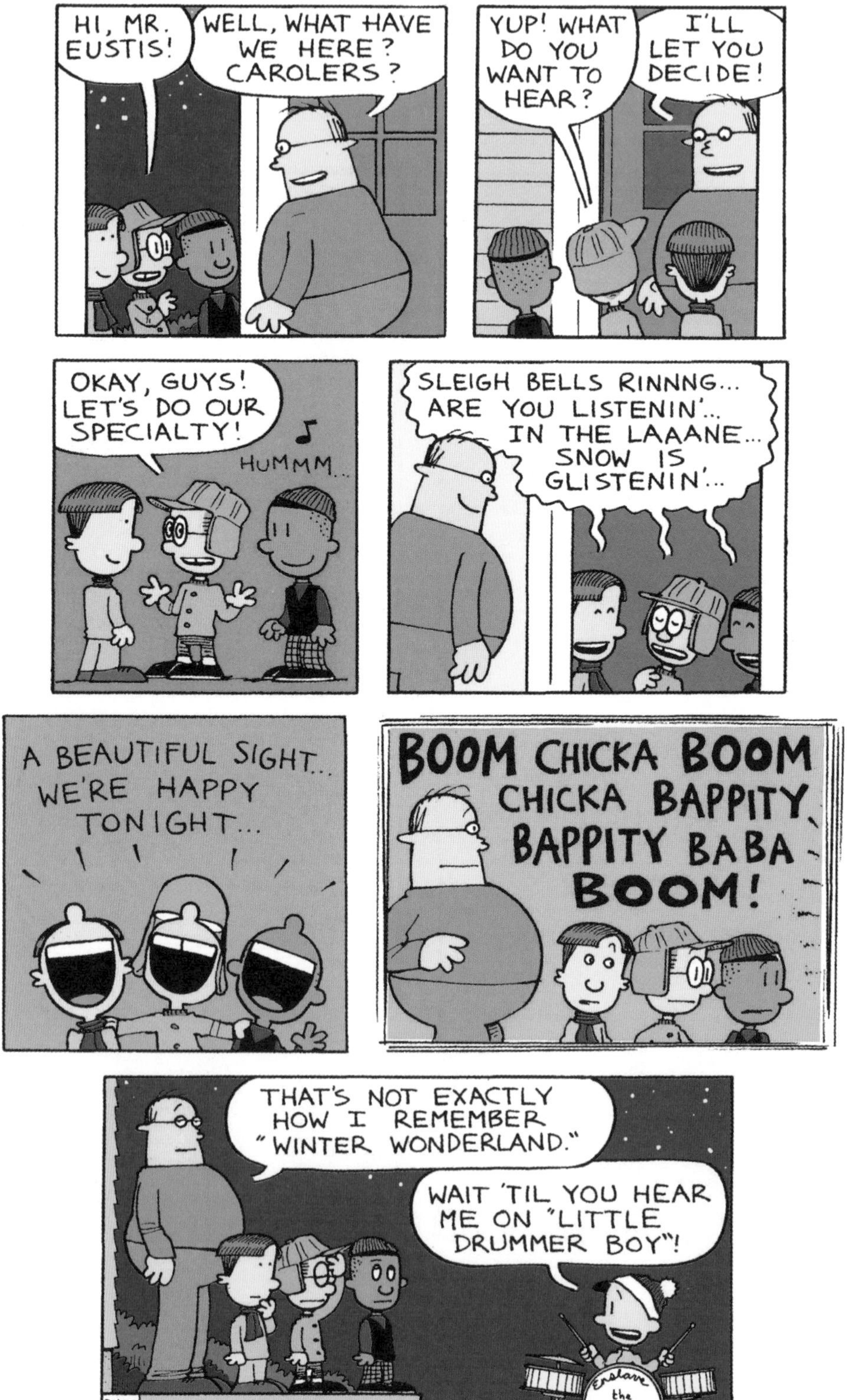
HI, MR. EUSTIS!
WELL, WHAT HAVE WE HERE? CAROLERS?
YUP! WHAT DO YOU WANT TO HEAR?
I'LL LET YOU DECIDE!
OKAY, GUYS! LET'S DO OUR SPECIALTY!
HUMMM...
SLEIGH BELLS RINNNG... ARE YOU LISTENIN'... IN THE LAAANE... SNOW IS GLISTENIN'...
A BEAUTIFUL SIGHT... WE'RE HAPPY TONIGHT...
BOOM CHICKA BOOM CHICKA BAPPITY BAPPITY BABA BOOM!
THAT'S NOT EXACTLY HOW I REMEMBER "WINTER WONDERLAND."
WAIT 'TIL YOU HEAR ME ON "LITTLE DRUMMER BOY"!
Enslave the
Peirce

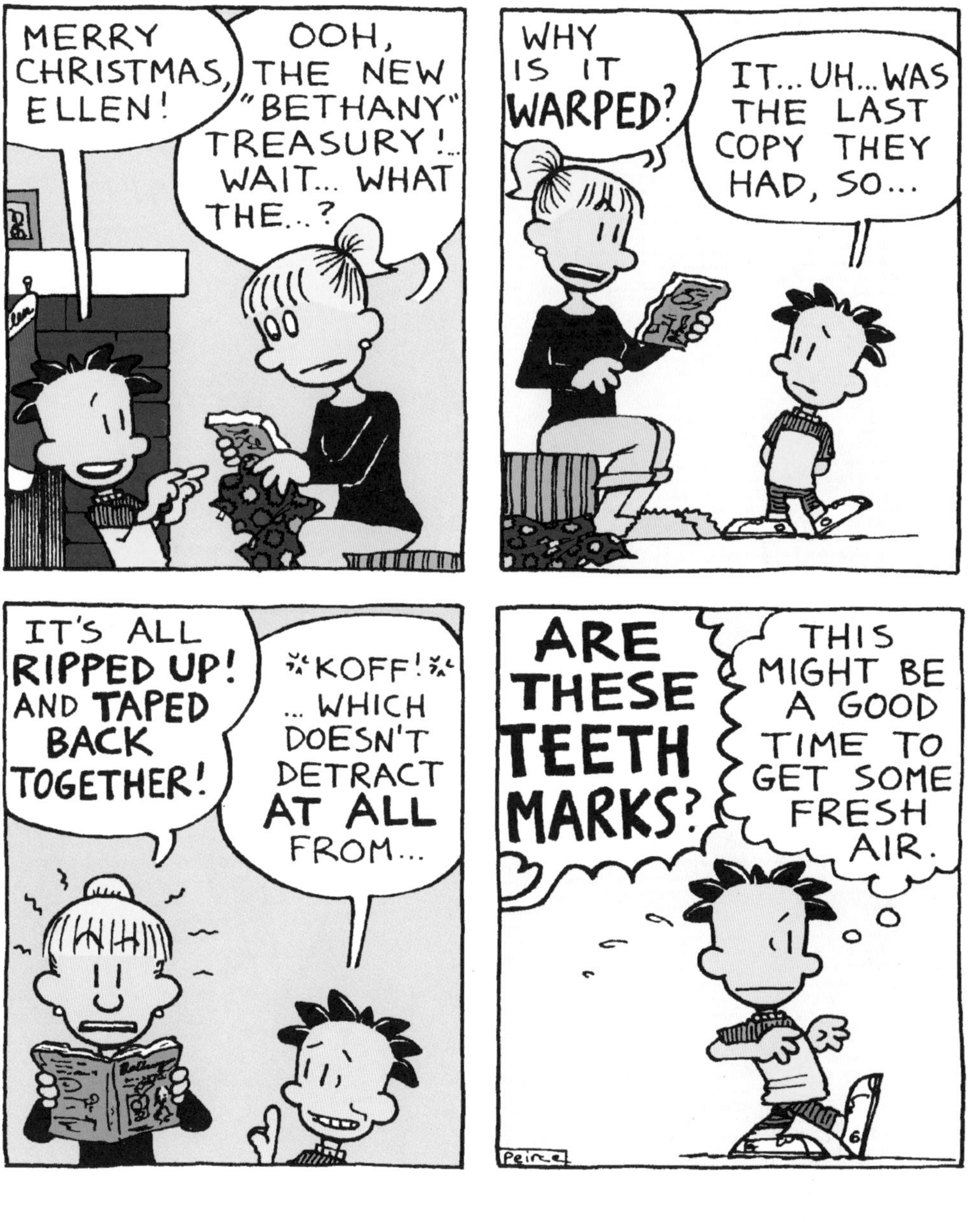
MERRY CHRISTMAS, ELLEN!
OOH, THE NEW "BETHANY" TREASURY!... WAIT... WHAT THE...?
WHY IS IT **WARPED**?
IT... UH... WAS THE LAST COPY THEY HAD, SO...
IT'S ALL **RIPPED UP**! AND **TAPED BACK TOGETHER**!
KOFF! ... WHICH DOESN'T DETRACT **AT ALL** FROM...
ARE THESE TEETH MARKS?
THIS MIGHT BE A GOOD TIME TO GET SOME FRESH AIR.
PEIRCE

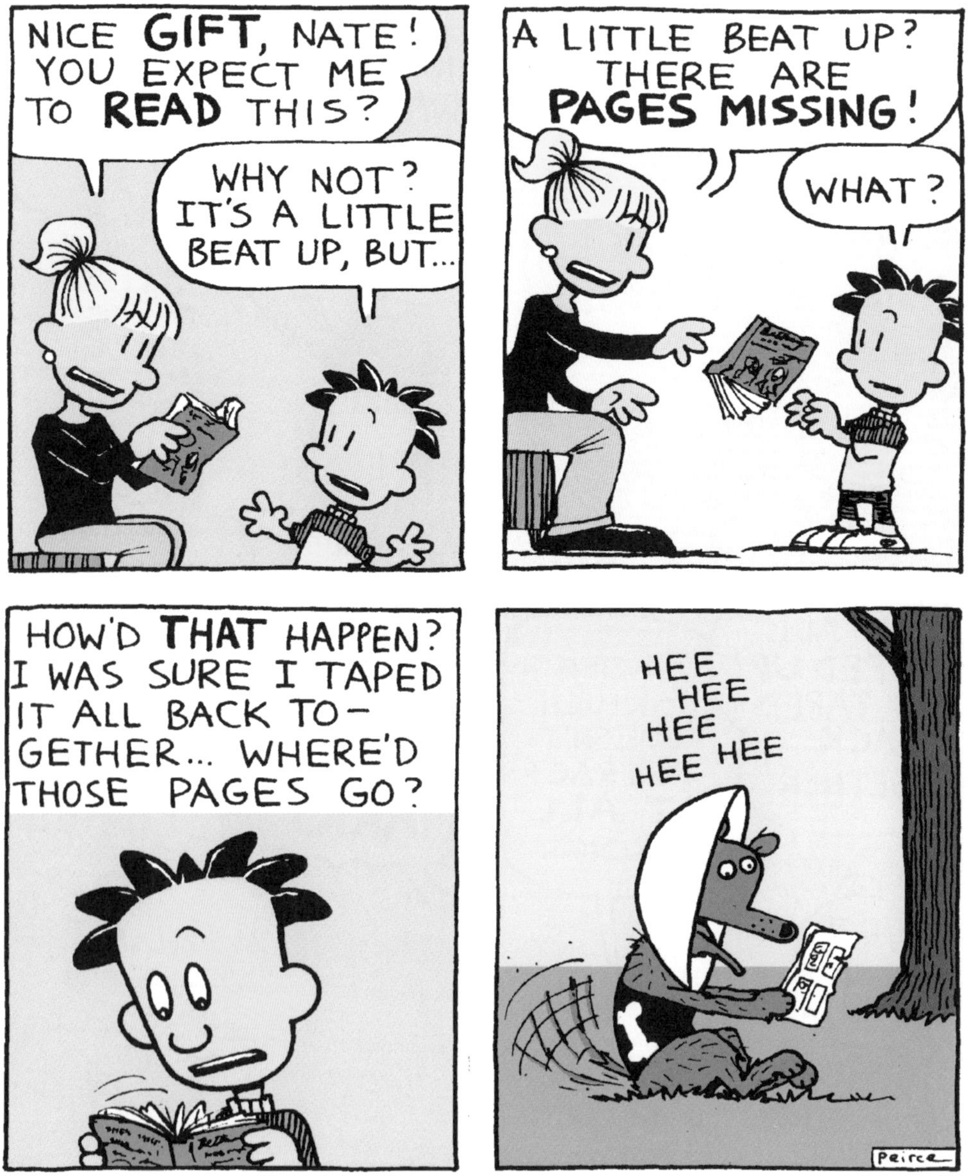
NICE **GIFT**, NATE! YOU EXPECT ME TO **READ** THIS?
WHY NOT? IT'S A LITTLE BEAT UP, BUT...
A LITTLE BEAT UP? THERE ARE **PAGES MISSING**!
WHAT?
HOW'D **THAT** HAPPEN? I WAS SURE I TAPED IT ALL BACK TOGETHER... WHERE'D THOSE PAGES GO?
HEE HEE HEE HEE HEE
Peirce

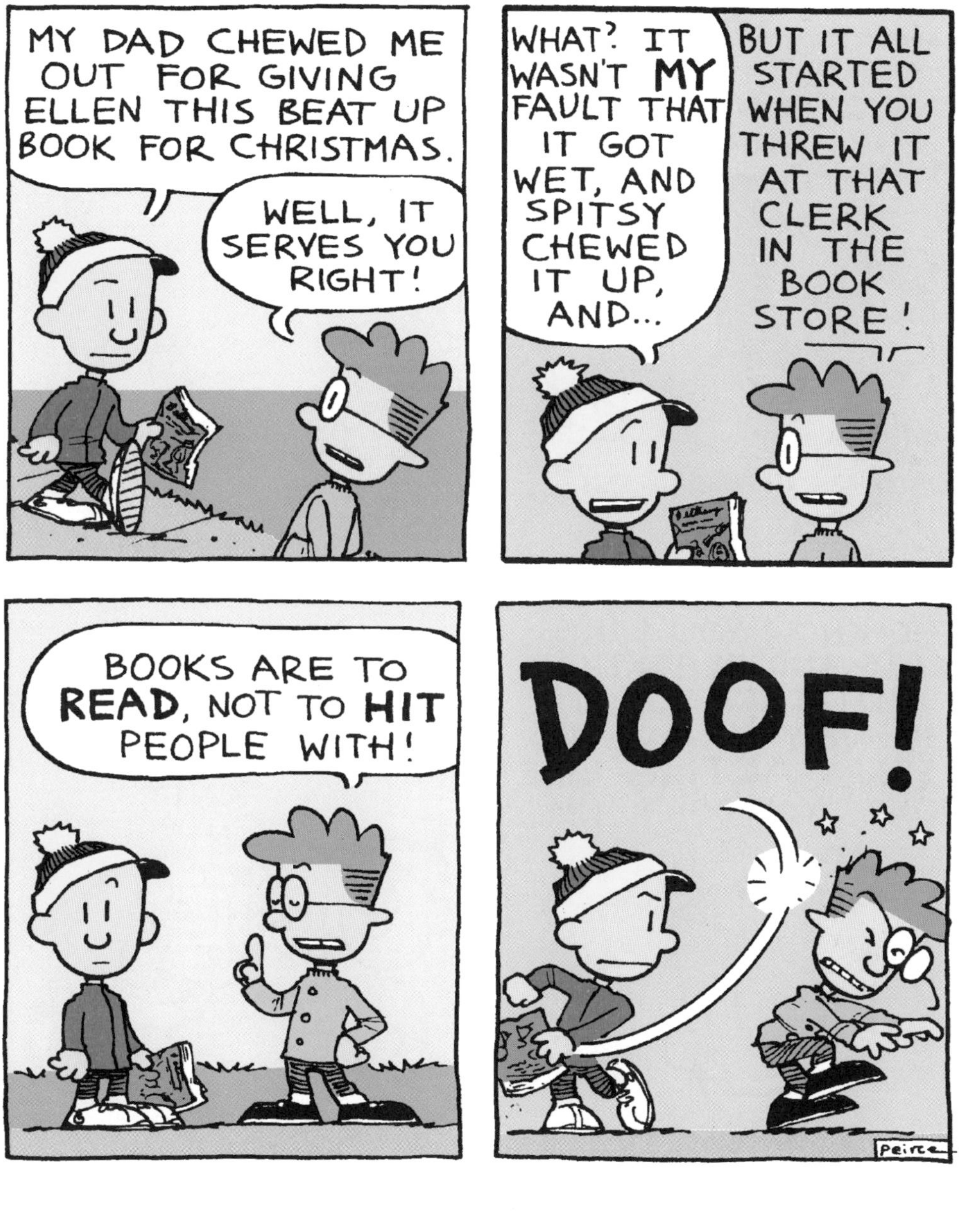
MY DAD CHEWED ME OUT FOR GIVING ELLEN THIS BEAT UP BOOK FOR CHRISTMAS.
WELL, IT SERVES YOU RIGHT!
WHAT? IT WASN'T **MY** FAULT THAT IT GOT WET, AND SPITSY CHEWED IT UP, AND...
BUT IT ALL STARTED WHEN YOU THREW IT AT THAT CLERK IN THE BOOK STORE!
BOOKS ARE TO **READ**, NOT TO **HIT** PEOPLE WITH!
DOOF!
Peirce

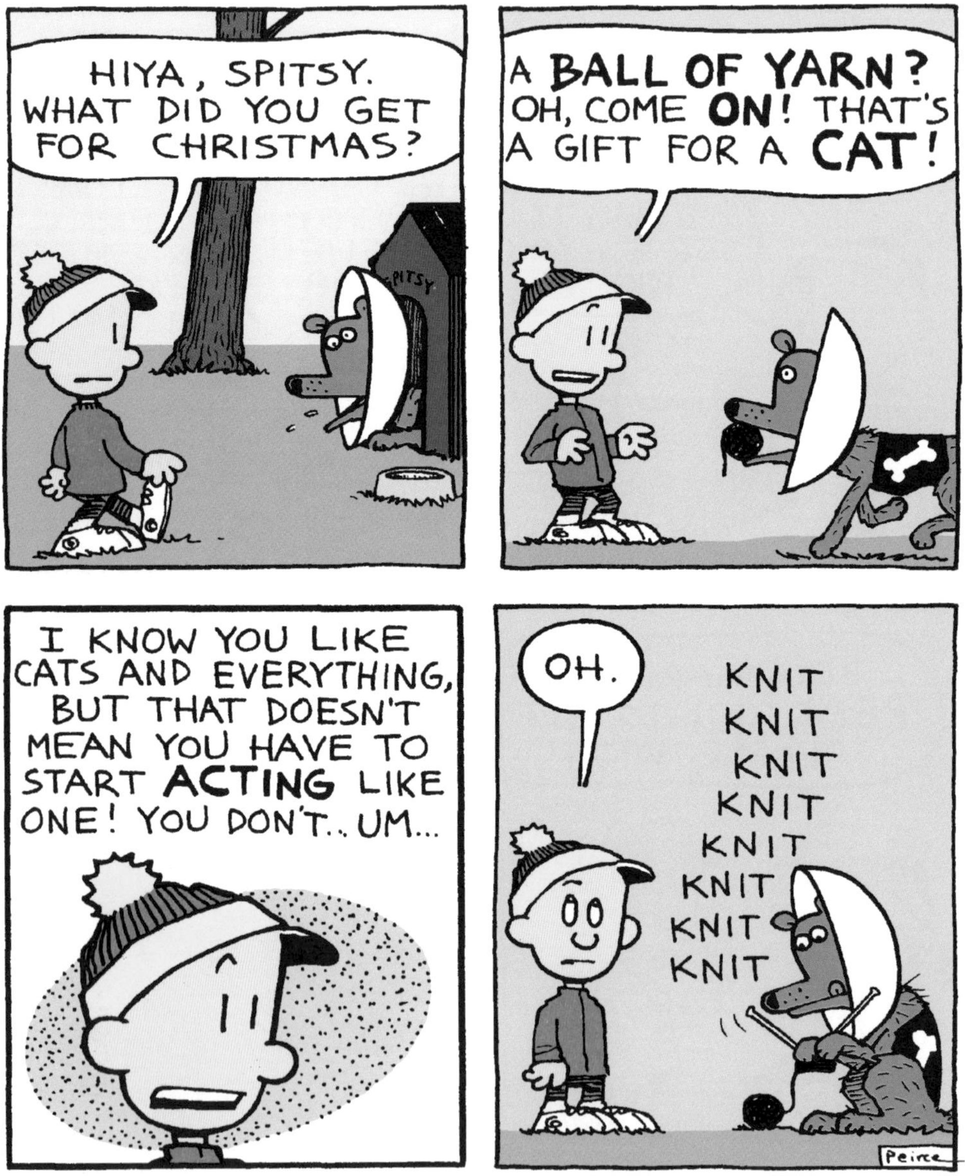
HIYA, SPITSY. WHAT DID YOU GET FOR CHRISTMAS?
SPITSY
A BALL OF YARN? OH, COME ON! THAT'S A GIFT FOR A CAT!
I KNOW YOU LIKE CATS AND EVERYTHING, BUT THAT DOESN'T MEAN YOU HAVE TO START ACTING LIKE ONE! YOU DON'T... UM...
OH.
KNIT KNIT KNIT KNIT KNIT KNIT KNIT KNIT
Peirce

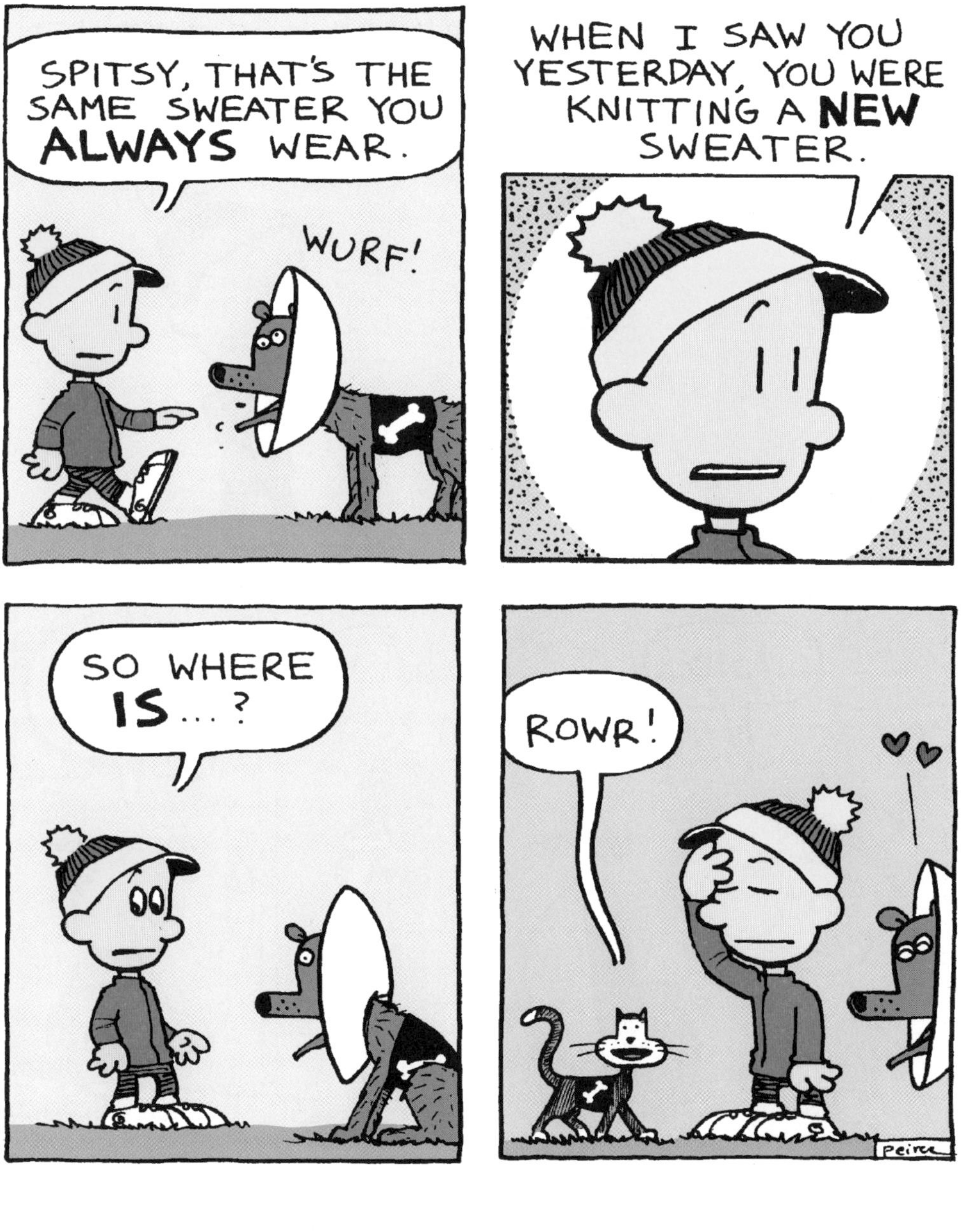
SPITSY, THAT'S THE SAME SWEATER YOU **ALWAYS** WEAR.
WURF!
WHEN I SAW YOU YESTERDAY, YOU WERE KNITTING A **NEW** SWEATER.
SO WHERE **IS**... ?
ROWR!
peirce

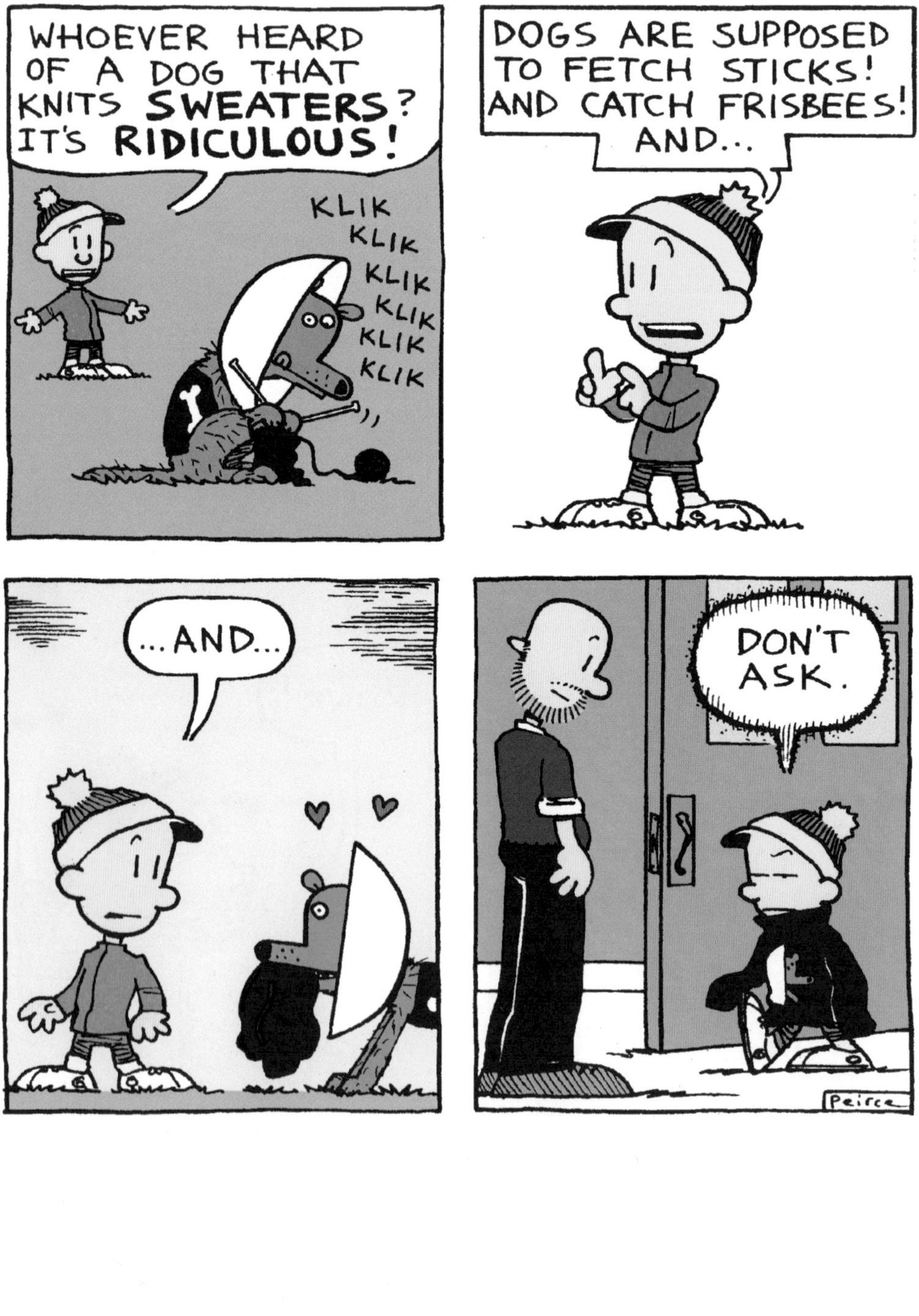
WHOEVER HEARD OF A DOG THAT KNITS SWEATERS? IT'S RIDICULOUS!
KLIK KLIK KLIK KLIK KLIK KLIK
DOGS ARE SUPPOSED TO FETCH STICKS! AND CATCH FRISBEES! AND...
...AND...
DON'T ASK.
Peirce

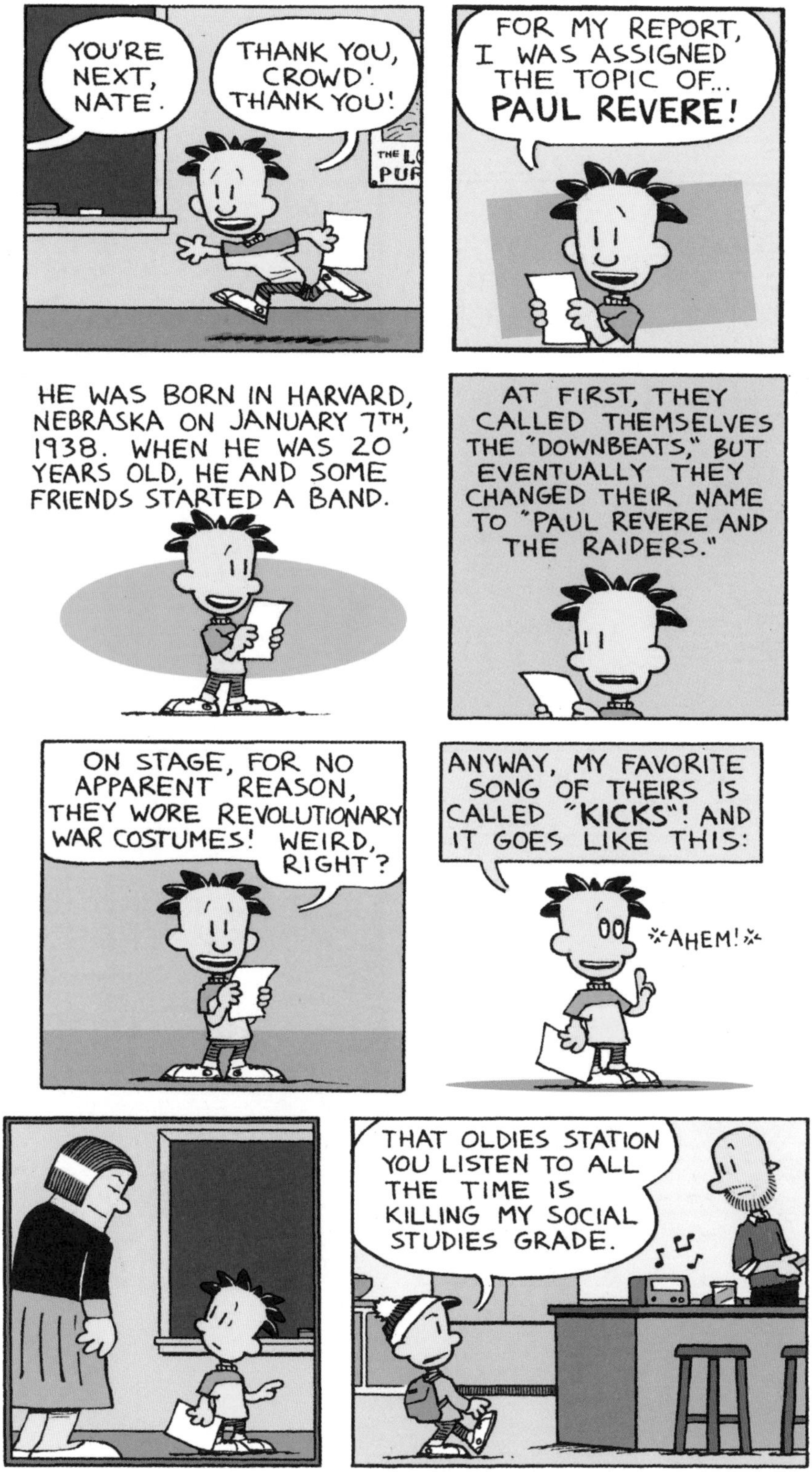
YOU'RE NEXT, NATE.
THANK YOU, CROWD! THANK YOU!
THE LO PUR
FOR MY REPORT, I WAS ASSIGNED THE TOPIC OF... PAUL REVERE!
HE WAS BORN IN HARVARD, NEBRASKA ON JANUARY 7TH, 1938. WHEN HE WAS 20 YEARS OLD, HE AND SOME FRIENDS STARTED A BAND.
AT FIRST, THEY CALLED THEMSELVES THE "DOWNBEATS," BUT EVENTUALLY THEY CHANGED THEIR NAME TO "PAUL REVERE AND THE RAIDERS."
ON STAGE, FOR NO APPARENT REASON, THEY WORE REVOLUTIONARY WAR COSTUMES! WEIRD, RIGHT?
ANYWAY, MY FAVORITE SONG OF THEIRS IS CALLED "KICKS"! AND IT GOES LIKE THIS:
AHEM!
THAT OLDIES STATION YOU LISTEN TO ALL THE TIME IS KILLING MY SOCIAL STUDIES GRADE.

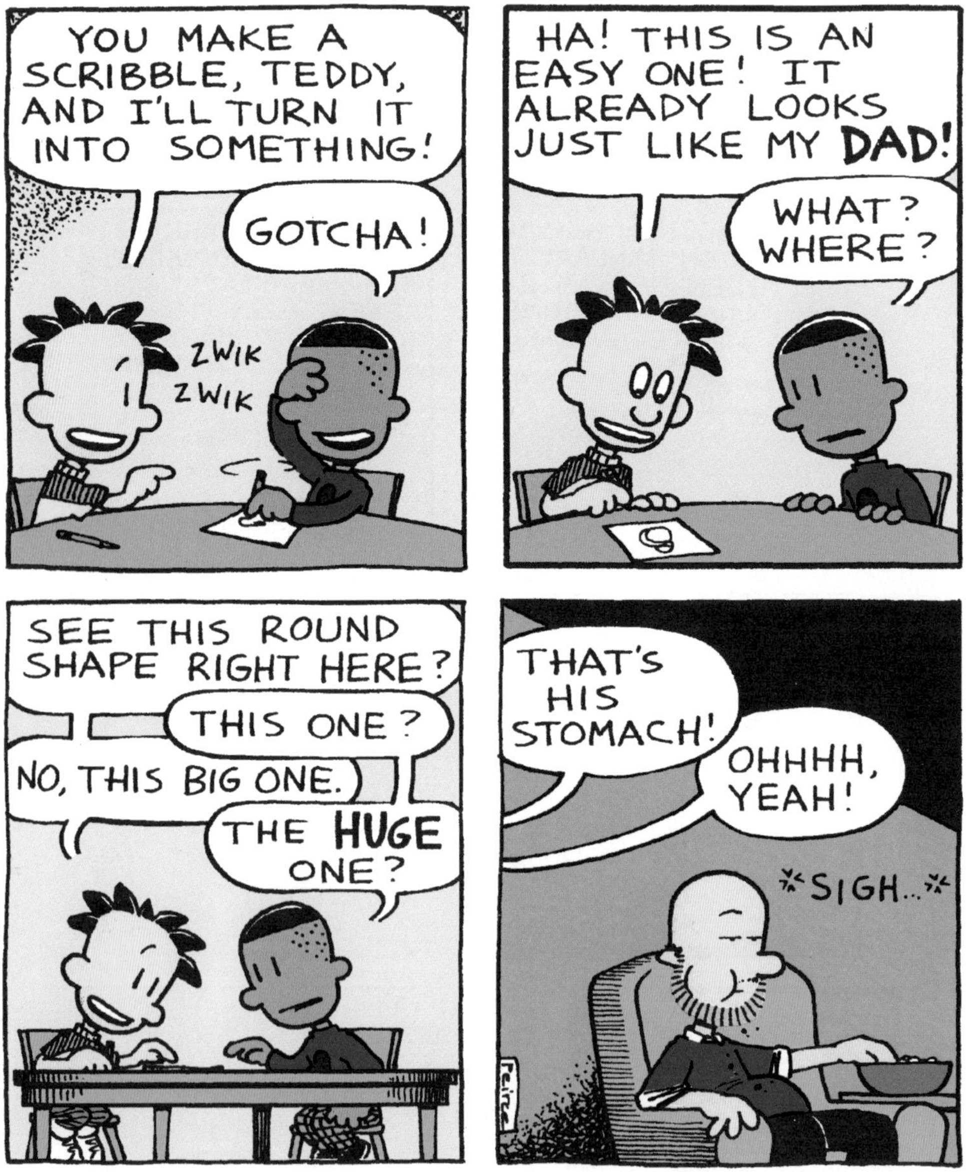
YOU MAKE A SCRIBBLE, TEDDY, AND I'LL TURN IT INTO SOMETHING!
GOTCHA!
ZWIK ZWIK
HA! THIS IS AN EASY ONE! IT ALREADY LOOKS JUST LIKE MY DAD!
WHAT? WHERE?
SEE THIS ROUND SHAPE RIGHT HERE?
THIS ONE?
NO, THIS BIG ONE.
THE HUGE ONE?
THAT'S HIS STOMACH!
OHHHH, YEAH!
SIGH...
Peirce

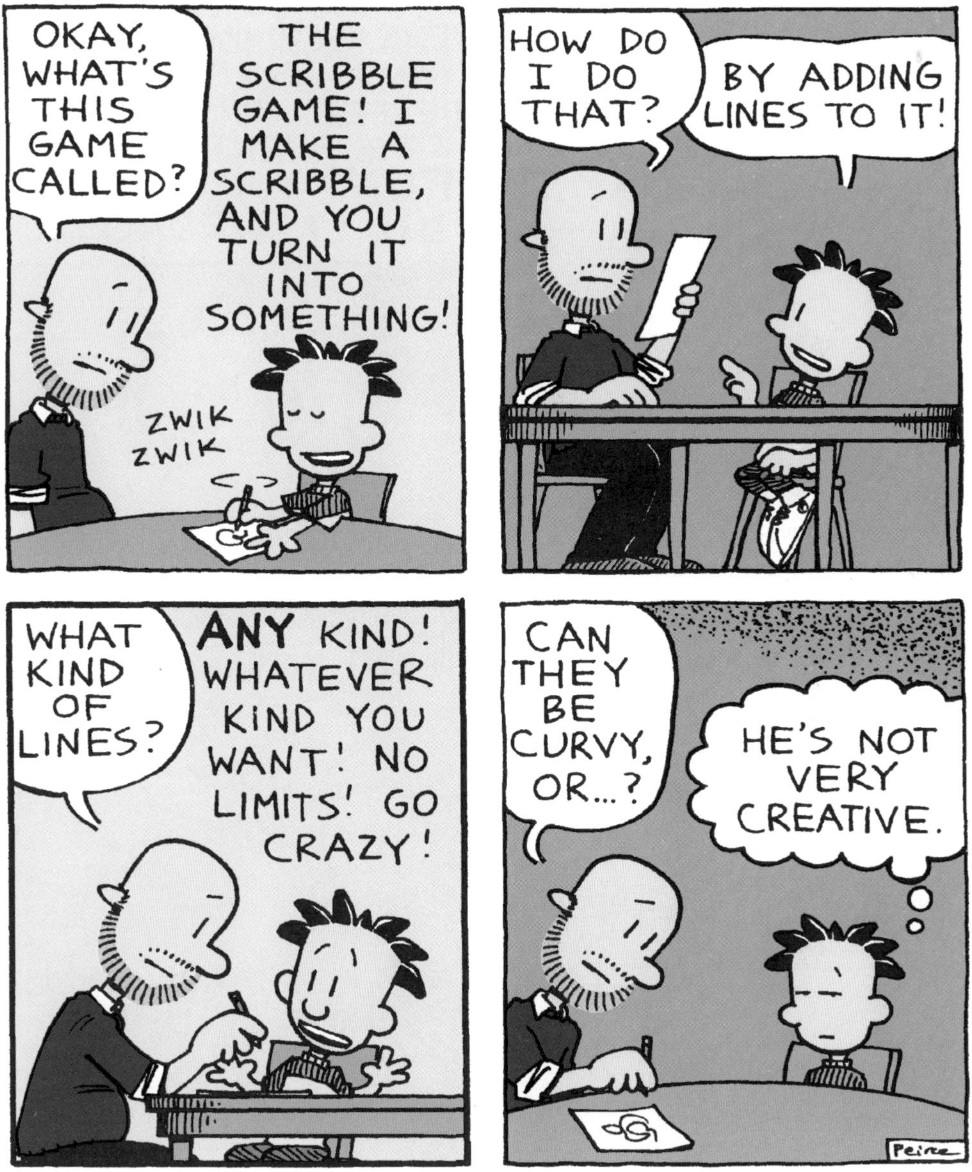
OKAY, WHAT'S THIS GAME CALLED?
THE SCRIBBLE GAME! I MAKE A SCRIBBLE, AND YOU TURN IT INTO SOMETHING!
ZWIK ZWIK
HOW DO I DO THAT?
BY ADDING LINES TO IT!
WHAT KIND OF LINES?
ANY KIND! WHATEVER KIND YOU WANT! NO LIMITS! GO CRAZY!
CAN THEY BE CURVY, OR...?
HE'S NOT VERY CREATIVE.
Peirce

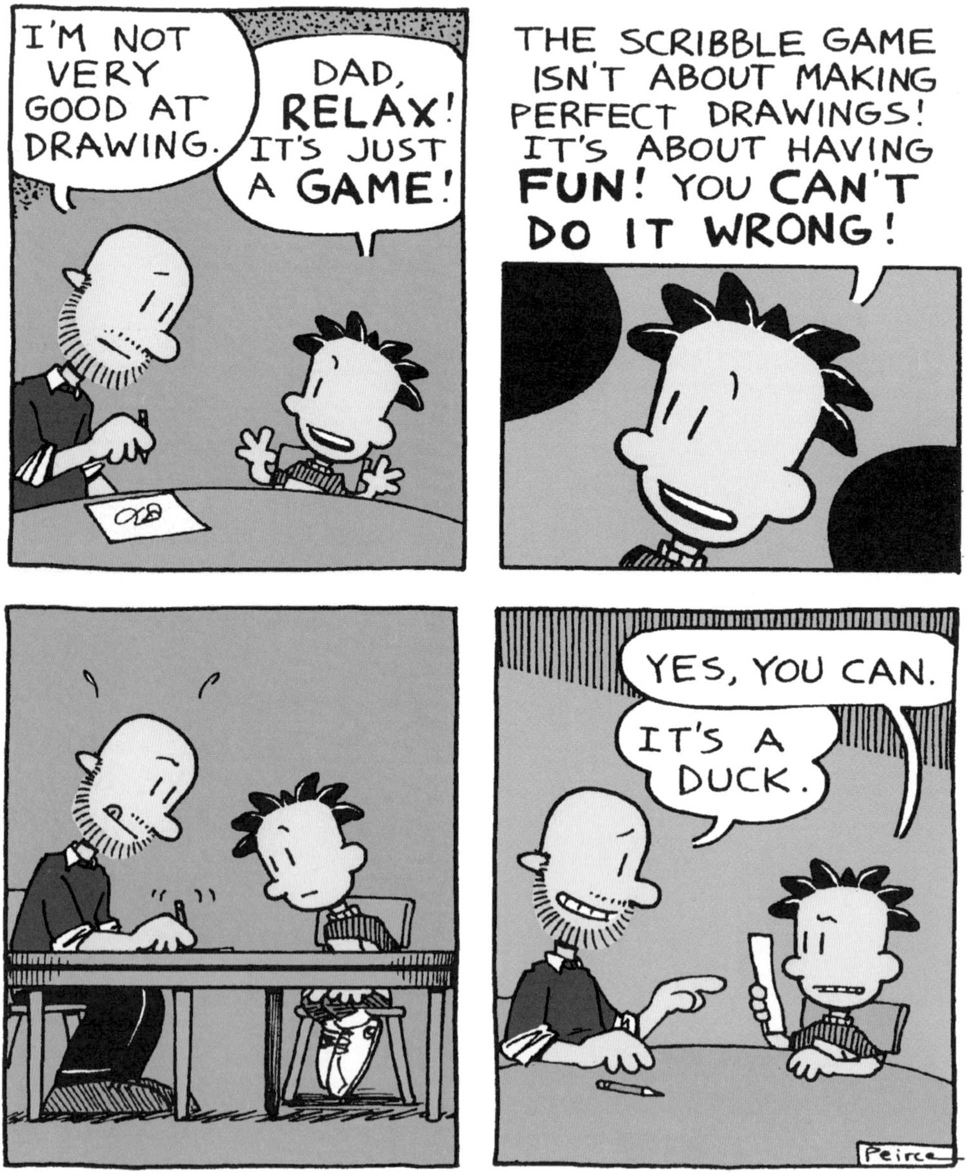
I'M NOT VERY GOOD AT DRAWING.
DAD, RELAX! IT'S JUST A GAME!
THE SCRIBBLE GAME ISN'T ABOUT MAKING PERFECT DRAWINGS! IT'S ABOUT HAVING FUN! YOU CAN'T DO IT WRONG!
YES, YOU CAN.
IT'S A DUCK.
Peirce

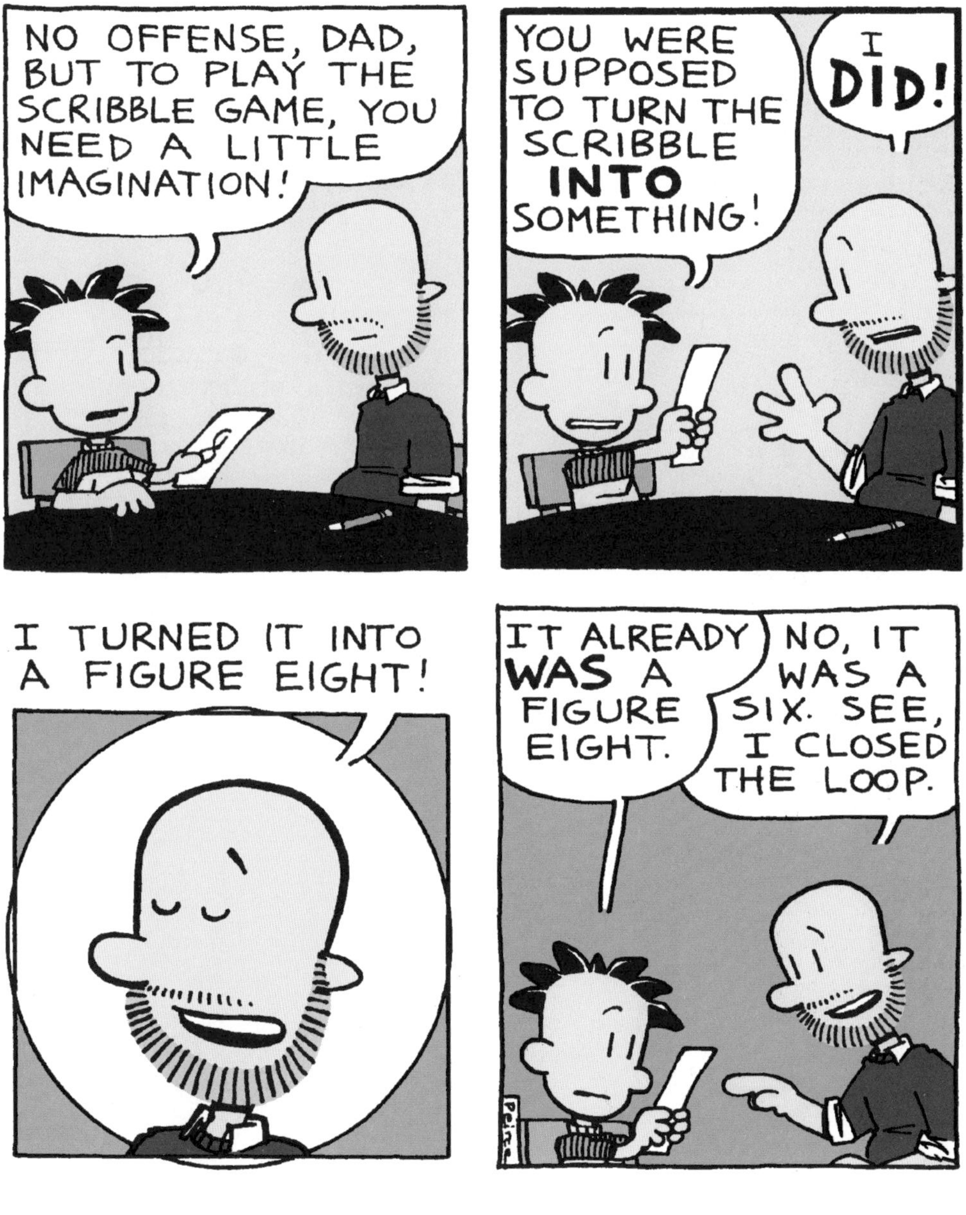
NO OFFENSE, DAD, BUT TO PLAY THE SCRIBBLE GAME, YOU NEED A LITTLE IMAGINATION!
YOU WERE SUPPOSED TO TURN THE SCRIBBLE **INTO** SOMETHING!
I **DID!**
I TURNED IT INTO A FIGURE EIGHT!
IT ALREADY **WAS** A FIGURE EIGHT.
NO, IT WAS A SIX. SEE, I CLOSED THE LOOP.
Peirce

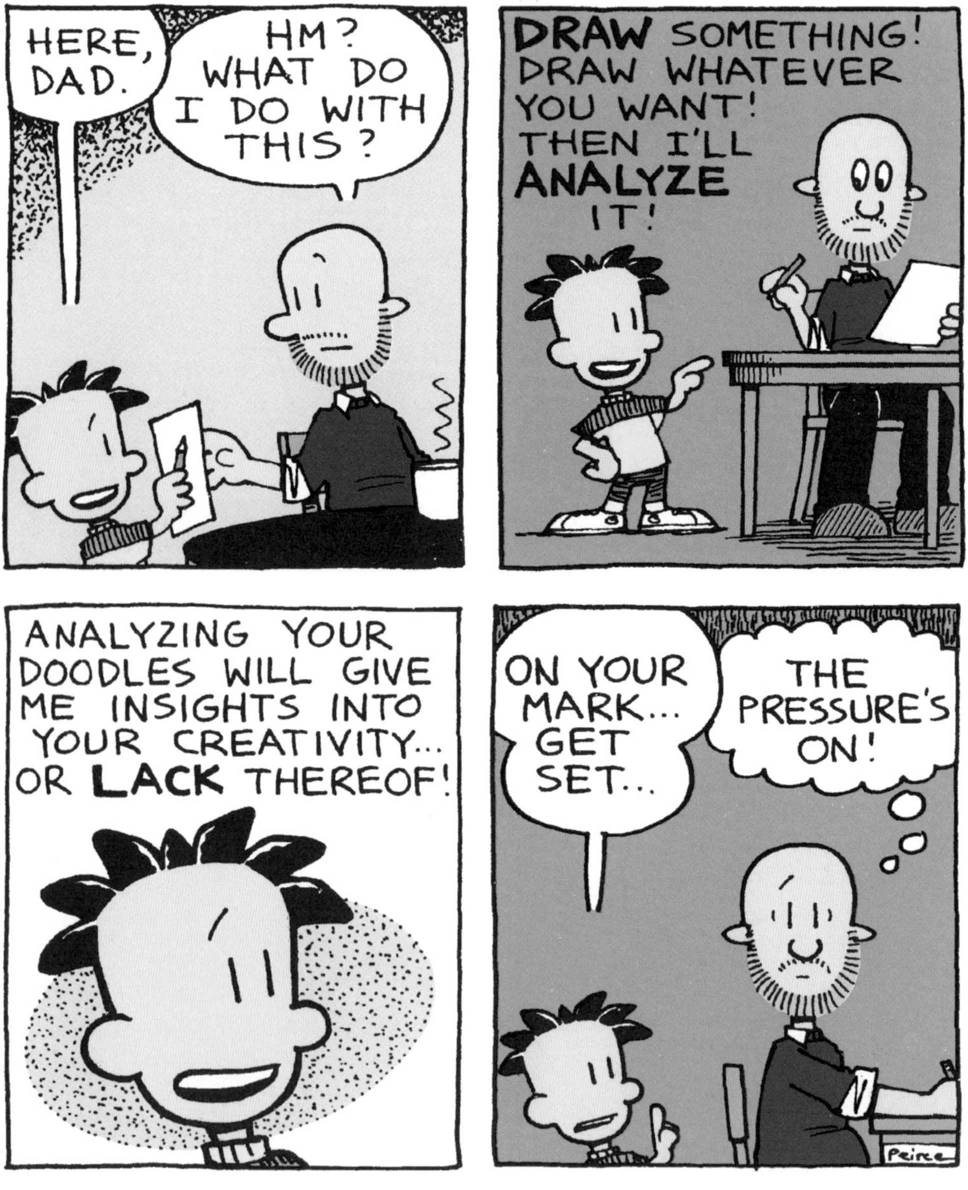
HERE, DAD.
HM? WHAT DO I DO WITH THIS?
DRAW SOMETHING! DRAW WHATEVER YOU WANT! THEN I'LL ANALYZE IT!
ANALYZING YOUR DOODLES WILL GIVE ME INSIGHTS INTO YOUR CREATIVITY... OR LACK THEREOF!
ON YOUR MARK... GET SET...
THE PRESSURE'S ON!
Peirce

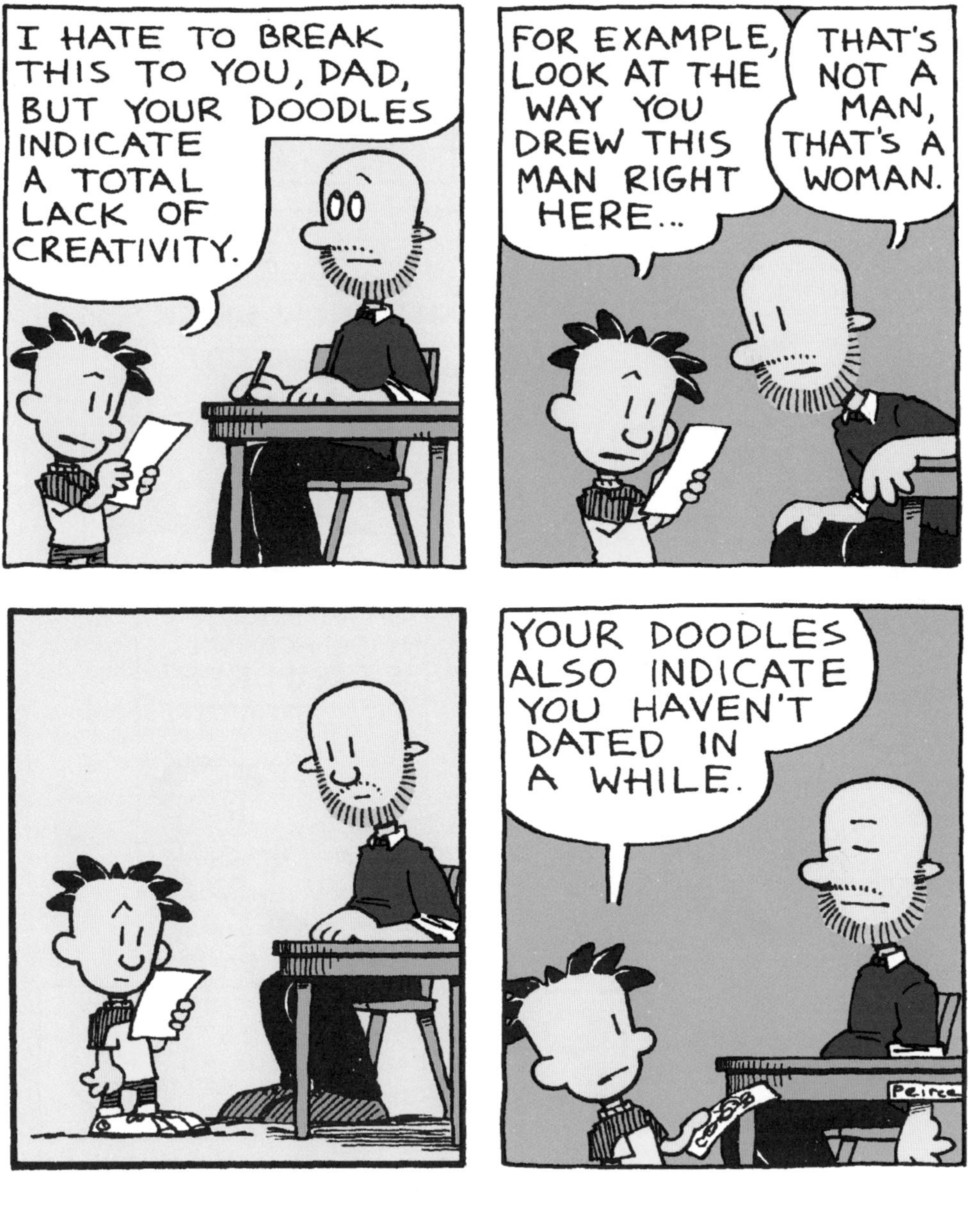
I HATE TO BREAK THIS TO YOU, DAD, BUT YOUR DOODLES INDICATE A TOTAL LACK OF CREATIVITY.
FOR EXAMPLE, LOOK AT THE WAY YOU DREW THIS MAN RIGHT HERE...
THAT'S NOT A MAN, THAT'S A WOMAN.
YOUR DOODLES ALSO INDICATE YOU HAVEN'T DATED IN A WHILE.
Peirce

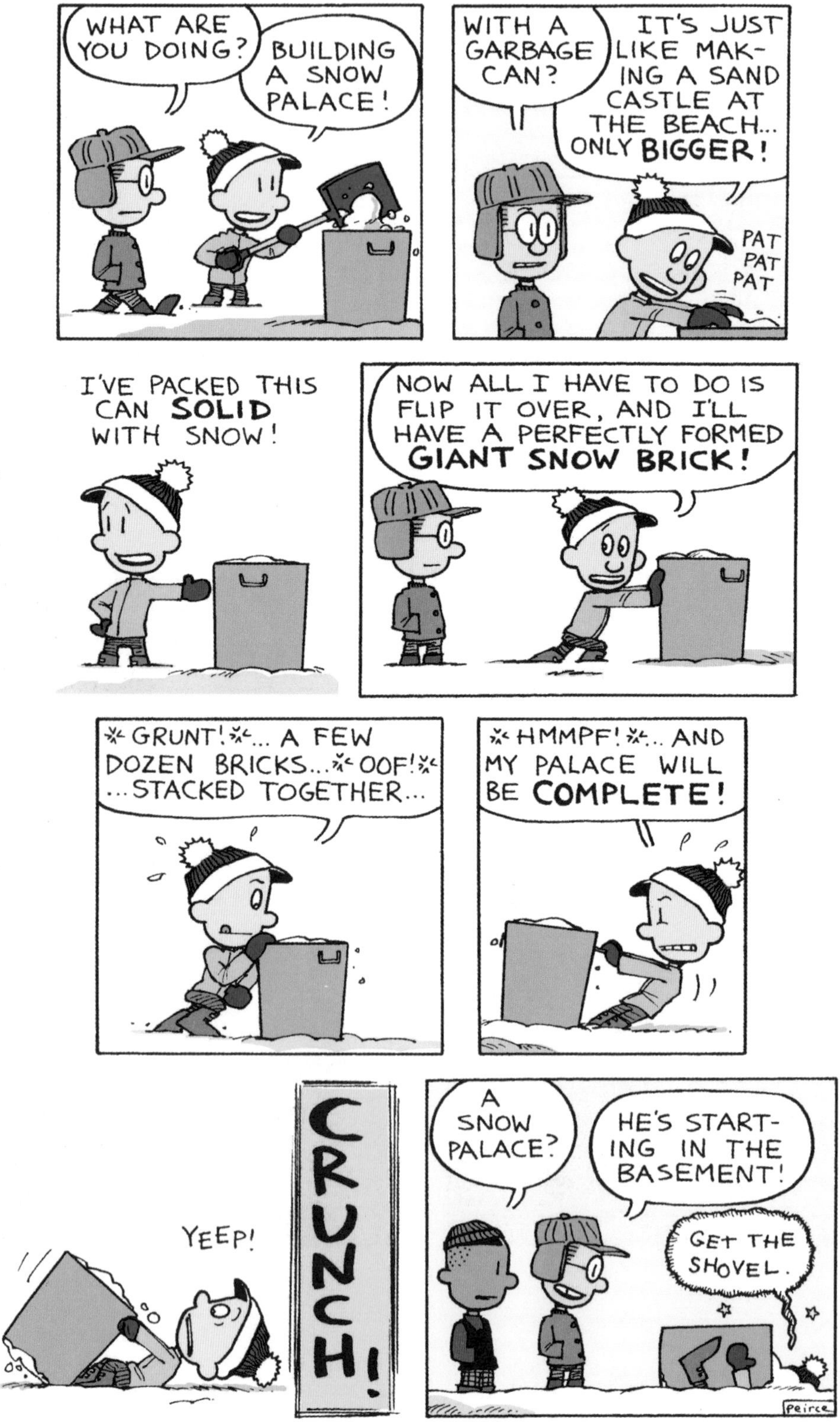
WHAT ARE YOU DOING?
BUILDING A SNOW PALACE!
WITH A GARBAGE CAN?
IT'S JUST LIKE MAKING A SAND CASTLE AT THE BEACH... ONLY BIGGER!
PAT PAT PAT
I'VE PACKED THIS CAN SOLID WITH SNOW!
NOW ALL I HAVE TO DO IS FLIP IT OVER, AND I'LL HAVE A PERFECTLY FORMED GIANT SNOW BRICK!
GRUNT!... A FEW DOZEN BRICKS... OOF! ...STACKED TOGETHER...
HMMPF!... AND MY PALACE WILL BE COMPLETE!
YEEP!
CRUNCH!
A SNOW PALACE?
HE'S STARTING IN THE BASEMENT!
GET THE SHOVEL.
peirce

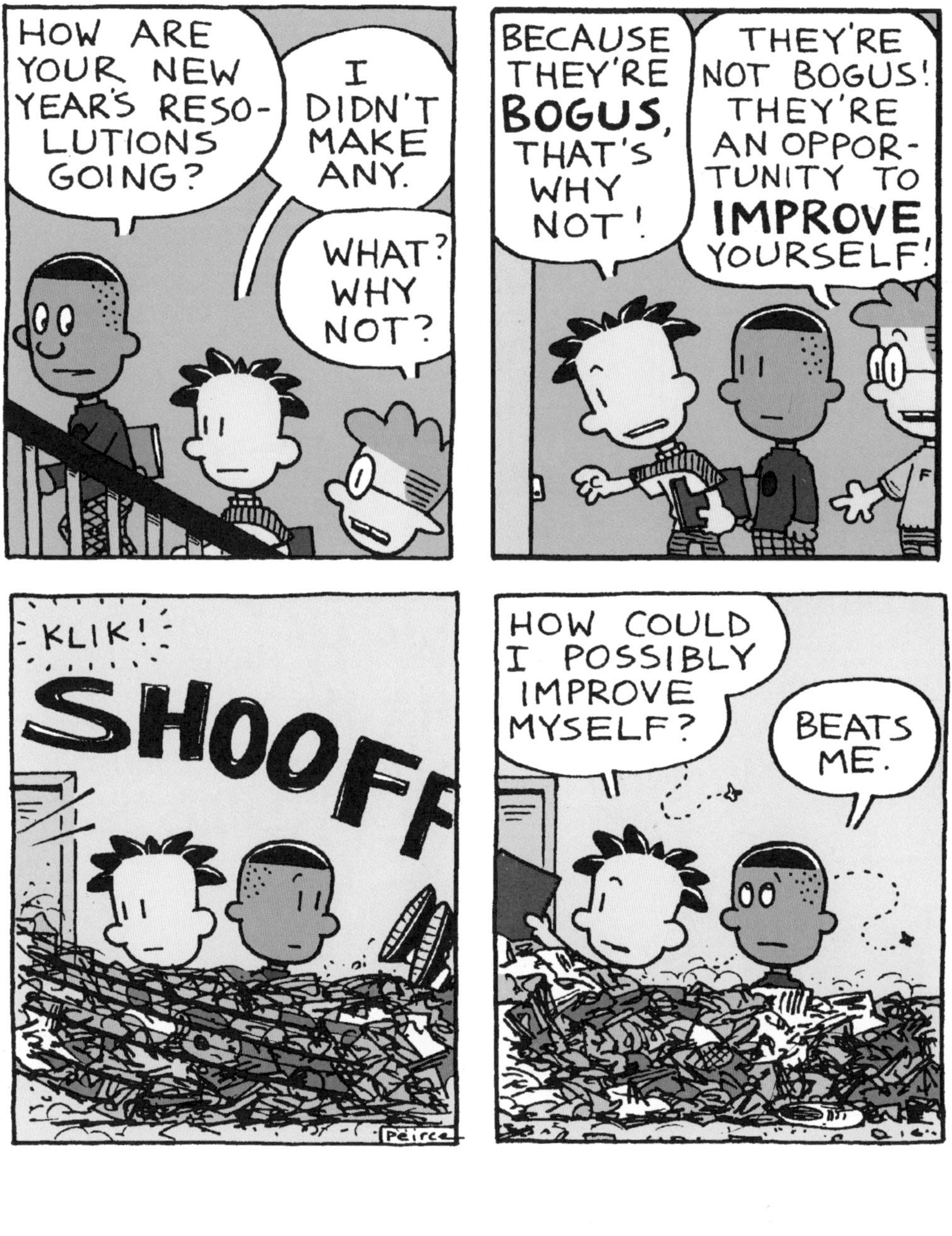
HOW ARE YOUR NEW YEAR'S RESO-LUTIONS GOING?
I DIDN'T MAKE ANY.
WHAT? WHY NOT?
BECAUSE THEY'RE BOGUS, THAT'S WHY NOT!
THEY'RE NOT BOGUS! THEY'RE AN OPPOR-TUNITY TO IMPROVE YOURSELF!
KLIK!
SHOOFF
HOW COULD I POSSIBLY IMPROVE MYSELF?
BEATS ME.
PEIRCE

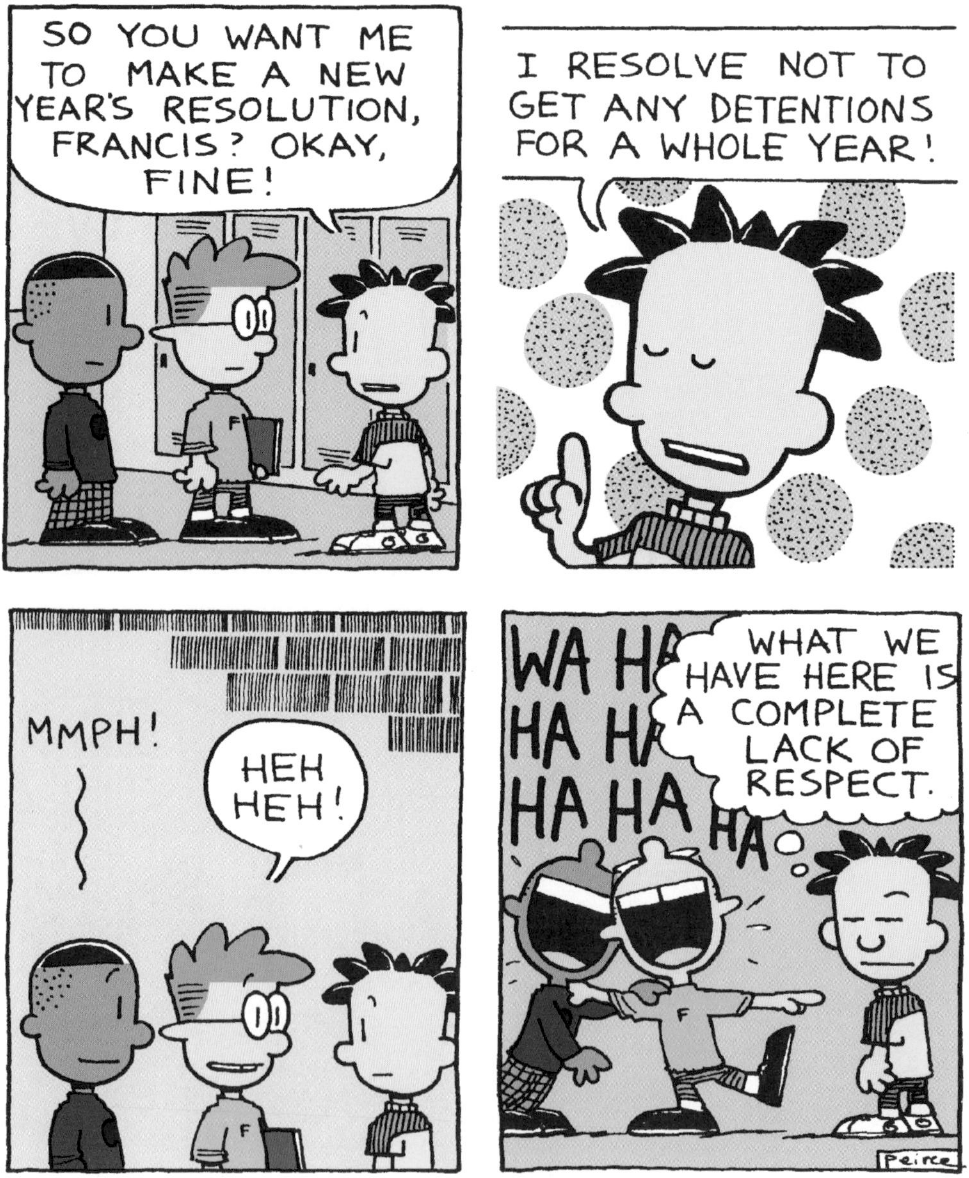
SO YOU WANT ME TO MAKE A NEW YEAR'S RESOLUTION, FRANCIS? OKAY, FINE!
I RESOLVE NOT TO GET ANY DETENTIONS FOR A WHOLE YEAR!
MMPH!
HEH HEH!
WA HA HA HA HA HA HA HA
WHAT WE HAVE HERE IS A COMPLETE LACK OF RESPECT.
Peirce

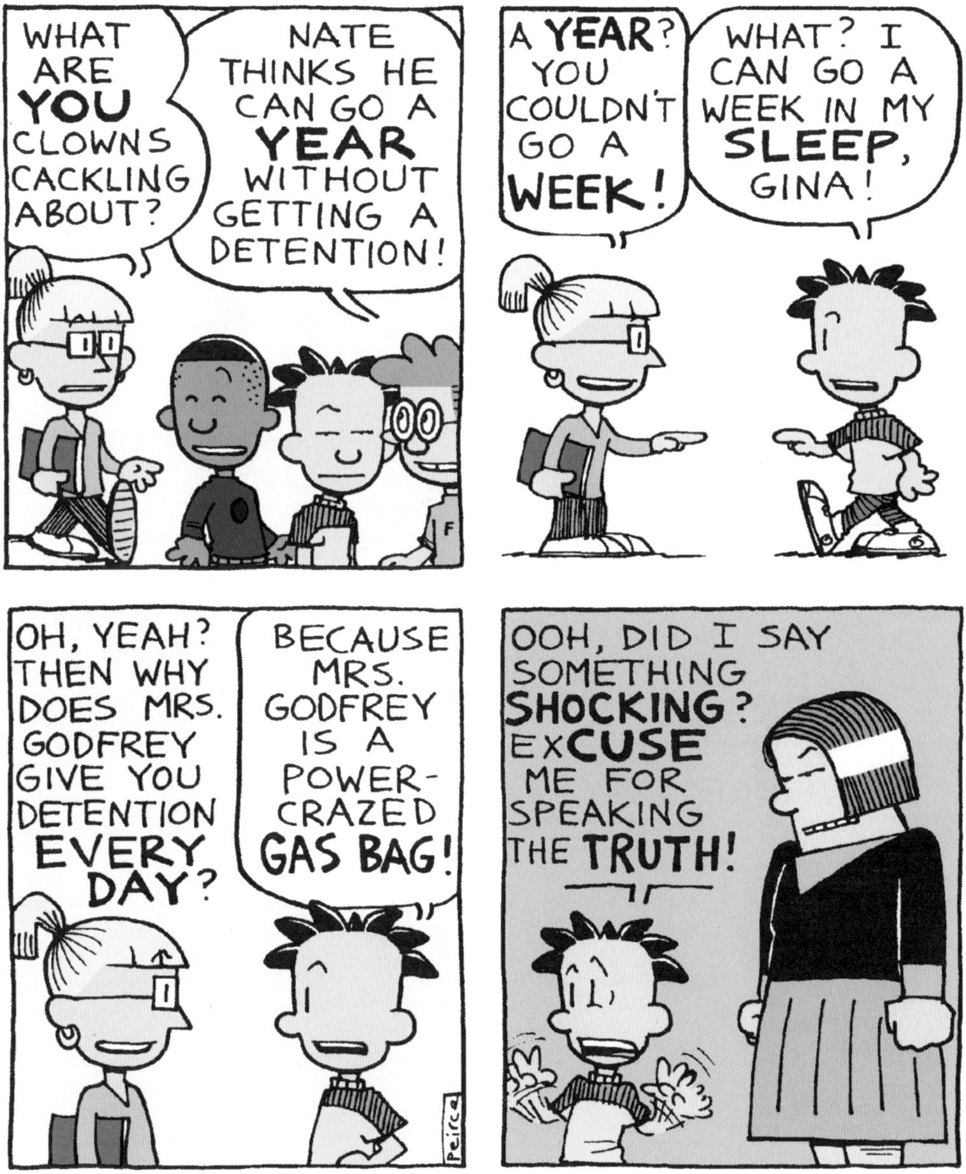
WHAT ARE YOU CLOWNS CACKLING ABOUT?
NATE THINKS HE CAN GO A YEAR WITHOUT GETTING A DETENTION!
A YEAR? YOU COULDN'T GO A WEEK!
WHAT? I CAN GO A WEEK IN MY SLEEP, GINA!
OH, YEAH? THEN WHY DOES MRS. GODFREY GIVE YOU DETENTION EVERY DAY?
BECAUSE MRS. GODFREY IS A POWER-CRAZED GAS BAG!
OOH, DID I SAY SOMETHING SHOCKING? EXCUSE ME FOR SPEAKING THE TRUTH!
Peirce

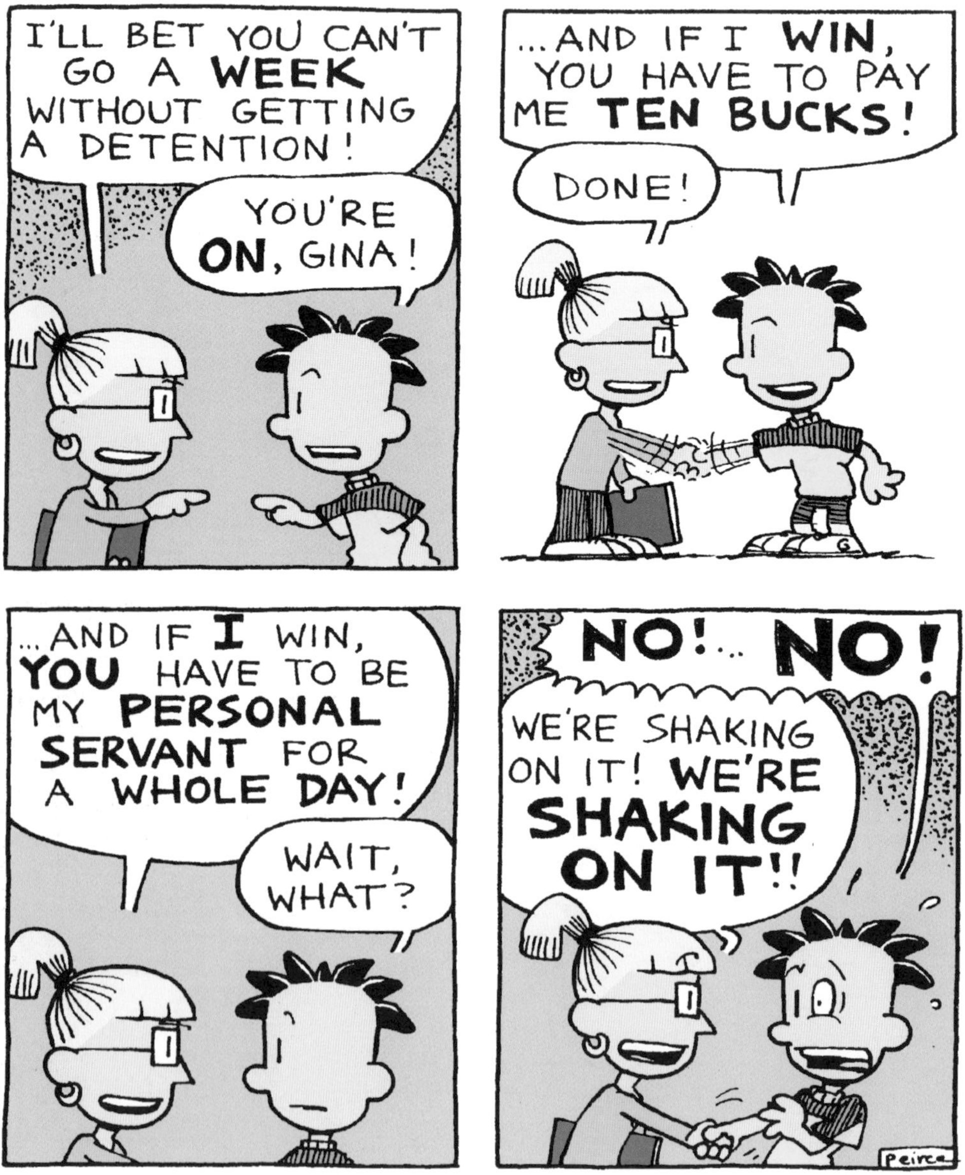
I'LL BET YOU CAN'T GO A WEEK WITHOUT GETTING A DETENTION!
YOU'RE ON, GINA!
...AND IF I WIN, YOU HAVE TO PAY ME TEN BUCKS!
DONE!
...AND IF I WIN, YOU HAVE TO BE MY PERSONAL SERVANT FOR A WHOLE DAY!
WAIT, WHAT?
NO!... NO!
WE'RE SHAKING ON IT! WE'RE SHAKING ON IT!!
Peirce

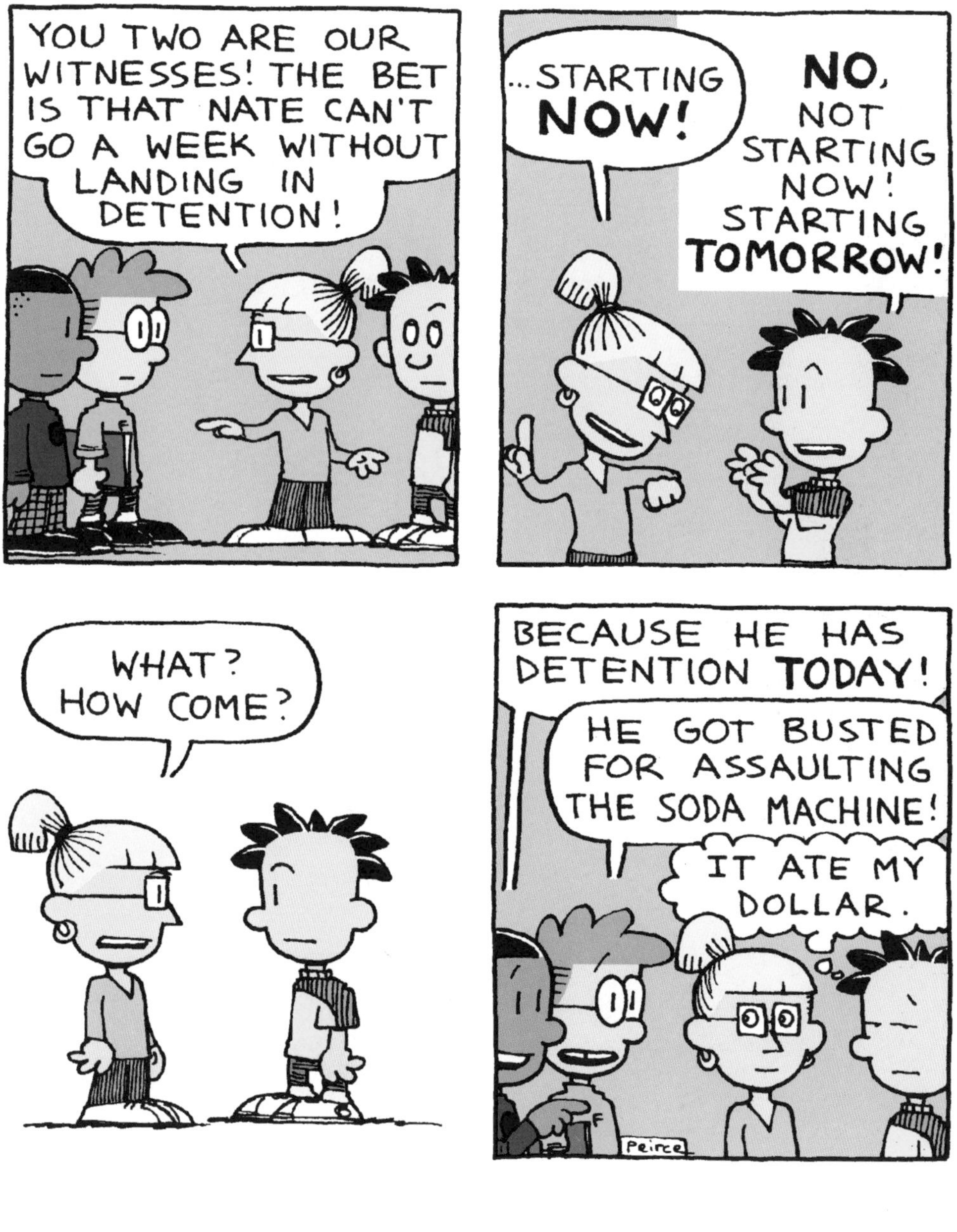
YOU TWO ARE OUR WITNESSES! THE BET IS THAT NATE CAN'T GO A WEEK WITHOUT LANDING IN DETENTION!
...STARTING NOW!
NO, NOT STARTING NOW! STARTING TOMORROW!
WHAT? HOW COME?
BECAUSE HE HAS DETENTION TODAY!
HE GOT BUSTED FOR ASSAULTING THE SODA MACHINE!
IT ATE MY DOLLAR.
Peirce

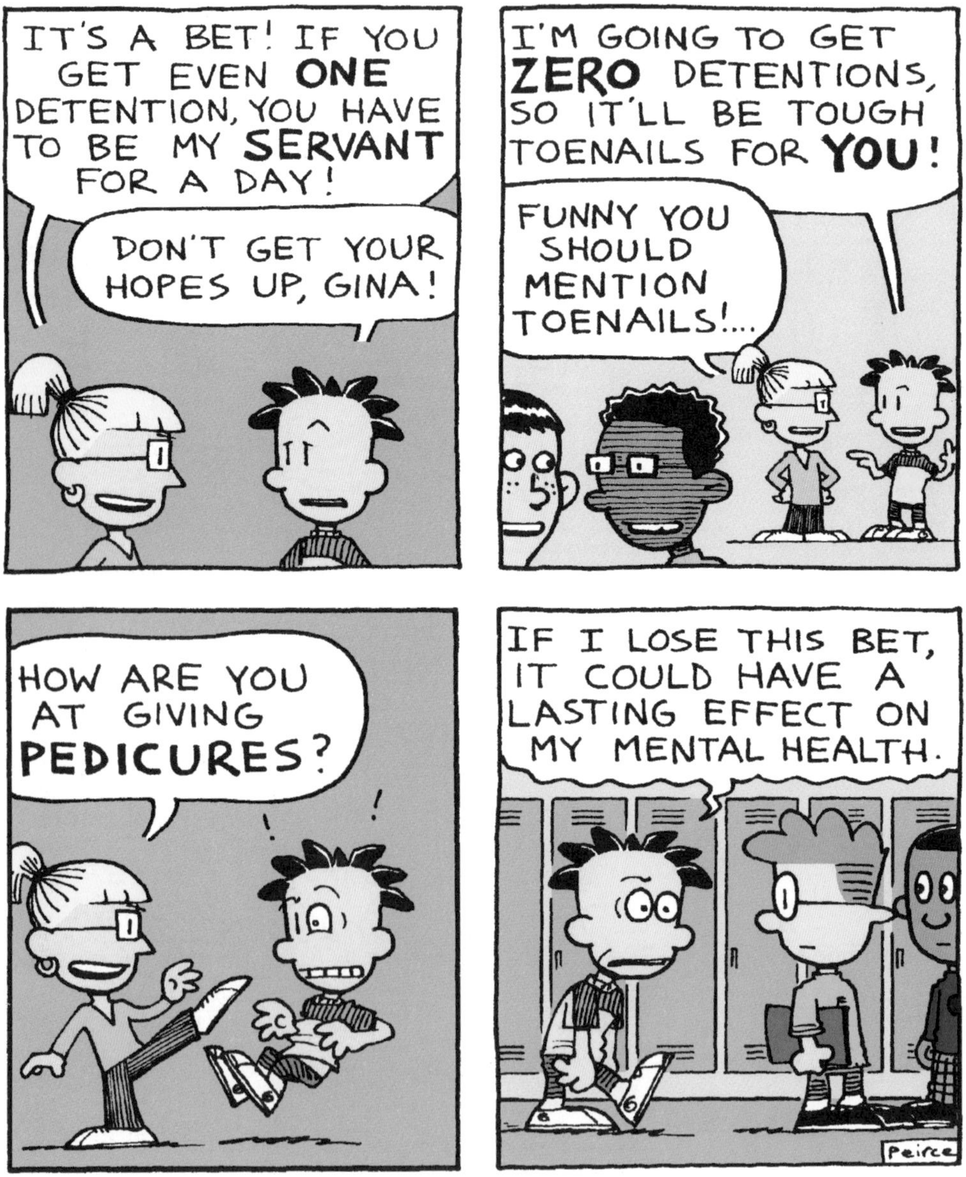
IT'S A BET! IF YOU GET EVEN ONE DETENTION, YOU HAVE TO BE MY SERVANT FOR A DAY!
DON'T GET YOUR HOPES UP, GINA!
I'M GOING TO GET ZERO DETENTIONS, SO IT'LL BE TOUGH TOENAILS FOR YOU!
FUNNY YOU SHOULD MENTION TOENAILS!...
HOW ARE YOU AT GIVING PEDICURES?
!
!
IF I LOSE THIS BET, IT COULD HAVE A LASTING EFFECT ON MY MENTAL HEALTH.
Peirce

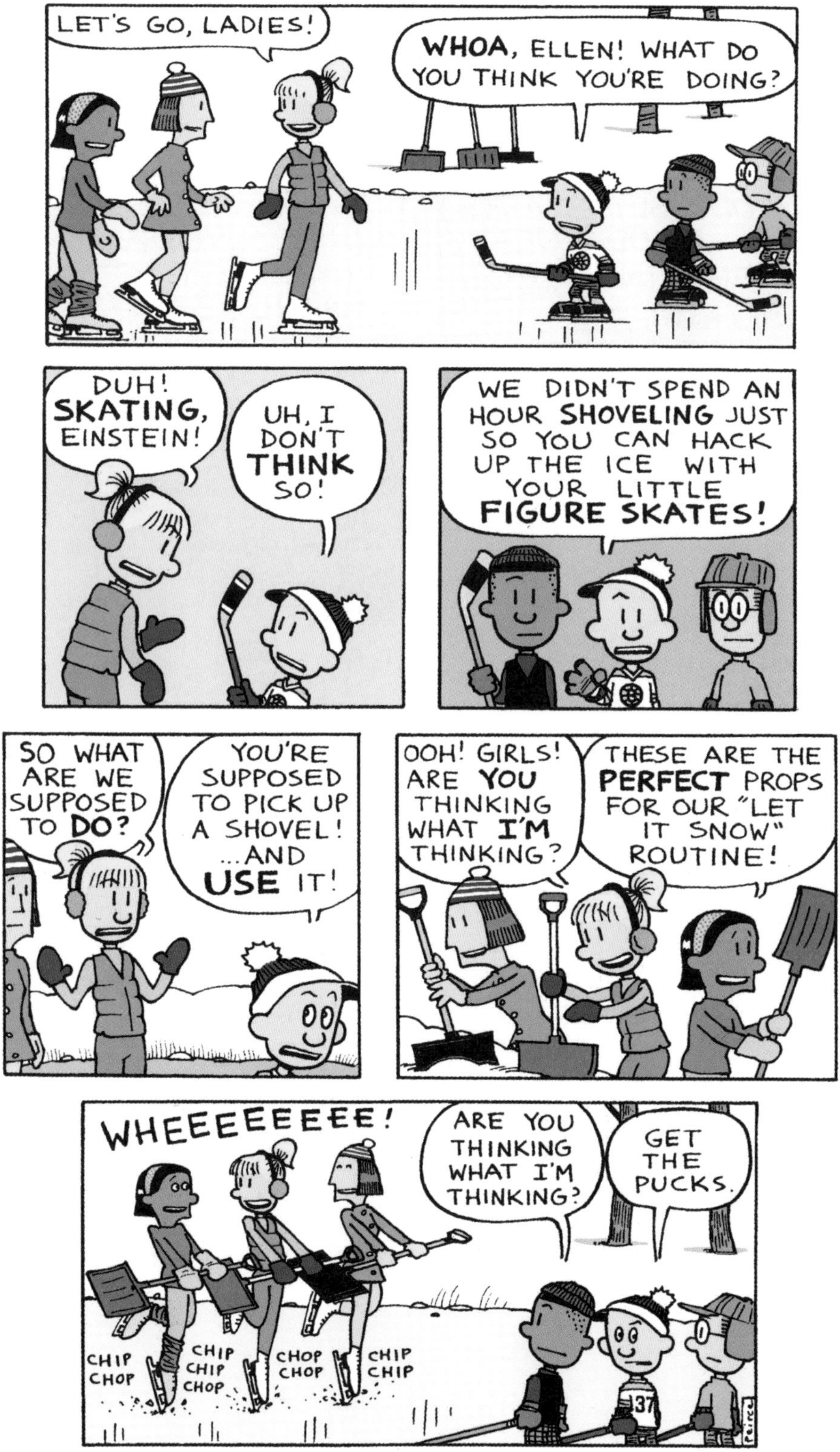

LET'S GO, LADIES!
WHOA, ELLEN! WHAT DO YOU THINK YOU'RE DOING?
DUH! SKATING, EINSTEIN!
UH, I DON'T THINK SO!
WE DIDN'T SPEND AN HOUR SHOVELING JUST SO YOU CAN HACK UP THE ICE WITH YOUR LITTLE FIGURE SKATES!
SO WHAT ARE WE SUPPOSED TO DO?
YOU'RE SUPPOSED TO PICK UP A SHOVEL! ...AND USE IT!
OOH! GIRLS! ARE YOU THINKING WHAT I'M THINKING?
THESE ARE THE PERFECT PROPS FOR OUR "LET IT SNOW" ROUTINE!
WHEEEEEEEE!
CHIP CHOP
CHIP CHIP CHOP
CHOP CHOP
CHIP CHIP
ARE YOU THINKING WHAT I'M THINKING?
GET THE PUCKS.
37
Peirce

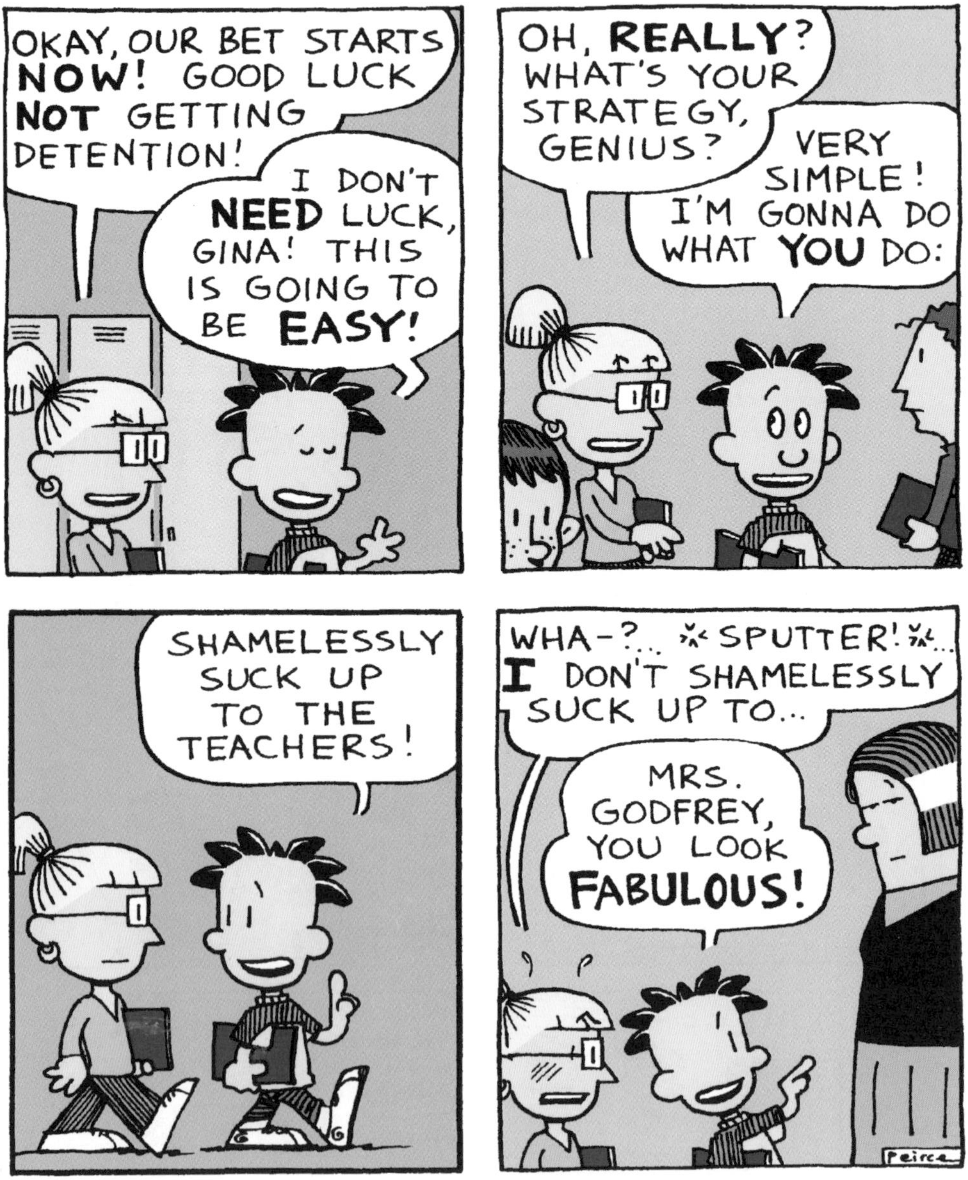
OKAY, OUR BET STARTS **NOW**! GOOD LUCK **NOT** GETTING DETENTION!
I DON'T **NEED** LUCK, GINA! THIS IS GOING TO BE **EASY**!
OH, **REALLY**? WHAT'S YOUR STRATEGY, GENIUS?
VERY SIMPLE! I'M GONNA DO WHAT **YOU** DO:
SHAMELESSLY SUCK UP TO THE TEACHERS!
WHA-?... *SPUTTER!*... **I** DON'T SHAMELESSLY SUCK UP TO...
MRS. GODFREY, YOU LOOK **FABULOUS**!
Peirce

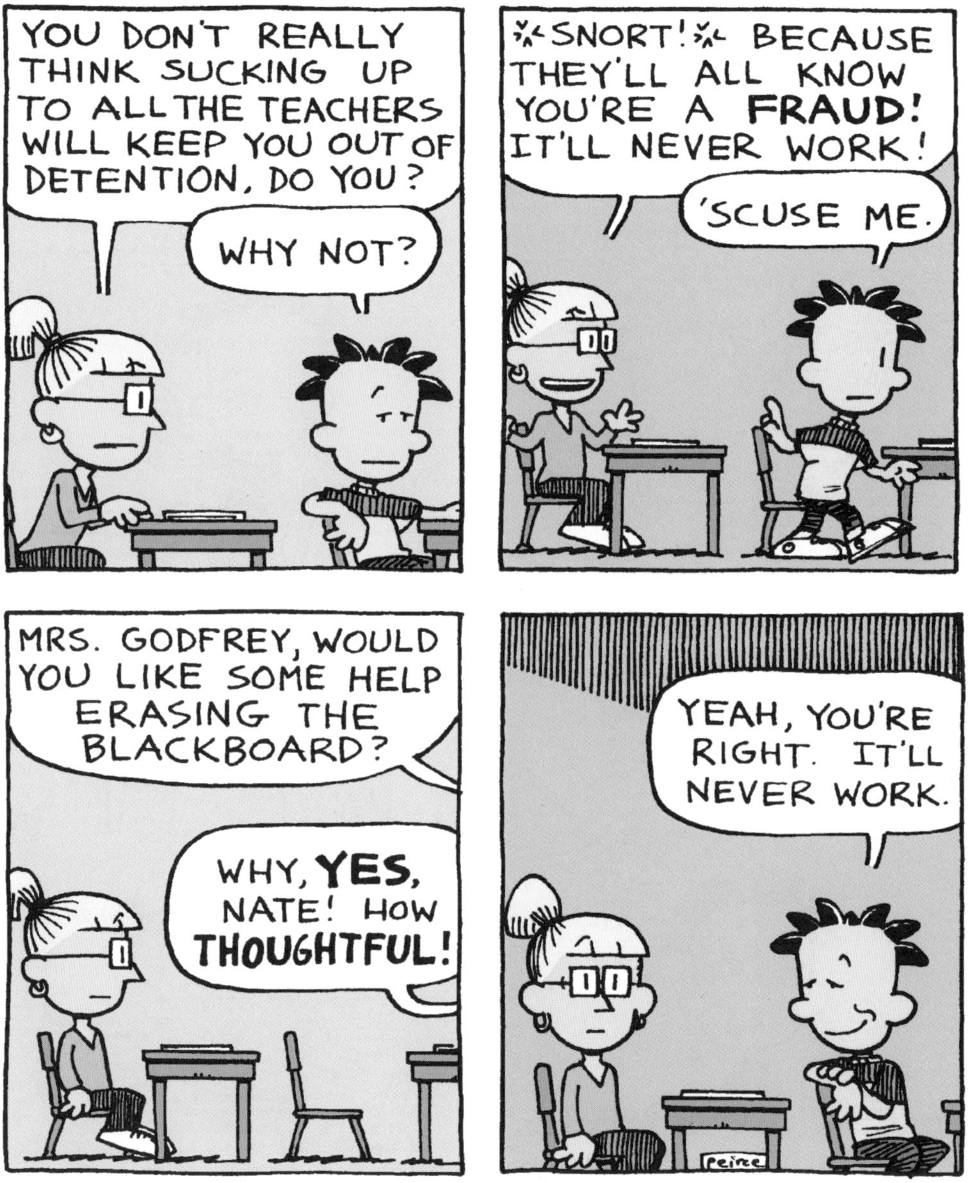
YOU DON'T REALLY THINK SUCKING UP TO ALL THE TEACHERS WILL KEEP YOU OUT OF DETENTION, DO YOU?
WHY NOT?
SNORT! BECAUSE THEY'LL ALL KNOW YOU'RE A **FRAUD!** IT'LL NEVER WORK!
'SCUSE ME.
MRS. GODFREY, WOULD YOU LIKE SOME HELP ERASING THE BLACKBOARD?
WHY, **YES,** NATE! HOW **THOUGHTFUL!**
YEAH, YOU'RE RIGHT. IT'LL NEVER WORK.
Peirce

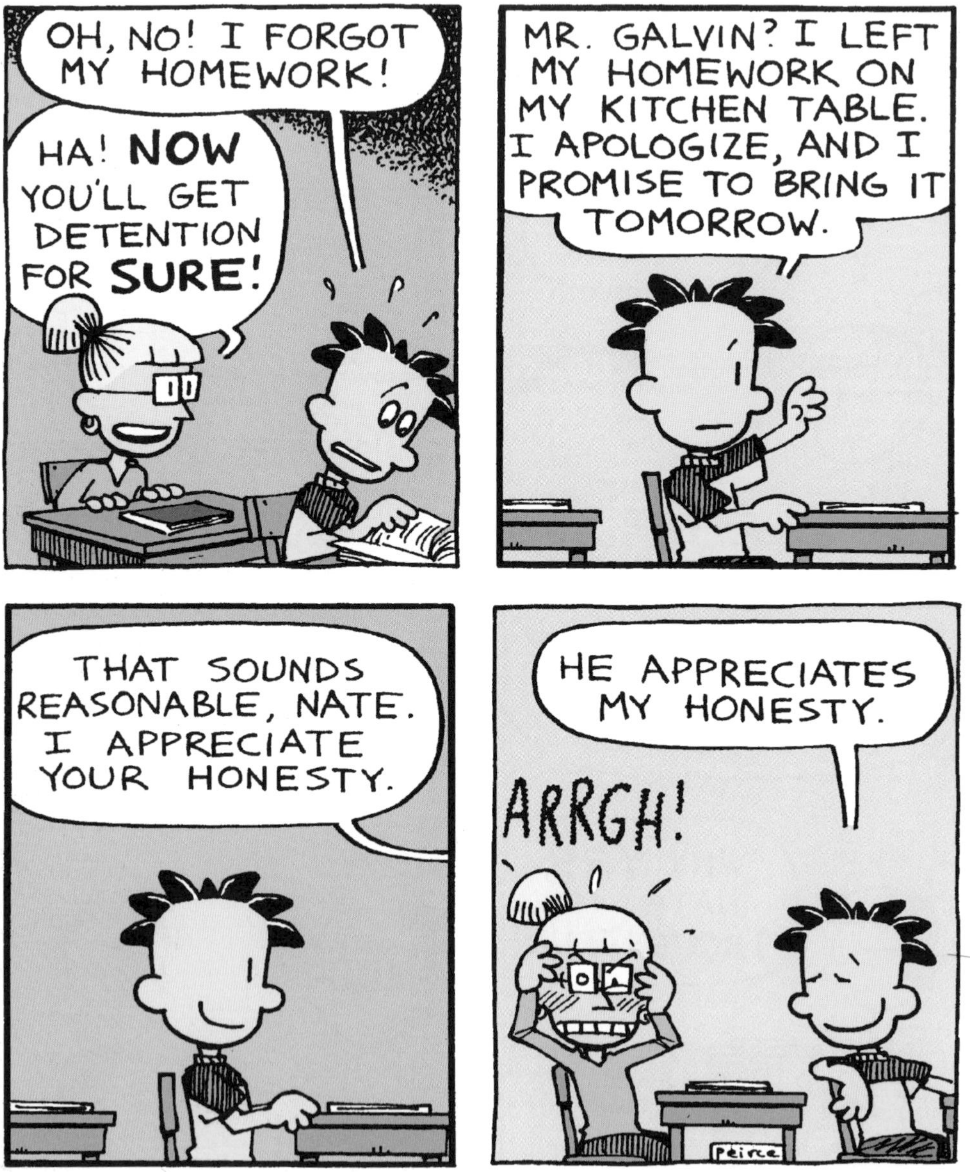
OH, NO! I FORGOT MY HOMEWORK!
HA! NOW YOU'LL GET DETENTION FOR SURE!
MR. GALVIN? I LEFT MY HOMEWORK ON MY KITCHEN TABLE. I APOLOGIZE, AND I PROMISE TO BRING IT TOMORROW.
THAT SOUNDS REASONABLE, NATE. I APPRECIATE YOUR HONESTY.
HE APPRECIATES MY HONESTY.
ARRGH!
peirce

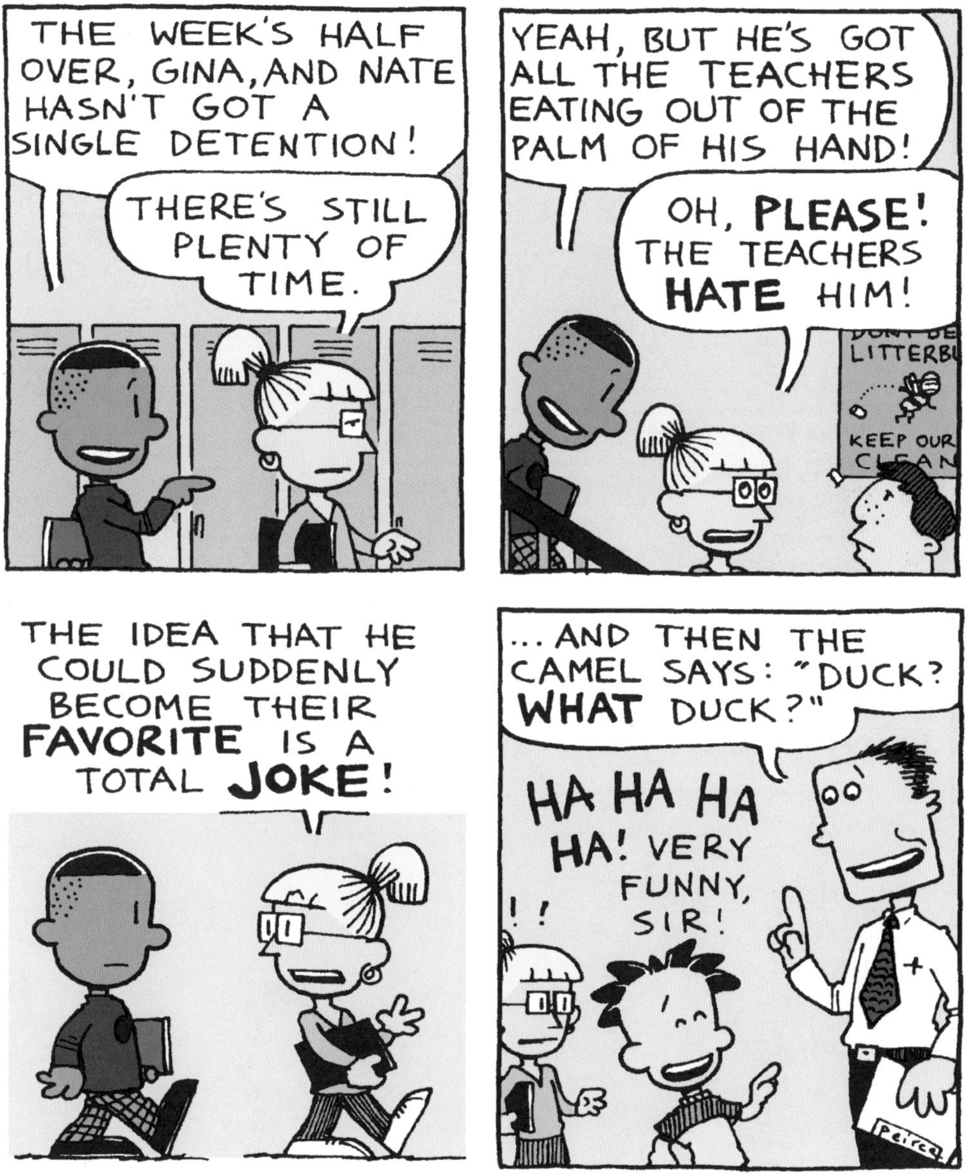
THE WEEK'S HALF OVER, GINA, AND NATE HASN'T GOT A SINGLE DETENTION!
THERE'S STILL PLENTY OF TIME.
YEAH, BUT HE'S GOT ALL THE TEACHERS EATING OUT OF THE PALM OF HIS HAND!
OH, **PLEASE**! THE TEACHERS **HATE** HIM!
KEEP OUR
THE IDEA THAT HE COULD SUDDENLY BECOME THEIR **FAVORITE** IS A TOTAL **JOKE**!
...AND THEN THE CAMEL SAYS: "DUCK? **WHAT** DUCK?"
HA HA HA HA! VERY FUNNY, SIR!
! !
peirce

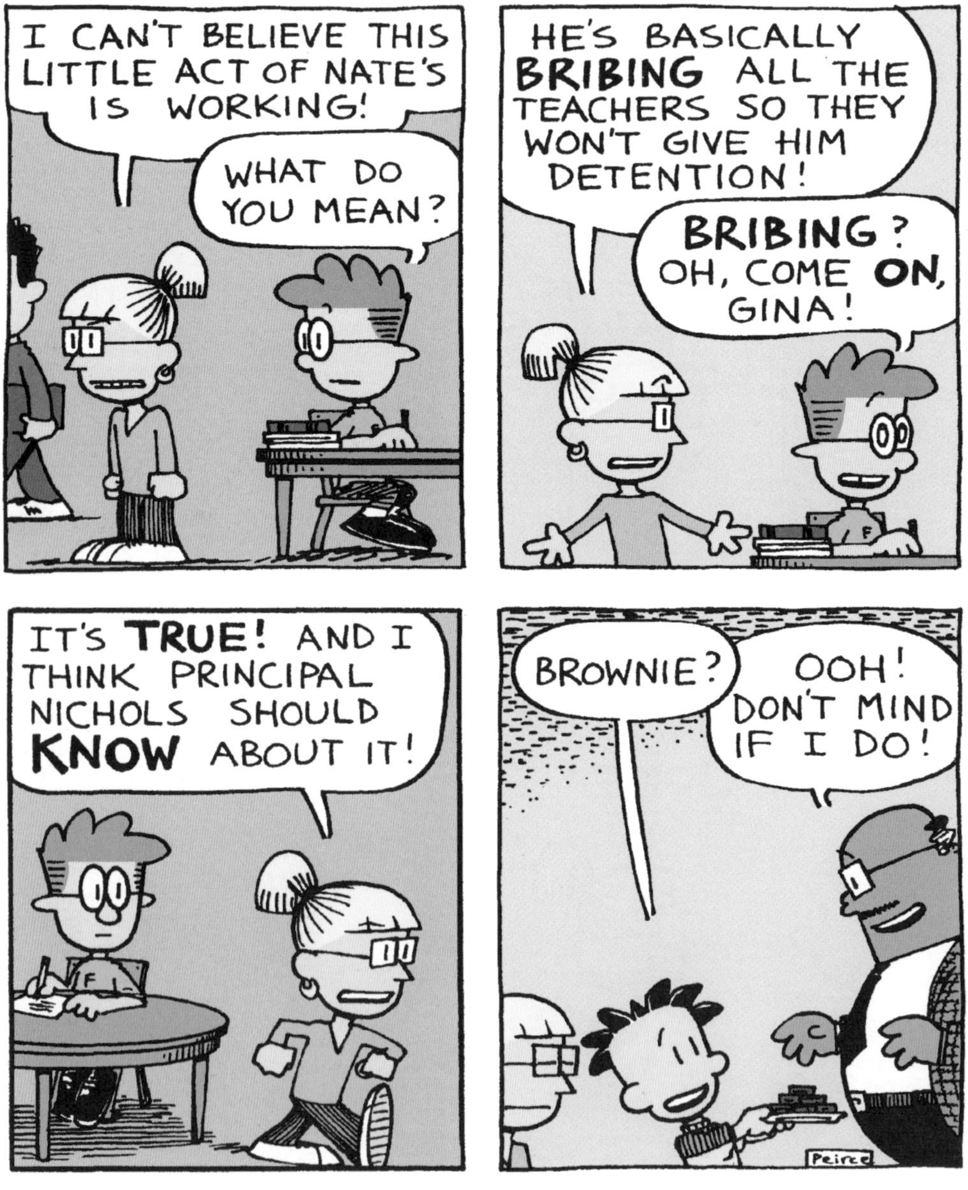
I CAN'T BELIEVE THIS LITTLE ACT OF NATE'S IS WORKING!
WHAT DO YOU MEAN?
HE'S BASICALLY BRIBING ALL THE TEACHERS SO THEY WON'T GIVE HIM DETENTION!
BRIBING? OH, COME ON, GINA!
IT'S TRUE! AND I THINK PRINCIPAL NICHOLS SHOULD KNOW ABOUT IT!
BROWNIE?
OOH! DON'T MIND IF I DO!
Peirce

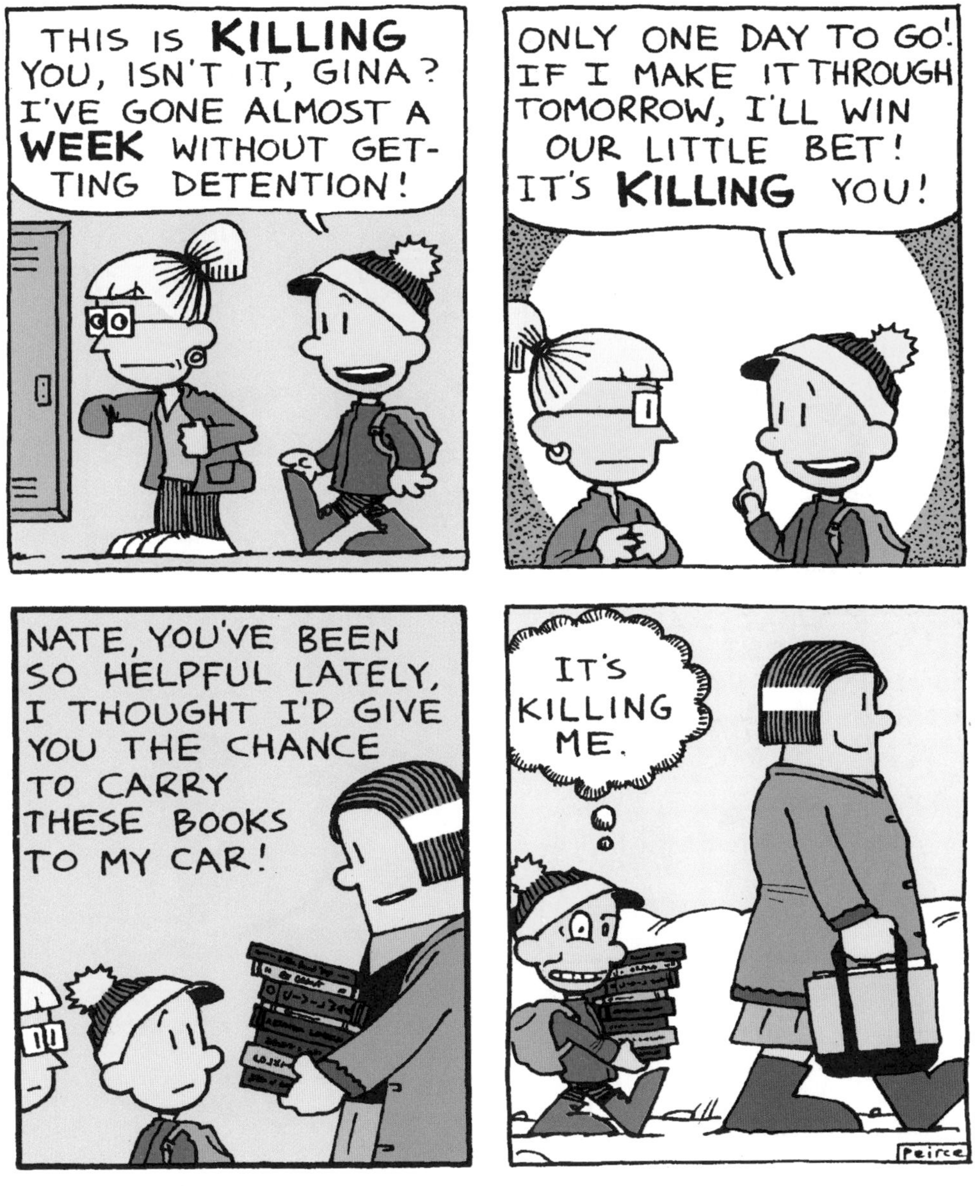
THIS IS KILLING YOU, ISN'T IT, GINA? I'VE GONE ALMOST A WEEK WITHOUT GET-TING DETENTION!
ONLY ONE DAY TO GO! IF I MAKE IT THROUGH TOMORROW, I'LL WIN OUR LITTLE BET! IT'S KILLING YOU!
NATE, YOU'VE BEEN SO HELPFUL LATELY, I THOUGHT I'D GIVE YOU THE CHANCE TO CARRY THESE BOOKS TO MY CAR!
IT'S KILLING ME.
Peirce

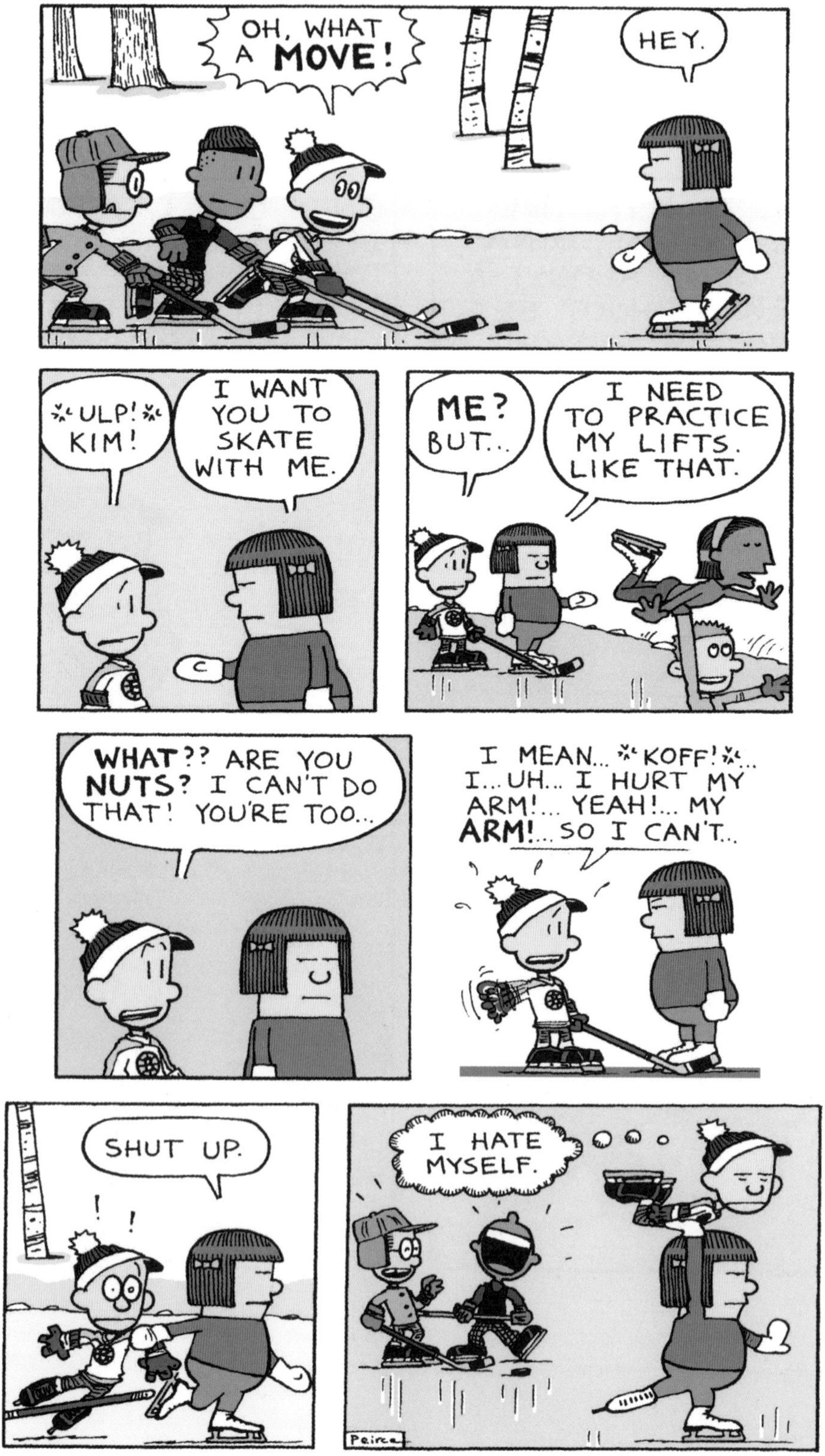
OH, WHAT A MOVE!
HEY.
ULP! KIM!
I WANT YOU TO SKATE WITH ME.
ME? BUT...
I NEED TO PRACTICE MY LIFTS. LIKE THAT.
WHAT?? ARE YOU NUTS? I CAN'T DO THAT! YOU'RE TOO...
I MEAN... *KOFF!*... I... UH... I HURT MY ARM!... YEAH!... MY ARM!... SO I CAN'T...
SHUT UP.
! !
I HATE MYSELF.
Peirce

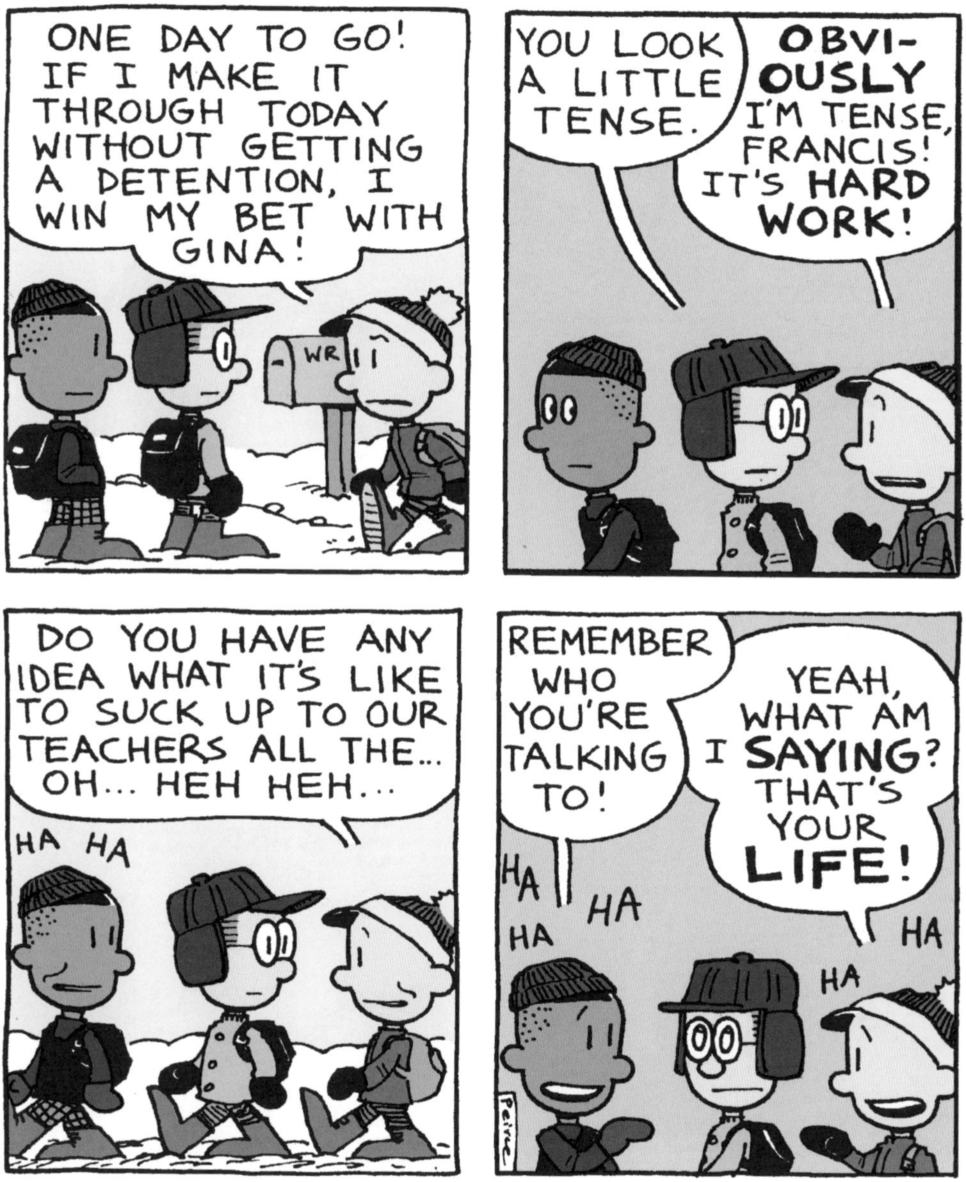
ONE DAY TO GO! IF I MAKE IT THROUGH TODAY WITHOUT GETTING A DETENTION, I WIN MY BET WITH GINA!
WR
YOU LOOK A LITTLE TENSE.
OBVIOUSLY I'M TENSE, FRANCIS! IT'S HARD WORK!
DO YOU HAVE ANY IDEA WHAT IT'S LIKE TO SUCK UP TO OUR TEACHERS ALL THE... OH... HEH HEH...
HA HA
REMEMBER WHO YOU'RE TALKING TO!
YEAH, WHAT AM I SAYING? THAT'S YOUR LIFE!
HA HA HA
HA HA
Peirce

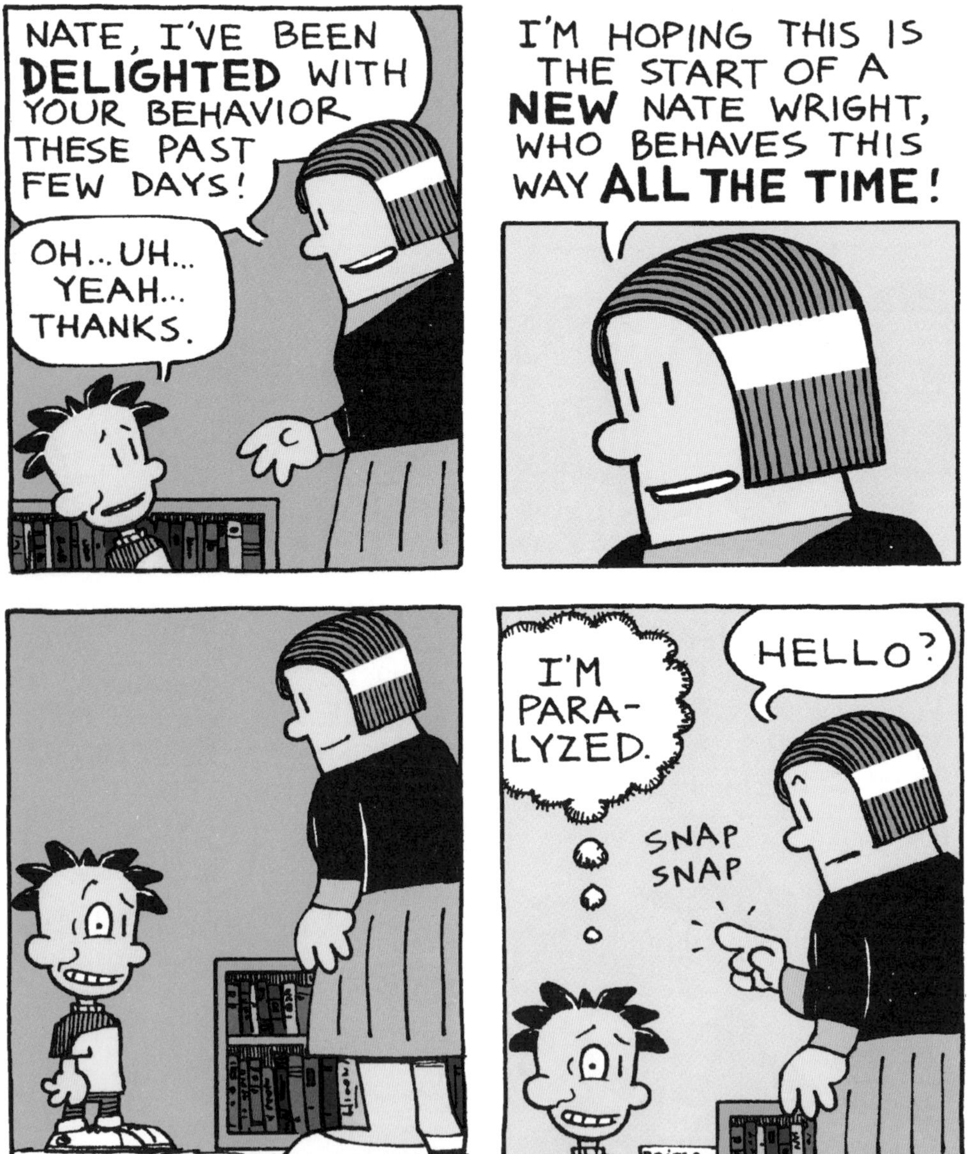
NATE, I'VE BEEN DELIGHTED WITH YOUR BEHAVIOR THESE PAST FEW DAYS!
OH... UH... YEAH... THANKS.
I'M HOPING THIS IS THE START OF A NEW NATE WRIGHT, WHO BEHAVES THIS WAY ALL THE TIME!
I'M PARA-LYZED.
HELLO?
SNAP SNAP
Peirce

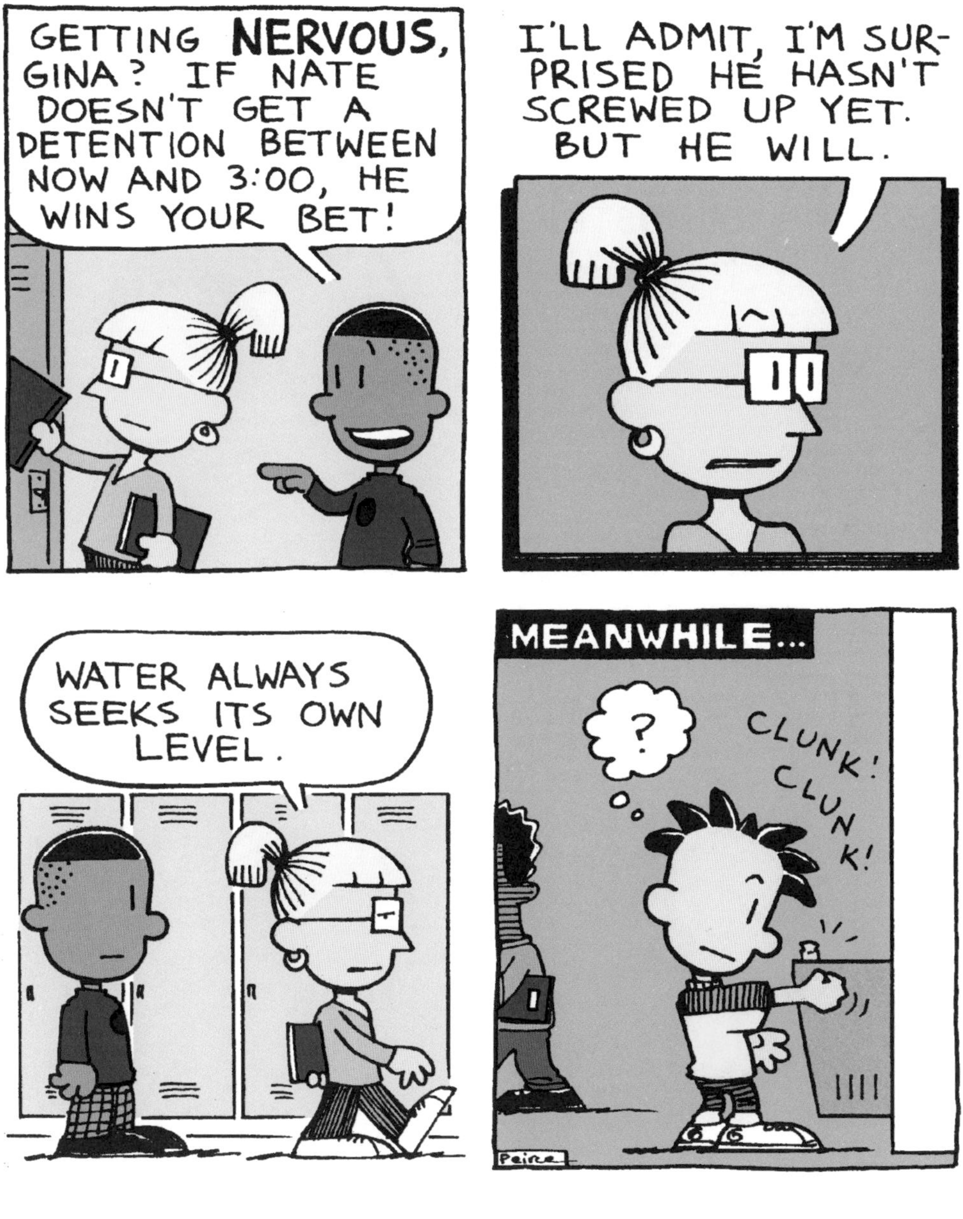
GETTING **NERVOUS**, GINA? IF NATE DOESN'T GET A DETENTION BETWEEN NOW AND 3:00, HE WINS YOUR BET!
I'LL ADMIT, I'M SURPRISED HE HASN'T SCREWED UP YET. BUT HE WILL.
WATER ALWAYS SEEKS ITS OWN LEVEL.
MEANWHILE...
?
CLUNK! CLUNK!
Peirce

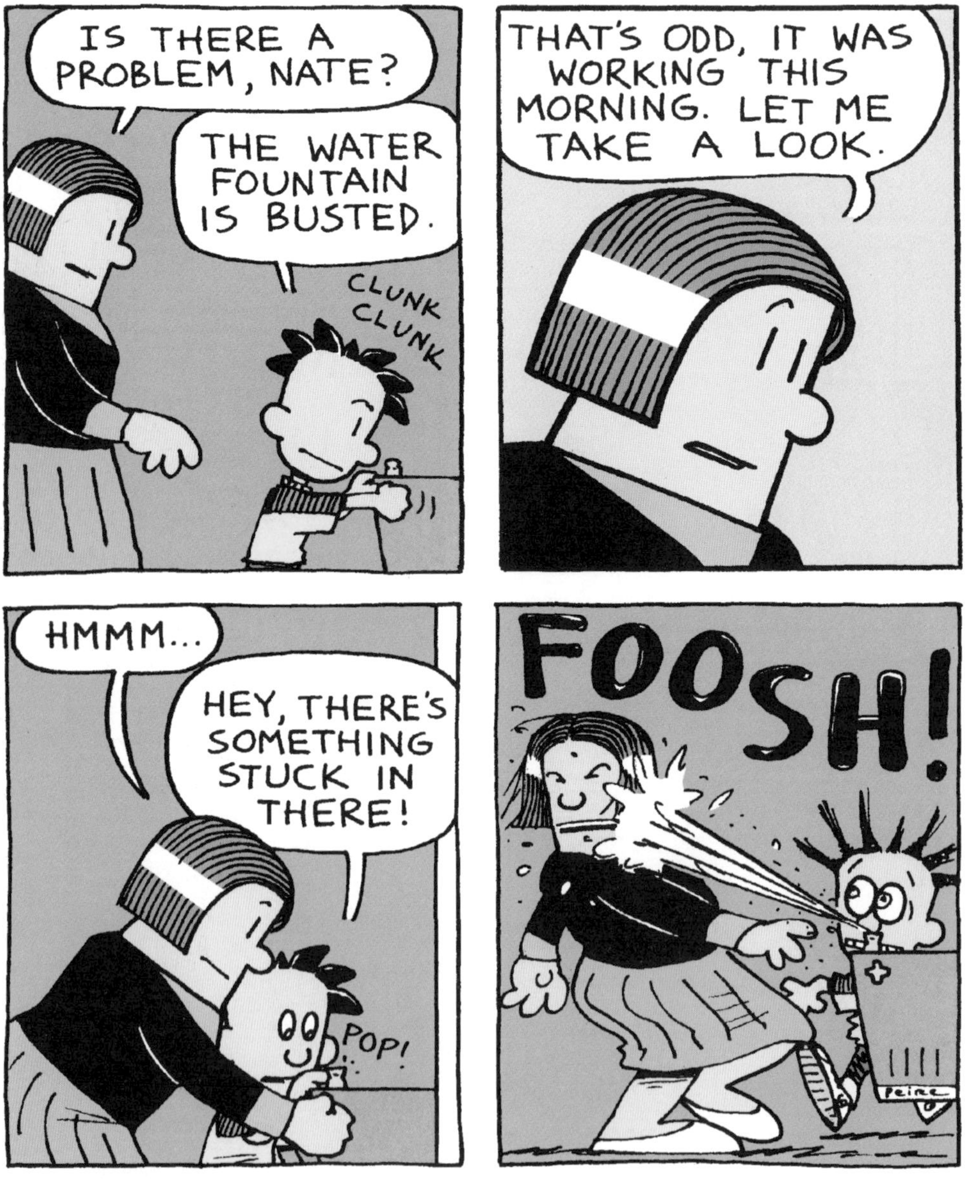
IS THERE A PROBLEM, NATE?
THE WATER FOUNTAIN IS BUSTED.
CLUNK CLUNK CLUNK
THAT'S ODD, IT WAS WORKING THIS MORNING. LET ME TAKE A LOOK.
HMMM...
HEY, THERE'S SOMETHING STUCK IN THERE!
POP!
FOOSH!
Peirce

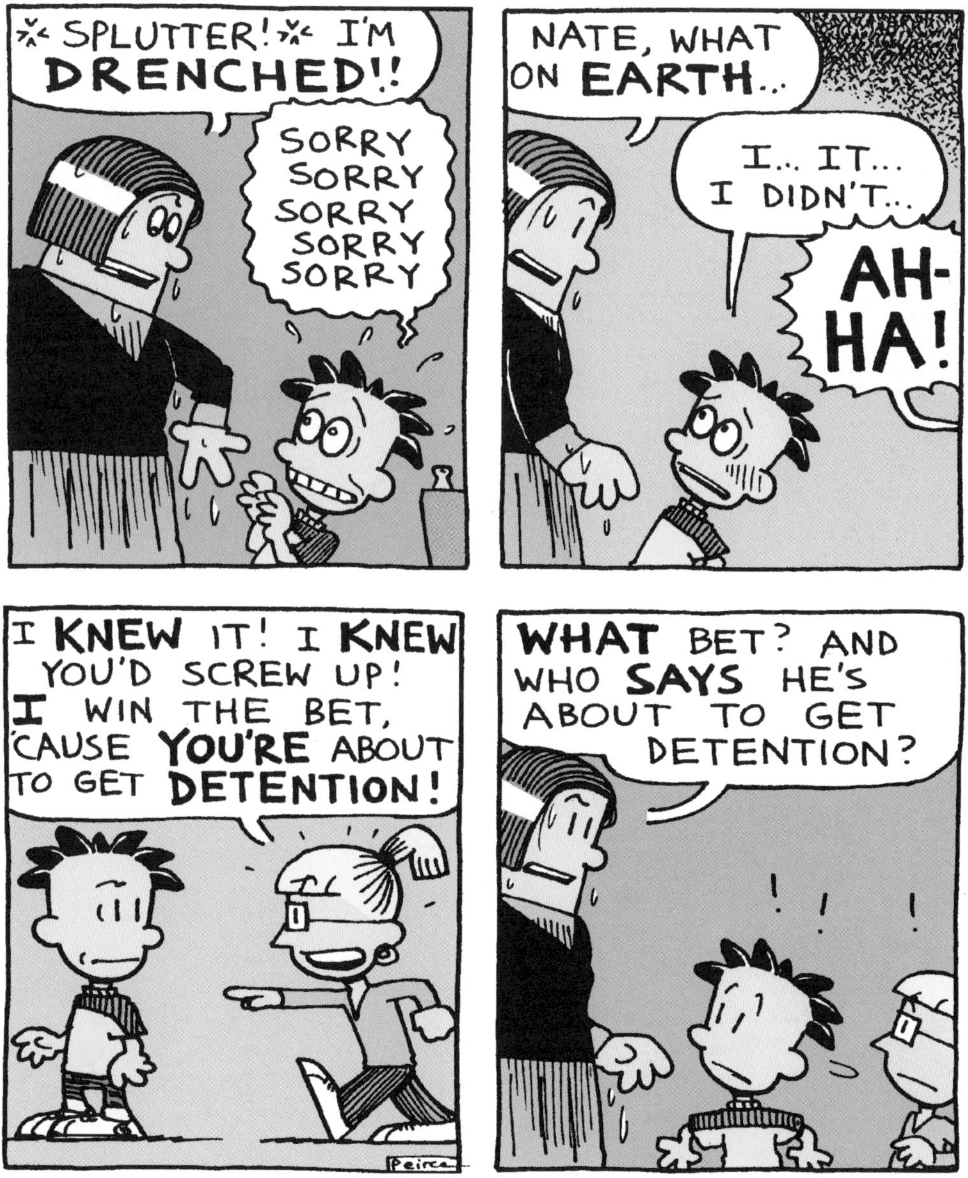
SPLUTTER! I'M DRENCHED!!
SORRY SORRY SORRY SORRY SORRY
NATE, WHAT ON EARTH...
I... IT... I DIDN'T...
AH-HA!
I KNEW IT! I KNEW YOU'D SCREW UP! I WIN THE BET, 'CAUSE YOU'RE ABOUT TO GET DETENTION!
WHAT BET? AND WHO SAYS HE'S ABOUT TO GET DETENTION?
! ! !
Peirce

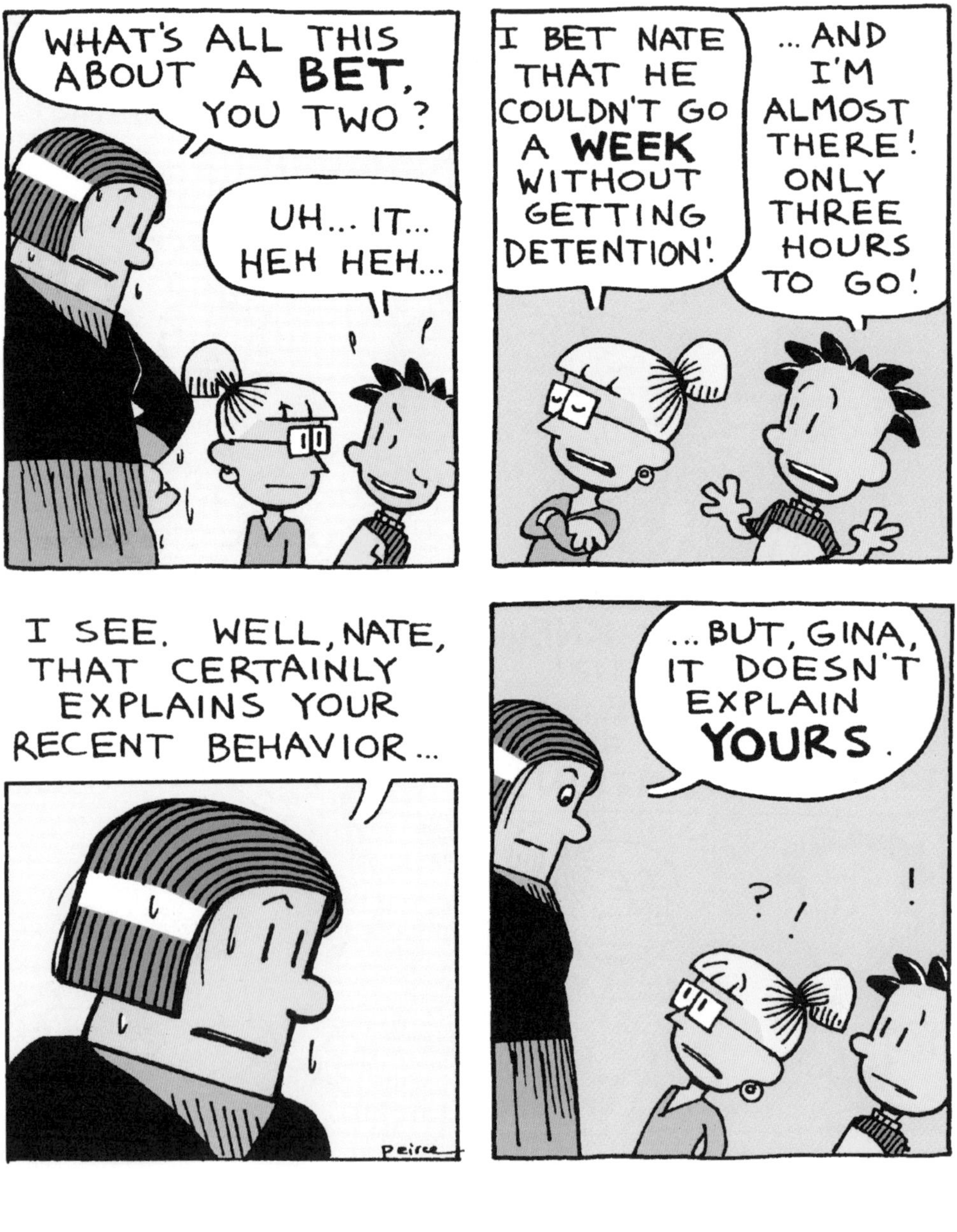
WHAT'S ALL THIS ABOUT A **BET**, YOU TWO?
UH... IT... HEH HEH...
I BET NATE THAT HE COULDN'T GO A **WEEK** WITHOUT GETTING DETENTION!
... AND I'M ALMOST THERE! ONLY THREE HOURS TO GO!
I SEE. WELL, NATE, THAT CERTAINLY EXPLAINS YOUR RECENT BEHAVIOR...
... BUT, GINA, IT DOESN'T EXPLAIN **YOURS**.
?!
!
peirce

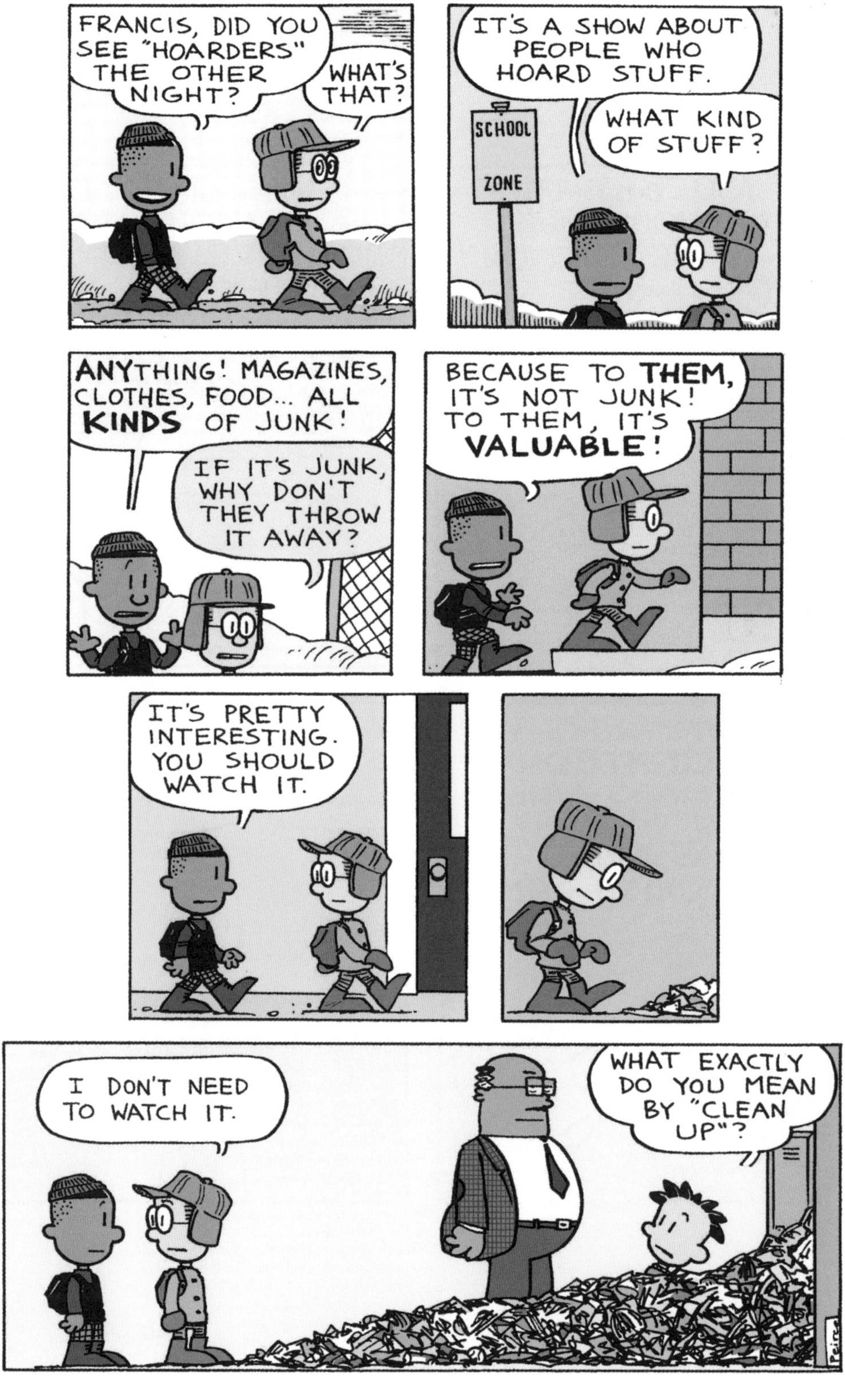
FRANCIS, DID YOU SEE "HOARDERS" THE OTHER NIGHT?
WHAT'S THAT?
IT'S A SHOW ABOUT PEOPLE WHO HOARD STUFF.
SCHOOL ZONE
WHAT KIND OF STUFF?
ANYTHING! MAGAZINES, CLOTHES, FOOD... ALL KINDS OF JUNK!
IF IT'S JUNK, WHY DON'T THEY THROW IT AWAY?
BECAUSE TO THEM, IT'S NOT JUNK! TO THEM, IT'S VALUABLE!
IT'S PRETTY INTERESTING. YOU SHOULD WATCH IT.
I DON'T NEED TO WATCH IT.
WHAT EXACTLY DO YOU MEAN BY "CLEAN UP"?
Peirce

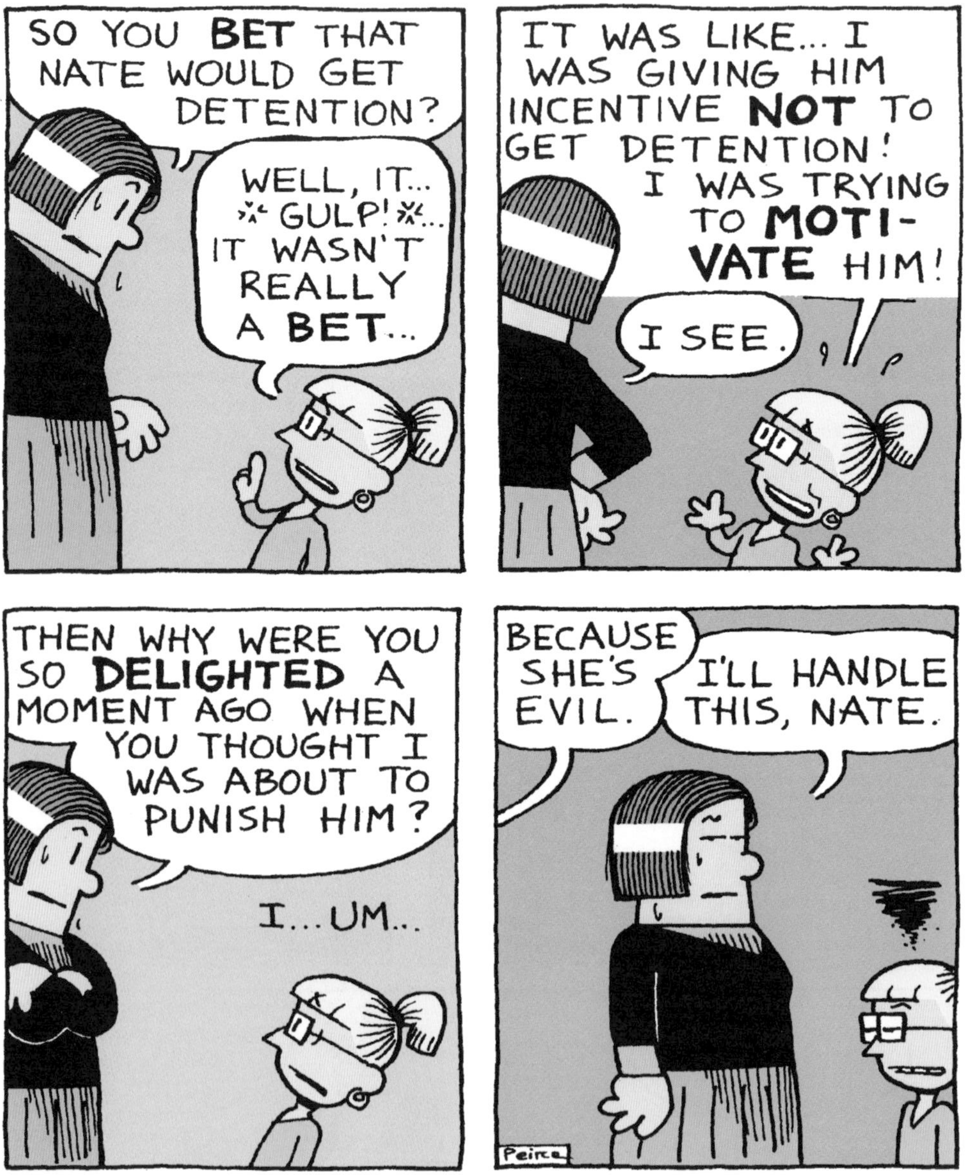
SO YOU **BET** THAT NATE WOULD GET DETENTION?
WELL, IT... *GULP!*... IT WASN'T REALLY A **BET**...
IT WAS LIKE... I WAS GIVING HIM INCENTIVE **NOT** TO GET DETENTION! I WAS TRYING TO **MOTI-VATE** HIM!
I SEE.
THEN WHY WERE YOU SO **DELIGHTED** A MOMENT AGO WHEN YOU THOUGHT I WAS ABOUT TO PUNISH HIM?
I... UM...
BECAUSE SHE'S EVIL.
I'LL HANDLE THIS, NATE.
Peirce

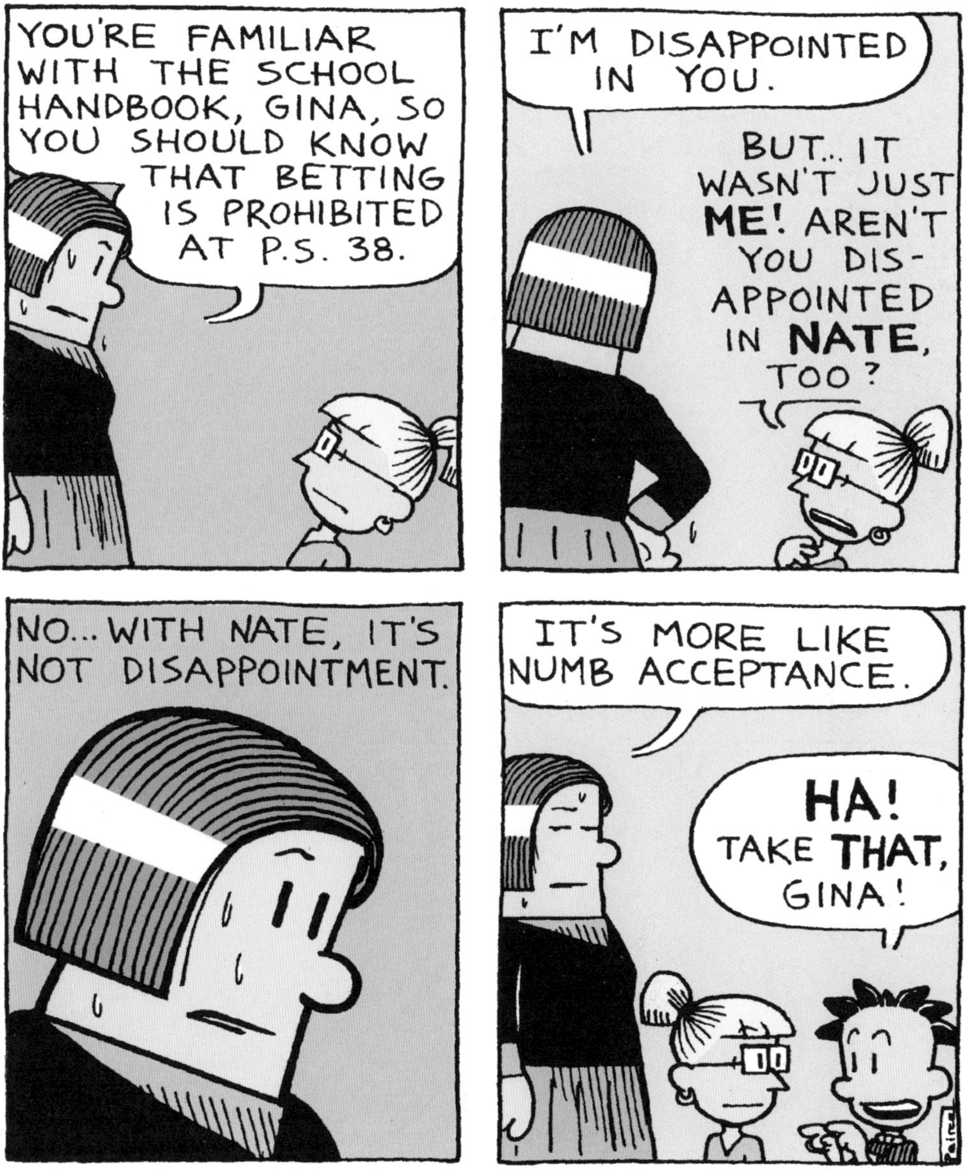
YOU'RE FAMILIAR WITH THE SCHOOL HANDBOOK, GINA, SO YOU SHOULD KNOW THAT BETTING IS PROHIBITED AT P.S. 38.
I'M DISAPPOINTED IN YOU.
BUT... IT WASN'T JUST **ME**! AREN'T YOU DIS-APPOINTED IN **NATE**, TOO?
NO... WITH NATE, IT'S NOT DISAPPOINTMENT.
IT'S MORE LIKE NUMB ACCEPTANCE.
HA! TAKE **THAT**, GINA!

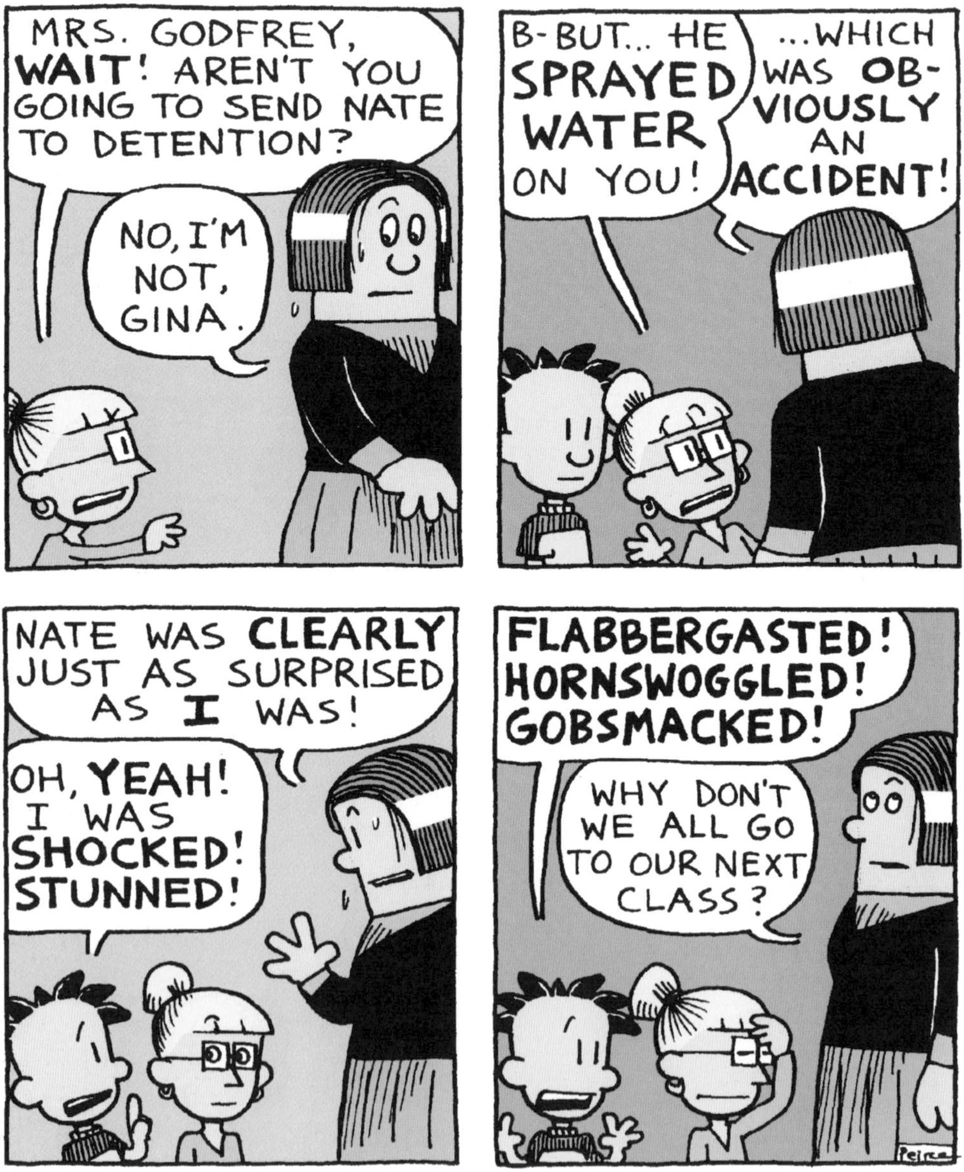
MRS. GODFREY, **WAIT**! AREN'T YOU GOING TO SEND NATE TO DETENTION?
NO, I'M NOT, GINA.
B-BUT... HE **SPRAYED WATER** ON YOU!
...WHICH WAS **OB-VIOUSLY** AN **ACCIDENT**!
NATE WAS **CLEARLY** JUST AS SURPRISED AS **I** WAS!
OH, **YEAH**! I WAS **SHOCKED**! **STUNNED**!
FLABBERGASTED! HORNSWOGGLED! GOBSMACKED!
WHY DON'T WE ALL GO TO OUR NEXT CLASS?
Peirce

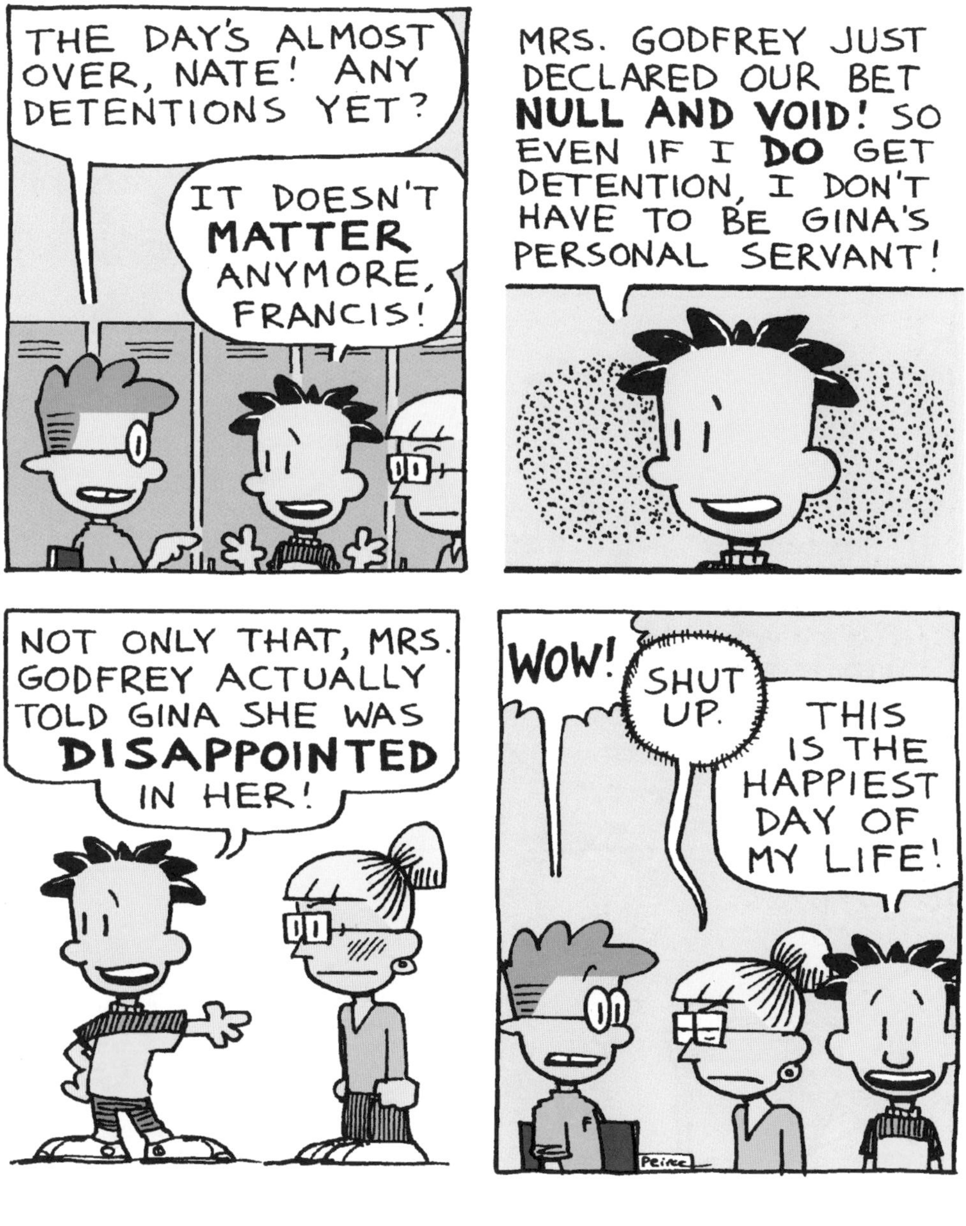
THE DAY'S ALMOST OVER, NATE! ANY DETENTIONS YET?
IT DOESN'T MATTER ANYMORE, FRANCIS!
MRS. GODFREY JUST DECLARED OUR BET NULL AND VOID! SO EVEN IF I DO GET DETENTION, I DON'T HAVE TO BE GINA'S PERSONAL SERVANT!
NOT ONLY THAT, MRS. GODFREY ACTUALLY TOLD GINA SHE WAS DISAPPOINTED IN HER!
WOW!
SHUT UP.
THIS IS THE HAPPIEST DAY OF MY LIFE!
Peirce

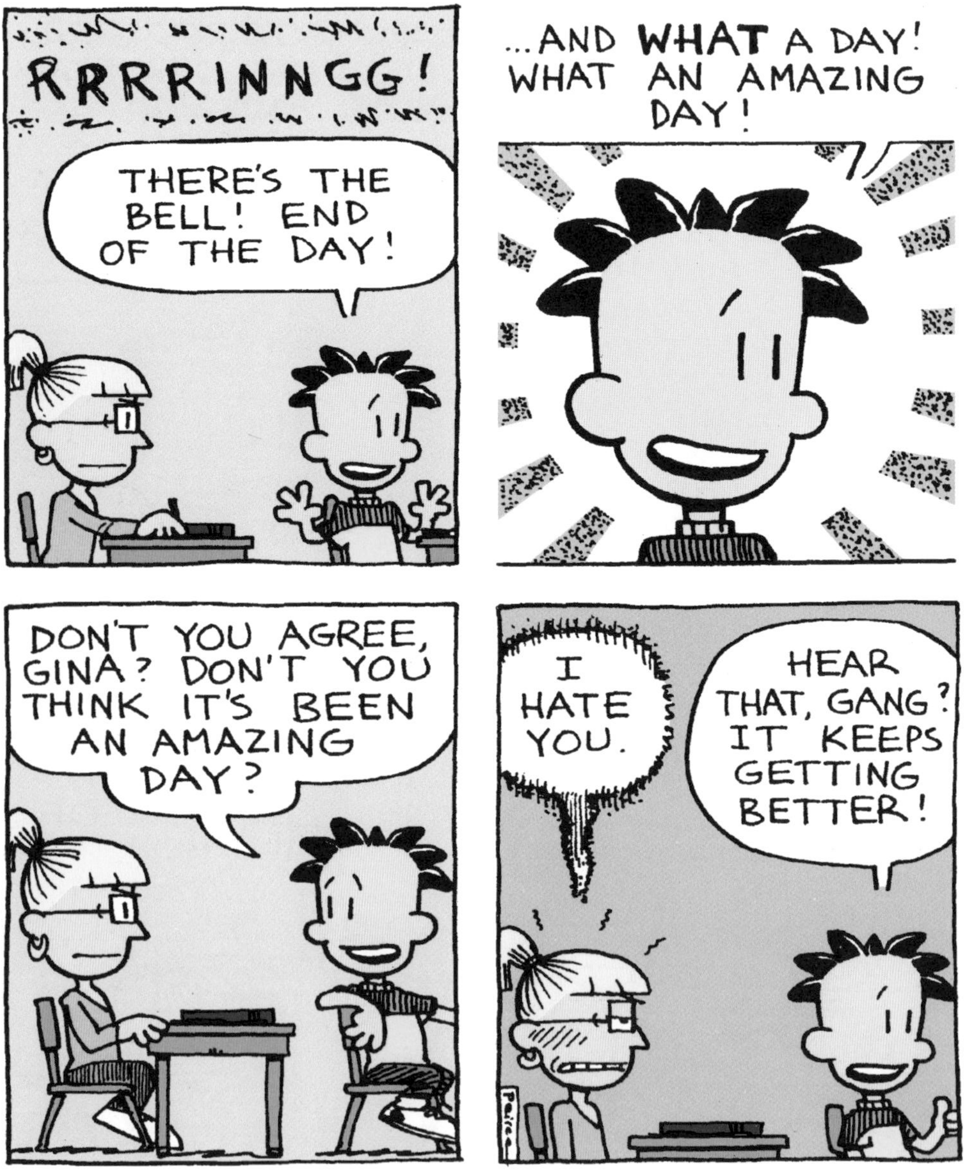
RRRRINNGG!
THERE'S THE BELL! END OF THE DAY!
...AND WHAT A DAY! WHAT AN AMAZING DAY!
DON'T YOU AGREE, GINA? DON'T YOU THINK IT'S BEEN AN AMAZING DAY?
I HATE YOU.
HEAR THAT, GANG? IT KEEPS GETTING BETTER!
Peirce

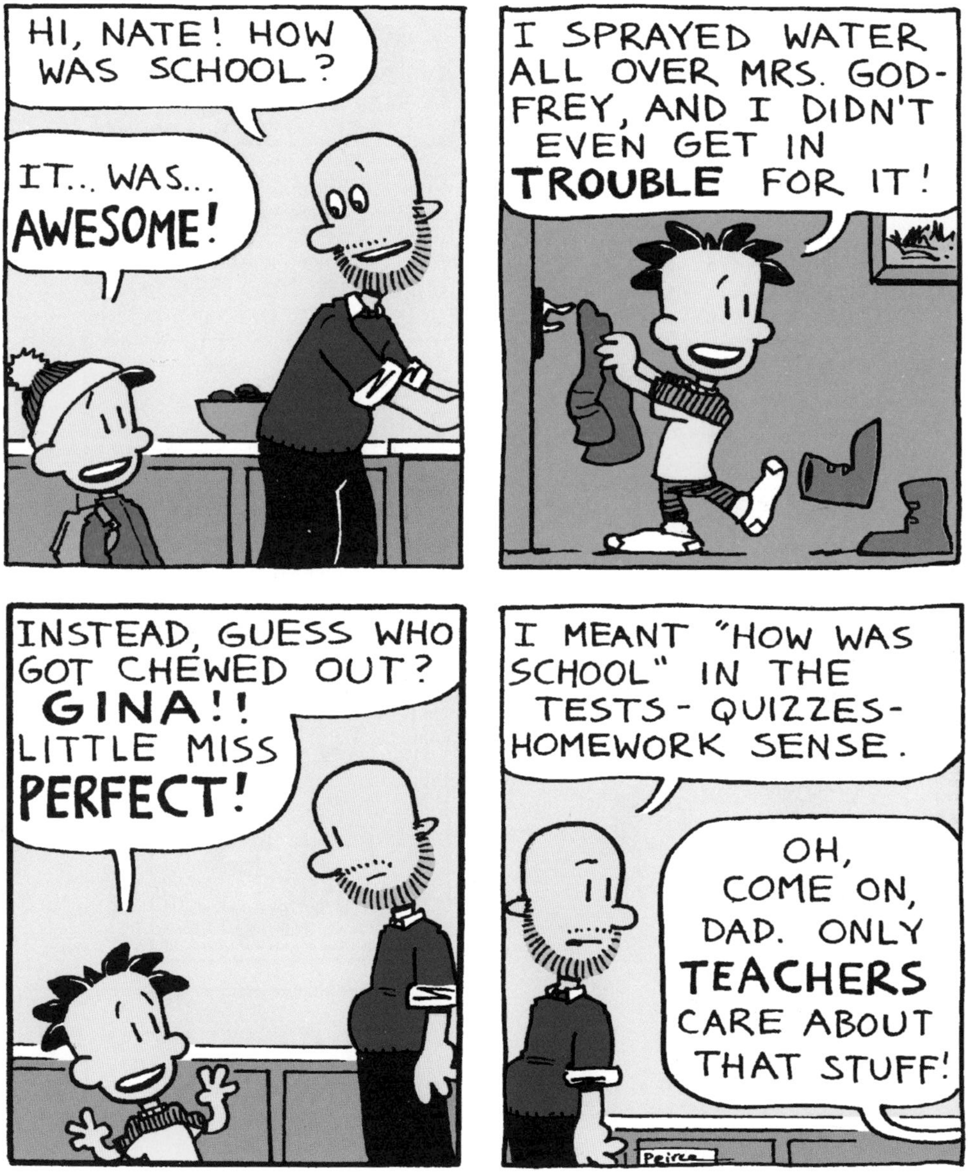
HI, NATE! HOW WAS SCHOOL?
IT... WAS... AWESOME!
I SPRAYED WATER ALL OVER MRS. GOD-FREY, AND I DIDN'T EVEN GET IN TROUBLE FOR IT!
INSTEAD, GUESS WHO GOT CHEWED OUT? GINA!! LITTLE MISS PERFECT!
I MEANT "HOW WAS SCHOOL" IN THE TESTS-QUIZZES-HOMEWORK SENSE.
OH, COME ON, DAD. ONLY TEACHERS CARE ABOUT THAT STUFF!
Peirce

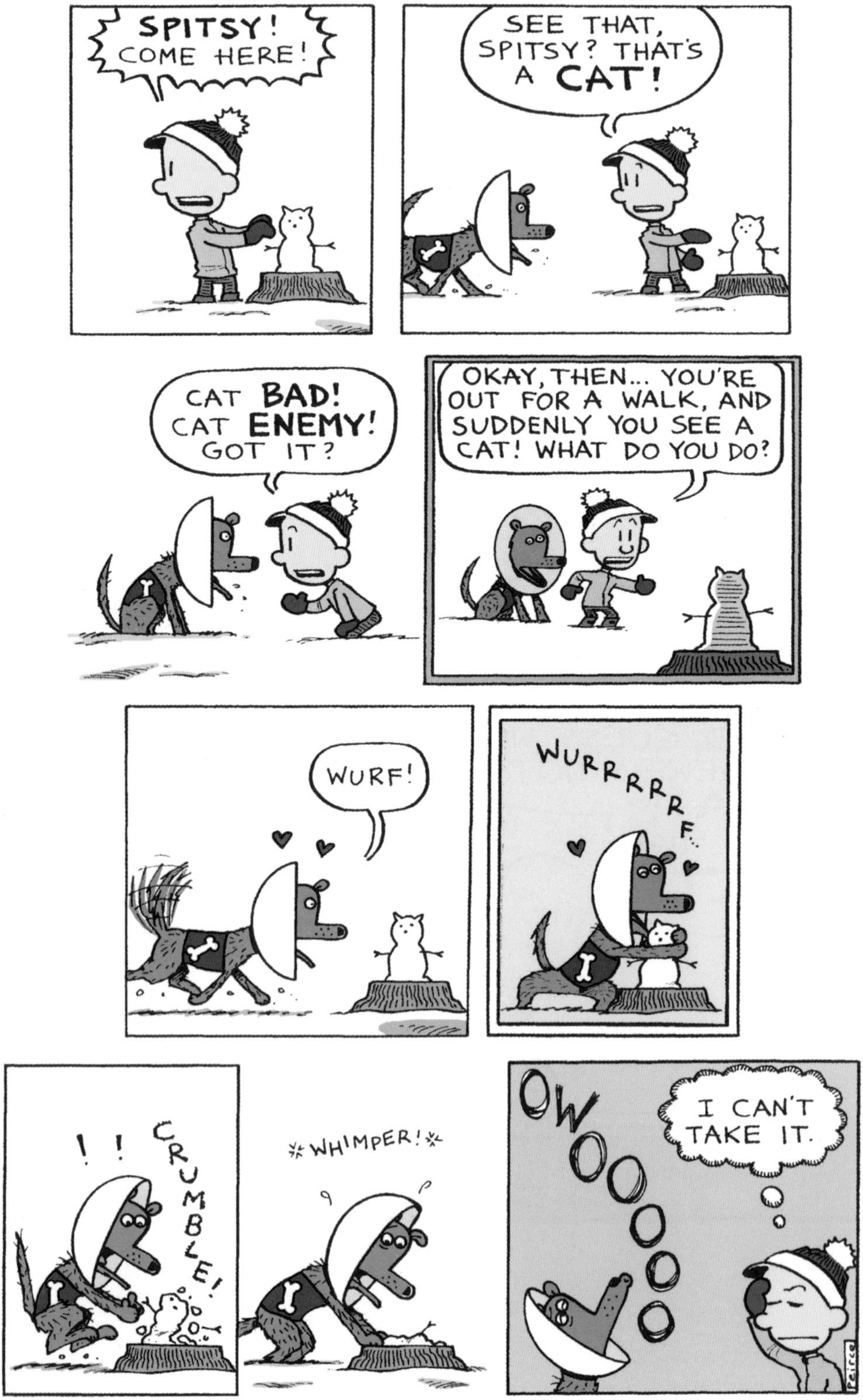
SPITSY! COME HERE!
SEE THAT, SPITSY? THAT'S A CAT!
CAT BAD! CAT ENEMY! GOT IT?
OKAY, THEN... YOU'RE OUT FOR A WALK, AND SUDDENLY YOU SEE A CAT! WHAT DO YOU DO?
WURF!
WURRRRRRF...
! !
CRUMBLE!
WHIMPER!
OWOOOOOO
I CAN'T TAKE IT.
Peirce

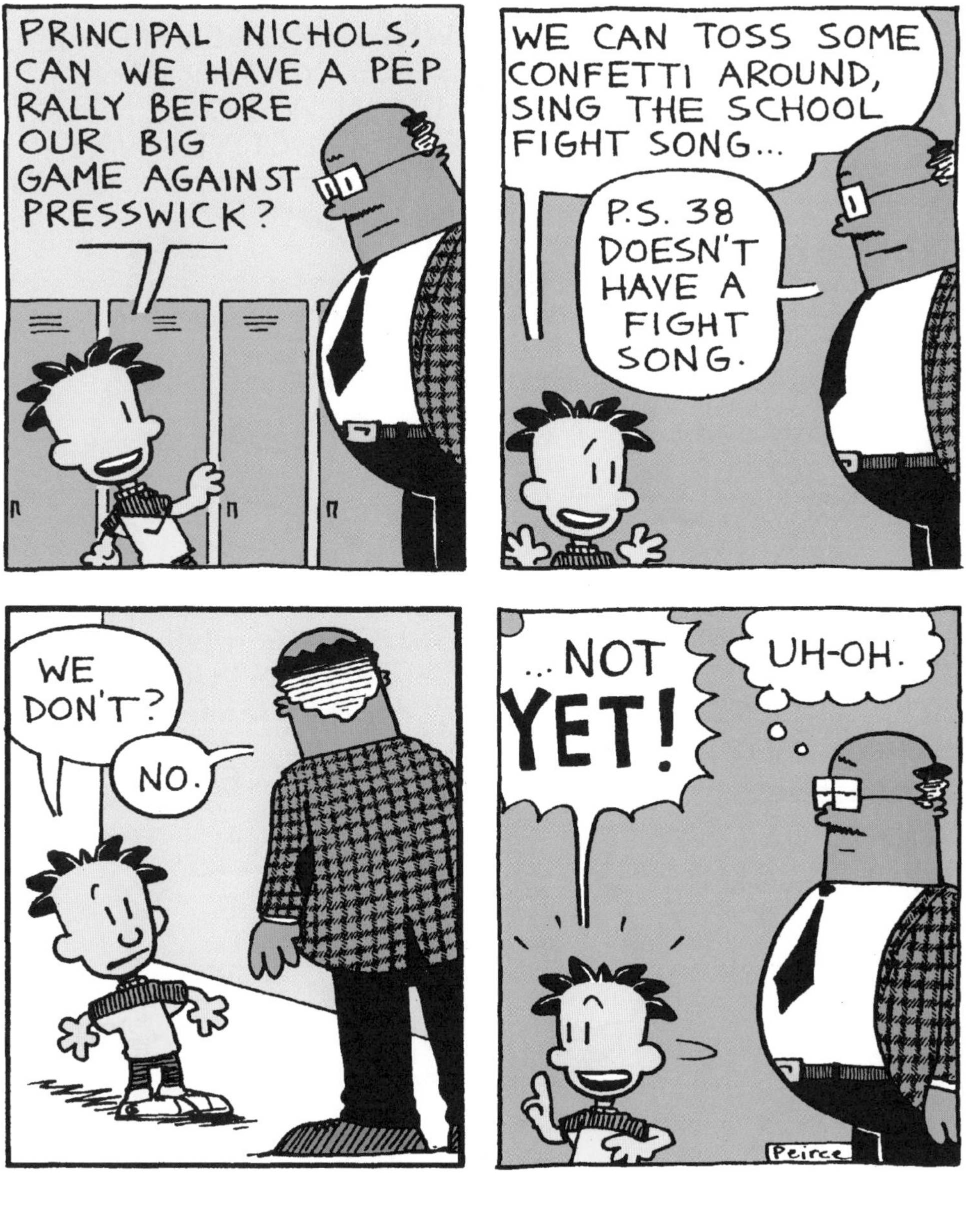
PRINCIPAL NICHOLS, CAN WE HAVE A PEP RALLY BEFORE OUR BIG GAME AGAINST PRESSWICK?
WE CAN TOSS SOME CONFETTI AROUND, SING THE SCHOOL FIGHT SONG...
P.S. 38 DOESN'T HAVE A FIGHT SONG.
WE DON'T?
NO.
...NOT YET!
UH-OH.
Peirce

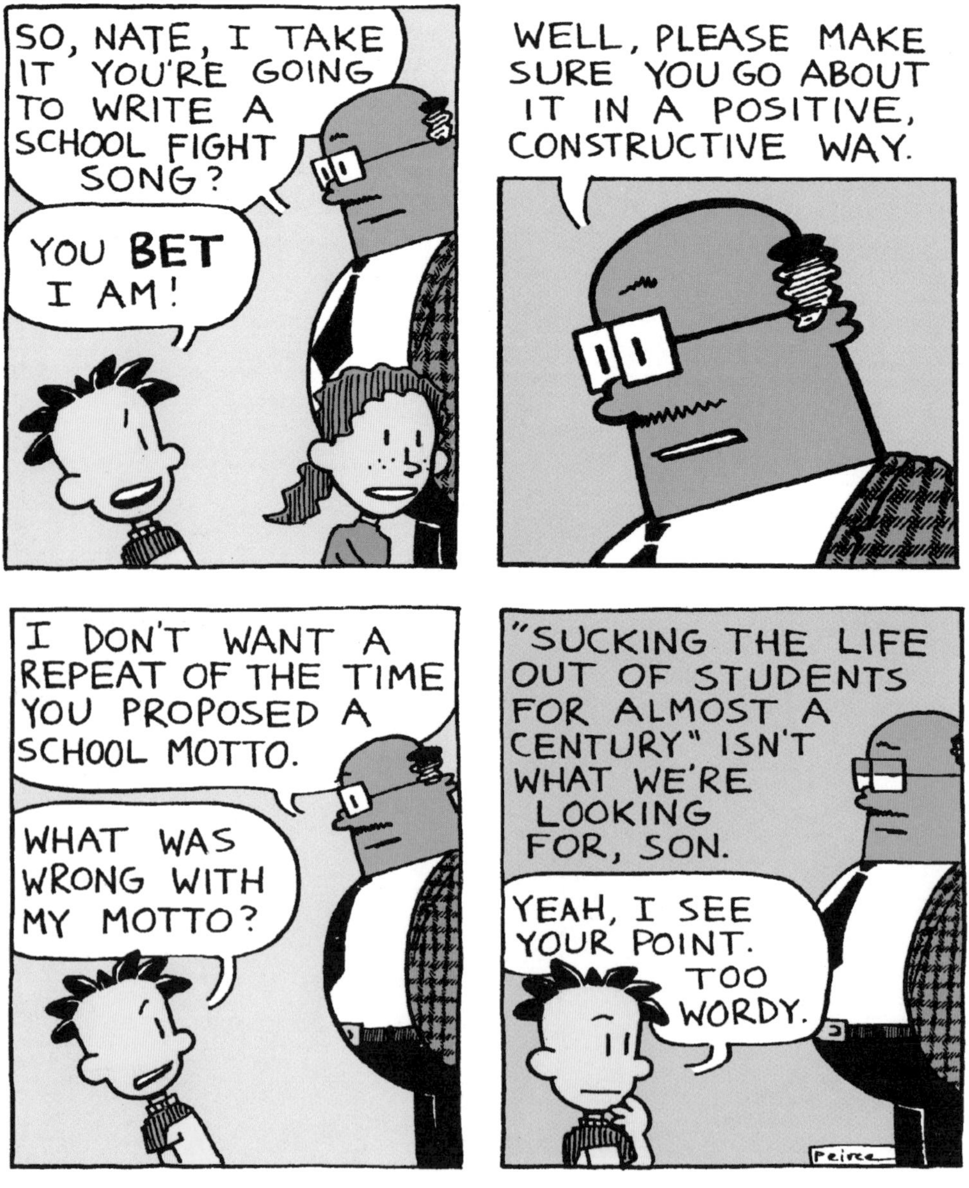
SO, NATE, I TAKE IT YOU'RE GOING TO WRITE A SCHOOL FIGHT SONG?
YOU **BET** I AM!
WELL, PLEASE MAKE SURE YOU GO ABOUT IT IN A POSITIVE, CONSTRUCTIVE WAY.
I DON'T WANT A REPEAT OF THE TIME YOU PROPOSED A SCHOOL MOTTO.
WHAT WAS WRONG WITH MY MOTTO?
"SUCKING THE LIFE OUT OF STUDENTS FOR ALMOST A CENTURY" ISN'T WHAT WE'RE LOOKING FOR, SON.
YEAH, I SEE YOUR POINT.
TOO WORDY.
Peirce

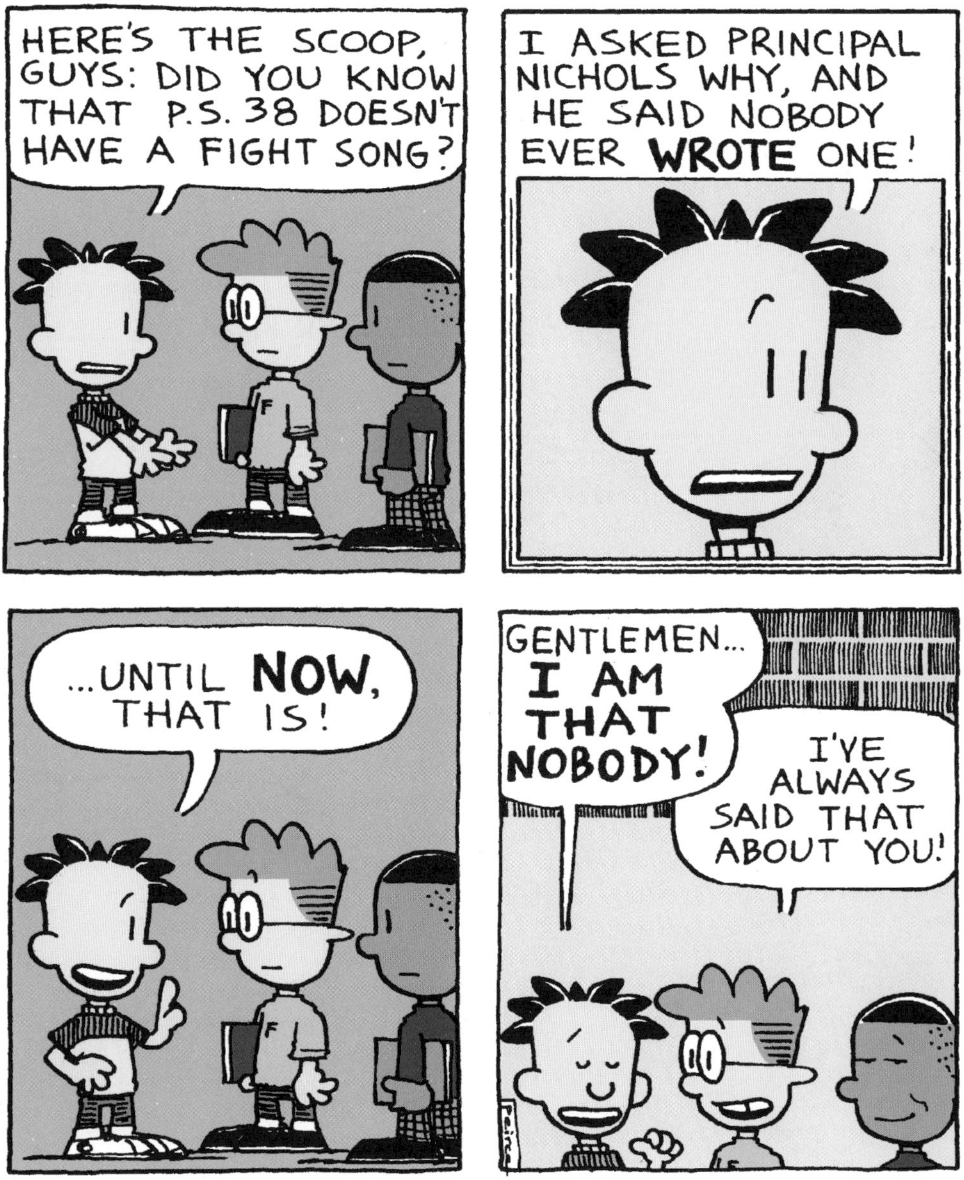
HERE'S THE SCOOP, GUYS: DID YOU KNOW THAT P.S. 38 DOESN'T HAVE A FIGHT SONG?
I ASKED PRINCIPAL NICHOLS WHY, AND HE SAID NOBODY EVER **WROTE** ONE!
...UNTIL **NOW**, THAT IS!
GENTLEMEN... **I AM THAT NOBODY!**
I'VE ALWAYS SAID THAT ABOUT YOU!
Peirce

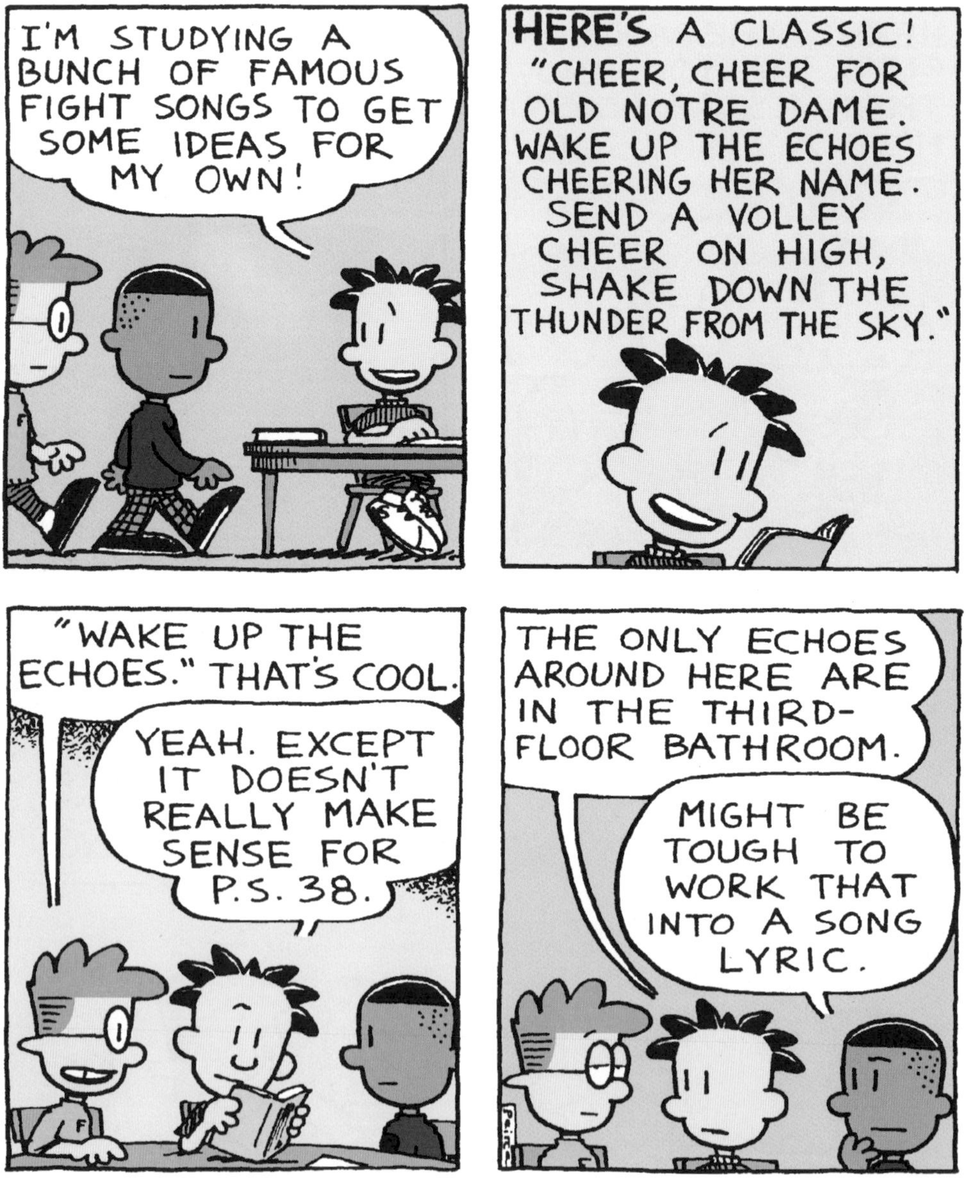
I'M STUDYING A BUNCH OF FAMOUS FIGHT SONGS TO GET SOME IDEAS FOR MY OWN!
HERE'S A CLASSIC! "CHEER, CHEER FOR OLD NOTRE DAME. WAKE UP THE ECHOES CHEERING HER NAME. SEND A VOLLEY CHEER ON HIGH, SHAKE DOWN THE THUNDER FROM THE SKY."
"WAKE UP THE ECHOES." THAT'S COOL.
YEAH. EXCEPT IT DOESN'T REALLY MAKE SENSE FOR P.S. 38.
THE ONLY ECHOES AROUND HERE ARE IN THE THIRD-FLOOR BATHROOM.
MIGHT BE TOUGH TO WORK THAT INTO A SONG LYRIC.
PEIRCE

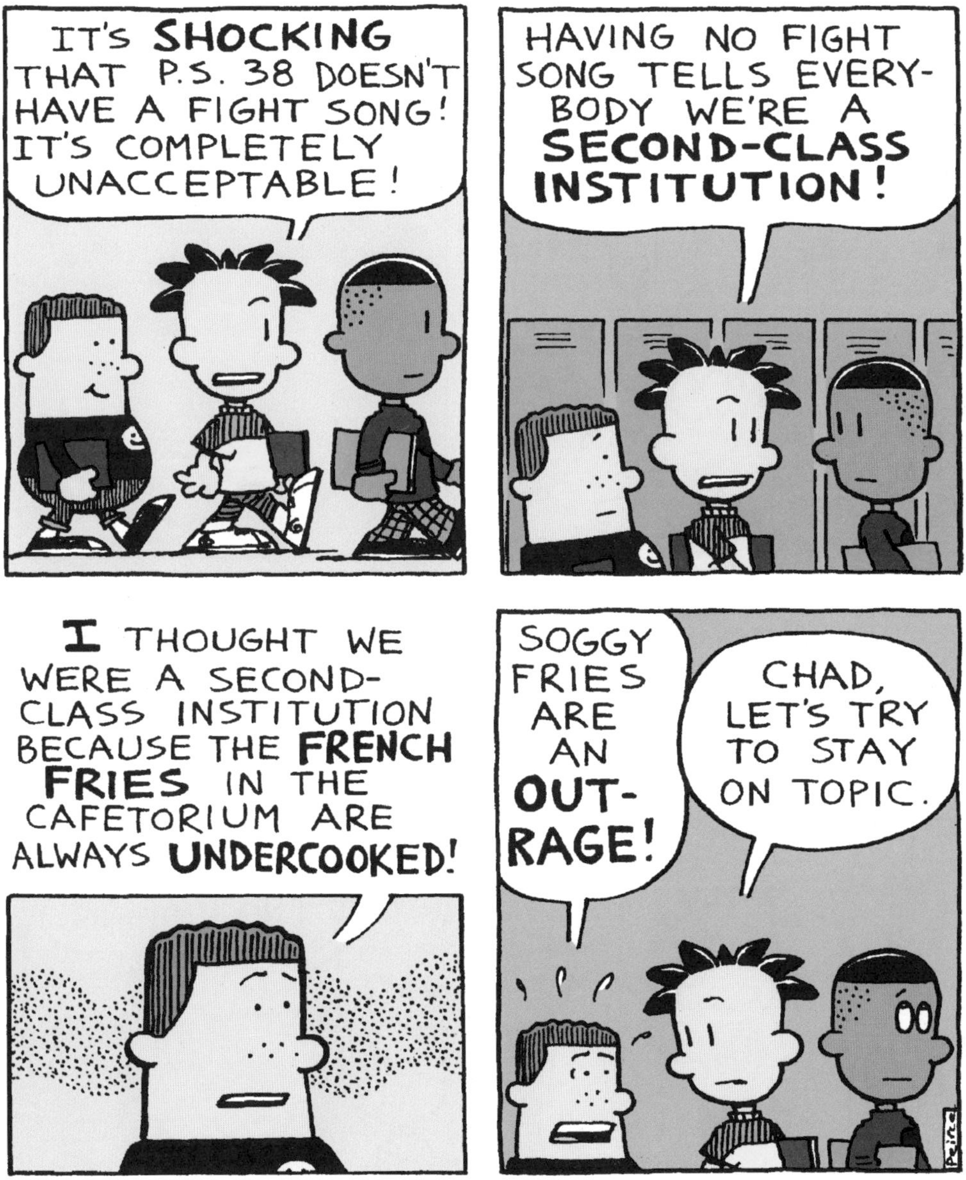
IT'S SHOCKING THAT P.S. 38 DOESN'T HAVE A FIGHT SONG! IT'S COMPLETELY UNACCEPTABLE!
HAVING NO FIGHT SONG TELLS EVERYBODY WE'RE A SECOND-CLASS INSTITUTION!
I THOUGHT WE WERE A SECOND-CLASS INSTITUTION BECAUSE THE FRENCH FRIES IN THE CAFETORIUM ARE ALWAYS UNDERCOOKED!
SOGGY FRIES ARE AN OUT-RAGE!
CHAD, LET'S TRY TO STAY ON TOPIC.
Peirce

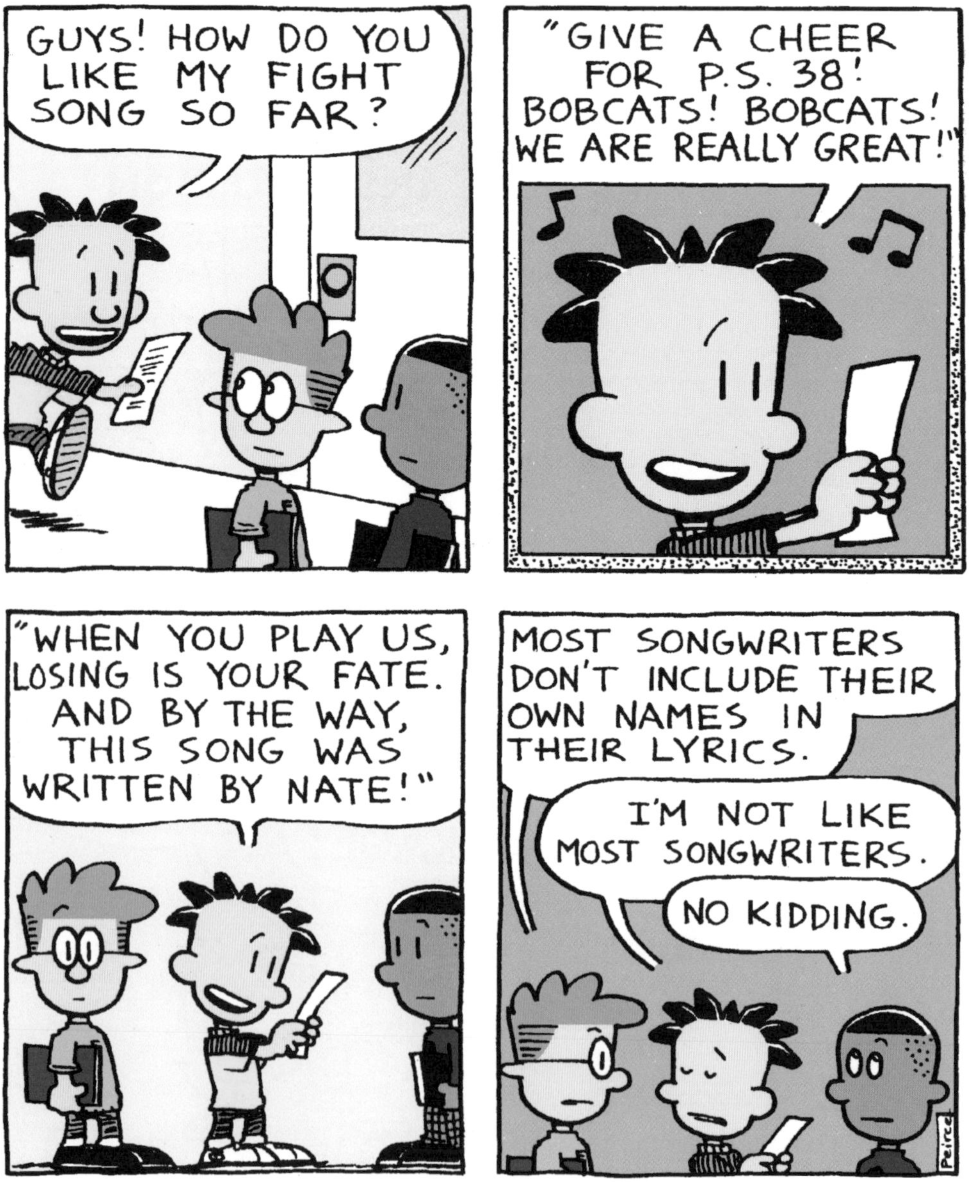
GUYS! HOW DO YOU LIKE MY FIGHT SONG SO FAR?
"GIVE A CHEER FOR P.S. 38! BOBCATS! BOBCATS! WE ARE REALLY GREAT!"
"WHEN YOU PLAY US, LOSING IS YOUR FATE. AND BY THE WAY, THIS SONG WAS WRITTEN BY NATE!"
MOST SONGWRITERS DON'T INCLUDE THEIR OWN NAMES IN THEIR LYRICS.
I'M NOT LIKE MOST SONGWRITERS.
NO KIDDING.
Peirce

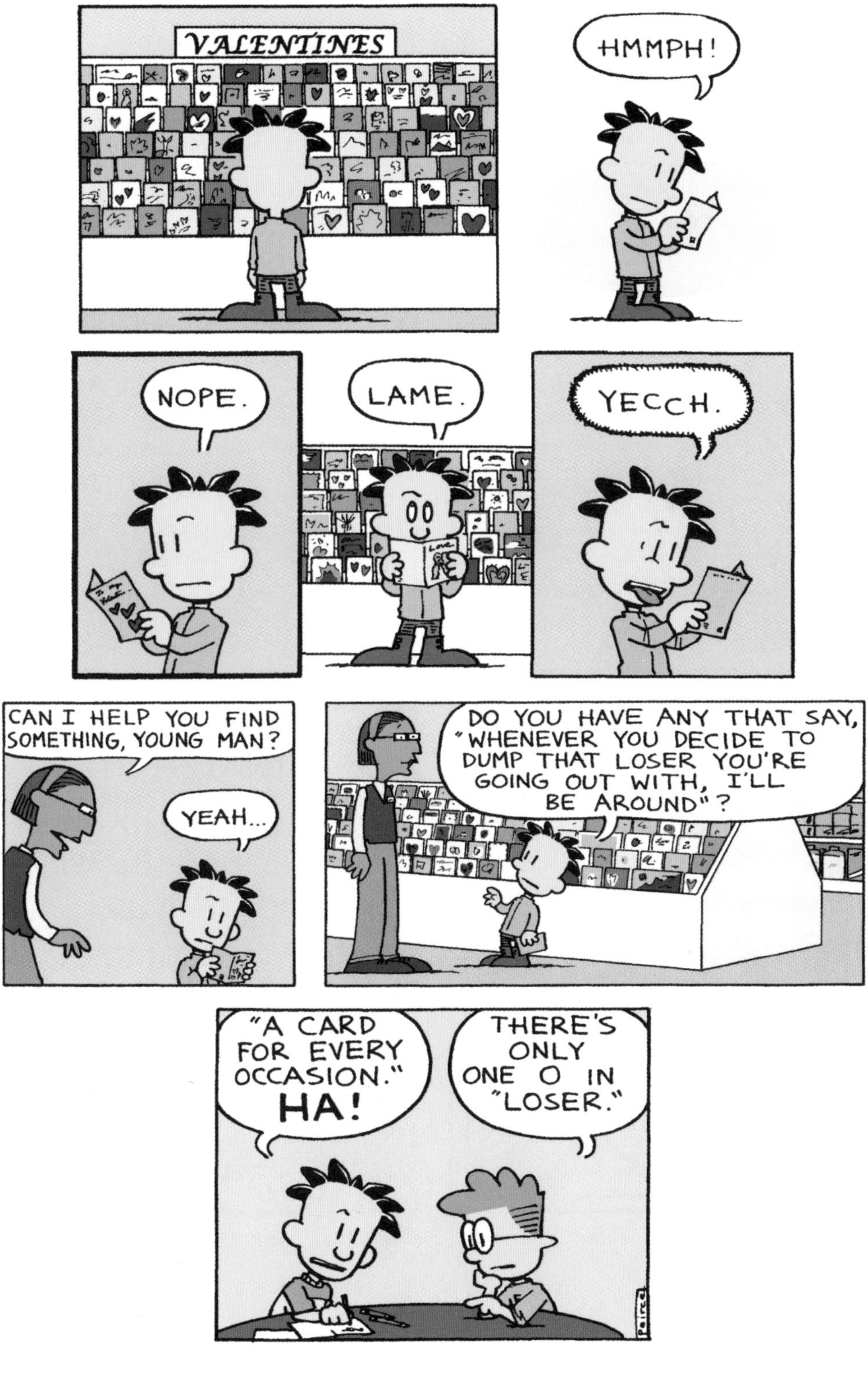
VALENTINES
HMMPH!
NOPE.
LAME.
YECCH.
CAN I HELP YOU FIND SOMETHING, YOUNG MAN?
YEAH...
DO YOU HAVE ANY THAT SAY, "WHENEVER YOU DECIDE TO DUMP THAT LOSER YOU'RE GOING OUT WITH, I'LL BE AROUND"?
"A CARD FOR EVERY OCCASION." HA!
THERE'S ONLY ONE O IN "LOSER."

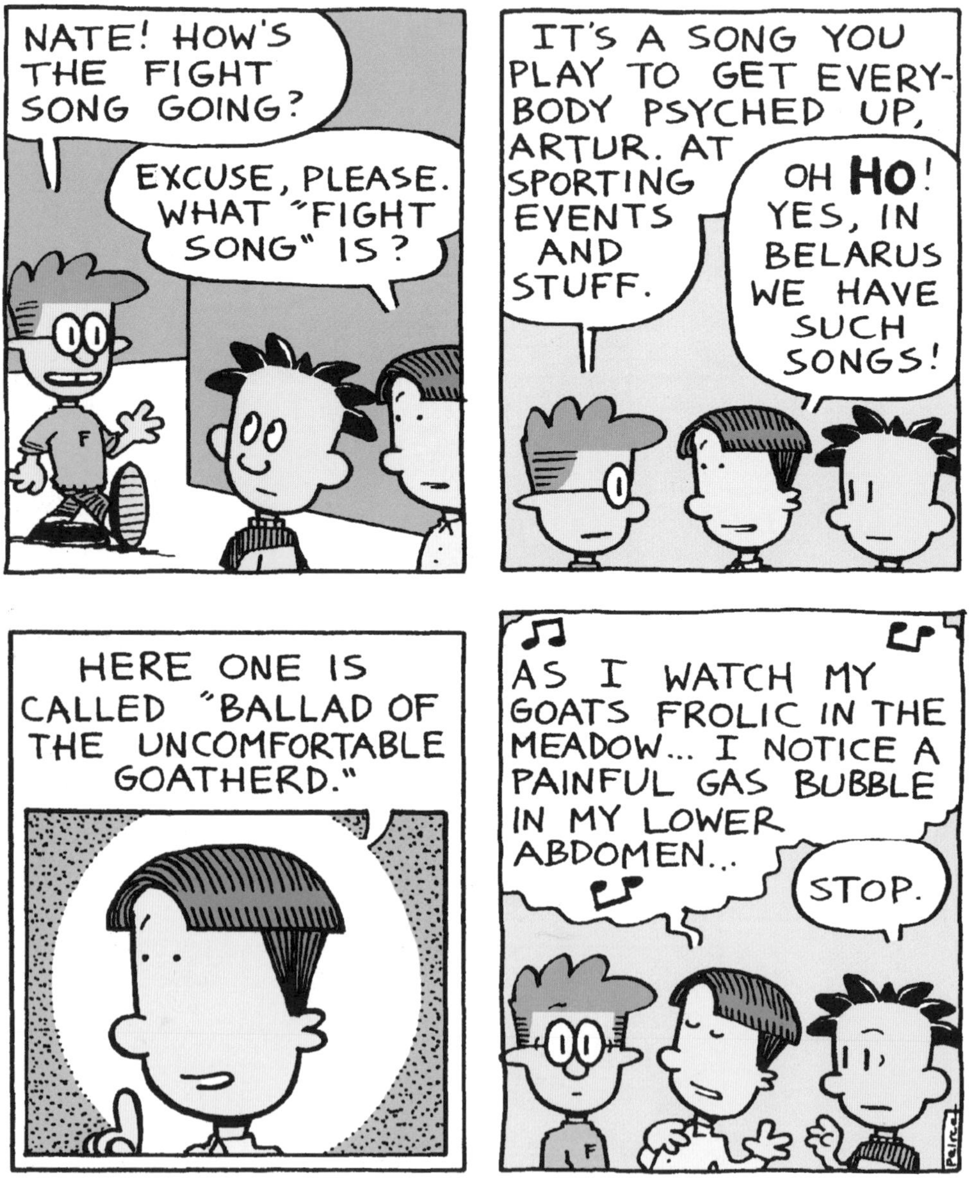
NATE! HOW'S THE FIGHT SONG GOING?
EXCUSE, PLEASE. WHAT "FIGHT SONG" IS?
IT'S A SONG YOU PLAY TO GET EVERY-BODY PSYCHED UP, ARTUR. AT SPORTING EVENTS AND STUFF.
OH **HO**! YES, IN BELARUS WE HAVE SUCH SONGS!
HERE ONE IS CALLED "BALLAD OF THE UNCOMFORTABLE GOATHERD."
AS I WATCH MY GOATS FROLIC IN THE MEADOW... I NOTICE A PAINFUL GAS BUBBLE IN MY LOWER ABDOMEN...
STOP.

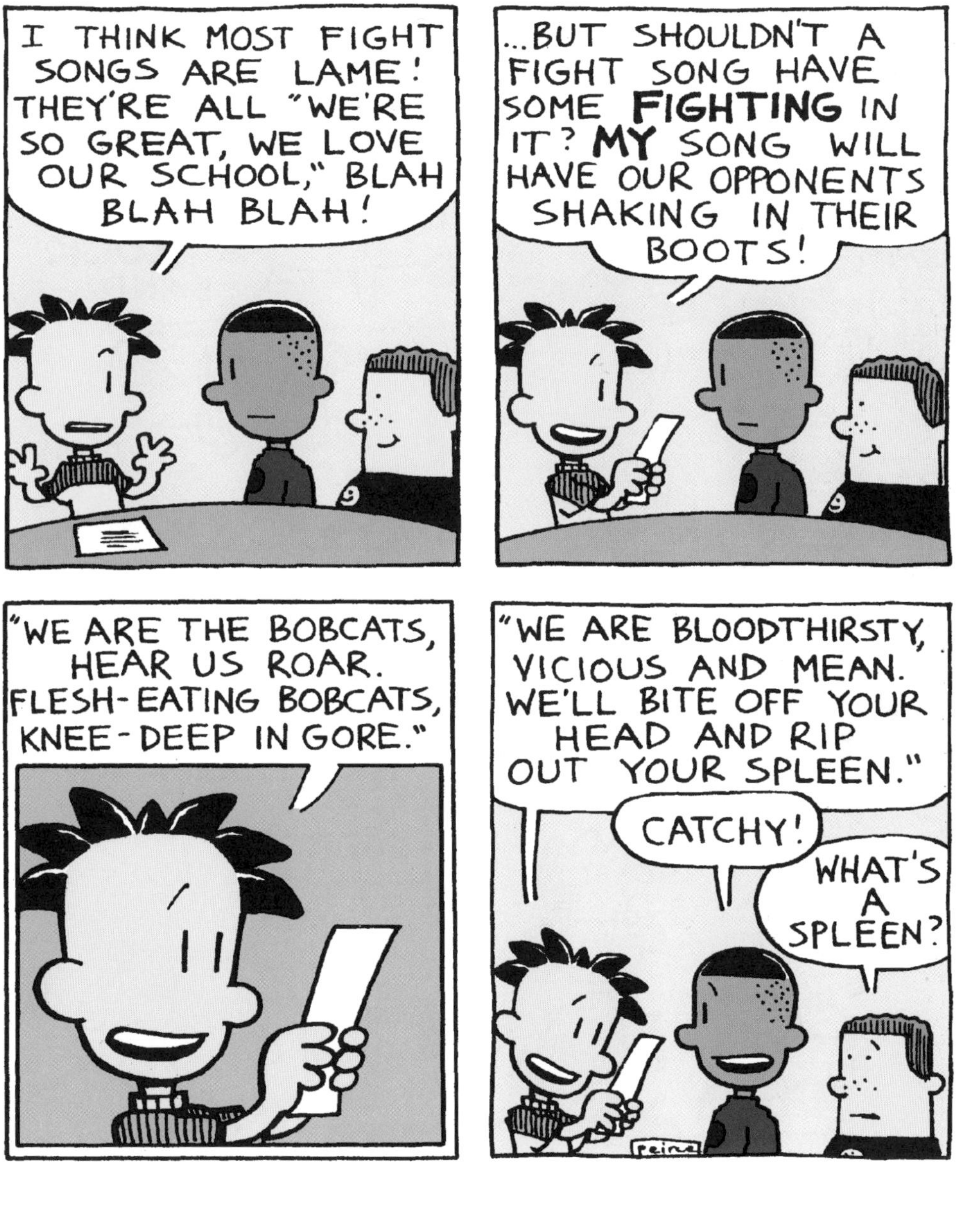
I THINK MOST FIGHT SONGS ARE LAME! THEY'RE ALL "WE'RE SO GREAT, WE LOVE OUR SCHOOL," BLAH BLAH BLAH!
...BUT SHOULDN'T A FIGHT SONG HAVE SOME FIGHTING IN IT? MY SONG WILL HAVE OUR OPPONENTS SHAKING IN THEIR BOOTS!
"WE ARE THE BOBCATS, HEAR US ROAR. FLESH-EATING BOBCATS, KNEE-DEEP IN GORE."
"WE ARE BLOODTHIRSTY, VICIOUS AND MEAN. WE'LL BITE OFF YOUR HEAD AND RIP OUT YOUR SPLEEN."
CATCHY!
WHAT'S A SPLEEN?
peirce

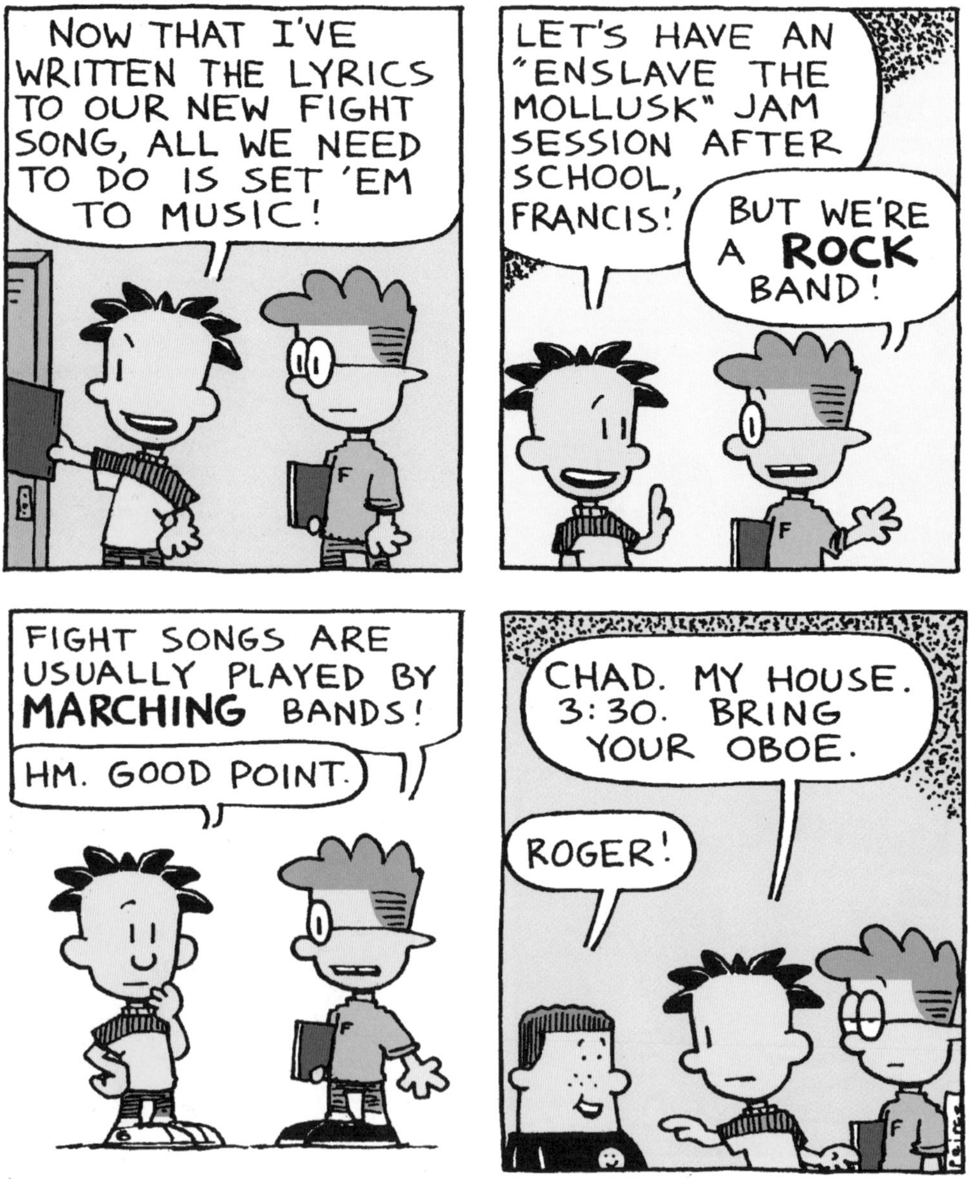
NOW THAT I'VE WRITTEN THE LYRICS TO OUR NEW FIGHT SONG, ALL WE NEED TO DO IS SET 'EM TO MUSIC!
LET'S HAVE AN "ENSLAVE THE MOLLUSK" JAM SESSION AFTER SCHOOL, FRANCIS!
BUT WE'RE A **ROCK** BAND!
FIGHT SONGS ARE USUALLY PLAYED BY **MARCHING** BANDS!
HM. GOOD POINT.
CHAD. MY HOUSE. 3:30. BRING YOUR OBOE.
ROGER!

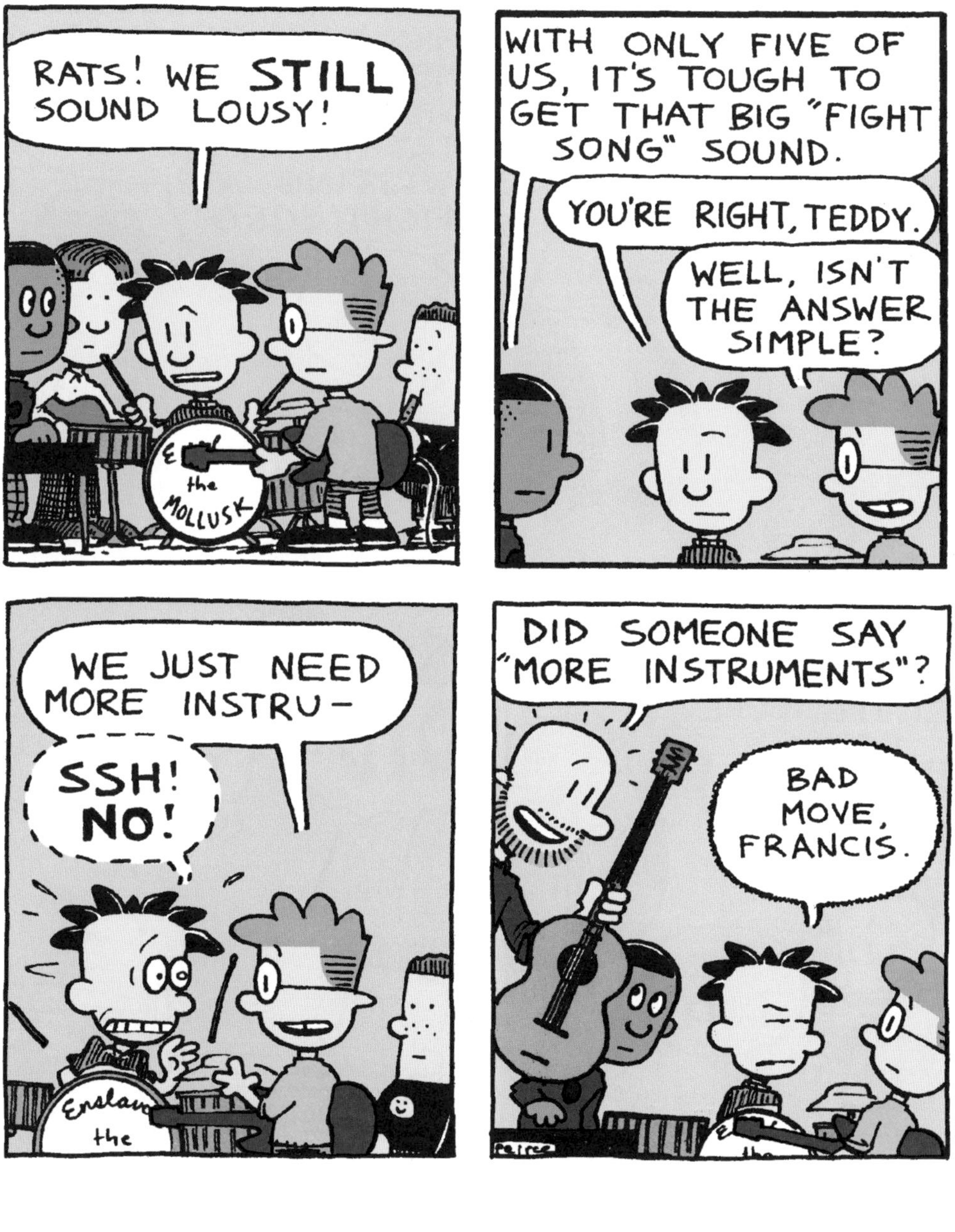
RATS! WE STILL SOUND LOUSY!
WITH ONLY FIVE OF US, IT'S TOUGH TO GET THAT BIG "FIGHT SONG" SOUND.
YOU'RE RIGHT, TEDDY.
WELL, ISN'T THE ANSWER SIMPLE?
WE JUST NEED MORE INSTRU-
SSH! NO!
DID SOMEONE SAY "MORE INSTRUMENTS"?
BAD MOVE, FRANCIS.

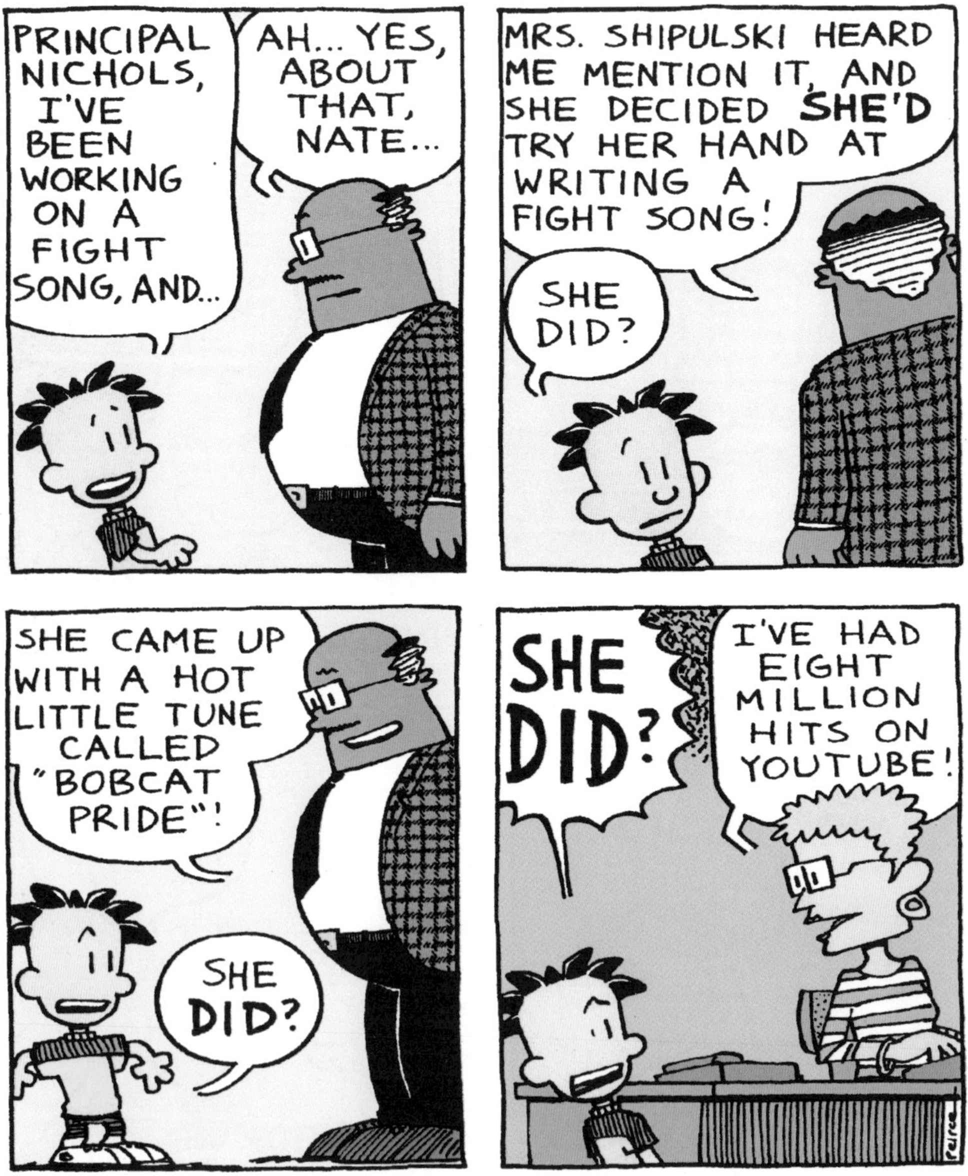
PRINCIPAL NICHOLS, I'VE BEEN WORKING ON A FIGHT SONG, AND...
AH... YES, ABOUT THAT, NATE...
MRS. SHIPULSKI HEARD ME MENTION IT, AND SHE DECIDED SHE'D TRY HER HAND AT WRITING A FIGHT SONG!
SHE DID?
SHE CAME UP WITH A HOT LITTLE TUNE CALLED "BOBCAT PRIDE"!
SHE DID?
SHE DID?
I'VE HAD EIGHT MILLION HITS ON YOUTUBE!

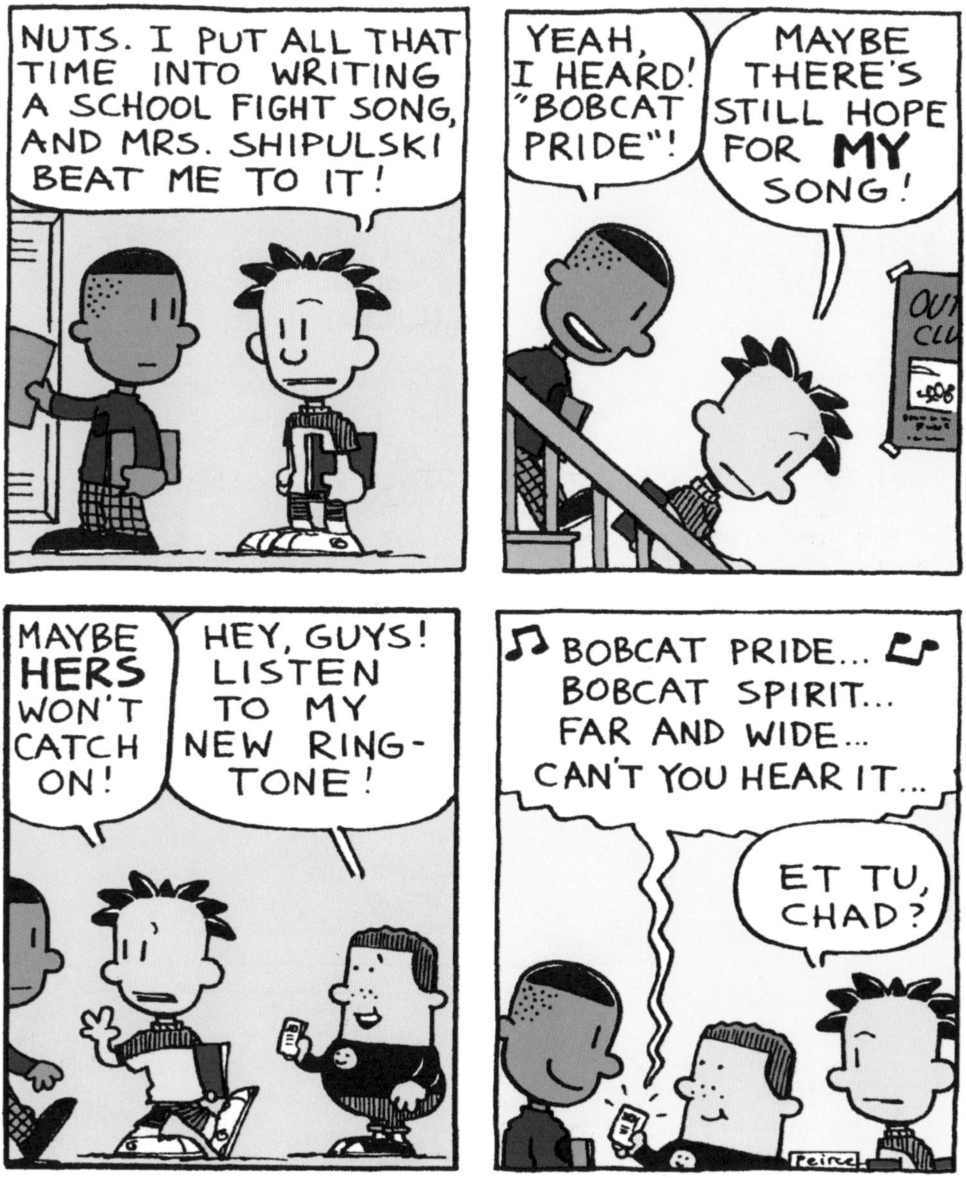
NUTS. I PUT ALL THAT TIME INTO WRITING A SCHOOL FIGHT SONG, AND MRS. SHIPULSKI BEAT ME TO IT!
YEAH, I HEARD! "BOBCAT PRIDE"!
MAYBE THERE'S STILL HOPE FOR MY SONG!
MAYBE HERS WON'T CATCH ON!
HEY, GUYS! LISTEN TO MY NEW RING-TONE!
BOBCAT PRIDE... BOBCAT SPIRIT... FAR AND WIDE... CAN'T YOU HEAR IT...
ET TU, CHAD?
Peirce

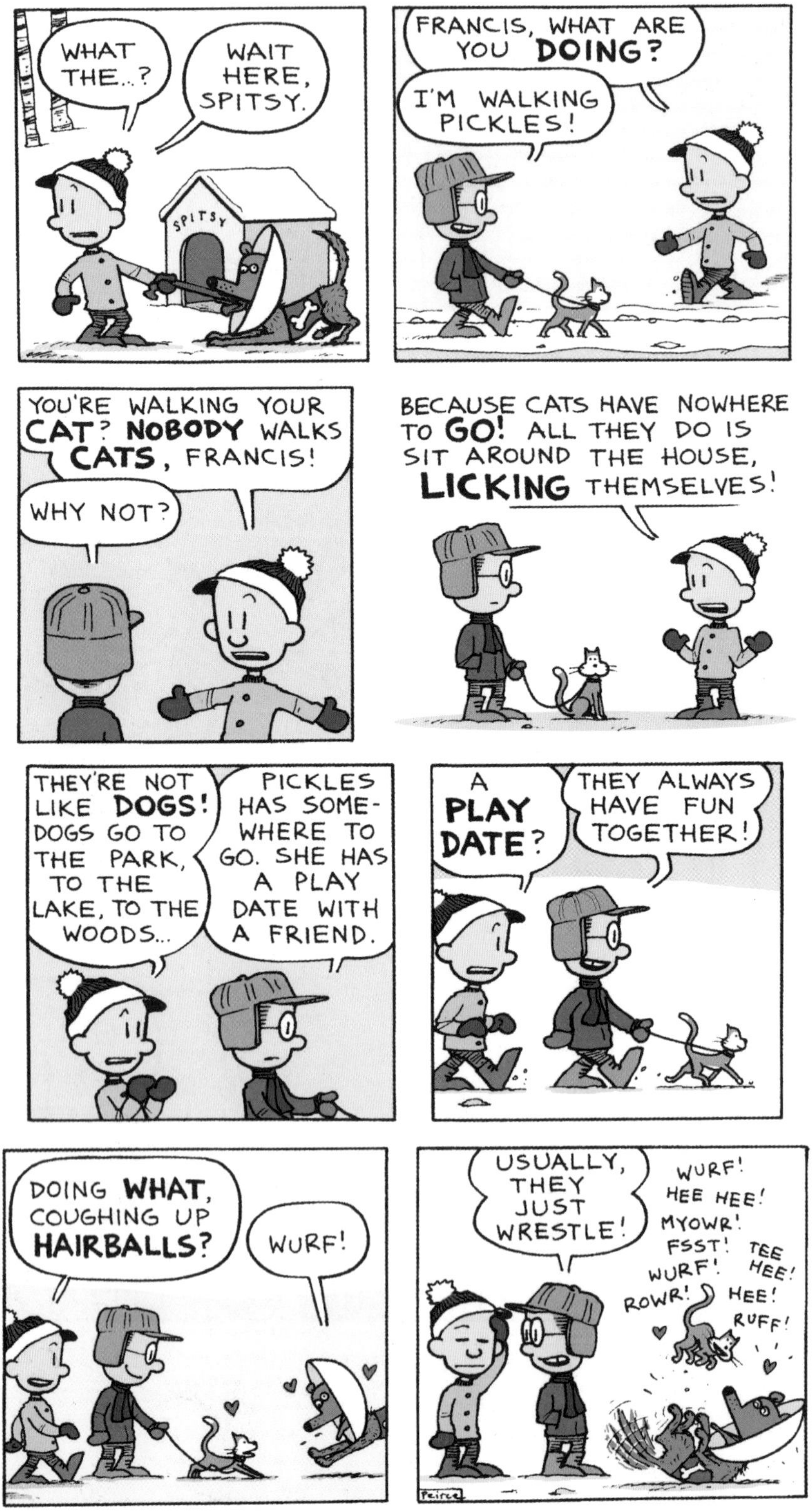

WHAT THE...?
WAIT HERE, SPITSY.
SPITSY
FRANCIS, WHAT ARE YOU **DOING**?
I'M WALKING PICKLES!
YOU'RE WALKING YOUR **CAT**? **NOBODY** WALKS **CATS**, FRANCIS!
WHY NOT?
BECAUSE CATS HAVE NOWHERE TO **GO**! ALL THEY DO IS SIT AROUND THE HOUSE, **LICKING** THEMSELVES!
THEY'RE NOT LIKE **DOGS**! DOGS GO TO THE PARK, TO THE LAKE, TO THE WOODS...
PICKLES HAS SOMEWHERE TO GO. SHE HAS A PLAY DATE WITH A FRIEND.
A **PLAY DATE**?
THEY ALWAYS HAVE FUN TOGETHER!
DOING **WHAT**, COUGHING UP **HAIRBALLS**?
WURF!
USUALLY, THEY JUST WRESTLE!
WURF!
HEE HEE!
MYOWR!
FSST!
TEE HEE!
WURF!
ROWR!
HEE!
RUFF!
Peirce

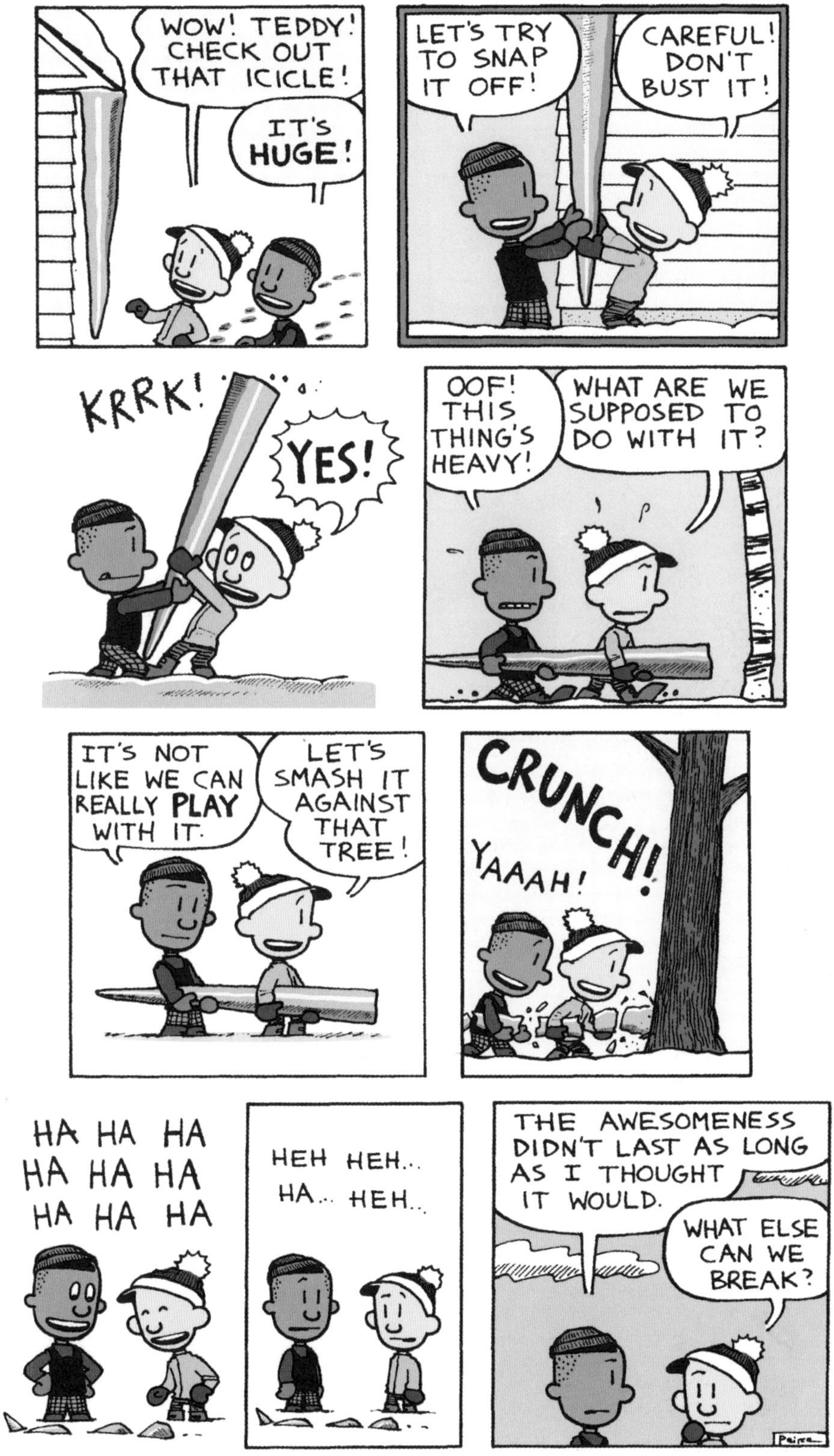
WOW! TEDDY! CHECK OUT THAT ICICLE!
IT'S HUGE!
LET'S TRY TO SNAP IT OFF!
CAREFUL! DON'T BUST IT!
KRRK!
YES!
OOF! THIS THING'S HEAVY!
WHAT ARE WE SUPPOSED TO DO WITH IT?
IT'S NOT LIKE WE CAN REALLY PLAY WITH IT.
LET'S SMASH IT AGAINST THAT TREE!
CRUNCH!
YAAAH!
HA HA HA HA HA HA HA HA HA
HEH HEH... HA... HEH...
THE AWESOMENESS DIDN'T LAST AS LONG AS I THOUGHT IT WOULD.
WHAT ELSE CAN WE BREAK?
Peirce

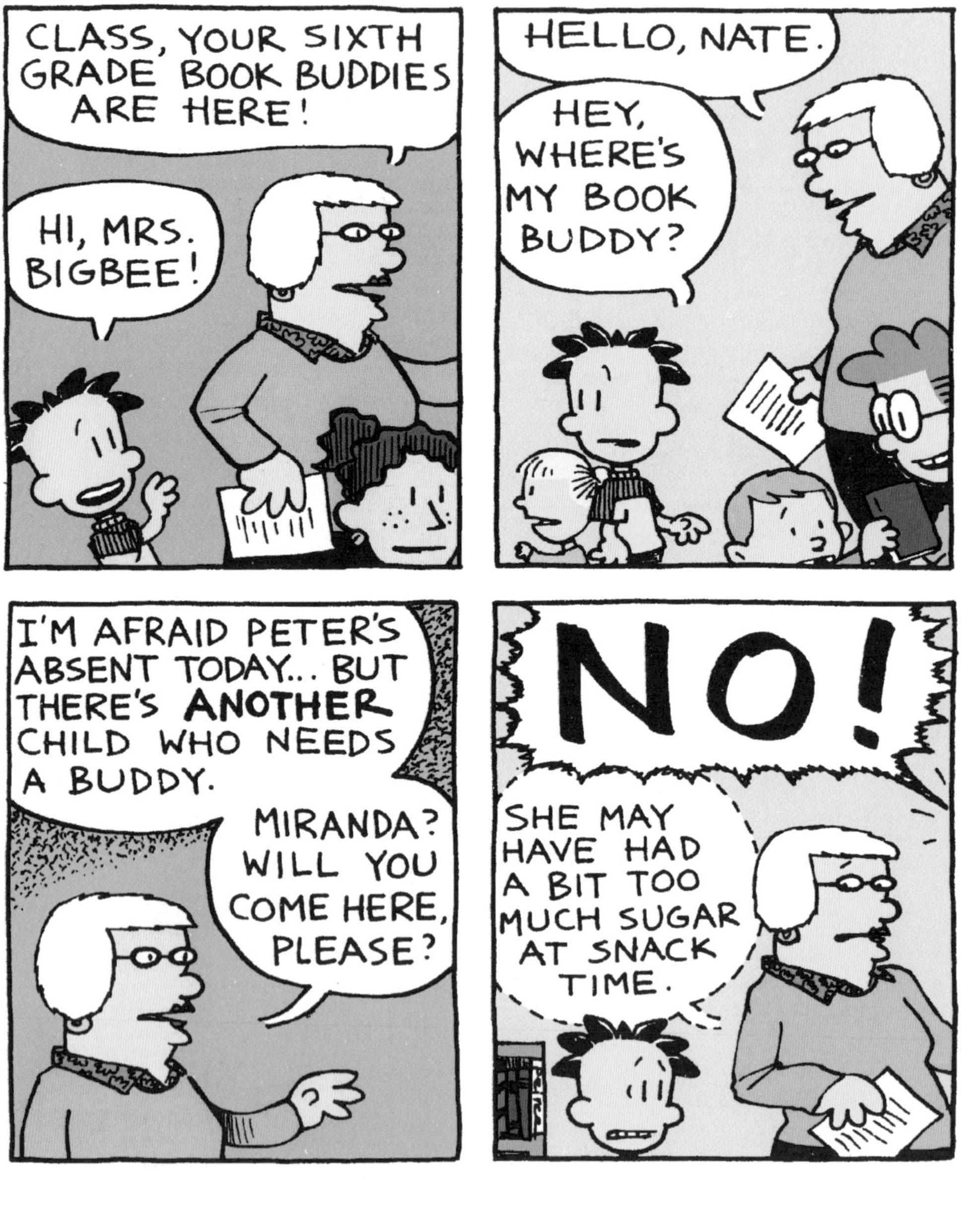
CLASS, YOUR SIXTH GRADE BOOK BUDDIES ARE HERE!
HI, MRS. BIGBEE!
HELLO, NATE.
HEY, WHERE'S MY BOOK BUDDY?
I'M AFRAID PETER'S ABSENT TODAY... BUT THERE'S **ANOTHER** CHILD WHO NEEDS A BUDDY.
MIRANDA? WILL YOU COME HERE, PLEASE?
NO!
SHE MAY HAVE HAD A BIT TOO MUCH SUGAR AT SNACK TIME.

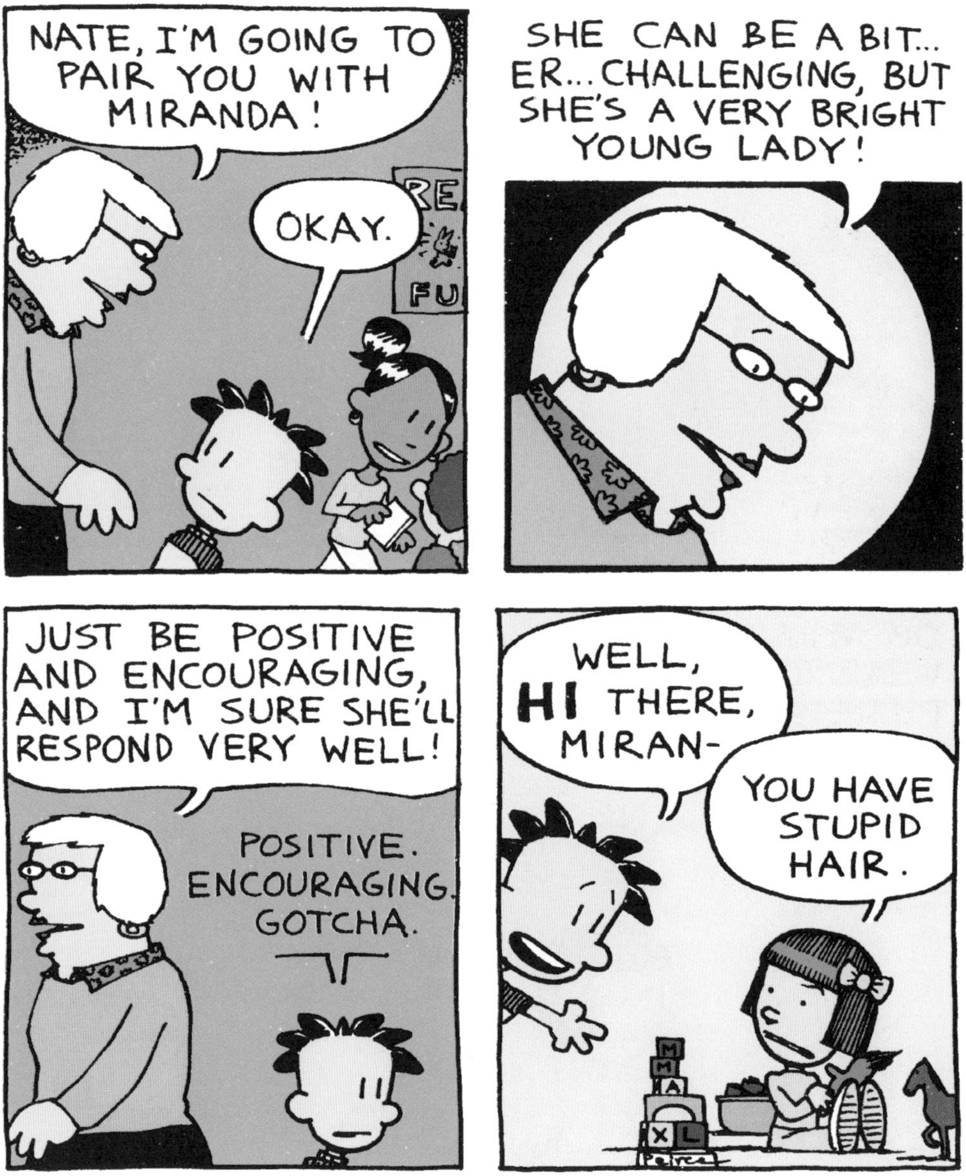
NATE, I'M GOING TO PAIR YOU WITH MIRANDA!
OKAY.
SHE CAN BE A BIT... ER... CHALLENGING, BUT SHE'S A VERY BRIGHT YOUNG LADY!
JUST BE POSITIVE AND ENCOURAGING, AND I'M SURE SHE'LL RESPOND VERY WELL!
POSITIVE. ENCOURAGING. GOTCHA.
WELL, HI THERE, MIRAN-
YOU HAVE STUPID HAIR.

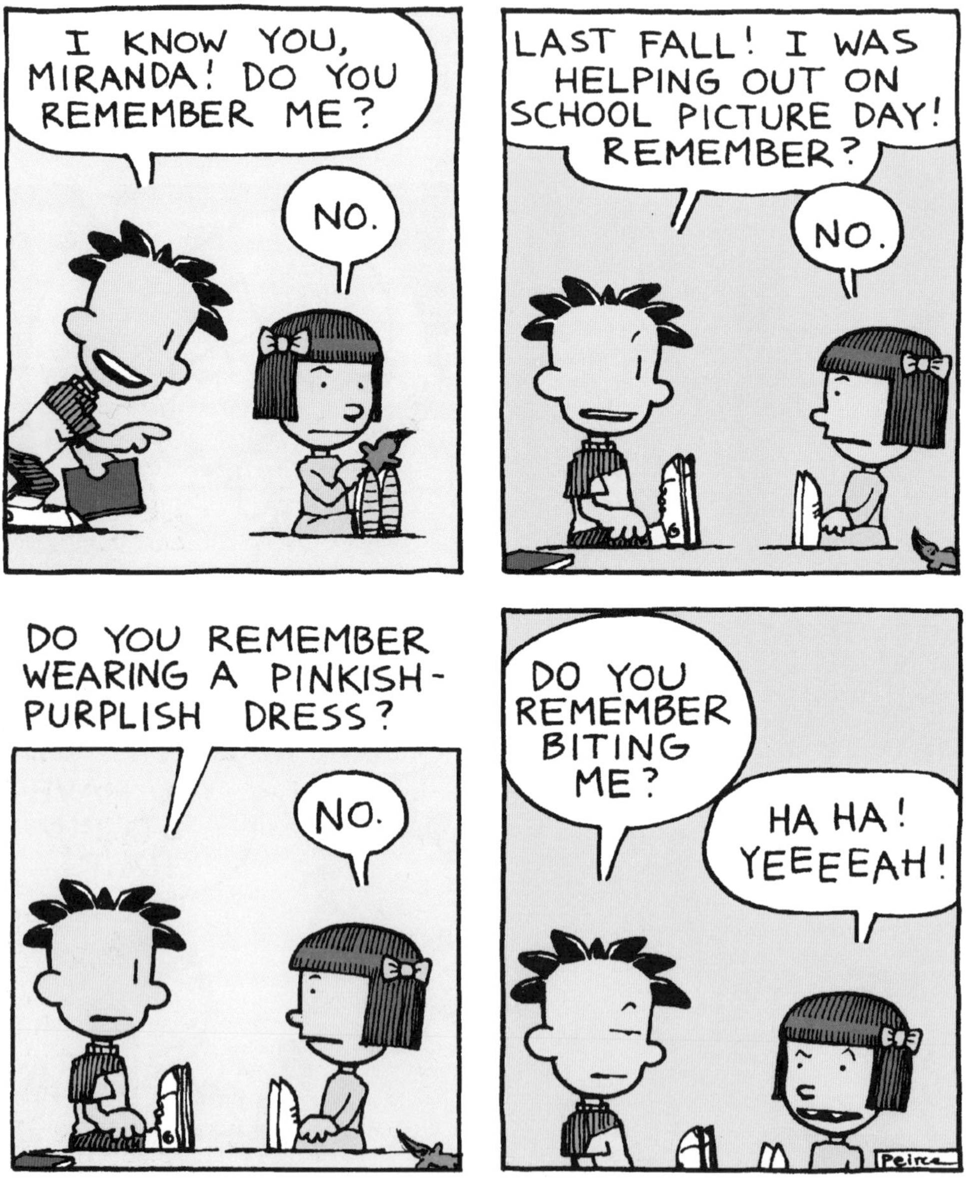
I KNOW YOU, MIRANDA! DO YOU REMEMBER ME?
NO.
LAST FALL! I WAS HELPING OUT ON SCHOOL PICTURE DAY! REMEMBER?
NO.
DO YOU REMEMBER WEARING A PINKISH-PURPLISH DRESS?
NO.
DO YOU REMEMBER BITING ME?
HA HA! YEEEEAH!
Peirce

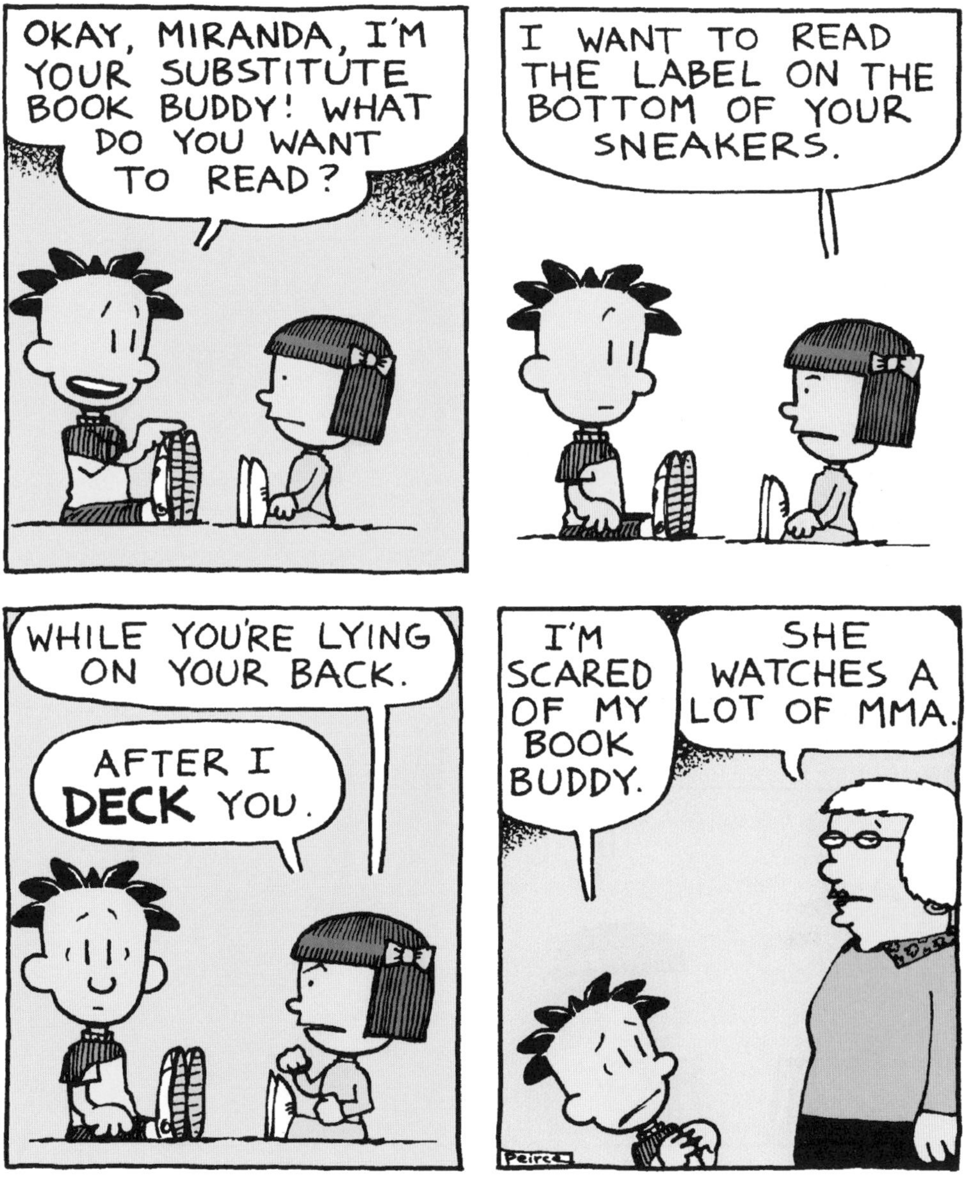
OKAY, MIRANDA, I'M YOUR SUBSTITUTE BOOK BUDDY! WHAT DO YOU WANT TO READ?
I WANT TO READ THE LABEL ON THE BOTTOM OF YOUR SNEAKERS.
WHILE YOU'RE LYING ON YOUR BACK.
AFTER I DECK YOU.
I'M SCARED OF MY BOOK BUDDY.
SHE WATCHES A LOT OF MMA.
Peirce

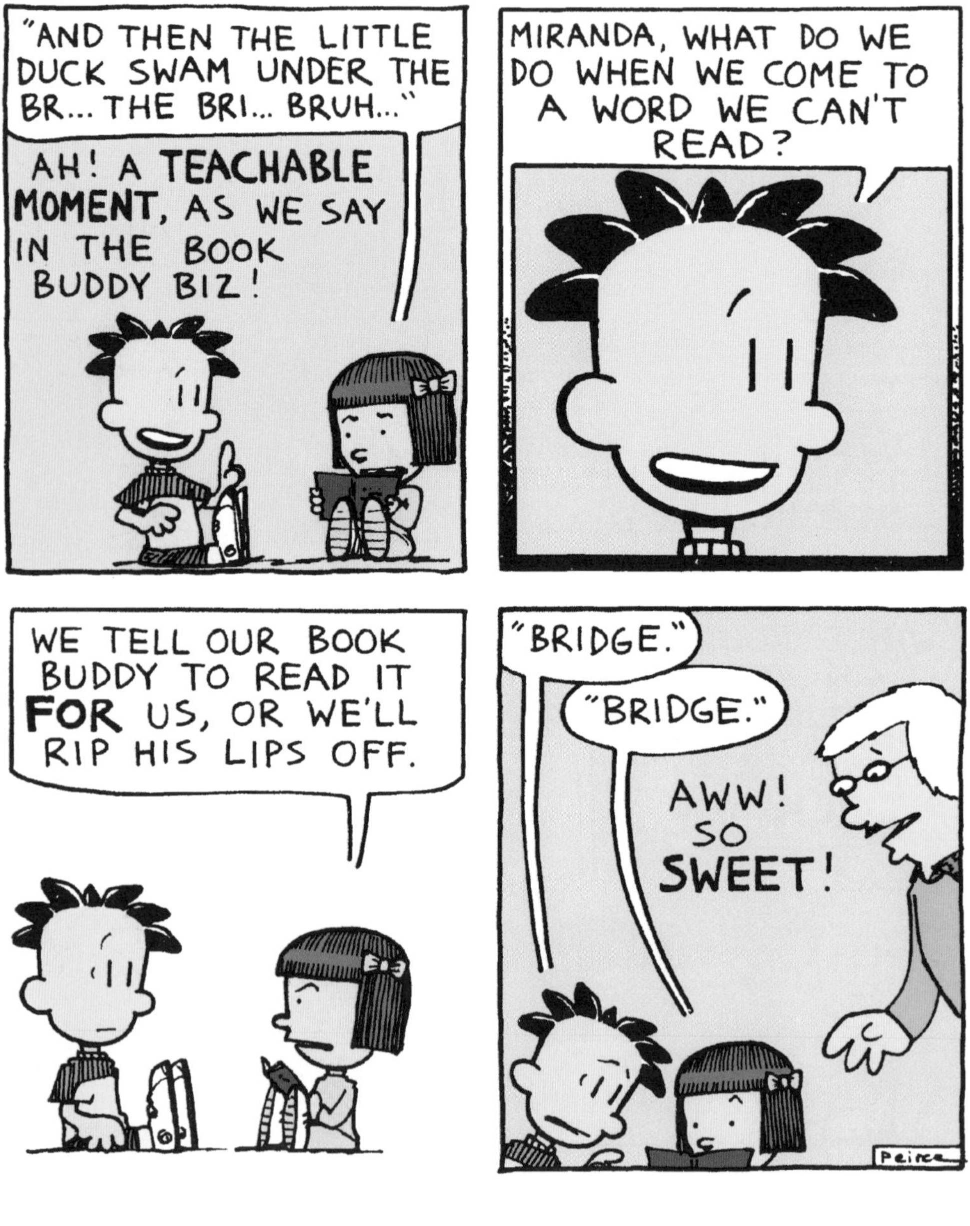
"AND THEN THE LITTLE DUCK SWAM UNDER THE BR... THE BRI... BRUH..."
AH! A **TEACHABLE MOMENT**, AS WE SAY IN THE BOOK BUDDY BIZ!
MIRANDA, WHAT DO WE DO WHEN WE COME TO A WORD WE CAN'T READ?
WE TELL OUR BOOK BUDDY TO READ IT **FOR** US, OR WE'LL RIP HIS LIPS OFF.
"BRIDGE."
"BRIDGE."
AWW! SO **SWEET**!
Peirce

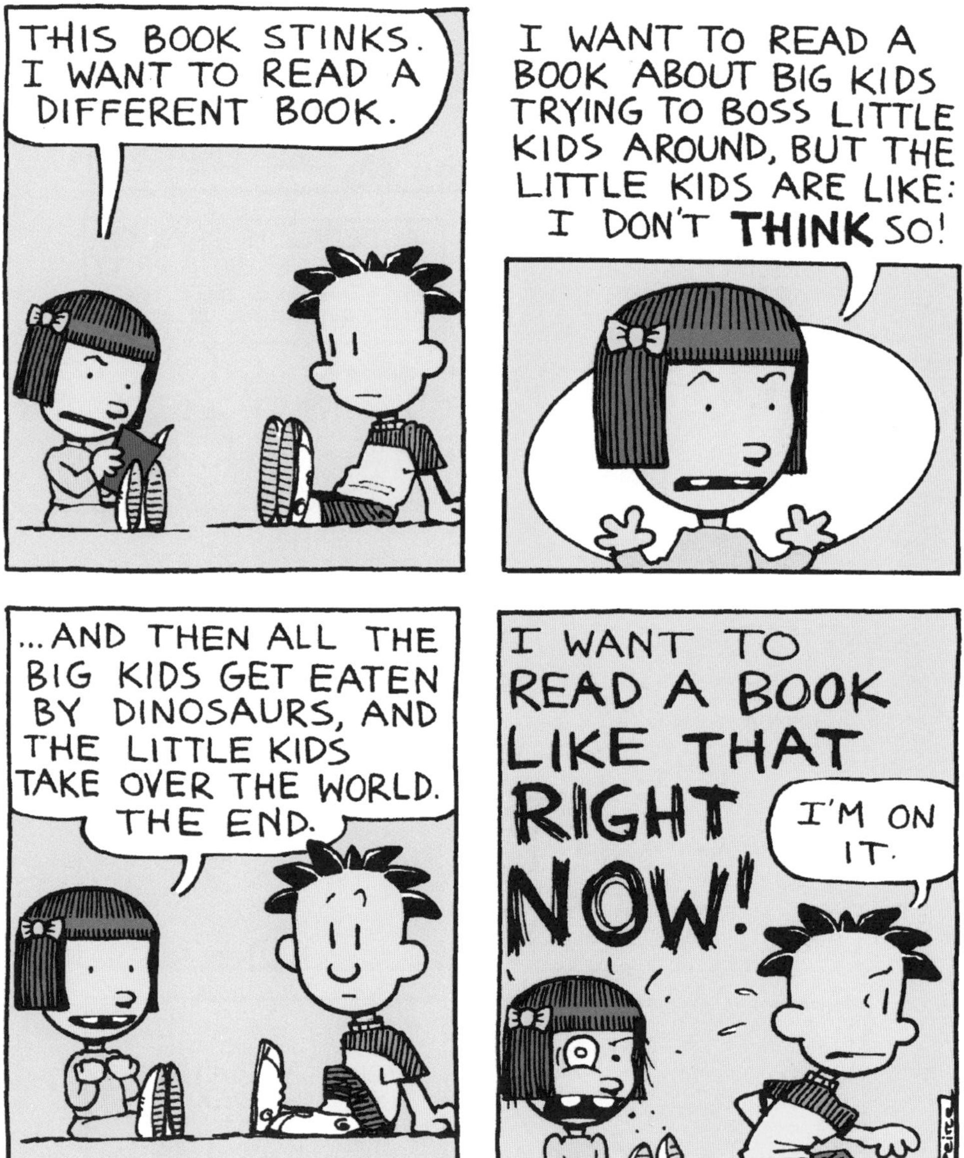
THIS BOOK STINKS. I WANT TO READ A DIFFERENT BOOK.
I WANT TO READ A BOOK ABOUT BIG KIDS TRYING TO BOSS LITTLE KIDS AROUND, BUT THE LITTLE KIDS ARE LIKE: I DON'T THINK SO!
...AND THEN ALL THE BIG KIDS GET EATEN BY DINOSAURS, AND THE LITTLE KIDS TAKE OVER THE WORLD. THE END.
I WANT TO READ A BOOK LIKE THAT RIGHT NOW!
I'M ON IT.
Peirce

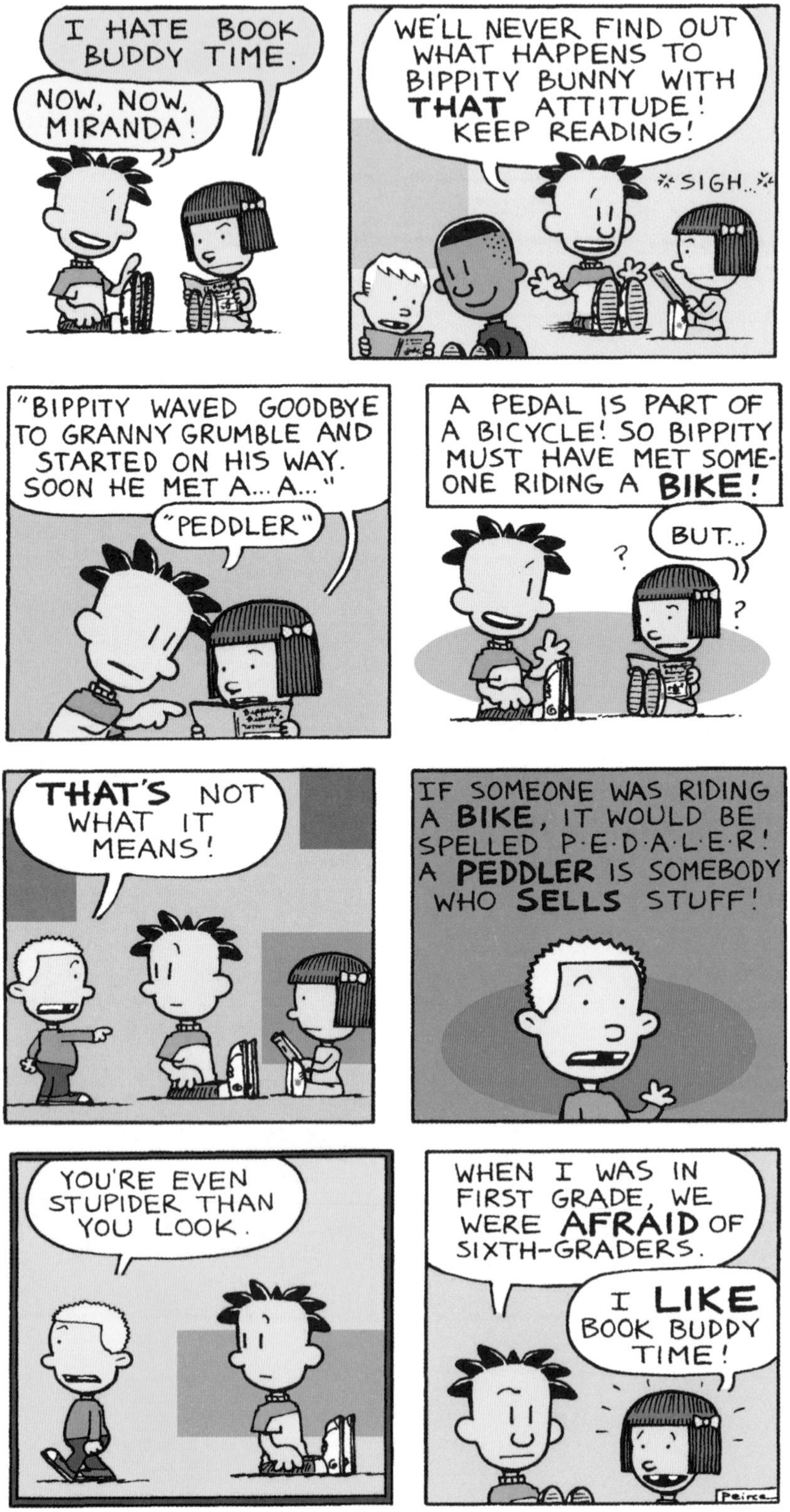
I HATE BOOK BUDDY TIME.
NOW, NOW, MIRANDA!
WE'LL NEVER FIND OUT WHAT HAPPENS TO BIPPITY BUNNY WITH THAT ATTITUDE! KEEP READING!
SIGH..
"BIPPITY WAVED GOODBYE TO GRANNY GRUMBLE AND STARTED ON HIS WAY. SOON HE MET A... A..."
"PEDDLER"
A PEDAL IS PART OF A BICYCLE! SO BIPPITY MUST HAVE MET SOMEONE RIDING A BIKE!
BUT..
THAT'S NOT WHAT IT MEANS!
IF SOMEONE WAS RIDING A BIKE, IT WOULD BE SPELLED P·E·D·A·L·E·R! A PEDDLER IS SOMEBODY WHO SELLS STUFF!
YOU'RE EVEN STUPIDER THAN YOU LOOK.
WHEN I WAS IN FIRST GRADE, WE WERE AFRAID OF SIXTH-GRADERS.
I LIKE BOOK BUDDY TIME!
Peirce

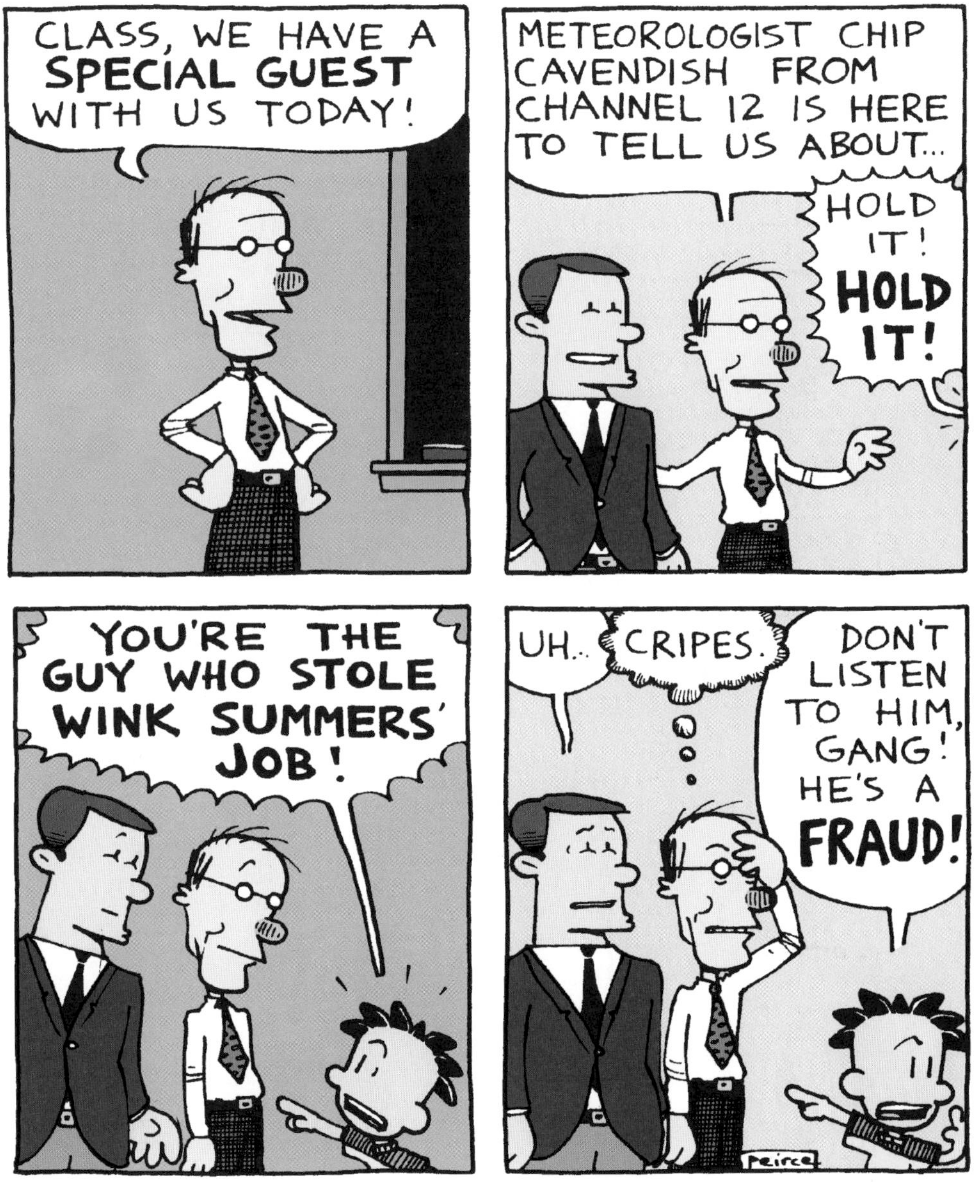
CLASS, WE HAVE A **SPECIAL GUEST** WITH US TODAY!
METEOROLOGIST CHIP CAVENDISH FROM CHANNEL 12 IS HERE TO TELL US ABOUT...
HOLD IT! **HOLD IT!**
YOU'RE THE GUY WHO STOLE WINK SUMMERS' JOB!
UH...
CRIPES.
DON'T LISTEN TO HIM, GANG! HE'S A **FRAUD!**
PEIRCE

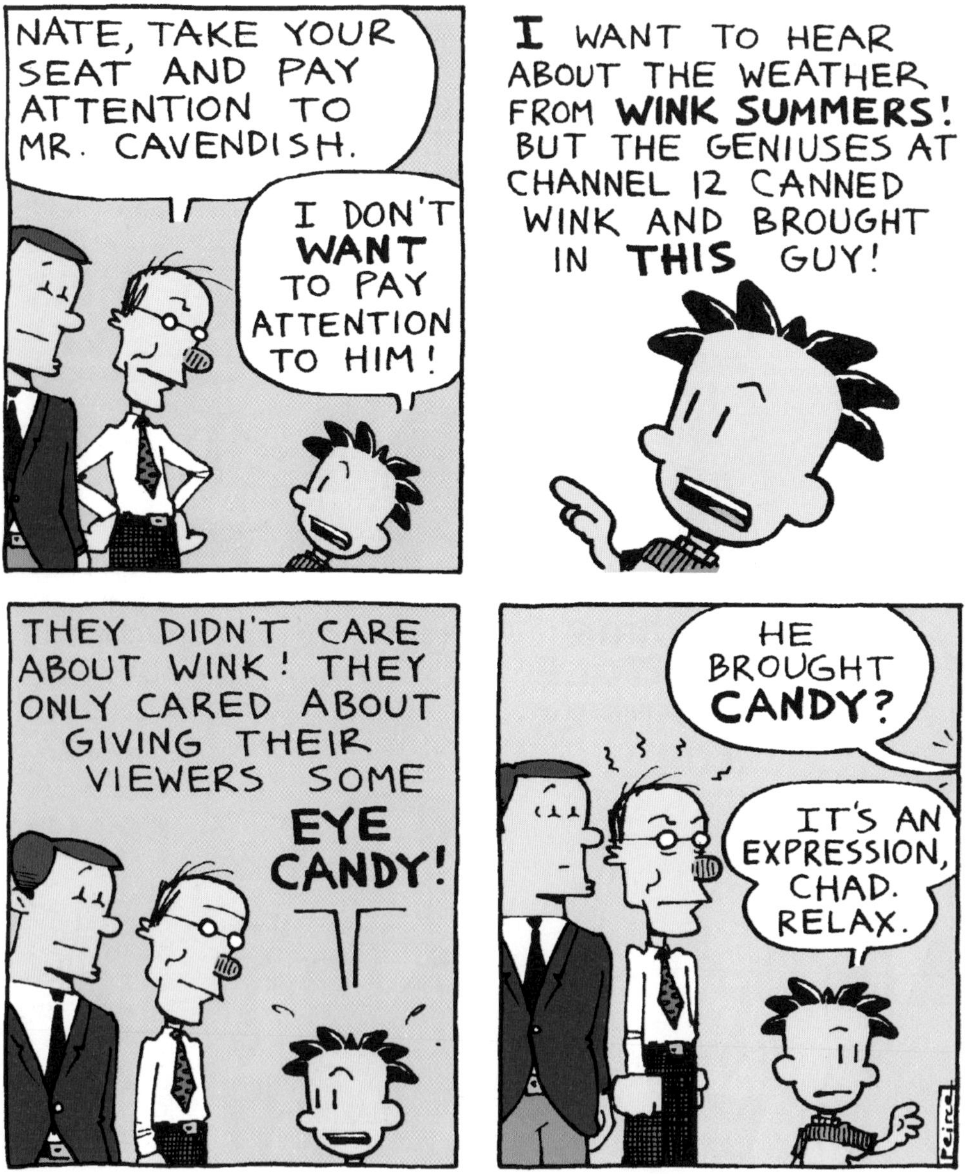
NATE, TAKE YOUR SEAT AND PAY ATTENTION TO MR. CAVENDISH.
I DON'T WANT TO PAY ATTENTION TO HIM!
I WANT TO HEAR ABOUT THE WEATHER FROM WINK SUMMERS! BUT THE GENIUSES AT CHANNEL 12 CANNED WINK AND BROUGHT IN THIS GUY!
THEY DIDN'T CARE ABOUT WINK! THEY ONLY CARED ABOUT GIVING THEIR VIEWERS SOME EYE CANDY!
HE BROUGHT CANDY?
IT'S AN EXPRESSION, CHAD. RELAX.

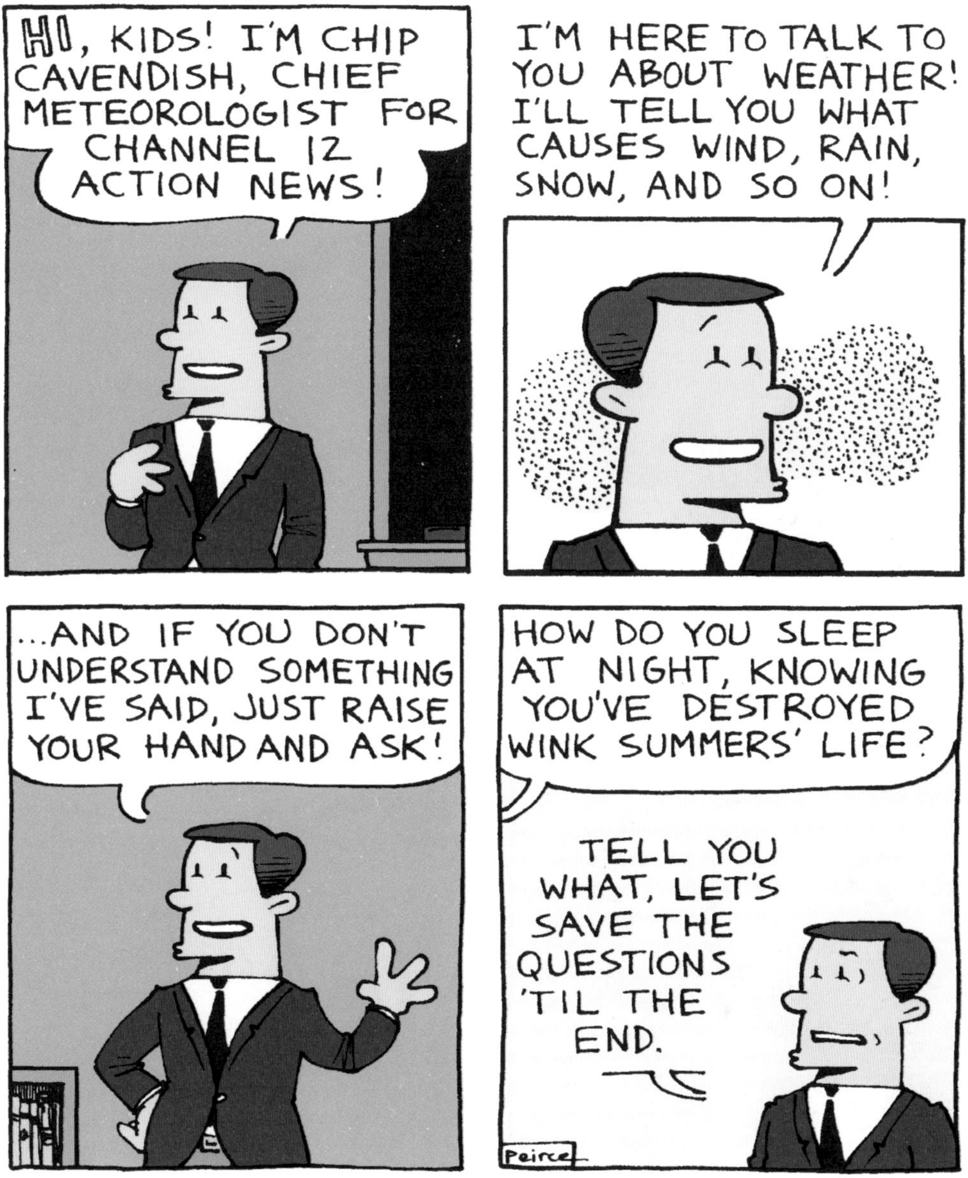
HI, KIDS! I'M CHIP CAVENDISH, CHIEF METEOROLOGIST FOR CHANNEL 12 ACTION NEWS!
I'M HERE TO TALK TO YOU ABOUT WEATHER! I'LL TELL YOU WHAT CAUSES WIND, RAIN, SNOW, AND SO ON!
...AND IF YOU DON'T UNDERSTAND SOMETHING I'VE SAID, JUST RAISE YOUR HAND AND ASK!
HOW DO YOU SLEEP AT NIGHT, KNOWING YOU'VE DESTROYED WINK SUMMERS' LIFE?
TELL YOU WHAT, LET'S SAVE THE QUESTIONS 'TIL THE END.
Peirce

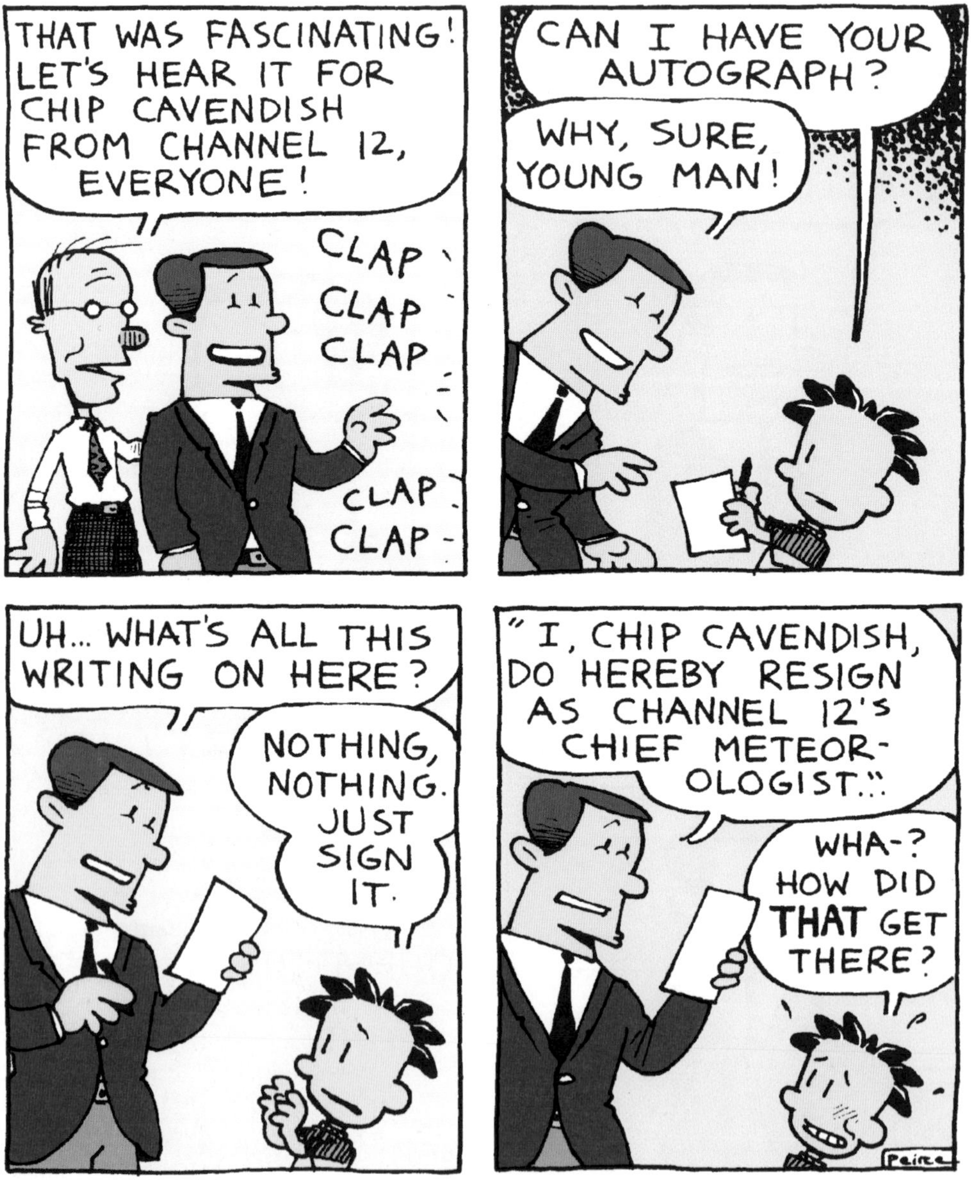
THAT WAS FASCINATING! LET'S HEAR IT FOR CHIP CAVENDISH FROM CHANNEL 12, EVERYONE!
CLAP CLAP CLAP
CLAP CLAP
CAN I HAVE YOUR AUTOGRAPH?
WHY, SURE, YOUNG MAN!
UH... WHAT'S ALL THIS WRITING ON HERE?
NOTHING, NOTHING. JUST SIGN IT.
"I, CHIP CAVENDISH, DO HEREBY RESIGN AS CHANNEL 12's CHIEF METEOR-OLOGIST..."
WHA-? HOW DID **THAT** GET THERE?
Peirce

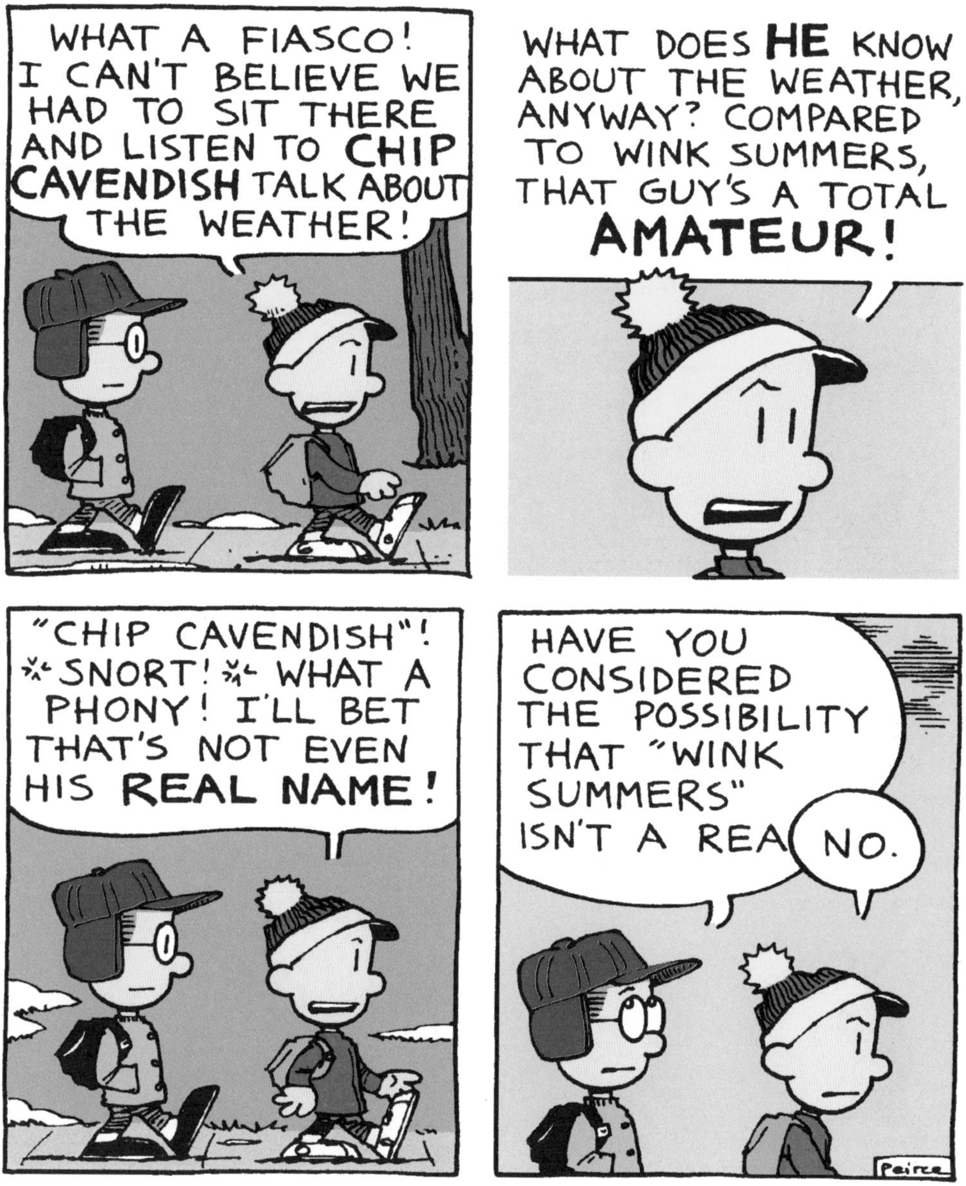
WHAT A FIASCO! I CAN'T BELIEVE WE HAD TO SIT THERE AND LISTEN TO CHIP CAVENDISH TALK ABOUT THE WEATHER!
WHAT DOES HE KNOW ABOUT THE WEATHER, ANYWAY? COMPARED TO WINK SUMMERS, THAT GUY'S A TOTAL AMATEUR!
"CHIP CAVENDISH"! *SNORT!* WHAT A PHONY! I'LL BET THAT'S NOT EVEN HIS REAL NAME!
HAVE YOU CONSIDERED THE POSSIBILITY THAT "WINK SUMMERS" ISN'T A REA
NO.
Peirce

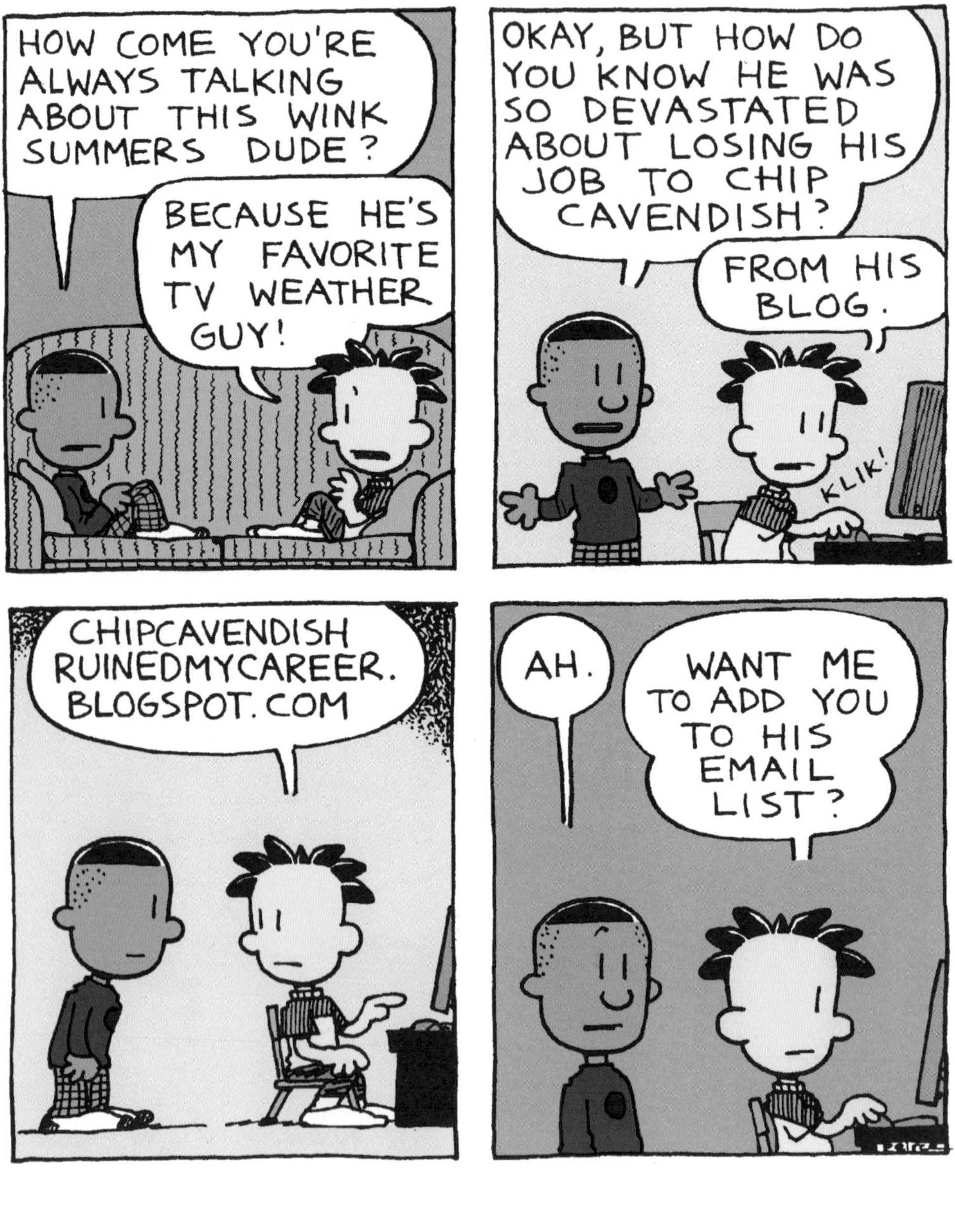
HOW COME YOU'RE ALWAYS TALKING ABOUT THIS WINK SUMMERS DUDE?
BECAUSE HE'S MY FAVORITE TV WEATHER GUY!
OKAY, BUT HOW DO YOU KNOW HE WAS SO DEVASTATED ABOUT LOSING HIS JOB TO CHIP CAVENDISH?
FROM HIS BLOG.
KLIK!
CHIPCAVENDISH RUINEDMYCAREER. BLOGSPOT.COM
AH.
WANT ME TO ADD YOU TO HIS EMAIL LIST?

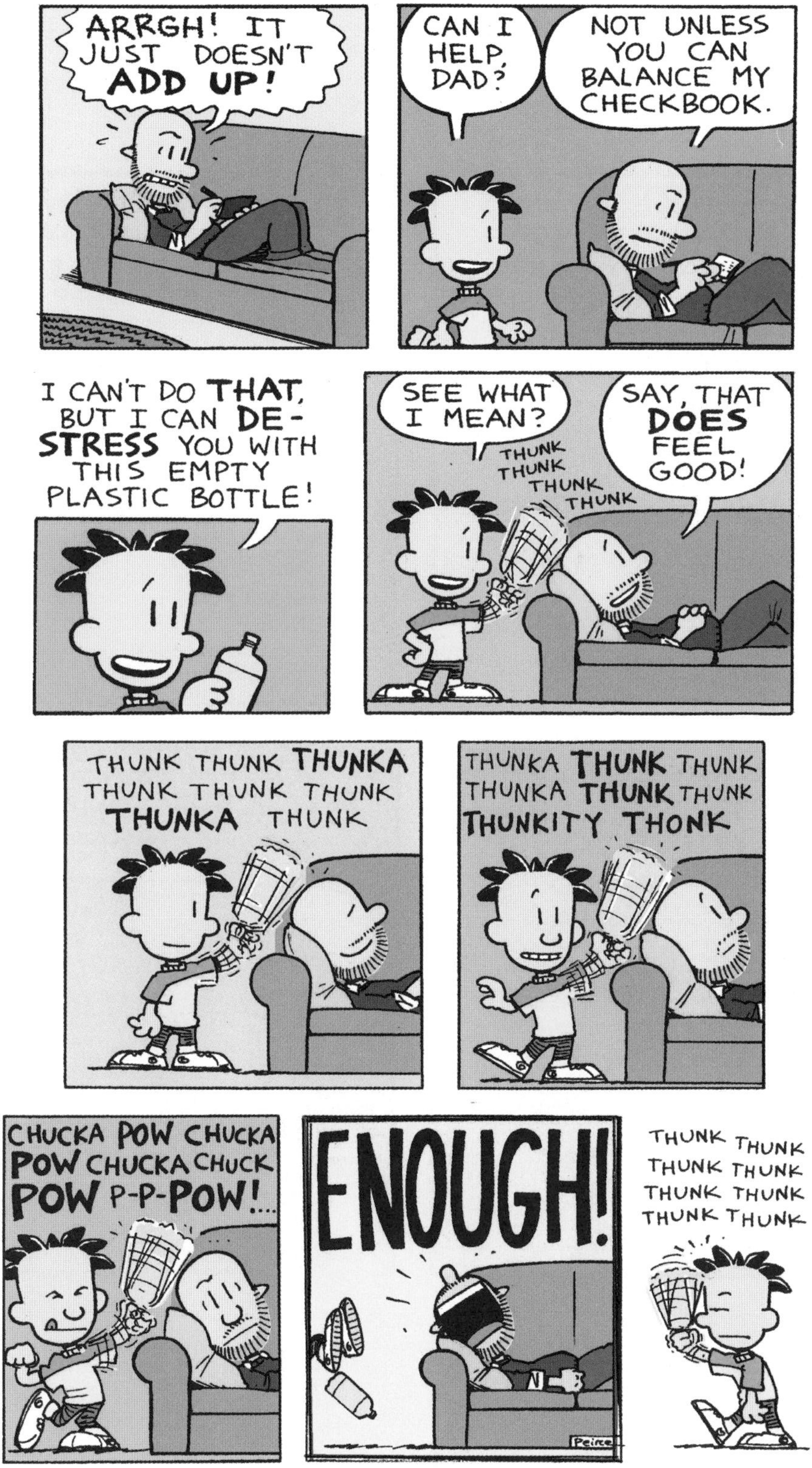
ARRGH! IT JUST DOESN'T ADD UP!
CAN I HELP, DAD?
NOT UNLESS YOU CAN BALANCE MY CHECKBOOK.
I CAN'T DO THAT, BUT I CAN DE-STRESS YOU WITH THIS EMPTY PLASTIC BOTTLE!
SEE WHAT I MEAN?
THUNK THUNK THUNK THUNK
SAY, THAT DOES FEEL GOOD!
THUNK THUNK THUNKA THUNK THUNK THUNK THUNKA THUNK
THUNKA THUNK THUNK THUNKA THUNK THUNK THUNKITY THONK
CHUCKA POW CHUCKA POW CHUCKA CHUCK POW P-P-POW!...
ENOUGH!
Peirce
THUNK THUNK THUNK THUNK THUNK THUNK THUNK THUNK

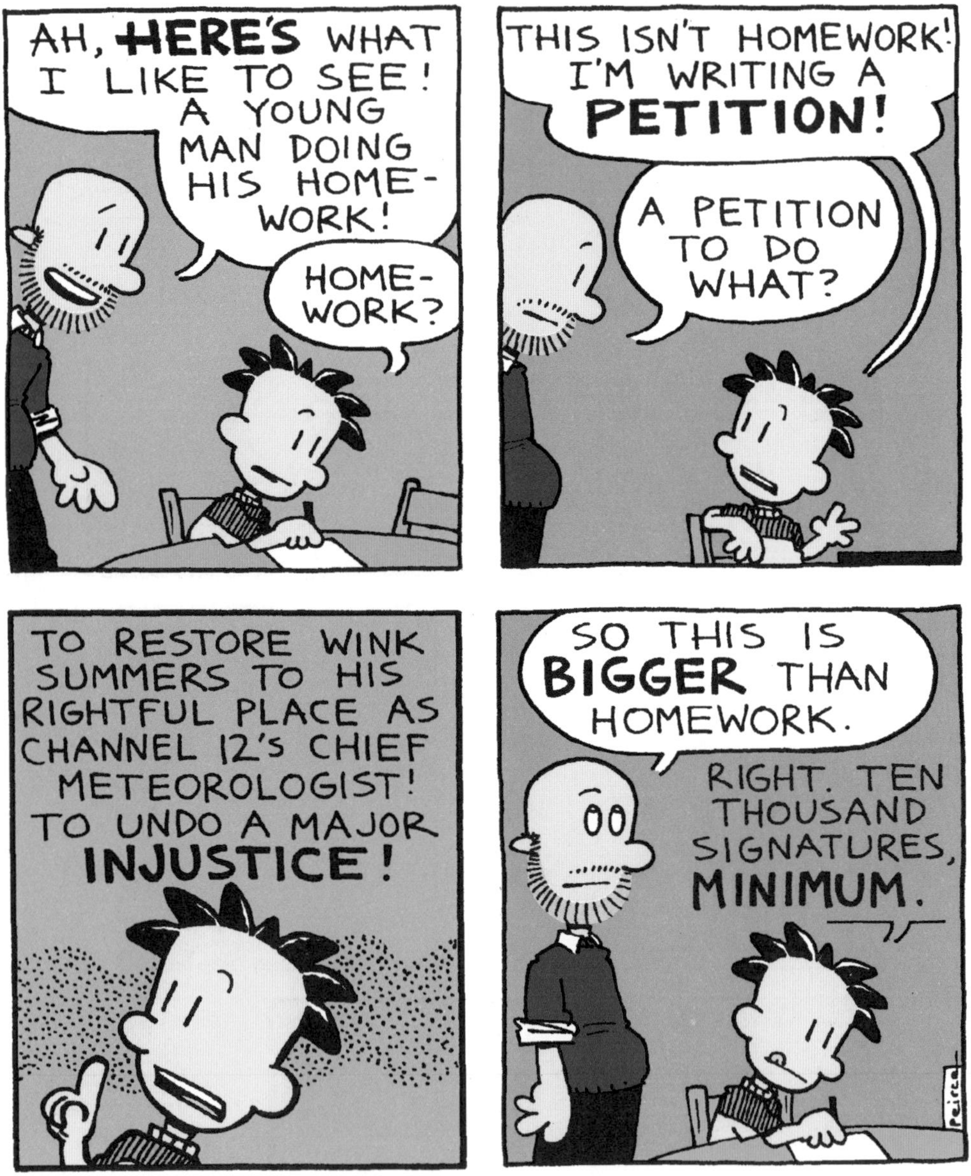
AH, **HERE'S** WHAT I LIKE TO SEE! A YOUNG MAN DOING HIS HOMEWORK!
HOMEWORK?
THIS ISN'T HOMEWORK! I'M WRITING A **PETITION**!
A PETITION TO DO WHAT?
TO RESTORE WINK SUMMERS TO HIS RIGHTFUL PLACE AS CHANNEL 12'S CHIEF METEOROLOGIST! TO UNDO A MAJOR **INJUSTICE**!
SO THIS IS **BIGGER** THAN HOMEWORK.
RIGHT. TEN THOUSAND SIGNATURES, **MINIMUM**.
Peirce

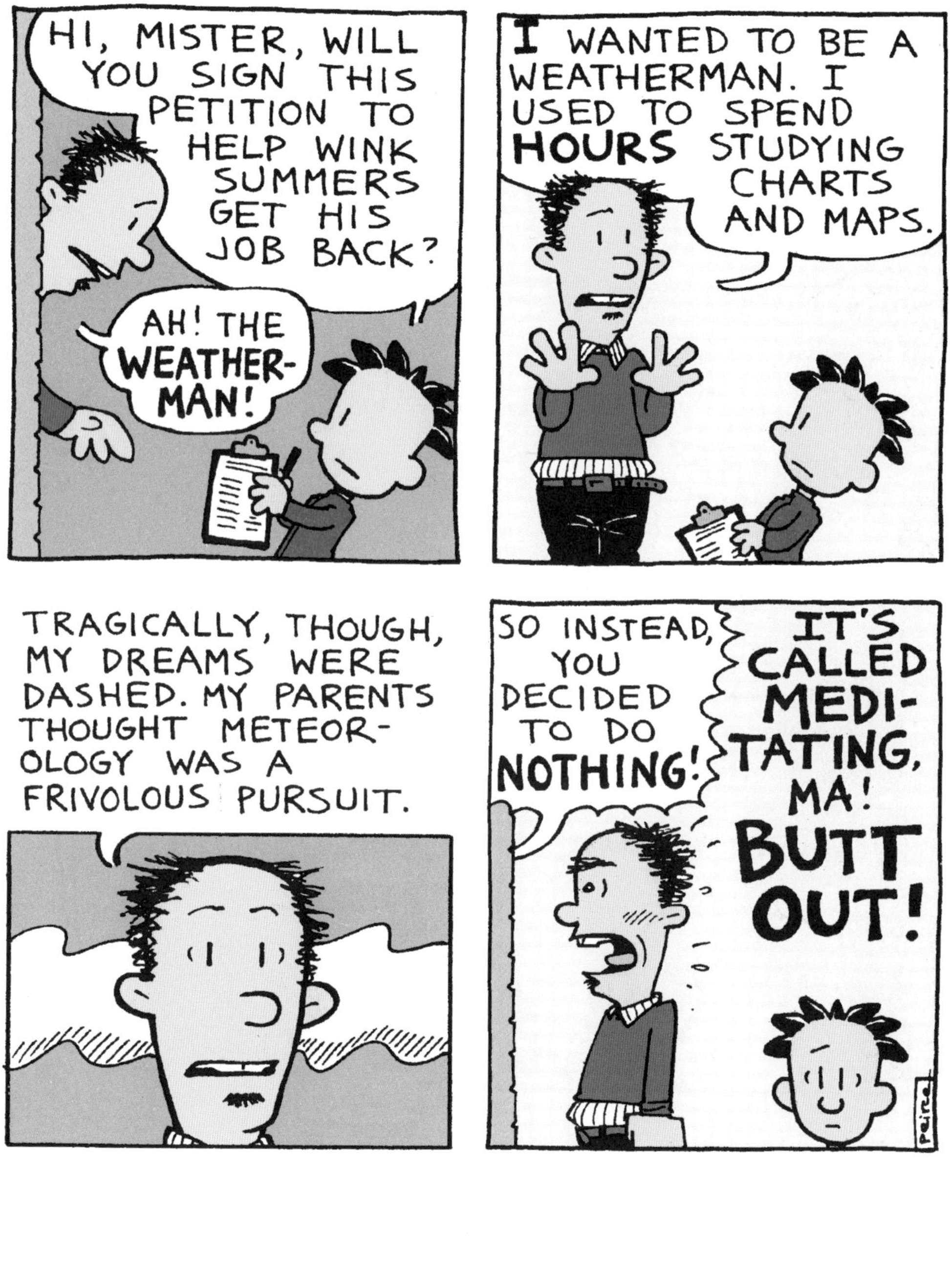

HI, MISTER, WILL YOU SIGN THIS PETITION TO HELP WINK SUMMERS GET HIS JOB BACK?
AH! THE **WEATHER-MAN!**
I WANTED TO BE A WEATHERMAN. I USED TO SPEND **HOURS** STUDYING CHARTS AND MAPS.
TRAGICALLY, THOUGH, MY DREAMS WERE DASHED. MY PARENTS THOUGHT METEOR-OLOGY WAS A FRIVOLOUS PURSUIT.
SO INSTEAD, YOU DECIDED TO DO **NOTHING!**
IT'S CALLED MEDI-TATING, MA! BUTT OUT!
peirce

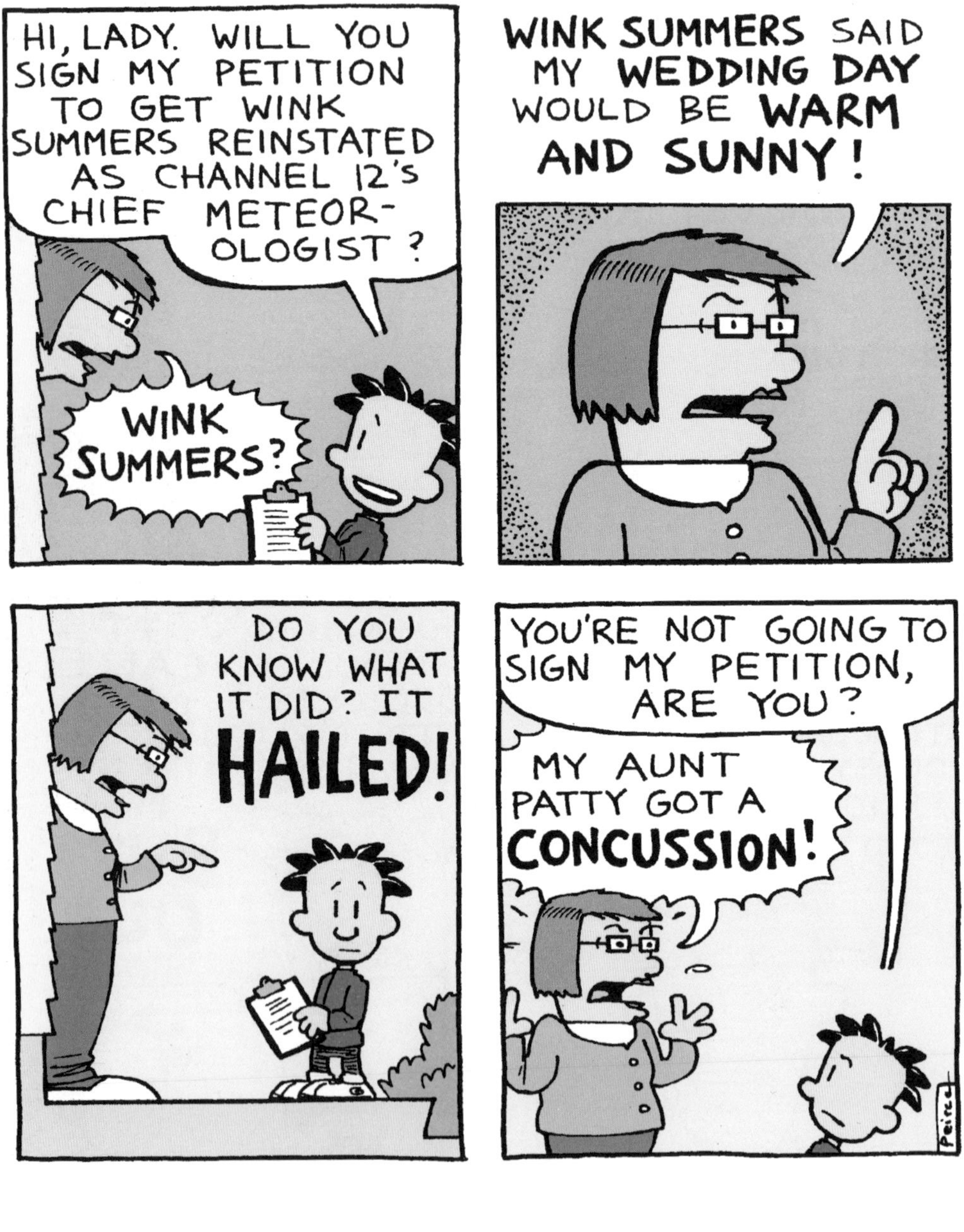
HI, LADY. WILL YOU SIGN MY PETITION TO GET WINK SUMMERS REINSTATED AS CHANNEL 12'S CHIEF METEOROLOGIST ?
WINK SUMMERS?
WINK SUMMERS SAID MY WEDDING DAY WOULD BE WARM AND SUNNY!
DO YOU KNOW WHAT IT DID? IT HAILED!
YOU'RE NOT GOING TO SIGN MY PETITION, ARE YOU?
MY AUNT PATTY GOT A CONCUSSION!
Peirce

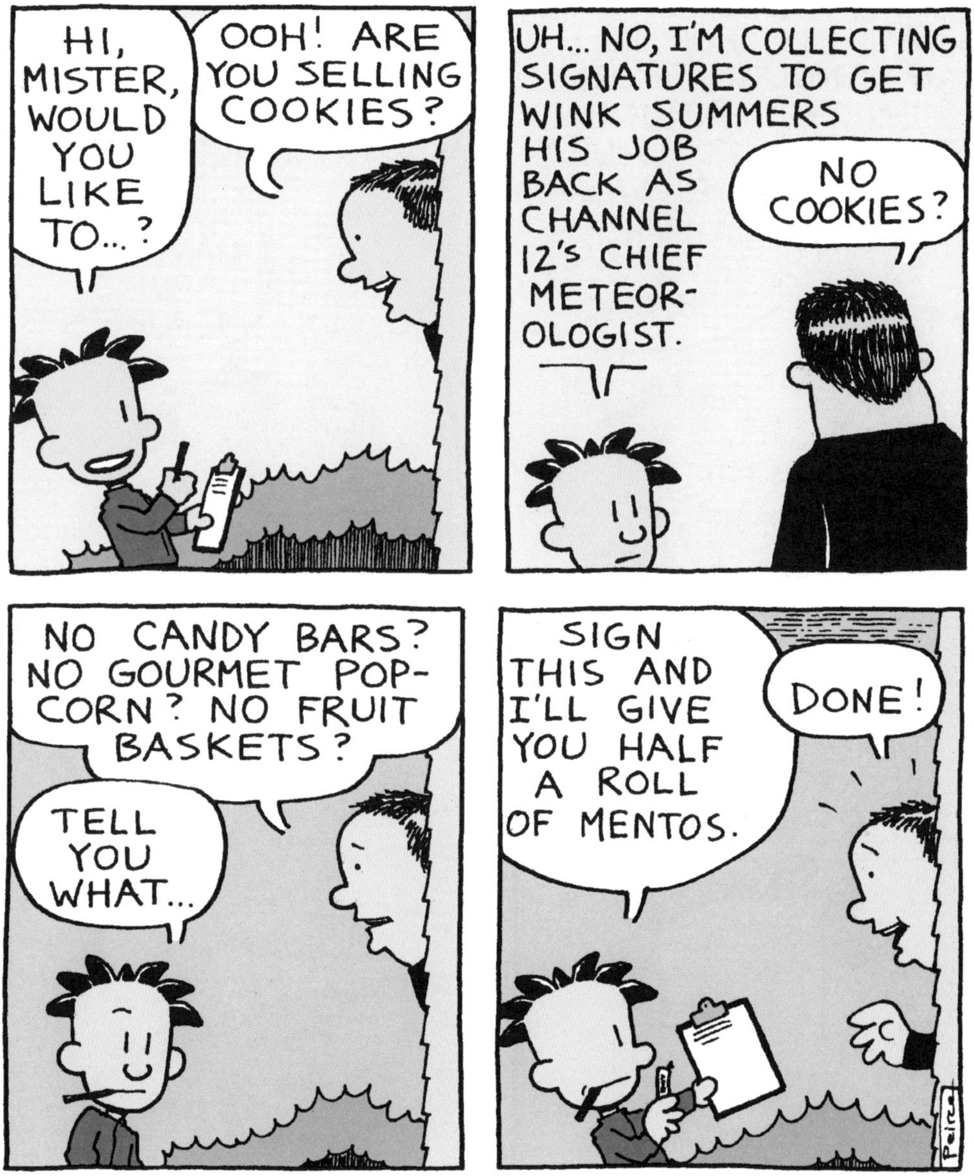
HI, MISTER, WOULD YOU LIKE TO...?
OOH! ARE YOU SELLING COOKIES?
UH... NO, I'M COLLECTING SIGNATURES TO GET WINK SUMMERS HIS JOB BACK AS CHANNEL 12'S CHIEF METEOR-OLOGIST.
NO COOKIES?
NO CANDY BARS? NO GOURMET POP-CORN? NO FRUIT BASKETS?
TELL YOU WHAT...
SIGN THIS AND I'LL GIVE YOU HALF A ROLL OF MENTOS.
DONE!
Peirce

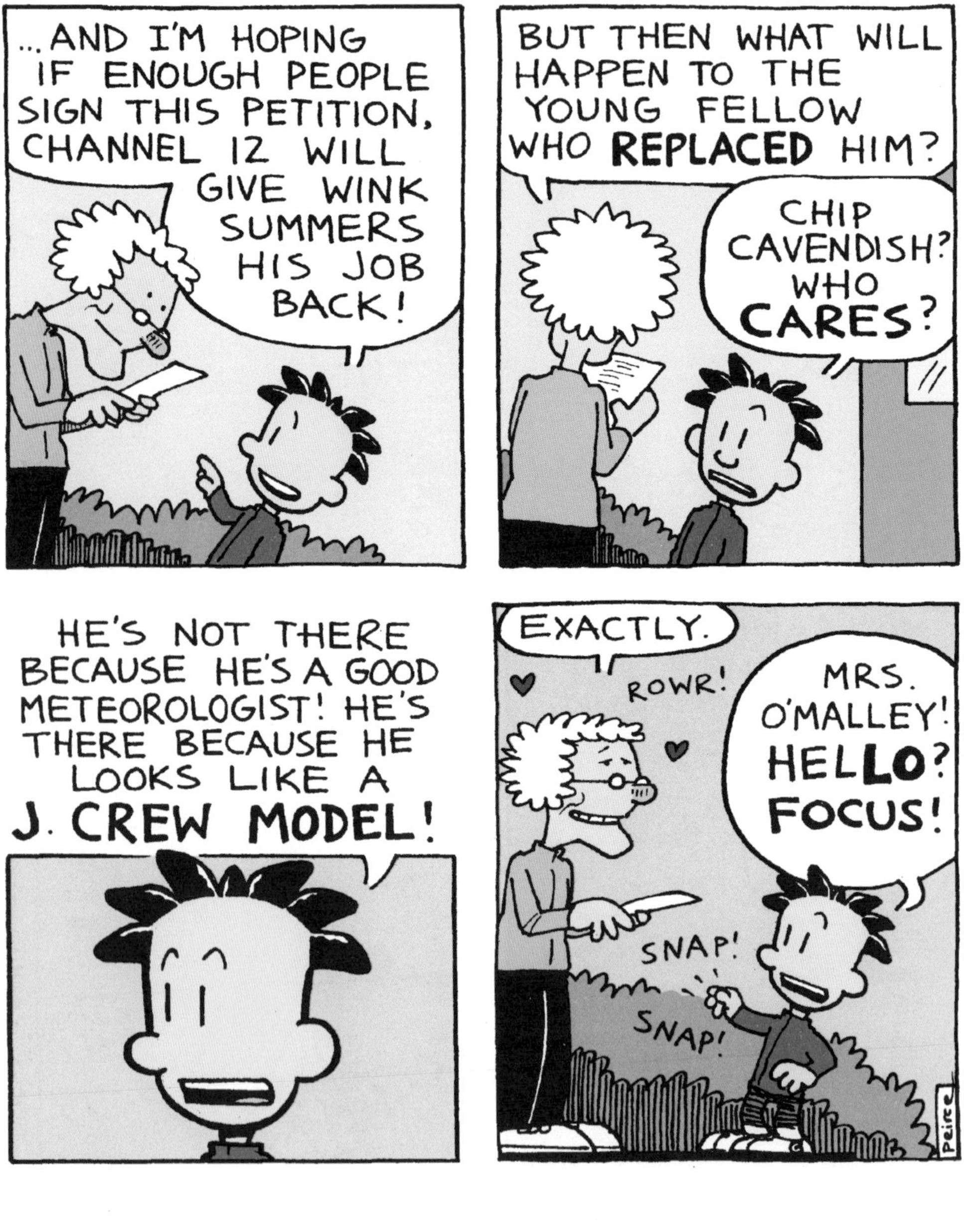
...AND I'M HOPING IF ENOUGH PEOPLE SIGN THIS PETITION, CHANNEL 12 WILL GIVE WINK SUMMERS HIS JOB BACK!
BUT THEN WHAT WILL HAPPEN TO THE YOUNG FELLOW WHO REPLACED HIM?
CHIP CAVENDISH? WHO CARES?
HE'S NOT THERE BECAUSE HE'S A GOOD METEOROLOGIST! HE'S THERE BECAUSE HE LOOKS LIKE A J. CREW MODEL!
EXACTLY.
ROWR!
MRS. O'MALLEY! HELLO? FOCUS!
SNAP!
SNAP!
Peirce

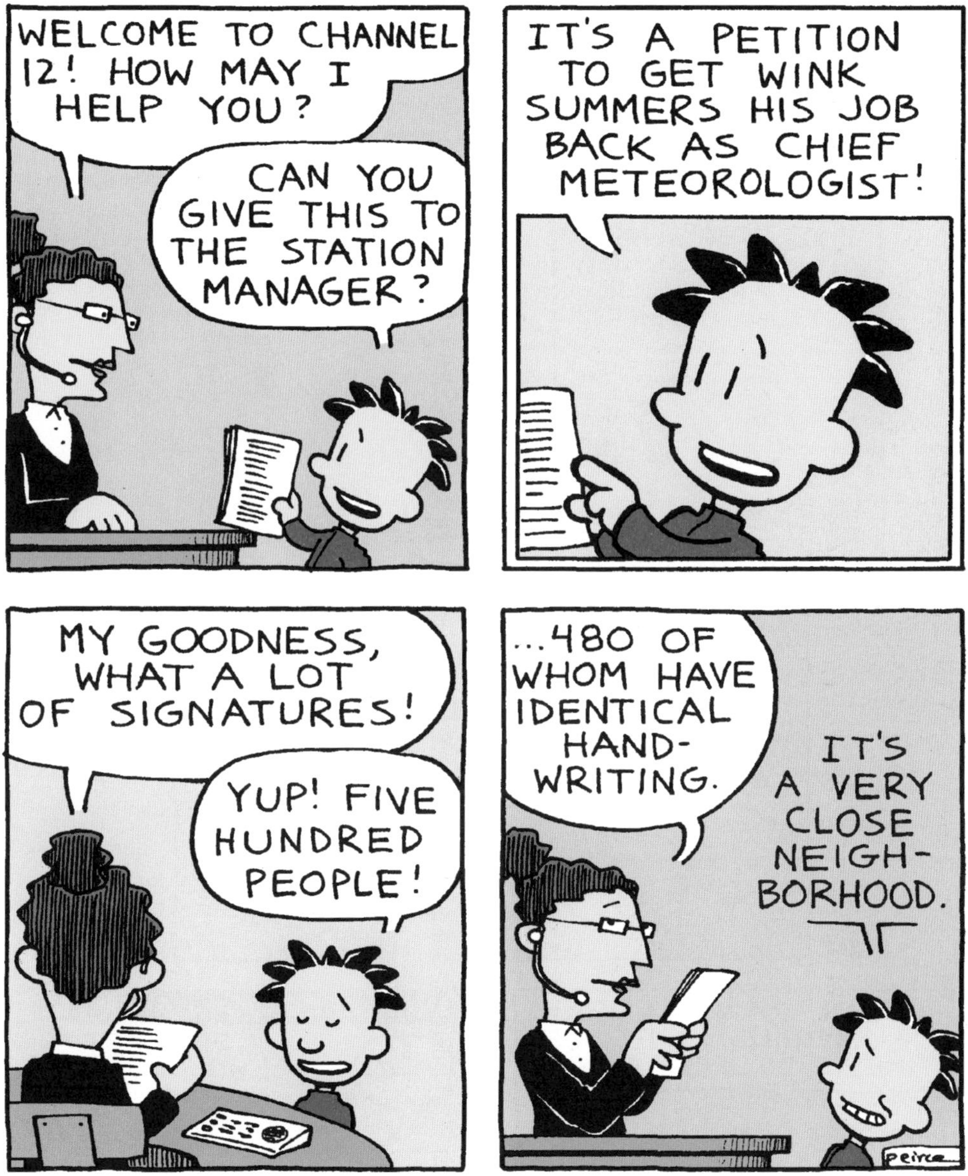
WELCOME TO CHANNEL 12! HOW MAY I HELP YOU?
CAN YOU GIVE THIS TO THE STATION MANAGER?
IT'S A PETITION TO GET WINK SUMMERS HIS JOB BACK AS CHIEF METEOROLOGIST!
MY GOODNESS, WHAT A LOT OF SIGNATURES!
YUP! FIVE HUNDRED PEOPLE!
...480 OF WHOM HAVE IDENTICAL HAND-WRITING.
IT'S A VERY CLOSE NEIGH-BORHOOD.
peirce

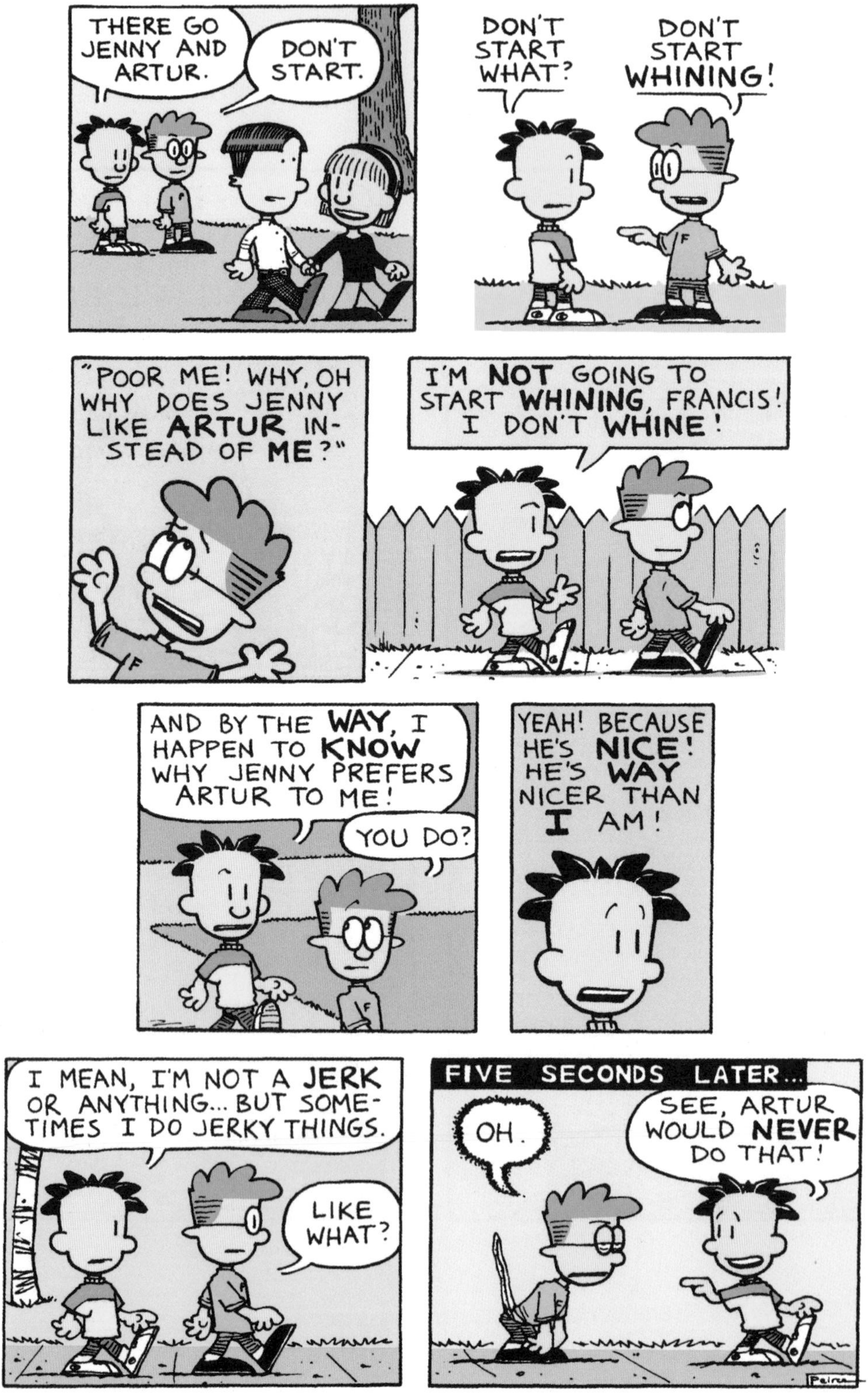
THERE GO JENNY AND ARTUR.
DON'T START.
DON'T START WHAT?
DON'T START WHINING!
"POOR ME! WHY, OH WHY DOES JENNY LIKE ARTUR INSTEAD OF ME?"
I'M NOT GOING TO START WHINING, FRANCIS! I DON'T WHINE!
AND BY THE WAY, I HAPPEN TO KNOW WHY JENNY PREFERS ARTUR TO ME!
YOU DO?
YEAH! BECAUSE HE'S NICE! HE'S WAY NICER THAN I AM!
I MEAN, I'M NOT A JERK OR ANYTHING... BUT SOMETIMES I DO JERKY THINGS.
LIKE WHAT?
FIVE SECONDS LATER...
OH.
SEE, ARTUR WOULD NEVER DO THAT!

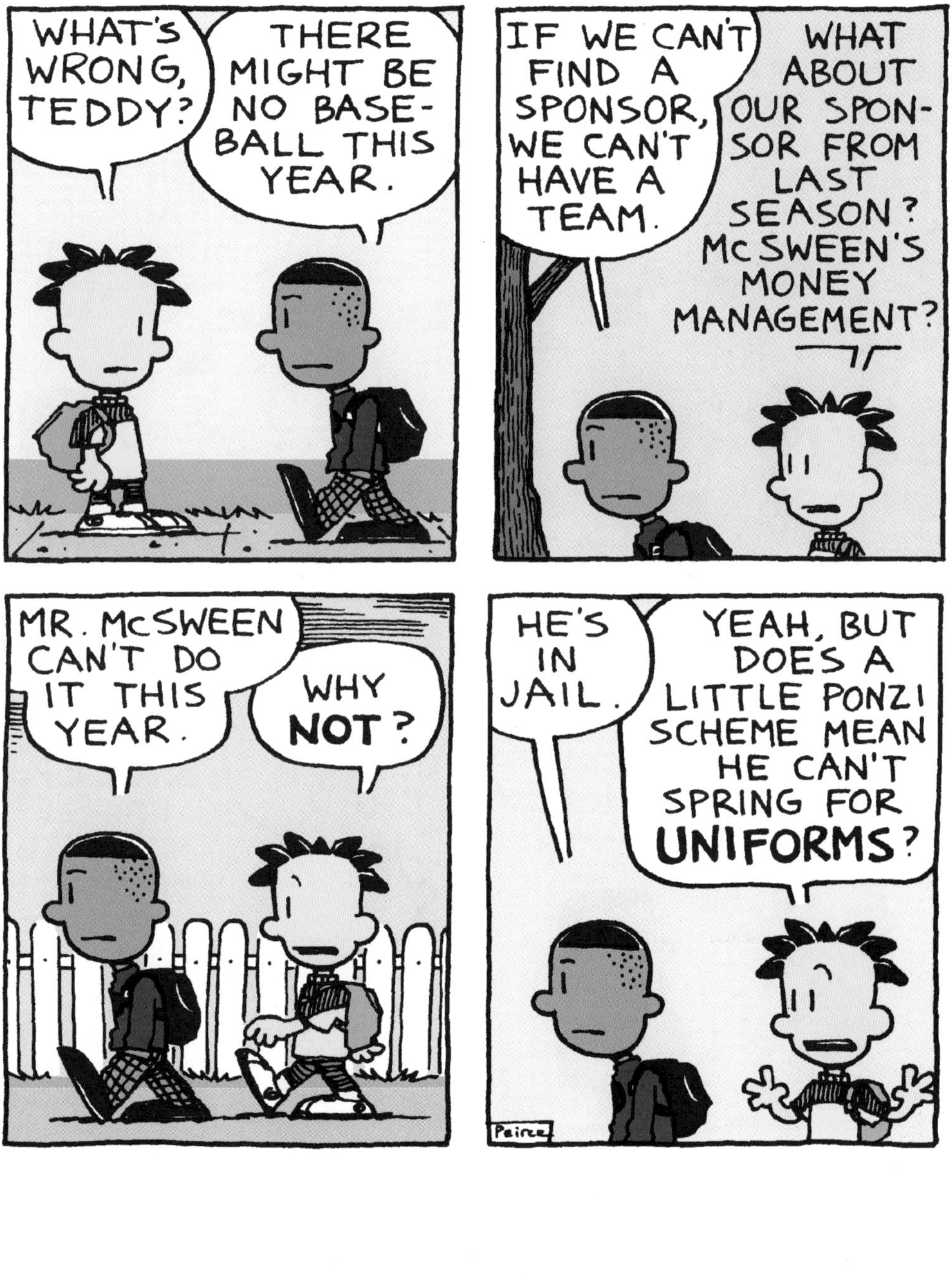
WHAT'S WRONG, TEDDY?
THERE MIGHT BE NO BASE-BALL THIS YEAR.
IF WE CAN'T FIND A SPONSOR, WE CAN'T HAVE A TEAM.
WHAT ABOUT OUR SPON-SOR FROM LAST SEASON? McSWEEN'S MONEY MANAGEMENT?
MR. McSWEEN CAN'T DO IT THIS YEAR.
WHY **NOT**?
HE'S IN JAIL.
YEAH, BUT DOES A LITTLE PONZI SCHEME MEAN HE CAN'T SPRING FOR **UNIFORMS**?
Peirce

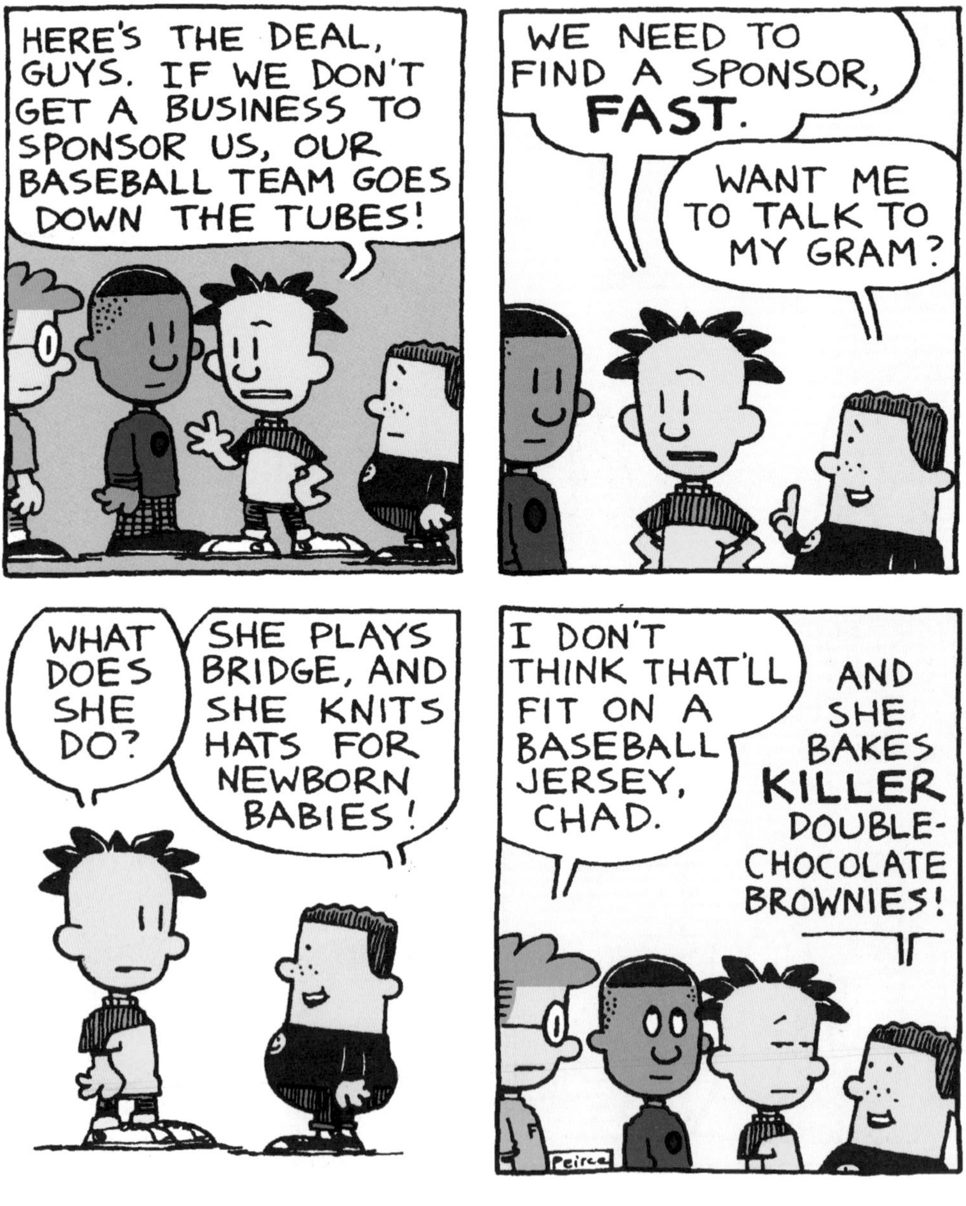
HERE'S THE DEAL, GUYS. IF WE DON'T GET A BUSINESS TO SPONSOR US, OUR BASEBALL TEAM GOES DOWN THE TUBES!
WE NEED TO FIND A SPONSOR, FAST.
WANT ME TO TALK TO MY GRAM?
WHAT DOES SHE DO?
SHE PLAYS BRIDGE, AND SHE KNITS HATS FOR NEWBORN BABIES!
I DON'T THINK THAT'LL FIT ON A BASEBALL JERSEY, CHAD.
AND SHE BAKES KILLER DOUBLE-CHOCOLATE BROWNIES!
Peirce

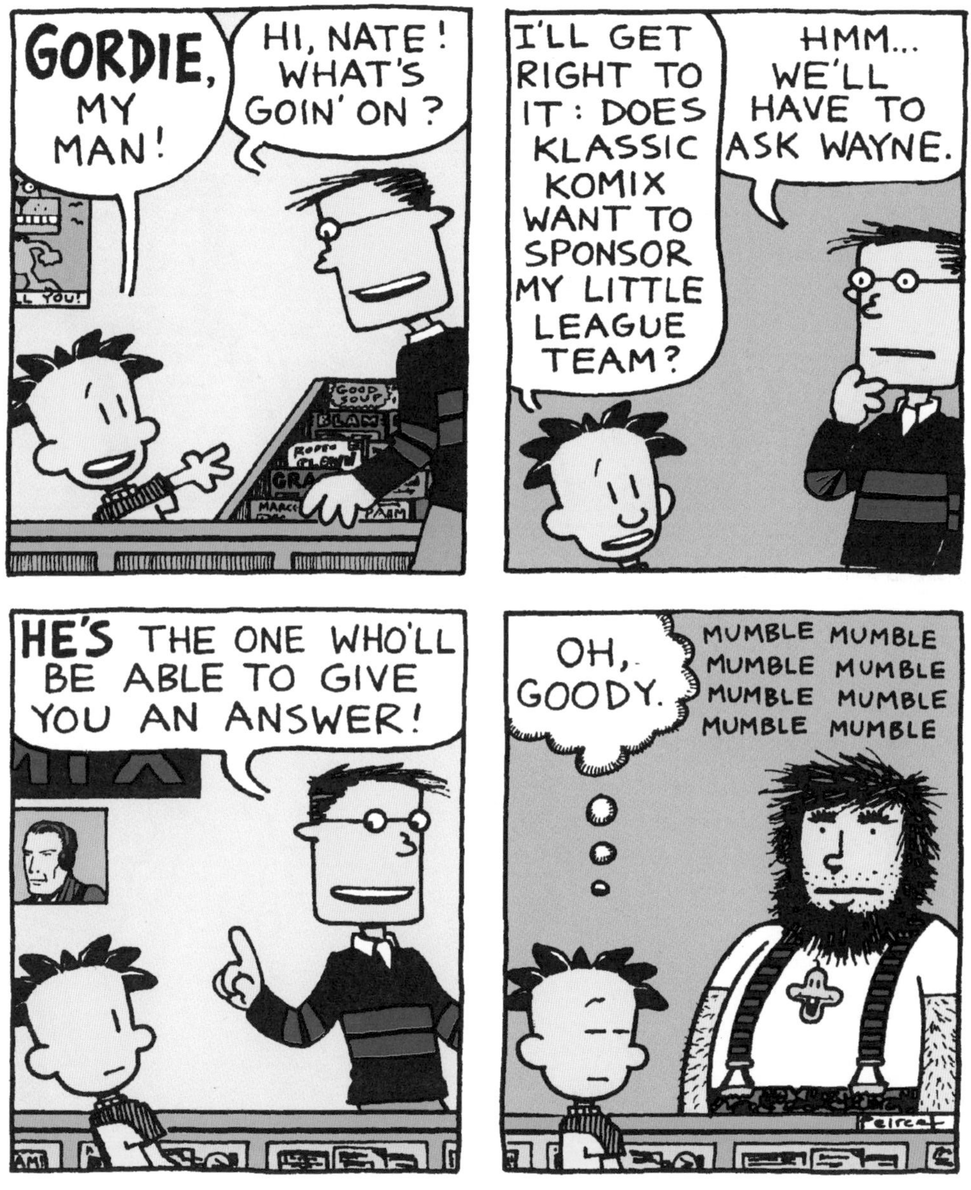
GORDIE, MY MAN!
HI, NATE! WHAT'S GOIN' ON?
I'LL GET RIGHT TO IT: DOES KLASSIC KOMIX WANT TO SPONSOR MY LITTLE LEAGUE TEAM?
HMM... WE'LL HAVE TO ASK WAYNE.
HE'S THE ONE WHO'LL BE ABLE TO GIVE YOU AN ANSWER!
OH, GOODY.
MUMBLE MUMBLE MUMBLE MUMBLE MUMBLE MUMBLE MUMBLE MUMBLE

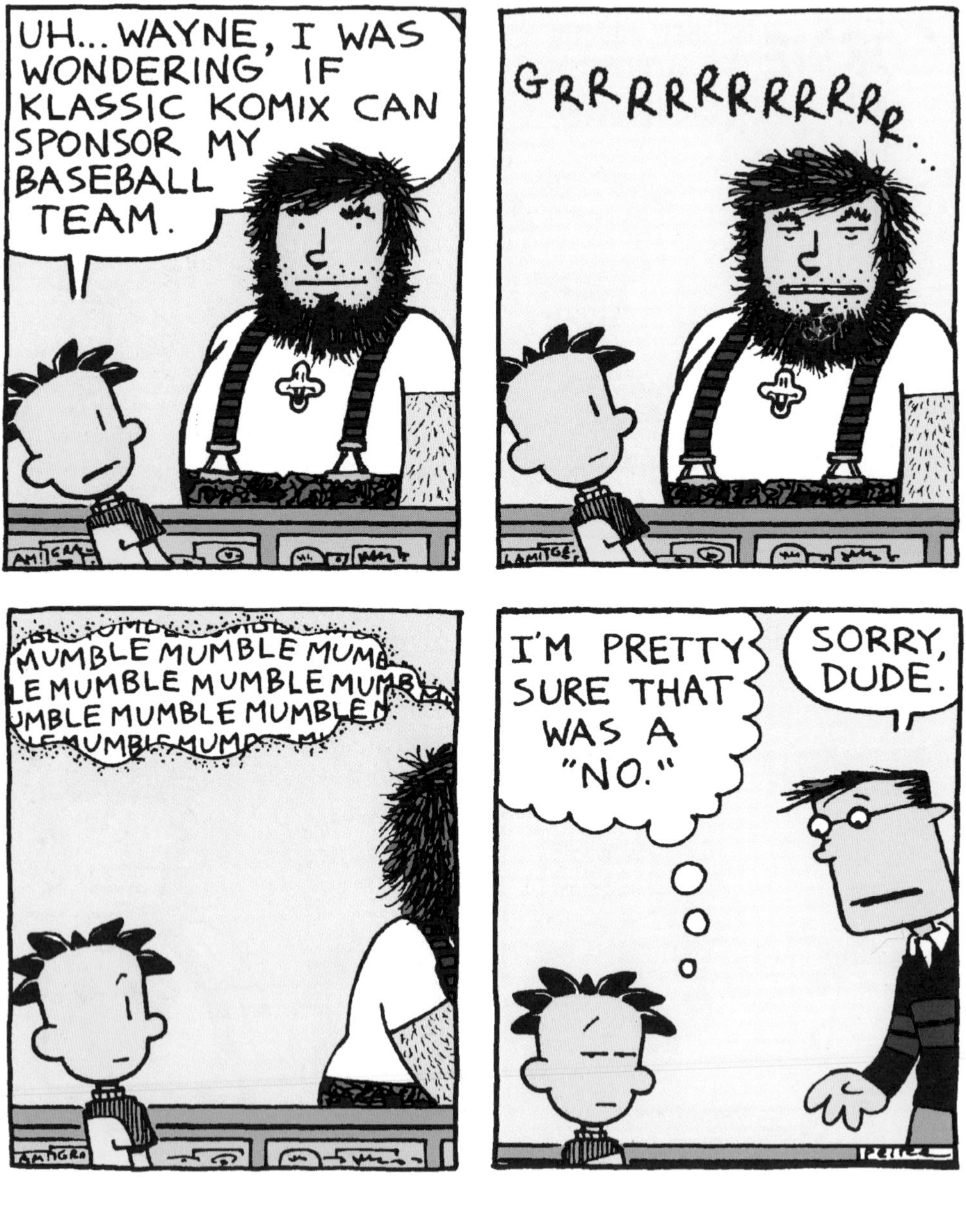
UH... WAYNE, I WAS WONDERING IF KLASSIC KOMIX CAN SPONSOR MY BASEBALL TEAM.
GRRRRRRRRRRR...
MUMBLE MUMBLE MUMB
LE MUMBLE MUMBLE MUMB
UMBLE MUMBLE MUMBLE
I'M PRETTY SURE THAT WAS A "NO."
SORRY, DUDE.

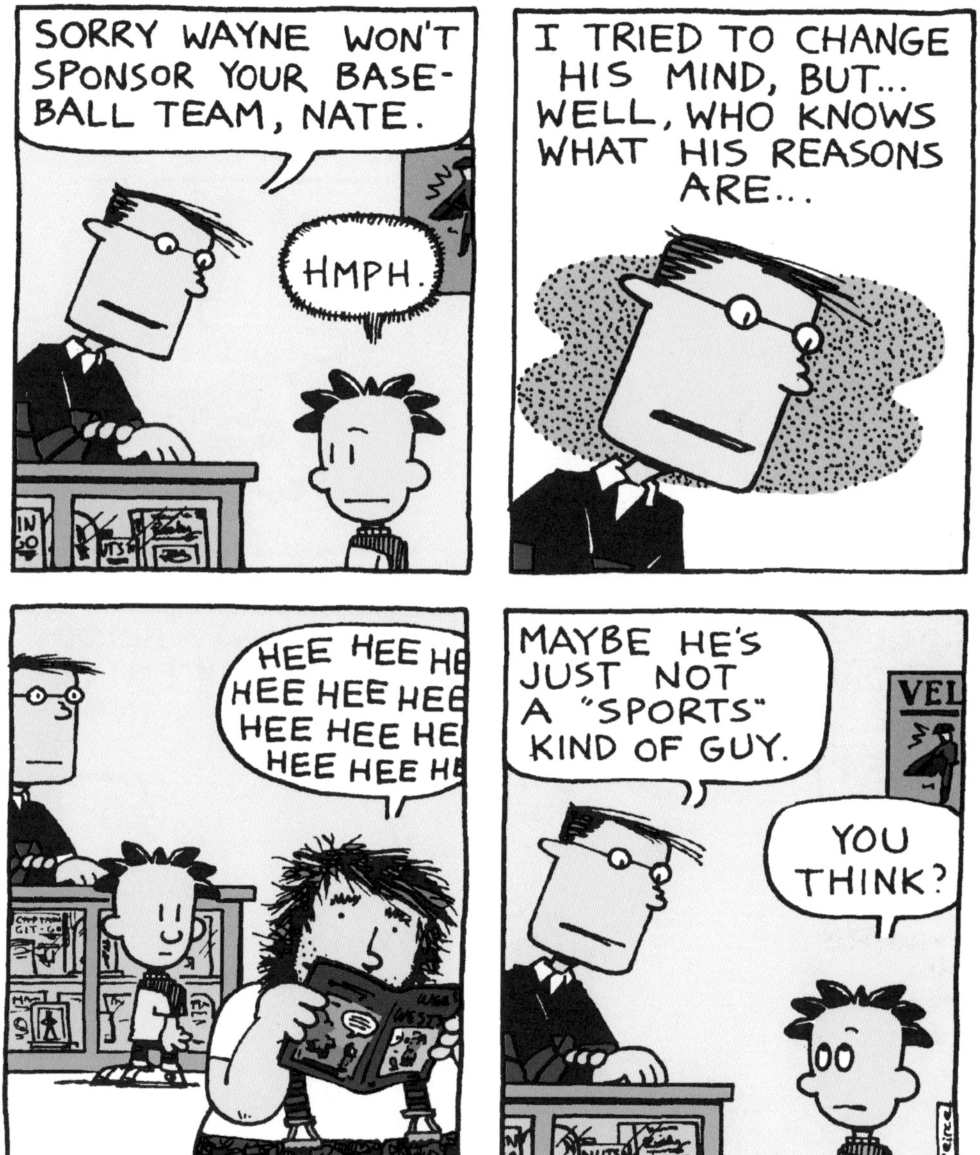
SORRY WAYNE WON'T SPONSOR YOUR BASE-BALL TEAM, NATE.
HMPH.
I TRIED TO CHANGE HIS MIND, BUT... WELL, WHO KNOWS WHAT HIS REASONS ARE...
HEE HEE HE HEE HEE HEE HEE HEE HE HEE HEE H
MAYBE HE'S JUST NOT A "SPORTS" KIND OF GUY.
YOU THINK?

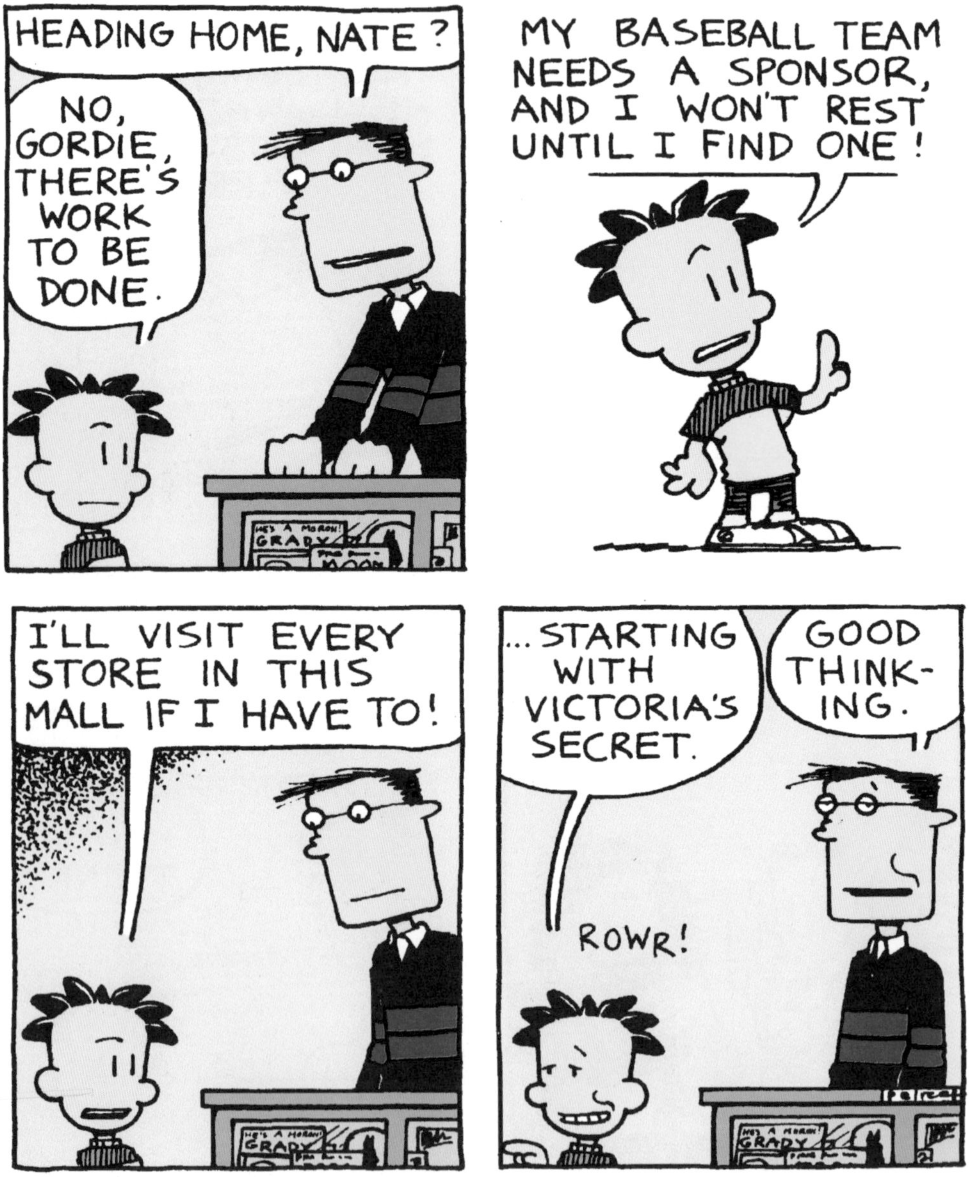
HEADING HOME, NATE?
NO, GORDIE, THERE'S WORK TO BE DONE.
MY BASEBALL TEAM NEEDS A SPONSOR, AND I WON'T REST UNTIL I FIND ONE!
I'LL VISIT EVERY STORE IN THIS MALL IF I HAVE TO!
...STARTING WITH VICTORIA'S SECRET.
GOOD THINKING.
ROWR!

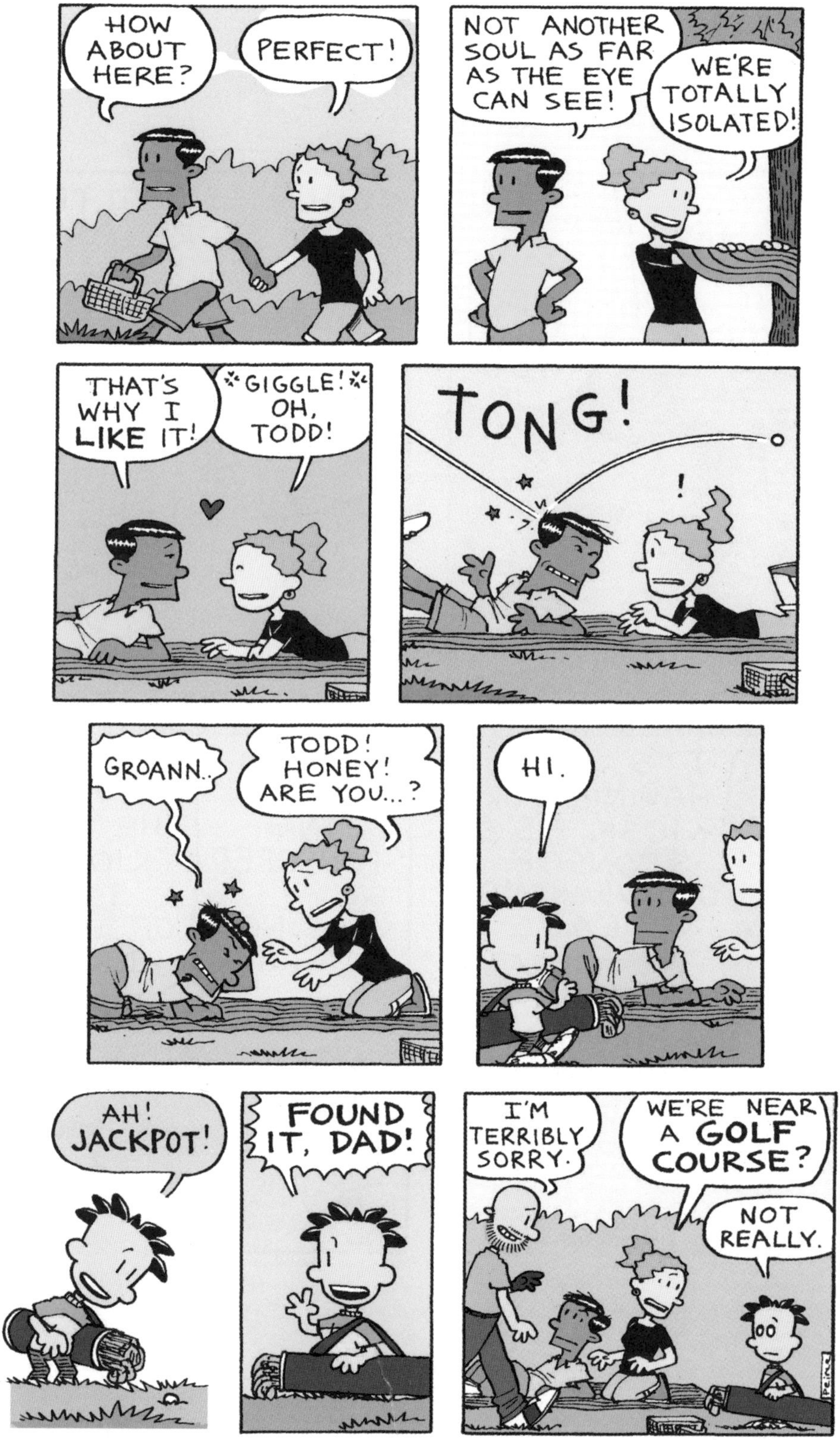
HOW ABOUT HERE?
PERFECT!
NOT ANOTHER SOUL AS FAR AS THE EYE CAN SEE!
WE'RE TOTALLY ISOLATED!
THAT'S WHY I **LIKE** IT!
GIGGLE! OH, TODD!
TONG!
!
GROANN..
TODD! HONEY! ARE YOU...?
HI.
AH! JACKPOT!
FOUND IT, DAD!
I'M TERRIBLY SORRY.
WE'RE NEAR A **GOLF COURSE**?
NOT REALLY.
PEIRCE

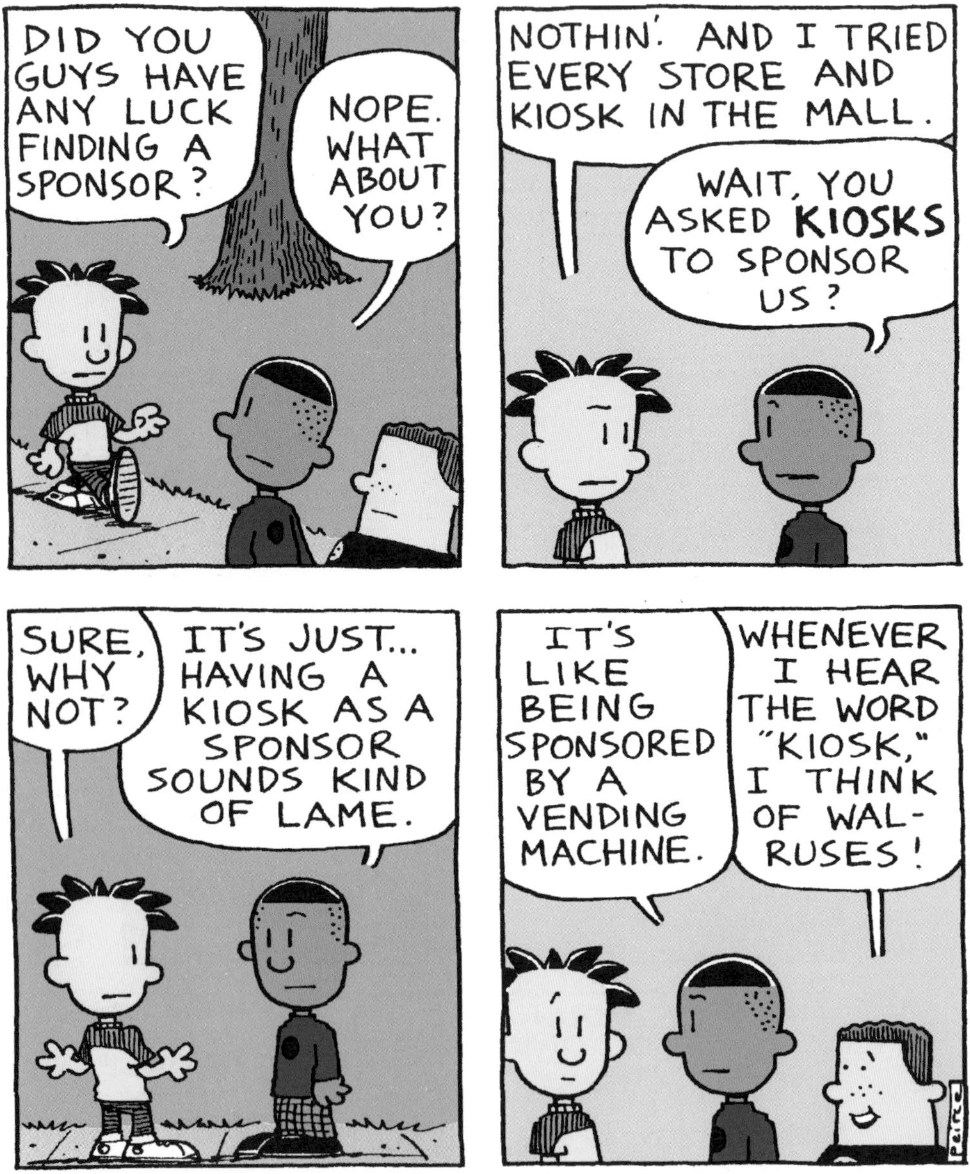
DID YOU GUYS HAVE ANY LUCK FINDING A SPONSOR?
NOPE. WHAT ABOUT YOU?
NOTHIN'. AND I TRIED EVERY STORE AND KIOSK IN THE MALL.
WAIT, YOU ASKED **KIOSKS** TO SPONSOR US?
SURE, WHY NOT?
IT'S JUST... HAVING A KIOSK AS A SPONSOR SOUNDS KIND OF LAME.
IT'S LIKE BEING SPONSORED BY A VENDING MACHINE.
WHENEVER I HEAR THE WORD "KIOSK," I THINK OF WALRUSES!
PEIRCE

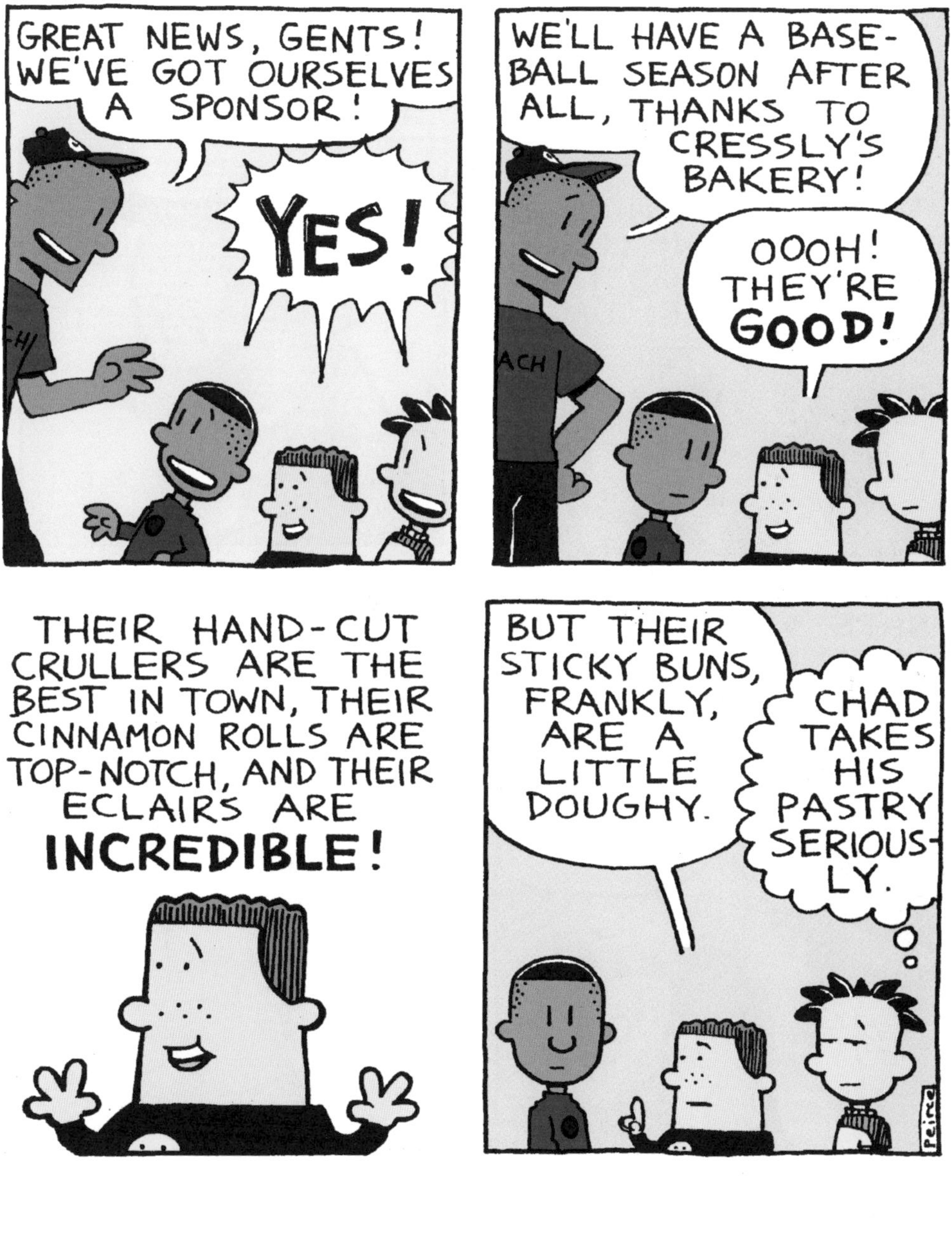
GREAT NEWS, GENTS! WE'VE GOT OURSELVES A SPONSOR!
YES!
WE'LL HAVE A BASE-BALL SEASON AFTER ALL, THANKS TO CRESSLY'S BAKERY!
OOOH! THEY'RE GOOD!
THEIR HAND-CUT CRULLERS ARE THE BEST IN TOWN, THEIR CINNAMON ROLLS ARE TOP-NOTCH, AND THEIR ECLAIRS ARE INCREDIBLE!
BUT THEIR STICKY BUNS, FRANKLY, ARE A LITTLE DOUGHY.
CHAD TAKES HIS PASTRY SERIOUS-LY.
Peirce

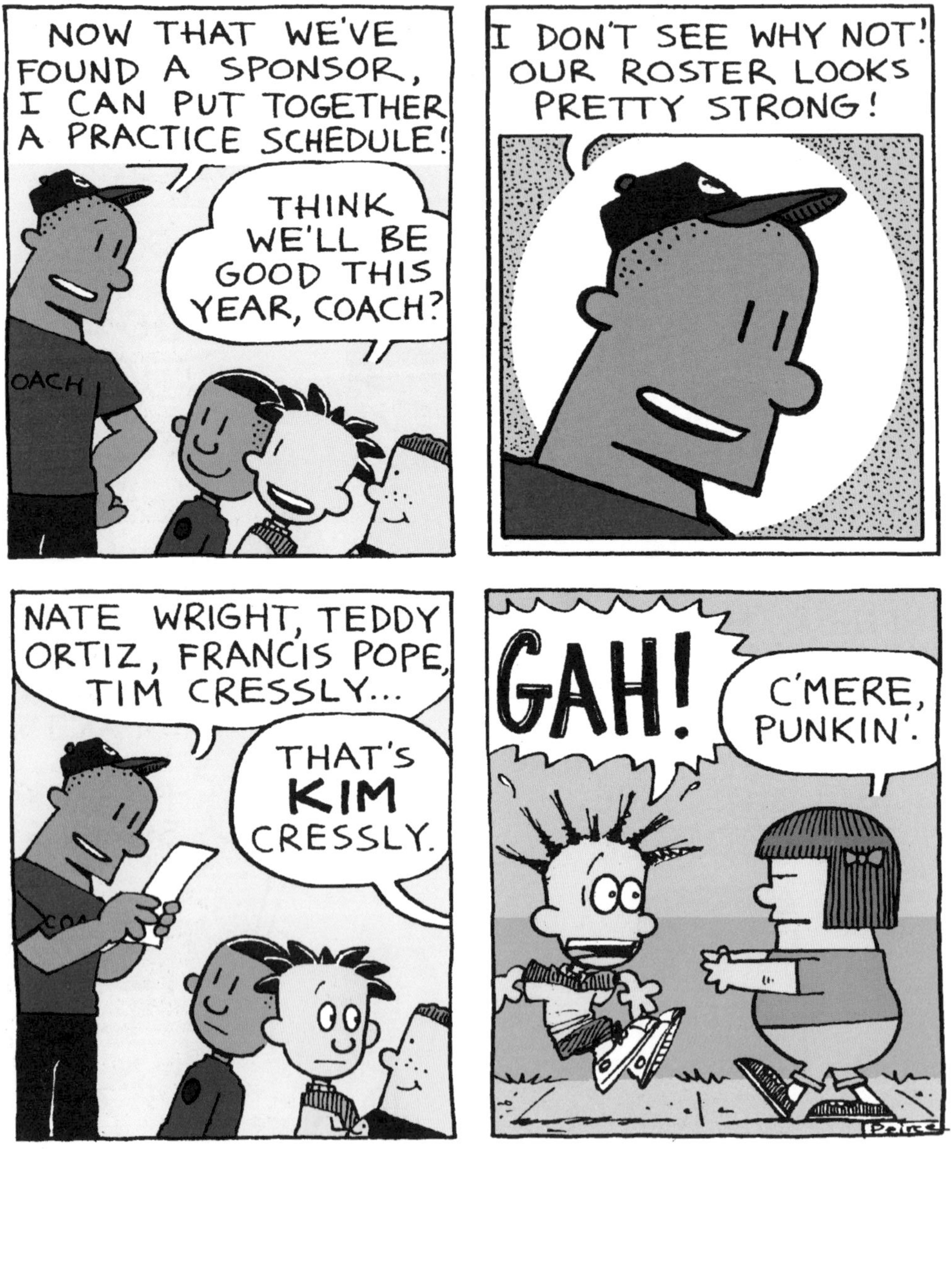
NOW THAT WE'VE FOUND A SPONSOR, I CAN PUT TOGETHER A PRACTICE SCHEDULE!
THINK WE'LL BE GOOD THIS YEAR, COACH?
OACH
I DON'T SEE WHY NOT! OUR ROSTER LOOKS PRETTY STRONG!
NATE WRIGHT, TEDDY ORTIZ, FRANCIS POPE, TIM CRESSLY...
THAT'S **KIM** CRESSLY.
GAH!
C'MERE, PUNKIN'.

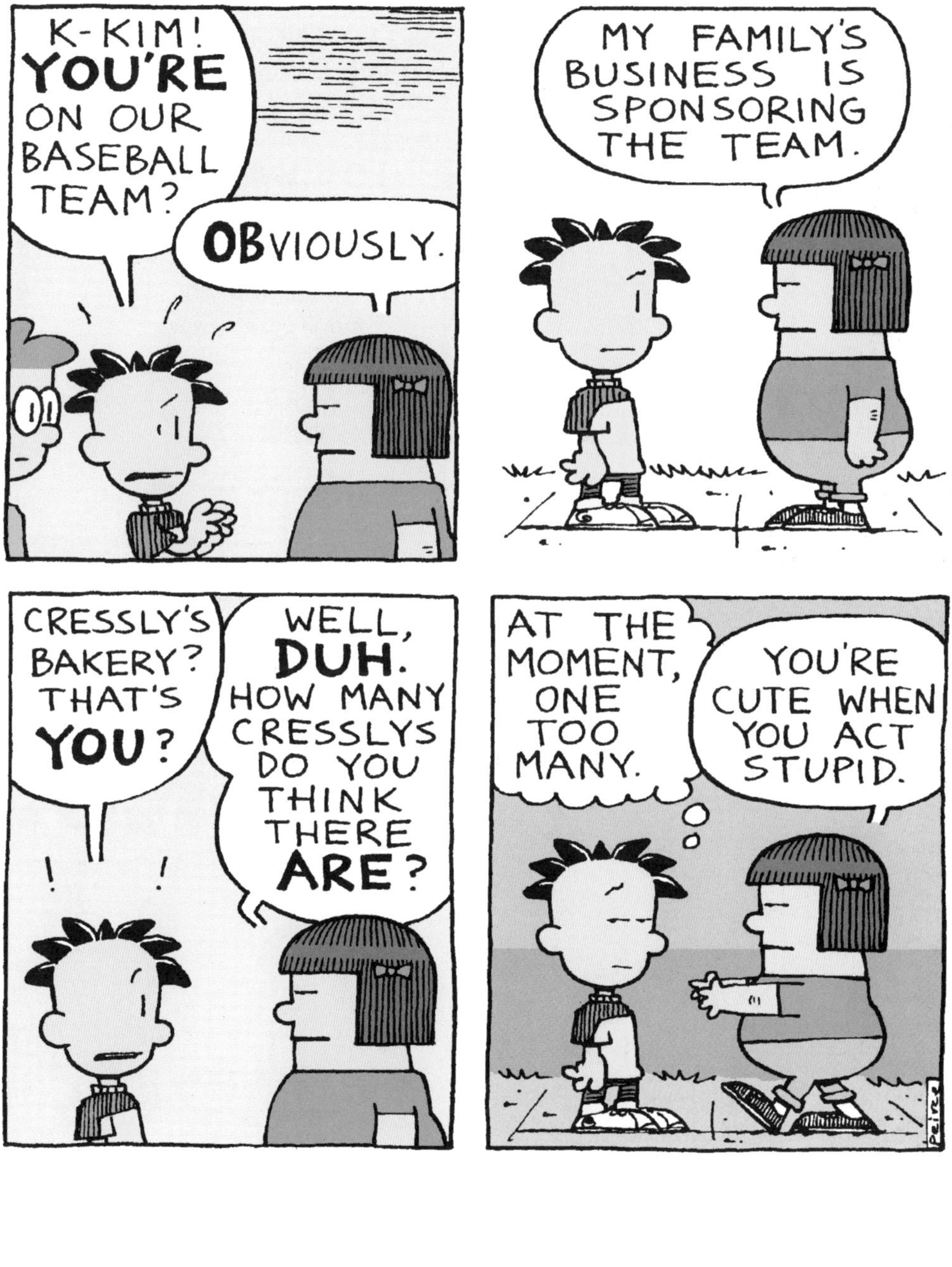
K-KIM! YOU'RE ON OUR BASEBALL TEAM?
OBVIOUSLY.
MY FAMILY'S BUSINESS IS SPONSORING THE TEAM.
CRESSLY'S BAKERY? THAT'S YOU?
WELL, DUH. HOW MANY CRESSLYS DO YOU THINK THERE ARE?
AT THE MOMENT, ONE TOO MANY.
YOU'RE CUTE WHEN YOU ACT STUPID.

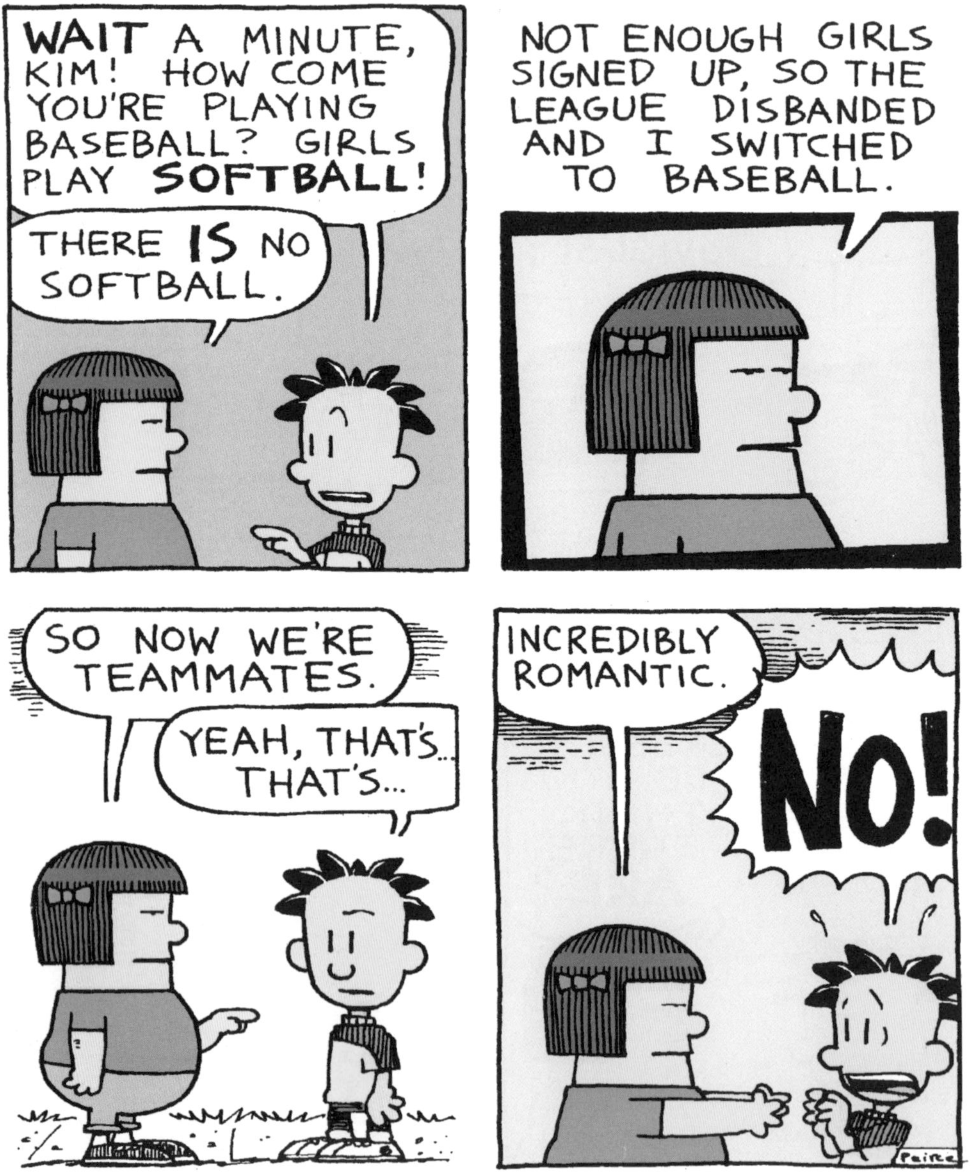
WAIT A MINUTE, KIM! HOW COME YOU'RE PLAYING BASEBALL? GIRLS PLAY SOFTBALL!
THERE IS NO SOFTBALL.
NOT ENOUGH GIRLS SIGNED UP, SO THE LEAGUE DISBANDED AND I SWITCHED TO BASEBALL.
SO NOW WE'RE TEAMMATES.
YEAH, THAT'S... THAT'S...
INCREDIBLY ROMANTIC.
NO!
Peirce

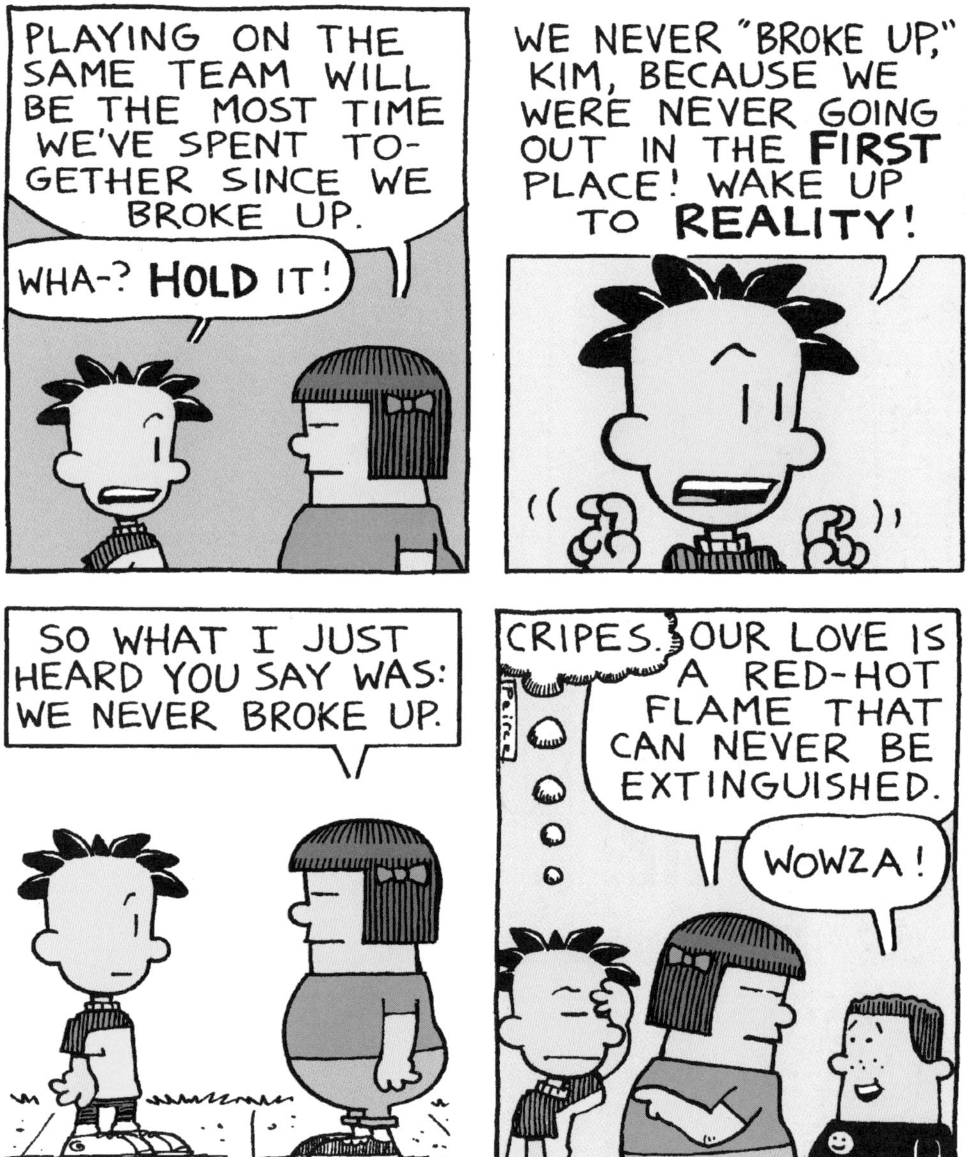
PLAYING ON THE SAME TEAM WILL BE THE MOST TIME WE'VE SPENT TOGETHER SINCE WE BROKE UP.
WHA-? **HOLD** IT!
WE NEVER "BROKE UP," KIM, BECAUSE WE WERE NEVER GOING OUT IN THE **FIRST** PLACE! WAKE UP TO **REALITY**!
SO WHAT I JUST HEARD YOU SAY WAS: WE NEVER BROKE UP.
CRIPES.
OUR LOVE IS A RED-HOT FLAME THAT CAN NEVER BE EXTINGUISHED.
WOWZA!
Peirce

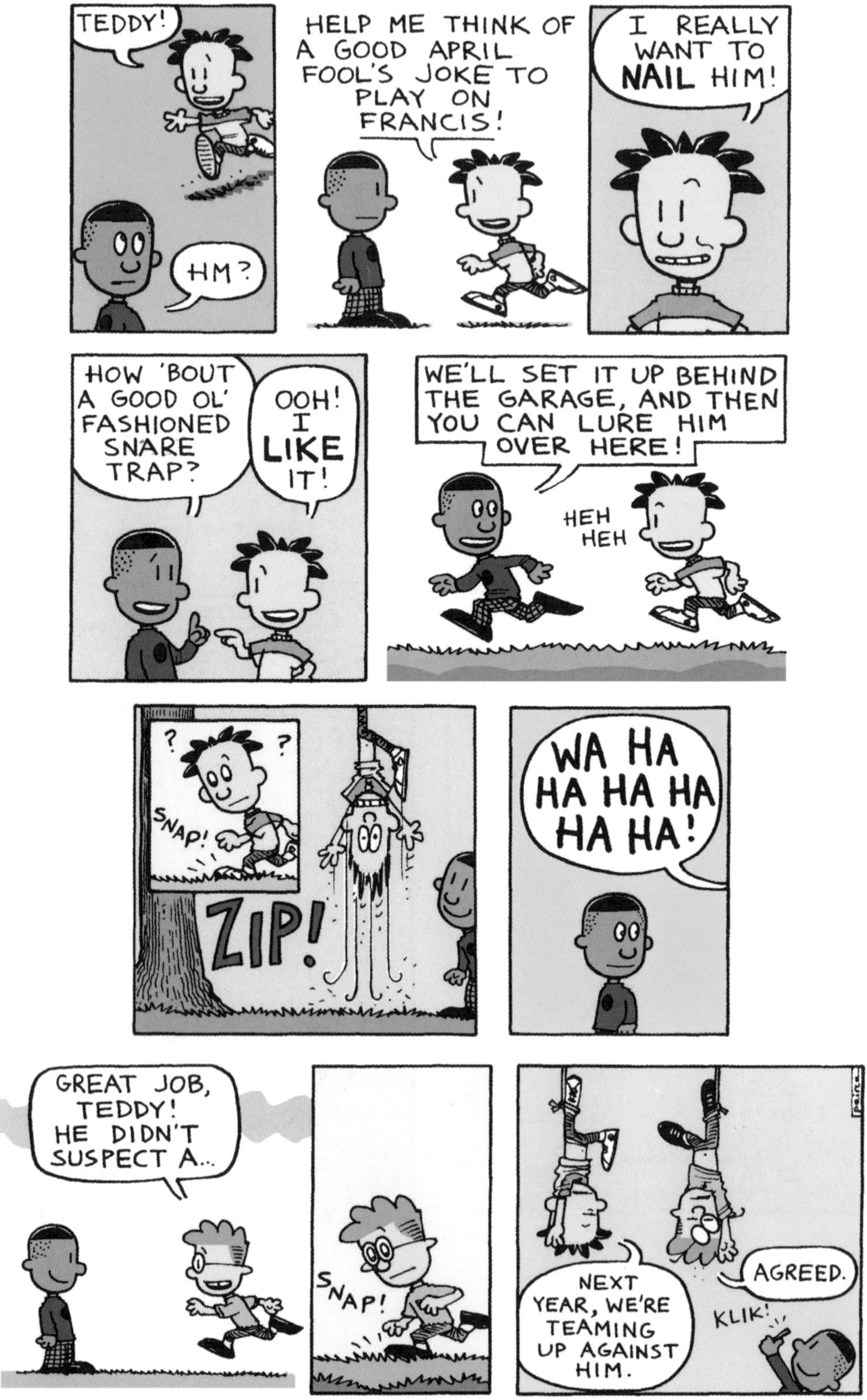
TEDDY!
HM?
HELP ME THINK OF A GOOD APRIL FOOL'S JOKE TO PLAY ON FRANCIS!
I REALLY WANT TO NAIL HIM!
HOW 'BOUT A GOOD OL' FASHIONED SNARE TRAP?
OOH! I LIKE IT!
WE'LL SET IT UP BEHIND THE GARAGE, AND THEN YOU CAN LURE HIM OVER HERE!
HEH HEH
? ?
SNAP!
ZIP!
WA HA HA HA HA HA HA!
GREAT JOB, TEDDY! HE DIDN'T SUSPECT A...
SNAP!
NEXT YEAR, WE'RE TEAMING UP AGAINST HIM.
AGREED.
KLIK!
peirce

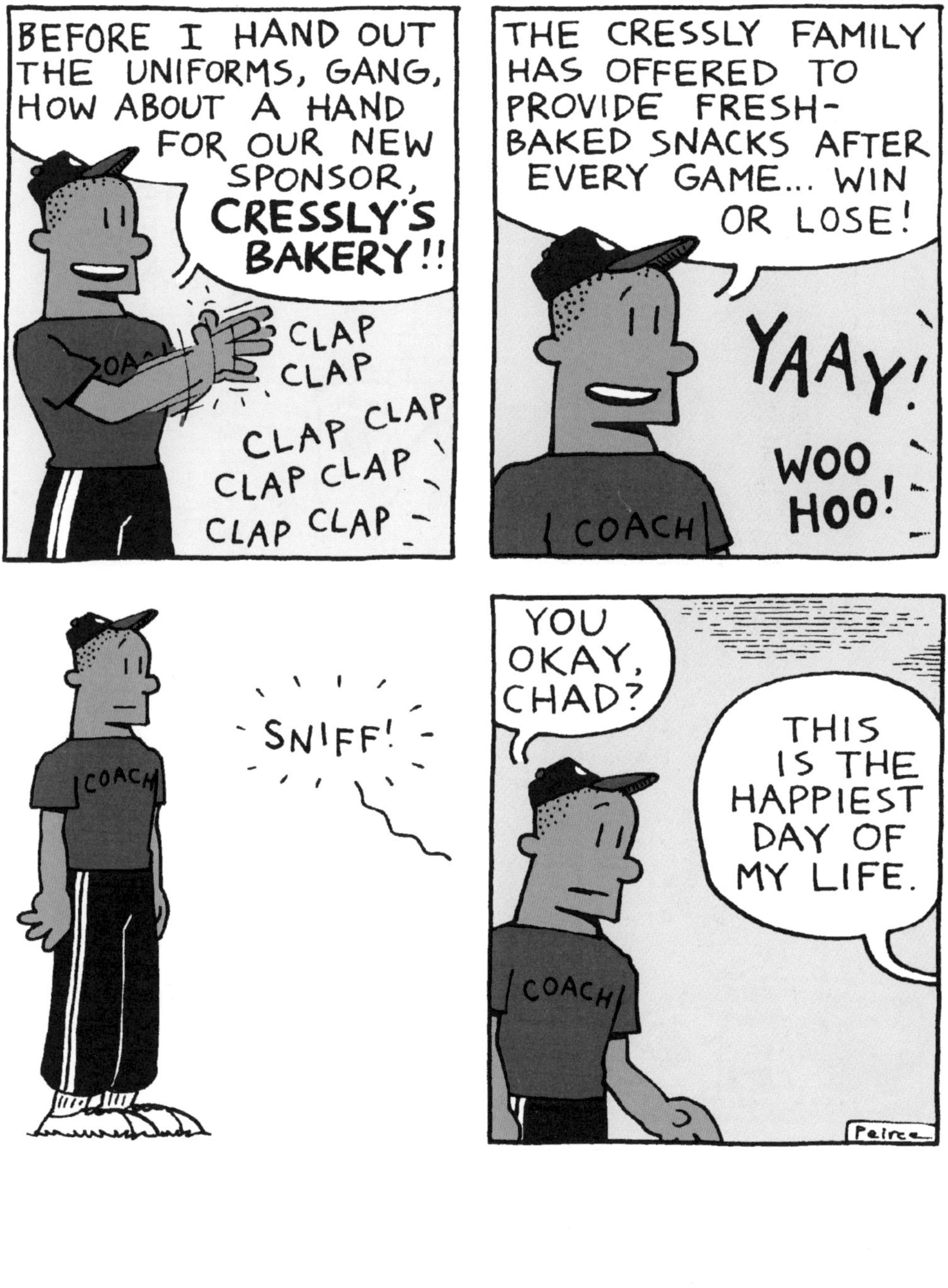
BEFORE I HAND OUT THE UNIFORMS, GANG, HOW ABOUT A HAND FOR OUR NEW SPONSOR, **CRESSLY'S BAKERY**!!
CLAP CLAP
CLAP CLAP
CLAP CLAP
CLAP CLAP
COACH
THE CRESSLY FAMILY HAS OFFERED TO PROVIDE FRESH-BAKED SNACKS AFTER EVERY GAME... WIN OR LOSE!
YAAY!
WOO HOO!
COACH
SNIFF!
COACH
YOU OKAY, CHAD?
THIS IS THE HAPPIEST DAY OF MY LIFE.
COACH
Peirce

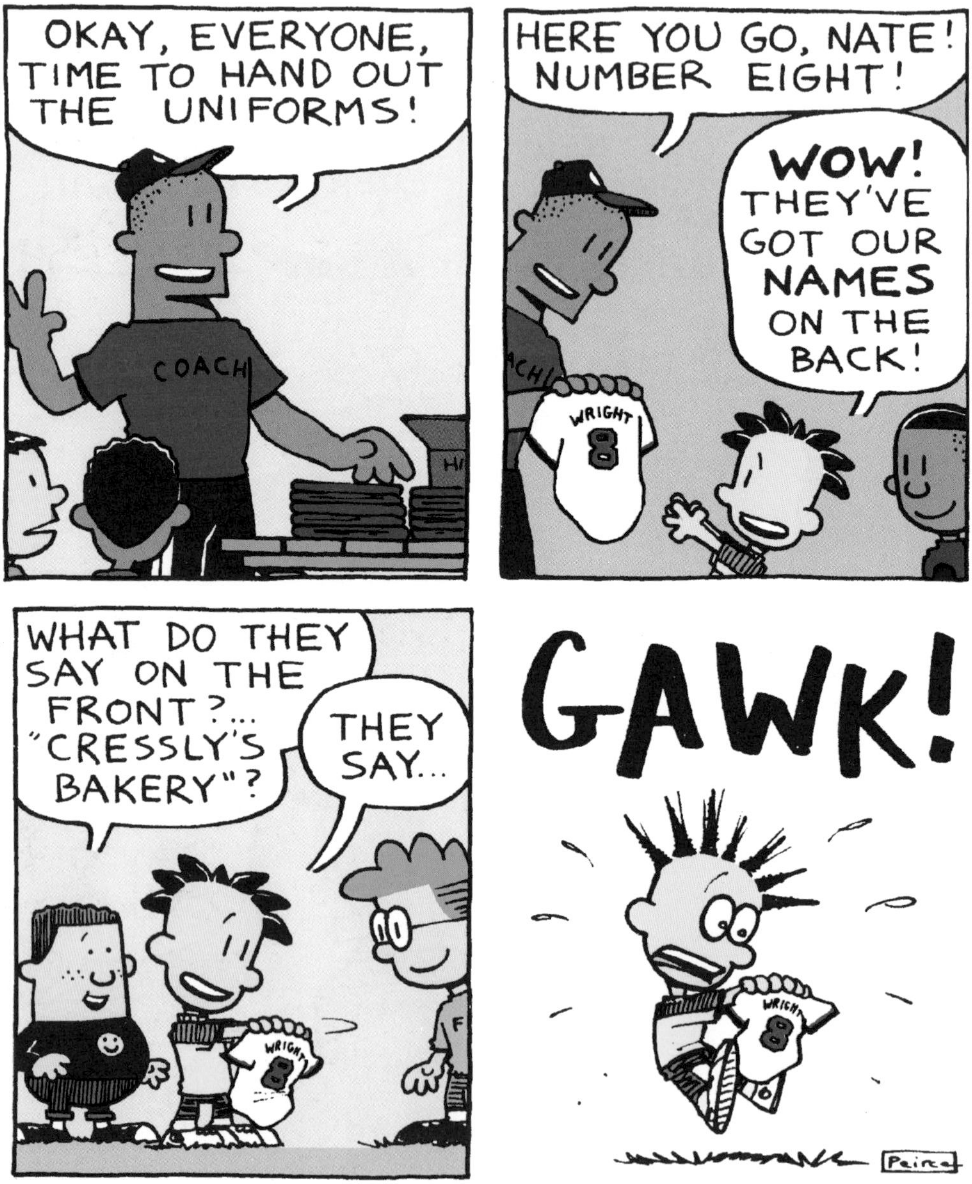
OKAY, EVERYONE, TIME TO HAND OUT THE UNIFORMS!
COACH
HERE YOU GO, NATE! NUMBER EIGHT!
WOW! THEY'VE GOT OUR NAMES ON THE BACK!
WRIGHT 8
WHAT DO THEY SAY ON THE FRONT?... "CRESSLY'S BAKERY"?
THEY SAY...
GAWK!
Peirce

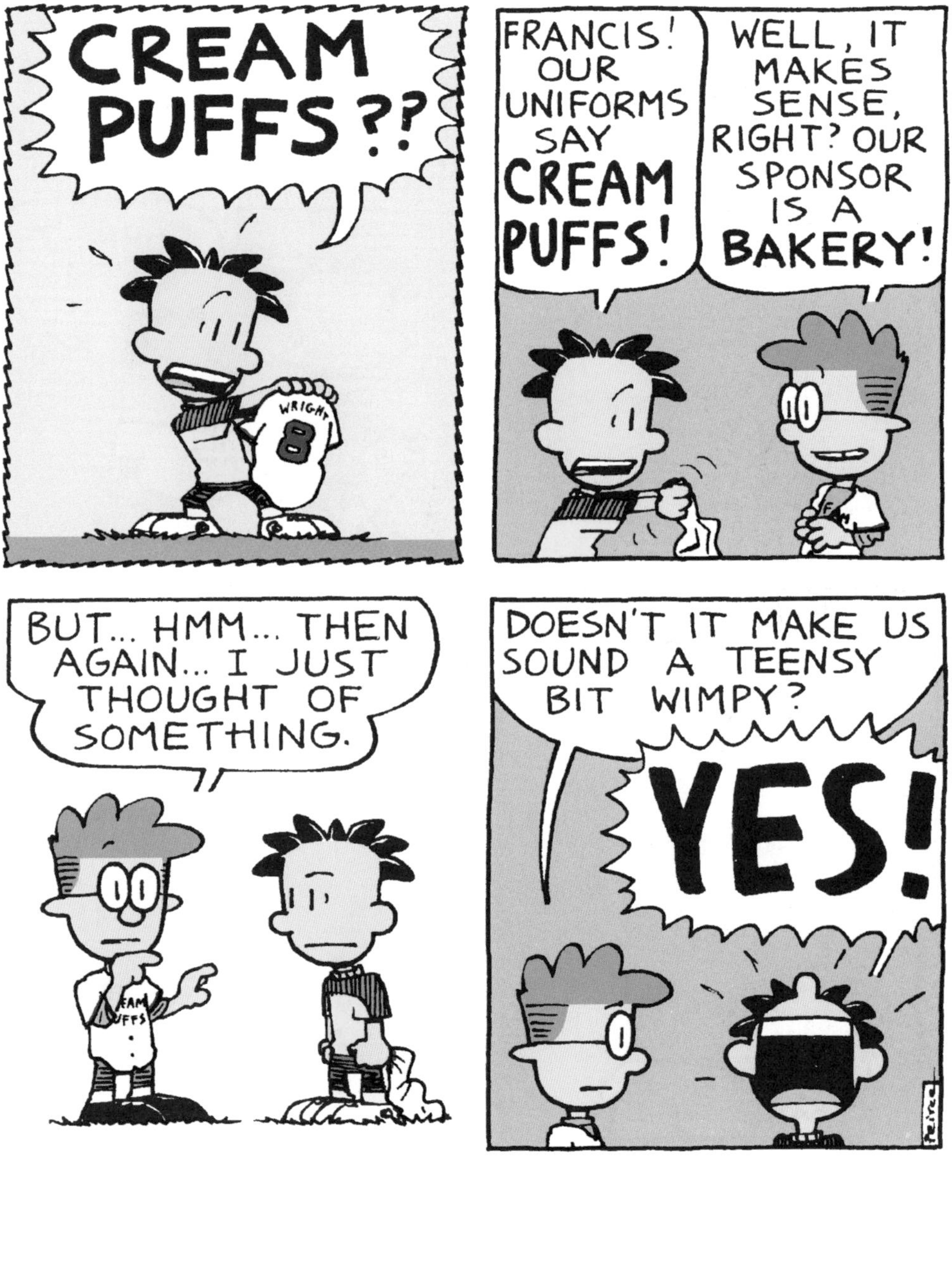
CREAM PUFFS??
WRIGHT
8
FRANCIS! OUR UNIFORMS SAY CREAM PUFFS!
WELL, IT MAKES SENSE, RIGHT? OUR SPONSOR IS A BAKERY!
BUT... HMM... THEN AGAIN... I JUST THOUGHT OF SOMETHING.
DOESN'T IT MAKE US SOUND A TEENSY BIT WIMPY?
YES!

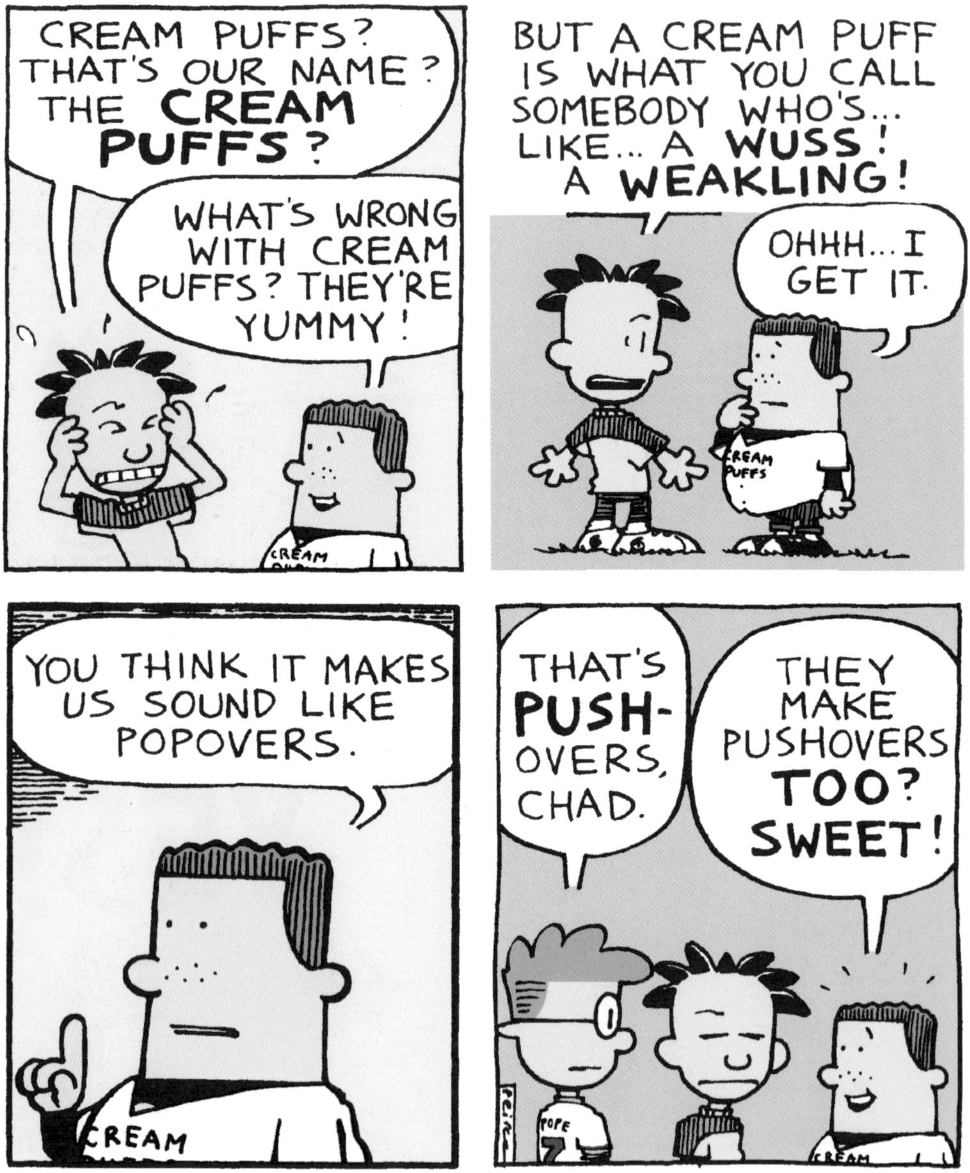
CREAM PUFFS? THAT'S OUR NAME? THE CREAM PUFFS?
WHAT'S WRONG WITH CREAM PUFFS? THEY'RE YUMMY!
BUT A CREAM PUFF IS WHAT YOU CALL SOMEBODY WHO'S... LIKE... A WUSS! A WEAKLING!
OHHH... I GET IT.
YOU THINK IT MAKES US SOUND LIKE POPOVERS.
THAT'S PUSH-OVERS, CHAD.
THEY MAKE PUSHOVERS TOO? SWEET!

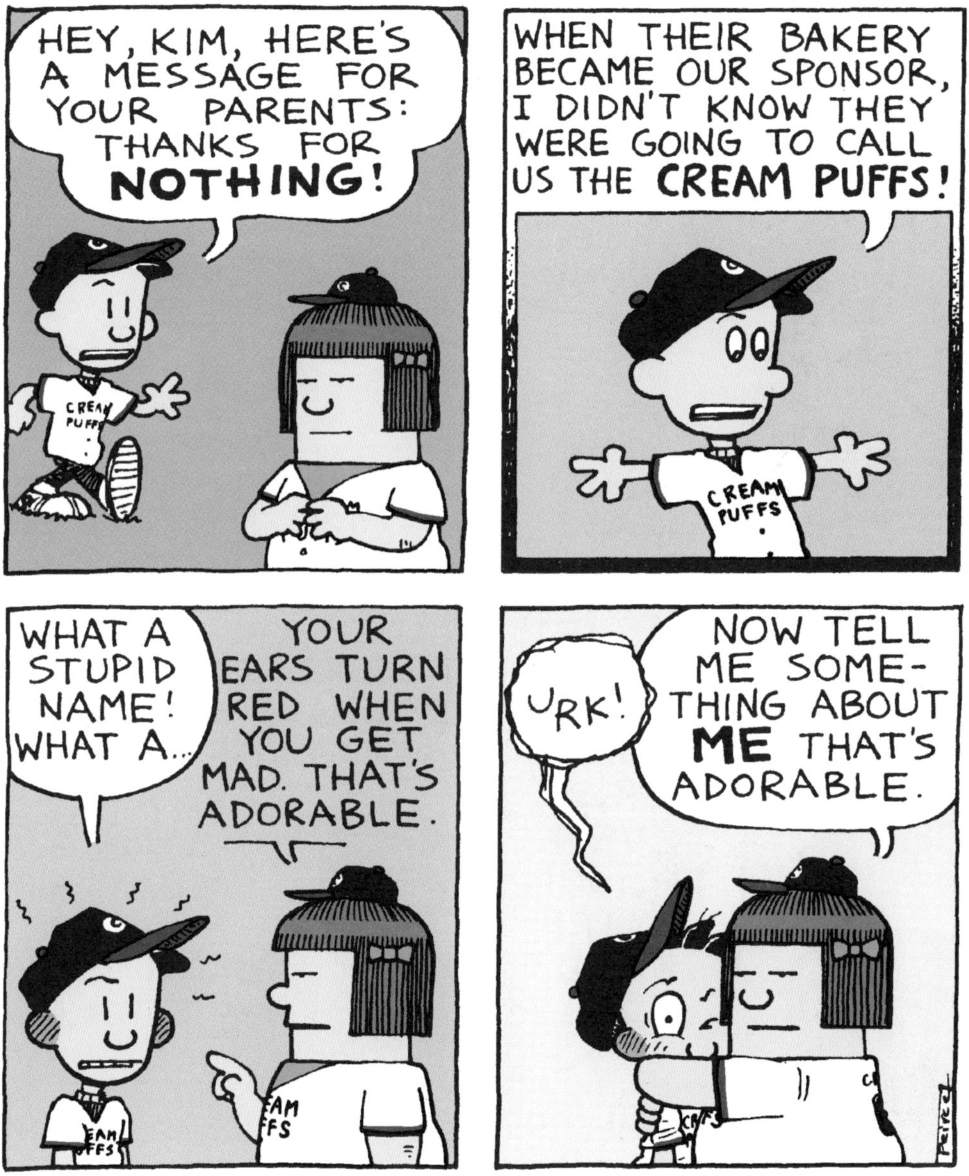

HEY, KIM, HERE'S A MESSAGE FOR YOUR PARENTS: THANKS FOR **NOTHING**!
CREAM PUFFS
WHEN THEIR BAKERY BECAME OUR SPONSOR, I DIDN'T KNOW THEY WERE GOING TO CALL US THE **CREAM PUFFS**!
CREAM PUFFS
WHAT A STUPID NAME! WHAT A...
YOUR EARS TURN RED WHEN YOU GET MAD. THAT'S ADORABLE.
URK!
NOW TELL ME SOME-THING ABOUT **ME** THAT'S ADORABLE.
PEIRCE

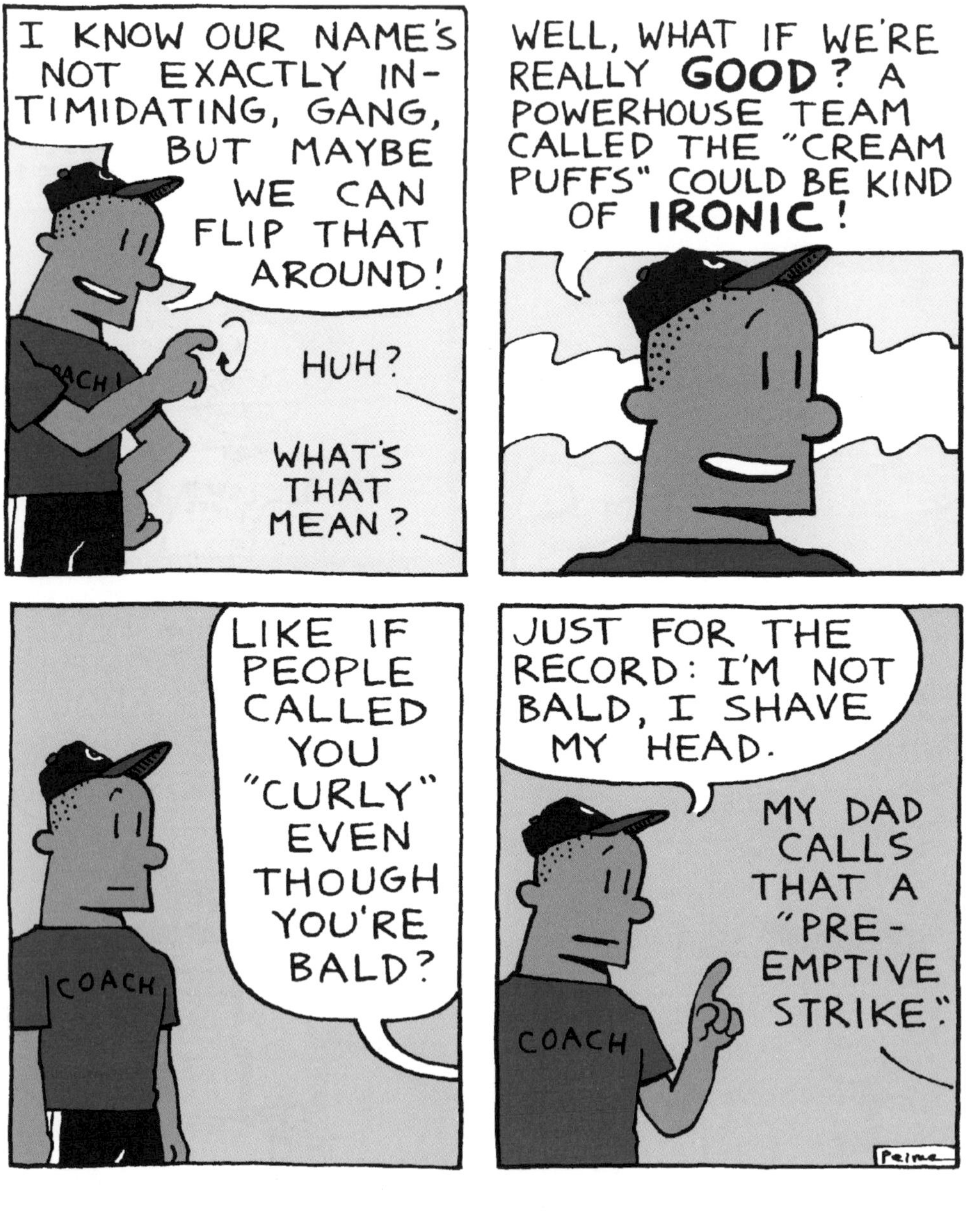
I KNOW OUR NAME'S NOT EXACTLY IN-TIMIDATING, GANG, BUT MAYBE WE CAN FLIP THAT AROUND!
HUH?
WHAT'S THAT MEAN?
WELL, WHAT IF WE'RE REALLY **GOOD**? A POWERHOUSE TEAM CALLED THE "CREAM PUFFS" COULD BE KIND OF **IRONIC**!
LIKE IF PEOPLE CALLED YOU "CURLY" EVEN THOUGH YOU'RE BALD?
JUST FOR THE RECORD: I'M NOT BALD, I SHAVE MY HEAD.
MY DAD CALLS THAT A "PRE-EMPTIVE STRIKE."
COACH
COACH
COACH
Peirce

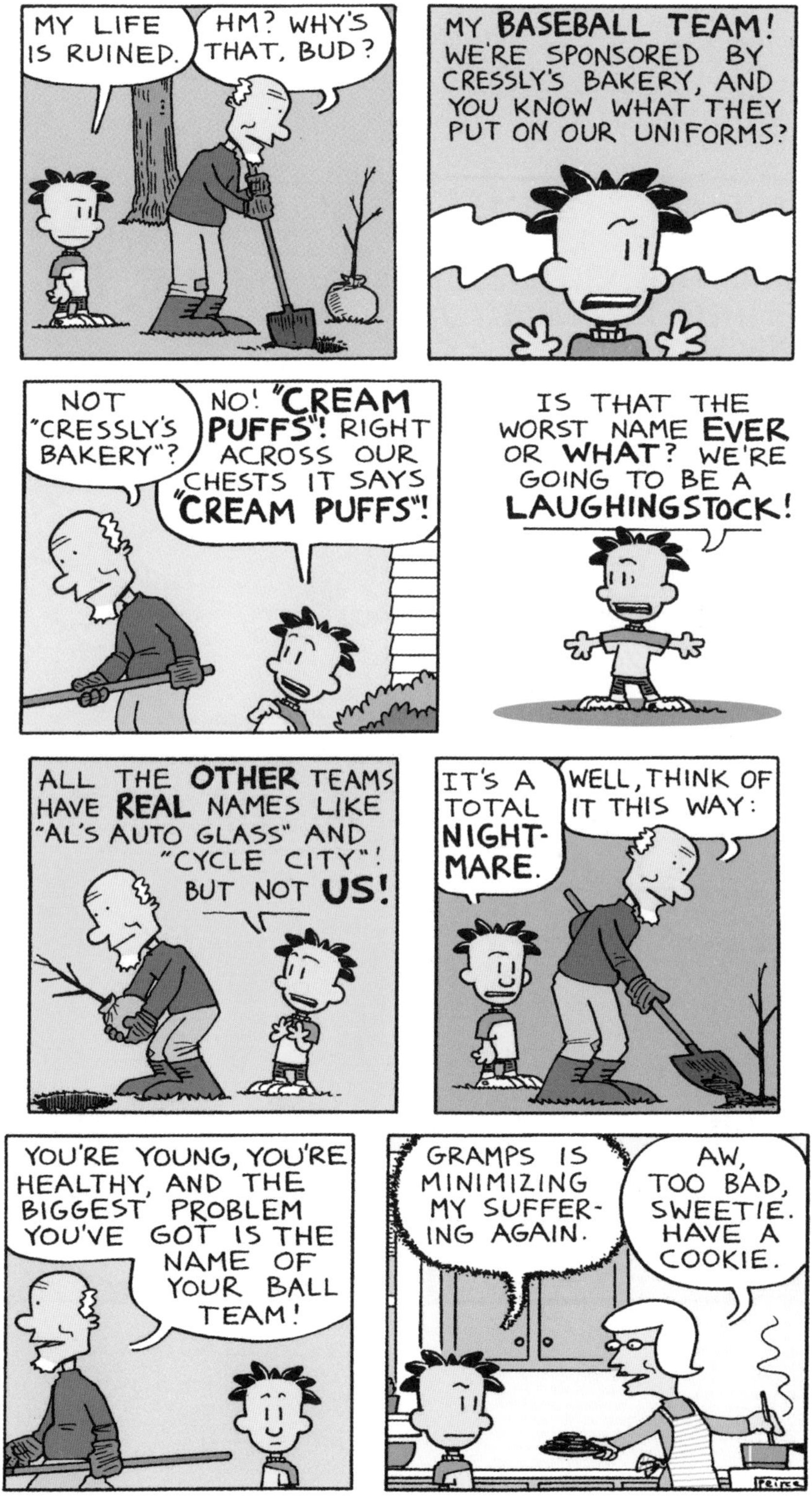
MY LIFE IS RUINED.
HM? WHY'S THAT, BUD?
MY BASEBALL TEAM! WE'RE SPONSORED BY CRESSLY'S BAKERY, AND YOU KNOW WHAT THEY PUT ON OUR UNIFORMS?
NOT "CRESSLY'S BAKERY"?
NO! "CREAM PUFFS"! RIGHT ACROSS OUR CHESTS IT SAYS "CREAM PUFFS"!
IS THAT THE WORST NAME EVER OR WHAT? WE'RE GOING TO BE A LAUGHINGSTOCK!
ALL THE OTHER TEAMS HAVE REAL NAMES LIKE "AL'S AUTO GLASS" AND "CYCLE CITY"! BUT NOT US!
IT'S A TOTAL NIGHT-MARE.
WELL, THINK OF IT THIS WAY:
YOU'RE YOUNG, YOU'RE HEALTHY, AND THE BIGGEST PROBLEM YOU'VE GOT IS THE NAME OF YOUR BALL TEAM!
GRAMPS IS MINIMIZING MY SUFFER-ING AGAIN.
AW, TOO BAD, SWEETIE. HAVE A COOKIE.
PEIRCE

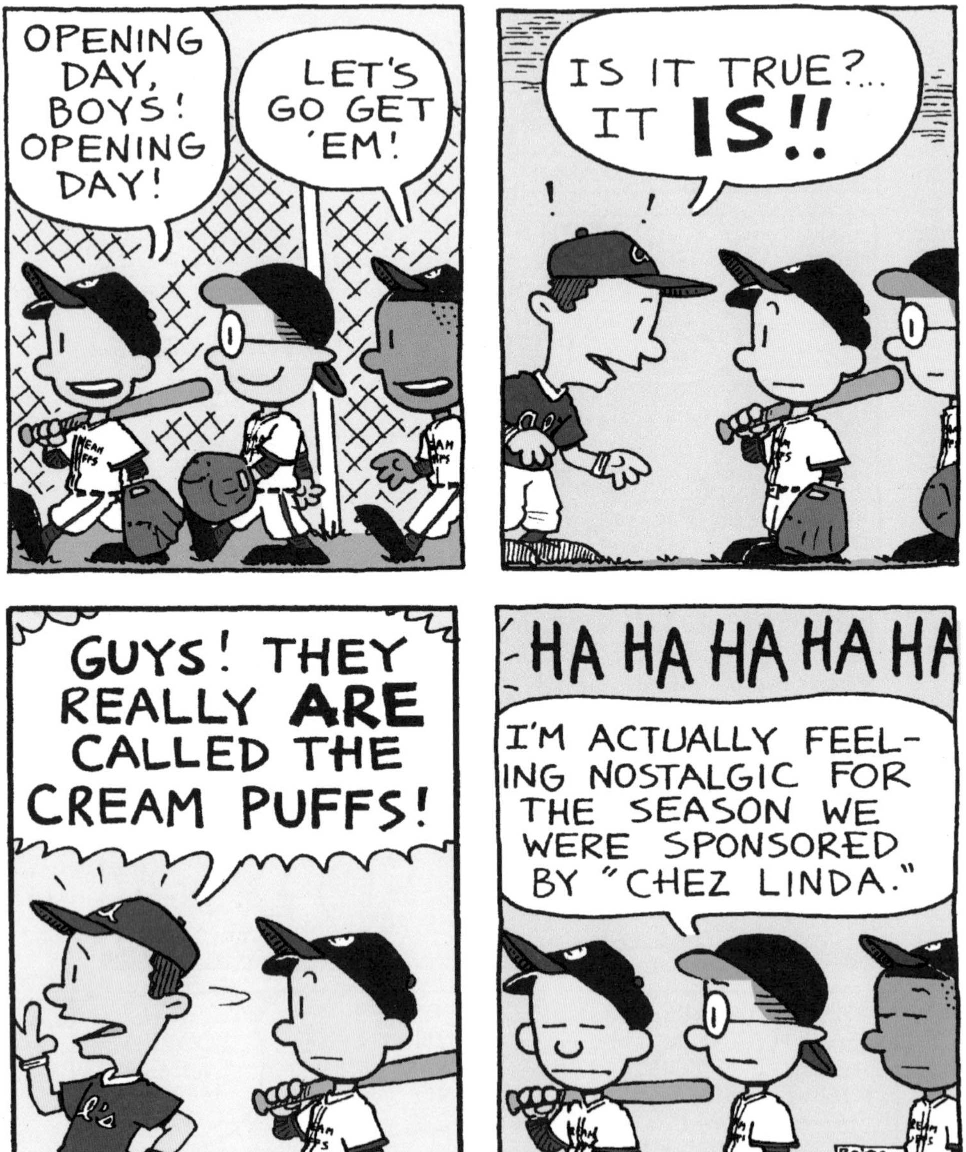
OPENING DAY, BOYS! OPENING DAY!
LET'S GO GET 'EM!
IS IT TRUE?... IT IS!!
GUYS! THEY REALLY ARE CALLED THE CREAM PUFFS!
HA HA HA HA HA HA
I'M ACTUALLY FEELING NOSTALGIC FOR THE SEASON WE WERE SPONSORED BY "CHEZ LINDA."

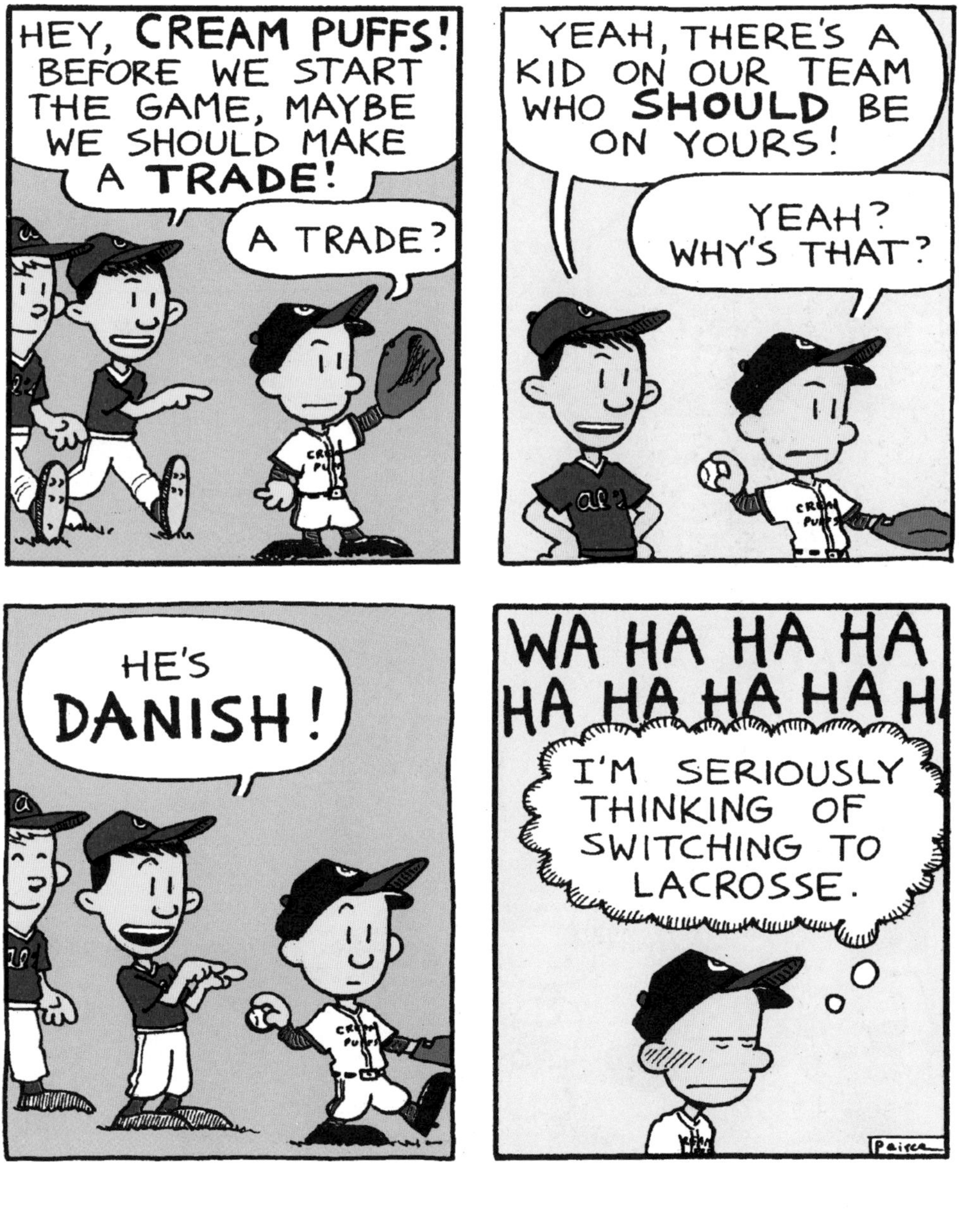
HEY, CREAM PUFFS! BEFORE WE START THE GAME, MAYBE WE SHOULD MAKE A TRADE!
A TRADE?
YEAH, THERE'S A KID ON OUR TEAM WHO SHOULD BE ON YOURS!
YEAH? WHY'S THAT?
HE'S DANISH!
WA HA HA HA HA HA HA HA H
I'M SERIOUSLY THINKING OF SWITCHING TO LACROSSE.
Pairce

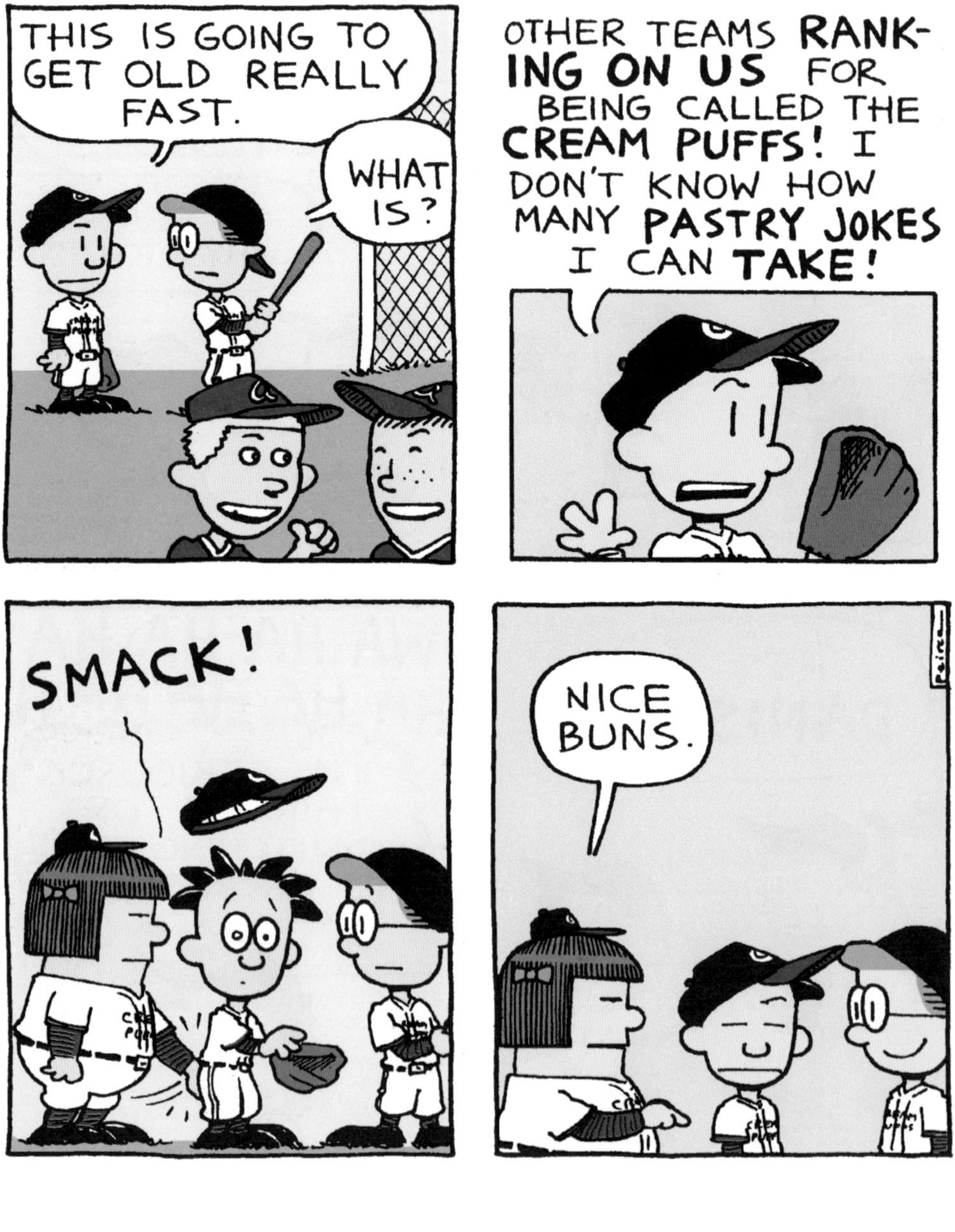
THIS IS GOING TO GET OLD REALLY FAST.
WHAT IS?
OTHER TEAMS RANKING ON US FOR BEING CALLED THE CREAM PUFFS! I DON'T KNOW HOW MANY PASTRY JOKES I CAN TAKE!
SMACK!
NICE BUNS.

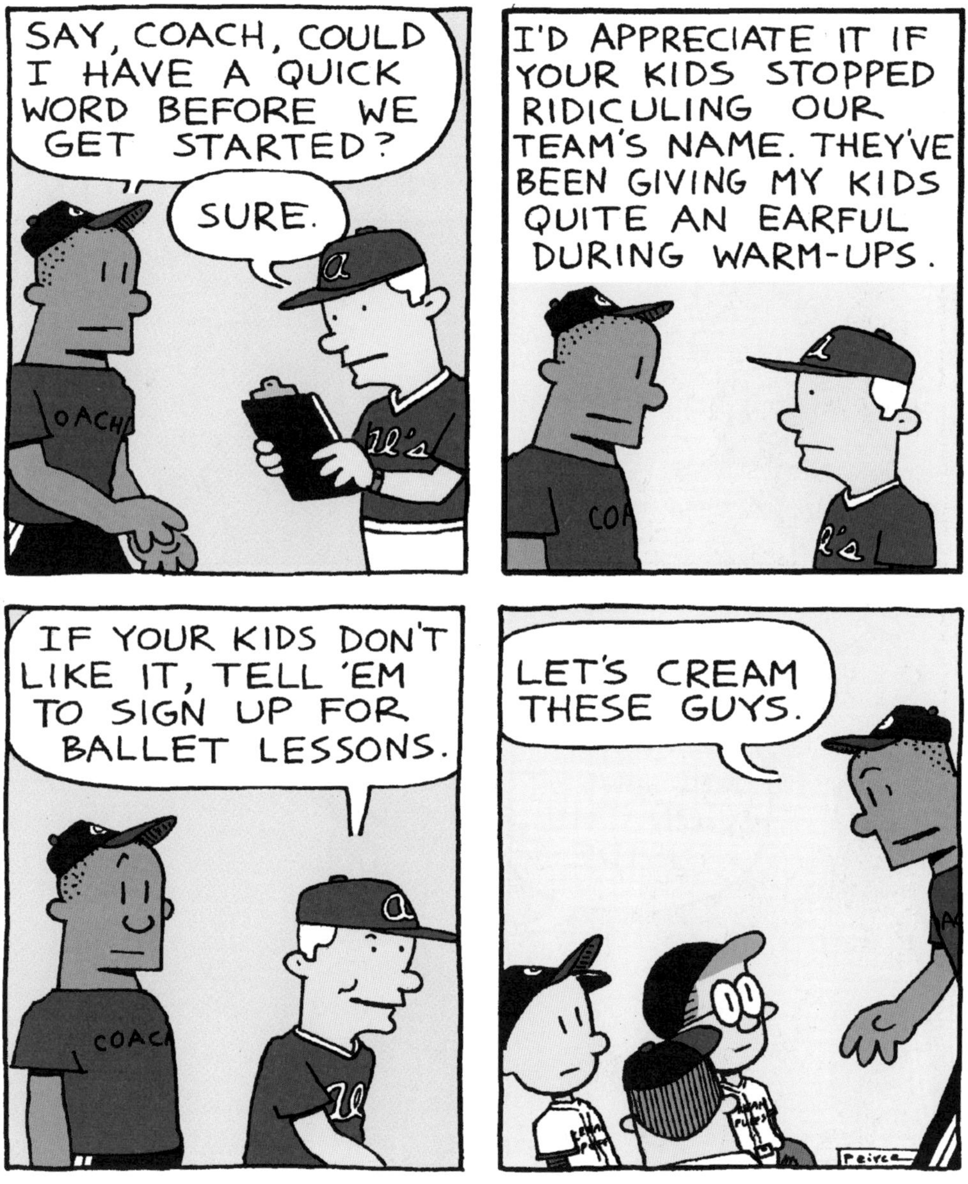
SAY, COACH, COULD I HAVE A QUICK WORD BEFORE WE GET STARTED?
SURE.
I'D APPRECIATE IT IF YOUR KIDS STOPPED RIDICULING OUR TEAM'S NAME. THEY'VE BEEN GIVING MY KIDS QUITE AN EARFUL DURING WARM-UPS.
IF YOUR KIDS DON'T LIKE IT, TELL 'EM TO SIGN UP FOR BALLET LESSONS.
LET'S CREAM THESE GUYS.

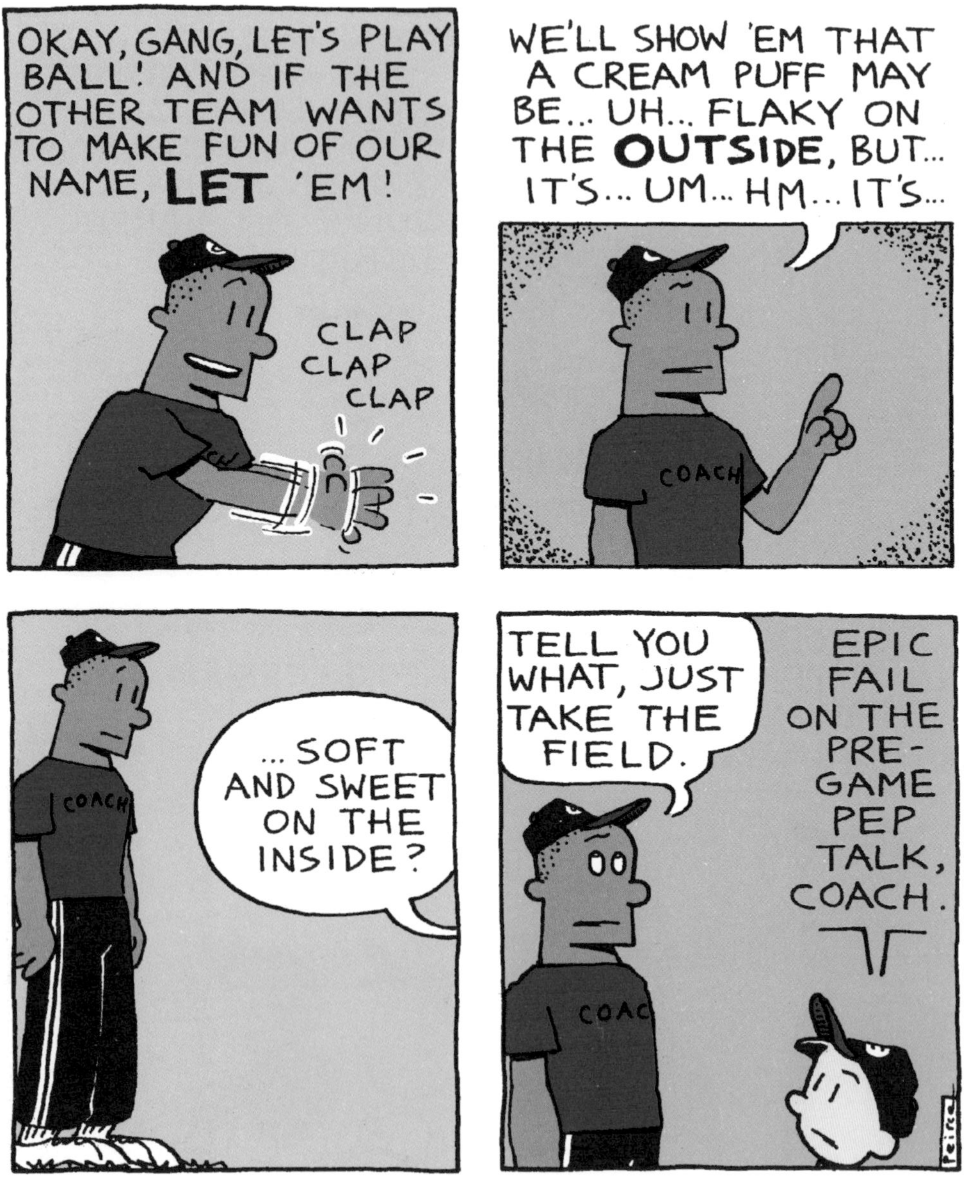
OKAY, GANG, LET'S PLAY BALL! AND IF THE OTHER TEAM WANTS TO MAKE FUN OF OUR NAME, **LET** 'EM!
CLAP CLAP CLAP
WE'LL SHOW 'EM THAT A CREAM PUFF MAY BE... UH... FLAKY ON THE **OUTSIDE**, BUT... IT'S... UM... HM... IT'S...
COACH
COACH
... SOFT AND SWEET ON THE INSIDE?
TELL YOU WHAT, JUST TAKE THE FIELD.
EPIC FAIL ON THE PRE-GAME PEP TALK, COACH.
COAC
Peirce

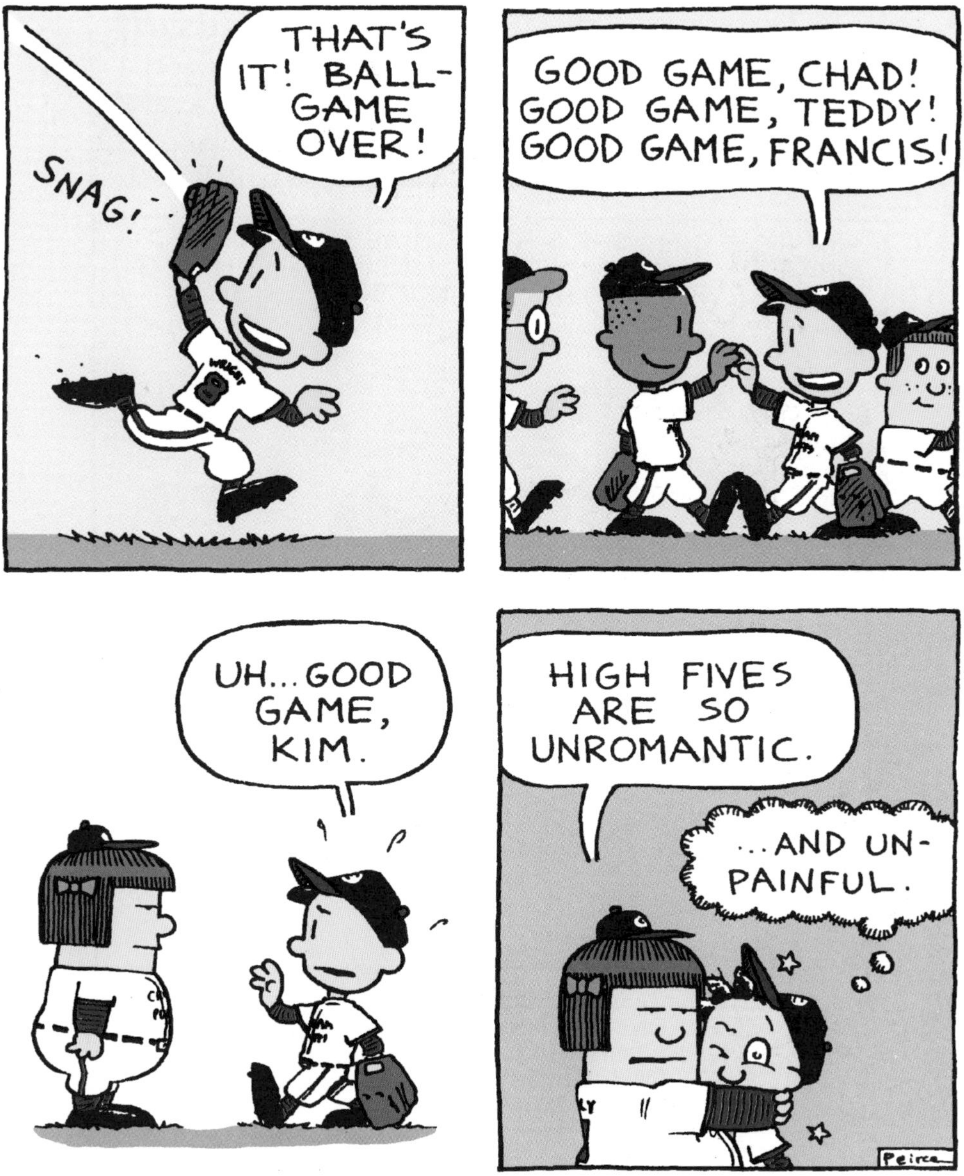
THAT'S IT! BALL-GAME OVER!
SNAG!
GOOD GAME, CHAD! GOOD GAME, TEDDY! GOOD GAME, FRANCIS!
UH...GOOD GAME, KIM.
HIGH FIVES ARE SO UNROMANTIC.
...AND UN-PAINFUL.
Peirce

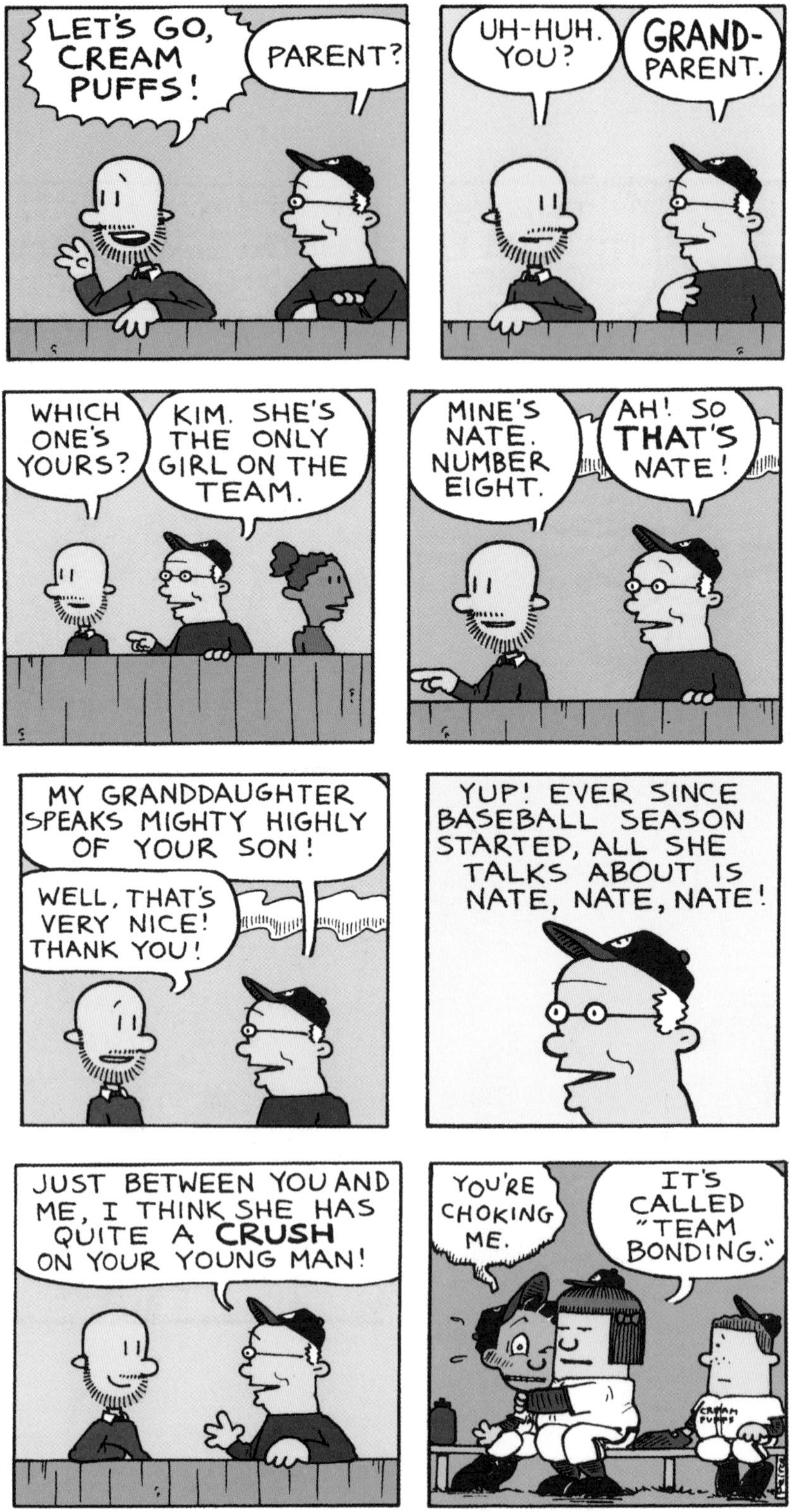
LET'S GO, CREAM PUFFS!
PARENT?
UH-HUH. YOU?
GRAND-PARENT.
WHICH ONE'S YOURS?
KIM. SHE'S THE ONLY GIRL ON THE TEAM.
MINE'S NATE. NUMBER EIGHT.
AH! SO THAT'S NATE!
MY GRANDDAUGHTER SPEAKS MIGHTY HIGHLY OF YOUR SON!
WELL, THAT'S VERY NICE! THANK YOU!
YUP! EVER SINCE BASEBALL SEASON STARTED, ALL SHE TALKS ABOUT IS NATE, NATE, NATE!
JUST BETWEEN YOU AND ME, I THINK SHE HAS QUITE A CRUSH ON YOUR YOUNG MAN!
YOU'RE CHOKING ME.
IT'S CALLED "TEAM BONDING."

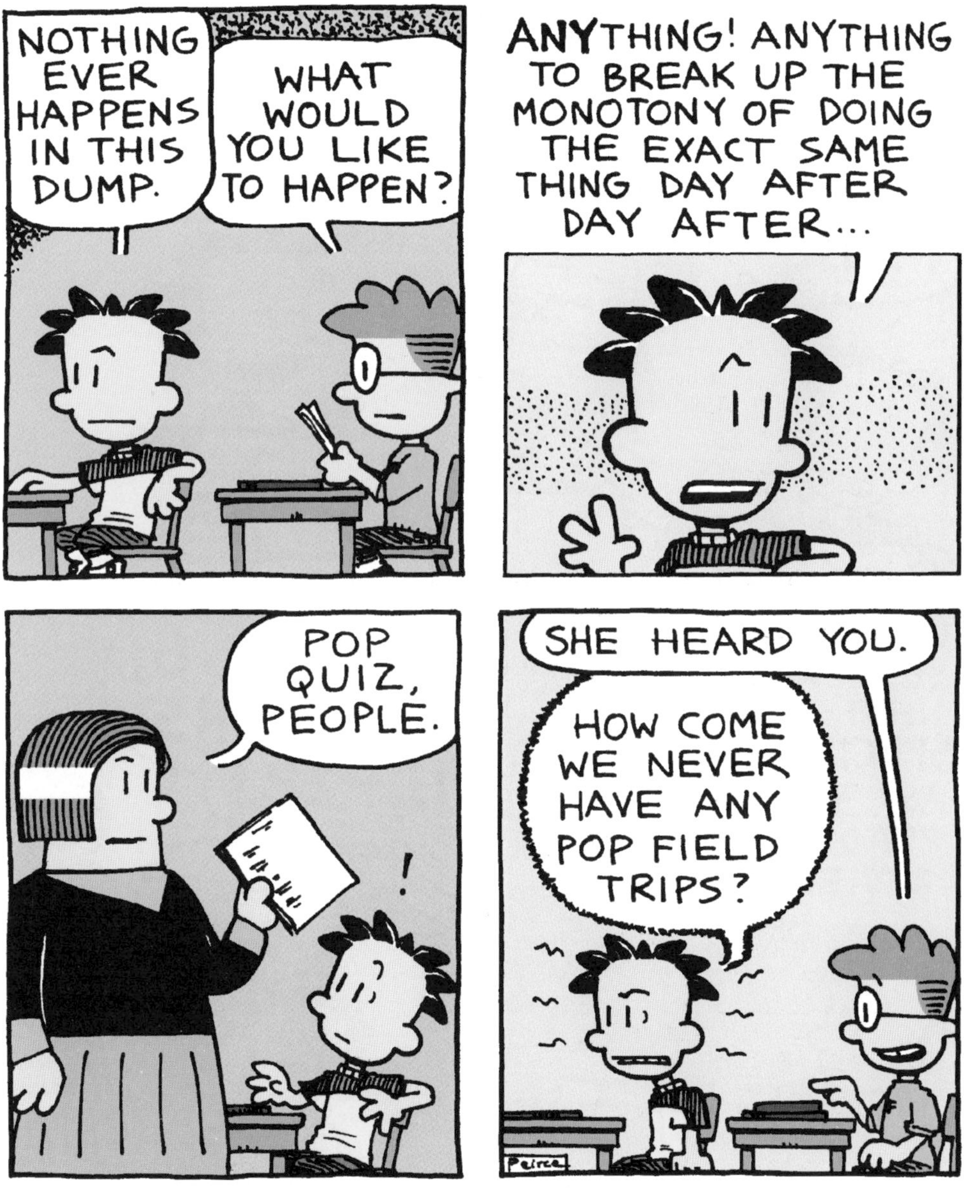
NOTHING EVER HAPPENS IN THIS DUMP.
WHAT WOULD YOU LIKE TO HAPPEN?
ANYTHING! ANYTHING TO BREAK UP THE MONOTONY OF DOING THE EXACT SAME THING DAY AFTER DAY AFTER...
POP QUIZ, PEOPLE.
!
SHE HEARD YOU.
HOW COME WE NEVER HAVE ANY POP FIELD TRIPS?
Peirce

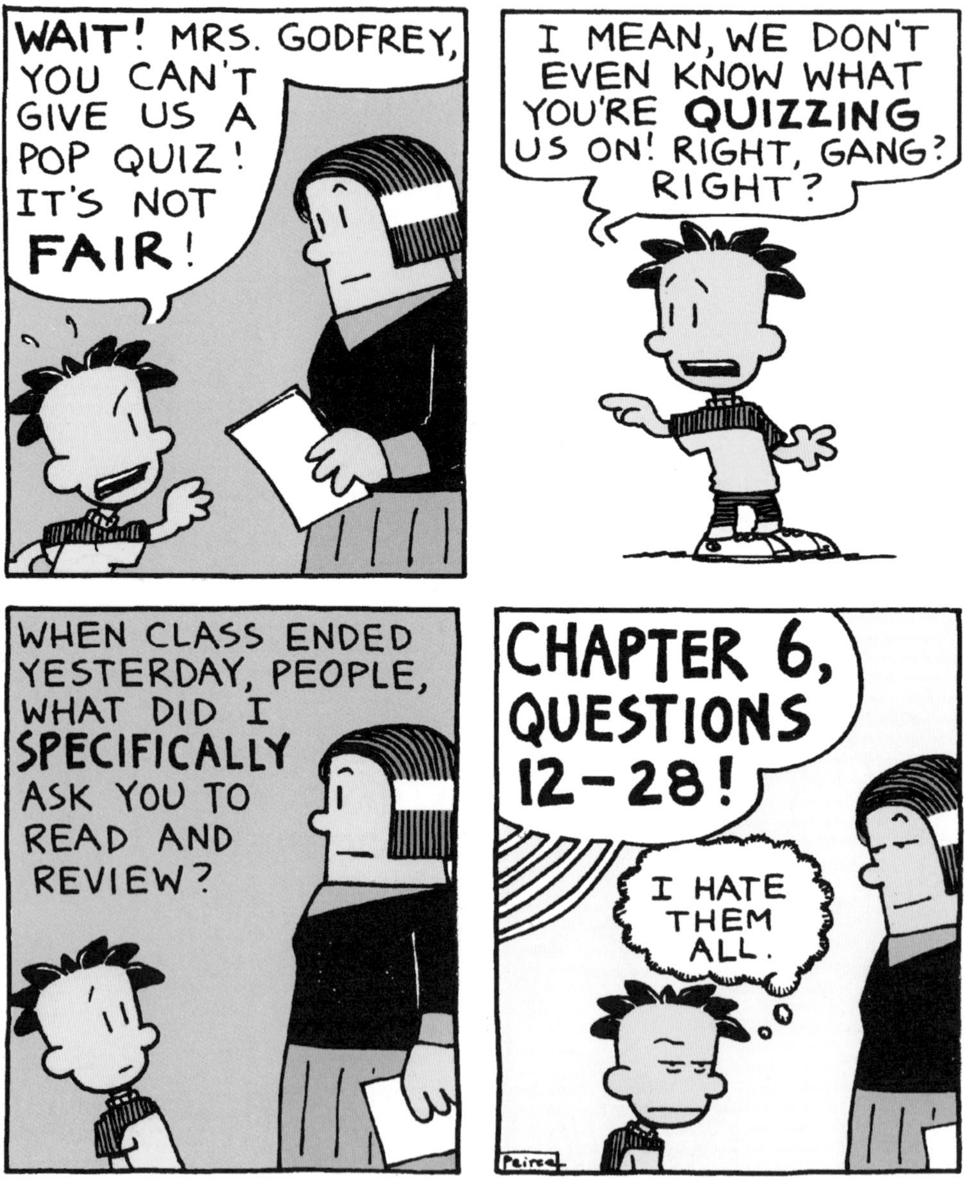
WAIT! MRS. GODFREY, YOU CAN'T GIVE US A POP QUIZ! IT'S NOT FAIR!
I MEAN, WE DON'T EVEN KNOW WHAT YOU'RE QUIZZING US ON! RIGHT, GANG? RIGHT?
WHEN CLASS ENDED YESTERDAY, PEOPLE, WHAT DID I SPECIFICALLY ASK YOU TO READ AND REVIEW?
CHAPTER 6, QUESTIONS 12-28!
I HATE THEM ALL.
Peirce

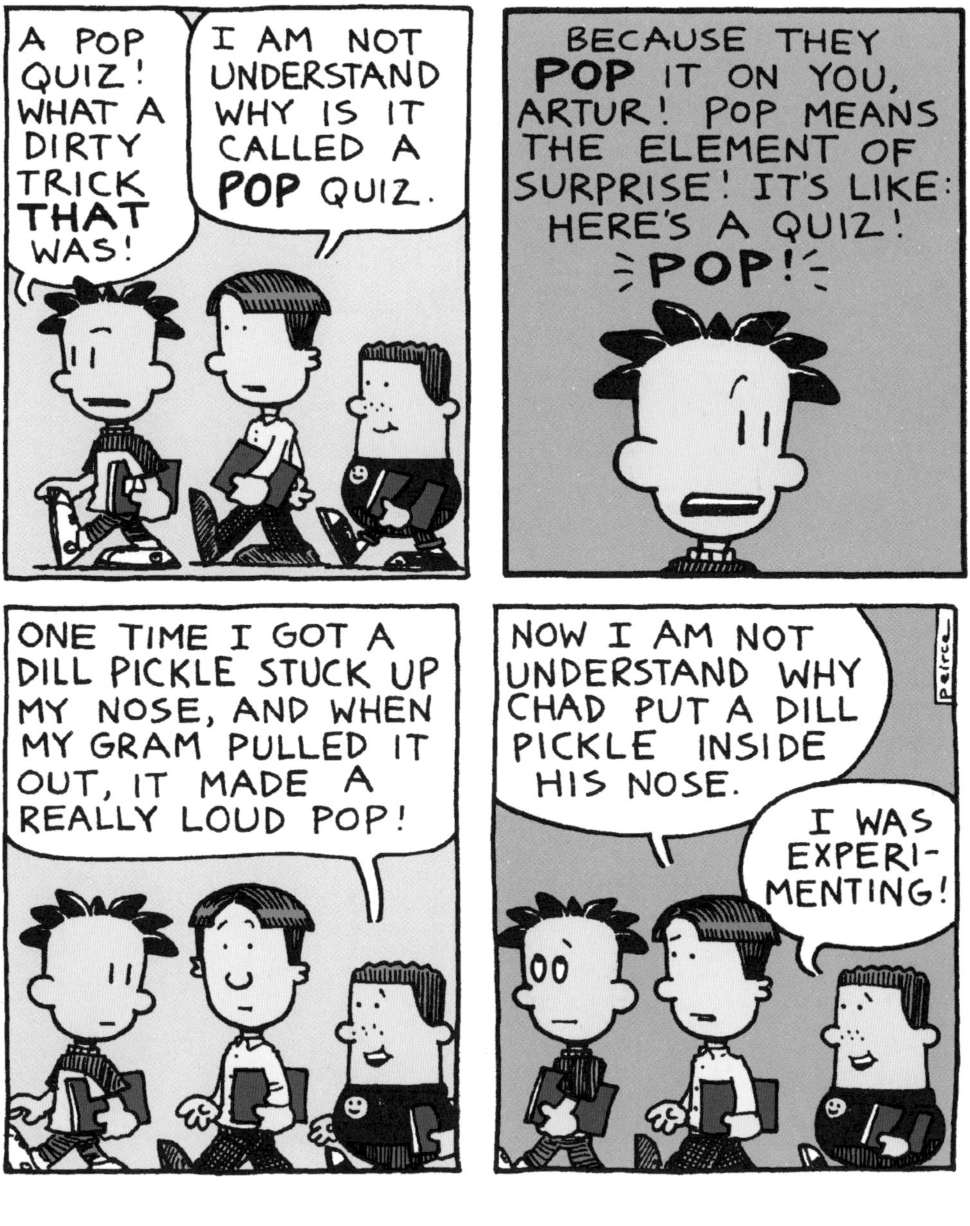
A POP QUIZ! WHAT A DIRTY TRICK **THAT** WAS!
I AM NOT UNDERSTAND WHY IS IT CALLED A **POP** QUIZ.
BECAUSE THEY **POP** IT ON YOU, ARTUR! POP MEANS THE ELEMENT OF SURPRISE! IT'S LIKE: HERE'S A QUIZ! **POP!**
ONE TIME I GOT A DILL PICKLE STUCK UP MY NOSE, AND WHEN MY GRAM PULLED IT OUT, IT MADE A REALLY LOUD POP!
NOW I AM NOT UNDERSTAND WHY CHAD PUT A DILL PICKLE INSIDE HIS NOSE.
I WAS EXPERI-MENTING!
peirce

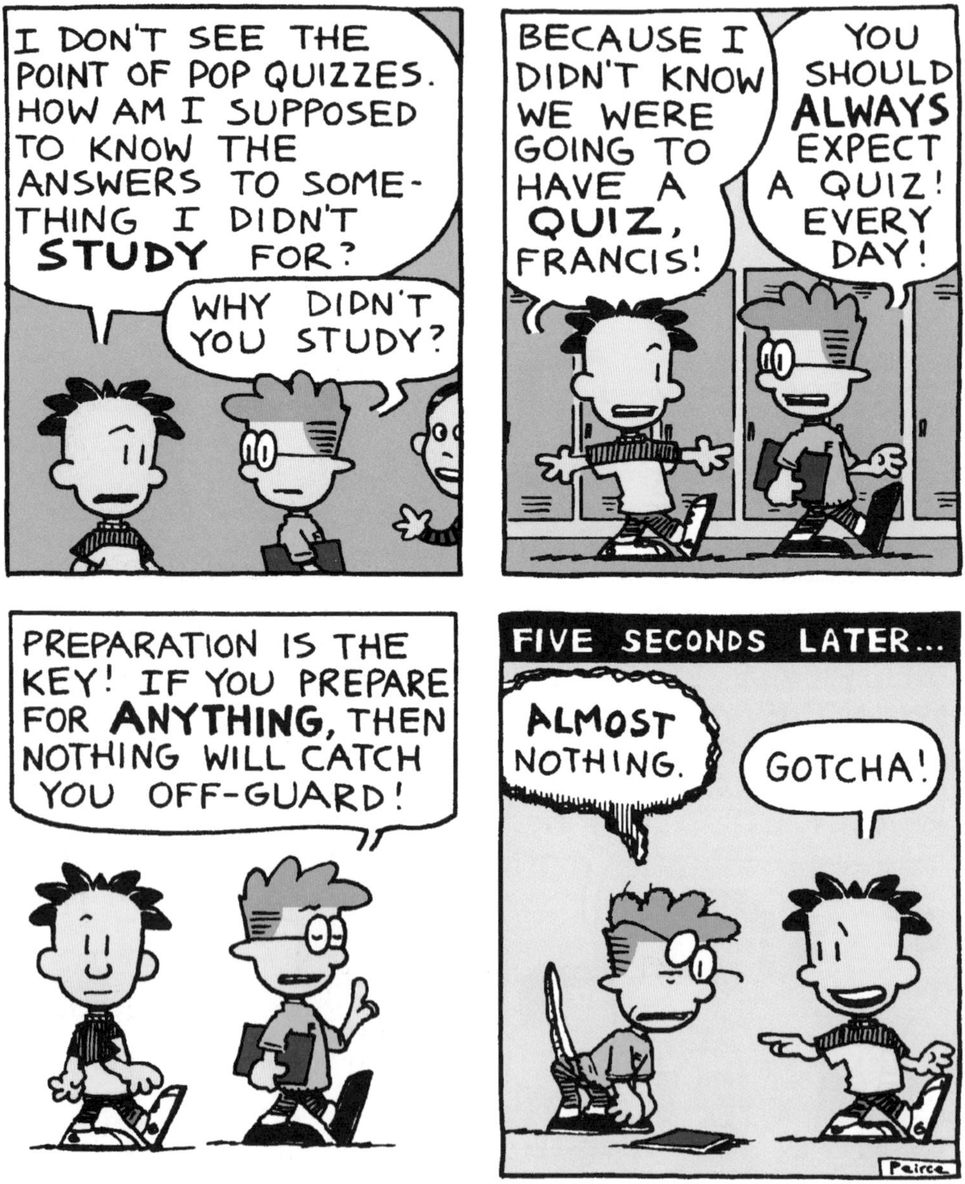
I DON'T SEE THE POINT OF POP QUIZZES. HOW AM I SUPPOSED TO KNOW THE ANSWERS TO SOMETHING I DIDN'T STUDY FOR?
WHY DIDN'T YOU STUDY?
BECAUSE I DIDN'T KNOW WE WERE GOING TO HAVE A QUIZ, FRANCIS!
YOU SHOULD ALWAYS EXPECT A QUIZ! EVERY DAY!
PREPARATION IS THE KEY! IF YOU PREPARE FOR ANYTHING, THEN NOTHING WILL CATCH YOU OFF-GUARD!
FIVE SECONDS LATER...
ALMOST NOTHING.
GOTCHA!
Peirce

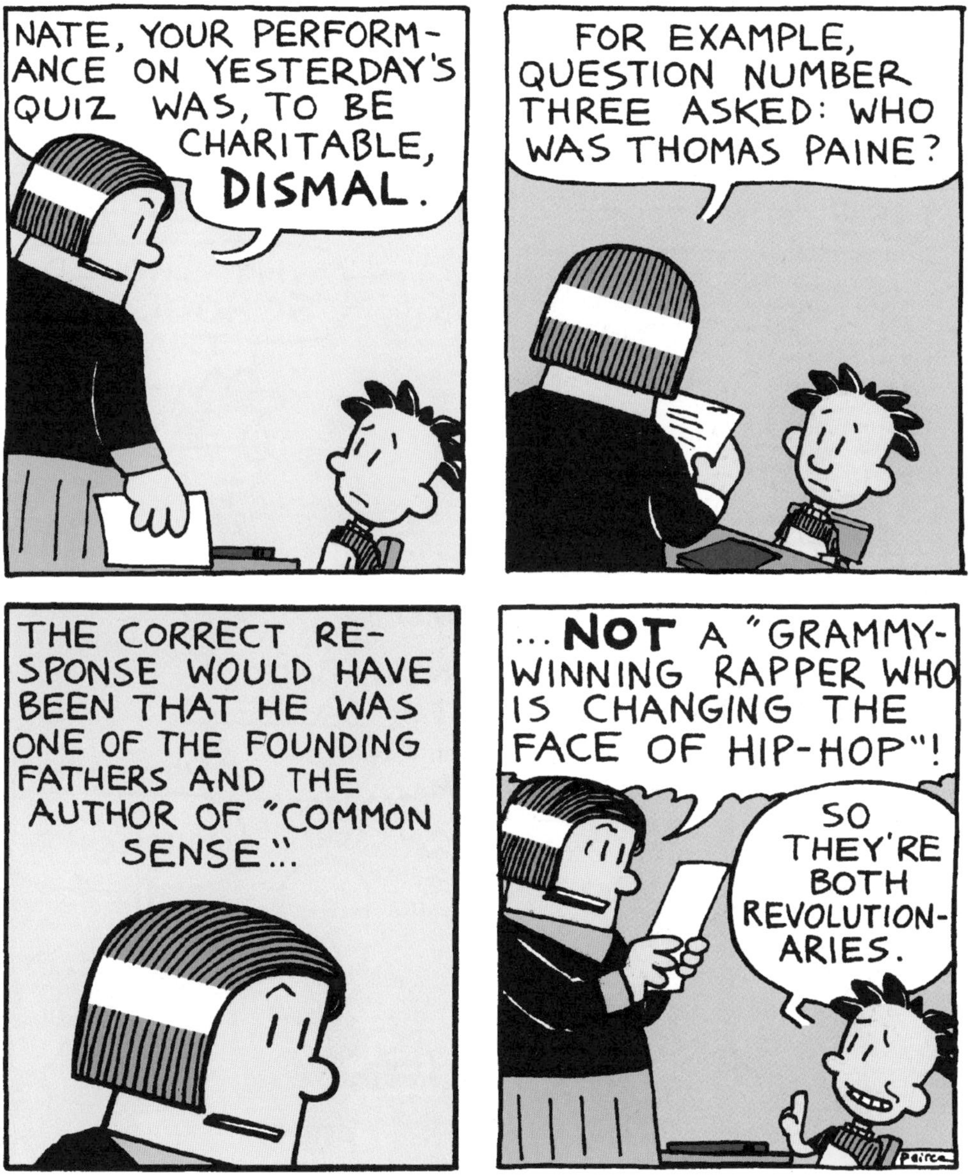
NATE, YOUR PERFORMANCE ON YESTERDAY'S QUIZ WAS, TO BE CHARITABLE, DISMAL.
FOR EXAMPLE, QUESTION NUMBER THREE ASKED: WHO WAS THOMAS PAINE?
THE CORRECT RESPONSE WOULD HAVE BEEN THAT HE WAS ONE OF THE FOUNDING FATHERS AND THE AUTHOR OF "COMMON SENSE."...
...NOT A "GRAMMY-WINNING RAPPER WHO IS CHANGING THE FACE OF HIP-HOP"!
SO THEY'RE BOTH REVOLUTIONARIES.

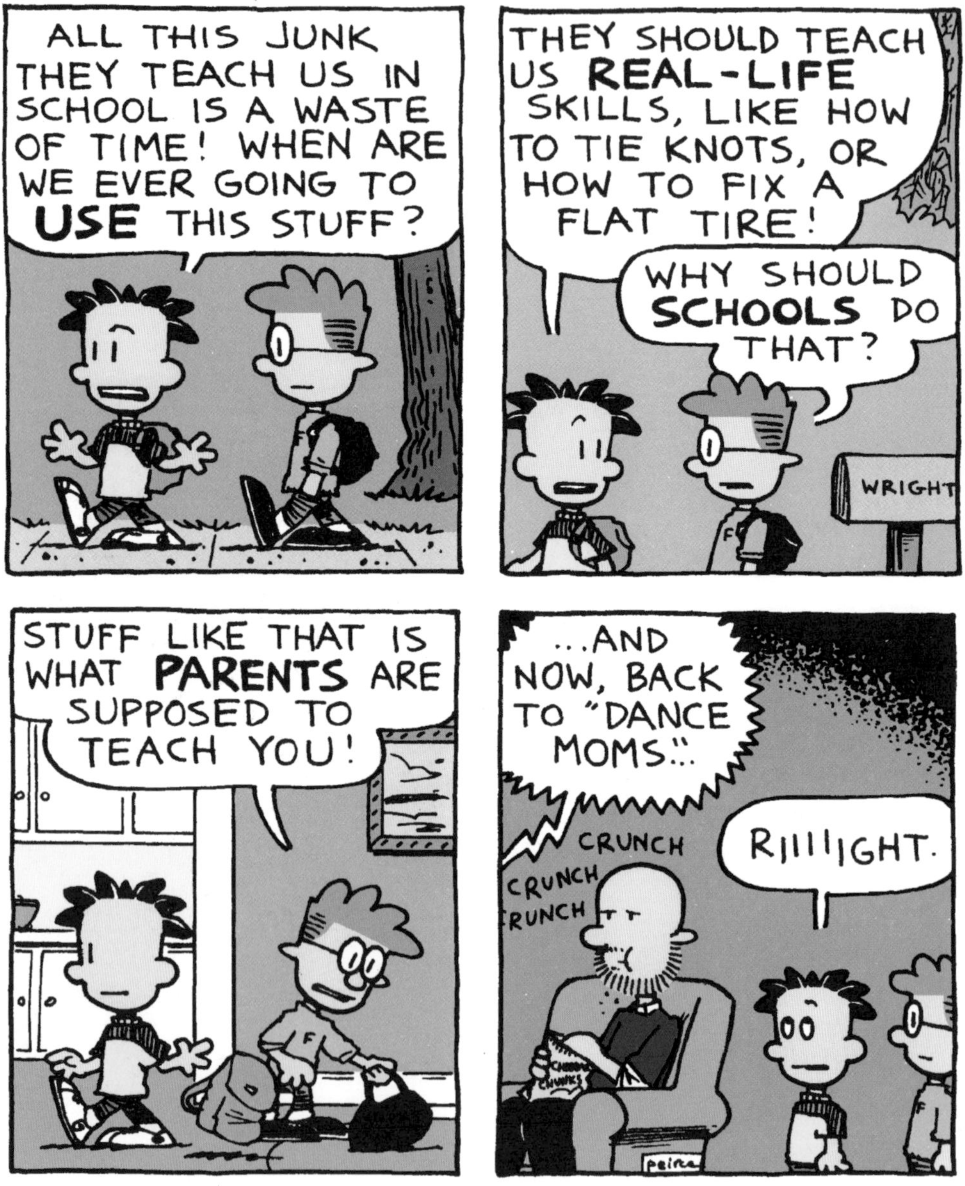
ALL THIS JUNK THEY TEACH US IN SCHOOL IS A WASTE OF TIME! WHEN ARE WE EVER GOING TO USE THIS STUFF?
THEY SHOULD TEACH US REAL-LIFE SKILLS, LIKE HOW TO TIE KNOTS, OR HOW TO FIX A FLAT TIRE!
WHY SHOULD SCHOOLS DO THAT?
WRIGHT
STUFF LIKE THAT IS WHAT PARENTS ARE SUPPOSED TO TEACH YOU!
...AND NOW, BACK TO "DANCE MOMS."
CRUNCH
CRUNCH
RUNCH
RIIIIGHT.
peirce

Look for these books!

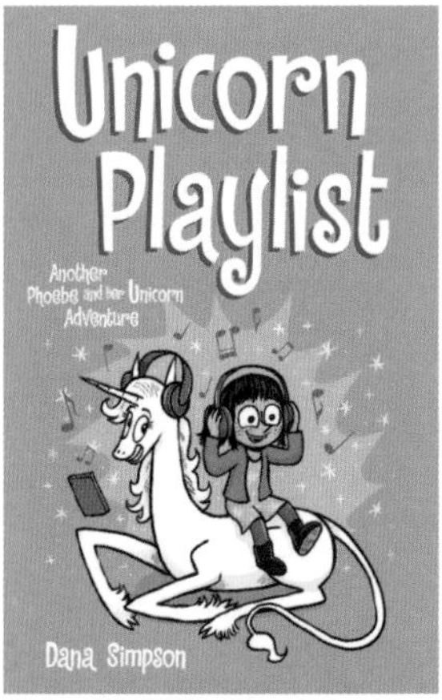
Unicorn Playlist
Another Phoebe and her Unicorn Adventure
Dana Simpson

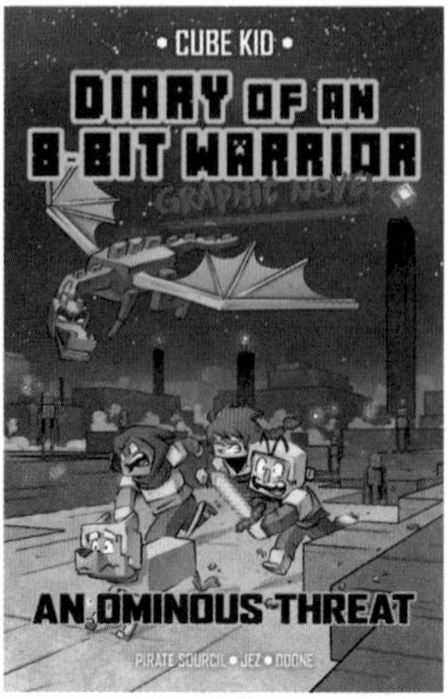
• CUBE KID •
DIARY OF AN 8-BIT WARRIOR
GRAPHIC NOVEL
AN OMINOUS THREAT
PIRATE SOURCIL • JEZ • ODONE

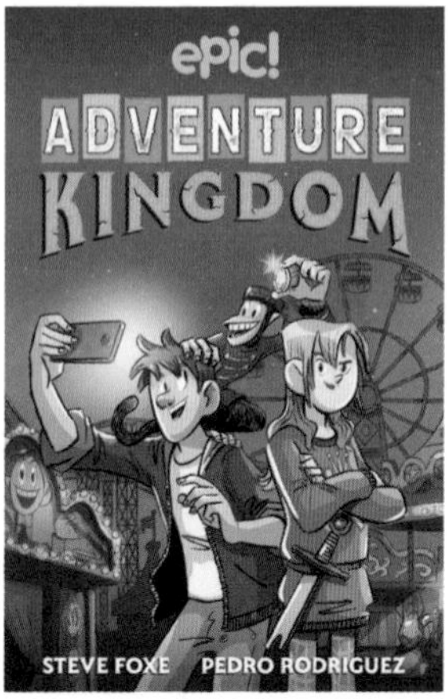
epic!
ADVENTURE KINGDOM
STEVE FOXE
PEDRO RODRIGUEZ

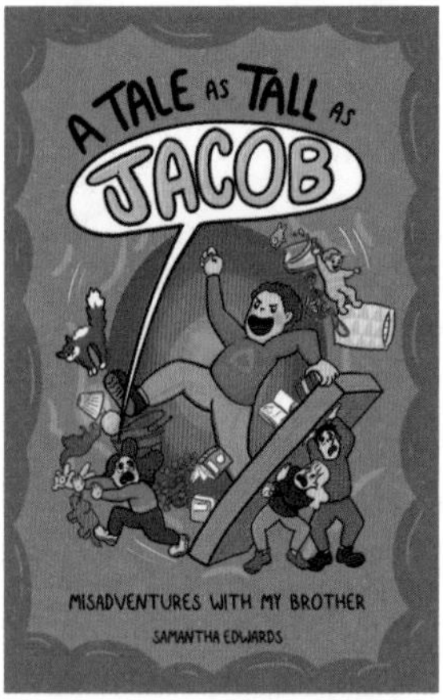
A TALE AS TALL AS JACOB
MISADVENTURES WITH MY BROTHER
SAMANTHA EDWARDS

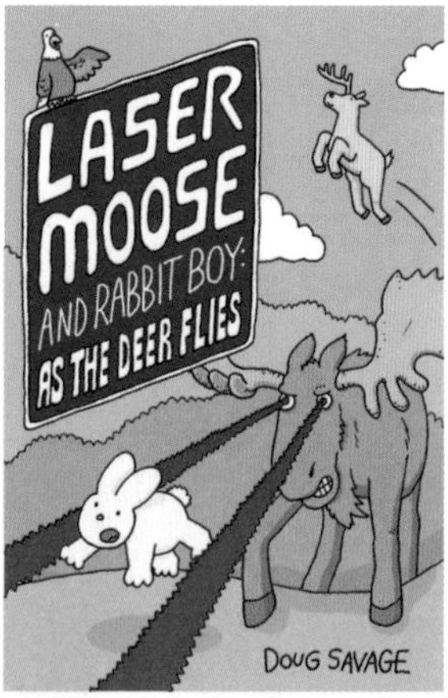
LASER MOOSE AND RABBIT BOY: AS THE DEER FLIES
DOUG SAVAGE

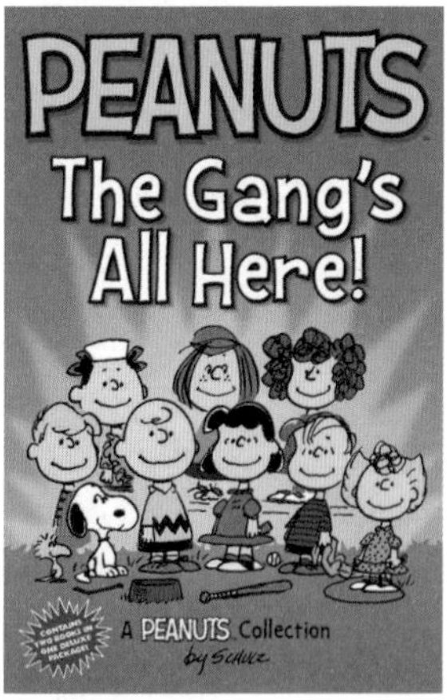
PEANUTS
The Gang's All Here!
A PEANUTS Collection
by Schulz

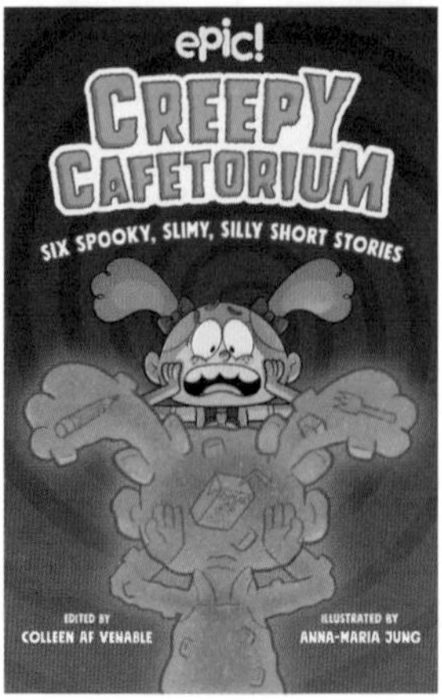
epic!
CREEPY CAFETORIUM
SIX SPOOKY, SLIMY, SILLY SHORT STORIES
EDITED BY
COLLEEN AF VENABLE
ILLUSTRATED BY
ANNA-MARIA JUNG

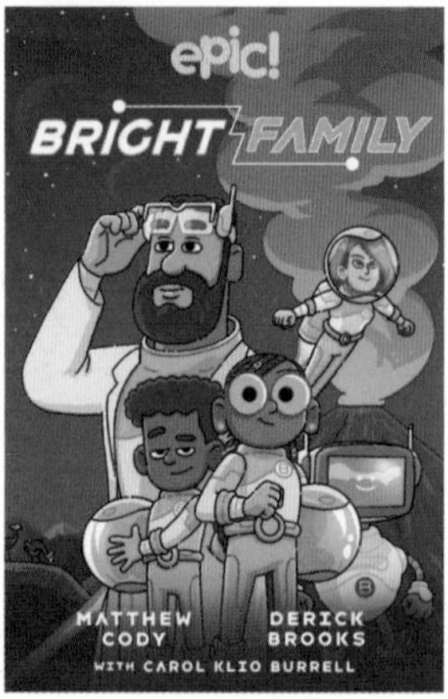
epic!
BRIGHT FAMILY
MATTHEW CODY
DERICK BROOKS
WITH CAROL KLIO BURRELL

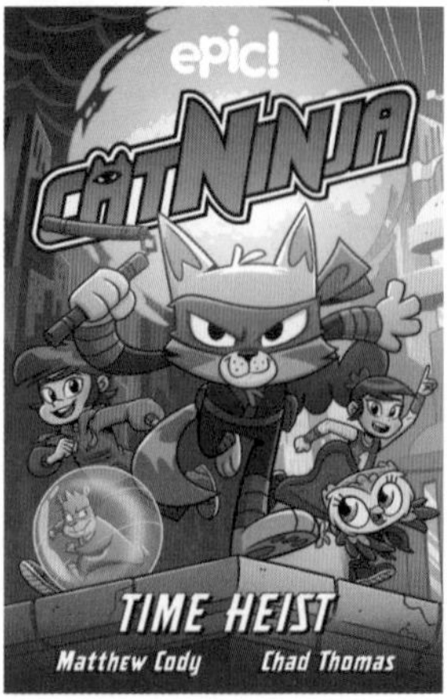
epic!
CATNINJA
TIME HEIST
Matthew Cody
Chad Thomas

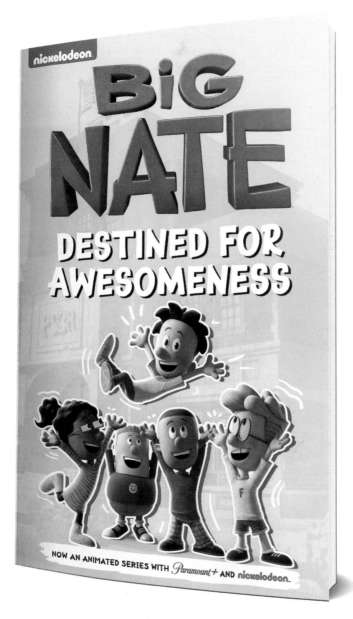

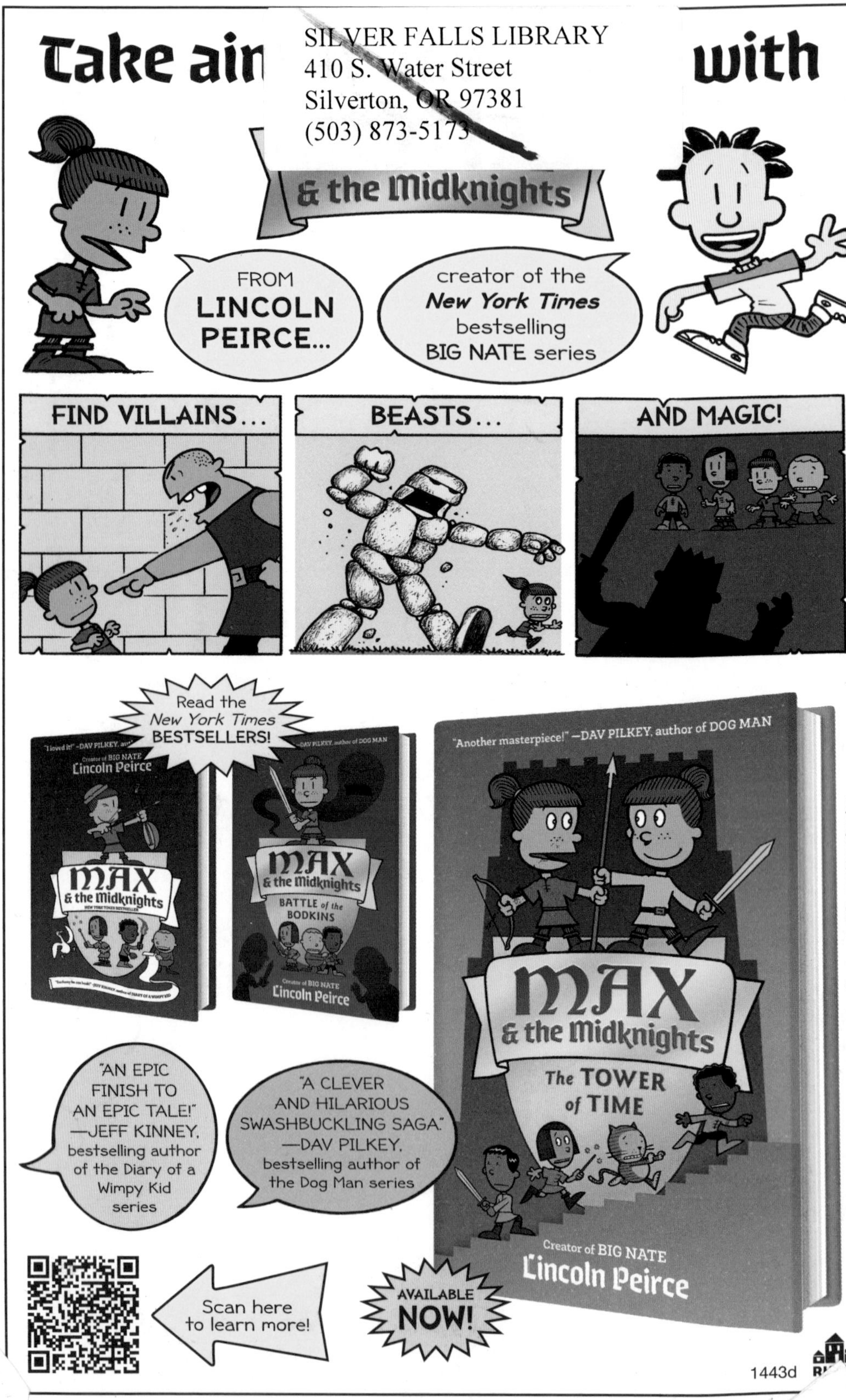
Take ai
with
& the Midknights
FROM LINCOLN PEIRCE...
creator of the New York Times bestselling BIG NATE series
FIND VILLAINS...
BEASTS...
AND MAGIC!
Read the New York Times BESTSELLERS!
"Another masterpiece!" —DAV PILKEY, author of DOG MAN
MAX & the Midknights
BATTLE of the BODKINS
The TOWER of TIME
Creator of BIG NATE
Lincoln Peirce
"AN EPIC FINISH TO AN EPIC TALE!" —JEFF KINNEY, bestselling author of the Diary of a Wimpy Kid series
"A CLEVER AND HILARIOUS SWASHBUCKLING SAGA." —DAV PILKEY, bestselling author of the Dog Man series
Scan here to learn more!
AVAILABLE NOW!
1443d